P9-BJG-960

Alice la Fée

David Shannon

Texte français d'Hélène Rioux

Éditions
SCHOLASTIC

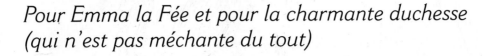

*Pour Emma la Fée et pour la charmante duchesse
(qui n'est pas méchante du tout)*

Catalogage avant publication de Bibliothèque et Archives Canada
Shannon, David, 1959-
Alice la Fée / David Shannon; texte français d'Hélène Rioux.
Traduction de : *Alice the Fairy*.
Pour enfants de 4 à 7 ans.
ISBN 0-439-96275-7
I. Rioux, Hélène, 1949- II. Titre.
PZ23.S485Ali 2004   j813'.54   C2004-904154-1
ISBN 13 978-0-439-96275-9

Lettrage créé par Monique Fauteux

Copyright © David Shannon, 2004.
Copyright © Éditions Scholastic, 2004, pour le texte français.
Tous droits réservés.

Il est interdit de reproduire, d'enregistrer ou de diffuser, en tout ou en partie,
le présent ouvrage par quelque procédé que ce soit, électronique, mécanique,
photographique, sonore, magnétique ou autre, sans avoir obtenu au préalable
l'autorisation écrite de l'éditeur. Pour toute information concernant les droits,
s'adresser à Scholastic Inc., 557 Broadway, New York, NY 10012.

Édition publiée par les Éditions Scholastic,
604, rue King Ouest, Toronto (Ontario) M5V 1E1.

7 6 5 4 3   Imprimé au Canada   08 09 10 11 12

Je m'appelle Alice. Je suis une fée.

Je ne suis pas une fée permanente. Je suis une fée temporaire. Il faut passer toute une série de tests avant de devenir une fée permanente.

Comme j'ai des ailes, je suis capable de voler.

Je ne vole pas encore très haut,

mais je vole très

Très viTe !

Voici ma
baguette magique

Et voici ma doudou.

Avec leur baguette magique, les fées peuvent changer les grenouilles en princes.

Moi, j'ai changé mon papa en cheval.

Une fois, maman a préparé des biscuits pour papa.

Ce n'était pas bien gentil, alors j'ai pensé faire apparaître un nouvel habit pour lui. T'ai-je dit que mon papa est le duc des Trois-Montagnes? Eh bien, c'est vrai!

Chemise en velours à carreaux

Pantalon doré avec des brillants

Souliers mauve rosé (ma couleur préférée)

Mais c'était trop difficile de faire apparaître des vêtements, alors je lui ai fabriqué une nouvelle couronne.

Avec ma baguette magique, je peux faire Tomber les feuilles des arbres.

Et je peux dessiner des images dans l'eau.

Parfois, j'utilise
ma baguette
pour disparaître

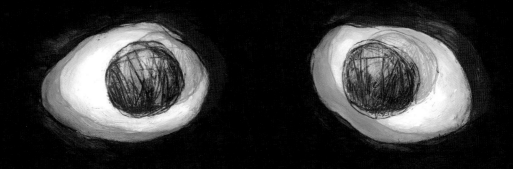

Mais c'est un peu terrifiant.

Je préfère

me servir de ma doudou !

Bien entendu, j'ai aussi un miroir magique.

Miroir, miroir,
du salon,
Qui est la meilleure
fée des environs ?

tiens, tiens ! C'est moi, Alice !
Merci, miroir !

La poudre de fée
est très utile. Je m'en sers
pour Transformer
mon gruau en gâteau.

Une fée peu aussi jeter des sorts. Regarde-moi faire flotter mon chien au plafond.

Abracadabra au plafond tu voleras!

Abracadabra, vole au plafond!

Abracadabra, envole-toi tête de **mule!**

Bon... Je crois que j'ai besoin d'un peu d'entraînement.

se montrer très prudente quand elle fait de la magie. Une fois, sans le vouloir, j'ai changé ma robe **blanche** en robe **rouge**.

La duchesse était très fâchée et elle m'a enfermée dans la tour pour **Toujours** !

(Mais j'ai réussi à m'échapper.)

La vie d'une fée est pleine de dangers.
Il ne faut jamais manger de
brocoli parce qu'il est souvent
empoisonné par la méchante duchesse.

Les fées détestent prendre leur bain. J'aimerais bien transformer l'eau en Jell-O à la fraise. Ce serait amusant!

Mais je ne sais pas encore faire ça.

Pour réussir ces tours de magie,
il faut être une fée permanente.

Elles suivent des cours de féerie avancée dans une école privée.

Je suis censée apprendre à faire voler mes vêtements, et à les faire danser et se ranger tout seuls dans le placard.

Je ne suis pas encore très habile

pour ce genre de tour.

Je vais probablement être une fée
Temporaire Toute ma vie.

P9-BJG-975

THE SHADOW LINE

DEVIANCE AND CRIME IN CANADA

UNIVERSITY
RECEIVED
APR 2 5 2003
UNIVERSITY
CALGARY BOOKSTORE
OF CALGARY

THE
SHADOW
LINE

DEVIANCE AND CRIME IN CANADA

THIRD EDITION

IAN MCDERMID GOMME

NELSON

THOMSON LEARNING

Australia • Canada • Mexico • Singapore • Spain • United Kingdom • United States

NELSON

THOMSON LEARNING

™

**The Shadow Line: Deviance and
Crime in Canada
Third Edition**
by Ian McDermid Gomme

Editorial Director and Publisher:
Evelyn Veitch

Acquisitions Editor:
Brad Lambertus

Marketing Manager:
Murray Moman

Developmental Editor:
Eliza Marciniak

Production Editor:
Laurie Thomas

Production Coordinators:
Cheri Westra/Helen Jager Locsin

Copy Editor:
Stacey Balakofsky

Proofreader:
Gilda Mekler

Creative Director:
Angela Cluer

Cover and Interior Design:
The Brookview Group Inc.

Cover Image:
Untitled photograph by Emily Miller. © 1999. Reproduced by permission of the artist.

Compositor:
Bookman Typesetting Co.

Indexer:
Elizabeth Bell—Pinpoint Indexing

Printer:
Victor Graphics

COPYRIGHT © 2002 by Nelson Thomson Learning, a division of Thomson Canada Limited. Nelson Thomson Learning is a registered trademark used herein under license.

Printed and bound in the United States
1 2 3 4 04 03 02 01

For more information contact Nelson Thomson Learning, 1120 Birchmount Road, Toronto, Ontario, M1K 5G4. Or you can visit our internet site at http://www.nelson.com

ALL RIGHTS RESERVED. No part of this work covered by the copyright hereon may be reproduced, transcribed, or used in any form or by any means—graphic, electronic, or mechanical, including photocopying, recording, taping, web distribution or information storage and retrieval systems—without the written permission of the publisher.

For permission to use material from this text or product, contact us by
Tel 1-800-730-2214
Fax 1-800-730-2215
www.thomsonrights.com

National Library of Canada Cataloguing in Publication Data

Gomme, Ian McDermid, 1949–

The shadow line: deviance and crime in Canada

3rd ed.
ISBN 0-7747-3730-1

1. Criminal behavior — Canada.
2. Deviant behavior. 3. Criminal behavior. I. Title.

HV6035.G65 2001   364.2
C2001-930696-2

For Sid
Happy trails, my friend, until .....

In writing *The Shadow Line*, I have assumed that its readers have little or no background in sociology and no previous training in the sociology of deviance and crime. The book is designed to provide a good grounding in the basic principles of sociology while generating further interest in sociology, criminology, and criminal justice.

The Shadow Line is organized into four parts. The first part focuses on how sociologists define deviance and crime, and on some of the pitfalls of this seemingly straightforward undertaking.

The second part discusses explanatory frameworks. It begins by developing a general appreciation of what sociological theory is and how it is used. This is followed by a brief historical summary outlining the development of explanatory frameworks from medieval times to the close of the nineteenth century. Most of the theory section assesses the principal twentieth-century positivist and humanist theories of deviance and crime. A detailed description and balanced assessment is offered for five major perspectives: the Chicago school, structural functionalism, social control and deterrence, symbolic interactionism and labelling, and conflict theory. Each of the five theory chapters describes the theory's mechanics and articulates its central recommendations for the development and implementation of social policy. Each chapter concludes by evaluating the logical and empirical criticisms that have been levelled at a particular perspective and by assessing its principal contributions to the development of sociological insight and imagination. The final theory chapter introduces several very recent theoretical formulations and includes discussions of routine activities analysis, left realism, feminism, power–control theory, self-control theory, peacemaking criminology, reintegrative shaming, and postmodernism.

The third part of this book outlines the prominent research and measurement techniques used to examine deviant and criminal activity. I stress that official records, surveys, and participant observation techniques, like the theories presented before them, answer some questions better than they do others. Each data-collection strategy has its strengths and deficiencies.

The fourth part of this book contains seven substantive chapters that emphasize Canadian research and policy. I have chosen to provide lengthy and detailed discussions of a few selected forms of deviance and crime rather than to opt for more comprehensive coverage with less depth. My purpose in such a vast field is not to be exhaustive, but rather to raise issues and sensitize readers to important debates.

Although data from other countries, principally the United States, are used sparingly for comparative purposes, the emphasis of the book is clearly Canadian and reflects the imagination and expertise of researchers and academics from across this country. The chapters describing the nature and dynamics of particular forms of deviance are relatively uniform. Each contains discussions of definitional problems, social and economic costs, sources of data, empirical description, sociological theory, and the complexities of social control.

The *Shadow Line* makes complicated questions and issues accessible by adopting a straightforward and animated style and by using concrete examples to facilitate comprehension and understanding. To promote learning and retention, chapters are structured similarly and include special-interest topics and illustrations in clearly defined boxes. Each chapter begins with a detailed set of learning objectives and ends with a comprehensive summary and a list of review questions. To encourage students to think independently and to read on their own, each chapter includes discussion questions and a list of recommended readings.

ACKNOWLEDGEMENTS

I wish to express my appreciation to those at Harcourt Canada who have contributed to the development of *The Shadow Line* over the years. Keith Thompson, Heather McWhinney, Laura Paterson Pratt, Semareh Al-Hillal, Jacqueline Faubert, Megan Mueller, Eliza Marciniak, and Brad Lambertus have kept me motivated and focused at various stages in the process and have helped immeasurably in bringing all three editions to fruition. I am grateful as well for the fine job of copy editing done by John Eerkes for the first edition, Darlene Zeleney for the second edition, and Stacey Balakofsky for the third.

John Nicholson, Ron Hinch, and Brian Burtch reviewed the manuscript for the first edition and their assessments were extremely helpful. David Ryan, Richard Gilbert, Aaron Doyle, Dorothy Pawluch, Oliver Stoetzer, and Kevin Wong provided reviews of the subsequent edition and offered many excellent suggestions for improvement. Kevin Wong's extremely detailed assessment of the manuscript for the third edition is especially appreciated. Anthony Micucci once again provided considerable assistance with the collection of material for this edition. His friendship and interest in my work over our years together at both York and Memorial are much appreciated.

Joining Memorial's Department of Sociology in 1985 was truly a fortunate development in my career. To say that I have benefited greatly from the intellectual environment, the camaraderie, and the friendship afforded by this milieu significantly understates the case. Those in the department deserving special commendations for their assistance, support, and singular senses of humour are Peter Sinclair, Larry Felt, Bob Hill, Barbara Neis, and Judi Smith. Outside the sociology department, Terry Murphy and Terry Murphy, in their own unique ways, have added immeasurably to my enjoyment of life on the Rock. South of the border, Will Wright has exerted considerable effort to provide the resources necessary for the completion of this project. Russ Meyer, Dean of the College of Humanities and Social Sciences at the University of Southern Colorado, has provided the kind of moral, intellectual, and material support that fosters productive and enjoyable academic enterprise.

Dick Carlton hooked me on teaching in 1963, Jack Puntis hooked me on Joseph Conrad in 1966, Alan King hooked me on sociology in 1973, and Gordon West hooked me on deviance in 1981. Without their contributions to my intellectual and pedagogical development, *The Shadow Line* would never have seen the light of day. Many of us can point to a single individual who has truly enriched our personal and professional lives. Without Sid Gilbert's encouragement, guidance, and friendship over my years as a graduate student and fledgling academic, I might well have lived up to my high school guidance counsellor's prediction of my future prospects ... not good. His knocking off at least some of the rough edges for which I am so well known has made me a better scholar, a better teacher, and, most of all, a better person.

There are others whose support and encouragement at different points in my life deserve mention. I thank Mary Hall for her insight, kindness, good humour, and indefatigable optimism. Max and Barbara Wallis provided shelter from the storm when it was much needed. Helen and Gordon Hopkins have offered constant support and encouragement. Helen Gomme inculcated in me, at an early age, an enthusiasm for learning, an appreciation of the written word, and a desire to understand opposing points of view. Whether in the flesh or in spirit, Clement Gomme is truly one of a kind. I owe him more than I can express.

Free spirits Linda Richardson and Jane Foster have graciously allowed me to serve as "sidekick" off and on during the past 30 years. Without them, I might be living a normal life.

A Note from the Publisher

Thank you for selecting *The Shadow Line: Deviance and Crime in Canada*, Third Edition, by Ian McDermid Gomme. The author and publisher have devoted considerable time to the careful development of this book. We appreciate your recognition of this effort and accomplishment.

BRIEF CONTENTS

CONTENTS

The "**shadow line**" is a multidimensional image borrowed from the work of British writer Joseph Conrad (1857–1924). Many of Conrad's tales were spun from his early experiences as a sailor, and much of his imagery reflects the sea's haunting beauty and seductive allure while at the same time portraying its ominous power and disquieting unpredictability. The shadow line is the horizon in high seas, the illusive and transient boundary that separates the grey shade of the sea from the grey shade of the sky. In the failing light of a stormy night, the shadow line is especially dark, amorphous, and difficult to pinpoint. In the abstract, it marks the point that distinguishes sunlight from shadow, right from wrong, and good from evil. In Conrad's terms, the shadow line separates humanity from its own heart of darkness. It can be thin indeed. Things on the shadow line are seldom what they seem, and the harder one looks, the more difficult it becomes to see clearly and to chart one's course with certainty.

The metaphor of "the line" is particularly appropriate for a book about **deviance**. Many people take for granted that there is a hard and fast boundary that separates conformity and law-abiding behaviour from deviant and criminal activity. With the line crystal clear and carved in stone, they have little difficulty separating the good from the bad and the ugly, the true and just from the crooked and underhanded, the hearts of gold from the hearts of darkness, the saints from the sinners, and the law-abiding from the bandits.

The Shadow Line examines the length and the width of this dividing line and the ease with which it can be crossed. It looks at who treads over the edge, how they take their first fateful steps, and why they become disreputable. It explores the fates of those who find themselves on the dark side and the fortunes of those who try to return. Where and how the line is drawn, who lays it down and why, and the ways in which people are made to toe the mark are also examined. *The Shadow Line* evaluates the efficacy of various anti-deviance bonds and barriers and considers the extent to which the boundary separating conformity from deviance drifts from time to time and shifts from place to place. Last, but by no means least,

the book continually confronts the issue of whether the line is as clear as day or whether it is, indeed, cloaked in shadow.

The Shadow Line has been written with several related aims in mind. First, deviance, **crime**, and control are discussed as social creations: their causes, consequences, and forms are variable, complex, and deeply imbedded in the social, moral, economic, and political fabric of Canadian society. There is much more to defining, measuring, describing, and explaining deviance, crime, and their control than first meets the eye. Second, folk wisdom, media portrayals, and so-called common sense are riddled with perceptions about the nature of deviant and criminal conduct that are frequently inaccurate if not dead wrong. In recognition of this problem, *The Shadow Line* continues the time-honoured sociological tradition of "debunking" (Berger, 1963), in which carefully collected sociological data routinely call into question some of people's most deeply entrenched ideas about "weirdos," "outlaws," and their "dastardly deeds."

Third, most Canadians view many forms of deviant and criminal behaviour as serious problems. Consequently, a great deal of attention is devoted to setting out clearly the major sociological frameworks that explain and provide solutions to social deviance and criminality.

Finally, *The Shadow Line* takes issue with simplistic and ill-conceived notions about how society ought to deal with such troublesome phenomena as murder, sexual assault, prostitution, drug abuse, organized crime, business crime, and mental illness. Effective treatment and control are neither straightforward nor inexpensive. Social and state-mandated responses to nonconformity and crime have significant impacts on both the individual and society. At the individual level, reactions affect both psychological and material well-being. On the societal plane, while the authors of social control policies inevitably endeavour to mend tears in the moral, economic, and political fabric of the nation, their initiatives are almost always double-edged swords. It is by no means unusual for "new" corrective strategies to produce more harm than good. Reactions to deviance and crime on the parts of individual Canadians, legislators, and social-control agencies demand consideration and reflection from all citizens.

Murder, sexual assault, prostitution, drug abuse, organized crime, business crime, and mental illness have been chosen for discussion because they differ on several important dimensions. The deviant statuses of some of the types of deviance and crime discussed in *The Shadow Line* enjoy considerable consensus. Virtually all Canadians strongly disapprove of terrorist activity. The attack on Air India Flight 182, which originated in Canada and killed several hundred Canadians in 1985, was universally condemned in this country as a heinous act. It remains one of the largest mass murders in history. About other forms of nonconformity and illegal conduct such as mental illness, drug abuse, and prostitution, however, there is much less consensus.

Some forms of deviance and crime such as murder and sexual assault involve physical aggression while others such as selling sex, shooting heroin, and embezzlement do not. Most *Criminal Code* violations and almost all noncriminal deviant acts are nonviolent. Other forms of deviance and crime thought to be nonviolent can be and often are violent. White-collar workers and business organizations do not confine themselves exclusively to fraud, price fixing, and conducting illegal mergers. When they violate laws governing consumer protection, worker health and safety, and pollution, they frequently maim and kill.

In some forms of deviant and criminal behaviour the targets are people, while in others the targets are material goods and property. Canadian serial murderer Clifford Olson stalked and killed at least eleven humans. Brian Molony, in perhaps the most costly embezzlement in Canadian history, relieved the Canadian Imperial Bank of Commerce of millions of dollars to finance his passion for gambling. On the other hand, for some forms of deviant and criminal activity, it is difficult, at least in the usual sense of the word, to find a victim at all. The identity of the victim in incidents of prostitution, narcotics use, and gambling is not entirely clear. Those on the receiving end of these sorts of shady dealings are usually customers and clients who are willing if not enthusiastic participants in the illicit transactions.

Some types of deviance and crime, such as murder and sexual assault, involve individuals both as perpetrators and as victims, while some involve organizations on one or both of these dimensions. Illegitimate organized criminal groups engage in racketeering, a practice that victimizes both legitimate business organizations and the labour unions representing their employees. Legitimate business corporations engage in espionage against their lawful competitors. They also knowingly victimize individuals: consumers buying their products; employees working in their mines, mills, and factories; and members of the public who find it necessary to drink water and breathe air.

Some types of nonconformity and illegality take place in an ongoing, careerlike fashion. Alcoholism, drug addiction, and mental illness can be analyzed by using the career as an orienting framework. Some forms of deviance and crime are not only careers in the informal sense, they represent occupations in which deviance is a core component. Providing sex or drugs for material reward is the cornerstone of a prostitute's or drug trafficker's livelihood. Furthermore, even some legitimate occupations in business and government virtually require deviance as part of their job descriptions.

Some deviant and criminal activity is sporadic, compulsive, and occasional. Most murders conform to this pattern; they occur more or less on the spur of the moment. Other crimes, both violent and nonviolent, are more rational and premeditated. Many sexual assaults, most robberies, and virtually all business crimes are planned in advance.

The nature of deviant and criminal behaviours varies by the social standing of perpetrators. "Street crime" — *Criminal Code* offences against persons and property (e.g., murder, assault, robbery, theft) — occur mostly among the lower classes and disadvantaged ethnic minorities. Alternatively, "suite crimes" such as anticompetitive practices and securities violations are perpetrated by the only people with the opportunity to do so — the rich and the powerful.

Canadian **criminal law** prohibits some of the illicit activities discussed in *The Shadow Line* and ignores others. Murder, sexual assault, arson, and fraud are prohibited by the *Criminal Code*. The harmful activities of businesses such as the restriction of trade or false advertising are prohibited by regulatory enactments. Although they are deviant, other behaviours such as those resulting from mental illness are not so directly regulated by Canadian statute. In some jurisdictions, socially harmful activities such as industrial pollution are not governed by *any* laws whatsoever.

Different forms of deviance and crime elicit different reactions. Some are responded to with control strategies advocating treatment; mental illness, drug addiction, and alcoholism are prime examples. On the other end of the continuum, other forms of deviance and, in particular, street crime are greeted with highly punitive sanctions. In many cases, criminal convictions involve lengthy prison sentences or, in some countries, the death penalty.

On one aspect of the control dimension, however, there is little variation. The forms of deviant and criminal conduct discussed in *The Shadow Line* are neither readily nor inexpensively amenable to reduction, let alone elimination. In recognition of this unsettling truth, the book assesses the nature and effectiveness of the efforts being made to keep these "problems" in check through means as disparate as education, moral dissuasion, treatment, and law enforcement.

Coping with deviance and crime in a liberal democracy raises enormously complicated issues. Nonetheless, authorities and lay people alike routinely overlook many of these complexities. Social control initiatives can be immensely costly economically, politically, and socially. Moreover, they can create more social ills than they stamp out. Many Canadians remain oblivious to these pitfalls as they clamour for the broadening of criminal laws, the expansion of police forces and prisons, the institution of higher fines and harsher sentences, and even a return to capital punishment. It is important to investigate both how Canada tries to control deviance and crime and the problems and prospects inherent in these measures.

Several themes woven into Conrad's symbolic framework bear repeating. First, casual glances seldom, if ever, suffice. We must peer long and hard to identify, understand, and respond sensibly to the vagaries of life on or beyond the shadow line. Second, the shadow comes and goes as we come and go within it. The darkness is, from time to time and from place to place, as much in our own hearts as in the hearts of others.

PART ONE

DEFINING DEVIANCE AND CRIME

CHAPTER 1

DEFINING DEVIANCE AND CRIME

The aims of this chapter are to familiarize the reader with:

- a definition of deviance as a negative reaction to behaviours, ideas, attributes
- informal and formal as well as external and internal reactions, and their relationship to processes of social control
- issues in the definition of deviance: the tension between **objectivism** and **subjectivism**, connections between deviance and rarity, links between deviance and crime, and voluntary and involuntary deviance
- the importance of social context — audiences, actors, and settings — in the definitions of deviance and crime
- the nature of criminal law: politicality, specificity, uniformity, and penal sanction
- the elements of criminal law: *actus reus*, *mens rea*, and motive
- criminal defences: mistake of law, mistake of fact, justification, necessity, consent, duress, provocation, intoxication, automatism, insanity, and entrapment.

INTRODUCTION

Deviants? Criminals? "We" know who "they" are. "They" are the highwaymen, pirates, and quacks, the rapists, gamblers, robbers, and axe killers, the satanists, hunchbacks, and gangsters, the winos, child molesters, and nut cases, the pushers, potheads, and psychos, the con artists, hookers, and assassins — misfits or soldiers of fortune at best, sinners and out-

laws at worst. These are "the children of the night," the denizens of an underworld we read about and see on television but know little of personally. They are the stuff of myth, legend, and romance.

Our fascination with deviance, crime, and especially violence is as glaring as it is boundless. Brutal killers Gary Gilmore and Ted Bundy died by executioners' hands while faithful and enchanted onlookers held candlelight vigils just beyond their prison walls. Albert De Salvo, Charles Manson, and others like them have become the protagonists in popular movies and bestselling books (*The Boston Strangler* and *Helter Skelter*). Lizzie Borden, Jack the Ripper, Billy the Kid, and Robin Hood have spawned veritable industries. Contemporary songwriters from rocker Bruce Springsteen to singing cowboy Ian Tyson have provided lyric portrayals of the dastardly deeds of modern-day outlaws like Charlie Starkweather and Claude Dallas.

Common sense and popular culture tell us that what makes people shady characters and outlaws is that they have traversed the line between conformity and deviance. "They" have crossed the thin line that separates the rather ordinary realms in which "we" go about our daily lives from the shadowy and exotic worlds in which "they" get high, buy and sell kinky sex, and prey upon innocent victims. Where we conform, follow the rules, and obey the law, they do not. They deviate from the straight and narrow; they lurk in the shadows along dimly lit city streets. They live outside the law.

Deciding what is and what is not deviance, however, is not nearly so straightforward as it appears. In their efforts to cast light through the haze that envelops this twilight zone, sociologists and criminologists subject deviance in its various forms to meticulous examination. They focus on questions concerning its definition, incidence, patterns, causes, consequences, and costs, as well as on its control. Their enterprise and resolve call common sense into question. Some of the images of deviance so deeply imbedded in popular culture are cracked if not altogether shattered when subjected to such close scrutiny.

The questions confronting sociologists interested in studying deviance are legion, and their answers — although complicated and a shade obtuse — are absolutely fascinating. First and foremost, what is deviance? What is the relationship between deviance and crime? By what means and with what degree of accuracy can we count such disparate incidents as sexual assault, environmental crime, illegal gambling, alcoholism, devil worship, and group sex?

Once deviance and crime have been defined, counted, and described, other aspects demand explanation. Why are most murderers, burglars, and mafia members male? Why has bank robbery become the domain of amateurs when, during the early part of this century, it was a thriving criminal profession? Why does prostitution continue to flourish in the face of continuous and determined efforts by concerned citizens and law enforcement agencies to stamp it out? Why are crime rates lower in Newfoundland than in southern Ontario? Why can being caught in your own home getting high on a marijuana cigarette land you with a fine and a criminal record while getting drunk on a bottle of Canadian Club whisky, in the same circumstances, cannot? Despite the tremendous potential for lethal harm, why are industries able to continue dumping toxic chemicals into lakes, rivers, oceans, and air? This book explores these and other issues in the study of deviance and criminality. It begins by examining the complexities inherent in defining deviance and crime.

DEFINING DEVIANCE

The understanding of deviance rests in the reactions of observers. Something is deviant because an individual, group, or society takes offence and reacts negatively (Cohen, 1966; Lofland, 1969). Consider an inebriated professor babbling on in a lecture hall filled with students. Think of a group of teenagers frolicking naked in a city park on a hot summer afternoon or of a young father on an airplane beating his screaming infant. Onlookers would almost certainly disapprove of all three acts. These are behaviours that most people would designate as deviant.

While deviance is usually thought of as a certain type of behaviour, this need not be the case. Deviance can encompass both ideas and attributes (Sagarin, 1975). Many Canadians and Americans think it deviant for someone to worship Satan or swear allegiance to the Communist Manifesto. People's attributes can also be the source of shunning and rejection. Although they might be unaware of it or deny it, many Canadians treat as deviant those who are disfigured, obese, ugly, crippled, or mentally handicapped. While most of this book focuses on deviant action, nonconformity is much broader than behaviour.

Negative reactions occur because onlookers interpret what they see and hear as wrong, bad, crazy, disgusting, strange, immoral or some combination of these (Higgins and Butler, 1982). A large segment of Canadian society views mate-swapping for the purposes of sexual recreation as wrong. Virtually everyone believes that the sexual molestation of children is bad. Most people think that adults who talk to trees are crazy and that men who masturbate during strip shows are disgusting.

Negative responses do more than simply demarcate deviance; they serve as **mechanisms of social control**. Negative responses and the social controls they represent vary in intensity from mild to severe and in conventionality from informal to formal. Informal negative reactions include epithets, avoidance, ridicule, criticism, and gossip. Consider some examples. Those who have been standing in line patiently for hours greet latecomers who butt in with derogatory comments that may or may not be uttered under their breath. Residents of a small community gossip about a teacher having an extramarital affair with a student. People with physical abnormalities are frequently avoided and excluded from get-togethers because others feel awkward in the company of the disabled.

These examples of informal punitive responses are external to the individual, but such responses need not be so. Negative reactions often are internal. In such cases, people in a very real sense represent their own audience. Many spouses who covertly cheat on their partners react negatively to their own infidelity, despite the fact that their deceptions remain hidden. Many closeted homosexuals worry about their sexual preference, clandestine activities, and secret identities. Shame and a guilty conscience define as deviant our

BOX 1.1
EDITOR CALLS 'VIRTUAL ADULTERY' A SIN

Forget about phone sex. That's stone age stuff. What has the editors of an Italian Catholic magazine worried these days is "adultery" over the Internet.

Adultery is adultery, even if it is virtual, according to *Famiglia Cristiana* (Christian Family) a magazine close to the Vatican. It is just as sinful as the real thing.

The question of the morality of flirting, falling in love and perhaps betraying a spouse via the World Wide Web surfaced in the advice column of the latest issue of Italy's largest-circulation weekly news magazine.

A woman from the northern city of Varese wrote to the magazine, asking for moral guidance as she surfed the Web.

"On the Internet you can fall in love, you can seek, you can think, you can truly desire. And you can commit adultery without leaving your home," she wrote in a long letter.

"I ask myself what difference there is for the Church between a real extramarital affair and a virtual one. I ask myself how long this new (Internet) reality, which is so tangible, can be underestimated."

The magazine's editor wrote in his "Conversations with the Priest" column that there is no difference.

"Virtual reality can be just as much of a vice as reality made up of facts and actions...," Father Antonio Sciortino wrote in his response.

"Gospel morals attach a premium to what is inside a person and are just as concerned with bad thoughts as they are with bad actions," he explained.

The priest recalled Christ's phrase in the Bible that if a man looks at a woman with lust he has already committed "adultery in his heart."

The story received wide coverage in Italy, where more than 97 per cent of the population is nominally Roman Catholic.

One newspaper, *Il Giornale*, published a poll that said 40 per cent of Italian women interviewed for it said they feared their husbands might find a woman more fascinating than them while surfing the Web.

Discussion Question

Can virtual reality be just as much of a vice as reality made up of facts and actions? Discuss the implications of using morality as a reference for what is or is not deviance.

Source: *Toronto Star,* June 8, 2000, p. A19. Copyright Reuters Limited 2000.

surreptitious actions, our hidden ideas, and our concealed traits. At the same time, guilt and shame compel us to desist or cover up (Douglas, 1977).

Formal negative reactions are by definition external. They include official warnings, legal punishments, and various forms of treatment. The police, and later the courts, may formally penalize the drunken party-goer stopped in a roadside spot check. Not only may she spend a night in jail, pay a $500 fine, and enrol in a rehabilitation program for drunk drivers, but she may suffer the indignity of having her name published in the newspaper and endure an enormous increase in her car insurance premium. Physicians addicted to drugs, corporate executives hooked on three-martini lunches, and many designated as mentally ill may be officially and involuntarily required to undergo various forms of corrective therapy.

Whether informal or formal, negative and potentially coercive reactions such as these define conduct, beliefs, and personal traits as deviance and define the people doing the behaving, believing, and appearing as deviants. At the same time, these responses serve as social controls. Varying in their power, these controls may or may not limit or drive underground the occurrence, appearance, or expression of deviance. Fundamentally, behaviours, ideas, and attributes that fail to elicit negative responses from audiences cannot be considered deviant.

Although the basic elements of a definition of deviance have been introduced, an understanding of deviance is fraught with complexities that warrant further consideration. Among the more important issues to be considered are the tension between positivist and humanist conceptualizations, the connection between deviance and statistical rarity, the relation of deviance to crime, and the role of voluntariness in the definition of certain acts, ideas, and traits as deviant (Higgins and Butler, 1982).

> ## BOX 1.2
> ## MOTHER STICKS UP FOR SON EXPELLED FROM
> ## SCHOOL AFTER TAKING SWISS ARMY KNIFE INTO CLASS
>
> The mother of a Grade 10 student expelled from his Edmonton high school for bringing a Swiss Army knife to class says his sentence was too severe. Mickey Legault took out the knife, which has a four-centimetre blade and a variety of tools, to cut paper in his mechanics class on May 29. He was removed from class, suspended for five days and the school's principal recommended expulsion. "He was in mechanics class. If he wanted to stab someone, he could have reached over and grabbed a screwdriver,"
>
> said Peggy Legault, his mother. "I was willing to acknowledge he did something wrong, but they're treating him as a common criminal." School board officials would not comment on the case, but said their policy on weapons has been in place for five years and should be well known.
>
> ### Discussion Question
>
> Does the punishment fit the crime in this case?
>
> Source: *National Post*, June 29, 2000, p. A8. Reprinted from the *Edmonton Journal* with permission from the *Edmonton Journal*.

ISSUES IN THE DEFINITION OF DEVIANCE

OBJECTIVISM AND SUBJECTIVISM

Sociologists have for years debated to what degree deviance is a matter of objective fact or of subjective interpretation. Early sociological discussions tended to treat deviance as the simple violation of pre-existing and concrete societal **norms**. This conceptualization rested squarely on the conviction that social norms were somehow given, external to individuals, and therefore objective. Initially objectivists viewed norms as absolute. They assumed that within society there was widespread consensus about the behaviours, ideas, and attributes that were proper, acceptable, and conformist and those that were improper, objectionable, and nonconformist. Conformity meant adhering to pre-existing societal expectations and rules, while nonconformity meant violating them (Parsons, 1951; Merton, 1971).

On the consensus issue, virtually all Canadians consider murder, rape, robbery, and theft intolerable and deviant. The same cannot be said of smoking marijuana, having an abortion, hiring out as a prostitute, selling pornographic materials, or making love to a person of the same sex. People simply disagree on the extent to which these latter activities are reprehensible. In recent decades, sociologists have begun to pay a great deal of attention to the nature of these dis-

agreements and to the implications of a lack of consensus for the definition and explanation of deviance. Those working in a subjectivist or humanist tradition emphasize the problems associated with the social construction of societal norms and the differential application of social rules.

Subjectivist or humanist sociologists point out that rules do not appear out of thin air. People create and interpret the standards that determine whether behaviours, ideas, and attributes are acceptable or unacceptable. Deviance, they maintain, is a social construction and as such is a relative concept. Like beauty, it is in the eye of the beholder. Deviance from one vantage point could well be conformity from another (Erikson, 1962; Becker, 1963).

Contemporary sociologists of deviance reside in two camps: objective positivists on one hand and subjective humanists on the other. Neither group totally denies the validity of the other's position; their differences in perspective are more a matter of degree. Many social scientists continue to work in the objectivist, positivist, and "scientific" tradition. While they recognize that rules do vary by place and over time, especially in heterogeneous societies such as Canada, objectivists focus most of their attention on explaining why people violate social norms and how they can be dissuaded from doing so. Alternatively, sociologists working in the humanist tradition do not take social norms as given. Rather, they emphasize their origins, implementation, and impacts. They particularly emphasize the critical roles of social definition and social power in the creation of deviance.

THE LINK BETWEEN DEVIANCE AND RARITY

There is a certain intuitive appeal in the notion that part of defining something as deviant depends on the rarity with which it occurs (Higgins and Butler, 1982). After all, murder, rape, homosexuality, prostitution, and mental disorder are infrequent when compared with other human events, activities, and conditions. The first difficulty with this idea is that many rare occurrences produce positive rather than negative public responses. Being the fastest person on two feet and being adept in directing a black disk at high speed and with deadly accuracy are not the stuff of which deviants are made. Indeed, rather than condemning their exploits, Canadians hail Olympic gold-medalist Simon Whitfield as a conquering hero, and affectionately refer to Wayne Gretzky as "the Great One." Rarity is not a critical component in defining acts, beliefs, or traits as deviant.

What happens routinely can also be considered deviant. There are, for example, certain behaviours in which virtually everyone engages but which people treat as deviant nonetheless. In the early 1980s, despite research suggesting that virtually all male and many female Canadian university students masturbated regularly, many participants felt guilt and shame about this covert sexual activity (Knox, 1984). More so than with other widespread and perfectly healthy forms of sexual release, masturbation was forbidden. Comments made by Canadian young people surveyed by Edward Herold (1984) reflect these sentiments. Two of Herold's respondents summed up their feelings:

> Masturbation is about the only taboo subject still remaining among my women friends at university. (p. 29)

> Masturbation had been a major source of guilt throughout my sexual development and I blamed many of my problems such as delayed physical development and lack of enjoyment of my initial heterosexual experiences as punishment from God for being "perverted." (p. 30)

THE LINK BETWEEN DEVIANCE AND CRIME

Most people consider crime a serious violation of formal rules that are designed to protect people from being harmed by others. From this standpoint, crime is deviance in its gravest form. Talk of rising crime rates usually conjures up images of ever more frequent murders, rapes, robberies, and thefts. Compared with crime, deviance is generally considered to be less serious, more frequent, and more pervasive. This view implies that while not all deviant acts are criminal, all criminal acts are deviant. Again, this conceptualization of the deviance–crime relationship is simplistic. It is true that many forms of deviance can by no means be thought of as crimes. Wearing a Hawaiian shirt to a funeral may cause a commotion, but it is not a violation of Canadian law. There can be no crime, technically, without a law prohibiting an act.

Even where laws prohibit certain actions, however, not all contraventions of legal codes elicit much in the way of negative response. Speeding on the highway, cheating on income taxes, and pirating computer software are all technically illegal. Even so, enormous numbers of Canadians habitually engage in these acts without being penalized either formally or informally. Crime is not always deviant.

Neither is there a hard and fast connection between an act's harmful consequences and its designation as criminal or deviant. Many actions that result in the serious injury and death of large numbers of people are not prohibited by law. Corporate executives routinely decide to market unsafe products to consumers, to place workers in unnecessarily dangerous environments, and to contaminate the biosphere with toxic pollutants. Many countries have no laws whatsoever that forbid such actions (Gomme and Richardson, 1991).

Since the relationship of deviance to crime is not hard and fast, sociologists work with a variety of definitions of criminal conduct (Hagan, 1991). Some restrict their definitions of crime to a violation of the *Criminal Code*. Others extend the definitional boundaries to include the violation of other statutes intended to protect the public. For example, laws outside the *Criminal Code* shield Canadians from the deleterious impacts of the restriction of competition in the marketplace, the operation of unsafe workplaces, and the pollution of the environment. At the other end of the spectrum, a few sociologists and criminologists broaden their definition of crime to include virtually any socially harmful activity. Human rights and human justice, they contend, are socially and not legally defined. From this perspective, corporations laying off workers and thereby increasing

BOX 1.3
JUDGE REFUSES TO BAN SPANKING OF CHILDREN

Spanking does not violate the constitutional rights of children, an Ontario judge has ruled.

But it may be time for Parliament to amend the Criminal Code, which allows using reasonable force when disciplining children, "to provide specific criteria to guide parents, teachers and law enforcement officials," Mr. Justice David McCombs said yesterday.

"The evidence shows that public attitudes toward corporal punishment of children are changing." Judge McCombs, of Ontario Superior Court, wrote in his decision.

Children's-rights advocates had wanted Judge McCombs to repeal the corporal-punishment law, Section 43 of the Criminal Code. The Canadian Foundation for Children, Youth and Law argued the section provides a convenient legal defence for adults who go far beyond spanking to abuse.

The section has been part of the Criminal Code since 1892.

The judge said parents must have a protected sphere in which to raise their children. But he was quick to point out that reasonable force must be used with the best interests of the child at heart.

"In a very real sense, parental liberty interests and the best interests of children are opposite sides of the same coin."

There were some areas both sides agreed upon, Judge McCombs said in his ruling, including that "corporal punishment should never involve a slap or blow to the head," and if corporal punishment causes injury it is considered child abuse.

Their main source of disagreement, according to the judge, was "the limits of acceptable parental and teacher discipline, and in particular, whether mild forms of corporal punishment are acceptable forms of discipline."

The foundation was most disappointed that the judge did not clarify the term "reasonable force," something all parties in the matter had wanted.

"We intend to appeal the decision. It is not what we were seeking," said Cheryl Milne, one of the lawyers for the foundation.

Superior Court is Ontario's second-highest level in criminal cases.

Ms. Milne said it was encouraging the judge said corporal punishment is wrong, but "viewing Section 43 as desirable contradicts that finding," she said.

In Vancouver, parent Kathy Lynn, head of the B.C. branch of the Repeal 43 Committee, said she was dismayed by the Ontario court ruling.

"In Canada today, a dog has greater legal protection from violence than a child does, and that's intolerable," Mrs. Lynn said.

She said the majority of convicted child abuse cases are simply examples of child discipline run amok.

Mrs. Lynn called on the federal government to fund special courses for parents having difficulty with their children.

"The kind of physical violence against children which Section 43 condones is illegal for adults. It is totally unnecessary as a means of discipline, and is counterproductive in raising responsible children."

Roslyn Levine, the lawyer for the federal government, said she was "very pleased" with yesterday's ruling as it "struck the right balance for parents and children."

"We discourage physical discipline, but what we said was don't criminalize that narrow range of behaviour that includes light spanking."

Keeping Section 43 unchanged is of great concern for Dawn Walker, executive director of the Canadian Institute of Child Health, who is firmly against hitting children in any circumstances.

"Children are the only group in society that we are allowed to hit. You can't hit a spouse, but you can hit a child, the most vulnerable in society," she said.

She added many other discipline techniques exist instead of spanking.

She said a common scenario faced by parents involves children who refuse to sit in their car seats. The reaction she advises: Stay put until your child buckles up.

"Alternatives to spanking and slapping are more time-consuming, but hitting breeds hitting," said the mother of six and grandmother of four.

Nadia Poreari-Lavoie, an Ottawa mother of two-year-old Juliana, said when her daughter refuses to sit in her car seat, or throws a tantrum in a busy store, she gives her child "time-outs" or talks to her.

"My main priority is to raise Juliana to be confident with high self-esteem. If I smack her, or spank her, she won't turn out that way," said the part-time bank employee.

An October, 1999, study by the Canadian Centre for Studies of Children at Risk and McMaster University found people who were often or sometimes spanked as youngsters were more likely to develop a psychiatric illness or abuse drugs or alcohol.

Discussion Question

Discuss ways in which issues raised in the court ruling on spanking are relevant to the definition of acts as deviant.

Source: Natalie Southworth, *Globe and Mail*, July 6, 2000, pp. A1 and A8. Reprinted with permission from the *Globe and Mail*.

unemployment and poverty violate human entitlements. Similarly, a government's failure to adequately fund health care — thereby inflicting pain and premature death on its citizens — is socially harmful and therefore criminal.

The main difficulty presented by a definition as broad as the latter one is that it transforms virtually *all* social problems and issues into crime (Schwendinger and Schwendinger, 1975). For our purposes, the intermediary definition of crime is most useful. In this book, "crime" generally means a violation of law, although not necessarily of criminal law. Most of the criminal activities discussed in this book are violations of the *Criminal Code*. Many of the criminal activities discussed in the chapter on business crime, while harmful, are under-regulated or totally uncontrolled. In this area, as in many others, the simple existence of a law is no guarantee that it will be enforced.

VOLUNTARY AND INVOLUNTARY DEVIANCE

People who voluntarily commit a deviant act are more likely to be punished than are people whose deviance is beyond their control (Higgins and Butler, 1982). Involuntary deviance increases the probability of a helping response. Killing one's rival in a love triangle or selling drugs for a living are voluntary acts. Consequently, perpetrators tend to be held fully responsible for these crimes. On the other hand, few consider the mentally ill or the physically disabled to be deviant by choice. Because members of these latter groups are not considered responsible for their deviance, other people's reactions tend to be more sympathetic and treatment oriented.

Falling between the poles that separate punitive from rehabilitative responses are cases such as drug addiction and alcoholism. People hold addicts and alcoholics partially responsible for their deviance because their initial decisions to use drugs or to drink

to excess are matters of choice (Verdun-Jones, 1989). Once initiated, however, these practices can lose the quality of voluntariness when physiological or psychological dependence sets in. In such cases, the importance of therapy (as opposed to pure punishment) increases. When substance use contravenes statutes, it is not unusual for court judgements to require "involuntary treatment." For example, courts often force persons convicted of drunk driving or cocaine possession to enrol in addict rehabilitation programs.

Perhaps the most extreme and controversial cases in which voluntariness figures prominently are those involving people found not guilty of a crime "by reason of insanity." Legal and medical authorities often forcibly "admit" these "patients" into treatment programs. The state deprives the criminally insane of their liberty, and, regardless of the seriousness of their offence, refuses to release them until they are "cured" (Carrithers, 1985; Menzies, 1991). Convincing psychiatrists and judges that one is no longer mentally ill is extremely difficult.

People with physical and psychological defects are not the only ones for whom criminal responsibility is reduced. The nonconformity and illegal conduct of children and youths produce different responses than do identical behaviours on the part of adults. Modern society considers the young as immature, malleable, and subject to worldly if not corrupt influences. When the young err, their parents, other adults, or society at large assume at least part of the responsibility. In cases where convicted adults are likely to face punishment, similarly circumstanced juveniles are more likely to be the objects of rehabilitative programs (West, 1984).

Canadian law considers children under the age of 12 incapable of committing a crime. Older children are held more accountable for their actions by the *Young Offenders Act*, which deals with lawbreaking by Canadian youth from the ages of 12 through 17. Maximum penalties contained in the *Young Offenders*

BOX 1.4
YOUTHS SERVE LONGER SENTENCES THAN ADULTS

Young offenders placed into custody in Canada are more likely to serve longer terms than adults sent to prison for the same crimes, according to a study by Statistics Canada.

This is happening despite the Young Offenders Act saying teenagers should receive shorter sentences than adults for similar offences.

Statistics Canada examined the sentences meted out on nine common offence categories, including robbery, break-and-enter, assault, and possession of stolen property. If convicted, teenagers are less likely than adults to be incarcerated – about half of all young offenders end up on probation.

But of those young people that are incarcerated – more than 25,000 cases in the 1998/1999 fiscal year – their terms are longer than adults in all nine crime categories except robbery.

For example, of all Canadians convicted of minor theft last year, 27% of adults were jailed compared with 15% of youths. But among those two groups, only 38% of adults spent more than one month in custody compared with 58% of young people.

In the case of common assault, 45% of incarcerated adults spent more than a month in custody, compared with 65% of young offenders.

Statistics Canada says one reason for the difference is that parole and other early release provisions are not available to young offenders. Adds Trevor Sanders, a Statistics Canada analyst: "As a whole, adults are still more likely to receive custody than young people."

Among young offenders placed in custody last year, about half were jailed. The other half were sent to an open facility such as a group home.

Only 35% of the young offenders aged 12 to 17 who were convicted last year were placed in some form of custody, compared with 48% who were allowed back into the community and put on probation – a consistent trend since 1992. The remainder were given fines or community service.

Chuck Cadman, a Canadian Alliance MP whose 16-year-old son was killed by a teenager, says he does not object to the fact that so many young offenders are not incarcerated for first time offences.

"I don't have a big problem with probation, except that when young people violate their probation they're usually just given more probation," he says. "Probation can be helpful, but only if it's used in an effective way."

In other findings, the young offender study says the youth crime rate is dropping in Canada. There were 106,665 cases in the country's youth courts in the 1998/1999 fiscal year, a 4% decrease from the previous year and a 7% drop from 1992.

Youth property crime cases have fallen dramatically over the same period, dropping 31% since 1992. However, the rate of violent crime cases has increased by 2% since 1992.

The percentage of female offenders is on the rise. In 1992, females accounted for 16% of all offenders compared with 21% last year. Females are now responsible for 32% of all minor assault crimes committed by young people. In the Northwest Territories, teenage women account for 27% of youth convictions compared with 9% in Quebec.

Discussion Question

To what degree does the information provided in this article support the development and implementation of a more punitive juvenile justice system of the sort articulated in the new *Youth Criminal Justice Act?*

Source: Richard Foot, *National Post*, August 2, 2000, p. A6. Reprinted with permission from the *National Post*.

Act differ markedly from those set out in the *Criminal Code* for adults. While the maximum sentence under the *Young Offenders Act* is generally two years, it can be extended to three years for crimes that would normally entail a maximum of life imprisonment in adult court or for cases that involve multiple offences. Grown-ups convicted of murder may spend the remainder of their lives behind prison walls. Assuming that homicide cases involving young offenders are not transferred to adult court, a conviction for first-degree murder carries a maximum sentence of six years in custody accompanied by four years of conditional supervision. For a second-degree murder, the maximum sentence is a four-year custodial term followed by three years of conditional supervision (Carriere, 2000). However, since youth crime, and youth violent crime in particular, is foremost in the minds of many Canadians and since there is widespread dissatisfaction with the *Young Offenders Act*, the federal government is proposing new legislation. The new *Youth Criminal Justice Act* would increase alternative sanctions for young offenders committing minor offences. It would also expand the number of violent offences automatically transferred to adult court, thereby making such offences subject to more severe penalties (Tremblay, 2000).

DEVIANCE AND SOCIAL CONTEXT

The importance of social context in defining deviance was hinted at in the previous discussion of the tension between the positions of objective positivism and subjective **humanism**. Deviance for a person at a certain time and place can — if person, time, or context changes — become conformity. For example, the statement "I'll fucking well change the channel when I'm good and ready!" scarcely raises an eyebrow among a group of young men lounging around a recreation room in a university residence. Indeed, the use of the word "fuck" signifies different things to different people. For many university students, the frequent and routine use of this descriptor may facilitate their integration into a desired group. The use of similarly colourful and descriptive language in front of one's parents at home is normally much less conducive to reinforcing feelings of belonging. The deviant status of an act depends on the context in which it occurs. The composition of the audience, the traits of actors, and the characteristics of the situation each affect the degree to which people define something as either deviant or conforming. Moreover, whatever is considered deviant or conforming fluctuates over time (Higgins and Butler, 1982).

The audience that differentiates the disreputable from the respectable can be an entire society or, as is more often the case, a segment of a society. Although individuals may define deviance, it is the societal segment and the entire society that are of greatest interest to sociologists. Societies vary in what they treat as deviant. In Ontario, women were not permitted to lounge about bare-breasted on public beaches until recently, and even now, few appear to be taking the opportunity that the 1996 court ruling provides. By contrast, in many European nations, this is accepted practice, and in some African societies, women rarely cover their breasts in public. In much of the world, the moderate consumption of alcohol is common-

place and accepted. In Saudi Arabia, however, drinking alcoholic beverages is prohibited by law and the penalties are quite severe. However, for a few types of behaviour, there is little variation from one society or time period to another. Virtually all societies condemn sexual relations among siblings and between parents and their children. The incest taboo is and has been virtually universal (Middleton, 1962).

Whether the defining audience is a society or a social segment is to a large extent a reflection of the size and complexity of the society. Size and complexity affect the degree of consensus surrounding the reprehensibility of particular behaviours, beliefs, and traits. Within large and heterogeneous societies like Canada, consensus on what is and what is not acceptable frequently varies according to the societal segment or subcultural group to which one belongs. Different subcultures may or may not view as deviant smoking marijuana, polluting a stream, purchasing a sexual service, striking a child, or marrying two women. Intolerance of alcoholism and violence, for example, varies by ethnicity and social class. Alcohol abuse among some ethnic groups is very high, while in others it is virtually unheard of. The Irish, for example, drink heavily and accept public drunkenness (Bales, 1962). Among other ethnic groups, such as Jews or Chinese, cultural norms stringently regulate alcohol consumption and prohibit overindulgence (Glassner and Berg, 1980). Similarly, "discipline" in one subculture is considered "battering" in another.

Different age groups have different conceptions of deviance. Adults have almost always viewed many of young people's customs and behaviours as disturbing. There was considerable turmoil surrounding the popularity of rock and roll in the 1950s and 1960s. Parents and teachers expended a good deal of energy in encouraging softer music, longer skirts, and haircuts. Ironically, the now-respectable "rockers" of this bygone era, some of them sociology professors, cringe at the sight of children of both sexes with green and orange hair, painted faces, and razor blade earrings. To these relics of the sixties, rap music and "spinning" at a rave are simply noise.

Definitions of what is deviant vary not only across societies and subcultures but over time as well. In Canada, narcotics were both widely accepted and legal before the beginning of this century (Comack, 1985). Now, many Canadians are very concerned about heroin and cocaine use and support stiff penalties for their possession. On the other hand, since the

BOX 1.5
TOPLESS OK IN OTTAWA

City council voted yesterday to prohibit women from swimming topless at indoor city pools but to make no rule for outdoor pools and beaches.

Councillor Allan Higdon was behind the motion to stop women from topless swimming indoors. "At least people know now if they really want to go topless they can go to a beach, not an indoor pool," he said.

"Nobody's sunbathing in a pool, so they tend to be used for swimming lessons, all year round with kids. I don't think toplessness is appropriate there. So this deals with that problem."

Councillors call the bylaw a compromise that will allow women to choose where and how they want to swim. They said it is neither an invitation nor a deterrent to women's going topless outdoors.

Last December, in a widely publicized challenge by Gwen Jacob of Guelph, the Ontario Court of Appeal ruled women have the right to go topless in public. Ms Jacob was successful in having her indecency conviction overturned. She had been fined after taking a topless stroll on a hot day in July 1991.

Ottawa city councillors agreed they could prescribe what swimmers wear inside city facilities, but couldn't legally do the same at outdoor parks and pools.

Signs will be posted about the indoor bylaw. They will say: "Women 10 years of age or older must wear tops. Violators will be asked to leave."

Mr. Higdon said the bylaw protects family use of the city's indoor pools. "There's an appropriate time to introduce sexuality to young children," he said.

Discussion Questions

The by-law prohibits women from going topless at indoor pools but not at outdoor pools. In light of this, does Councillor Higdon's admonition that "there's an appropriate time to introduce sexuality to young children" make sense? What course of action do you think is likely if bare-breasted women at indoor pools refuse to cover up and refuse to leave? Given the decision of the Ontario Court of Appeal that women have the right to go topless in public, does the Ottawa by-law abridge that right?

Source: *Globe and Mail*, May 22, 1997, p. A3. Reprinted with permission from Canadian Press.

1960s the use of soft drugs across North America has become more acceptable. Canada and the United States have both reduced penalties for the simple possession of marijuana. Several American states have followed Oregon's lead and legalized the possession of small amounts of marijuana for personal consumption (Inciardi, 1986).

Tolerance of homosexuality in North America increased during the late 1960s and the 1970s. Canada and many American states repealed statutes prohibiting homosexual acts in private between consenting adults. There is some indication, however, that intolerance toward homosexuals is once again growing. One reason for this hostility is the widespread but inaccurate perception that AIDS is a gay disease and that homosexuality is responsible for its spread.

Tobacco smoking is perhaps the most recent example of a behaviour once accepted and encouraged but now labelled deviant. Smokers are being asked to butt out in some cases and forced to butt out in others.

Another aspect of context that affects deviant designations involves the statuses of the actors (Higgins and Butler, 1982). If someone present at a dinner defecates in his or her pants, the determination of this action as deviant is likely to be strongly influenced by the miscreant's age. For toddlers, this sort of impropriety is acceptable; for adult guests it is not.

Sex too affects the definition of deviance. The range of circumstances in which males can publicly shed tears without recrimination is much more restricted than it is for females. As for fistfights, while "boys will be boys," the same violent exchanges among females are more likely to result in a trip to the psychiatrist. Wearing a skirt is an acceptable practice for women, but for men (Scots aside) it is deviance.

The economic and occupational statuses of the actors also influence the degree to which certain behaviours are considered deviant. The Canadian Medical Association admits that there are physicians who misuse alcohol and other drugs to survive the rigours of their work days. When caught, these physicians are

BOX 1.6
LET'S CURB CURSING, AUTHOR PLEADS

First, all swearing is an art.

It is a unique form of expression in which the practitioner is bounded solely by his or her ability to weave off-colour language into a stunning tapestry.

Sadly, however, the medium has been taken over by a paint-by-numbers crowd totally lacking in creativity, nuance and, most annoyingly, discretion.

James O'Connor is out to change that.

The Illinois public relations executive wants to curb the pervasive cursing he says has wiggled its way into every corner of our culture. To this end, he has written a book called *Cuss Control: The Complete Book On How to Curb Your Cursing* (Three Rivers Press).

"I think more people are offended by swearing than we think," O'Connor says. "That's because it is rare for someone to go up to someone else and ask them not to swear. So, as a consequence, people tend to think it is all right. But I don't think swearing is accepted as much as it is tolerated.

"Your choice of words determines whether you are viewed as mature, intelligent, polite and pleasant or rude, crude, insensitive and abrasive."

It might be tempting to dismiss O'Connor as just some crusading blankety-blank. He has done some 400 radio interviews, as well as several television shows, including *The Oprah Winfrey Show*.

But in conversation he comes across as even-keeled, rational and down to earth, with an easy sense of humour.

"I'm not a big preacher," he says. "There is nothing you can do about other people's swearing. You have to be concerned about yourself."

And what of O'Connor?

"I think 'recovering' is a good word to use in regard to me," he says. "I still swear from time to time, but I try to be more discreet about it. Usually no one hears me, but if they do, it doesn't matter. I'm just trying to break the habit.

O'Connor says he was inspired to write *Cuss Control* after making the decision to curb his own cursing.

"I decided I was going to stop swearing, but I found it was a difficult habit to break... I thought there were probably other people out there who wished they didn't swear. And seeing there were no books on the subject, I decided I would be the one to write one."

O'Connor divides swearing into categories: casual and causal.

"I think causal swearing is the more defensible of the two," he says, "because it is usually provoked by an emotion and is very hard to resist.

"Casual swearing is just lazy language. You just do it out of habit without even trying to think of a better word."

O'Connor says one key to breaking the cussing habit is learning to cope with situations – to be more patient, more tolerant. He points to his own driving as an example.

"I think this is the one area in which I have made the most improvement," he says. "Men, in general, tend to take driving personally. You know: 'That guy cut me off.' Well, he didn't cut you off, he cut your car off. Something like that happens to me now, I let it go."

In terms of the generation gap, O'Connor says youths today are more foul-mouthed than ever.

"Kids today are growing up in a cursing culture," O'Connor says. "They hear it among their friends, in the movies, on cable and network television. Many even hear it coming from their parents. It is difficult for them to see anything wrong with it when they hear it everywhere they turn.

I speak at a lot of high schools, and when I ask the kids how many of them swear, 90 to 95 per cent of them raise their hands. When I ask how many of their parents swear, 60 to 70 per cent raise their hands. When I ask about their grandparents, it's about 40 per cent.

If there is a weak point in O'Connor's quest, it rests in his advocacy for substitutions. If, for example, one says "bull-spit," does not a listener still think of the obvious curse?

O'Connor agrees that is probably the case, but adds, "I still think it is better than the actual swear. Instead of saying 'bull,' why not say 'bunkum' or 'balderdash'? It softens the effect significantly."

While having no illusions about totally eliminating cursing, O'Connor believes a significant dent can be made.

"We are almost at the saturation point in regard to swearing, and I think the book is helping to create an awareness... I know a lot of people receive this book anonymously. Someone buys it for them and it makes them think.

"Take ethnic slurs. We've definitely reduced the number you hear now. They've become politically incorrect. So there's hope."

Quick Facts
The progress of profanity

Profanity has gotten progressively worse in the 20th century, says James O'Connor, author of *Cuss Control*. Here are some examples from the *Washington Post*, with polite substitutions in italics:

- In the 1939 film *Gone with the Wind*, Rhett Butler caused a cataclysmic linguistic shift by uttering: "Frankly, my dear, I don't give a damn."

- In the rebel-rousing '60s, Vietnam protesters started shouting at authority figures. But who would have listened had they shouted: "Blazes no, we won't go!"? In 1969, the year of Woodstock, Country Joe led millions of young people in the cheer: "Give me an F, gimme a U... What's that spell?"

- Richard Nixon spent hours blacking out the Watergate transcripts, seemingly more worried about the curse words than the cover-up.

- During a fiery live interview on CBS in 1988, Dan Rather asked U.S. vice-president George Bush about his role in the Iran-Contra arms scandal. After Bush thought the microphone had been turned off, he said: "The *child of an unmarried mother* didn't lay a glove on me."

- World leaders apparently cuss out people a lot. In 1991, prime minister Brian Mulroney allegedly called a critic a *friggin' child of an unwed mother* – out loud on the floor of the House of Commons. He later denied the comment. Almost 21 years earlier, prime minister Pierre Trudeau muttered to the Opposition: "*Go away.*" He insisted he had said: "fuddle duddle."

Discussion Questions

How is swearing a cultural phenomenon? How does its reprehensibility vary historically and contextually?

Source: Jim Shea, *The Toronto Star*, June 24, 2000, p. M4. Copyright © Jim Shea, *The Hartford Courant*. Reprinted with permission.

---

treated with greater sympathy than skid-row drunks and street junkies. There is a tendency to see the former as the victims of stress and worthy of rehabilitation, while viewing the latter as worthless "bums" deserving incarceration. Where the poor and the unemployed tend to receive fines or serve time for their addictions, the affluent and the employed are more likely to receive psychological counselling and medical care.

Many forms of deviance involve interactions among the actors. The ties connecting performers in social interactions can influence the extent to which audiences conceive of an interchange as deviant. When a man strikes a child, the status of the victim may modify onlookers' definitions of the situation. It is one thing for parents to "discipline" their misbehaving children, but quite another matter for them to strike the child of another. Similarly, when a man sexually attacks a woman, public reaction may depend upon whether or not she is his wife. Indeed, until recently, Canadian law considered husbands incapable of raping their own wives; by legal definition, women could be raped only by men to whom they were not married.

The settings in which we behave, in which we express our ideas, and in which we display certain attributes can also shape conceptions of deviance. If someone unexpectedly walks into a friend's home and discovers the friend walking around nude in the bedroom, it is unlikely that the visitor would consider the homeowner a deviant. But, if a student inadvertently opened the door to her sociology professor's office and found her sitting stark naked at her desk marking papers, she might think twice about hanging around to discuss Marx, Durkheim, and Weber. Setting is important.

In most cases, if one man were to beat another with his fists, the action would be considered an assault. If the victim were to bleed profusely, the assault might be upgraded to "aggravated." Were the assailant to use a stick, the action could be construed as assault with a deadly weapon. If the clubbing took place in front of thousands of witnesses and someone recorded the incident on videotape, our initial reaction might be to consider this circumstance a police officer's dream and a cakewalk conviction for even the most inept Crown prosecutor. Nonetheless, if the thousands of witnesses were cheering hockey fans and

BOX 1.7
HAVING HIS CAKE AND EATING IT TOO

The greatest of last month's Great Literary Dinners organized by the Writers' Development Trust was undoubtedly the party hosted by food writer Cynthia Wine. As guest of honor at the $200-a-plate repast, the irrepressible Farley Mowat shocked and delighted the guests by climbing onto the dinner table and burying his face in a chocolate cake intended for dessert. Mowat insists that he could not resist. "Bob Rae was sitting on one side of me," he said, "and I was really trying to be serious." Mowat also insists that he was sober. "I just got infatuated with a chocolate cake," he said, "so I climbed onto the table and, without disturbing so much as a salt cellar, I pounced. It was the most profound culinary delight I have ever laid a lip on." Said Wine:"If such a thing is possible, he crawled across the table like a gentleman. We loved it."

Discussion Questions

How might the audience's reactions have differed if this incident had involved someone of a different status than the irrepressible Mowat? What might the public's response have been if Bob Rae, Premier of Ontario, had embarked upon a similar course of action? Would Premier Rae have been considered more deviant than Farley Mowat? Why or why not?

Source: *Maclean's*, January 14, 1991, p. 8. Reprinted with permission of *Maclean's*.

if the location of the assault were the ice in Maple Leaf Gardens, we might wisely revise our prediction of an easy conviction. Over the years, such incidents have occurred many times in NHL buildings. In only a few instances have stick-swingers been charged, let alone convicted. A recent exception to this trend was Marty McSorley's conviction for assault with a weapon. On October 6, 2000, he was found guilty in a British Columbia courtroom for administering a blow to the head that injured a Vancouver Canucks player.

Most Canadians believe that taking the life of another human being is the gravest human action. Few would dispute, on first thought, that this form of behaviour is almost universally prohibited. Killings are severely sanctioned as a matter of routine, with culprits suffering either life imprisonment in Canada or, in 38 American states, death. Canadians do not view all who kill in the same light, however. The child who inadvertently runs in front of a car and is killed by a sober driver dies by accident. If someone attacks another person with a knife and is killed by the intended victim, many Canadians would consider the killing self-defence and judge the homicide justifiable. Indeed, some who served in the Persian Gulf war in 1991 and killed a great many Iraqis have been hailed as conquering heroes.

The definition of actions, beliefs, and attributes as deviant is a complex matter. Consideration must be given not only to the nature of the act, the idea, or the personal trait but also to the composition of the audience, the characteristics of the actors and their connections with one another, and the quality of the circumstance and setting.

While many of the acts of deviance and crime discussed in this book are committed by individuals and are governed by the *Criminal Code* of Canada, many are not. Many of the harmful acts examined in later chapters are perpetrated either by criminal organizations or by law-abiding businesses and fall outside the purview of the *Criminal Code*. Moreover, for some maleficent deeds, certain features of the Code make it an ineffective means of social control.

The discussions of formal social control in subsequent chapters require an introduction to the fundamentals of criminal law. The following sections outline the basic elements of criminal law and examine the principal defences available to persons accused of committing crimes.

CRIMINAL LAW IN CANADA

The *Criminal Code* of Canada defines crime as the intentional violation of criminal law without defence or excuse. Criminal law is a set of rules legislated by the state in the name of society and enforced by the state through the threat or application of punishment. It has four important characteristics: **polit-**

BOX 1.8
NHL GOONS ON SKATES

It's good that Thursday night's brawl between the Toronto Maple Leafs and the Chicago Blackhawks broke out late in the hockey game: fewer kids probably saw it on TV.

Hawk defenceman Steve Smith's bloodied and pulpy face and the pile of writhing bodies on the ice were, of course, nothing new for the National Hockey League.

But the sight of Hawk Stu Grimson, a thug on skates if ever there was one, running amok — with the home crowd roaring approval — was unforgettable.

As the fight subsided on the ice, Grimson, glassy-eyed and stripped down to his sweat-soaked under-shirt, simply came unglued.

Suddenly, his own coach, Mike Keenan, couldn't hold him back at the bench.

Breaking from Keenan's grasp, Grimson first tracked down, then grabbed one of the linesmen by the head as if hoping to dash his brains out against the glass.

When Grimson finally went to the showers, there was a telling moment when teammate Ed Belfour gave him a congratulatory send-off tap on the rear with his goalstick.

It was disgusting.

And someone could have been seriously hurt.

A night of half-decent hockey — a couple of pretty goals by the Hawks, classic goaltending by the Leafs' Grant Fuhr in a losing cause — ruined by 40 minutes of mayhem.

Starting with this episode of goonery, the NHL must clamp down on the violence that gives hockey a bad name.

Sitting in the comfort of their living rooms, Don Cherry-types may covet this kind of rock-'em, sock-'em stuff on skates.

But if it ever happened in a bar or a back alley somewhere, there'd be criminal charges — and maybe even a trip to the cooler.

Discussion Questions

Explain why violent actions such as those alluded to in this editorial are neither considered nor treated as crimes. Why do law-abiding fans condone such behaviour? Why does it go unchecked? What outcomes would you predict for the game of hockey if such actions were prosecuted in court? What outcomes would you predict if similar acts of violence in back alleys and bars were responded to in a similar fashion?

Source: *The Toronto Star* editorial, January 18, 1992, p. D2.

icality, specificity, uniformity, and penal sanctions (Vaz and Lodhi, 1979).

POLITICALITY

Because it is legislated by the state, the creation of criminal law is fundamentally a political process. In Canada, the federal Parliament enacts statutes that prohibit a variety of violent and property crimes such as murder, sexual assault, arson, and fraud. Judges appointed by Parliament and provincial legislatures frequently modify criminal statutes through **case law**. Case law sets legal precedent through court decisions and, in so doing, clarifies rules that are insufficiently precise or are not fully codified (Parker, 1987a).

Some criminal laws enjoy high levels of consensus. They concern offences known as *mala in se* or "bad in themselves," such as murder, rape, robbery, and theft. Almost all Canadians believe that these crimes are serious wrongs. Surrounding some criminal laws, however, there is much less consensus. Criminologists refer to these nonconsensus crimes as *mala prohibita* offences, meaning that they are illegal simply because the law says they are. The best examples of *mala prohibita* crimes are "morality offences," such as pornography, prostitution, drug use, and public drunkenness.

The large number of *mala prohibita* offences enumerated in the *Criminal Code* raises the spectre of overcriminalization. Criminalizing activities that much of society sees as legitimate runs the risk of undermining respect for the criminal law. Criminologists cite a host of problems stemming from attempts to legislate and regulate public morals. Laws about which there is a low degree of consensus, because they are not respected, are much more difficult to enforce.

Their existence paves the way for discriminatory enforcement, for the corruption of the police and the courts, and for the draining of resources away from the regulation of more serious misconduct (Hagan, 1986).

A critical issue in the sociology of law is the extent to which laws truly represent the best interests of the majority of the population (Cotterrill, 1984). The consensus approach envisages law as effectively mediating between the vested and competing interests of society's rival factions. This perspective conceives of the elected government of the state as autonomous. The state enacts legislation with the aim of striking a balance among competing interest groups in order to preserve the well-being of the greatest number of its citizens. The law, in short, protects the common good.

The conflict approach to the role of law in society holds that the law disproportionately reflects the best interests, not of the majority of citizens, but of a minority of affluent and powerful people who form the economic elite. Viewed from this perspective, the state is not entirely autonomous. Elected governments must rely on the goodwill of powerful economic elites in order to stay in power. The conflict perspective maintains that the state must cater to these elites and ensure that their positions of advantage are preserved. When push comes to shove, the laws created by the government and the laws enforced by the state serve the interests of the powerful.

In sum, the debate between the consensus and conflict approaches revolves around the question of who benefits from the existence and enforcement of a law. Is the beneficiary society at large or only its more privileged segments?

SPECIFICITY

Canadian criminal law has two major objectives: crime control and the preservation of **due process**. The crime-control function of law involves ensuring the safety of citizens' lives and the security of their property. In the pursuit of these goals, **substantive law** specifies both what constitutes a crime and what its punishment will be. Criminal law also sets out rules of due process. Through procedural law, it protects the rights of the accused. Among other things, procedural criminal law specifies the kinds of proof required for conviction, the legality of searches and seizures, and the rights of accused persons to counsel and bail.

From the standpoint of substantive law, **specificity** is key, as the exact nature of prohibited acts must be clearly specified. While in legal terms there can be no

crime without law, laws appear and disappear over time. This means that certain acts can be unlawful at some times and perfectly legal at others. While spirits could be consumed legally in Prince Edward Island in 1906, it became illegal to do so the following year. In Alberta and Ontario in 1915 drinking was lawful, but it became a crime in both provinces in 1916. With the repeal of Prohibition, the consumption of alcohol once again became lawful in Ontario in 1923 and in Alberta in 1924. Prince Edward Island, however, remained "dry" until 1948 (Smart and Ogborne, 1986).

Not only does criminal law specify what acts are and are not criminal, it also specifies the nature of punishment for a particular act. In all cases, criminal law clearly states maximum penalties, and for some offences it also states minimum penalties. Someone convicted of sexual assault with a weapon can receive as much as fourteen years' imprisonment. Someone found guilty of a second offence of impaired driving can receive no less than fourteen days behind bars (Sauvé, 1999). These legal specifications limit the discretion of courts. Judges cannot imprison someone for twenty years upon a first conviction for marijuana possession, nor can they institute a fine and probation for someone pleading guilty to first-degree murder.

There is considerable tension between the objectives of crime control and due process. Controlling crime at all costs is made easier by limiting the rights of accused persons. In such cases, the likelihood of mistakenly punishing at least some innocent people increases. Conversely, going to great lengths to enshrine defendants' rights to freedom from unwarranted intrusion by the law makes it more difficult to control crime. In these circumstances, the scales of justice are tipped toward freeing some who are guilty. Striking an acceptable balance is not always easy. Compared with the criminal justice systems of the United States, Canada has leaned more toward crime control than toward ensuring due process (Brannigan, 1984).

UNIFORMITY

Uniformly administering the law requires that the police, the courts, and the corrections system apply it equally to all citizens. **Extralegal characteristics** such as the sex, ethnicity, or social class of a suspect, an accused, or a convicted felon are not supposed to influence the application of criminal law. Uniformity requires that decisions by criminal-justice personnel be made solely on the basis of legal factors such as the nature of the crime, its seriousness, and the perpetrator's prior record. The extent to which legal and extralegal factors affect the application of criminal law is a matter of some dispute among criminologists.

PENAL SANCTIONS

The application of the penal sanctions meted out by the courts to those found guilty of an offence is the responsibility of the Canadian corrections system. Imbedded in Canadian criminal law is the notion that the severity of the punishment should reflect the seriousness of the crime.

Although there is a growing movement in Canadian criminal justice toward various forms of victim compensation, Canadian criminal law places little emphasis on restitution. For the most part, restitution falls within the domain of civil law. When drunk drivers kill, they commit a criminal offence and are punished under criminal law. Nonetheless, the families of victims may seek monetary compensation from offenders through suits in Canada's civil courts.

THE ELEMENTS OF CRIMINAL LAW

For Crown prosecutors to establish criminal liability under criminal law, they must prove three fundamental conditions: **actus reus**, **mens rea**, and the concurrence in time of *actus reus* and *mens rea*. *Actus reus* signifies the requirement of an act. Criminal law normally forbids doing, not being or thinking. One can *be* an addict. One can identify oneself as a prostitute. Only the *acts* of drug possession and "communication for the purposes of prostitution" are crimes. Similarly, one can contemplate a theft or sexual assault, but only when the plan is put into action does a crime occur.

Criminal acts are of two basic types: commission or omission. Commission implies doing something prohibited, such as assaulting or breaking and entering. Alternatively, omission signifies failing to do something required by law, such as filing one's income tax or caring for someone to whom one has a legal obligation. People are responsible, for example, for their own children and spouses (Verdun-Jones, 1989). Under Canadian law, the needs of children and adults to whom one is not legally attached can often be ignored without liability.

Mens rea translates as "the guilty mind." Criminal law requires that, to be convicted of a crime, one must be capable of forming intent, and capable of knowing that an action is illegal. *Mens rea* operates on the assumption that people behave on the basis of their own free will. In other words, the law considers people able to govern their own actions through unencumbered choice and therefore holds them responsible for their deeds.

Intent means purposefully and knowingly wanting to act and accurately foreseeing the act's immediate consequences. For example, intentionally pointing a loaded gun at a person's head and pulling the trigger will almost certainly cause his or her death.

Situations in which the law holds accountable people who lack intent include negligence and recklessness. In cases involving negligence or recklessness, the law considers the accused to have disregarded consequences that should have been foreseen by any "**reasonable man**" or "reasonable person." Where the possibility of plausible foresight is less clear-cut, the crime is carelessness. Where the courts deem foresight entirely reasonable and consider the risks completely without justification, the illegal act is recklessness. Where a person is injured or dies as a result of someone racing a car down a crowded street or sighting in a rifle behind a school yard, the criminal charge would likely be recklessness.

There are a few instances in which prosecutors need not establish intent to prove that someone committed a crime. In such cases, proof of an act alone is sufficient to establish guilt through "**absolute liability**" (Parker, 1987b). In some jurisdictions, for example, having sex with a minor is a crime even if the accused honestly believed that the "victim" was an adult (there was no intent).

People's blameworthiness and subsequently the severity of their punishments increase with malice aforethought. For accidents, there is no malice aforethought and no punishment. The courts punish carelessness and recklessness less severely than they do crimes with clear intent because blameworthiness and malice aforethought are lesser in degree. Of intentional crimes, the criminal justice system sanctions those occurring with little premeditation, in the heat of the moment (such as homicide in a fit of jealous rage) less severely than those that are rationally premeditated (such as hiring a paid killer to murder on one's behalf).

Criminal law draws an important distinction between **intent** and **motive**. Intent involves the anticipated direct outcome of an act, in the specific and immediate sense. Motive, on the other hand, is the underlying rationale for committing a crime. In shooting his wife twice in the head, the husband's intent is to end her life. Suppose that she were terminally ill and suffering great pain. Motivated by his love and by the agony of seeing her suffering prolonged endlessly, he pulls the trigger — twice. His motive may be kindness and mercy, but his intent is to kill. Putting money belonging to another into your pocket and running away betrays an intent to steal. The thief's motive might vary from getting rich quick to staving off the starvation of his or her children. In court, motive is normally only corroborative. While motive may affect sentencing, a conviction hinges on the proof of an act, of intent, and of the coincidence of the two.

CRIMINAL DEFENCES

Many standard defence tactics are available to accused persons (Parker, 1987b; Inciardi, 1987), including mistake of law, mistake of fact, justification, necessity, consent, **duress**, provocation, intoxication, automatism, insanity, and entrapment. While most cases are defended on these grounds, defence lawyers occasionally initiate more unique and celebrated tactics.

The "**mistake of law**" defence, in which those charged argue that they did not know that their action was against the law, is almost never effective. Canadian courts subscribe to the old adage that ignorance of the law is no excuse. Everyone, resident and alien alike, is presumed to know the laws of the land, even though federal, provincial, and municipal laws number in the thousands.

If suspected criminals try to establish innocence on the basis of "**mistake of fact**," they must prove that their crimes occurred as a consequence of honest errors. The accused must convince the court that when he took the victim's umbrella, for example, he truly believed it to be his own. The use of violence to defend oneself or others from physical attack is a common example of the "justification" defence. Justification is valid when someone perpetrates an act that, without its representing a pressing imperative, would otherwise be a crime.

Another defence available for acts that otherwise would be crimes were they not necessary to ensure the well-being of the accused is "necessity." Some people have successfully invoked the necessity defence by arguing that they used marijuana only as a painkiller, broke jail only to preserve their own safety, or engaged in cannibalism only to avoid starvation.

The "consent of the victim" defence requires the suspect to convince the court that the victim freely and willingly acquiesced to a request or demand. In cases of car theft or sexual assault, for example, absolution depends on persuading the judge or jury that authorization to take the car was given voluntarily by the owner or that permission to have sexual intercourse was granted without protest. Persons giving consent must be legally capable of doing so, which means that they cannot be insane, retarded, or under age.

The crime must also be "consentable." Murder, for example, is not a crime for which consent can be used as a defence. The fact that a terminally ill husband gives his wife permission to end his life is not an acceptable defence for homicide. Furthermore, consent cannot be obtained by fraud. Mechanics who misrepresent to car owners the state of their transmissions and subsequently perform unnecessary and expensive repair work cannot use as a defence the fact that their customers willingly signed contracts to have the jobs done. Finally, the person giving consent must have the authority to do so. One person cannot give consent to sell property that belongs to another.

To use the "duress" defence, accused persons must prove that they were coerced by someone else into committing the crime. Their costs for refusing to execute the illegal act must be immediate (not several days hence) and must involve the threat of personal rather than property victimization. The classic example is that of the bank president whose wife is kidnapped in the morning by thieves who threaten to murder her in the early afternoon if the manager refuses to steal on their behalf.

Both "provocation" and "intoxication" are partial defences. While they do not absolve the accused from responsibility for the offence, they do reduce accountability. A man who returns home to find his wife in bed with another man might argue that, in killing his wife, he was provoked beyond the tolerance of a reasonable person. A convincing defence to murder would hinge on persuading a jury that the killing took place in the heat of passion. Success would result not in an acquittal but in a conviction for the lesser charge of manslaughter. Intoxication also reduces responsibility because it diminishes the capacity of an accused to form intent. In a controversial decision in 1995, the Supreme Court permitted a defence of extreme drunkenness in a sexual assault case. Parliament responded shortly thereafter, however, with a law prohibiting its use. Another defence, "**automatism**," applies where accused persons commit criminal acts without free will because they are acting as automatons. Crimes involuntarily carried out while sleepwalking, as a consequence of epilepsy, or as a result of some other physical condition qualify for this rare but by no means unheard-of defence (Parker, 1987a; Verdun-Jones, 1989).

Defendants can use the "insanity defence" if they can show that they were in a "state of natural imbecility" or suffered from a "disease of the mind" at the time of the crime. Accused persons would also have to convince the court that one of these conditions left them incapable of appreciating "the nature and quality" of their act or omission or of knowing that their act or omission was wrong. The insanity defence is fraught with ambiguities such as the definitions of natural imbecility and disease of the mind.

Pleading insanity has not been a common defence strategy, although, at least for murder, it appears to be becoming more frequent. Part of the reason for this change involves the very lengthy sentences now meted out for homicide. Convincing the psychiatric community and the courts that sanity has been regained has historically been a very time-consuming activity. During the 1980s, however, sentences of life imprisonment for murder have made the risk of long-term confinement in a hospital for the criminally insane less of a deterrent to the use of the insanity defence (Menzies, 1991).

The "**entrapment**" defence hinges on the ability of accused persons to convince the court that they were induced by law-enforcement agents to commit a crime that they would not otherwise have contemplated. This defence occurs most frequently in cases of "**victimless crime**," such as drug dealing and prostitution, in which the "victim" is a willing purchaser of the prohibited good (drugs) or service (sex). Since willing victims rarely complain to the authorities, police must engage in "proactive" crime control efforts. When undercover police approach pushers and prostitutes, they run the risk of being overly enticing in their bids to trap their unsuspecting prey.

SUMMARY

Deviance is a behaviour, an idea, or a trait that elicits negative responses. Most of this book emphasizes the behavioural dimension. Negative reactions that define something as deviant may be both internal and external, both informal and formal. In many cases, negative reactions both define something as deviant and simultaneously serve as mechanisms of social control designed to suppress, eliminate, or drive underground an act, idea, or personal characteristic.

A number of complexities must be explored when developing a conceptualization of what is and what is not deviant. First, there is the tension between objective positivist and subjective humanist definitions. Objectivists see deviance as the violation of pre-existing and given social norms. Subjectivists emphasize that norms are socially constructed, and they view deviance as a quality conferred by some upon others. Those conferring deviant status usually differ from those upon whom deviant status is being conferred on the basis of social power. Deviance, humanists argue, is in the eye of the beholder.

Deviance should not be confused with actions that are statistically rare. What is deviant is determined not by infrequency but by the negativity of the response. Furthermore, deviance and crime are not related in a straightforward way. The popular conception of crime as deviance serious enough to be prohibited by law is faulty. Although it is true that much deviance is noncriminal, some crime is not deviant. It is also true that some noncriminal deviance is much more harmful to society than are many acts prohibited by the *Criminal Code*. Indeed, some noncriminal deviance is far more damaging to society than are the most serious *Criminal Code* offences.

Some deviance is voluntary and some is not. When people are voluntarily deviant, their decisions to violate rules are frequently punished. When deviance is less a matter of choice and more beyond the control of the offending individual, the response is likely to be more treatment-oriented. Nonetheless, treatment may be, and frequently is, coercive.

What gets defined as deviant is not inherent in the conduct, the belief, or the trait. Rather, the degree to which something is defined as deviant varies according to context. Within a particular context, deviant designations are also affected by the nature and composition of audiences, the characteristics of the actors (perpetrators and victims), and social context.

To set the scene for the discussions of social control contained in the following substantive chapters, several important features of criminal law have been examined (politicality, specificity, uniformity, and the requirement of sanction). Also discussed were the fundamental elements of criminal law (*actus reus* and *mens rea*) and the major criminal defences (mistake of law, mistake of fact, justification, necessity, consent, duress, provocation, intoxication, automatism, insanity, and entrapment).

Deviance is pervasive in Canadian society, both in terms of the range of phenomena represented and in terms of where these phenomena occur. Sex, violence, addiction, deception, theft, deformity, disease, Satanism, and many other behaviours, beliefs, and conditions elicit negative reactions from at least some Canadians. Deviance is not confined to the "dark side," to the seamy downtown vice districts of large cities, or to the "other side of the tracks." It exists in our homes and schools, where we work, and where we play.

DISCUSSION QUESTIONS

1. Discuss the essential components of a definition of deviance.

2. Explain how deviance and crime are conceptually related to one another.

3. Illustrate the difference between voluntary and involuntary deviance. How might the public and the authorities (police, psychiatrists, social workers, etc.) respond differently to involuntary and voluntary deviant behaviour?

4. Discuss the impact of social context on the designation of behaviours, ideas, or traits as deviant.

5. Under which circumstances could acts, ideas, or traits that are generally highly valued in society be defined as deviant?

WEB LINKS

Online Dictionary of the Social Sciences
http://bitbucket.icaap.org/cgi-bin/glossary/SocialDict?
> This on-line dictionary, prepared by Robert Drislane and Gary Parkinson and hosted by Athabasca University, has approximately one thousand entries related to sociology, criminology, political science, and women's studies. Many of the concepts discussed in this chapter are covered.

Deviance: Online Demo Course
http://dl.miramichi.nbcc.nb.ca/courses/demo/default.html
> This on-line demo course provides an interactive, engaging introduction to the concept and study of deviance. It was developed by the Distributed Learning Centre in New Brunswick. Click on "Begin the Course" and then use the navigation menu at the top to complete units and lessons.

Criminal Code of Canada
http://canada.justice.gc.ca/en/C-46/
> Full text of the *Criminal Code* of Canada.

First Line Criminal Law Information
http://firstlinelaw.com/indexfl.html
> This site, maintained by the Bastion Law Corporation, provides an overview of the Canadian criminal law system. It covers issues such as arrest and charge, bail, pleas, the trial, sentencing, and appeals.

The Great Young Offenders Act Debate
http://www.lawyers.ca/tgyad/
> This site, run by Stephen R. Biss, features extensive resources related to legislation dealing with young offenders.

RECOMMENDED READINGS

Adler, P.A., and P. Adler. (1997). *Constructions of Deviance: Social Power, Context, and Interaction.* Belmont, CA: Wadsworth.
> Sets out a variety of issues concerning the way in which power and context affect the definition of behaviours as deviant or conforming.

Ferrell, J. and N. Websdale. (1999). *Making Trouble: Cultural Constructions of Crime, Deviance and Control*. Hawthorne, NY: Aldine de Gruyter.
> A collection of articles examining the importance of image, meaning, and representation to both official and public understandings of deviance, crime, and social control. Emphasizes the emerging perspective of "cultural criminology" and its relativistic approach.

Lemert, E.M. (1997) *The Trouble with Evil: Social Control at the Edge of Morality*. Albany, NY: SUNY Press.
> Focuses on cross-cultural studies of activities described as evil. Examines the extent to which the study of evil clarifies sociological concerns about deviance and social control.

Pfohl, S. (1985). *Images of Deviance and Social Control: A Social History*. New York: McGraw Hill.
> Examines the transformation of images of deviance and social control as they are affected by historical factors.

Sasson, T. (1995). *Crime Talk: How Citizens Construct a Social Problem*. New York: Aldine de Gruyter.
> Explores the social construction of the crime problem around people's ideas concerning issues of law and order. Examines the complexity of "crime talk," emphasizing its ambivalent and contradictory nature.

Verdun-Jones, S. (2001). *Criminal Law in Canada* (3rd ed.). Toronto: Harcourt Canada.
> Provides a comprehensive and very readable introduction to Canadian criminal law.

PART TWO

THEORIES OF DEVIANCE AND CRIME

CHAPTER 2

AN OVERVIEW OF SOCIAL THEORY

The aims of this chapter are to familiarize the reader with:

- three components of sociological theory: explanation, empirical testing, and policy
- differences between sociological theory and both biological and psychological theories: levels of analysis, norm violation, and social definition
- differences among structural, process, and integrated theoretical explanations
- basic assumptions underlying sociological theories: human nature, social order, and the link between individual and society
- the historical development of theories of deviance and crime: demonology, classical theory, neoclassical theory, early ecological perspectives, and positivism
- the contributions and deficiencies of early ecological and positivist approaches

INTRODUCTION

Three interrelated components make up social science theories generally and sociological theories of deviance specifically. These fundamental components, as shown in Figure 2.1, are an explanatory framework, a strategy for assessing whether the observed facts fit the proposed explanation, and a body of recommendations or policies mapping out effective courses of action to respond to the types of deviance being explained (Liska, 1987). In setting out an explanatory framework, theories invariably nominate underlying mechanisms that do one of two things: precipitate the violation of social norms or instigate the designation

of certain behaviours as deviant or criminal. These underpinning principles may be stated explicitly or implicitly in the theory, and they may involve relative combinations of precipitating factors such as family disintegration (Nye, 1958), substandard educational and occupational performance (Polk and Schafer, 1972; Gomme, 1986b), undesirable companions (Warr and Stafford, 1991), poverty (Watts and Watts, 1981), unemployment (Parker and Horwitz, 1986), the reactions of meaningful others (Glassner, 1982), the uneven distribution of power in society, or the inequitable creation and application of criminal law (Chambliss and Seidman, 1982).

Once theorists have specified the key precipitating mechanisms, their theories describe the ways in which these structures either produce deviant behaviour or bring about the definition of certain phenomena as deviant. For example, a theory might explain a teenager's delinquent behaviour as a function of the expectations and pressures emanating from his or her involvement in peer groups disproportionately composed of delinquent youth (Empey, 1982). It might account for the relationship between the leanings of one's companions and one's own rule-breaking as follows: Associating with youth who violate norms provides opportunities to learn necessary skills and rationalizations for delinquent acts. The novice thief, for example, learns from his or her more experienced associates how to work in teams to shoplift CD's from music stores. The rationalizations justifying this behaviour include the challenge of the undertaking, the exorbitant prices of the items stolen, and the enormous wealth of record shops.

FIGURE 2.1

PRINCIPAL COMPONENTS OF SOCIAL SCIENTIFIC THEORIES OF DEVIANCE

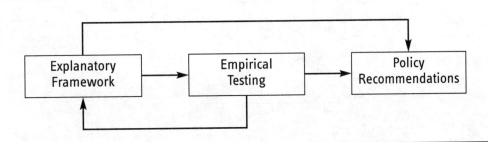

The social scientist might test this "bad companions" or reference group theory by examining the friendship patterns of delinquents and nondelinquents. If it were found that delinquents usually associate with friends who are also delinquent while nondelinquent youth affiliate primarily with law-abiding friends, then the facts support the theory.

Social control policies grounded in this reference group perspective would likely involve reducing delinquents' associations with one another while promoting their fraternization with nondelinquent peers. The reference group perspective might recommend that young people convicted of minor offences (e.g., shoplifting and soft drug possession) be diverted out of institutions where association with more hardened teenage criminals is inevitable and where the tricks of criminal trades are learned. It would advocate placing juvenile lawbreakers in more conventional settings such as foster homes and halfway houses, because exposure to hardened criminals would be limited in such settings and developing ties to law-abiding youth would be more feasible (West, 1984).

Before the major sociological theories of deviance, crime, and social control are examined, some fundamentals of social science theory should be introduced. A closer look at the development of theories of deviance, their empirical assessment, and their policy relevance will be followed by an examination of pre–twentieth century theories of nonconformity and lawbreaking.

THEORY AS EXPLANATION

The examination of **theory** as **explanation** focuses on three central points: the differences between sociology and other approaches to the explanation of deviance, the tension between sociological theories emphasizing structure and those that emphasize process, and the importance of several basic assumptions that provide the foundations of sociological theories of deviance (Liska, 1987).

BIOLOGICAL, PSYCHOLOGICAL, AND SOCIOLOGICAL THEORIES

Biology and psychology offer explanations of deviance that differ from sociological perspectives in two important ways. First, both biological and psychological interpretations concentrate on the nonconforming and illegal conduct of individuals. Sociological explanations, alternatively, concentrate on deviance at both the individual level and the group and aggregate levels. Second, biological and psychological explanations view deviance exclusively as the violation of established social norms. (See Table 2.1.) Sociological explanations, by contrast, encompass both objective norm violation and subjective social definition in their conceptualizations of nonconformity. Some sociological theories, unlike biological and psychological theories, explain deviance as a process of active designation in which the more powerful can actively define the less powerful as deviants (Liska, 1987).

To show how the biological and psychological approaches focus on the individual, consider the case of Clifford Olson, who sexually assaulted, murdered, and mutilated at least eleven children and teenagers in the lower mainland of British Columbia in the early 1980s. Biological explanations of the factors motivating a serial killer like Olson focus on incriminating physiological traits, such as chromosomal

TABLE 2.1

DISCIPLINARY APPROACHES TO THE ANALYSIS OF DEVIANCE AND CRIME

		Discipline		
		Biology	Psychology	Sociology
unit of analysis	individual (micro level)	yes	yes	yes
	group (meso level)	no	no	yes
	aggregate (macro level)	no	no	yes
definition of deviance	violation of norms	yes	yes	yes
	social definition	no	no	yes

defects, brain disorders, biochemical imbalances, and nerve damage (Hippchen, 1978). Psychological interpretations focus on personality deficiency, psychopathology, or psychosis (Leyton, 1986). Psychologists usually locate the origins of these maladies in the deviant's background, citing as **causes** such factors as maternal deprivation during childhood, Freudian conditions like penis envy and the **Oedipal complex**, and variations in behavioural conditioning. They believe that conditions like these are the foundations of personality disorders, some of which manifest themselves in deviant and criminal conduct (Laufer and Day, 1983).

Sociologists refer to the individual, group, and aggregate **levels of analysis** as "micro," "meso," and "macro," respectively (Brantingham and Brantingham, 1984). These three levels are a continuum, along which human behaviour varies both in breadth and in detail. **Micro-level analysis** can be thought of as a close-up shot revealing the minute traits of individuals, while **macro-level analysis** can be thought of as a distant, wide-angle panoramic shot encompassing the general characteristics of entire populations. Macro perspectives sacrifice intricate detail for a composite vision of broader social patterns. **Meso-level analysis** falls in between.

Micro sociological theories examine social learning and social interaction by focusing on the processes through which individuals learn to deviate and to develop deviant self-concepts. Mastering the skills of a prostitute (Bryan, 1965), finding out how to enjoy the sensations produced by drugs (Becker, 1963), and learning to be proud of one's homosexuality (Troiden, 1979) are examples of processes investigated through micro-level analyses.

Meso sociological theories provide explanations of behaviour at the intermediary level and concentrate upon the subcultural group as the **unit of analysis**. Groups are relatively small collectivities of individuals who communicate and interact with one another in the pursuit of common goals and ways of living. The reasons why groups engage in deviant and criminal activity and the ways in which they are organized in these pursuits are the focuses of meso-level investigations. Deviant groups such as delinquent gangs (Maxson, Gordon, and Klein, 1985), outlaw motorcycle clubs (Thompson, 1972; Wolf, 1991), and organized crime families (Ianni, 1972) are the targets of meso-level approaches.

Macro sociological theories do not focus on the performance of individuals or the collective behaviour or social organization of groups, but on the distribution of actions and attitudes across aggregates. In comparison with groups, aggregates are very large collectivities of individuals who share one or more common characteristics but who, because of the large numbers of people involved, may not interact, communicate, or work together to pursue common goals.

They may share attributes such as gender, age, socioeconomic status, ethnicity, and regional affiliation. Women, teenagers, the poor, Canada's Native people, and Cape Bretoners are examples of aggregates.

Macro-level analysis concentrates on explaining large-scale social (age, sex, income, ethnicity), temporal (rates over time), and geographical (national, provincial, municipal) patterns in the distribution of deviance and crime, either within a single society or across different societies. The following questions are typical of those addressed in macro-level theorizing. Why are more males than females involved in virtually all types of deviant behaviour, with the possible exceptions of shoplifting and prostitution (Hendrick, 1996)? Why are elderly people more fearful of crime but less frequently directly victimized than younger people (Gomme, 1986a)? How and why does the criminal conduct of the poor differ from the criminal conduct of the rich (Clinard and Yeager, 1980)?

Besides differing from biological and psychological theories in terms of the levels of analyses employed, sociological theory differs in another critical respect: it does not necessarily conceive of deviance as the violation of existing, agreed-upon social norms. Some sociological theories envision deviance and crime as social constructions and argue that being a deviant or a criminal is a matter of social definition (Becker, 1963); that is, some people label others as deviant, delinquent, or criminal. These nonconsensus or conflict-oriented perspectives point out that certain segments in society have more power than others to influence the design, implementation, and enforcement of rules or laws that transform some people into nonconformists or criminals. Definition as "deviant" or "criminal" represents a devalued status into which the more powerful in society categorize, contain, and control the weaker. In this view, both the creation and the enforcement of laws are discriminatory and serve the vested interests of society's wealthier and more powerful elements (Ermann and Lundman, 1982).

To illustrate this view, consider two common actions that result in different degrees of destruction to communal assets. Vandalizing public property is illegal and likely to elicit swift and punitive responses from both the police and the courts (Ellis, 1987). Apprehension for laying siege to a public park with a chain saw, a can of gasoline, and a lighter would cost a vandal dearly in terms of money, time, and reputation. On the other hand, knowingly dumping mercury and other lethal chemicals into rivers and lakes that provide food and drinking water for large numbers of Canadians is unlikely to mobilize authorities in a similar way (Gordon and Suzuki, 1990). Often, governments have failed to prohibit these acts, and even where regulations have been in place, enforcement has rarely been rigorous (Gomme and Richardson, 1991). Although chemical pollution causes far more damage to public "property" than vandalism does, legislation forbidding large-scale destruction of the environment remains ineffectual, underenforced, or nonexistent (Gomme and Richardson, 1991).

The social definition or social reaction approach seeks, among other things, to explain why the relatively minor destruction of public property through petty vandalism is likely to result in a fine or short jail term (and a criminal record) while the continuing destruction of the environment is likely to go unpunished. The typical vandal is young, from the lower classes, and lacking in resources (Ellis, 1987). Those ultimately responsible for decisions regarding the discharge of chemical wastes into fresh water supplies are older, from the higher social classes, and have the backing of their companies' financial resources, legal expertise, and political connections (Clinard and Yeager, 1980). Power affects exactly what is prohibited by law, how that law is enforced, and, consequently, who gets defined as criminal.

STRUCTURE AND PROCESS IN SOCIOLOGICAL THEORY

In their explanation of various aspects of deviance, sociological theories differ in their emphasis on structure on one hand and on process on the other. Some provide structural accounts, while others emphasize the process through which people are designated "deviant" and how, as a result of this designation, they develop deviant identities. Structural explanations focus on the impacts of external social and economic factors over which the individual has little or no control (Menzies, 1982). Among other things, the way in which age, sex, income, family and work statuses, educational and employment opportunities, and power are distributed within a society defines its structure. These structural determinants ultimately affect whether the attitudes, values, beliefs, and behaviours of individuals, groups, and aggregates conform to social expectations or deviate from them.

Other sociological theories of deviance focus on the process of becoming a deviant and of developing a deviant self-concept. Process approaches examine how individuals learn to define their particular situations and how their culture socializes them to develop deviant identities that facilitate long-term involvement in deviant careers (Becker, 1963). Negative responses to individuals emanating not only from their personal associates but from the powerful machinery of the justice system assume primacy in social process explanations.

A recent trend in theorizing about deviant and criminal behaviour is the construction of integrated theoretical models. Integrated approaches incorporate variables from both the structural and the process traditions. For any individual, location in the **social structure** affects his or her involvement in certain subcultural groups. This involvement in turn influences the development of definitions of the situation that affect self-concept and either support or undermine participation in deviant activity. Such models have become quite popular in research on juvenile delinquency (Linden and Fillmore, 1981; Gomme, 1985a; Hagan, Gillis, and Simpson, 1985; Hagan, Simpson, and Gillis, 1979, 1987).

Consider an example of a model incorporating structural and process variables, shown in Figure 2.2. Youth with origins in lower socioeconomic status groups and disadvantaged minorities grow up in broken homes more frequently. Because of the breakup of the mother and the father, children are subject to less supervision than if the family were "intact." With free time on their hands, "latchkey" teenagers are more likely to become involved in groups of wayward peers. In these youthful peer groups, teenagers internalize norms and values that support various forms of delinquency, including skipping school, smoking, drinking under-age, and using soft drugs. Eventually they come to *do* deviant acts because they *are* deviants. Identity affects behaviour.

BASIC ASSUMPTIONS OF SOCIOLOGICAL THEORY

Although assumptions are the foundations of all theories, they are often unstated and implicit. Three assumptions underlie sociological theories: basic assertions about human nature, about the degree of order in society, and about the nature of the connection between the individual and society (Liska, 1987). (See Table 2.2.)

Sociological theories tend to envisage human nature as either intrinsically good or inherently bad. In the former view, people deviate either because structural forces beyond their control compel them to violate social norms or because more powerful persons or groups define them as deviant. The notion is that people would be good if they could but that, for some, circumstances dictate otherwise. Alternatively, in the latter view, theories conceive of humans as inherently evil. The question for these theories is not why some people *do* engage in deviance, but rather why everyone *does not*. The implication, from this perspective, is that nonconformity is natural, more exciting, and more rewarding than conformity and that all people would be deviants if they were not held in check by some combination of informal and formal controlling forces (Gottfredson and Hirschi, 1990).

The degree to which society is characterized by order or disorder forms the second fundamental assumption integral to social theory. Some approaches view society as being held together by a series of

FIGURE 2.2

AN EXAMPLE OF AN INTEGRATED SOCIOLOGICAL THEORY OF DEVIANCE AND CRIME

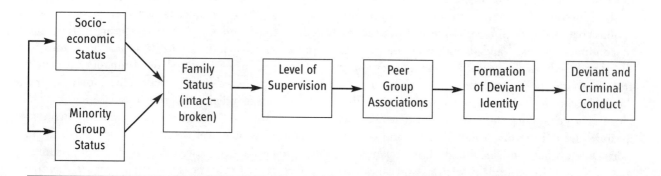

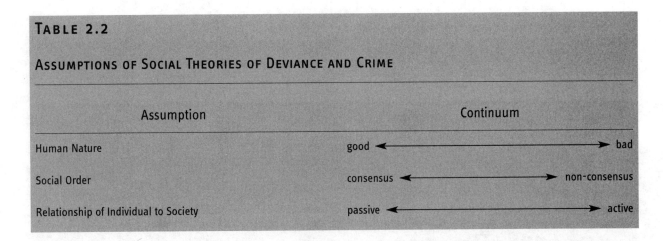

TABLE 2.2

ASSUMPTIONS OF SOCIAL THEORIES OF DEVIANCE AND CRIME

Assumption	Continuum	
Human Nature	good ←——————————————→ bad	
Social Order	consensus ←——————————→ non-consensus	
Relationship of Individual to Society	passive ←————————————————→ active	

norms, values, and beliefs, around which there is considerable consensus. Adherents of these approaches see rules about appropriate behaviour as relatively clear, stable, and unchanging. Deviance is simply the violation of these consensual norms (Merton, 1938; Hirschi, 1969).

Another group of theories conceives of society as containing competing groups, each with different conceptions of conformity. Given the diversity of these vested interests, the pre-eminence of which may shift over time, behavioural norms become unclear and unstable. Deviance is a matter of definition, and some behaviours of the relatively **powerless** will eventually become violations of the rules. While consensus theories emphasize reasons why people break rules, nonconsensus or conflict theories emphasize the source of the rules, the ways in which these rules are differentially applied, and consequently the ways in which certain individuals become rule violators by definition (Taylor, Walton, and Young, 1973).

Finally, the various theories of deviance express different notions about the link between individuals and their society. Some sociological theories portray people as largely passive, with forces in their environment and beyond their control shaping their conduct (Parsons, 1951; Merton, 1957). Others pay greater attention to the individual's capacity for action, whereby he or she interprets, reacts to, and acts upon the social environment in an attempt to change it (Blumer, 1969).

EMPIRICAL ASSESSMENT IN SOCIOLOGICAL THEORY

In addition to providing explanations, theories in social science typically include an empirical component that makes them amenable to systematic assess-

ment on the basis of evidence. Evidence must be something observable (Rosenberg, 1968). A theory might suggest that people steal because they do not have much money and that they do not have much money because they are unemployed. Assessing the rates of theft among unemployed persons and comparing those rates with the rates for employed persons would permit the confirmation or the rejection of the **hypothesis**. Another way of assessing the adequacy of this explanation is to compare rates of theft for regions of Canada characterized by high and low unemployment. Is there a **correlation** between unemployment rates and theft rates? Are rates of theft greater in Newfoundland, where unemployment is high, than in Ontario, where unemployment is considerably lower? The evidence in this case would not support the initial contention, and theorists would have to account for why it did not.

In studying social deviance, there are a variety of sources of evidence or empirical data. The more common of these are discussed in Chapter 9. Whether the sources of data are **quantitative** (e.g., official records, surveys of victims and perpetrators, and experiments) or **qualitative** (e.g., observation studies, historical analyses), sociological theory should be testable. Logical consistency is not sufficient to ensure the adequacy of the explanation (Menzies, 1982). Some sociological theorists argue that theory that cannot be evaluated by data is not theory at all, but rather ideology.

SOCIAL POLICY AND SOCIOLOGICAL THEORY

In providing an explanation of the occurrence of various forms of deviant and criminal activity, theory also

BOX 2.1
'READY-MADE SOLUTIONS' AREN'T FOR US, ADDICTS SAY

Rick W. has no plans to take his welfare cheque and inject it.

For one thing, he's no longer on welfare. He's living in the shelter system and surviving on a Personal Needs Allowance of $3.75 daily.

The other reason is that he doesn't use heroin. He smokes crack – even though his addiction brings with it an inevitable self-loathing.

"I hate myself, I kick myself, every time I break down and do it," says the 35-year-old, who's been struggling with the drug for years.

Rick has tried, through treatment programs and on his own, to stop. Sometimes he's successful, going days or weeks without feeding his addiction. Sometimes, his abstinence is measured in scant hours.

When he's broke, which is often, he helps other people score crack in return for a little kickback. It's never too hard to find someone with cash – doctors, lawyers, teenagers – who cruise the downtown core looking to buy a few rocks.

"There's always people up and coming," he says, "new addicts all the time."

Ultimately, Rick W. says he'll beat this. But that victory, and he stresses this, can only come when he's ready – and living in a stable environment.

"There are no ready-made solutions to addictions," he says. "It's a life-long battle. For social services to tell someone – boom - stop using it, it's impossible.

On Nov. 14, the minister of community and social services announced plans to screen welfare recipients to identify those addicted to substances. Those people would then be required to take part in treatment or lose their benefits. The rationale, John Baird said at the time, was that the province doesn't want recipients "shooting their welfare cheques up their arms."

The announcement prompted an immediate outcry from many professionals in the addictions, health and social justice fields. They argued such a policy would target the poor and vulnerable, increase the stigma of addictions and lead to additional homelessness. Many suggested it reflected, at best, a simplistic view of the complex nature of substance dependence. The *Canadian Medical Association Journal* confirms an upcoming editorial will condemn the plan.

"The people I know in this field are completely outraged by this," says Dr. Philip Berger, chief of Family and Community Medicine at St. Michael's Hospital. "I hate imputing motivation, but in this one it's very difficult to resist, because it appears punitive, vindictive and meant to humiliate sick and poor people. And I'm not alone in that opinion."

The minister doesn't see it that way. Quite the opposite, in fact.

"Our basic motive, I think, is one of compassion," he says.

Baird says addiction can be a "barrier to employment," and that people successfully treated will be able to rejoin the workforce. He sees the proposed plan as being analogous to Ontario Works – where welfare recipients participate in skills training and job placements in exchange for their cheque.

"The fundamental premise of our welfare program is that there's not just an expectation, but a requirement for you to participate," he says. "it's not a money-for-nothing welfare policy. That's a fundamental shift in thinking, and I don't take issue with people who honestly disagree with that policy."

When it comes to applying that concept to addictions, however, many do disagree. Health authorities say addictions are an illness, a disability, that significantly alters the way in which decisions are made. Choosing to participate in a jobs program, they say, cannot be equated with choosing to take part in treatment.

"This policy suggests drug use, on a day-to-day basis, is a choice," says Dr. David Marsh, clinical director for addiction medicine at the Centre for Addiction and Mental Health.

"For someone who's dependent on drugs, their brain chemistry changes in a way that they feel a strong compulsion to use drugs, the same kind of compulsion that we feel to eat food when we're hungry. And for them, it's not a simple matter of choosing: 'Okay, today I won't use heroin or cocaine.'"

"People don't understand the seriousness of addictions," says Beric German of Street Health. "They think it's like a virus that you would give some drug or treatment to and you get over it. And that isn't the case."

Nor is it the case that addictions are usually a barrier to work, say professionals. Given that substance dependence exists at all rungs of the socioeconomic ladder, they say the theory is the exception rather than the rule.

"The premise that addiction causes unemployment is the biggest fallacy around," says Ginette Goulet, associate director of the Ontario Federation of Community Mental Health and Addiction Programs. "How many people right now are addicted to something and are working? Many. Most people who have a substance abuse problem are working – and in all kinds of fields."

Goulet and others expressed grave concern that the minister's announcement further stigmatized both welfare recipients and those with problems of addiction. A poster unveiled for the program depicted a man injecting himself.

"The image of a person injecting drugs does not raise compassion, it raises fear," states a federation position paper opposing the plan.

There's also the problem that the infrastructure for mandatory treatment simply does not exist in Ontario. Waiting lists are chronic — and that's for people who *want* to take part. Baird says he'll fix it.

"We need to put a significant new investment into this, probably in the tens of millions of dollars," he says. "I recognize that and I'm prepared to go to bat and to fight for that money."

But will it work? Can someone with a serious addiction be forced into treatment and successfully kick their habit?

The ministry says 'Yes,' and points to a handful of U.S. studies indicating positive outcomes with mandatory treatment. But the majority of subjects in those studies were incarcerated populations, or women faced with a choice between treatment and having their children taken away.

"In all of those (studies), you're talking about mandatory treatment based on something that's black or white – you're either incarcerated or you're not, you either have your children or you don't," says March. "I don't know of any studies looking at mandatory treatment in this context, where someone's welfare benefits are dependent on their participation in treatment."

Nor, in the few U.S. states that apply mandatory treatment, is it quite as mandatory as the word implies. In Oregon, some welfare case managers do not support – or follow – the policy. At least one state applies its sanctions by degree, rather than the all-or-nothing approach pitched here.

"In some aspects, I suspect we'll be the first in what we do," says Baird.

Despite widespread concern among professionals, the plan does have supporters. One of them is Dr.

Suan-Seh Foo, an addictions specialist with the non-profit Canterbury Clinic.

"I appreciate their (colleague's) concern; it sounds punitive," he says. "But what is the alternative? I ask you, is it right for the government to knowingly give out $3, $6 or even $900, knowing full well that a portion of it is going to be used for drugs?... If you really want to help the individual you mandate the therapy – even if they don't want it."

Foo also agrees with those who've suggested that, if you're going to screen and treat those on welfare, why not screen and treat *all* individuals whose salaries are publicly paid.

"I have no problems with that," he says.

The minister says because mandatory treatment was a prominent plank in the 1999 election, there's already been a referendum of sorts on the issue. He also rejects the suggestion that the policy unfairly links welfare recipients with substance abuse.

"I don't think for a moment that anyone who's on social assistance is any more likely to be abusing drugs. I suspect there are more people on social assistance where their addiction is a barrier to employment," he says.

Those who work at street-level say that living on welfare, in and of itself, is so difficult that it may even contribute to the abuse of substances. A single person receives a total of $520 per month, $325 of which is to be used for accommodation. That leaves $195 for all other personal expenses – including food, clothing, transportation. Such an impoverished environment, say professionals, is not ideal for recovery from substance abuse.

"For anyone, but particularly for individuals with mental illness or substance use disorder, social environment is a key factor to their recovery," says addiction specialist Dr. Marsh. "The more that they're able to have reliable housing, a steady, well-balanced diet and a supportive social network, the more likely they are to recover."

Boris Rosolak, superintendent of Seaton House, one of the largest men's shelters in North America, suggests it's very difficult to survive on welfare – let alone complete a treatment program.

"If I was a single guy, living on $525 a month in the most expensive city in the country, I think I may be prone to some substance abuse just to escape the misery that I'm facing every day," he says.

Rosolak believes treatment would benefit some of the clients of Seaton House. But he doesn't think a coercive approach is the answer.

Rosolak and others suggest that a more positive approach would be to offer incentives over and above the regular welfare cheque. Maybe it's extra money, better housing, training for a career of choice — things that improve people's lives and offer hope. Incentives, even small ones, have been shown to improve outcomes with addiction treatment.

It's an approach Toronto's commissioner of community and neighbourhood services, Shirley Hoy, supports.

"From our experience in counselling people and a number of years in running the old general welfare programs, we have always found that positive incentives tend to be much more effective in encouraging people to get help, get treatment," she says.

Then there's the question of what impact, if any, the new policy might have on programs known as 'harm reduction.'

Services like needle exchanges or wet hostels do not offer 'traditional' treatment. These are non-judgmental programs that help people minimize the harm caused by their addiction. As clients of such programs engage over time with staff, many do eventually make the choice to seek help.

"Harm reduction is very important," says Dr. Patrick Smith, vice-president of addiction programs at the Centre for Addiction and Mental Health. "And Canada has been one of the international leaders."

Baird says he cannot yet say whether such programs would be considered a form of treatment for a welfare recipient. But he does emphasize there will be a firm expectation that people attempt, even repeatedly, to overcome their addiction. Refusal will lead to a cessation of welfare benefits.

"We're not, for a moment, saying that people have got to succeed. But they've got to try," he says.

That may be politically popular, but many say it's clinically unsound.

"The minister has an undeveloped, unevolved and unsophisticated analysis of addiction," says Dr. Philip Berger, who's also on the methadone committee of the College of Physicians and Surgeons of Ontario. "It's astonishing to me that we have people in leadership in government making very serious decisions who have a completely uninformed and unsubstantiated analysis of very profound and serious social problems."

What is undoubtedly the most troubling aspect of the plan, say critics, is that those unwilling or unable to embrace treatment will be at great risk of home-lessness. They may also turn to other, perhaps more harmful, ways of supporting their addiction.

"It just shows how out of touch our government is with the understanding of people with addictions," says Sister Susan Moran, co-founder of the Out of the Cold program.

Discussion Questions

To what degree is the Ontario government's proposed policy firmly based on the findings of empirical research? Is the proposed policy based upon expert opinion? Discuss the role of political considerations in policy formulation and implementation. Recall the direct connection depicted in Figure 2.1 between explanatory framework and policy.

Source: Scott Simmie, *Toronto Star*, December 3, 2000, pp. A1, A16, and A17. Reprinted with permission — The Toronto Star Syndicate.

provides advice for policymakers (Liska, 1987). Theory confirmed by evidence sheds light on the kinds of actions that can be taken in response to the problems under examination. Social policy may recommend either taking steps to alter the behaviour of perpetrators or changing the social structure in ways that will reduce or eliminate the deviant or criminal activity in question. What the process of policy formulation amounts to is the identification of crucial precipitating conditions and the subsequent altering of those conditions to produce the desired positive result.

For theories defining deviance as a matter of norm violation, policies are usually directed at the punishment, treatment, and rehabilitation of individual offenders. In this vein, theoretical insights have prescribed life in prison rather than capital punishment for convicted murderers (Fattah, 1972), chemotherapy rather than straitjackets for the mentally ill (Eaton, 1986), and vocational and literacy education rather than no training at all for prison inmates (Griffiths and Verdun-Jones, 1989). Where theories define deviance as a matter of social definition, policy recommendations typically relate to modifying laws and enforcement practices or eliminating them altogether. Policies based on these theories have advocated the creation and implementation of stricter laws for corporate crime (Goff and Reasons, 1978), the release of large numbers of patients from facilities for the mentally disturbed (Marshall, 1982), and the decriminalization of morality offences such as soft drug abuse, prostitution, and pornography (Solomon, 1983).

While virtually all social theories offer policy suggestions, many factors routinely constrain the implementation of policy initiatives. The principal impediments include social technology, societal values, and the distribution of power across social groups (Liska, 1987). Suppose that a decline in the strength of people's ties to their community, for example, contributes to the commission of a variety of property and violent crimes. Identifying the causal factor is one thing, but altering it is quite another. Researchers and legislators may simply not possess the social technology to encourage bonding at this level. Certain theories indicate that strong family attachments discourage suicide (Durkheim, 1951). Requiring everyone to marry and have children might reduce the suicide rate in Canada, but this strategy would not be accepted because it would dramatically contravene our societal values of freedom and democracy. Finally, there is more than a hint that material and social inequality contributes greatly to the commission of property crimes (Crutchfield, Geerken, and Gove, 1982). Sharing material resources equally among all members of society is likely to be met with considerable resistance by the wealthy and powerful. Policy, regardless of the soundness of the theory and research upon which it is based, is largely limited by what is technically feasible and by what people will accept. The adoption and implementation of policies are especially political processes. The fact that policy is often implemented without solid empirical support is illustrated in Figure 2.1 by the direct causal connection between explanatory framework and policy recommendations.

THE HISTORICAL DEVELOPMENT OF EXPLANATIONS OF DEVIANCE AND CRIME

Chapters 3 to 8 examine in some detail sociological theories of deviance developed, tested, and modified in the twentieth century. The remainder of this chapter discusses several of their important and popular predecessors. (See Table 2.3.) Classical, neoclassical, ecological, and positivist approaches, in particular, have greatly influenced contemporary approaches to the understanding of deviance, crime, and social control. It is especially important to understand their contributions to modern social theories.

DEMONOLOGY

The earliest explanations of deviance had their bases both in the supernatural and in Christian theological doctrine (Vold and Bernard, 1979). Until the eighteenth century, many people considered the deviant to be possessed by Satan or damned by God. In league with the devil or suffering the wrath of God, the criminal was first and foremost a sinner. Heretics, witches, and criminals were often drowned in boiling water, drawn and quartered, burned alive at the stake, or otherwise tortured and painfully executed (Farrell and Swigert, 1982). These agonizing remedies were undertaken to rid the community of evil spectres that were thought to inhabit the bodies of humans and to ensure that the marauding spirits felt the wrath of God. Whether people saw the deviant attributes or behaviours as divine afflictions or as evidence of a pact with the forces of darkness was of no consequence. They viewed the crime and the criminal as inexorably entwined (Vold and Bernard, 1979).

CLASSICAL AND NEOCLASSICAL THEORY

During the middle ages and until the eighteenth century, punishments were cruel and capricious. However, as the liberal philosophies of the **Enlightenment** became established during the eighteenth century, both the savagery of these penalties and their erratic and unpredictable application came to be seen as unacceptable. Seventeenth- and eighteenth-century thinkers like Locke, Hobbes, and Rousseau espoused innovative ideas that emphasized the natural rights of human beings and the use of reason to guide behaviour. The two fundamental Enlightenment ideas of rights and reason radically challenged the existing powers of the clergy and the aristocracy. In so doing, the Enlightenment fuelled both the American and French revolutions (Venturi, 1972).

An Italian, Cesare Beccaria (1738–1794), and an Englishman, Jeremy Bentham (1748–1832), are the two major figures of the **classical school of criminology**, which began its rise to prominence during the Enlightenment. In 1764, in reaction to the judicial practices of his time, Beccaria published his famous essay "On Crimes and Punishments." In this

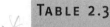

TABLE 2.3

EARLY THEORIES OF DEVIANCE AND CRIME

Theory	Theorist(s)	Central Premise	Key Concepts	Principal Contributions
demonology		Deviance results from possession by demons or from being damned by God. Deviant appearance and behaviour interpreted in terms of evil spirits and human sin.	demonic possession	
classical	Cesare Beccaria; Jeremy Bentham	Developed with rise of Enlightenment philosophy in which the ideas of reason and human rights held great importance. Crime is a consequence of a rational choice between pleasure and pain. Classical theory maintained that laws are means of benefiting the majority, that punishments should fit the crime, and that sanctions should apply equally to everyone.	free will; rational choice; felicific calculus	provided foundation for modern deterrence doctrine and due process provisions underpinning contemporary systems of criminal justice
neoclassical		Neoclassical thinking enhanced the classical approach with the idea that justice should be tailored to accommodate aggravating or mitigating circumstances.	aggravating or mitigating circumstances	added to classical theory the ideas of aggravation and mitigation that form the basis of current judicial discretion
ecology	Adolphe Quetelet; André Guerry	The advent of statistical data gave rise to the early ecological school. Ecologists linked geographical patterns and demographic characteristics to the distribution of criminal events.	statistics; geography; demographics	challenged the notions of free will as a cause of crime and provided the basis for contemporary ecological theories
positivism	Auguste Comte; Cesare Lombroso	Emphasized objectivity; stressed the importance of data in the development of explanations; highlighted the structural causes of deviance and crime. Crime is caused by factors beyond the individual's control. Positivism advocated the betterment of society through social engineering.	atavism; stigmata	promoted scientific approaches to the study of crime and pointed out that factors external to individuals and beyond free will can contribute to illegal conduct

document, he argued that where the individual can anticipate neither the nature of criminal law nor the penalty for violating it, the deterrent value of that law is negated. During this era, people were routinely ignorant of what acts the law prohibited. Even if they knew that a particular act contravened legal statutes, they often did not know what the punishment would be. Theft of a loaf of bread might result in an agonizing dip in boiling water on one day, the removal of a hand by an axe on the next day, and a warning a week later.

In reaction to the cruel and unpredictable punishments, Beccaria argued that the severity of punishments meted out by the state should be consistent and should fit the seriousness of the crime (Beccaria, 1963 [1764]). He also contended that laws ought to ensure that the greatest happiness be experienced by the largest possible number of people. Since at the time laws were drawn up specifically to protect the physical well-being and property of the privileged few, Beccaria's ideas departed considerably from the popular practices of the period (Monachesi, 1973).

In 1823, Jeremy Bentham built upon the ideas of Beccaria and of the then-popular utilitarian philosophy to develop his own version of utilitarian hedonism, "felicific calculus." Bentham argued that society is most properly based on people acting in ways that create the greatest possible ratio of good to evil for all concerned. He believed that individuals act on the basis of their own free will and that hedonism and self-interest heavily influence their choices of action. Bentham conceived of hedonism as a pleasure principle whereby rational men and women seek to maximize their pleasurable experiences while simultaneously minimizing life's more painful trials.

According to Bentham, people left to their own devices will formulate strategies and act in ways designed to result in their experience of the greatest possible pleasure. They will continue to engage in a broad range of activities so long as they believe that these activities will be enjoyable. In this way, each person makes a rational choice about engaging in a behaviour according to its benefits and costs. Some actions motivated by a person's desire for immediate self-gratification, however, contravene the best interests of other members of society. For this reason, laws reflecting the interests of the majority must ensure that the costs of self-interested acts that also cause harm outweigh their benefits. Through the use of law, individual choice can be channelled to result in behaviour that preserves the best interests of the largest number of citizens (Bondanello and Bondanello, 1979).

Classical theory suggested not only that the punishment should fit the crime, but also that punishments should be applied equally to all lawbreakers regardless of their economic and social status. The central problem with the latter tenet soon became clear. To what extent is it sensible to apply the same degree of punishment to children and adults, to the mentally competent and the insane, to the first offender and the repeat offender (Vold and Bernard, 1979)? Classical theory in its original form offered

room neither for mitigating or aggravating circumstances nor for judicial discretion.

Later nineteenth-century revisions of classical doctrine, the **neoclassical perspective**, incorporated the notion of mitigating circumstances such as youthfulness, insanity, and adverse environmental conditions. **Mitigating circumstances** differed from one criminal incident to another and required variations in punishments even where the charges (e.g., murder and robbery) were identical. Judicial discretion, introduced at this point in history, remains a cornerstone of the current justice system (Griffiths and Verdun-Jones, 1989).

THE ECOLOGICAL APPROACH

Perhaps the most ignored of the early approaches to understanding criminal activity was a perspective known as the **ecological**, statistical, or geographical school (Thomas and Hepburn, 1983). This school of thought relied heavily on crime statistics, which first became available in Europe in the 1820s.

Founders of the early ecological approach were André Guerry (1802–1866), a Frenchman, and Adolphe Quetelet (1796–1874), a Belgian. Both of these men focused their investigations on the relationship between humans and their physical environment. Using official data on crime, they pinpointed and mapped out geographical areas characterized by higher and lower crime rates. Assessing criminal behaviour at the aggregate rather than the individual level, they documented regularities in patterns of illegal activity not only by region but also by age, sex, and economic condition (Guerry, 1831; Quetelet, 1842).

Their discovery of consistencies in crime patterns severely challenged popular classical explanations of criminality that stressed free will and rational choice. That certain geographical areas, the young, and males were especially prone to crime contradicted the classical explanations of criminal behaviour that envisaged such activity solely in terms of individual hedonistic choice (Quetelet, 1842). According to pioneer ecologists, being a slum resident, young, or male predisposed individuals toward illegal behaviour.

The ecological and statistical school represented a shift from the purely logical approach of classical theorists like Beccaria and Bentham in incorporating an empirical base. This scientific emphasis became the forerunner of several schools of thought that emerged in the twentieth century. Nonetheless, while the ecological perspective was strong empirically, it was weak theoretically. It offered no real explanation for the observed variation in patterns of crime. This deficiency is one of the reasons why so little attention has been paid to the works of Guerry and Quetelet.

POSITIVISM

The founder of "positive" sociology was a Frenchman named Auguste Comte (1798–1857). Comte advocated the employment of empirical **scientific methods** to bring about progress and the improvement of society. In pursuit of social betterment, Comte's **positivism** emphasized measurement, objectivity, and a search for the root causes of social phenomena. These principles have had a profound effect on the development of social science (Lenzer, 1975).

From his positivist perspective, Comte claimed that measurement required the accumulation and assessment of data, which in turn permits the confirmation or rejection of a theory. Stressing objectivity, he called for the setting aside of researchers' own values so as to avoid biased judging of the behaviour being observed. Comte also argued that behaviour is determined by various causes, over which the individual has little control. Social betterment, he believed, depended on isolating the causal conditions underlying undesirable behaviour and modifying or eliminating them (Simpson, 1969).

Another considerable influence on late-nineteenth-century positivism was Charles Darwin, who heavily influenced the ideas of an Italian criminologist, Cesare Lombroso (1835–1909). Particularly important were Darwin's notions of evolutionary development, natural selection, survival of the fittest, and humankind's connection to a savage heritage (Darwin, 1927).

To explain criminality, Lombroso used Darwin's theory of evolution to develop the idea of biological **atavism** (Wolfgang, 1973). An atavist, Lombroso argued, was a born criminal, a throwback to an earlier, more primitive evolutionary period. Lombroso claimed that these atavistic individuals or evolutionary throwbacks could be identified by a variety of physical characteristics or "**stigmata.**" Physiological attributes such as protruding jaws and cheekbones, sloping foreheads, close-set eyes, and small skulls were associated with criminal inclinations. As far as Lombroso was concerned, these physical features clearly indicated inherent criminality (Lombroso, 1972).

Lombroso's theory of atavism has not been influential in the contemporary study of deviance. Critics of his own period pointed out a number of serious flaws in Lombroso's social Darwinist approach. First, attempts to find statistically significant differences between the physical characteristics of criminals and noncriminals proved fruitless. For example, Goring, a contemporary of Lombroso, was unable to discriminate between the physical characteristics of prison inmates and of students attending Oxford University (Goring, 1913). Second, Lombroso's samples were taken from populations of incarcerated convicts. The physical characteristics Lombroso believed indicative of innate criminal potential were likely created by the inclement and inhospitable conditions to which prisoners were subjected at that time. In short, the stigmata were the consequence of imprisonment rather than the cause of the criminal behaviour that precipitated incarceration in the first place. Finally, Lombroso's notion of atavism laid the blame for criminality on the individual. His theory deflected attention from the importance of conditions such as poverty and inequality as progenitors of deviance. For this reason, historians of crime frequently cite Lombroso's theory of atavism as a regressive step (Vold and Bernard, 1979).

Lombroso did, however, make some contributions to the social scientific study of criminality. He advocated careful observation and meticulous measurement in the study of criminal behaviour. He believed that pure theory alone was insufficient. Lombroso also suggested that the causes of deviance and crime lay in factors beyond the control of the individual. An important implication of this notion is that simply punishing a criminal made little sense. With this idea, the positivist position directly challenged classical doctrine. Classical theory proposed that punishment can deter crime because punitive sanctions make illegal conduct more painful than pleasurable. Positivists, in arguing that the causes of nonconforming behaviour were beyond the individual's control, underscored the futility of punishment by maintaining that people commit crimes not out of choice but because they are compelled to do so. In adopting this position, positivists directed attention toward the control of crime through means other than punishment. Positivism calls first for the treatment of criminals and second for remedies to **criminogenic social and economic conditions** (Vold and Bernard, 1979).

SUMMARY

Sociological theories consist of three basic components: explanation, empirical verification, and directives for social policy. Some theories seek to explain why some people violate agreed-upon norms and others do not. Other sociological perspectives focus on explaining why and how some people can designate others as deviant or criminal.

In explaining deviance, sociological theory differs from biological and psychological perspectives in two important ways. Sociological approaches move beyond discussions of individual nonconformity to examine deviance within and across social groups and aggregates. Sociology also extends the conceptualization of deviance beyond simple norm violation to include discussions of the social construction of deviance. Unlike biological and psychological theory, some sociological frameworks present deviance as a quality conferred upon the relatively powerless by the more powerful.

Structural explanations in sociology emphasize the contributions to deviant and criminal behaviour made by social and economic structures that people confront but about which they can do little. Process explanations concentrate upon explaining how people develop deviant identities and self-concepts and, in turn, how these identities and senses of self are shaped by and contribute to deviant careers. Integrated theoretical models represent relatively new approaches and contain both structural and process variables. In effect, they provide insights into how structure affects process.

All social theory is based on assumptions that are either explicit or implicit. Three important assumptions underpin theories of deviance and crime: whether humankind is naturally good or naturally bad; the degree of order in society; and the connection between individuals and their society. At issue is the extent to which human beings are relatively passive pawns in the grip of social structure or active shapers of their own social worlds.

Part of appreciating theory involves subjecting logical explanation to an empirical test. Do the facts fit the explanation? Facts may be quantitative, as is the case with official data or statistics generated from surveys. They may also come from qualitative historical data, the direct observation of events, or the extensive interviewing of deviants, criminals, or agents of social control.

Sociological theories of deviance either identify causes of norm violation (positivist approaches) or highlight the process of deviant designation (humanist approaches). In so doing, they also suggest remedies to problems posed by deviance and crime both for individuals and for society. Policy recommendations usually aim at changing individual perpetrators, altering social structure, or modifying law and legal processing. Constraints on the implementation of policy are inherent in existing social technology, societal values, and the distribution of social power. Regardless of the logic and the empirical support underlying a course of action, initiatives that are hard to implement, that contravene cultural and subcultural values, and that threaten the powerful are unlikely to be successful. Conversely, initiatives that are easy to implement, that are in line with social values, and that offer no threat to the privileged are likely to proceed even in the face of illogical suppositions and contrary evidence.

To understand twentieth-century thinking about deviant and criminal behaviour, several historical explanations were examined. Demonological approaches viewed deviant appearance and behaviour in terms of evil spirits and human sin. With the rise of Enlightenment philosophy, the ideas of reason and human rights grew in importance. The classical perspective presented crime as the consequence of a rational choice between pleasure and pain. It maintained that laws were means of benefiting the majority, that punishments should fit the crime, and that sanctions should apply equally to everyone. Neoclassical thinking added the notion that justice should be tailored to accommodate aggravating or mitigating circumstances.

The advent of statistical data gave rise to the early ecological school. Ecologists linked geographical patterns and demographic characteristics to the distribution of criminal events. For their part, positivists emphasized objectivity, stressed the importance of data in the development of explanations, highlighted the structural causes of deviance and crime, and advocated the betterment of society through social engineering.

DISCUSSION QUESTIONS

1. Discuss the three main components of any sociological theory of deviance.
2. Explain how theories that define deviance as norm violation differ from those that define deviance as social definition.

3. Demonstrate how neoclassical theory modified the classical philosophies of Beccaria and Bentham.

4. Discuss the major deficiencies and contributions of early ecological research on the distribution of deviance and crime in society.

5. How did positivism differ from the classical approach? What were the implications of these differences for the notion of punishment as deterrence?

WEB LINKS

Crime Theory
http://www.crimetheory.com
> Crimetheory.com is an educational resource for learning and teaching theoretical criminology. This extensive site features overviews of many theories, a gallery of criminologists, a glossary, an archive of early criminological texts, links, and much more.

Crime Times
http://www.crime-times.org/
> This American newsletter focuses on examining biological causes of criminal, violent, and psychopathic behaviour.

Cesare Beccaria's "Of Crimes and Punishments"
http://www.constitution.org/cb/crim_pun.htm
> This site includes the full text of Beccaria's famous treatise "Of Crimes and Punishments," as well as a biographical sketch of the author.

Jeremy's Labyrinth
http://www.la.utexas.edu/labyrinth/
> The site, maintained by Dan Bonevac, contains the full text of many of Jeremy Bentham's writings.

Cesare Lombroso
http://www.tld.jcu.edu.au/hist/stats/lomb/
> A brief look at Lombroso's theory of crime and his influence from the Pictures of Health site.

RECOMMENDED READINGS

Akers, R. (2000). *Criminological Theory: Introduction, Evaluation, and Application* (3rd ed.). Los Angeles: Roxbury.
> Provides a solid introduction to criminological theory.

Barlow, H.D. (1995). *Crime and Public Policy: Putting Theory to Work.* Boulder, CO: Westview.
> Collection of essays assessing the relevance of sociological theory to the formulation of crime control strategies. Leading proponents of various theoretical frameworks specify policy proposals while arguing against current reactionary approaches.

Martin, R., R.J. Mutchnick, and W.T. Austin. (1990). *Criminological Thought: Pioneers Past and Present.* New York: Macmillan.
> Presents the principal ideas of seminal thinkers in the criminological tradition.

Shoemaker, D.J. (2000). *Theories of Delinquency: An Examination of Explanations of Delinquent Behavior* (4th ed.). New York: Oxford University Press.
> Provides a comprehensive survey of major theoretical approaches to the understanding of delinquency.

Vold, G.B., T.J. Bernard, and J.B. Snipes. (2000). *Theoretical Criminology* (4th ed.). New York: Oxford University Press.
> A classic introduction to various forms of criminological theory, both old and new.

CHAPTER 3

THE CHICAGO SCHOOL

The aims of this chapter are to familiarize the reader with:

- the ways in which the early work of Guerry and Quetelet influenced the later work of Shaw and McKay
- the adaptation of ideas from plant and animal ecology in the explanation of deviant and criminal behaviour in urban settings
- the policy implications of human ecology
- points of evaluation for the ecological approaches
- connections between Sutherland's differential association and the ecological perspectives of the Chicago school
- the nine propositions of differential association
- the ways in which Glaser's differential identification and Burgess and Akers's differential reinforcement complement differential association
- the policy implications of human ecology and differential association
- deficiencies in the human ecology and differential association perspectives
- the contributions of the human ecology and differential association approaches to the understanding of deviance and crime

INTRODUCTION

A deeply rooted interest in the urban environment was perhaps the central concern of the sociological tradition that originated at the University of Chicago in 1892. Chicago's population grew at an impressive pace from 1850 to 1900, and the social fabric of this dynamic and changing city formed the basis of much of the school's empirical research. On the basis of their observations of city life and the process of **urbanization**, Chicago sociologists developed explanations for a variety of social phenomena, including deviance and crime (Park, 1952). Their approach resembles that of Guerry and Quetelet of the early ecological school, except that the Chicago ecologists used their empirical observations to develop explanations of deviance.

This chapter examines the **Chicago school's** contributions to the understanding of deviance and crime. Contained within the Chicago tradition are a macro theory (human ecology) and a micro theory (differential association). The discussion begins with the macro-level ecological theory in its general form and focuses on how ecological theories account for deviant and criminal behaviour. The micro approach — differential association — is then examined to show how it is rooted in the theory of human ecology. The chapter continues with a discussion of the policy strategies inherent in each of the Chicago school's approaches and concludes with an assessment of their deficiencies and contributions.

HUMAN ECOLOGY

One of the most noticeable patterns observed by social scientists at the University of Chicago was that city areas inhabited predominantly by the poor, by recent immigrants, and by ethnic minorities displayed high rates of nonconformity. Their task became to explain this relationship by modifying and applying ecological theory, a schematic framework borrowed from the biological sciences (Hawley, 1986).

The ecological approach to understanding the organization of living matter in natural environments focuses on the relationships of plants and animals both to each other and to their physical surroundings. This interaction strongly affects the activity and survival of all organisms. Human ecology likens human communities to plant and animal communities and, in the process, makes two simple observations: racial, class, and other groups affect one another's daily lives; and these groups are also affected by a variety of conditions in the urban environment, including land use, property values, the location of industry, and natural boundaries such as rivers, highways, and railroad lines.

Chicago sociologists argued that all these intricate relationships form a social system, or "web of life." They believed that the "normal" conditions of this complex system are equilibrium and order. They envisaged change as an evolutionary process involving the gradual adaptation of people and groups to alterations in the characteristics either of one another or of their physical surroundings (Faris, 1967).

In particular, two central and interrelated concepts from the science of plant ecology were adapted and applied to the sociological analysis of city life. The first was the notion of symbiosis, and the second was the idea of invasion, dominance, and succession (Vold and Bernard, 1986). Symbiosis refers to a condition of mutual interdependence among organisms in an environment that is necessary for their survival. Forms of life compatible with each other and with the environment survive. When species become incompatible with one another or when the nature of the environment changes, some forms of life inevitably suffer or perish. In the world of nature, plants produce oxygen that is vital to the survival of animals. Animals produce carbon dioxide that is equally essential to the survival of plants. This mutually dependent relationship among plants and animals exemplifies symbiosis. The slow destruction of large masses of plant life through industrial expansion and pollution, however, undermines this equilibrium. The ultimate loss of food and shelter caused by acid rain, for example, is dramatically changing the nature of animal and bird life in affected areas. The demolition of urban slums represents an analogous change in the physical surroundings of city dwellers. The elimination of housing affordable to disadvantaged class and ethnic groups requires both their adaptation and relocation.

An important point emphasized in the ecological approach is that change in one part of the system invariably affects other system components.

The sequential process of invasion, dominance, and succession in biology involves species competing with each other for scarce resources, thus changing the balance of relationships in any given geographical area. The balance of nature changes as new species drive out competitors, come to dominate the environment, and eventually form stable interdependencies themselves. After a forest fire, for example, weeds and grasses move in, followed by scrub brush, which eventually gives way first to coniferous and later to deciduous trees. These changes in plant life affect the distribution of animals, which depend on various plants for survival. In a similar process, industrial and commercial establishments reclaim slum areas. New and modern banks, business establishments, and government offices replace dilapidated housing. In the process, people living in these run-down areas are displaced to other locations.

An examination of Chicago's growth patterns suggested an evolutionary process whereby urban expansion occurs radially from the city core outward in a series of concentric bands, each of which is continually expanding (Burgess, 1925). (See Figure 3.1.) The Chicago school maintained that this series of concentric zones emerges from the ecological process of competition, in this instance, for valuable land. The Chicago ecologists noted that each concentric zone reflects a different land value, land use, residence pattern, and cultural character. They did not, however, believe that all cities necessarily perfectly exemplified the concentric zonal pattern. Rather, they employed this image as an ideal type against which to assess actual urban patterns.

According to Chicago ecologists, land is most expensive in the core of the city. Only commerce, industry, and government can afford the high prices there. They dominate the core by erecting banks, stores, theatres, hotels, public transportation centres, and government offices. The band immediately adjacent to the central business district is the transitional zone. Located next to the ever-expanding industrial core, the transitional zone's property values are sharply eroded. Since property owners believe that buildings in this sector will eventually be torn down to make room for industrial and commercial expansion, they do not maintain the buildings. Residential areas in this zone deteriorate as higher-status residents flee to

FIGURE 3.1

CHICAGO'S CONCENTRIC ZONES

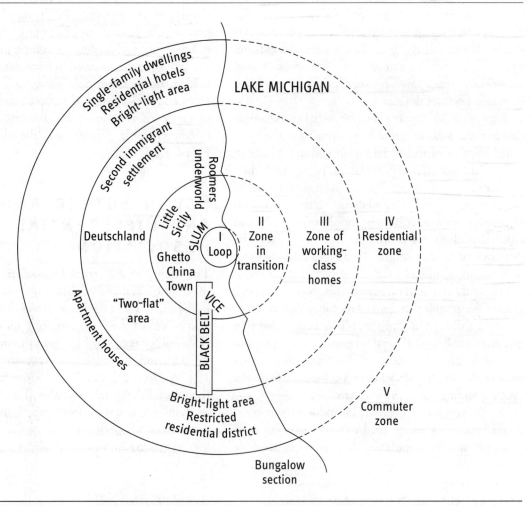

Source: Robert E. Park, Ernest W. Burgess, and R.D. McKenzie, *The City*. Chicago: University of Chicago Press, 1925. p. 55. Reprinted with permission of University of Chicago Press.

the suburbs. Their low rents make these dilapidated and run-down dwellings attractive to impoverished ethnic and immigrant populations.

The third zone contains relatively inexpensive two- and three-family dwellings inhabited by members of the working class, who had previously migrated outward from the transitional zone. In the fourth zone are the more expensive apartments and single-family dwellings occupied by the middle class. Small business and professional offices are also present in this ring. In the outermost sector are the residences of the more affluent commuter population. This outlying suburban area has more recently become the contemporary satellite city.

Each of the five zones contains "natural areas." In the transitional band, these natural areas are ghettos. In the third and fourth zones, the natural areas are communities united by ethnic or religious ties. Often physical boundaries such as railway tracks, rivers, or roads separate these areas from other parts of the city.

CLIFFORD SHAW AND HENRY McKAY AND SOCIAL DISORGANIZATION

While examining the geographical distributions of deviant and criminal activity in Chicago, Clifford Shaw and Henry McKay (1969 [1942]) noted that rates of nonconformity and illegal conduct are highest in the **transitional zone**. They contend that industrial growth and urban expansion erode the traditional social controls inherent in the family, the church, and the community, and they argue that this erosion is particularly severe in the transitional zone. Areas where social controls are weakened or severed are "disorganized" and consequently susceptible to increased levels of deviance.

Shaw and McKay explain the social disorganization in these neighbourhoods by referring to the combined impacts of industrialization and urbanization. Industrial expansion requires labour power, and when workers arrive to meet the employment needs of industry, population size and density increase. Groups of people with vastly different social backgrounds and cultural traditions are brought together. Given the diversity of ethnic origin, language, religion, and occupation, conflicts over differing values, norms, beliefs, and behaviours are inevitable. Moreover, high rates of geographical and social mobility also converge to weaken the ties binding people in a community to one another. Primary social relationships are particularly difficult to sustain in the transitional zone because this band is under constant pressure from the ever-expanding commercial centre.

As the spectre of invasion by industry and commerce becomes a reality, land values in adjacent areas plummet and the population flees for more desirable locations farther from the city core. Consequently, living conditions in the transitional area deteriorate, and the area fills with a heterogeneous mix of marginally employed or unemployed lower-class immigrant groups. The deleterious effects of diversity, geographical mobility, and conflict are compounded in the transitional zone by poverty, substandard housing, and inadequate social services, education, and recreation. Shaw and McKay argue that these conditions continue to erode traditional social controls and encourage unconventional activity and illegal conduct. (See Figure 3.2.)

EDWIN SUTHERLAND AND DIFFERENTIAL ASSOCIATION

The theory of **differential association** is one of the most influential and popular explanatory frameworks in the sociology of deviance. It was outlined by Edwin Sutherland of the University of Chicago in his 1934 criminology text, was first set out in proposition form in 1939, and was refined to its present structure in the 1947 edition of the textbook (Sutherland, 1947). The theory of differential association has remained largely unchanged since that time. (See Figure 3.3.)

Sutherland's perspective was influenced by the ecological approach. Shaw and McKay had provided an

FIGURE 3.2

SOCIAL DISORGANIZATION THEORY

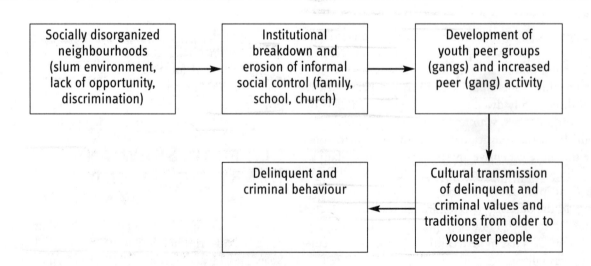

FIGURE 3.3

DIFFERENTIAL ASSOCIATION THEORY

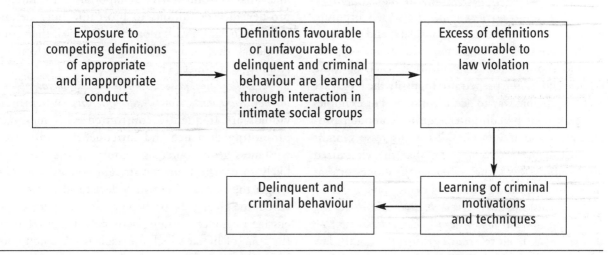

explanation of why crime rates varied across certain social groups. They had observed from official crime data that urban dwellers, nonwhites, members of the lower classes, and males were consistently more involved in crime than were rural residents, whites, the affluent, and females. In developing their explanation, Shaw and McKay (1931) observed that various geographical areas have different levels of social disorganization, which undermine traditional forces of social control and are the root cause of high rates of deviance. Once established in a particular area, the high rates of deviance and crime are transmitted from one generation of inhabitants to the next.

Sutherland, building on these ideas, suggests that some social groups possess pro-criminal traditions and that others have anti-criminal traditions. Both types of tradition, he maintains, are passed down through generations in a process of socialization. Groups with cultural traditions encouraging deviance (e.g., urbanites, blacks, the poor) have higher crime rates than groups with cultural traditions promoting conformity (e.g., rural inhabitants, whites, the rich). This part of Sutherland's thinking is a "cultural transmission" explanation of deviance and crime. According to cultural transmission theory, two primary factors affect deviant behaviour. The first is the degree to which cultural traditions stimulating nonconformity characterize the group. The second is the extent to which these traditions are passed on from generation to generation.

Sutherland's major concern, however, is to explain why participation in deviant and criminal activity varies from one individual to the next. Why are some people more criminal than others? To answer this question, Sutherland modifies ideas from the ecological and cultural transmission traditions and constructs his theory of differential association. He outlines his theory in nine propositions (Sutherland and Cressey, 1970).

1. Criminal behaviour is learned. People learn to act criminally in the same way as they learn other behaviours. The propensity for deviance is neither inherited nor the result of a personality defect. Stealing a car, using a computer to embezzle funds from a bank, driving a truck, and removing a brain tumour are all learned behaviours.

2. Criminal behaviour is learned in interaction with other persons in a process of communication. Through words and gestures exchanged with others, people learn how to perform criminal acts just as they learn conventional behaviours.

3. The principal part of learning criminal behaviour occurs in intimate personal groups. The greater the intimacy among group members, the more effective is the communication of the message. Sources of information can vary from the personal (e.g., family and friends) to the impersonal (e.g., television and newspapers). Personal sources of information, particularly families, are more powerful because of their higher degrees of intimacy.

*4. When criminal behaviour is learned, the learning includes (a) the techniques of committing the crime, which sometimes are very complicated and sometimes very simple, and (b) the specific direction of motives, drives, **rationalizations**, and attitudes.* Corporate price fixing, drug smuggling, burglary, and prostitution require skills varying tremendously in complexity and sophistication. In addition, each of these crimes requires the perpetrator to justify the illegal act as an acceptable way to acquire money. For example, embezzlement by computer requires computer programming and accounting skills. Transgressors might rationalize the act by arguing that the victimized organization "owes" the embezzler the money or that the embezzled funds are merely being "borrowed."

5. The specific directions of motives and drives are learned from definitions of legal codes as favourable or unfavourable. Their **reference group's** view of the law affects people's commitment to criminal or conforming behaviour. There is an increased probability that individuals will develop an aversion to criminal behaviour if their reference group respects the law. However, if the reference group has contempt for the law, the individual is more likely to engage in crime. Where members of the reference group have mixed feelings about legal codes, a person is more likely to be ambivalent about crime.

6. A person becomes criminal because of an excess of definitions favourable to violation of the law over definitions unfavourable to violation of the law. This proposition is the core of differential association theory. It states that if people associate more with patterns of ideas encouraging participation in deviance and crime, they are more likely to violate the rules. Two important points related to this proposition must be emphasized.

First, the notion of criminal patterns refers to ideas, not persons. Strictly speaking, proposition 6 does not state that if a person associates with criminals, he or she, on that basis alone, is more likely to become criminal. Rather, it refers to connections with *definitions of the situation* or with ideas that support the commission of crime. Thus, law-abiding persons may transmit definitions conducive to law violation. For example, law-abiding parents who complain about the unfairness of income tax may provide their children with a rationalization for cheating on their tax returns later in life.

Second, differential association comprises more than one type of association. The key word in proposition 6 is *excess*. People are exposed differentially to two types of definitions, criminal and law-abiding. While everyone is influenced to some degree by both types of definition, one type probably has greater primacy than the other. What is important is the ratio of pro-deviance definitions to pro-conformity definitions. Association with more criminal ideas than conventional ideas is the root source of nonconforming and illegal conduct (Thio, 1988).

7. Differential association varies in terms of frequency, duration, priority, and intensity. When individuals are frequently confronted with messages promoting deviance and infrequently confronted with messages encouraging conformity, they are more likely to deviate from the straight and narrow. The longer the time during which deviant ideas are conveyed, the greater the probability that the person will engage in nonconforming activity. Priority refers to the time of life at which a person is presented with ideas favouring deviance or conformity; the younger the person, the more influential the ideas are likely to be. Finally, the level of affectivity or emotional commitment between an individual and those persons providing the deviant and conforming definitions sways the person's behaviour. Intense bonds to deviant associates, combined with weak ties to conventional comrades, increases the likelihood that the person will choose a deviant path.

These four aspects of differential association are not entirely independent. Their effects may be cumulative. Where definitions favourable to violation of the law are relatively frequent, take place over a long period of time, are experienced early in life, and emanate from people held in high regard, the probability of nonconformity and illegal conduct increases significantly.

8. The process of learning criminal behaviour by association with criminal and anti-criminal patterns involves all the mechanisms involved with any other type of learning. Criminal and law-abiding patterns differ in terms of content but not in terms of the process through which knowledge is acquired. Learning how to research and write an essay, how to invest money wisely, how to cheat on exams, and how to rob banks all require the same learning process.

9. Although criminal behaviour is an expression of general needs and values, it cannot be explained by them, because noncriminal behaviour is an expression of the same needs and values. Most people value material acquisitions in general and money in particular. These motivations do not explain why some people commit burglary, robbery, or fraud since many other people choose legitimate ways to attain these same goals.

Rather than break the law to get what they want, they work overtime or take on a second job.

The ecological theory of Shaw and McKay and Sutherland's differential association approach are mutually complementary. Differential social organization across different social groups results in their embodying, to varying degrees, criminal or conventional traditions. Exposure by birth or by migration to these differing group traditions causes individuals to differentially associate with mainly criminal or mainly law-abiding definitions. This differential association with patterns of ideas in turn results in criminal or conforming behaviour, depending on the degree to which the balance of these associations is tipped one way or the other. Where the associations are mostly favourable to law violation, people will break the law. Where the associations are mostly unfavourable to law violation, people will obey the law. Individuals are more likely to engage in crime if they are members of groups with criminal traditions. Conversely, they are more likely to avoid participation in illegal action if they are members of groups with law-abiding traditions.

Differential association theory has spawned a good deal of research and much critical debate. Part of this debate concerns the generality of the theory. Some critics argue that the mechanisms through which differential association produces crime need to be specified in more detail. Consequently, refinements of the theory have been offered by Daniel Glaser in the form of differential identification and by Robert Burgess and Ronald Akers in the form of differential reinforcement.

Daniel Glaser and Differential Identification

Glaser (1956) criticizes Sutherland on two counts. He argues that differential association theory presents an overly mechanistic image of criminality, in which the individual is mechanically propelled into involvement with crime as a result of excessive association with criminal traditions. According to Glaser, Sutherland does not sufficiently emphasize individual role taking and choice making. He also points out that Sutherland's theory was developed when mass media were less influential than they now are. As a result, Sutherland does not take sufficient account of the potential impacts of indirect interactions.

To remedy these deficiencies, Glaser constructs a theory based on differential association but with an additional component that he terms "identification." Glaser maintains that, to be influenced by criminal traditions, the individual must identify with definitions of deviance conveyed by real or imaginary others who deem nonconforming behaviour acceptable. (See Figure 3.4.) Importantly, while **differential identification** operates in the context of both deviant and conforming groups, it does not necessarily involve groups of which the individual is actually a member. Criminal traditions need not be transmitted to the individual by persons in close proximity. Attachment may occur between an individual and either a real or a fictional character if that character is attractive and admirable. The notion of identification is useful in explaining media contributions to deviance and crime. Differential identification also provides an account of how a nonconformist might be part of a conforming group and how a conformist might belong to a nonconforming group.

Robert Burgess and Ronald Akers and Differential Reinforcement

Burgess and Akers's dissatisfaction with Sutherland's differential association theory stems from their feeling that it is not sufficiently specific about the nature of

Figure 3.4

Differential Identification Theory

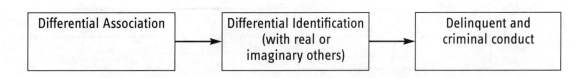

the learning process. They maintain that Sutherland fails to clearly demarcate the mechanisms alluded to in proposition 8, which refers to the way in which learning occurs. To correct this deficiency, they identify differential reinforcement as the necessary but missing link between the initial cause, excessive association with traditions encouraging deviance, and the effect — deviant behaviour (Burgess and Akers, 1966). Drawing on behavioural psychology, they introduce the concept of **operant conditioning** as an intermediary stage in the process, as shown in Figure 3.5.

Burgess and Akers claim that people engage in deviant conduct if and only if its social or material rewards outweigh those attached to conformity. In short, one continues activities that are rewarded and desists from activities that are punished. For example, through interactions with friends, teenagers learn the skills and rationalizations necessary for becoming "high" on drugs. To the extent that the sensations are pleasurable and rewarding, drug use is likely to continue. Conversely, feeling guilty or having a "bad trip" will likely reduce subsequent use.

THE CHICAGO SCHOOL AND SOCIAL POLICY

HUMAN ECOLOGY

Shaw and McKay cite as a key cause of deviance and crime the social disorganization that results from rapid industrialization and urbanization. Since it is impossible to halt industrial growth and urban expansion, human-ecology policy initiatives focus on countering the social disorganization that frequently accompanies this growth. Policymakers have attempted to provide communities in transitional areas with the means to encourage social organization. Community-building initiatives such as improving schools, building recreational facilities, and providing on-the-street social services are attempts to strengthen traditional social controls and improve the quality of neighbourhood life (Liska, 1987).

DIFFERENTIAL ASSOCIATION

Differential association states that nonconformity and crime are consequences of the excessive transmission, through group members, of an excess of deviant over conforming definitions. The policy implications are clear: to reduce deviance, the ratio of nondeviant to deviant associations must be increased. Since the theory identifies socialization in reference-group contexts as the principal conduit through which individuals internalize illegal traditions, much of the policy stemming from differential association theory aims at reducing contacts between individuals and criminal groups and increasing contact between individuals and law-abiding groups. Typical strategies include diverting individuals from the correctional system altogether or placing them in secure settings

FIGURE 3.5

DIFFERENTIAL REINFORCEMENT THEORY

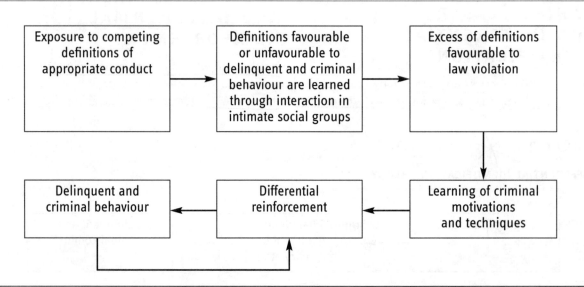

that limit their contact with hardened criminals. These initiatives stem from the widely held view that correctional institutions are training centres in which inmates refine their skills and motivations on the road to career criminality (West, 1984).

Other initiatives grounded in differential association theory include the use of helping professionals and the establishment of self-help groups. In the first instance, psychiatrists, social workers, and correctional personnel may serve as sources of conventional definitions. These professionals meet with clients regularly to provide advice, support, and treatment to assist rehabilitation and reintegration into conventional society. Self-help groups like Alcoholics Anonymous and Synanon, consisting of reformed alcoholics and former drug addicts, promote the development of nondeviant definitions through resocialization. Group members who have themselves experienced alcohol and drug addiction seek to help others break the habit and return to more productive lives.

The frequency, **duration**, and **intensity** of contacts between deviants and their pro-conformist referents affect the success of these efforts. These factors are likely to be less influential for the clientele of the helping professions than for the voluntary members of self-help organizations (Liska, 1987).

Table 3.1 summarizes the development of the Chicago School's ideas.

TABLE 3.1

THE CHICAGO SCHOOL

Theory	Theorist(s)	Central Premise	Key Concepts	Principal Contributors
① Human Ecology; Social Disorganization	Clifford Shaw and Henry McKay	Institutional breakdown and a lack of social control give rise to values and norms conducive to illegal conduct; older youth socialize their younger counterparts to law violation in stable slum environments	web of life; symbiosis; invasion, dominance, and succession; social disorganization; mobility, heterogeneity, and poverty; concentric zones (zone of transition); differential social organization	Explains enduring patterns of illegal behaviour in impoverished inner-city areas over time
② Differential Association	Edwin Sutherland	Individuals learn to commit crime from exposure to an excess of pro-deviant definitions	Differential association; learning; frequency, duration, priority, and necessity	Explains crime across the social structure
③ Differential Identification	Daniel Glaser	Individuals learn to commit crime through a process of identification with definitions of deviance conveyed by real or imagined others who favour rule violation	Differential identification	Explains potential for media contribution to deviant and criminal activity
④ Differential Reinforcement	Ronald Akers and Robert Burgess	Individuals' learning to commit crime is enhanced by having criminality more often rewarded than punished	Differential reinforcement; operant conditioning	Augments differential association with principles of learning theory (operant conditioning); incorporates psychological principles

EVALUATION OF THE CHICAGO SCHOOL

HUMAN ECOLOGY

Human ecology has been criticized for overemphasizing social disorganization. Critics argue that the terms "organizational diversity" or "differential social organization" better capture the reality of the situation. The essence of the critics' claim is that the transitional zone merely has different forms of social organization, which appear disorganized only from a staunchly middle-class point of view (Matza, 1966).

In addition to confusing differential social organization with disorganization, human ecologists display another middle-class bias. Shaw and McKay assume that middle-class areas of cities are more homogeneous and more cohesively organized (and hence less deviant) than inner-city neighbourhoods (Mills, 1943). However, these presumed high levels of social integration and cohesion do not always exist in affluent neighbourhoods. Moreover, while the official data used by Shaw and McKay reveal a strong concentration of deviance and crime in transitional zones, other sources such as crime surveys suggest that residents of middle-class neighbourhoods also perform large numbers of nonconforming and illegal acts (Jensen and Rojek, 1980). Furthermore, since police patrols tend to be more concentrated in impoverished slum neighbourhoods than in affluent middle-class districts and since the types of crime committed by the lower classes are of the more visible street variety, the profile of criminal activity is distorted. The essence of these criticisms is that crime is simply more easily detected in lower-class ghettos than in higher-class neighbourhoods.

Measurement problems have made the determination of cause and effect particularly problematic in earlier human ecology research. The theory holds that social disorganization results in higher rates of deviance. All too often, however, disorganization itself is measured by the existence of a high rate of rule violation. It is hardly surprising that social disorganization (measured by high rates of deviance) is highly predictive of deviance (measured by high rates of deviance). Since the measurements of cause and effect are virtually identical, the exercise represents a rather circular analysis (Kornhauser, 1978).

Recent assessments of the ecological approach have employed indicators other than rates of deviance as measures of social disorganization (Chilton, 1964).

These improved measures include degrees of ethnic differentiation, ratios of owners to renters, and ratios of singles to families. High degrees of ethnic difference, more renters than owners, and more singles than families are taken to indicate less social cohesion and community attachment. Conversely, ethnic homogeneity, home ownership, and resident families indicate greater cohesion.

The prediction is that less neighbourhood integration will result in more nonconformity. Research based on the ecological model has consistently supported this hypothesis. Deviance and crime, at least as it is measured in official data, are consistently concentrated in city areas characterized by poverty, transience, urban decline, and ethnic diversity (Brantingham and Brantingham, 1981).

The success of programs for improving the quality of life and reducing crime in disadvantaged urban areas is uncertain. Although many of these programs have operated for a long time, their impacts on crime reduction have not been subjected to methodologically rigorous research (Miller, 1962). While improved services and facilities may have many positive consequences, their direct relationship to the control of deviant and criminal activity is difficult to assess.

Critics have attacked the policy of the ecological approach by charging that it advocates treating symptoms rather than alleviating causes. They maintain that the problems in disadvantaged areas are consequences of an economy that advantages some groups at the expense of others. The ecological perspective advocates providing slum residents with sufficient resources to increase their educational and occupational opportunities and to otherwise adjust to the problems they face. Many sociologists argue that these efforts do not seriously address issues of inequality. Providing genuine solutions to the problem of urban decay, they maintain, requires more radical social and economic change (Vold and Bernard, 1986).

When it was introduced in the early part of this century, the ecological approach did much to counter the dominant biological and psychological theories of deviance and crime. Residents of disadvantaged urban neighbourhoods were widely considered deviant as a result of racially inherited biological and psychological deficiencies. What Shaw and McKay and others demonstrated was that various class and ethnic groups were deviant only while residing in slum areas. Once they abandoned the transitional zone for the more affluent outlying sectors, they joined the ranks of the law-abiding (Faris, 1967). This finding was powerful evidence that social and economic conditions associated with certain urban areas were more responsible for increased rates of drug addiction, alcoholism, mental illness, suicide, and crime than were the individual traits of residents.

DIFFERENTIAL ASSOCIATION

Both differential identification and differential reinforcement are supported by empirical testing. Differential identification, however, is unclear about whether identification consistently occurs before or after the deviant activity it is supposed to explain. If identification with a criminal figure, real or imaginary, occurs after the deviant or criminal act, it cannot be considered to have contributed to that act (Thio, 1988).

Burgess and Akers emphasize the positive experience of reward that results in deviant acts being repeated time and again. However, critics point out that the theory does not explain why someone would commit a deviant act in the first place (Thio, 1988).

Differential association emphasizes the learning of skills and motives in group contexts. Some sociologists have pointed out that much deviance and crime requires no special skills and that nonconformity comes naturally (Glueck, 1956). They cite violence, vandalism, and ordinary theft as examples of unsophisticated acts that often occur in the heat of passion or on impulse. Moreover, they argue that deviant acts for which there are no cultural or subcultural supports are not well accounted for by differential association. Incest and child molesting, for example, appear universally unsupported by the traditions of any group.

Developing concrete empirical measures has also been problematic for differential association theory. It is difficult to isolate and identify empirically the presence, in an individual, of too many definitions favouring either deviance or conformity. Similarly, indicators and accurate estimates of frequency, duration, priority, and intensity have proven elusive (Nettler, 1984).

The difficulty of measuring excesses of definitions has led researchers to employ a proxy indicator — group membership. Persons who are members of deviant groups are assumed to be associated with deviant traditions. This "bad companions" conceptualization of deviance causation, while departing significantly from Sutherland's initial conceptualization,

has received considerable empirical support (West, 1984).

While members of deviant groups are indeed more deviant than members of conforming groups, a major debate revolves around this fact. Differential association, as presented in this revision, suggests that membership in deviant groups results in the learning of skills and motivations that encourage and result in deviant behaviour. Several critics point out that an alternative sequence is equally plausible: deviants may seek out persons with similar predispositions. The question is which comes first — membership in deviant groups or deviant behaviour (Gomme, 1985b).

SUMMARY

Human ecology approaches examine the geographical distribution of deviance and crime in urban areas. Districts plagued by social and economic deprivation also experience more deviant and criminal activity. Ecologists explain this empirical association between deprivation and deviance by arguing that traditional forms of social control in these areas have broken down and left these neighbourhoods socially disorganized. This erosion of traditional social control is seen as a result of industrial expansion and urbanization. Human ecology recommends various forms of urban renewal and community building, but their effectiveness in reducing crime awaits methodologically rigorous evaluation.

The human ecology approach has been criticized for overemphasizing "disorganization," for unequivocally asserting that crime is concentrated among the lower classes, and for imprecisely measuring central concepts. The consistency of human ecology research findings and the challenge they presented to the established accounts of deviance are the major contributions of the human ecology approach.

Differential association builds on several of the tenets of the ecological approach, including the notion of cultural transmission, to explain how individuals are socialized to deviant behaviour by their reference groups. In nine propositions, the theory suggests that the skills and motives of deviance are learned from intimate others through various communication processes. When individuals, through social interaction, are exposed to more definitions favouring deviance than favouring conformity, rule breaking becomes likely. Two major extensions of differential association are the theories of differential identification and differential reinforcement. Differential identification explains how definitions favouring deviance develop in contexts other than face-to-face interaction. Differential reinforcement explains continuing deviant behaviour in terms of operant conditioning: the rewards and costs of most behaviours affect the extent to which they are continued. Differential reinforcement explains more specifically than does differential association the precise way in which people learn deviant and conforming behaviours. Policies grounded in differential association aim to reduce deviant associations and bolster conforming associations.

The deficiencies of differential association include its inadequate account of deviance engaged in alone or in the absence of cultural support, its imprecise measurements, and its uncertainty with respect to the sequence of cause and effect. That the theory spawned considerable research and challenged the conception of deviance as primarily a product of personality deficiencies are among its major contributions.

DISCUSSION QUESTIONS

1. Demonstrate how ideas from plant ecology were adapted to explain social deviance.

2. Discuss the relationship between the transitional zone and the other concentric zones.

3. Explain how differential identification and differential reinforcement represent extensions of differential association.

4. How can differential association and human ecology explanations be combined to explain deviance?

5. Discuss how the work of the Chicago school has contributed to an understanding of the causes of deviance and crime.

WEB LINKS

The Chicago School
http://www.crimetheory.com/Soc1/Chic1.htm
> This page from Crimetheory.com contains information on Park and Burgess's concentric zone model. Click on the link at the bottom to read about Shaw and McKay's application of that model.

The Ecological Approach and Social Disorganization
http://www.criminology.fsu.edu/crimtheory/week6.htm
> These lecture notes prepared by Professor Cecil E. Greek provide an introduction to the ecological approach in criminology.

Chicago's Pragmatic Planners
http://www.sociology.columbia.edu/faculty/venkatesh/papers/soc_sci_hist_paper.html
> In this paper, Professor Sudhir Venkatesh of Columbia University argues that the attempt by Ernest Burgess and his colleagues to uncover the human ecology of Chicago was a deliberate social construction of the city.

Differential Association Theory
http://www.indiana.edu/~theory/Kip/Edwin.htm
> This page offers a point-form synopsis of Edwin Sutherland's differential association theory.

The Theory of Differential Association
http://www.calvin.edu/academic/crijus/courses/suth1.htm
> This page, by J. Scott Richeson, puts the theory of differential association into context.

RECOMMENDED READINGS

Akers, R.L. (1998). *Social Learning and Social Structure: A General Theory of Crime and Deviance.* Boston: Northeastern University Press.
> Presents culmination of Akers's development and testing of social learning theory. Incorporates Skinnerian principles of operant conditioning. Concludes with outline of social structural theory that is consistent with social learning principles.

Burgess, R., and R.L. Akers. (1966). "A Differential Association-Reinforcement Theory of Criminal Behaviour." *Social Problems* 14:128–47.
Original formulation of social learning theory that has influenced contemporary thinking in the sociology and psychology of crime.

Glaser, D. (1956). "Criminality Theories and Behavioral Images." *American Journal of Sociology* 61:433–44.
Classic presentation of differential identification theory and its extension of Sutherland's ideas of differential association.

Shaw, C., and H.D. McKay. (1969). *Juvenile Delinquency and Urban Areas.* Chicago: University of Chicago Press.
Presents the fundamental thesis of social disorganization in Chicago that has strongly influenced contemporary analyses of crime in urban contexts.

Sutherland, E., and D. Cressey. (1978). *Criminology.* Philadelphia: Lippincott.
Contains Sutherland's classic articulation of the highly influential theory of differential association.

CHAPTER 4

FUNCTIONALISM

The aims of this chapter are to familiarize the reader with:

- the organic analogy, manifest and latent functions, and the idea of the social system
- the concept of anomie, developed by Durkheim to explain suicide and later modified by Merton to explain deviance and crime generally
- Merton's theory of anomie and the five adaptations to strain
- Cohen's extension of Merton's theory with his use of "status frustration"
- Cloward and Ohlin's extension of Merton's theory with their use of "differential illegitimate opportunity"
- the four functions of deviance
- the policy implications of functional theories
- the deficiencies of the functionalist perspective
- the contributions of the functionalist perspective to an understanding of deviance and crime

INTRODUCTION

Functionalism, like the ecological branch of the Chicago school, uses a biological analogy to explain how society operates. It draws parallels between organic life and the social order. This chapter begins by outlining the general mechanics of the functionalist perspective. The two central thematic frameworks applied to the explanation of deviant and illegal conduct, both of which originate in the work of Émile Durkheim, are described. The anomie approach emphasizes the violation of social norms, while the functions-of-deviance approach seeks to explain the contributions to the social order made by nonconformity and illegality.

THE FUNCTIONALIST APPROACH

Like a living organism, society is conceived of as a series of integrated parts, each of which plays a role in assuring the continuance of the system (Parsons, 1951). Just as the heart, lungs, stomach, and veins of an animal operate to keep it alive and well, society's parts — its social structures — function in an orderly manner to meet its goals — maintenance, solidarity, and survival. The parts of society that operate in harmony to sustain the entire system are usually called social structures and are analogous to parts of the body.

An elementary example of the functionalist perspective illustrates its central propositions. The family, the educational system, organized religion, and the economy are four parts of the social system that ensure the persistence of society and the well-being of its members. The family produces children and instils in them fundamental values, including respect for others, regard for their property, and belief in the merit of hard work. Later, the school provides the child with basic knowledge and work-related skills. Organized religion supports, in its teachings, many of the basic values learned at home and at school and provides a spiritual means of coping with life's problems. Then, properly socialized by the family, the school, and the church, the individual participates in the marketplace by working, earning, and spending. The healthier the parts of the social system, the more vital is society and the better off are its members.

Functionalism, like the organic analogy from which it derives, asserts that the ideal condition of any system is balance and stability. An important implication of equilibrium is that changes in one part of the system affect all other parts. Increased heart rates require arteries and veins to cope with a greater volume of blood. With regard to society, the same principle pertains. If families produce more children, the educational system must expand to accommodate more students, religious institutions must increase their services to youth, and the economy must incorporate an enlarged cohort of workers.

Functionalists assert that there are two types of function: manifest and latent (Merton, 1957). **Manifest functions** are those that society intends and that are often formally set out as institutional goals. For example, society seeks to punish criminals so that they and others will obey its laws. It tries to protect the public from continued criminal activity by incarcerating career criminals, and attempts to rehabilitate and reintegrate offenders by treating their psychological maladies, by instilling in them the values of diligence and honesty, and by training them for re-entry into the labour market and society at large (Griffiths and Verdun-Jones, 1989).

Latent functions differ from manifest functions in that they are unintended and almost always informal. Among the latent functions of the corrections system are the provision of an underground training school for criminals, which in turn creates an enormous number of jobs in crime control and related fields (Toch, 1977).

Functionalism assumes that society is integrated and orderly and that there is considerable consensus among its members regarding the form and nature of normative rules, values, and beliefs. Since functionalists presume that no pattern of behaviour perseveres unless it serves a function, they explain persisting social structures in terms of the functions they perform. Marriage, worship, and work are patterns of behaviour that have been around for a long time; so is crime. Functionalist analysis first identifies persistent societal patterns and then analyzes how they maintain the social system.

FUNCTIONALIST EXPLANATIONS OF DEVIANCE AND CRIME

Functionalism has two basic theories of deviance and crime, both of which originate in the writings of Émile Durkheim. The first perspective focuses on norm violations as a disruption of natural order and equilibrium. This approach includes the work of the anomie theorists Merton, Cohen, and Cloward and Ohlin. The second perspective argues that deviance is normal and functions to maintain society.

ÉMILE DURKHEIM AND ANOMIE

In explaining the incidence of one particular type of deviance — suicide — Durkheim emphasized the importance of variations in external social regulation. The relative absence of social regulation resulting in a state of normlessness is a condition Durkheim calls **anomie**. He considers it a pathological state indicating a breakdown in social order and solidarity (Durkheim, 1951).

In a healthy society where anomie does not exist, citizens know exactly what goals are appropriate for their particular social positions and precisely how they are supposed to realize those goals. Under normal conditions, social ethics and individuals' sense of what is morally proper limit their aspirations. Durkheim conceptualizes anomie as a state of confusion about the legitimacy of various social aspirations and the propriety of certain ways of pursuing those aspirations.

Using the concept of anomie, Durkheim develops his theory of suicide in the following fashion. He theorizes that a person's physical and social needs are governed differently. Nature regulates physical needs. For example, hungry people eat until they are full and then they stop; internal regulatory mechanisms automatically discourage people from eating too much. Social needs, however, are not regulated naturally. A person's desires for wealth, power, and prestige, for example, are unlimited if not checked by external and social constraints. Unregulated by external social norms, these goals escalate until they become virtually unattainable. The inability to satisfy unregulated and heightened desires for wealth, power, and prestige results in disappointment, unhappiness, and frustration. This disillusionment is accompanied by stress and subsequently by an increased propensity to commit suicide, as shown in Figure 4.1.

In explaining how anomie is produced, Durkheim focuses on the relationship between suicide and sudden dislocating changes in economic conditions. Noting that suicide rates are lowest when the economy is stable, he argues that under such conditions, both culturally defined goals and the rules relating to their attainment are closely governed by strong and unequivocal social norms. Both rapid economic contraction and rapid economic expansion, however,

FIGURE 4.1

DURKHEIM'S THEORY OF ANOMIE AND SUICIDE

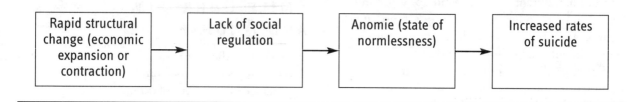

weaken the constraining power of normative regulation and produce anomie. During severe economic depressions, for example, individuals experience declining wages and increasing unemployment. They do not, however, reduce their wants to reflect the new economic realities. As the disparity increases between high aspirations and the failing economic means of realizing such aspirations, feelings of distress intensify. The resulting strain manifests itself, according to Durkheim, in higher rates of suicide.

The alternative case, unbridled economic growth and expansion, produces equally stressful conditions. Although individuals are able to achieve their long-standing goals more readily, at least initially, they are encouraged in the long run to aspire to increasingly lofty ends. Where rising expectations outstrip the opportunities for their realization, frustration and disillusionment increase and so does the frequency of suicide.

ROBERT MERTON – SOCIAL STRUCTURE AND ANOMIE

Robert Merton revised Durkheim's original discussion of anomie and suicide into a more general theory of social deviance (Merton, 1938).

From a very early age, according to Merton, people are taught the value of being successful. In North American society in particular, success means making money and acquiring material possessions. Under ideal conditions of structural integration, the culturally defined goals of success and material acquisition align sufficiently well with the institutionalized means of attaining them (e.g., education and work) that individuals are able to legitimately achieve the rewards to which society has encouraged them to aspire. Winners are regularly rewarded in school, on the job, in sports, and in other spheres of human activity. Media depictions reinforce this view; they often fea-

ture a rags-to-riches story wherein some downtrodden soul "makes good" through intelligence and effort. Indeed, individuals frequently assess their social worth mainly in terms of their material success.

Merton argues that what is implied in North American culture is that success is available to anyone who has the necessary intelligence and drive, regardless of social characteristics such as class, ethnicity, and gender. He suggests, however, that these ideal conditions do not exist in North American society rather, inequality produces **differential opportunity** for people of different circumstances.

According to Merton, the combined overemphasis on ends and underemphasis on means produces an imperfect state of affairs (anomie). With all their energies focused on winning (goals), the way people play the game (means) may lose much of its importance. Inattention to the rules eventually results in their becoming imprecise and less explicit. This lack of structural balance results in a condition of malintegration or anomie that in turn produces strain, which is most acutely felt by lower-status individuals. Legitimate mechanisms of attainment, mainly educational and occupational opportunities, are more restricted for these individuals. Compared with white people from the middle and upper classes, members of certain ethnic groups and of the lower classes are significantly disadvantaged in the competition to become successful. The dilemma facing lower-status individuals is that society has encouraged them to aspire highly while denying them equal access to legitimate avenues of opportunity (education and work). As a result, the disadvantaged experience frustrations and strains that encourage them to engage in deviance as a way of adapting to the gap separating social goals and the means of attaining them.

Merton specifies five modes of personal adaptation to anomie: conformity, innovation, **ritualism**,

retreatism, and rebellion. (See Figure 4.2.) All except conformity are deviant responses. Conformists accept the legitimacy of both social goals and the legitimate means of reaching them. They seek success through the socially acceptable avenues of educational and occupational advancement. Most middle- and lower-class people are conformists. Although members of the lower classes are less likely than members of the middle classes to attain their desired ends, most of them still obey the rules. While accepting both goals and means does not ensure that goals will be met, it does imply faith in the system. Conforming members of the lower classes who are less successful than they wish to be accept responsibility for their own poor showing and continue to strive by sticking with it and by encouraging their children to compete within the rules.

Innovation occurs when individuals experiencing strain adhere to the culturally defined goals of material success but abandon the legitimate ways of pursuing them. Seeking material gain through illegal means, innovators typically engage in a variety of predatory offences, including theft, burglary, and robbery.

The archetype of the innovator is the gangster (Liska, 1987). Stories abound of impoverished young immigrants coming to North America in search of a better life. Excluded from legitimate avenues of success by discrimination and prejudice, many young immigrants with considerable intelligence and ambition have turned their talents to organized crime and amassed considerable fortunes. The affluence of several wealthy and influential North American families began with alcohol trading in the Prohibition era.

Ritualists reduce strain by lowering their aspirations so that their goals correspond more closely with what is attainable in light of the insufficient legitimate means available. The ritualist is usually lower-middle class; a good example is the aging junior-level bureaucrat who gradually becomes aware that he or she will not be promoted. The ritualist accepts this worrisome reality, comes to work each day, and toils relatively compulsively as an honest employee. For ritualists, means become ends in themselves. While ritualists break no formal rules they do violate informal cultural norms, since everyone is expected to strive continuously for success. Since ritualism is only a minor social problem, this adaptation has received little attention from sociologists of deviance.

Retreatism is a deviant adaptation to stress that involves renouncing not only the legitimate means of attaining goals but the very goals themselves. Merton suggests that when an individual's socialization equally emphasizes success goals and the legitimate means of their attainment, and when the individual is unable to soothe feelings of strain by depreciating goals over means (ritualism) or means over goals (innovation), the solution is likely to be withdrawal. Those who retreat neither value success nor wish to actively pursue it. Retreatists include alcoholics, drug addicts, psychological misfits, tramps, and hippies.

FIGURE 4.2

MERTON'S THEORY OF SOCIAL STRUCTURE AND ANOMIE

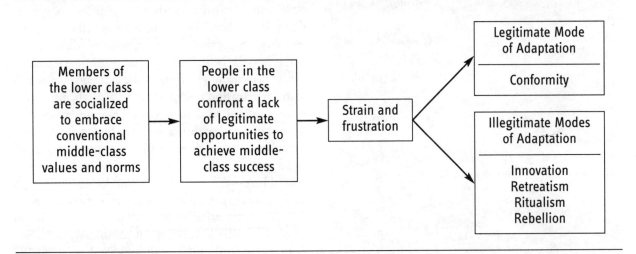

In rebellion, the rebel rejects both the goals and the legitimate means of their acquisition and seeks to replace them with new ones. Into this category fall revolutionaries and terrorists who seek radical change in the social order, perhaps by replacing one form of government (tyranny) with another (democracy).

In his typology of adaptations, shown in Table 4.1, Merton presents four deviant reactions to the structural malintegration of social goals and legitimate means, the latter of which he views as differently distributed among social segments. Innovation, ritualism, retreatism, and rebellion are not meant to represent personality types. An individual might vary his or her adaptive strategy from time to time or engage in more than one adaptation concurrently. In this way, Merton is somewhat vague as to why one adaptation might be selected over another. In explaining differing propensities for innovation and ritualism, however, he does point out that differing degrees of socialization against the use of illegitimate means affect the person's choice of adaptation. Lower-class individuals more frequently innovate because they are less likely to be socialized against the use of illegitimate means in the pursuit of success. Lower-middle- and middle-class individuals, because they are more effectively socialized to conformity, are reluctant to break the law to achieve success. As a result of their presumably more adequate

TABLE 4.1

MERTON'S THEORY OF ANOMIE

Mode of Adaptation	Cultural Goal	Institutionalized Means
Conformity	+	+
Innovation	+	−
Ritualism	−	+
Retreatism	−	−
Rebellion	+	+
	−	−

Source: Robert Merton (1938). "Social Structure and Anomie." *American Sociological Review* 3(1938):676.

socialization, lower-middle- and middle-class persons are more likely to adapt to strain by simply reducing their aspirations and becoming ritualists.

ALBERT COHEN AND STATUS FRUSTRATION

In 1955, Albert Cohen modified Merton's theory of anomie to explain higher rates of delinquency among lower-class youth. Cohen developed the idea that lower-class delinquency occurs as a subcultural adaptation to problems generated by the societal predominance of middle-class culture (Cohen, 1955).

Like Merton, Cohen argues that North American society encourages all its members to aspire highly but at the same time makes it very difficult for some groups to be successful. With compulsory attendance, the school becomes a competitive arena in which youth of all classes pursue the all-important goal of elevated social status. While both lower- and middle-class youth desire high status, lower-class boys are much more likely to fail in attaining the rewards commonly accorded to achievers in the public school system. In the competition for academic and social success in school, children from middle-class backgrounds have a decided advantage over their lower-class counterparts. Middle-class parents have already socialized their offspring into the system of values and behaviours represented, promoted, and rewarded in schools. Academically, middle-class children are more highly motivated, more diligent, more articulate, and better able to defer gratification. Behaviourally, they are more likely to be obedient, polite, and respectful.

Lower-class youths, having learned different norms and values, do not readily meet the standards of attitude and performance that the education system demands of them. Unable to compete effectively and faced with constant failure to achieve middle-class status, lower-class children experience considerable frustration. According to Cohen, the consequence of this **status frustration** is the formation of a subculture that incorporates a rival hierarchy of statuses through a process of reaction formation. (See Figure 4.3.) In this subculture, lower-class youth can compete on more equal terms for status that is meaningful in their own eyes. The criteria for status in the lower-class youth subculture are precisely the opposite of those valued in the dominant middle-class culture. Acts worthy of accolades in the lower-class subculture are, as Cohen puts it, "nonutilitarian, malicious, and negativistic."

FIGURE 4.3

STATUS FRUSTRATION THEORY

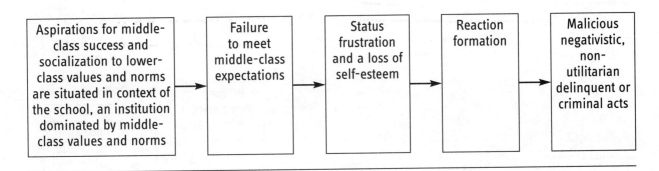

Performed not out of need but in pursuit of status, these acts symbolize the rejection of the middle-class value system. Stealing, fighting, and vandalizing property are intended to improve one's position in a delinquent subculture that itself defies conventional, law-abiding, middle-class behaviour.

For both Merton and Cohen, the decisive causal factor in the production of deviant behaviour is the disjunction between the social goals of material success and elevated status on the one hand, and the legitimate means of their attainment — occupational and educational achievement — on the other. The lower classes lack sufficient access to legitimate means and consequently engage in delinquent and criminal activity. Cohen extends the horizons of anomie theory by using it to explain nonutilitarian as opposed to utilitarian deviant acts. He also expands the explanatory framework by documenting the connection between status frustration and the formation of delinquent subcultures.

RICHARD CLOWARD AND LLOYD OHLIN AND DIFFERENTIAL ILLEGITIMATE OPPORTUNITY

Cloward and Ohlin (1960) extended Merton's theory by developing the concept of **differential illegitimate opportunity**. They agree with Merton that individuals are compelled to become deviant in circumstances where success goals are highly emphasized but where the legitimate strategies of attainment are severely restricted. Cloward and Ohlin differ from Merton in one major respect, however. They point out that while lower-class persons frequently lack access to socially acceptable ways of achieving success,

many are also denied equal access to the illegitimate ways of meeting their goals. As with the legitimate avenues to success, like education and work, illegitimate routes range from the highly restricted to the wide open. Cloward and Ohlin criticize Merton's implicit assumption that, faced with the disjunction between ends and legal means, all lower-class individuals enjoy equal access to illicit techniques of goal attainment. Rather, they assert that both the extent of deviance and the form it takes are strongly influenced by the availability of unlawful options.

The degree to which opportunities exist for people to learn illicit techniques and put them to use affects participation in deviant activity. To make a living as a burglar, one must have the opportunity to learn how to execute the crime and how to sell stolen merchandise without getting caught. These endeavours are likely to be greatly facilitated by the immediate presence of criminal role models, of instructors expert in the skills required for break, enter, and theft, and of a reliable "fence." The lack of such an illegitimate opportunity structure markedly reduces the likelihood of taking up burglary as a vocation.

Cloward and Ohlin outline three types of deviant subculture that offer different access to illicit opportunities: criminal, conflict, and retreatist. (See Figure 4.4.) A neighbourhood characterized by an illegitimate opportunity structure has developed a criminal subculture. Individuals learn the skills required for theft, burglary, robbery, and the like from more seasoned members of the neighbourhood subculture. Fences convert stolen goods into cash. Illegal conduct of this type is less likely if, for whatever reason, integration into the **criminal subculture** is impossible.

FIGURE 4.4

DIFFERENTIAL OPPORTUNITY THEORY

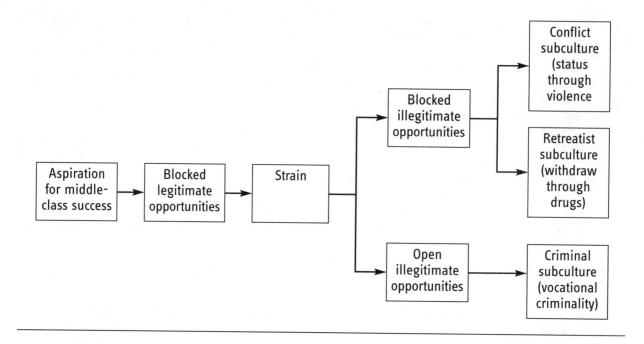

According to Cloward and Ohlin, the criminal subculture is most prevalent in established and stable slum areas of large cities, where various criminal organizations have become firmly entrenched.

Conflict subcultures characterize neighbourhoods that offer neither legitimate nor illegitimate routes to success. The only way to obtain high status in these cases is through violence. Combat skill, physical strength, and enthusiasm for risking one's safety form the bases of prestige in the violent gang. This type of subculture, Cloward and Ohlin suggest, is prevalent in the disorganized slum.

Membership in conflict subcultures has prerequisites that cannot be met by all. For those who lack the physical prowess and taste for violent action and for whom both legitimate and illegitimate opportunities are unavailable, retreat is a likely alternative. "**Double failures**," those who are not able to take advantage of either legitimate or illegitimate opportunity structures, form retreatist subcultures in which drugs and alcohol are used frequently to escape.

Cloward and Ohlin, like Cohen before them, extend Merton's theory of anomie by further specifying the way in which the gap between aspirations and opportunities translates into deviant behaviour. Cohen specifies the intervening mechanism as status

frustration, while for Cloward and Ohlin differential illegitimate opportunity is the mechanism through which the rift separating goals and means produces conduct that violates social norms.

THE FUNCTIONS OF DEVIANCE

Academic interest in Merton's anomie theory and its variants declined significantly in the early 1960s. The publication of K.T. Erikson's *Wayward Puritans* in 1966, however, renewed interest in functionalist theories of deviance. In this work, Erikson studies deviance in a seventeenth-century Massachusetts colony. He explains incidents of heresy and witchcraft in terms of their contributions to the social cohesion and social stability of the community. In developing the notion that deviant behaviour is functional for society and social groups within it, Erikson leans heavily on ideas developed by Durkheim (1962) in his *Rules of Sociological Method*. In this book, Durkheim further explores his interests in both the creation of social solidarity and the nature of legal sanctions.

Durkheim points out that while there is tremendous variation across societies with regard to what is considered crime, no society is entirely crime-free.

Given the considerable range of this variation, it cannot be said that anything intrinsically makes acts criminal. Rather, what defines an act as criminal in any society is the fact that it elicits social condemnation. An act is a crime, Durkheim maintains, "because it shocks the common conscience." Further, crime can be distinguished from minor social infractions by virtue of the fact that the social disapproval is intense. Crime and punishment, Durkheim notes, are universal and persistent features of human society. Since patterns of norm violation and their punishment are both widespread and enduring, he argues that they must perform vital functions for the social system.

Four functions are served for society by crime and by the social reactions it elicits (see Table 4.2) (Erikson, 1966). When community standards are seriously violated, the ensuing outrage and contempt felt by citizens brings them together in an expression of common indignation. Crime and the reaction it entails on the part of both citizens and the media promote the creation of social solidarity. For example, on April 16, 1992, St. Catharines teenager Kristen French disappeared in broad daylight while walking home from school. Her disappearance, the subsequent discovery of her body, and the search for her killer became the central focus of public and media attention for months following the incident. The horror and outrage people felt over this brutal killing were widely shared, and public emotions were communicated in such a way that common values of right and wrong and good and evil were reconfirmed. In this sense, crime functions to integrate members of a social system who unite with a common sentiment against a universal enemy.

The second **function of deviance** and its condemnation is the clarification of the moral boundaries of the community. The precise borders separating the

acceptable from the unacceptable are not always clear. Social reactions to behaviour that "crosses the line" clarify how far one can go in a particular direction. What constitutes an act of sexual harassment in the university? Can sexual harassment be a longing glance? Is a professor's compliment on a student's attire sexual harassment? Do requests by an instructor for a graduate-student assistant to work late, to go for a drink after work, or to share a room at a conference constitute sexual harassment? Is an overt request for sex necessary? Must a student be threatened with lower grades or the loss of a research position if sexual demands are not met? Is any sexual reference that makes a student feel uncomfortable equivalent to harassment? Cases in which complaints are formally examined and punitive actions taken do much to clarify the bounds of acceptable behaviour. In a celebrated case at the University of Toronto, for example, a tribunal held a professor responsible for harassing a female student. Wearing skin diving equipment, he had repeatedly followed and stared at her underwater in a university swimming pool.

Functionalists consider conformity to social values and norms on the part of the majority necessary for society to operate harmoniously. Conformity, they suggest, must be rewarded; saintly behaviour must be visibly condoned. By inflicting punishment on those who violate society's rules, those who obey them can compare themselves with deviants and feel virtuous. Fining the motorist who drinks and drives or jailing the executive who cheats on an income tax return allows law-abiding drivers and businesspeople to compare themselves with their lawbreaking counterparts and to feel respectable for having remained honest and upright. These penalties accent the rewards for conformity and reinforce the commitment to moral uprightness.

Finally, Durkheim argues that crime is a precondition of society's capacity for flexibility and change, and that it can sometimes promote progress:

> How many times, indeed, it is only an anticipation of future morality — a step toward what will be! According to Athenian law, Socrates was a criminal, and his condemnation was no more than just. However, his crime, namely, the independence of his thought, rendered a service not only to humanity but to his country. (Durkheim, 1962:71)

Many consider it progressive to defy certain laws if the cause is worthy. In recent years, various groups of Canadians have defied the law to promote an end to

TABLE 4.2

FUNCTIONS OF DEVIANCE AND REACTION TO DEVIANCE

Integrate members of the society

Clarify moral boundaries of communities

Reward and thereby motivate saintly behaviour

Provide avenue for social flexibility and change

wars and nuclear-weapons testing, discrimination against disadvantaged groups, and environmental destruction.

Crime, according to Durkheim, performs four functions for society: it increases social solidarity, clarifies norms, accents the rewards of conformity, and has the potential to stimulate social progress. Deviance is a normal, necessary, inescapable characteristic of society. Even in a "perfect" group, some behaviours will be considered criminal:

> Imagine a society of saints, a perfect cloister of exemplary individuals. Crimes, properly so called, will there be unknown: but faults which appear venal to the layman will create there the same scandal that the ordinary offence does in ordinary consciousness. If then, this society has the power to judge and punish, it will define these acts as criminal and will treat them as such. (Durkheim, 1962:69)

While some level of deviance can have positive consequences for society, too much nonconformity can be pathological and encourage social breakdown. The murder of a teenager in St. Catharines may result in increased solidarity among residents of south central Ontario, but the killing of hundreds of children in Beirut does not have the same effect. Excessive deviance and crime can fuel suspicion and fear and seriously undermine social order. Too much crime, in short, can be dysfunctional (Liska, 1987). Table 4.3 summarizes functionalist approaches.

FUNCTIONALISM AND SOCIAL POLICY

Durkheim identified several interrelated causes of deviance and crime: social disintegration, social deregulation, and rapid social and economic change. To reduce deviance, the integration and regulation of society must be increased and economic expansions and contractions stabilized.

The Mertonian version of anomie as a gap between cultural goals and means of achievement has led to policy initiatives aimed at either broadening access to lawful educational and occupational means or redistributing existing resources more equitably. Programs designed to provide more training and more jobs to members of socially and economically disadvantaged groups and to stimulate economic growth are offshoots of this perspective (Liska, 1987).

EVALUATION OF THE FUNCTIONALIST PERSPECTIVES

Critics have subjected both the anomie and functions-of-deviance approaches to careful scrutiny. Some argue that there is no evidence that individuals from lower-class backgrounds are more deviant than people from the middle and upper classes (Thio, 1975). In initially proposing his theory, Merton observed that official crime data demonstrate that illegal conduct is concentrated among the lower classes. However, official data on crime are obtained from police and court records. This information base produces a clear bias, because police are more likely to detect types of deviance perpetrated by members of the lower classes. Alternatively, they are much less likely to uncover and proceed against the deviant activities of the middle and especially of the upper classes. Murder, assault, and bank robbery are much more likely to be brought to police attention than are the marketing of unsafe products, the polluting of the environment, and theft by computer. Thus, critics charge that anomie theory, by dwelling on the explanation of lower-class deviance, effectively ignores the wide range of violations committed by more advantaged members of society (Taylor, Walton, and Young, 1973).

The assumption that the same aspirations are held by the lower, middle, and upper classes is questionable. Although society may encourage everyone to aspire highly, members of the lower classes may have more realistic expectations of what is achievable (Nettler, 1984; Kornhauser, 1978). Their aspirations may not be as high as those of members of the middle classes.

Sociologists have also questioned the notion of value consensus, which is central to the anomie framework. The heterogeneity and pluralism that are the hallmarks of Canadian and American postindustrial societies call into question the assertion that everyone is committed to material success. Divisions of class, ethnicity, region, age, and sex may promote competing sets of values. Thus, it is likely that various minority groups engage in different types of deviance for reasons other than frustration with their inability to reach material goals. For example, gambling, the use of prohibited drugs, and excessive alcohol consumption may be motivated not by strain but by the fact that they are a normal part of a culture (Lemert, 1967; Ribordy, 1980).

TABLE 4.3

FUNCTIONALIST APPROACHES TO EXPLAINING DEVIANCE AND CRIME

Theory	Theorist(s)	Central Premise	Key Concepts	Principal Contributions
Anomie	Émile Durkheim	Anomie or a breakdown in social regulation increases dissatisfaction, which produces stress and leads to suicide	Social regulation; anomie	Provides a social structural explanation for behaviour (suicide) that is often taken to be highly individualistic with purely psychological causes
Anomie	Robert Merton	Disjunction between ends and means produces strain, thereby increasing the probability of deviant behaviour	Structural integration: conformity; innovation; ritualism; retreatism; rebellion	Emphasizes the role of social structural conditions, as opposed to personality, in generation of illegal conduct
Status frustration	Albert Cohen	Lower-class males' experience of failure to achieve middle-class success creates a subculture in which status attainment involves engagement in nonconforming conduct that is nonutilitarian, malicious, and negativistic	Status frustration; reaction formation	Demonstrates mechanism by which lower-class living conditions produce illegal conduct that is violent and destructive and is often seen as senseless
Differential opportunity	Richard Cloward and Lloyd Ohlin	Blocked conventional and available illegitimate opportunity pressures lower-class youth to embrace a criminal subculture; blocked conventional and illegitimate opportunity pressures lower-class youth to embrace conflict or retreatist subcultures	Differential legitimate opportunity; differential illegitimate opportunity; criminal subculture; conflict subculture; retreatist subculture	Illustrates how the presence or absence of legitimate and illegitimate opportunities structures criminal involvement; indicates why one type of subculture activity is chosen over another
Functions of deviance and punishment	Émile Durkheim	Some level of deviance and crime are inevitable, necessary, and functional for the operation of society	Manifest function; latent function	Demonstrates the commonly overlooked fact that deviance and crime at a certain level are not without their positive aspects; emphasizes contribution of deviant behaviour, and reaction to it, to social solidarity and community

Anomie theory represents lower-class people as frustrated and miserable with their lives, but some critics suggest that this image is an exaggeration. In arguing that untenable conditions create strain that in turn forces basically good people to become deviants, anomie theory does not explain deviant and criminal activities that inject fun and excitement into otherwise routine and dull lives (Bordua, 1961).

Anomie theory fails to spell out adequately why lower-class persons choose one form of deviant adaptation over another. For example, it does not explain why, under the same conditions, one person innovates and one retreats while another rebels. While each of these three adaptations occurs as a result of restricted access to legitimate means of achieving success, innovators continue to pursue lofty ends (albeit illegally), retreatists give up the chase, and rebels seek to institute entirely new goals. The reasons for these choices are not explicitly articulated.

Anomie theory cites the gap separating ends and means as the primary source of deviant behaviour. It argues that this disjuncture is disproportionately experienced by lower-class persons. Given that the gap presumably endures over time, the prediction follows that deviant and criminal behaviour should also be continuous. However, evidence suggests that for many lower-class people who do engage in some illegal conduct, deviance is far more episodic than continuous. Why some lower-class persons never start, why some stop entirely, why some engage in deviant acts only occasionally, and why others perpetrate deviant acts systematically over long careers are questions not adequately addressed by the theory (Liska, 1987).

Violence is frequently more expressive than instrumental. Beating a child, killing a spouse, or assaulting a bar-room acquaintance are usually expressive acts of violence and, because they occur in the heat of the moment and do not involve the pursuit of material success, they are not well explained by anomie theory. Nonetheless, violence occasionally is used for material gain. Abduction, robbery, some murders (e.g., contract killing, homicide for insurance or inheritance money), and some terrorist activities are violent crimes rationally undertaken to enrich the lawbreaker.

Anomie theory also fails to take proper account of the impact upon individuals of their major reference groups (Farrell and Swigert, 1982). People compare their circumstances with the situations of those with whom they associate, who resemble them in terms of occupation and income. Thus, lower-class persons comparing themselves with others similarly circumstanced or possibly even worse off will not experience much strain.

Some commentators concede that anomie theorists are correct in assuming that the dissonance between one's goals and legitimate opportunities encourages deviance. Those who see themselves as deprived in comparison with their reference groups will experience greater strain and thus will be more likely to deviate. This mismatch of goals and opportunities, however, may not be entirely class-related. Anyone whose aspirations outstrip the legitimate means of their achievement may be prone to deviate, regardless of his or her class (Farrell and Swigert, 1982).

Cloward and Ohlin's version of anomie theory posits the existence of three subcultures that promote different forms of deviance. Researchers have attacked their presentation of three separate and distinct subcultures in light of data indicating that this threefold typology oversimplifies the varied and complex specialties of delinquent gangs and that it fails to consider shifting membership patterns across these subcultural forms (Schrag, 1962; Bernard, 1984).

Cohen's version of anomie focuses exclusively on nonutilitarian delinquency. This focus, say some critics, ignores the profit-making rationale for much delinquent behaviour (Bordua, 1961).

The functions-of-deviance branch of the functionalist perspective proposes that deviance and reactions to it promote social solidarity. Critics dispute that deviance and crime always produce consensus. Although the murder of a child may unite the community in indignation, the provision of abortion services on demand may result in considerable divisiveness. The opening of the Morgentaler abortion clinics across Canada is a case in point. The heated dispute about the legitimacy of these clinics has split public opinion, with each side of the controversy impassioned in its stance. Thus, while serious crimes like murder, rape, and robbery may produce community cohesion, acts upon which there is less consensus may have the opposite effect. Where there is less agreement on the wrongfulness of certain illegal practices like drug use, prostitution, and gambling, these illegal acts and reaction to them may undermine social solidarity (Box, 1981).

Functionalists have not clearly established the point at which the incidence of deviance and crime becomes dysfunctional. At some point (unspecified by the theory), the number of crimes may become so large that people's fears of victimization erode community integration (Liska, 1987).

Criticisms of the policy implications of anomie theory focus mainly on their feasibility. Significantly reducing the gap between goals and means would necessitate a radical redistribution of wealth and property in society. Meaningful redistributions of goods and services across social strata would negatively affect middle- and particularly upper-class groups, which are already affluent, privileged, and powerful. Even relatively conservative initiatives such as expanding unemployment-insurance benefits, increasing welfare payments, and developing guaranteed-income schemes are unpopular among those whose income taxes would support them. More drastic steps, such as compelling corporations to absorb the costs of keeping their workers employed despite fluctuations in markets, are costly and unlikely to be embraced by economic elites. For these reasons, policies based upon anomie theory that are aimed at dramatically reducing the disjuncture between material goals and legitimate means are unlikely to be widely implemented. More limited initiatives advocating the modest expansion of legitimate opportunities through job training and job creation are much more likely to be undertaken. Such measures are, however, less likely to have a significant impact on the reduction first of anomie and then of crime (Maris and Rein, 1973).

For obvious reasons, the argument that deviance is functional for society has not been reflected in social policy. Crime-creation programs to ensure social solidarity and clarify social norms would be met with less than enthusiasm by most people. In any case, such efforts are clearly unnecessary; the current volume of deviance and crime appears sufficient to meet these requirements.

Although it has been heavily criticized, anomie theory has made major contributions to the explanation of deviance and crime. Before Merton proposed his theory in the 1930s, scholars and laypersons alike commonly assumed that deviant behaviour resulted from personality deficiencies and psychopathologies. That the structure of society could cause deviant and criminal behaviour was a truly innovative insight. The fact that this premise is now commonplace is testimony to the importance of the idea (Bernard, 1984).

SUMMARY

Anomie theory and the functions-of-deviance approach are the two basic themes of functionalism. Durkheim's theory of anomie asserts that deregulation in society produces conditions wherein individuals' aspirations and the means of their achievement fall out of phase with one another. The widening gap between ends and means produces strain, which in turn increases rates of suicide. Durkheim cites both rapid economic expansion and rapid economic contraction as major forces in creating the disjunction between ends and means.

While Durkheim argues that both ends and means fluctuate, Merton maintains that goals are firmly set at high levels for all social groups. He argues that the means through which these goals may be legitimately attained, however, are differentially distributed, with the poor having restricted access. As a result, deprived groups adapt in five distinct ways to anomic conditions: they conform, innovate, become ritualistic, retreat, or rebel.

Following Merton's lead, Cohen constructs a theory positing that delinquency occurs because lower-class youths lack the means to be successful in a world dominated by middle-class values. Faced with continual frustration over their failure to acquire middle-class status, they adapt by forming deviant subcultures that patently reject middle-class values and offer meaningful ways of attaining status in lower-class contexts.

Finally, Cloward and Ohlin extend Merton's anomie formulation by suggesting that illegitimate opportunity structures affect involvement in various forms of delinquency. The availability of illegal opportunities encourages people experiencing strain to become embroiled in criminal subcultures. The presence of neither legitimate nor illegitimate options increases the likelihood of involvement in violent-conflict subcultures or of entry into the retreatist world of drug use.

The functions-of-deviance approach maintains that some level of deviance in society is inevitable and that deviance serves several distinct functions. Central among these functions are the creation of social solidarity, the clarification of social norms, the emphasis on the rewards of conformity, and the stimulation of social change. Too much deviance and crime, however, can be dysfunctional in that they erode social cohesion.

Functional theories have been heavily criticized, partly because they have existed for a long time. Deficiencies of the anomie approach include the middle-class biases inherent in the theory, the ignoring of value pluralism in modern society, the lack of information as to why certain adaptations are chosen over others, the inability to account for episodic deviance among the lower classes, and the failure to consider deprivation as a relative concept. The functions-of-deviance point of view has been attacked for its naïve assumption that all deviance and crime produce an element of cohesion and for its failure to specify the point at which deviance becomes dysfunctional.

Anomie theory implies that social and economic resources should be redistributed more equitably to reduce the considerable gap between ends and means experienced by some groups in society. Radical change in this regard is unlikely to be accomplished because affluent and powerful groups with nothing to gain and something to lose would resist it.

The major contribution of functional theory is the idea that social structure profoundly affects the distribution of deviance and crime in society.

Discussion Questions

1. Explain how the organic analogy of functionalism applied to understanding the social system.

2. Illustrate how Merton's theory of anomie represents a modification of Durkheim's original formulation.

3. Demonstrate how Cohen and Cloward and Ohlin extend Merton's theory to explain lower-class delinquency.

4. Discuss policy recommendations that stem from functionalist perspectives.

5. Show how functionalist perspectives have contributed to an understanding of deviant and criminal activities.

WEB LINKS

The Durkheim Pages
http://www.relst.uiuc.edu/durkheim/
> Devoted to the work of Émile Durkheim, this site features a brief biography, a time line, summaries, and discussions of some of Durkheim's works, and much more.

The Émile Durkheim Archive
http://www.durkheim.itgo.com/
> This archive includes a brief biography of Durkheim, a summary of his views on various subjects (including crime), and a useful glossary.

Merton's Strain Theory
http://www.hewett.norfolk.sch.uk/curric/soc/mert_str.htm
> A summary of Robert K. Merton's strain theory.

Robert K. Merton's "Dream Machine"
http://www.crimetheory.com/Merton/index.html
> An explanation of Merton's "Social Structure and Anomie" (1938) by Bruce Hoffman.

Recommended Readings

Cloward, R., and L. Ohlin. (1960). *Delinquency and Opportunity*. New York: Free Press.
> Provides the seminal account of the role of illegitimate opportunity structures in understanding the formation and reinforcement of criminal, conflict, and retreatist subcultures and gangs.

Cohen, A. (1955). *Delinquent Boys: The Culture of the Gang*. New York: Free Press.
> Sets out influential ideas concerning development of delinquency among lower-class youth in middle-class-dominated schools.

Merton, Robert. (1968). *Social Structure and Anomie*. New York: Free Press.
> Represents an expansion and refinement of Merton's classic formulation of anomie and its relation to various forms of lower-class criminality in America.

Passas, N. and R. Agnew. (1997). *The Future of Anomie Theory*. Boston: Northeastern University Press.
> Re-examines empirical research based on anomie theory and finds support for the original formulation. The authors provide responses to criticism and attempt to extend the theory.

Messner, S. and R. Rosenfeld. (1997). *Crime and the American Dream* (2nd ed.). Belmont, CA: Wadsworth.
> Presents a contemporary version of anomie or strain theory that incorporates the idea of the American Dream and its pursuit in an era of weakened societal connections that might have constrained illegality more effectively in the past.

CHAPTER 5

SOCIAL CONTROL THEORY

The aims of this chapter are to familiarize the reader with:

- the differences between inner and outer controls
- the differences between informal and formal controls
- the major elements of Reckless's containment, Nye's family ties, and Hirschi's social bonding versions of social control theory
- the fundamentals of the deterrence perspective
- the similarities and differences among the versions of the theory presented by Reckless, Nye, and Hirschi
- the historical antecedents of deterrence theory
- the concepts of specific and general deterrence
- the three major elements of the deterrence perspective
- the policy implications of social control theories that stress informal and formal controls
- the deficiencies of the social control perspectives
- the contributions of the social control perspectives to the understanding of deviance and crime

INTRODUCTION

Social control theory differs fundamentally from the human ecology, differential association, and anomie theories by asking not what causes people to violate social norms but rather what causes them to conform to the rules. It accepts the Freudian notion that the natural state of humankind is base and animalistic and that, if not inhibited or constrained by social controls, these inborn animal impulses will burst forth in free expression (Freud, 1961 [1930]). Deviant behav-

iour, then, requires no special motivation. Incentives to deviate need not be created by structural malintegration, and they need not be learned. Without social controls, everyone would succumb to the enjoyment, excitement, and profit that frequently accompany deviant and criminal conduct.

This chapter begins by examining the broad divisions between the two basic themes of social control theory, inner control and outer control. The remainder of the chapter discusses particular versions of the social control perspective: containment theory, the family ties approach, the social bonding perspective, and deterrence theory. The policy implications of **informal** and **formal control** perspectives are examined, and the strengths and shortcomings of these perspectives are assessed.

INNER AND OUTER CONTROL

Social control theory outlined in Figure 5.1, focuses on two types of control: inner and outer. Inner social controls consist of norms internalized through the socialization process. People learn most rules of proper behaviour in the family during the formative years of childhood.

INNER CONTROLS

Subjected to **inner controls**, people conform because doing so makes them feel good about themselves. Children first learn to be honest in order to curry favour with their parents. Continuous socialization during childhood and adolescence gradually transforms honesty into an internal value that guides exchanges with other people. Being honest and forth-

FIGURE 5.1

GENERAL MODEL OF INFORMAL SOCIAL CONTROL THEORY

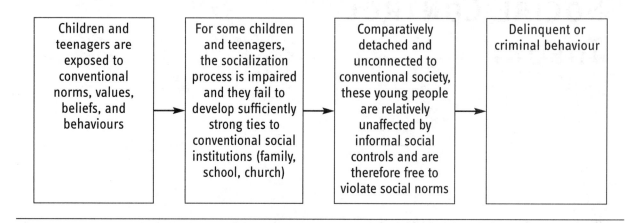

| Children and teenagers are exposed to conventional norms, values, beliefs, and behaviours | → | For some children and teenagers, the socialization process is impaired and they fail to develop sufficiently strong ties to conventional social institutions (family, school, church) | → | Comparatively detached and unconnected to conventional society, these young people are relatively unaffected by informal social controls and are therefore free to violate social norms | → | Delinquent or criminal behaviour |

right in dealings with others bolsters self-worth and creates a feeling of personal moral satisfaction. Dishonesty, alternatively, gives rise to feelings of guilt and self-deprecation. Preferring feelings of personal satisfaction to feelings of guilt, the individual conforms to a fundamental social value — honesty. In this sense, constraints internalized in the personality control the person. The process of socialization is extremely important to the development of internal social controls. Not surprisingly, control theorists frequently cite inadequate socialization as the primary reason for weak social controls and consequently for deviance.

OUTER CONTROLS

Outer controls manifest themselves in the potential loss of social or economic rewards experienced by a norm violator. They can be both informal and formal. Informal outer controls include concerns about what friends and relatives will think, about being the subject of gossip, and about being ostracized. The threat of apprehension, conviction, and "correction" with legally imposed fines and jail terms are examples of formal outer controls. Operating together, informal and formal external controls can be powerful suppressors of behaviour that violates community standards.

For example, in an effort to deal more effectively with intoxicated drivers in St. John's, Newfoundland, authorities not only subjected violators to the punishments provided by the *Criminal Code* but also published the names of miscreants in the newspaper. This strategy used informal social control mechanisms to

bolster the existing formal ones to more effectively deter drinking and driving. Although this practice has been discontinued, rumour has it that this column was avidly read. According to the social control perspective, when both inner and outer controls are strong, levels of deviance will be low. Alternatively, where both inner and outer controls are weak or absent, rates of deviance will be high.

Social control theory has several variations, each of which differs somewhat in the degree of emphasis it places on inner and outer informal and formal controls.

WALTER RECKLESS AND CONTAINMENT THEORY

Walter Reckless developed one of the earliest and best-known versions of the social control perspective (Reckless, 1973). In his **containment theory**, outlined in Figure 5.2, Reckless points out that many powerful societal and psychological forces propel individuals into nonconforming acts. Social forces that push and pull people toward deviant behaviour include poverty, membership in an ethnic minority, restricted access to legitimate opportunities, involvement in deviant subcultures, and exposure to media influences. Reckless calls these mechanisms external forces because they reside outside the individual personality. Inner psychological pressures that promote deviant activity include motives, desires, hostilities, and feelings of inferiority and inadequacy. While Reckless views these outer and inner forces as

FIGURE 5.2

RECKLESS'S CONTAINMENT THEORY

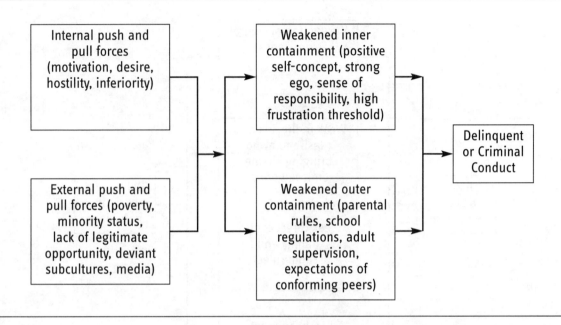

impelling people to violate rules, he notes that not everyone becomes deviant. Reckless answers the question of why some become rule breakers while others do not with the concept of containment.

While internal and external forces promote deviance, inner and outer containments insulate people from these pressures. According to Reckless, **inner containments** are qualities of personality acting as impediments to deviance. These include a positive self-concept, a strong **ego**, an intense sense of personal responsibility, and a high frustration threshold. People acquire these components of **self** largely during childhood through socialization to the "proper" social values. **Outer containments**, on the other hand, are external to the individual and take the form of parental rules, school regulations, supervision by adults, and the expectations of rule-abiding friends.

Deviant behaviour, Reckless argues, is a function of the interaction of inner and outer pro-deviance pressures on the one hand and the internal and external anti-deviance containing forces on the other. When predisposing factors are strong and containing forces are weak, deviant behaviour will result. Conversely, where predisposing factors are weak and containing forces are strong, the outcome will be conformity. This framework predicts that moderate involvement in deviant activity might be produced by intermediary combinations such as strong external pressures but weak internal pressures coupled with weak inner constraints but strong outer constraints.

IVAN NYE AND FAMILY TIES

Ivan Nye's version of social control theory, outlined in Figure 5.3, emphasizes the family's role as an agent of socialization (Nye, 1958). Drawing on Freudian psychology, Nye accounts for pro-deviance motivations by pointing to the baser animal instincts ingrained in the human psyche. Nye, in short, assumes that all humans are born with the same tendencies toward deviance. He explains why only a few actually violate social norms by identifying four types of social control stemming from the family environment: internal control, indirect control, direct control, and legitimate need satisfaction. Nye contends that each type mitigates the negative forces exerted by people's natural animal instincts.

Children acquire internal control through a process of socialization wherein they learn from their parents the values and norms governing acceptable social conduct. Conditioned through rewards and punishments, children over time internalize family

FIGURE 5.3

NYE'S THEORY OF FAMILY TIES

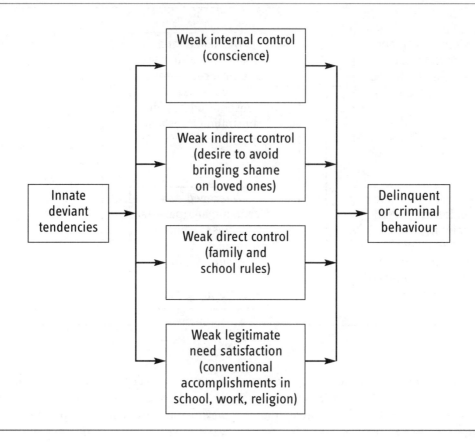

and social values and in so doing develop a conscience. If families properly socialize their progeny at this stage, children's consciences will exert considerable controlling power over them as they mature. People with healthy consciences will feel good when they conform to social rules; they will feel bad when they do not.

In addition to being guided by internalized notions of right and wrong, behaviour is also governed by indirect control. Most people do not wish to shame, hurt, or heap disrespect on those for whom they care deeply. The feeling that being observed or apprehended while engaging in deviance might distress loved ones, Nye suggests, is a strong inhibitor.

Direct controls are the efforts of conventional groups like the family and the school to restrict the activities of youth. Rules concerning curfew, leisure time use, studying, and the company one keeps are examples of direct controls. The threat and application of informal and formal sanctions can be powerful inhibitors of deviant conduct. The child who plays hooky faces not only parental disapproval but also the legalistic penalties handed down by an irate principal or a disgruntled truant officer.

Nye's final form of social control is need satisfaction. If families prepare children to become successful in school and at work and society enables individuals to find affection, security, and recognition, their legitimate needs will be satisfied. The satisfaction of these legitimate needs by family, friendship circles, the school, and organized religion knits the individual securely into the social fabric.

Variation in the strengths of these controls results in variations in conduct ranging from conformity to deviance. Strong controls overcome people's baser instincts and produce obedience to social regulations. Weak controls, alternatively, permit innate animal impulses to surface and to be more freely expressed.

TRAVIS HIRSCHI AND SOCIAL BONDING

Travis Hirschi, like Reckless and Nye before him, also takes the position that people's natural predisposition is to behave deviantly. Despite this, few conduct themselves reprehensibly. For the most part, they conform. According to Hirschi, people obey the rules because they are tied to conventional society by **social bonds**, which are similar to the inner and outer controls identified earlier by Reckless and Nye. Specifically, Hirschi (1969) presents four strands constituting the ties that bind: **attachment**, **commitment**, and **involvement**, which are analogous to outer controls; and **belief**, which is comparable to inner control. (See Figure 5.4.)

Attachment refers to the connection between individuals and other conventional people and institutions. Sensitivity to the wishes and expectations of conforming others whose opinions are valued is the main idea behind attachment. Children and adoles-

FIGURE 5.4

HIRSCHI'S SOCIAL BONDING THEORY

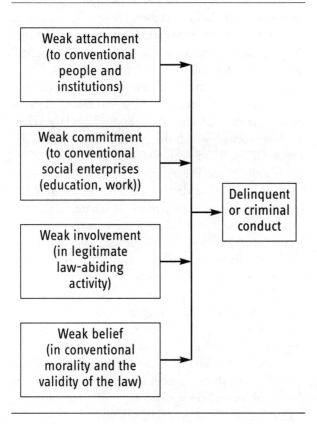

cents who love their parents, who respect their teachers, who admire their conventional friends, and who care deeply about what these people think, are attached. Conversely, a person who does not care about the degrees of affection or respect accorded by others is detached. High degrees of detachment make rule violation possible if not likely.

Acquiring an education, securing a challenging and well-paying job, and otherwise building a good reputation in the community are conventional achievements that require considerable time and energy. Hirschi suggests that those who enjoy the rewards of these and other conformist activities are unwilling to risk their loss. Consequently, they avoid being publicly identified as deviant. Working long and hard at building a conventional way of life, enjoying present rewards, and anticipating bright prospects in the future increase one's stake in conformity. With vested social and economic interests such as these, many people have considerably more to lose by deviant action than they have to gain. Strong commitments to the social system reduce the probability of deviant behaviour.

The idea that idle hands are the devil's helper is the central point of Hirschi's third social bond. Involvement refers to the amount of time spent pursuing legitimate undertakings. Taken to its extreme, if conformist activities consume every waking minute, no time remains for hatching plots and getting into mischief. Adolescents who are heavily involved in school, extracurricular activities, and homework during the week, who work at a part-time job on Saturday, and who spend Sunday morning in church and Sunday afternoon at home, entertaining younger brothers and sisters, have little time for delinquency.

While attachment, commitment, and involvement are external to the individual, belief is an internal control. Intense beliefs in the rightness of conventional morality and in the legitimacy of social norms reduce the likelihood of misconduct. Hirschi's notion of belief is comparable to Nye's idea of internalized control. One is likely to be bothered by one's conscience if one were to break a rule that one believed should be obeyed. Those whose internalized beliefs support conventional social values and norms are morally constrained from committing anti-social acts. Those who do not feel these moral obligations are free to deviate as they wish.

The social control theories discussed thus far concentrate largely on informal inner and outer controls.

The discussion of social control theory will now focus on formal external controls.

DETERRENCE THEORY

The threat or application of punishment can deter behaviour that violates formal norms. Formal codes governing proper conduct characterize many formal organizations, including the military, industry, the professions, mental hospitals, and universities. Formal normative systems also characterize nations. The *Criminal Code* of Canada, for instance, governs the proper conduct of its citizens.

Contemporary deterrence theory, outlined in Figure 5.5, has its roots in the works of the classical theorists, principally Beccaria and Bentham. Deterrence theory views people as rational beings capable of calculating the costs and benefits of breaking the law (Cook, 1980; Gibbs, 1975; Zimring and Hawkins, 1973). If an individual believes that the benefits of committing a crime outweigh the potential liabilities of detection, apprehension, and punishment, criminal action is encouraged. Conversely, when the costs of punishment appear to outweigh the benefits of committing a crime, the probability of obeying the law increases. For example, the average "take" for a bank robbery in Canada is less than $4000 (Ballard, 1987). Clearance rates for this offence are typically less than 30 percent (Brannigan, 1984). Conviction for robbery in Canada carries a maximum sentence of life imprisonment. A potential robber of a Canadian bank who is aware of these facts and who decides that the risks of the crime outweigh its benefits demonstrates the deterrent value of the criminal law pertaining to bank robbery.

There are two types of **deterrence**, specific and general. **Specific deterrence** embodies the idea that the direct experience of punishment will dissuade those convicted from repeating their crimes. The ideal for the deterrence enthusiast is that the person convicted of fraud, who must repay the amount owing to the government and who must serve a two-month jail sentence, will be reluctant to repeat this action. In **general deterrence**, the punishment of the criminal serves a symbolic purpose. It warns members of the public about the potential costs that they might incur if they were to commit the same offence. This warning signal, transmitted through the criminal justice system, operates to deter those who might be contemplating but who have not yet committed the crime. Affluent businesspeople and influential politicians whose marriages are deteriorating may be reluctant to hire killers to dispatch their spouses, given the dismal track records of Peter Demeter, Helmuth Buxbaum, and Colin Thatcher. Those of lesser means may be even more strongly deterred by the knowledge that it is difficult for even the rich to terminate marriages in this fashion.

Three dimensions of punishment affect the efficacy of deterrence: the severity of the sanctions, the **certainty** that the sanctions will be applied, and the **celerity** or speed with which they are administered (Cook, 1980; Gibbs, 1975; Zimring and Hawkins, 1973). According to the theory, more severe punishments increase the level of deterrence. The more costly the fines and the longer the periods of incarceration, the less likely is the commission of the crime.

Certainty refers to the risk of being punished. If a potential culprit is virtually certain of receiving a fine or a jail term, his or her likelihood of committing the crime decreases commensurately. Deterrence theory also hypothesizes that the speed with which one is punished increases the deterrent value of a particular sanction. A short time interval between the crime and the punishment heightens the deterrent value of the sanction. The thinking underlying this proposition is that more immediate punishments are somehow more real in the minds of potential offenders.

FIGURE 5.5

DETERRENCE THEORY

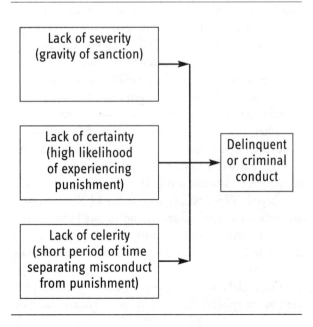

Interest in deterrence theory and its applications declined after World War II as the emphasis in Canadian corrections shifted to a concern for rehabilitating and reintegrating prisoners. Rehabilitation and reintegration, however, have been very costly and, in the opinion of much of the Canadian public, have failed (Moore, 1985; Gomme, 1987). The widespread perception of rapidly increasing crime rates, despite being erroneous, has generated considerable interest in a return to punishment as the primary if not sole function of Canadian prisons. In light of these contemporary correctional trends in Canada and the United States, deterrence theory has recently undergone a rejuvenation.

SOCIAL CONTROL THEORY AND SOCIAL POLICY

Some social control theories call for the implementation of strategies designed to curb deviant behaviour by increasing the strengths of inner and outer informal controls. In this vein, various intervention techniques, including individual, group, and family counselling, have been undertaken to increase intrafamily unity and develop a stronger sense of right and wrong in youth. Social service agencies have also promoted education and work projects designed to involve youths in conventional activities, thereby fostering greater conformity in them. These initiatives enjoy a good deal of popularity because they fit nicely with commonsense notions that delinquency and crime originate in the poor upbringing of the young (Vold and Bernard, 1986).

Policy based on deterrence theory is equally straightforward in principle. Deterrence theory predicts that increases in the severity, certainty, and celerity of punishment will reduce criminal infractions. Recommendations favouring harsher punishments enjoy considerable public support because they coincide with the public's conception of better crime control. Efforts to increase the punitiveness and efficiency of criminal justice are not merely popular, they are simpler to implement and easier to evaluate than are alterations in informal social control mechanisms. Lengthening sentences and hiring more police are much more straightforward undertakings than altering belief systems, strengthening ties to family and conventional peers, and instilling commitment to school and work (Liska, 1987).

Table 5.1 presents a summary of social control theories.

THE EVALUATION OF SOCIAL CONTROL THEORIES

INFORMAL SOCIAL CONTROL THEORIES

Critics point out that informal social control theories (such as those of Reckless, Nye, and Hirschi) contain concepts that are vague and overlap conceptually (Nettler, 1984). For example, it is difficult to separate analytically some of Hirschi's elements of the social bond. An adolescent's investment of a great deal of time in homework and study projects could indicate involvement in conventional activities, attachment to a charismatic teacher, belief in the values of knowledge and diligence, or commitment to a conventional course of action. These elements are neither theoretically nor empirically distinct.

The relative importance of the various forms of inner and outer controls remains largely undetermined (West, 1984). Does an inner control, such as a person's conscience, have a greater impact on deterring deviant behaviour than an external control, such as ostracism? Also, control theorists have paid insufficient attention to the way in which the various dimensions of informal social control interact with one another. Does a highly developed self-concept (inner containment) render the individual more or less susceptible to external controls such as parental expectations and levels of supervision?

Researchers have extensively tested containment, family ties, and social bond explanations of deviance with data gathered primarily on adolescents. These tests support the hypothesis that strong controls foster conformity and that weak or nonexistent controls unleash deviant impulses (Hagan, 1985).

Theories emphasizing informal controls have not been carefully tested with adults and the utility of the theories of informal social control in explaining adult deviance is dubious. As control theorists present it, the world of children and adolescents is comparatively simple — rules regarding right and wrong are relatively clear-cut. Parents socialize their offspring to the basic values and norms of society. The young learn to eat and dress properly, to observe the rights of others, to respect property, to be honest, and to work hard. With some variations, in the early stages of life social values are comparatively straightforward and the norms governing conduct are relatively simple. Moreover, the child is subject to socialization in only a few groups. In the earliest formative years, the family alone is responsible for inculcating a single set of norms, values, and beliefs.

TABLE 5.1

THEORIES OF SOCIAL CONTROL

Theory	Theorist(s)	Central Premise	Key Concepts	Principal Contributions
Containment	Walter Reckless	Different levels of external and internal social and psychological pressures to deviate are neutralized by different levels of inner and outer containment; high internal and external pressures and weak inner and outer containments result in delinquent and criminal behaviour	External pressure; internal pressure; inner containment; outer containment	Emphasis on societal and psychological forces in encouraging conformity or deviance
Family ties	Ivan Nye	While everyone is innately inclined to deviate, strong connections to the family through internal, indirect, and direct control and high need satisfaction encourage conformity; weak controls facilitate deviant behaviour	Internal control; indirect control; direct control; need satisfaction	Focuses attention on the family as the primary institution of socialization to conformity or deviant behaviour
Social bonding	Travis Hirschi	Non-conformity is impeded by attachment to conventional people and institutions, commitment to conventional social enterprises, involvement in legitimate undertakings, and belief in conventional morality	Attachment; commitment; involvement; belief	Presents a popular reformulation of informal social control theory that has been widely tested and empirically supported
Deterrence theory		Severe, certain, and swift punishment deters crime; certainty of punishment is more important than its severity	Specific deterrence; general deterrence; severity; certainty; celerity	Forms the cornerstone of crime control and correctional policy in many countries, including Canada and the United States

As a person grows older, the surrounding world becomes increasingly complex. Right and wrong become more equivocal, and the norms governing proper conduct become more ambiguous. The combination of occupying more roles, holding memberships in a larger number of groups, and playing for higher stakes renders the adult world more complicated, confusing, and conflict-ridden (Thio, 1988).

The manner in which external controls like Hirschi's attachment and commitment channel the adolescent into conforming conduct has already been examined. Attachment refers to the child's love and respect for and desire to please parents, while com-

mitment refers to the investment of the child's time and energy in conventional activities like doing well in school. Consider, however, how attachment and commitment might operate in the world of adults.

Intense affective attachments to their families often place adults in difficult moral positions. Executives who inform the media about their companies' violations of pollution regulations and who later testify in court may be worthy of our commendation for their honesty and courage. The consequences of whistle-blowing, however, might very well be the denial of promotion or the loss of a job. Attachment to family members might well preclude ensuring that one's company be forced to follow anti-pollution legislation to the letter. Being a good parent and spouse in one's own eyes and in the eyes of family members might mean keeping one's job and maintaining family security, or it might mean being honest and preserving the environment for future generations. Either choice has major ethical implications.

Presumably, a highly committed adult would be one who worked very hard and who sought to improve his or her status. For example, for the well-educated, high-performing, ambitious executive employed by General Motors, promotion requires diligence, intelligence, and following the instructions of superiors. It is not impossible that company directives might involve carrying out morally debatable actions. Suppose the executive is required to assist in the speedy marketing of an unsafe vehicle. To refuse to do so might have dire consequences for a person with an immense stake in the conventional occupational world. Life becomes complicated when consensus on what is good and what is evil declines and when commitment to conventional success necessitates participating in actions that may be harmful to others.

Being highly committed to conventional courses of social action can encourage deviant and criminal activity in another manner. Committed and successful people may climb to positions of higher status and greater power in the conventional occupational hierarchy. Many sociologists of deviance seriously question the notion that lower-class people are more frequently involved in deviant and criminal activity than are higher-status people. They maintain that what varies by status is not the frequency of wrongdoing but the type of misconduct. Put simply, people from all status groups, in more or less equal proportions, commit acts that harm others. The type of rule violation or the manner in which it is carried out, however, differs as a consequence of status in general and occupational status in particular. Assembly-line workers steal tools, salespeople abscond with merchandise and pad expense accounts, physicians overbill government health-insurance plans, and oil executives conspire and fix prices (Snider and West, 1980). Broadly construed, each of these acts is theft.

Consider another example. People near the bottom of the status hierarchy kill. The act is usually performed swiftly, in anger, at home or in a bar, and often in the presence of witnesses. However, those at the top of the status hierarchy are also responsible for the deaths of others (Hills, 1987). Industrial safety standards that are not observed (Frank, 1987; Reasons, Ross, and Paterson, 1981), potentially unsafe automobiles and pharmaceutical drugs that are marketed nonetheless (Braithwaite, 1984; Dowie, 1977), and toxic chemicals that are improperly disposed of (Tallmer, 1987) have killed, are killing, and will kill — albeit without anger — slowly and from a considerable distance. Safety standards, marketing strategies, and waste disposal practices are frequently matters of policy. They are rational, planned decisions made by "responsible" people. As a final point, of course, status is related not only to the type and means of commission of certain illegitimate acts but also to the chances of being detected, prosecuted, and convicted. All such probabilities tend to be greater for members of the lower classes.

While there are many acts of deviance and crime for which social controls may not serve as constraints for adults, there are some for which controls do curb participation. Social control theory may inform our understanding of adult involvement in such activities as shoplifting, petty theft, and certain sex offences. Fear of apprehension and the ensuing embarrassment and shame effectively deter the commission of these offences.

The social control theories elaborated by Reckless, Nye, and Hirschi have been very well received, for two reasons. First, empirical research strongly confirms them. Second, they provide logical explanations for the ways in which a large number of variables are associated with deviance and lawbreaking. School, family, peer group, community, and religion are all subsumed under the social control umbrella. Common sense has long suggested that these factors are important in accounting for delinquency.

FORMAL SOCIAL CONTROL THEORIES

Deterrence theory applies specifically to the formalized efforts of the state to enforce the conformity of its citizens. Attempts to evaluate the impacts of criminal laws and the dimensions of deterrence (e.g., severity, certainty, and celerity) have resulted in findings that are neither entirely consistent nor easily synthesized (Liska, 1987). That all types of crime are equally affected by deterrence seems unlikely. The idea of deterrence assumes that individuals rationally calculate the costs and benefits of committing a particular illegal act. Rational calculation requires a period of thought. People commit certain crimes, some of them serious, on the spur of the moment and often under considerable emotional strain. Most assaults and murders are unpremeditated and, as such, are prime examples of acts of passion.

While there is a low probability of deterring crimes that are not carefully thought through, the same may be less true of predatory offences such as robbery, burglary, consumer fraud, and restriction of trade, all of which require planning. Planned crimes leave time for contemplation. To the extent that people perceive the costs of apprehension to outweigh the profits of crime, penalties may have some deterrent impact. Deterrence is especially the case where there is a high probability that sanctions will be administered (Avio and Clark, 1976, 1978; Tittle and Rowe, 1974).

For any punishment to accomplish the goal of general deterrence, a knowledgeable public is required. The citizenry must know about the potential liabilities of committing a particular crime in order to properly calculate its costs and benefits. Some critics of deterrence theory maintain that potential offenders do not understand the penalty structure (Liska, 1987). To be properly informed, a potential offender should be able to answer, for the jurisdiction in which the crime is to be carried out, the following questions. For the proposed crime, what is the rate of offence cleared by charge (that is, in how many instances are charges laid)? What are the minimum and maximum sentences set out in the *Criminal Code*? What is the average sentence actually meted out? To bring this point home, do you yourself know the answers to these questions for any of the following crimes: selling narcotics, impaired driving, burglary, forgery, or armed robbery?

Theories of formal social control tend to ignore the idea that the control efforts of police forces may actually cause some criminal activity (Marx, 1981). Police often assume false identities to trap criminals. They may pose as drug buyers, sellers of stolen goods, and "johns" in search of sexual services from prostitutes. In some instances, through tempting the unaware, crime-control strategies induce criminal acts where they would not otherwise have taken place. Unofficially, informal aspects of police–citizen encounters may result in lawbreaking. The demeanour with which police treat citizens may either encourage co-operation or provoke flight or retaliation, both of which are illegal.

The idea of specific deterrence implies that if someone commits a crime and is apprehended and punished, the direct experience of negative sanctions decreases the likelihood of re-offending. That incarceration reduces a person's lawbreaking, given the recidivism rates reported for Canadian correctional facilities, seems questionable. Despite punishment, many ex-inmates re-offend, are re-convicted, and return to serve time in a correctional institution (Ekstadt and Griffiths, 1988).

It has long been recognized that lengthy prison sentences may have effects opposite to those intended. There are two reasons why this may be the case. Time served in prison in the company of more experienced and more hardened criminals provides a setting in which crime-oriented skills and values can be learned (Ekstadt and Griffiths, 1988). The incarcerated find it easy to learn how to "case" a house, how to gain entry efficiently, what to steal, and how to turn a profit on the goods. In this context, incarcerated persons also develop the beliefs that they are downtrodden, that they have been unfairly treated by "the system," and that "society" owes them a living by whatever means.

The second reason offered for the frequent re-commission of crime by ex-inmates is that they emerge from prison with a criminal record (Ekstadt and Griffiths, 1988). The socially devalued status of ex-convicts has a number of very real implications. Ex-offenders often face both rejection by family and former conventional associates and exclusion from the job market. Branded in this fashion, many ex-convicts renew acquaintances with lawbreaking friends and return to making a living through illegal enterprise. Socialization in the correctional institution and the social stigma after release may outweigh or totally negate the power of punishment as a specific deterrent.

Deterrence theory specifies neither the relative strengths of severity, certainty, and celerity nor the nature of interactions among these dimensions (Gibbs, 1975). On the first point, the theory offers no reasons why one of these three elements might be more powerful than the others. On the second point, explanations as to why certain combinations of elements might have different deterrent effects have not been forthcoming. Is the impact of severity reduced or eliminated for crimes for which punishment is rarely meted out (lack of certainty) or where considerable time elapses between the commission of the act and the experience of negative sanction (lack of celerity)?

While some variations exist from one research study to the next, empirical findings generally suggest that increasing the severity of punishments does not increase deterrence (Tittle, 1969). Comparing jurisdictions where the lengths of sentences differ for the same offence indicates that more severe penalties produce no greater deterrent impact. Similarly, comparisons of regions in which the penalty for murder is execution with those in which it is life imprisonment show that capital punishment does nothing to reduce the rates of homicide (Bailey, 1974; Fattah, 1972).

Although increasing severity does not appear to curb criminal activity, increasing the certainty of arrest does seem to have some deterrent effect (Avio and Clark, 1976, 1978). Jurisdictions in which arrests more frequently result in charges seem to have lower crime rates than those in which arrests do not so often lead to the laying of charges. The effects of celerity of the negative sanction have, to date, not been seriously investigated.

Research concerning the elements of deterrence presents an interesting dilemma for policymakers. Increasing severity as a crime-control strategy is unsupported by the data but widely called for by the public. Alternatively, making punishment more certain might, according to research findings, heighten the impact of punitive sanctions. Increasing the certainty of punishment, however, would require restructuring and expanding the various agencies of the criminal justice system, including police, courts, and corrections. By comparison, lengthening sentences is much less expensive, disturbs fewer vested interests, and incurs less resistance from justice-system personnel. The coping strategies called for by political expediency do not coincide with the best advice offered by existing research.

Finally, the theory and research on social control have yet to carefully assess the relative impacts and interactions of informal and formal controls. Are informal controls more or less important than formal controls in enforcing conformity? What levels of informal control (conscience and attachment) must exist for formal controls (threat or application of punishment) to deter deviant acts?

SUMMARY

Social control theory posits that people are not propelled into deviance by external forces beyond their control. Rather, control theorists argue that everyone would be deviant if they were not constrained by inner and outer controls. The impacts of informal controls are emphasized by Reckless (containment), Nye (family ties), and Hirschi (social bonds). Deterrence theory concerns itself with formal controls and, in so doing, directs attention to the impacts of three dimensions of punishment, namely, severity, certainty, and celerity.

Criminologists criticize informal control theories on the bases of conceptual overlap, measurement deficiencies, the failure to specify the relative impacts and interactions of different types of informal control, and the dubious ability of these theories to explain adult deviance and crime. Approaches stressing informal social control have two strengths: juvenile-delinquency research confirms many of their principal propositions, and these theories convincingly incorporate many variables empirically associated with delinquency.

The deterrence perspective, which examines the formal aspects of social control, has been criticized on a number of grounds. First, deterrence theory does not explain passionate or impulsive crime. Second, since many people are unfamiliar with the penalties for a variety of crimes, finer distinctions regarding the deterrent values of particular sanctions are difficult to determine. Third, the deterrence approach fails to consider that crime-control efforts can produce rather than deter crime. Incarceration provides exposure to criminal learning opportunities, and a criminal record results in the experience of stigma; both these factors may negate the deterrent value of sanctions. Finally, the relative impacts or interactions of severity, certainty, and celerity are unspecified by the theory. Research casts doubt on the overall efficacy of deterrence, particularly increases in the severity of punishment.

Social control theories prescribe the strengthening of inner and outer social ties through socialization. This objective is unlikely to be accomplished easily. Deterrence research indicates that an increased certainty of punishment may reduce crime, while increasing severity is unlikely to have this effect. Increasing the severity of punishment, although unsupported by research, is nonetheless heavily favoured by the public.

DISCUSSION QUESTIONS

1. Demonstrate how inner and outer controls are linked to informal and formal controls.

2. To what extent are the versions of social control theory articulated by Reckless, Nye, and Hirschi different from one another?

3. Discuss the three major elements of deterrence theory. How do they interact with one another?

4. Evaluate the major criticisms that have been directed at theories of social control.

5. How have the theories of informal and formal social control contributed to an understanding of the causes of deviance and crime?

WEB LINKS

Theories of Criminal Behaviour
http://mulerider.saumag.edu/~milford/crime/crime1.html
> This page contains a chart summarizing some criminological theories. Click on "Containment Theory" and "Social Control Theory" to read about contributions made by Walter Reckless and Travis Hirschi.

Social Control Theories
http://www.indiana.edu/~theory/Kip/Control.htm
> A point-form summary of several strands of social control theory.

Ivan Nye's Theory
http://www.d.umr.edu/~jhamlin1/nye.html
> A point-form summary of Nye's version of social control theory.

Travis Hirschi's Theory
http://www.d.umn.edu/~jhamlin1/hirschi.html
> A point-form summary of Hirschi's theory of social bonding.

Rational Choice and Deterrence Theory
http://www.umsl.edu/~rkeel/200/ratchoc.html
> An overview of deterrence theory by Robert Keel.

RECOMMENDED READINGS

Hirschi, T. (1969). *Causes of Delinquency*. Berkeley: University of California Press.
> Provides the classic statement of social bonding theory. Hirschi explains the approach in detail and convincingly emphasizes its superiority to competing frameworks.

Nye, F.I. (1958). *Family Relationships and Delinquent Behaviour*. New York: John Wiley.
> Nye sets out his version of informal social control in the context of family relationships and their power to constrain delinquent conduct.

Reckless, W.C. (1973). *The Crime Problem* (3rd ed.). New York: Appleton Century Crofts.
> Contains the fundamentals of a version of social control theory that emphasizes the importance of inner and outer containments in the constraint of adolescent misconduct.

Varma, K.N. and A.N. Doob. (1998). "Deterring Economic Crime: The Case of Tax Evasion." *Canadian Journal of Criminology* 40:165–184.
> Study of tax evasion in Canada suggesting that severity is less important in deterring crime than certainty.

CHAPTER 6

SYMBOLIC INTERACTIONISM

The aims of this chapter are to familiarize the reader with:

- the bases of symbolic interactionism: verbal and nonverbal symbols and communication through interaction
- self-image, self-concept, and identity as social constructs
- Blumer's propositions on symbolic interaction: the importance of meaning, the origin of meaning, and the active creation of meaning
- definitions of self: Mead's "self as a social construct" and Cooley's "looking-glass self"
- definitions of society
- definitions of situations
- the links between the general theory of symbolic interaction and the labelling perspective on deviance and crime
- labelling approaches: Tannenbaum's dramatization of evil, Lemert's primary and secondary deviance, and Becker's deviant career
- the policy implications of the symbolic interactionist perspective
- the deficiencies of the interactionist framework
- the contributions of symbolic interactionism to an understanding of deviance and crime

INTRODUCTION

The two basic concepts providing the foundation for symbolic interactionist theory are, not surprisingly, symbols and interaction. This chapter explores the interactionist framework and its contribution to an understanding of deviance and crime. It begins with a discussion of the general principles of symbolic interactionism as developed by philosopher George Herbert Mead and sociologists Charles Horton Cooley and Herbert Blumer. It then examines the development of the labelling perspective, an orientation focusing on deviance and heavily grounded in symbolic interactionism. Subsequent sections discuss the policy implications of labelling theory, its deficiencies, and its contributions to an understanding of deviance, crime, and social control.

THE THEORY OF SYMBOLIC INTERACTIONISM

Symbols are signs that stand for things. They can be either nonverbal or verbal. The red light in front of many old houses in the seedier districts of turn-of-the-century Canadian cities is a good example of a nonverbal symbol; it ensured that all who passed by understood the service available from the establishment. Similarly, hoisting one's arms over one's head, shaking one's clenched fist, or holding the gaze of another are nonverbal symbols intended to communicate surrender, displeasure, or sexual interest, respectively. As verbal symbols, words provide representation for objects, emotions, and behaviours. The words *gun*, *car*, and *mask* are abstract signs that stand for concrete objects. *Fear* is a word representing a real feeling, while *shoot*, *drive*, and *hide* are verbal symbols representing different kinds of behaviour. Moans, screams, and whistles, although they are not words, are verbal signs nonetheless.

To the extent that people have internalized symbols and share their meanings, symbolic interactionists say that society and culture exist. From the symbolic interactionist perspective, society is a large collectivity of people held together by a common culture that itself is composed of shared symbols. That people interpret red lights, arms held above the head, and screams in approximately the same way and that they attach similar meanings to words like *shoot*, *drive*, and *hide* indicate that they share the same basic culture.

People use symbols to communicate, and communication requires interaction. Prominently displaying the red lantern allows the madam to communicate a marketing idea to the passerby with a sexual desire. The robber pointing a .45-calibre pistol at an unarmed man on a deserted street clearly communicates a desire for his money. In the process of interaction, people use symbols to convey meanings. Madam and robber interact with john and victim and in so doing communicate intentions through both verbal symbols ("Need a date, honey?", "Give me the money!") and nonverbal symbols (red light, gun).

The context in which interaction occurs affects the way in which people interpret symbols. A red light on a doorway on December 25, a red light on a post at an intersection, and a red light on the bow of a houseboat convey different meanings, none of which has anything to do with the sale of sexual services. As the context changes, so too does the meaning attached to the symbol.

A central focus of **symbolic interactionism** is the development of self-image, self-concept, and identity. Interactionists view a person's self-concept as the product of long-term social interaction during which an individual develops a positive or negative sense of self in response to the perceived reactions of others who surround and are important to the individual. Being able to date physically attractive persons is a symbol of worth in our society. People whose phones ring constantly and whose date books are filled are likely to interpret this enthusiasm for their company as a sign of extraordinary personal value. Alternatively, those for whom the phone never rings, for whom the answer is always no, and for whom owning a date book is entirely superfluous are equally likely to interpret this continuous indifference as unflattering. Interactionists claim that the long-term experience of either favourable or unfavourable responses produces varying degrees of positive or negative self-image.

Philosopher George Herbert Mead is generally acknowledged as the founder of symbolic interactionism (Mead, 1943). Although Mead wrote little, many of his ideas have been widely disseminated by his students. One such student, Herbert Blumer, has written extensively on symbolic interactionism. Blumer (1969) summarizes the perspective more formally in the following manner.

First, Blumer stresses the importance of social meaning. He states that humans act toward things on the basis of the meanings that those things have for them and not simply as a consequence of something inherent in those things. Other theoretical explanations of deviance suggest that factors such as economic hardship, involvement in deviant groups, or severed social bonds produce deviance. Symbolic interactionists, alternatively, take the position that it is not the existence of these conditions per se but rather the meaning that people attach to them that is vital in explaining deviance. People interpret things differently. Some see growing up in poverty, being surrounded by a neighbourhood full of delinquents, or having a parent die an untimely death as intolerably stressful. Others view these same circumstances as great personal challenges. According to symbolic interactionists, behaviour is not simply determined in any straightforward way by conditions; rather, it is affected by the variable meanings that a condition has for a particular individual in a particular context.

Second, having asserted that meaning affects action, Blumer addresses the issue of where the meanings that people attach to things originate. He contends that the meaning of things arises out of social interaction with others. Neither the thing itself nor the person alone provides meaning. Rather, people create, modify, and transmit meaning through a process of social interaction in social and cultural contexts. The precise meanings attached to specific objects and actions in the multitude of contexts in which deviance occurs develop in this way. Observing and interpreting the verbal and nonverbal symbols manipulated by others communicates the meanings of objects (e.g., crowbars, marijuana cigarettes, pool tables, submachine guns), conditions (e.g., poverty, broken homes, unemployment), and acts (e.g., murder, robbery, prostitution). People observe and interpret the actions and reactions of others in relation to objects, conditions, and acts such as these. In the process, they acquire and internalize, in their cultures and subcultures, much of the meaning attached to things, to circumstances, and to behaviours.

Finally, Blumer notes that people take an active part in creating meaning. Meanings, he claims, are handled and modified through an active interpretive process invoked by individuals as they deal with the things that they encounter. The person is not simply a receptor for meaning. Because people actively interpret symbols, they may see slightly or even radically different meanings than others would under the same circumstances. People are partly passive receivers of meaning and partly its active creators.

Out of the meanings arising from interaction, people construct three important definitions that greatly affect their current and future actions, both conforming and deviant. From past interaction and the interpretation of meanings in those past interactions, the person constructs definitions of self, society, and situation. Each of these definitions significantly influences subsequent behaviour. The following sections consider each definition in detail.

DEFINING SELF

A person constructs a conception of **self** through interaction with others. The reactions of others provide the person with symbolic information that, once interpreted, provides the individual with crucial details about the nature of his or her personal identity. For example, our conceptions of ourselves as attractive, kind, cowardly, or worthless arise from our interpretations of the symbolic reactions directed to us by those in our social environment. Our positive and negative evaluations of ourselves originate in our interpretations of the ways in which others react to us. In the long term, the positive and negative meanings that we attach to our senses of self come to affect more and more how we act both toward ourselves and toward others. Mead called this process of identity formation "the self as a social construct" (Mead, 1943). Another pioneer in sociology, Charles Horton Cooley, spoke of identity formation in terms of "the **looking-glass self**" (Cooley, 1902).

According to Mead, people make objects out of the self. They do so, he contends, by taking on the attitudes toward themselves that are expressed by the people with whom they interact. One's self, in these terms, is created by stepping out of one's own shoes and into the shoes of an onlooker. In this way, people make efforts to see themselves "objectively." The sociology professor who considers turning off the lights, leaping onto a desk with candle in hand, and reciting the Shakespearean soliloquy on the demise of Lady Macbeth to make a point about death in the family is a case in point.

The professor, before this dramatic performance, momentarily steps outside of himself and into the shoes of his youthful audience. If he were a student, he reflects, would he see himself as a brilliant lecturer or a raving idiot? This reflection suggests the former and it motivates him to undertake this flamboyant action. A class moved to tears allows the professor to see himself, on reflection, in positive terms, as a gifted pedagogue. Why? Because if someone had moved him to tears under the same circumstances, he would have been profoundly impressed by the eloquence and emotion of a fine though unconventional performance. A class rolling in the aisles in hysterical laughter, however, would force the instructor to reflect that his technique, if not he himself, was a failure. Why? Because if he as a student had laughed under similar circumstances, he would have done so because he had been appalled by the ridiculous, inept, and immature display.

Mead separates the self into three components: the "**I**," the "**me**," and the "**generalized other**." The I is the action-oriented behavioural part of the individual, while the me is the person's contemplative reflective component. As such, the me reflects the attitudes and beliefs that people have about their own social and physical characteristics. The generalized other represents what people imagine others will think about them and their actions. When people ask themselves "What would people think?", they are invoking in themselves the generalized other. The generalized other is a composite of all the "significant others" who have made up or continue to make up our social world. Those whom people love and cherish and whose respect they keenly desire represent their significant others. When the child contemplating lighting up a cigarette wonders "What would Mom and Dad think?" or when a spouse considering adultery reflects "What would my children think?", they are taking account of significant others.

The me part of the self is particularly important to symbolic interactionism, and it is to the me that symbolic interactionists have devoted most of their attention. Understanding the conceptualization of the me offers an explanation of how one develops self-concept and identity. Charles Horton Cooley explains the development of this part of one's self with a rather catchy metaphor, "the looking-glass self."

Just as people's perfections and imperfections are reflected in a mirror, or looking-glass, so are their finer points and deficiencies reflected symbolically in the faces, voices, and even movements of those who make up their social environment. Cooley conceives of the looking-glass process in three stages: the initial conception, the test, and the feeling of pride or mortification. Cooley contends that, at first, people have an initial idea of how they and their actions will appear to others. Consider the child who voluntarily confesses to stealing an apple from the teacher's desk. The child confesses because he or she believes that the teacher's and other students' reactions to the confession will confirm his or her identity as a basically honest but ever-so-human person.

Cooley suggests that people's initial conception of how they will appear to others is subjected to a test as soon as they act and as soon as the act is observed. If the admission of theft is made and the teacher commends the child for honesty and inflicts a minor punishment, this confirms the child's self-conception as honest but perhaps subject to temptation now and then. If, on the other hand, the teacher brings out the strap and the other students begin to chant "You're a thief," the culprit will conclude that his or her image has been "spoiled."

Cooley argues that people feel pride or mortification as a result of their interpretations of others' responses to them. If the teacher commends the student, the student's positive image of the self as honest takes precedence over the negative image of the self as disreputable. If the teacher goes for the strap, the negative reaction emphasizes the child's disreputable image over his or her image as the honest person who made a little mistake. Feelings about self created by spoiled identity are unlikely to be positive. The dark reflection from the looking-glass produces mortification. The audience, according to Cooley, is a social mirror. Positive cues from others make people feel good about themselves, while negative cues make them feel bad. Cooley maintains that what the audience reflects in the long run profoundly shapes a person's sense of self.

DEFINING SOCIETY

Communication through symbols in the process of interaction shapes not only one's definition of self but also one's definition of society in general and of a variety of social situations in particular. For example, the individual's perception of society as either full of opportunity or inhospitable develops in interaction with various agents of socialization, including family members, friends, co-workers, and the media. Once this perception is created, it subsequently affects the way in which people behave. Perceiving social and economic opportunities as plentiful, whether or not this is true, results in the person happily working hard to get ahead. Conversely, the perception of restricted opportunities may produce unhappiness, disenchantment, and withdrawal despite the reality of economic well-being.

DEFINING SITUATIONS

People also **define situations** according to how the interaction process unfolds. Once the situation is defined in a certain way, its meaning influences people's actions. Consider, for example, how differences in the definition of the same situation can produce law-abiding behaviour in some and law-breaking behaviour in others. A motorist stops for a red light in the centre lane of a three-lane street. The driver repeatedly revs the car's engine. The car's windows are heavily shaded, hiding the person behind the wheel. Two other cars pull up on either side and also stop for the light. The driver of the centre vehicle continues to rev the engine. The light turns green. The car in the right lane pulls away slowly, while the car in the left lane crosses the intersection sideways, blue smoke rising from its squealing tires. The car in the centre lane stalls.

Each driver defined the situation differently and acted accordingly. The driver of the car on the right was a middle-aged executive on her way home from the office. Behind the wheel of the car on the left was a young male construction worker. For the businesswoman, the centre car and the sound of its engine are irrelevant. Her socialization left her ears untuned to the subtle variations in the tones emanating from idling engines. The construction worker, alternatively, interpreted the revving engine as a challenge to see who could cross the intersection first. For the driver of the centre car, the constantly revving engine was simply evidence of an annoyingly bad tune-up. How might the definitions of this situation and the drivers' subsequent actions have been affected by different times of day, different makes of cars, and, of course, different driver characteristics?

Symbolic interactionism makes several distinct points worth reviewing. Definitions of self, of society, and of situation are the product of symbolic exchanges that occur in one's interaction with oneself, when one thinks and reflects, with others when one communicates with them, and with external inanimate sources like books and newspapers when one absorbs information from them. Once created, the way in which people conceive of themselves, of society, and of specific situations affects their behaviour. Since individuals vary in the way in which they interpret things and since people actively engage their social world by thinking and responding, symbolic interactionism views behavioural outcomes as less deterministic in terms of cause and effect than do the causal theories presented in previous chapters.

THE SYMBOLIC INTERACTIONIST LABELLING PERSPECTIVE ON DEVIANCE

Symbolic interactionist theory as it is applied to the study of deviance is commonly referred to as the **labelling perspective** (Schur, 1971) and is outlined in Figure 6.1. Labelling theory does not define deviance as a straightforward violation of social norms in the way that human ecology, functional, differential association, and social control theories do. Rather, labelling theorists stress that it is not the act itself but the contextual meaning attached to it that defines whether or not it is deviant. According to interactionists, deviance, like beauty, is in the eye of the beholder. In developing an understanding of deviance, interactionists focus on three basic questions. Who gets defined or labelled deviant? How does this process occur? Finally, what are the consequences of being designated deviant?

The defined tend to differ from their definers on one significant dimension. Those who are either informally or formally labelled as deviant tend to occupy lower social statuses and to wield less social power than do those who successfully apply the labels. Possessing power means that dominant groups can force the less powerful to do their bidding. Power, however, is a matter of degree. The difference in power between those who define and those who are defined affects the ease with which deviant designations can be applied.

The degree of power wielded by individuals and groups frequently depends upon their statuses. Differences in income, occupation, property ownership, age, sex, ethnicity, and regional and national affiliation define social position and hence, to a large extent, determine social power. For example, all other things being equal, earners of high incomes, workers in "professional" occupations, owners of property, the middle-aged, men, whites, Ontarians, and Canadians are likely to be more powerful than the poor, blue-collar workers, renters, the very old and the very young, nonwhites, Newfoundlanders, and Ethiopians.

Furthermore, some in Canadian society are given special status with regard to power. The state invests

FIGURE 6.1

GENERAL TENETS OF THE LABELLING PERSPECTIVE

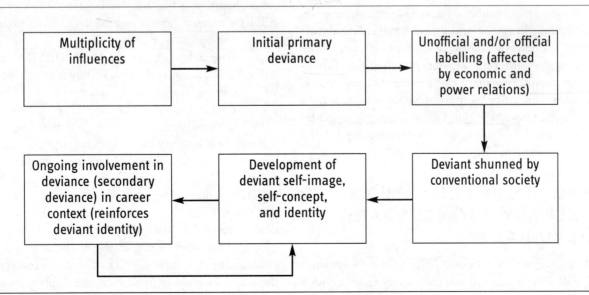

those in officially mandated positions of legitimate authority with special legal power to assign deviant and criminal labels. Agents of the criminal justice system (e.g., police, Crown prosecutors, judges, and correctional workers), psychiatrists and psychologists, and workers in alcohol and drug rehabilitation centres are among those whose formal statuses and roles have attached to them this kind of special power.

FRANK TANNENBAUM AND THE DRAMATIZATION OF EVIL

The process by which the more powerful attach labels to the less powerful was initially outlined during the 1930s by a historian, Frank Tannenbaum. In his discussion of crime in the community, Tannenbaum (1938) developed an account of the way in which adolescents become delinquents. According to Tannenbaum, children participate in a wide range of activities every day. Many of these activities comprise behaviours that adults frequently find objectionable. Smoking cigarettes, flooding school washrooms, cutting classes, and throwing stones at passing trains are some of the joys of adolescent life. Not only do adults informally disapprove of such behaviours, regulations and laws prohibit and specify sanctions for each of these acts. If apprehended by teachers, parents, or police officers, miscreants can be and often are punished. According to Tannenbaum, severe sanctions represent a "dramatization of evil" that can easily stimulate the young to engage in more of the same misconduct.

Over the years, symbolic interactionists interested in explaining deviance and crime have enlarged this basic framework considerably. Various approaches emphasize different aspects of labelling. Edwin Lemert conceptualizes the process of labelling as a transition from primary deviance to secondary deviance. Howard Becker follows suit with an explanation of the labelling process that focuses on the deviant career model.

EDWIN LEMERT – FROM PRIMARY TO SECONDARY DEVIANCE

According to Edwin Lemert (1967), society comprises a wide variety of social and cultural segments divided along such lines as age, ethnicity, and class. These societal segments can be differentiated from one another, at least to some extent, by their unique norms, values, beliefs, and behaviours. Given this social diversity and given that power also varies along these lines, it is inevitable that some social segments come into conflict with other social segments. When this happens, the rules of the more dominant segments, more broadly construed as society's norms, will be violated from time to time as a matter of course. Lemert (1967) calls these initial acts, wherein individuals violate social rules, primary deviance.

A multitude of factors, many of which are identified as causes in the theories discussed in previous chapters, act alone or together to promote specific individual acts of deviant and illegal conduct. Deviant acts produced by accident, by unusual situations, by a desire to experiment, or by pressure from deviant associates, Lemert maintains, are common occurrences in the lives of virtually everyone. Deviance remains primary so long as it is occasional or hidden and so long as it does not result in strong and continuous negative social reaction.

Lemert argues that without a strong and continuous punitive response, the norm violator's sense of self is unlikely to be affected. Primary deviance implies that rulebreakers, for several reasons, have not closely identified themselves with their deviant actions. In some cases, deviance goes undetected by others and the violator has no mirror to reflect the dark image necessary to develop a deviant identity. In other cases, the deviant act is noticed and elicits a negative sanction. On such occasions, a mirror is provided to reflect negative self-image. Nonetheless, rulebreakers still have at hand several possible techniques to neutralize a repugnant self-image.

Gresham Sykes and David Matza (1957) specify five **neutralization techniques**, shown in Table 6.1, whereby those confronted with a deviant self-image may maintain a nondeviant self-concept. They may deny responsibility for their act, deny that injury to others is real, or deny that a victim is really a victim. They may also condemn those who are condemning them, and they may appeal to higher loyalties to justify their actions. The unemployed parent who peddles drugs, claiming to be forced to do so by poverty, denies personal responsibility for the illegal conduct. The poacher who bags a moose without a licence, maintaining that there are plenty of the creatures out there in the woods, denies that illegal hunting is inju-

TABLE 6.1

TECHNIQUES OF NEUTRALIZATION

Technique	Examples
Deny responsibility	I had to do it. I had no choice. It was me or him.
Deny injury	They have insurance. What's one CD to a store like Walmart?
Deny victim	They had it coming. She shouldn't have talked back to me.
Condemn condemners	Everyone is on the take. If I don't do it to them, they'll do it to me.
Appeal to a higher loyalty	Only cowards back down. I have to feed my family. National security required this action.

rious. Police officers who administer violent doses of curbside justice to "street scum" deny that there is a "victim" in this assault. The "woman of the night" condemns her condemners when she dismisses her more conventional female critics as hypocrites, charging that they too exchange sexual favours in return for material considerations. Finally, high-ranking RCMP officials appeal to higher loyalties when they claim that concerns for national security required them to approve barn burnings, illegal wiretapping, and unlawful mail openings. In each of these situations, the actors make considerable effort to avoid self-definition as a deviant or lawbreaker.

Primary deviance is incidental to the perpetrator's self-concept because labels have not been successfully attached through a process of negative reflection. In many cases, however, negative responses may be strong and enduring because people persist in their nonconforming acts, because they are relatively powerless, or both. As the intensity of negative responses increases, efforts to maintain a nondeviant self-concept through neutralization or some other means become sorely taxed. When stigma is successfully applied and becomes all-encompassing, it can have negative effects on a person's social relations and economic opportunities. As someone becomes more and more broadly labelled as deviant, family members may withdraw their support, former friends may avoid social contact, employers may deny or take away jobs, and strangers may react with hostility. Moreover, official agents of social control may increase surveillance and harassment. The application of derogatory labels and the severing of connections to conventional spheres intensify the construction of a deviant identity by forcing the devalued person to seek out others in similar situations who can provide more favourable reflections of the self.

To retain a reasonably positive identity, to accept oneself as a "normal" person of some value, and to recast one's self-image in a more favourable light, the stigmatized person reorganizes life around the deviant status and the deviant role. When people transform their psychological outlooks and role performances into a defence from, attack against, or deep adjustment to negative labelling, **secondary deviance** has occurred (Lemert, 1967). The secondary deviant is a person with a deviant self-concept who participates fully in and is heavily committed to the deviant role. Deviant behaviour, for such persons, comes to be generated to a large extent by their definitions of self. The prostitute, the con artist, and the assassin who speak of their work in terms of professionalism and pride are secondary deviants. Their concepts of self are inexorably entwined with their statuses and their roles. They "are," therefore they "do."

HOWARD BECKER, MORAL ENTREPRENEURSHIP, AND THE DEVIANT CAREER

— Becker

Howard Becker develops two lines of reasoning to extend the labelling perspective — moral entrepreneurship and the deviant career (Becker, 1963). Moral entrepreneurs are people with the power to create or enforce moral norms that are often translated into legal statutes and prohibitions. Becker emphasizes that some individual or group must actively focus public attention on social wrongdoing. He sees deviance as the outcome of an enterprise in which those with vested moral or economic interests act accordingly to create and apply rules against those with less social and economic power. From this perspective, offenders are, in essence, created by rules that result in their being identified, apprehended, convicted, and, in the process, labelled.

Moral entrepreneurs are often successful at mobilizing support for social and legal sanctions developed and implemented in defence of what are they view as core moral values. When they are successful, moral entrepreneurs can create full-blown moral panics out of incidents and events that represent relatively minor acts of non-conformity. Moral panics involve overreactions on the part of media, police, courts, the legislature, and the public. Far from eliminating deviant behaviour, such reactions tend to amplify it. Examples of moral entrepreneurship and the creation of moral panics include various forms of vice and morality violations, such as smoking marijuana, drinking alcohol, gambling, accessing pornography, and visiting prostitutes.

Becker also examines the process of becoming deviant by using the sociological concept of the career (Becker, 1963). While normally thought of in terms of occupations, people can have legitimate careers as students, parents, religious devotees, and golfers or illegitimate careers as drug users, gamblers, prostitutes, and shoplifters.

Sociologists define a career as a sequence of social statuses through which people pass in some sphere of their lives. In the most general of terms, the stages are novice, new recruit, veteran, and retiree. Using an occupation as an example, the typical career of an upwardly mobile police officer might involve working up through the ranks from patrol officer to sergeant, lieutenant, captain, inspector, superintendent, and perhaps even chief. Each career stage represents a social status in which the occupant is reacted to differently both by proximate and distant audiences. Reactions of others to one's status, Becker points out, affect, to varying degrees, one's self-esteem, self-concept, and identity.

Becker suggests that many forms of deviance can be seen as careers through which people pass on their way to becoming full-fledged "outsiders." Prostitutes, alcoholics, and the mentally ill, as well as the majority of professional criminals, pass through a recognizable pattern of stages beginning with the initiate, progressing with the confirmed, and ending with retirement or death. Becker suggests that at each stage in a **deviant career**, some observers subject potential deviants to a variety of stigmatizing processes, while others, already committed to the devalued activity themselves, promote the redefinition of the deviant role in a more positive light. As a result of widespread homophobic attitudes, people wrestling with the thought that they might be gay often begin the homosexual career with feelings of anxiety, guilt, and shame. These repugnant feelings, in turn, promote a negative self-concept. In later stages of the career, some gays come into contact and interact with homosexuals in the context of a cohesive and supportive subculture. The gay subculture promotes homosexual identity, thereby encouraging gays to accept their sexuality, to "come out," and to declare their sexual orientation publicly and with pride (Troiden, 1979).

Another aspect of the career concept with which Becker deals is the notion of "**master status**." Essentially, a master status overrides other statuses regardless of the context in which the person is located when he or she is the subject of reaction. Someone at a party may occupy a number of different statuses, each of which might affect how other guests respond. For example, a party-goer might simultaneously occupy the statuses of wife, mother, president of a charitable organization, squash player, and physician. Occupying some statuses (e.g., being a doctor) can affect the reactions of others, regardless of the setting. Whether or not the context involves the delivery of health care, people tend to defer to doctors. If one status that a person occupies overrides all others, it is a master status.

Many deviants, when their devalued status becomes public knowledge, accordingly receive a negative response regardless of the context. Being homosexual and being mentally ill are often master statuses. Perhaps the best example is the "ex-con." People routinely treat with suspicion and distrust those who have served time in prison, regardless of their other status characteristics. Continuous negative reactions experienced by people with some form of deviant master status include gossip, ridicule, avoidance, and discrimination in housing and employment.

INTERACTIONIST THEORY AND SOCIAL POLICY

Interactionist approaches cite labelling and stigmatization, particularly by official agents of social control, as key precipitators in the development of an identity that promotes further deviance. The policy initiatives stemming from the labelling perspective call for a reduction in the degree to which official agents of social control negatively label and stigmatize the people whom they process. Strategies include a variety of undertakings aimed at limiting or eliminating the institutionalization of deviants. Diversion programs try to redirect accused persons out of the criminal justice system before official processing begins. Community-service orders seek to minimize official labelling by channelling those convicted of minor offences out of prisons and into court-mandated work in the community. Similarly, probation and parole programs aim to reduce stigma by minimizing periods of incarceration (Ekstadt and Griffiths, 1988).

The criminal justice system is not the only organization that has sought to incorporate the tenets of the labelling perspective. Many institutions for the mentally ill routinely release into the community people who are considered capable of functioning at an acceptable level on their own. Psychiatric centres have also moved toward reducing their admissions of persons with less serious mental problems (Marshall, 1982). Both these policy initiatives reflect efforts to reduce stigmatization.

Some labelling theorists have advocated more radical steps. Radical noninterventionists would limit official intervention to only the most serious forms of deviance (Schur, 1973). Decriminalization advocates would eliminate many forms of nonserious violation from the *Criminal Code* (Solomon, 1983); widespread illegalities such as the use of soft drugs, prostitution, and gambling would simply be dropped from the statutes. Reducing the numbers of minor but frequent offences would reduce the likelihood of someone becoming the object of official processing.

Table 6.2 summarizes the labelling perspective.

THE EVALUATION OF INTERACTIONIST THEORY

Micro theories in general and symbolic interactionism in particular have been criticized for paying little if any attention to history. Interactionists ignore the links between who or what is labelled deviant in the present and events that have occurred in the past. Moreover, interactionism downplays the importance, in the labelling process, of the social impacts of political and economic forces.

Another criticism levelled at labelling theorists is that they tend to ignore the causes of primary deviance (Gibbs, 1966). Consequently, they fail to offer adequate explanations for many forms of misconduct. Furthermore, types of deviance that do not lend themselves to incorporation in the career model cannot, in most cases, be adequately understood from the vantage point of labelling. Nevertheless, such acts (the majority of murders, assaults, and suicides) are significant problems in Canadian society.

Some people demonstrate real personality and behavioural differences long before deviant labels are applied to them. Not only do people become deviant without ever having been labelled as such, the application of stigma in itself often does not produce deviant behaviour. For some, the application of a negative label deters further nonconformity (West, 1980). While punishment may provoke the powerless to further acts of deviance, executives and professionals may be discouraged by punitive responses, especially when they receive public attention.

Labelling theory focuses on the powerful only as labellers; it pays little attention to the deviant behaviour of the socially privileged and economically advantaged (Thio, 1973). This emphasis, critics charge, is misplaced and perpetuates the conventional but mistaken belief that the disadvantaged in society are more deviant than the privileged. Ignoring the misconduct of the segments of society whose resources allow them to resist being labelled is a serious shortcoming.

The labelling perspective tends to treat the deviant as a passive receptor of the stigma that it holds ultimately produces secondary deviance (Piven, 1981). Some people, however, vigorously reject the imposition of these labels (Rogers and Buffalo, 1974). At least some prostitutes, mental patients, and homosexuals, for example, remain primary deviants in the sense that the stigma attached to their behaviours is not incorporated into their self-concepts and personal identities. As Nettler (1984) points out, the perspective is imprecise. It does not, for example, specify what behaviours and what kinds of personality are most susceptible to the application of labels. Nor does it indicate the stage in a person's life at which he or she is most easily labelled. Furthermore, labelling theory does not spell out how the kind of response, the type of actor responding, or the nature of the situation affects the likelihood that a label will stick.

The interactionist theory of deviance has strongly emphasized the importance of official labelling by the criminal justice system but has largely ignored the reactions of those within a person's own reference group (Vold and Bernard, 1986). Significant others play powerful roles in the development of deviant identity, in two ways. For those designated deviant by official agents, significant others may attach the

TABLE 6.2

LABELLING PERSPECTIVES ON DEVIANCE

Theory	Theorist	Central Premise	Key Concepts	Principal Contributions
Dramatization of Evil	Frank Tannenbaum	Children participate in a variety of acts to which adults object. Severe sanctions dramatize evil and stimulate youth to do more of the same	Dramatization of evil	Sensitization to the possibility that sanctions meant to deter may actually encourage deviant conduct.
Primary and Secondary Deviance	Edwin Lemert	A variety of factors produce initial or primary deviance. Strong persistent negative sanctions isolate deviants and produce deviant identities. Those who are stigmatized recast their identities in more favourable ways and organize their lives around deviant statuses and roles and continue deviant conduct as a process of secondary deviance.	Primary deviance; secondary deviance; neutralization; stigma	Emphasizes role of negative sanction in amplification as opposed to deterrence of non-conformity; stresses role of identity and self-concept as facilitators of deviance.
Deviant Careers	Howard Becker	Moral entrepreneurs create or enforce moral norms that are translated into legal statutes and prohibitions that label as deviant those with less social and economic power. Deviance persists over time and may result in development of deviant self-concept; this process can be analyzed using the career model (entry, novice, veteran, exit).	Moral entrepreneur, moral panic, career; master status	Provides a coherent analysis of criminal occupations; emphasizes the role of social control agents in the creation of devalued master statuses.

official label even more securely. Alternatively, where deviants fall into the company of similarly predisposed comrades, these significant others may help recast stigma into a more positive mould.

The labelling perspective depicts the stigmatized as resistant to the application of derogatory labels. There are, however, occasions where this is not the case. Rather than struggle to avoid a label, some deviants seek out and embrace stigma (Vold and Bernard, 1986). Juvenile gang members, for example, frequently view their newly acquired disrepute as a badge of honour and a sign of group acceptance.

Attempts to empirically test labelling theory show mixed results (Gove, 1980). Some studies suggest that labelling does promote career deviance, while others fail to demonstrate the link.

From a policy perspective, labelling theory advocates that lawmakers reduce the number of offences and that the police, the courts, and the corrections system avoid officially processing accused persons wherever possible. It recommends that official intervention be initiated only for serious offences. However, decriminalization and nonintervention strategies are problematic in several ways. They may not work, and even if they do, they are too radical for a "law-and-order" oriented public to accept (West, 1984). Moreover, even when strategies such as diversion programs, community-service orders, and other efforts aimed at de-institutionalization are undertaken, some labelling is inevitable. The application of at least some stigma by officials or by the deviant's acquaintances, friends, and family members is difficult to avoid.

Despite some of the difficulties associated with the interactionist or labelling approach, this orientation has dramatically influenced recent thinking in the areas of deviance, crime, and social control. Labelling theory has focused badly needed attention both on the social reaction to deviance and on the problems faced by those to whom stigma is attached. It has also highlighted the difficulties of reintegrating ex-offenders into the community. Finally, it has encouraged the criminal justice community to apply tough sanctions only as a last resort and only in cases involving serious crime (Stebbins, 1987).

SUMMARY

Symbolic interactionists stress the importance of communicating meaning through verbal and nonverbal symbols in a process of interaction. To the extent that the meanings attached to and conveyed by symbols are shared, interactionists maintain that culture exists. A person's interpretation of symbolic messages in cultural contexts positively or negatively affects the development of identity and self-concept. The symbolic interpretations of the reactions of others act as a social mirror that reflects the actor's self.

Herbert Blumer, a sociologist, articulated the framework of symbolic interaction first set out by its founder, philosopher George Herbert Mead. Meaning is not inherent in things, but arises as people develop interpretations during their interaction with one another. Once developed, meanings affect people's actions and their definitions of self, of society, and of situation. The sense of self arises from how people interpret the reactions that others have to them. Mead termed the process "the self as a social construction," and Charles Horton Cooley called it "the looking-glass self." Mead partitioned the self into three components: the I, the me, and the generalized other. The me, the reflective part of the self, is central to an understanding of interactionism. In this vein, Cooley argued that through the looking-glass, the reflective social mirror represented by the audience, people test their initial conceptions of their selves. The results of these tests are either positive or negative, pride or mortification.

The generalized other has its origins in significant others, those whose opinions are of critical importance. Over time, the opinions of significant others like parents and immediate friends become internalized and transformed into the generalized other. The generalized other represents the ideas people have about what others would think of their actions. The generalized other represents a kind of conscience.

Definitions of society represent views of the social world as either hospitable and full of opportunity, or as hostile and unjust. Definitions of the situation refer to views of contexts. The way in which people define the same circumstances varies according to culture and background.

Out of this general framework of symbolic interaction, sociologists interested in deviance and crime developed the labelling perspective. The cornerstone of labelling is the notion that deviance, like beauty, rests in the eye of the beholder. Labelling proponents concern themselves with finding the answers to three fundamental questions: Who gets defined as deviant? How does this happen? What are the consequences for people who are designated as deviants? Labelling theorists point out that the designators can usually be differentiated from the designated on the basis of their more elevated status. In comparison with the labelled, labellers wield more social power.

The policy implications of labelling rest on the argument that labelling and stigmatization by official agents of social control promote deviant and criminal behaviour. Labelling theorists direct their policy initiatives at reducing or eliminating stigma by limiting or abolishing the formal processing and incarceration of offenders. The labelling perspective supports decriminalization, de-institutionalization, diversion, probation, parole, and community service orders.

Some critics point out that labelling is ahistorical and pays insufficient attention to the role of social and economic structures in generating deviance and crime. Others argue that labelling trivializes the causes of primary deviance and fails to provide an explanation of deviant acts, like murder, that do not fit the career model. In many cases, deviance precedes labelling and labelling discourages rather than encourages deviant and illegal conduct. Furthermore, empirical tests of the labelling process have produced mixed results.

Critics have also attacked labelling theory for its inability to explain the deviance of elites, for treating people as passive receptors, and for not paying sufficient attention to specifying the conditions under which labels are more or less likely to be successfully applied. Labelling has largely ignored the impacts of informal social groups on the development of negative self-concepts and deviant careers. Policy directives based on the labelling approach have fallen out of fashion of late because they tend to support noninterventionist, nonpunitive, and rehabilitative stances at a time when the corrections system is moving increasingly toward an exclusively punitive orientation.

Labelling approaches have made important contributions to the understanding of social deviance and crime. They focus attention on the negative impacts of formal processing by criminal justice agencies. In particular, labelling theory has highlighted the problems of reintegrating into society those bearing the stigma of institutionalization. Labelling theory has added additional credence to the idea that severe negative sanctions like imprisonment should be used sparingly and as a last resort.

DISCUSSION QUESTIONS

1. How do interactionists explain the development of self-concept and identity? Use Mead's "self as a social construct" and Cooley's "looking-glass self" as starting points.

2. Explain the relevance of the "definition of the situation" idea for the understanding of deviant and criminal activity.

3. Discuss the links between the general theory of symbolic interaction and the labelling perspective on deviance and crime.

4. What are the commonalities among Tannenbaum's dramatization of evil, Lemert's primary and secondary deviance, and Becker's deviant career? How can these approaches be combined to account for (1) a deviant act and (2) a deviant trait?

5. What are the central policy implications of the symbolic interactionist perspective? How influential has the labelling approach been in influencing government action?

WEB LINKS

George's Page: The Mead Project
http://paradigm.soci.brocku.ca/~lward/
   George's Page: The Mead Project Web site contains a wealth of information about George Herbert Mead, including documents about, by, and related to the famous philosopher, as well as timelines and other resources.

Symbolic Interactionism as Defined by Herbert Blumer
http://www.xrefer.com/entry/344835
   An overview of Herbert Blumer's formulation of symbolic interactionism.

Charles Horton Cooley's *Human Nature and the Social Order*
http://paradigm.soci.brocku.ca/~lward/Cooley/cooley_1toc.html
   Full text of Cooley's *Human Nature and the Social Order*, in which the author introduces the idea of "the looking-glass self," from The Mead Project site.

Labelling Theory
http://www.crimetheory.com/Archive/Response/SR2.htm#Title
   An introduction to the labelling theory, from Crimetheory.com. Use the links at the bottom of the page to put this theory in context.

Symbolic Interactionism and Howard Becker
http://www.criminology.fsu.edu/crimtheory/becker.htm
   This page provides an overview of several symbolic interactionist theories, with an emphasis on Howard Becker's contribution.

RECOMMENDED READINGS

Becker, H.S. (1963). *Outsiders: Studies in the Sociology of Deviance.* New York: Free Press.
   A collection of papers by Howard Becker that set out the foundation of his labelling framework. Among the concepts developed are deviant careers, master statuses, and moral entrepreneurship.

Charon, J.M. (1985). *Symbolic Interactionism* (2nd ed.). Englewood Cliffs, NJ: Prentice-Hall.
   This text provides a clear and very readable introduction to the basic ideas of symbolic interactionism as articulated by Mead, Blumer, and others.

Goffman, E. (1963). *Stigma.* Englewood Cliffs, NJ: Prentice Hall.
   This short book sets out Erving Goffman's conceptualization of stigma and its impacts on various types of deviants including the mentally disordered and the physically disadvantaged.

Lemert, E.M. (1972). *Human Deviance, Social Problems, and Social Control.* Englewood Cliffs, NJ: Prentice-Hall.
   This work contains a discussion of Lemert's articulation of primary and secondary deviance and their roles in understanding non-conforming and illegal conduct.

Rubington, E. and M.G. Weinberg. (1999). *Deviance: The Interactionist Perspective* (7th ed.). Boston: Allyn and Bacon.
   This is a longstanding anthology of pioneering and contemporary articles on a wide variety of forms of deviance, written from a symbolic interactionist perspective.

CHAPTER 7

CONFLICT THEORY

The aims of this chapter are to familiarize the reader with:

- liberal conflict perspectives: Sellin's culture conflict, Vold's group conflict, Turk's authority–subject conflict, and Quinney's social reality of crime
- the general fundamentals of Marxist conflict theory
- Marxist theories presenting deviance and crime as products of conditions: Bonger's foundation, Greenberg's age structure, and Friedrich's crisis of legitimacy
- Marxist perspectives emphasizing the role of the law in creating crime: instrumental Marxism and structural Marxism
- the policy implications of conflict theories
- deficiencies in the conflict framework
- the contributions of conflict approaches to an understanding of deviance and crime

INTRODUCTION

There are two types of conflict theories of crime: liberal conflict and **Marxism**. Both highlight the roles of social conflict and power in producing deviance and crime. (See Figure 7.1.) **Liberal conflict perspectives** view society as composed of a variety of competing groups with different and fluctuating sources of power. Marxist perspectives see society as comprising two competing groups, one of which owns or controls the economy while the other does not. The first section of this chapter considers several forms of liberal conflict theory as they have been applied to the understanding of deviance and crime: **culture conflict**, group conflict, authority–subject conflict, and the social construction of crime. The second section investigates Marxist approaches, beginning with an

examination of Marxist theory generally and then narrowing its focus to Marxist analyses of deviant behaviour and criminality.

LIBERAL CONFLICT PERSPECTIVES ON DEVIANCE AND CRIME

THORSTEN SELLIN AND CULTURE CONFLICT

In 1938, Thorsten Sellin proposed a theory of crime based on the notion of culture conflict (Sellin, 1938). Sellin noted that in societies where culture is homogeneous, the values to which people adhere and the norms to which they accede are essentially the same for all people. Cultures in which this sort of consensus reigns are governed by a single set of rules, which he termed "conduct norms." When different cultures come into contact with one another or when a variety of subcultures exists within a single society, the different groups will inevitably subscribe to different conduct norms. Where this is the case, the disparate groups are likely to come into conflict with one another.

Conflict increases in complex societies in which group norms overlap in some instances but are contradictory in others. Where the conduct norms of one group clash with those of another group, conflict ensues as each segment vies with the other for the right to have its norms recognized by competitors as legitimate. Most likely to be successful in this competition are the groups with access to the largest share of resources. Usually, Sellin points out, the dominant group in society translates its conduct norms into law. A society's laws, then, represent the conduct norms of the dominant cultural group or groups.

Figure 7.1

General Model of Conflict Theory

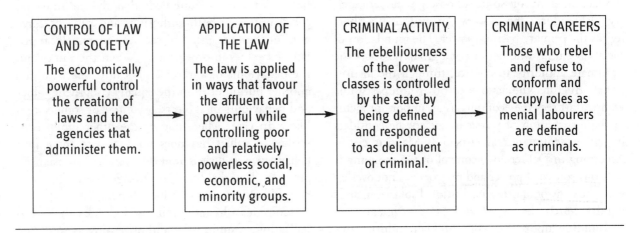

George Vold and Group Conflict

On the basis of some of Georg Simmel's ideas, George Vold in 1958 outlined another form of group conflict theory. Vold (1958) envisaged humans as compelled by necessity to become involved with one another in group contexts. Through working as individuals, people come to see that they can most effectively achieve their own best interests through collective action, so they form groups. When a number of different groups form and several of them pursue similar collective goals, it is common for one group to encroach upon the others' domains. When such encroachments occur, competition for scarce resources produces conflict.

Vold's view of society is one of competing groups locked in a continuing struggle to maintain or to improve their positions in relation to those of their competitors. Consequently, from Vold's perspective, conflict is an essential and endemic part of a functioning society. Social order emerges and continues at times when it is possible for groups to adjust to one another's demands. Vold argues that such adjustments are tenuous, however, and that social stability is fragile and quite often transitory.

According to Vold, when groups compete for scarce resources, they often seek the assistance of the state in achieving their goals. To protect or enhance its own interest, an ascendant group lobbies the state to create laws that will operate to its advantage and undermine the best interests of its competitors. This is a legislative political process. If some groups favour

a law and other groups do not, the group with the greatest political support carries the day. If a group in favour of enacting a particular law can command more votes than an opposing group, it wins. If not, the law will die and the sponsoring group loses. When legislators enact a law, its promoters are in a position both to obey the new law and, in defence of their interests, to insist that the state enforce it. Opposition groups, or to use Vold's term, "minority power groups," can either obey the new law or break it. If they violate it, they become subject to the punitive machinery of the state.

Vold limits his group conflict theory to the explanation of a narrow range of conflicts that can result in criminalization. The theory is not, as he points out, applicable to crimes that are unplanned, irrational, or occur in the heat of passion. Rather, Vold focuses on explaining criminalization that results from a relatively powerful group invoking the law against a less powerful group to maintain or further improve its social and economic position. Examples of such conflicts include those arising between management and labour, among various ethnic groups, and between the state and civil rights advocates.

Austin Turk and Conflict Between Authorities and Subjects

Austin Turk's conflict theory of crime (Turk, 1969) builds on the more general theory of conflict developed earlier by Ralf Dahrendorf (1959). Dahrendorf's theory of conflict emphasizes differences in power among various factions in society. Unlike Marxist theory, which cites ownership of the means of economic production as the sole source of power in modern society, Dahrendorf's theory views "institutional authority" as the primary basis of power. The foundation of social division is whether or not a group possesses the legitimate authority to control, through the institutional structure, the actions of other groups. While Dahrendorf sees the economy as an important factor in the distribution of power in society, he considers it neither central nor as critical as Marxists claim. According to Dahrendorf, control of the economy is only one source of power and may or may not overlap with the control of other institutional spheres including the church, the school, and the government.

Building upon the work of Dahrendorf, Turk divides society into two groups: those with power, "the authorities," and those without power, "the subjects." For Turk, social order emerges from the long-term institutionalized coordination of these two groups. To ensure coordination, authorities must maintain a delicate balance of consensus-building and coercion. There must be neither a preponderance of consensus-building nor a preponderance of coercion; balance is essential. According to Turk, the enduring maintenance of this balance psychologically conditions subjects to the social roles inherent in the authority–subject relationship. With successful conditioning, subjects do not question the legitimacy of their relationship to "super-ordinates." Like Dahrendorf, Turk believes power is invested in groups through their institutional authority rather than solely through their ownership of the means of economic productivity. Turk's focus also falls squarely on legal conflict and, in that context, upon criminalization.

When a balance exists between consensus-building and coercion and when social conditioning is successful, conflict in a society is minimal. Under certain conditions, however, group differences are likely to lead to social conflict and subjects are likely to be criminalized by active law enforcement. Turk specifies these conditions first by defining "cultural norms" and "social norms" and then by identifying the situations in which cultural and normative differences between authorities and subjects are most likely to result in conflict and criminalization. He defines cultural norms as verbal formulations of value, and social norms as actual behaviours. The former can be understood as laws on the books while the latter can be understood as laws as they are actually enforced.

Turk specifies three conditions under which cultural and normative differences between authorities and subjects lead to social conflict. The first condition begins with the requirement that the cultural and social norms of both authorities and subjects agree with one another; that is, each group actually translates its values into behaviour. When the values and the behaviours of authorities fall into line with one another but differ from the equally congruent values and behaviours of subjects, a contest of some sort is likely. In cases where one or the other group subscribes to values but does not translate them into behaviour, a struggle is unlikely. In such circumstances, groups will probably not deem significant the issues raised by differences in values alone.

Consider a hypothetical case in which the criminalization of subjects by authorities involves the use of soft drugs. Assume that authorities value industry, sobriety, and deferred gratification. Assume that they translate these cultural norms into behaviour by toiling in the mines, mills, and factories from dawn to dusk and by saving their hard-earned wages for the future. The cultural norms or values of the subject group, on the other hand, extol self-exploration, pleasure, and living for the moment. When subjects translate their cultural norms into social norms by actively dropping out, tuning in, and turning on with mind-altering drugs, the chances of conflict between the two groups and the criminalization of the latter escalate. Compare this situation with a circumstance in which either authorities or subjects, or both authorities and subjects, fail to translate their beliefs into action. Without both authorities and subjects translating cultural norms (values) into social norms (behaviour), the potential for conflict and criminalization is greatly reduced.

The second condition affecting the probability of conflict is the subject group's degree of social organization. Tightly organized subjects are in a better position to resist the subjugation efforts of authorities. Unorganized subject groups, by comparison, are much less capable of meaningful resistance.

The final condition contributing to the likelihood of conflict between authorities and subjects is the degree of sophistication demonstrated by the subjects in their attempts at resistance. The greater their sophistication, the less likely is overt conflict. Highly sophisticated subjects will be more likely to assess accurately the position taken by the authorities and, on the basis of that knowledge, will be able to manipulate them. Sophisticated subjects can frequently violate the norms of the authorities without engaging them in open conflict.

Having discussed the conditions precipitating conflict between authorities and subjects, Turk proceeds to outline three circumstances under which the authorities are most likely to enforce their legal norms, thereby criminalizing members of subject groups. First, when the authorities' cultural and social norms are not only congruent but also salient, authorities are likely to enforce legal norms. Within this context, Turk also points out that the meaning of a prohibited act for the first line of enforcement (the police) and for higher-level enforcers (the courts) is vital. If all levels of enforcement agree that a behaviour is offensive, a violation is likely to result both in high rates of arrest and conviction and in the imposition of severe penalties. In cases where the first line of enforcement finds a behaviour offensive but higher levels of enforcement do not, arrest rates will be high but convictions will be few and sentences lenient. Conversely, if the first line of enforcement views a violation as trivial while higher-level enforcers do not, arrest rates will be low but for those few arrested, conviction rates will be high and punishment severe.

Second, the relative power of authorities and subjects plays a role in determining whether subjects can successfully resist authorities' efforts to criminalize them. The criminalization of subjects is highest when they are powerless to resist the authorities. In such cases, authorities expend few resources because subjects muster little opposition. Where the distribution of power between authorities and subjects is more equal, authorities must expend more of their own resources to bring about criminalization. In such cases, the social and economic costs of criminalization temper their initiatives. Enforcers under these circumstances become more cautious in their efforts. In those rare instances in which subjects manage to acquire a great deal of power, they may change the laws that criminalize them.

Third, the degree of realism with which either authorities or subjects undertake action one against the other influences the extent to which the powerful will criminalize the powerless. Unrealistic moves by either party increase the likelihood that subjects will become criminals. Subjects, for example, rather than adopt the realistic stance of maintaining a low profile, sometimes flagrantly violate existing laws. In these instances, authorities who might otherwise ignore such violations have no recourse but to invoke and to enforce the law. For their part, authorities generally demonstrate realism by opting for restrained coercion rather than unrealistic measures that might later be construed as brutal.

RICHARD QUINNEY AND THE SOCIAL REALITY OF CRIME

Criminologists divide the theoretical contributions of Richard Quinney into two segments, depending upon whether the work dates from the period before 1970 or after 1970. Quinney (1970) outlines his initial conflict theory of criminality in his book *The Social Reality of Crime*, in which he elaborates the theory, in proposition form, as follows.

1. *Crime is a definition of human conduct that is created by authorized agents in a politically organized society.* With this statement, Quinney asserts that crime is a product of the way in which those in positions of authority choose to define it. Crime is not a product of some sort of individual pathology.

2. *Criminal definitions describe behaviours that conflict with the interests of the segments of society that have the power to shape public policy.* Quinney substitutes Vold's concept of "interest group" with his notion of "social segment." A social segment, according to Quinney, differs from a group in that it need not be comparatively small, organized, communicative, and in pursuit of a common goal through concerted action. He defines a segment as a broad statistical aggregate containing persons similarly disposed on certain characteristics such as age, sex, class, status, occupation, ethnicity, and religion.

3. *Criminal definitions are applied by the segments of society that have the power to shape the enforcement and administration of criminal law.* Some activities of relatively powerless segments become crimes because they aggravate or threaten those in possession of power. The powerful then mobilize to protect their vested interests. The preservation of privilege on the part of those with power produces intersegment conflict, the ultimate result of which is the criminalization of less powerful social segments. When Quinney links his third proposition to the one preceding it, he expands the range of criminal activity beyond that first outlined by Vold. For example, Quinney includes irrational and impulsive crimes in his framework. He sees these types of illegalities as individual acts of rebellion that members of disorganized segments direct against their more privileged oppressors.

4. *Behaviour patterns are structured in segmentally organized society in relation to criminal definitions, and*

within this context persons engage in actions that have relative probabilities of being defined as criminal. This proposition asserts that deciding what acts become violations of law depends on the power and influence of the segment engaging in them. If a social segment has little or no power, more of the behaviours of its members are likely to be legislated as crime. Alternatively, the more powerful a segment is, the smaller is the number of its behaviours that will be criminalized.

The final two propositions present a different conception of **criminogenesis**. 5. *Conceptions of crime are constructed and diffused in the segments of society by various means of communication.* 6. *The social reality of crime is constructed by the formulation and application of criminal definitions, the development of behaviour patterns related to criminal definitions, and the construction of criminal conceptions.* According to Quinney, crime is created and its essence is communicated so as to promote a set of values and interests that benefit the powerful. The media inculcate a social reality of crime as consisting of interpersonal violence and common property offences. Their message also conveys the image of rapidly increasing crime rates. By promoting these images of crime and by cultivating the widespread acceptance of their authority as legitimate, the powerful can implement, in the name of the common good, policies of social control that they themselves have created. The good, in Quinney's view, is far from truly "common," because these particularistic policies preserve the advantages of the privileged. In these last two propositions, Quinney explains why all segments of society, powerful and powerless alike, are inclined to view street crime as the real problem while ignoring the socially harmful acts of economic and political elites.

Table 7.1 summarizes liberal conflict theories.

Quinney's more recent theories are more distinctly Marxist. The contributions of Marx and the contemporary criminological theorists who have adapted his insights deserve discussion.

MARXIAN CONFLICT PERSPECTIVES ON SOCIAL CONTROL, DEVIANCE, AND CRIME

Karl Marx did not have a great deal to say about crime (Taylor, Walton, and Young, 1973). However, crimi-nologists working within the Marxist paradigm have tried to explain criminality by using as a foundation Marx's ideas about the exploitative nature of capitalist economy and about the way in which capitalist society is organized.

THE MARXIAN PERSPECTIVE IN GENERAL

To make sense of European society during the latter part of the nineteenth century, Marx adopted a historical perspective (Lefebvre, 1968). First, he argues that conflict has always been the basic element of social process. Second, he maintains that, for all eras in human history, **class** struggle is the critical factor in understanding both social structure and social process. Marx conceptualizes the principal historical social conflict as occurring between "the material forces of production" — the means by which the manufacture of goods is accomplished — and "the social relations of production" — the human contribution to this economic and material process, that is, the social organization of work.

In elaborating his vision of social conflict, Marx explains how the **material forces of production** (the mechanics of manufacturing goods) profoundly affect the **social relations of production** (the social organization of work). According to Marx, the social relations of production initially facilitate the material production of goods. When changes in the material forces of production (technology) occur so rapidly that changes in the social relations of production (work) cannot keep pace, the way in which work is socially organized impedes the efficient manufacture of goods. Such conditions result, Marx maintains, in abrupt and dramatic changes through which new social relations of production (new ways of organizing work) are established to better achieve efficient economic productivity. In his analysis of the events of the early industrial era, Marx argues that the social relations of production (organization of work), which functioned well during **feudalism**, came to impede the material forces of production during the process of **industrialization** in the nineteenth century. The result was the Industrial Revolution and the rapid restructuring of the social relations of production under capitalism.

The new social relations of production that emerged during and after the Industrial Revolution revolved around the development of private property

TABLE 7.1

LIBERAL CONFLICT THEORIES

Theory	Theorist(s)	Central Premise	Key Concepts	Principal Contributions
Cultural conflict	Thorsten Sellin	Different cultures subscribe to different conduct norms. Conflict arises over whose conduct norms will be accepted as legitimate. Those with access to resources become dominant and translate their conduct norms into law.	Conduct norms	An early (1938) formulation of liberal conflict theory that influenced more contemporary versions.
Group conflict theory	George Vold	Of necessity, groups come into contact with one another in competition for scarce resources. Social order involves groups adjusting to one another's demands. Groups seek to use their power and other resources to influence the creation of laws that favour them and disadvantage competitors who are relegated to the status of "minority power groups."	Group conflict; minority power group	Provides a good explanation of certain types of legal conflict and criminalization that arise from problems involving labour relations, ethnic strife, and civil rights disputes.
Authority-subject conflict	Austin Turk	Social order emerges from long-term institutionalized coordination between authority and subject groups through a balance of consensus building and/or coercion. Conflict arises where cultural norms (values) and social norms (behaviours) differ, where subject groups are organized, and where subject resistance is unsophisticated. Authorities are likely to criminalize subjects where cultural and social norms are salient, where subjects are powerless, and where either group responds to the other unrealistically.	Institutional authority; authorities and subjects; cultural norms; social norms	Offers a parsimonious articulation of the sociological thinking of Weber and Dahrendorf as it applies to law, power, and processes of criminalization.
Social reality of crime	Richard Quinney	Authorized agents in a politically organized society use power to create a definition of human conduct called crime. By virtue of differing behaviour patterns in a segmented society, some are more likely to be defined as criminal than others. The social reality of crime is a product of the construction of criminal conceptions through various means of communication.	Social segmentation; social reality of crime	Stresses the importance of communication through the media of a social reality of crime that benefits powerful social and economic interests.

under **capitalism**. For Marx, "private property" refers to resources used to generate wealth — land, machinery, and factories. Around the idea of private productive property, Marx develops his conception of a two-class system: the **bourgeoisie** (the haves) and the proletariat (the have-nots). The bourgeoisie are capitalists who own the land, the machinery, and the manufacturing plants. The proletariat are workers who must sell their labour to the capitalists and work in the mines, mills, and factories of the newly industrializing world.

Marx points out that the vested interests of the bourgeoisie and the proletariat are diametrically opposed. Capitalists strive to increase profits so that they can then reinvest this surplus wealth in additional capital-generating enterprises. Reinvestment of profits increases one capitalist's advantage over other capitalists. To build greater and greater surpluses of wealth, capitalists must maximize productivity while minimizing operating expenses. Since workers' salaries represent significant overhead costs, the bourgeoisie must keep wages as low as possible. Improvements to the workers' quality of life, on the other hand, depend largely on their ability to extract higher salaries from their capitalist employers. For either group to maximize its own economic interests, it must operate to the detriment of the other.

Capitalists, in addition to being in conflict with workers, must also compete with each other for increasingly larger shares of economic markets. As such, stronger capitalists put weaker capitalists out of business, in effect relegating them to the proletariat. As more and more unfit capitalists fail to survive the competition, the proletariat continues to increase in number and the private property of production becomes ever more concentrated in fewer hands. With increasing mechanization, capitalists need fewer workers to produce the same or greater amounts of goods. As the numbers of available workers grow while the demand for their labour tapers off, the bourgeoisie forces the proletariat to compete for fewer jobs at lower wages. This competition among labourers combines with rising rates of unemployment to make it possible for capitalists to easily replace one worker with another. All of these factors converge to erode the bargaining position of workers, thereby allowing capitalists to keep wages low.

Marx claimed that, in time, the number of capitalists would shrink. With smaller numbers, the wealth of individual capitalists would grow markedly.

On the other hand, Marx predicted that the numbers of workers would expand dramatically while their incomes and standards of living would decline. He believed that members of the proletariat would become ever more concentrated in cities and that, as a result, their mutual awareness of a common plight would emerge. He predicted that periods of economic crisis would exacerbate the predicament of workers as capitalists cut costs by laying them off. Layoffs would increase poverty among the workers and accordingly result in a **polarization of classes** as the bourgeoisie's and proletariat's positions grew increasingly divergent. Marx argued that such a severe rift between the haves and have-nots would ignite a revolutionary restructuring wherein socialism would eventually replace capitalism. Under socialism, a **classless society** would emerge.

In elaborating his notion of dominance and self-interest, Marx discusses the importance of society's "**superstructure**" and "**infrastructure**." He defines the superstructure of society as its ideology and institutional structure. **Ideology** is the set of ideas that effectively govern people's lives — law, science and knowledge, popular beliefs, and religion. The institutional structure comprises the social organizations that promulgate these ideas — state, school, mass media, and church. Marx argues that society's superstructure (ideology and institutional structure) would impede the revolutionary transition from capitalism to socialism. The foundation or infrastructure of a society is its economy. While Marx views the relationship between a society's superstructure (ideas and institutions) and infrastructure (economy) as reciprocal, he makes it clear that both serve the interests of the capitalist class and enable capitalists to maintain their dominance over the proletariat.

The central ideas of any society, Marx points out, are the ideas of that society's ruling class. Under capitalism, the central ideas assert that freedom, opportunity, individualism, and equality are the cornerstones of modern society. All segments of the superstructure (political, legal, religious, educational and mass communication) disseminate these precepts. Marx observes that the bourgeoisie and proletariat both believe in these precepts, but that such beliefs favour the capitalists.

Marx makes the point that, should the internalization of the dominant ideology falter or fail, certain branches of the state — the police and the army — are ready to force compliance. In *The Communist*

Manifesto (written by Marx and Friedrich Engels), Marx states that the central justification of the political system under capitalism is to develop and administer a society's laws, using force if necessary. To the extent that the proletariat embrace society's ideological underpinnings, however, the creation and enforcement of law appear to reflect the common good of the entire society. Nonetheless, according to Marx, the enactment and the enforcement of statutes support the vested interests of those who own and control the economy.

Marx deals directly with deviance and crime only in passing (Taylor, Walton, and Young, 1973). He suggests that a productive and satisfying work life is essential both to human nature and to the realization of the human self. He presents underemployment and unemployment as unproductive and dissatisfying to the individual. According to Marx, marginalization and the demoralization associated with powerlessness, alienation, and low self-esteem produce strains. These pressures in turn result in the venting of frustration among the lowest class, the "**lumpenproletariat**," in the form of crime and other vices.

Despite this rendition of the cause of crime, Marx shows little sympathy for the criminal class. He sees members of the lumpenproletariat as social parasites who make little contribution to society, who undermine labour as a potentially potent force, and who impede social change. Moreover, he argues that the deviance and crime of the lumpenproletariat simply expand and strengthen the power of the state's police forces, which may then be used to control legitimate labour unrest and insurrection.

Another theme emerging from Marx's discussion of crime and criminalization is the unequal distribution of wealth in capitalist society and, with it, the unequal distribution of power. Wealth provides power, and the wielding of power allows the wealthy to preserve their own interests. Marx hints that deviance and crime may be thought of as isolated expressions of rebellion against the deprivations inherent in oppressive circumstances.

To summarize, capitalism and private property give rise to a social system comprising two antagonistic classes. The bourgeoisie own productive property, while the proletariat who work for them do not. Marx predicted that the ever-worsening plight of the workers would eventually draw them together in a revolution that would replace capitalism with socialism. According to Marx, in situations where the ideology and the institutions promoting capitalist values and interests break down, society's wealthy and powerful elites use law and agents of social control to force the proletariat to comply. It is upon the themes of deprived circumstances and of the inequitable creation and application of law that Marx's followers have concentrated.

MARXIST THEORIES OF DEVIANCE AND CRIME

Modern Marxist theorists have not concentrated upon expanding the little that Marx had to say about deviance and crime. Rather, they have attempted to construct their explanations around central Marxian tenets about the nature of social conflict. Theories building upon Marx's ideas seek to provide insights into why some social norms are translated into law, why some laws are enforced while others are not, and why laws that are enforced are not applied equally to all social segments. Answering these questions, Marxists maintain, depends on a fundamental understanding of the way in which elites employ power both to create law and to criminalize people.

WILLEM BONGER'S MARXIST CRIMINOLOGY

Willem Bonger, whose work dates from the early part of this century, was the first criminologist to employ the Marxian approach. His argument is that while capitalism produces greed and selfishness in all members of society, only the avarice of the poor is criminalized. The acquisitiveness of the affluent, conversely, receives legitimate support. Bonger claims that a move to socialism would eliminate a great deal of criminal activity because legal biases favouring the wealthy would be removed (Bonger, 1916). After Bonger's early foray into the use of Marxist thought to explain crime, Marxist approaches did not resurface until the early 1970s.

CONTEMPORARY MARXIST APPROACHES

Contemporary Marxist scholars attempt to account for deviance and crime in two principal ways. Some concern themselves with the ways in which certain conditions inherent in capitalism generate nonconforming behaviour, while others direct their attention toward the social origins of law and the criminalization process. The first approach, the "reaction to deprivation" thesis, views deviance and crime as calculated responses on the parts of rational individuals who must confront daily the miserable conditions endemic in the social relations of capitalism. People generally and in the long term think and behave in their own economic interests. Acquisitive property crime becomes a means of earning or supplementing income for those who are unemployed or who toil in low-paying, demeaning jobs. Violent crime, on the other hand, is either an unsophisticated means of stealing (e.g., robbery) or a venting of the frustrations (e.g., wife battering) produced by occupying an economically marginal position. In a similar vein, this brand of Marxist thought views more-organized criminal endeavours as larger-scale rational responses of the poor to black markets and to their exclusion from legitimate money-making opportunities.

Against this ubiquitous backdrop of deprivation, marginalization, and strain, several Marxist criminologists, including David Greenberg and David Friedrichs, have developed more specialized theoretical frameworks. Greenberg (1980) offers an analysis of juvenile delinquency that begins by noting that today's youth are systematically excluded from the paid labour market. This exclusion, he suggests, results in severe strain for adolescents who find themselves unable to finance the leisure activities that have become such an integral part of teenage subcultures. The acute experience of strain induces adolescents to steal, while the daily negative experiences and degrading atmosphere that they confront in school encourage hostile responses to authority.

In another application of the Marxian model, Friedrichs (1980) views crime as a product of what he calls a "**crisis of legitimacy**." Social order, he maintains, is based on the perceived legitimacy of authority relations in society. According to Friedrichs, an erosion of faith in political leaders and governmental institutions has created a crisis of legitimacy, which itself has produced a breakdown in social control. Increasingly disillusioned with basic values, citizens come to perceive social institutions as ineffective. Loss of faith and disillusionment have spurred increases in crime, social protest, and rebellion. Under such circumstances, the government has little choice but to be ever more coercive to reinforce social order. This continued coercion has, according to Friedrichs, merely worsened the existing crisis of legitimacy, which continues to spiral out of control.

Some contemporary Marxist frameworks focus on the origin and application of law. There are two principal variants of this approach. The **instrumental theory of Marxism**, developed in the late 1960s and the 1970s, was replaced by the structural perspective in the 1980s. **Structural Marxism** was a response to criticisms levelled at the earlier instrumental approach. Instrumental and structural Marxist criminological theories present different views both of the law and of the ruling class (Chambliss and Seidman, 1982).

Instrumental Marxist Theories of Social Control

For instrumentalists, the ruling class is a unified and monolithic social group. The law, for this powerful elite, is designed to preserve and expand the group's economic and social interests (Smandych, 1985). The image of the ruling elite is one of a conspiratorial group plotting its own advantage at the expense of other social classes.

Quinney's theorizing in the early 1970s is an example of the instrumental position. Quinney claims that the fundamental conflict in society is between those who own the means of economic production and those who do not. The owners comprise a ruling elite that also controls relations in other spheres of social life, including politics, education, and religion. The state, in its authority to enact and enforce criminal law, is an important instrument used by the ruling class to perpetuate an economic and social order that reflects its own best interests. The economic elite influences the actions of the state either directly by affecting the legislative process or indirectly by bringing to bear various forms of economic pressure. On behalf of the ruling class, the state creates and selectively enforces the law when elite interests are threatened. Quinney argues that in those rare instances when statutes contravene ruling-class interests and the ruling class itself violates the law, the state seldom undertakes active enforcement. Instances of nonenforcement commonly arise where laws protect consumers and employees or where they preserve the environment at the expense of economic elites.

Quinney explains lower-class **over-representation** and upper-class under-representation in crime statistics by pointing to differences both in their economic roles and in their relative power to resist the encroachment of the state. He suggests that certain societal groups are susceptible to special strains that drive them toward higher rates of criminal activity. Street crime occurs because those breaking the law in this fashion are brutalizing their victims as they themselves have been brutalized under capitalism. To ensure its continued contribution to the capitalistic enterprise, the lower class becomes the target of law enforcement. By comparison, because the privileged have the capacity to resist enforcers, the upper classes tend not to become objects of legal control.

Quinney maintains that institutional structures buttress crime control in capitalist society. The ruling class establishes and maintains institutional structures specifically to provide definitions of morality that reinforce the existing domestic order. Schools teach people to obey statutes, claiming that they represent the common good. News and entertainment media present an image of harmful wrongdoing that situates the crime problem squarely in the laps both of the lower classes and of certain ethnic minorities. Religious teachings preach the sanctity of hard work and personal sacrifice, both of which will be rewarded, if not in this life, in the next. Religion, as a famous statement from Marx points out, is the "opium of the people." It dulls their senses to their predicament and, by putting a damper on the sparks of rebellion, supports the status quo.

Quinney argues that contradictions inherent in advanced capitalism fuel the oppression of subordinate classes. Competition among the bourgeoisie and the failure of many capitalists expand the ranks of the proletariat. Along with this expansion, the introduction of technology and the cyclical nature of the economy swell the ranks of the unemployed. The resultant growth in the numbers of the dispossessed in itself contains a potential threat to the established order that must be dealt with. Quinney points out that one strategy of mollifying the masses is to expand programs of social welfare. Another tactic is to escalate the coerciveness of society's main mechanism of formal social control, the criminal justice system (Quinney, 1970, 1973).

Structural Marxist Theories of Social Control

Like the instrumental approach, the structural perspective views the bourgeoisie and the proletariat as social segments occupying different positions in the social structure and, as a consequence, as having different values, beliefs, and behaviours. Structuralists differ from instrumentalists in that they do not view the ruling class as a cohesive group organized in conspiratorial fashion to defend its own economic and social interests. Moreover, they do not view governments simply as instruments in the hands of conspiratorial elites. While structuralists see the state as relatively more autonomous than do instrumentalists, they point out that the material well-being of a society and ultimately of the state itself depends upon the economic vitality of the industrial enterprises owned and controlled by the ruling class. If it is to survive, the state has little choice, in the long term, but to protect and enhance the overall interests of economic elites regardless of the consequences for other societal groups.

Structural Marxism takes account of different and competing factions or "**class factions**" among the ruling class. Because some capitalist interests compete and interfere with other capitalist interests, structuralists portray the ruling class as highly factionalized, even though all capitalists occupy a similar structural position in relation to the means of production and, as a result, possess similar values and beliefs. The role of the state when factionalism occurs is to mediate between the competitive groups in the ruling class to protect the long-term interests of the entire capitalist class. From the state's perspective, the promotion of capital accumulation and social harmony is more important than the unbridled pursuit of self-interests by capitalist class factions.

The structural position is an advance over instrumentalism because it explains how certain laws appear to contravene the best interests of the capitalist class (Smandych, 1985). Occasionally the state must serve the best interests of the proletariat, but only in the short term. It does this in order that the long-term interests of capitalists will not be undermined. By occasionally protecting proletariat interests in the short run, the state prevents the development of conditions that might eventually fuel the disruption or eventual disintegration of the capitalist economy. Governments pass laws designed to ensure consumer protection, worker health and safety, and environmental preservation. The existence and occasional enforcement of these laws lull citizens into believing that they are adequately protected. While the laws are without any real teeth, their existence quells protest and rebellion by consumers, employees, and the public. Thus, from the structuralist perspective, some laws may serve interests other than those of the capitalist elite but only on occasion and in the short run. (See Table 7.2.)

TABLE 7.2

TWO VERSIONS OF MARXIST CONFLICT THEORIES

Theory	Theorist(s)	Central Premise	Key Concepts	Principal Contributions
Instrumental Marxism	Richard Quinney	A unified ruling class affects the creation and application of law to pursue its own interests and to preserve an economic and social order that reflects those vested interests. The state serves as an instrument of the ruling class. People in the lower classes commit crime as a consequence of deprivation and criminalization at the hands of powerful economic interest groups. The status quo is reinforced by social institutions (education, religion, media). The lower classes are controlled through social programs (welfare) and coercion (police, courts, corrections).	Instrumental Marxism	Represents the initial articulation of Marxist theory as an explanation of crime, class relations, and the operation of criminal justice systems.
Structural Marxism		The structural approach differs from the instrumental in two ways: the ruling class is not cohesive and conspiratorial, and the state is more autonomous. The ruling class is split into competing class factions but shares similar values and beliefs. The state mediates between competitive elite groups to promote overall capital accumulation and social harmony in the face of the potential for unbridled pursuit of self-interest by elite groups, but only in the short term.	Bourgeoisie; proletariat; class factions	Explains the origin and application of laws that do not serve directly the best interests of the entire capitalist class.

CONFLICT THEORIES AND SOCIAL POLICY

Conflict theorists advocate responding to crime either by changing the way in which governments create and enforce criminal laws or by altering the economic and political structure of capitalist society. Theories in the liberal conflict tradition advocate a greater balance of power among factions with competing interests. Advocates of liberal conflict theory champion greater participation in political decision making for all social segments and greater equality in treatment under the law. One policy initiative is the decriminalization of many nonviolent street crimes that have no direct vic-

tims and that are disproportionately enforced against the underprivileged. In addition to calling for the legalization of some offences, liberal conflict theorists advocate the criminalization of certain harmful actions that are the exclusive domain of the rich and the powerful. They also promote more vigorous enforcement of existing laws prohibiting white-collar and corporate offences.

Liberal conflict theorists emphasize the importance of increasing access to lawmakers for the poor and the underprivileged while reducing the advantage of the affluent in this regard. Suggestions include creating and enforcing laws directed at controlling the lobbying of politicians and the making of political campaign donations. Other strategies aim at strengthening the capabilities of disadvantaged groups to resist the incursion into their lives of criminal justice agencies. Such undertakings include bolstering legal-aid programs, fostering inner-city community organizations, and strengthening the powers of independent boards that investigate and discipline police misconduct.

While liberal conflict theories advocate change from within the existing social and economic system, Marxist theories of deviance and crime assume that meaningful social change is impossible without a massive restructuring of society from capitalism to socialism. Marxists advocate dismantling the capitalist economy and restructuring society on a socialist model wherein there is meaningful equality in economic and political decision making. When the pro-capitalist state is dismantled and the power to criminalize is eliminated, crime will disappear or at least be substantially reduced.

Marxists believe that the disintegration of capitalism and the emergence of socialism is inevitable. First, they predict that a massive proletariat will develop in the cities of the capitalist world. Members of this dispossessed class will communicate with one another and see their common plight. In the face of growing crises of unemployment, poverty, and crime and with their consciousness raised, the lower classes will become ever more troublesome for the capitalist class and the state's law-enforcement agencies. To control the masses and keep the capitalist state operating, the government will implement more restrictive crime-control initiatives, which will be enormously costly and will bring about major violations of human justice. The situation will degenerate and increase in volatility until the masses eventually revolt and replace a capitalist economy and government with socialist institutions. The equality of human relations under socialism, according to Marxists, will eliminate the need to criminalize and in so doing will substantially reduce if not eradicate crime.

THE EVALUATION OF CONFLICT THEORIES

The early instrumental approaches drew much criticism from non-Marxists and Marxists alike. In response, Marxists developed the structural perspective, which continues to be refined. Several critiques of the more rudimentary instrumental position exist. First, instrumentalists' portrayal of the ruling class as a unified, monolithic elite is a gross oversimplification of reality: elites are divided and disagree about their economic and political interests. Moreover, instrumental Marxist claims of institutionalized elite conspiracies were both difficult to believe and unsubstantiated by data (Klockars, 1979). Evidence suggests that the state is not a simple instrument of the economic elite (Denisoff and MacQuarie, 1975). For example, the state has often contravened the position of the dominant class by passing legislation that undermines its economic interests in favour of the lower classes' interests. Laws governing minimum wage, worker health and safety, restriction of trade, and pollution control are examples.

Critics dispute instrumentalist claims that laws always serve only the interests of ruling elites. They cite laws prohibiting murder, sexual assault, robbery, and theft, while emphasizing the consensus surrounding the legal definition of these acts as crimes (Rossi, Waite, Bose, and Berk, 1974). Not only do such statutes reflect the best interests of all, but those most frequently victimized by these crimes are the underprivileged.

Some instrumental Marxists have asserted that violent and predatory criminal activity is a political response to oppression, marginalization, and exploitation. Critics say these claims are overly romantic caricatures; killers, robbers, and thieves are not Robin Hoods and freedom fighters (Toby, 1980). Less extreme Marxist positions still present street crime as at least partly a response to deprivation, but they make no claims regarding the political nature of this sort of rebellion.

On the social policy dimension, both liberal conflict and Marxist theories have been criticized for their lack of realism (Wilson, 1975). Liberals require the privileged to forsake their advantage in the name of increased tolerance and equality. Critics, particularly of the liberal position, point out that efforts to transfer more power to the disadvantaged have been largely cosmetic and that the powerful have strongly resisted the erosion of their already advantaged position.

Instrumental Marxists' claims that crime will disappear under socialism have been assailed on two grounds. First, crime not only existed in pre-capitalist societies, but it was a major problem. Second, crime thrives and presents a serious dilemma for socialist republics such as China and, until it was dismantled, the USSR. Marxists retort that truly socialist states are nonexistent in the world today; they point out that the state bureaucracies of contemporary communist nations alienate and exploit their citizens. Other Marxists respond to the criticism of utopian expectations under socialism by suggesting that crime, while not entirely eradicated, would be substantially reduced under a more egalitarian economic and political system. They admit that the claim that crime would disappear is extreme and suggest instead that the criminality of the poor would, under conditions approaching equality, more closely resemble the criminality of the more affluent in contemporary capitalist nations.

Structural Marxism explains how elites are neither unified nor necessarily conspiratorial, how the state is often autonomous and not a simple instrument of the ruling class, and how the law can and does undermine the vested interests of the powerful economic elite. It fails, however, to solve the classic criticism of Marxist social theory — that it is a vague and untestable *ex post facto* explanation.

Ex post facto means explanation after the fact. Instrumentalists first observe that a law exists and then set about showing how that legislation benefits the powerful. Their argument is that a law on the books must serve the interests of the powerful, or it would not have been passed in the first place. It is easy to make theories fit facts when the facts are already known. Such propositions are untestable, in the sense that they cannot be disproved scientifically (Jacobs, 1980).

Structuralists are as vague as their instrumental predecessors. After structuralists document the existence of a law, they show that the law either contravenes or supports the ruling elite. In the former case, structuralists argue that the law will undermine the position of the elite only in the short term. In the latter case, they contend that the law protects the powerful in the long term. *Ex post facto* explanations have no tests to establish whether they are right or wrong.

One of the difficulties of evaluating Marxist theories of deviance and crime is the different notion of theory in Marxist thought. Marxists emphasize that the purpose of theory is to raise consciousness. Consciousness-raising entails making the world aware of inequality, of its unfairness, and of the harm it engenders. Theory raises consciousness, and consciousness-raising in turn encourages action to remedy social inequality and the pains it produces. Marxist theory is less concerned with scientifically testing the adequacy of its propositions than with

praxis — action to change the world. Critics from the more conventional perspectives, of course, maintain that theories that cannot be tested are more ideological than explanatory.

Unlike the theories discussed in previous chapters, conflict perspectives on deviance and crime are relatively new, dating mostly from the late 1960s. Since their rejuvenation, they have contributed substantially to sociological insights into inequality and the uses and misuses of legal power. Conflict frameworks focus attention on the origins of laws and the degree to which criminal statutes apply equally to all social segments. They have focused attention on the malfeasance of justice systems around the world and have fuelled initiatives to reform aspects of policing, the courts, and corrections. In a similar vein, the insufficiencies of law governing certain socially and economically harmful activities have also been seriously questioned. Moreover, conflict criminology has generated intense interest in research on the illegal conduct of business and political elites (Akers, 1985).

The conflict tradition has focused attention on ideology's previously ignored role in shaping both societal consensus and the social reality of crime. Conflict-oriented theorists have admonished positivistic criminologists for seeking both the causes and remedies of crime in the wrong places. According to Marxists, criminologists who cite strain, differential associations, or broken social bonds as precipitators of deviance and crime support the status quo. By ignoring issues of power and oppression, their analyses deflect attention from the wrongdoing of elites and thus reinforce their positions of advantage.

Liberal conflict and Marxist theories of deviance and crime and their critics' responses have enlivened sociological debates linking power, law, and social control. These approaches have given birth to new forms of critical thinking and have encouraged sociologists and criminologists to reflect on their role vis-à-vis the criminal justice industry.

SUMMARY

Liberal and Marxist conflict theories differ about the number of competing groups in society and the importance of economic resources as the basis of power. Liberal conflict theorists view society as being composed of a variety of groups vying to maximize their own interests. Moreover, they see power bases as potentially involving more than economic advantage.

Sellin emphasizes conflict among groups having different cultures. Vold focuses on the role of the state and the political enactment of law in power disputes involving labour, ethnic, and civil rights groups. Turk builds upon Dahrendorf's "institutional authority" as the basis of power. Turk sees society as comprising two competing groups: authorities and subjects. According to Turk, their coming into conflict depends on the congruence of their values and behaviours, the degree to which subjects are socially organized, and the subjects' level of sophistication in responding to authorities. Turk further specifies three circumstances wherein authorities are likely to actively enforce legal norms. Enforcement is most likely where norms are salient, where the discrepancy in power between authorities and subjects is large, and where the degree of realism demonstrated in the potential conflict is low.

Quinney's initial conflict theory of crime can be placed in the liberal conflict tradition, while his later theorizing is more Marxist. He understands crime as a definition of human behaviour that authorities create in a political framework. Crime is socially constructed to benefit the powerful. Quinney observes that public images of crime are created through interpersonal and media communications that direct attention toward street crime. The socially and economically harmful activities orchestrated in the executive suites of the powerful are ignored.

While Marx had little to say about crime, contemporary conflict criminologists have adapted many of his themes. Marx notes the development of private productive property, or what he calls the material means of production, following the Industrial Revolution. Around the development of productive property there arose a two-class system. One small class, the bourgeoisie, owns or controls the means of producing material goods, while another, much larger class of workers, the proletariat, sells its labour for wages. Marx points out that these groups' vested self-interests — profits and earning a decent living — conflict. As conditions worsened for the less powerful proletariat, Marx foresaw revolution and the replacement of capitalism with socialism and a classless society.

For Marx, the driving force of society was its infrastructure — the economy. Society's superstructure comprised the political, legal, religious, educational, and media systems controlled by capitalists. The superstructure's purpose is to promote pro-capitalist ideology. Marx suggested that when the institutions promoting ideology failed to communicate the pro-capitalist message effectively, capitalists would use coercion to preserve their dominance. In such cases, the law and agents of social control such as the police and the military would maintain order. Contemporary Marxist criminologists have echoed the Marxian themes of deprived social and economic conditions and the exercise of coercion.

Greenberg's theory shows how the conditions experienced by youth in modern capitalist societies produce strain and cause acquisitive crime. Friedrichs argues that social and economic conditions have undermined people's faith in social institutions and have stimulated deviance and crime. The nonconformity and violation of the law produced by this crisis of legitimacy are answered by the state's coercive responses. But coercion only escalates over time, as the need to maintain order and control becomes more critical.

Other Marxist approaches directly address the creation and application of laws. Primary among these perspectives are instrumental and structural Marxism. Instrumentalists present the ruling class as a unified and monolithic social group. The law and the state are instruments designed to preserve or expand its economic and social interests. The ruling elite is a conspiratorial group actively plotting its own advantage at the expense of other social classes. Structural Marxism builds upon its predecessor to take account of evidence indicating that the elite class is fractionalized, that the state enjoys a significant degree of autonomy from the economic elite, and that laws do not always directly serve elite interests.

Policy recommendations springing out of liberal conflict perspectives call for balancing the power between the privileged and the underprivileged by providing the latter groups with better political and economic access to the mechanisms of creation and administration of the law. Liberal theorists advocate change from within the existing system. Conversely, Marxist theorists see the dismantling of capitalism as an essential step in eliminating social and economic inequality and the crime and criminalization stemming from that inequity.

Conflict theory, particularly the instrumental version of Marxism, has received a barrage of criticism. Among the more important critiques are those concerning the degree of unity among powerful elites, the degree of conspiratorial action, and the extent to which the law always and only serves the interests of the privileged. Other criticisms include the romanticization of crime and criminals, the lack of realism in social policy, and the dubiousness of the claim that socialism would eliminate crime. While the structural perspective has remedied some of these concerns, it continues the Marxist failing of *ex post facto* theorizing, or explanation after the fact. Part of this deficiency, however, stems from the different purposes of theory envisaged by Marxists on the one hand and by their more positivistic critics on the other. For Marxists, the goals of theory are consciousness-raising and praxis. Unlike positivists, they are less concerned with explaining and predicting events on the basis of theories emphasizing cause and effect.

Liberal and Marxist conflict theorists have since the 1960s contributed immensely to the understanding of deviance and crime. Their work has greatly sharpened the social scientific and criminological community's focus on such important areas as social and economic inequality, the use and abuse of power, the workings and shortcomings of the criminal justice system, and elite deviance.

DISCUSSION QUESTIONS

1. Discuss the similarities of and differences between Sellin's culture conflict theory and Vold's group conflict theory.

2. Explain how Turk's authority–subject conflict perspective and Quinney's social reality of crime approach differ. Do these two theories share any common ground?

3. Demonstrate how structural Marxism addresses some of the criticisms levelled at the earlier instrumental perspective.

4. How do the policy recommendations of liberal conflict and Marxist theories differ? What type of recommendation has the best chance of implementation?

5. What are the contributions of the conflict approaches to the understanding of deviance and crime in modern capitalist societies?

WEB LINKS

Ralf Dahrendorf's Views on Class and Conflict
http://raven.jmu.edu/~ridenelr/courses/DAHREND1.html
    An excerpt from Ralf Dahrendorf's *Class and Class Conflict in Industrial Society*.

Marx and Engels's Writings
http://eserver.org/marx/
    This site offers searchable, full-text versions of many writings by Marx and Engels, including *The Communist Manifesto*.

Marxists Internet Archive
http://www.marxists.org/
    This extensive archive, presented in over twenty languages, offers information on Marxist ideas, Marxist writers, Marxist history, and more. For an introduction to Marxism, click on "Subject Archive" and scroll down to the Student's Section.

A Marxian Theory of Crime
http://www.tryoung.com/archives/116marxtheorycrime.html
    In this paper, T.R. Young outlines a Marxian approach to crime and offers a critique of American criminological theory.

Conflict Theory(ies)
http://www.umsl.edu/~rkeel/200/conflict.html
    Notes on the main ideas of several strands of conflict theory.

RECOMMENDED READINGS

Hinch, R. (1994). *Readings in Critical Criminology*. Scarborough: Prentice-Hall.
  Canadian criminologist Ron Hinch's collection of readings in the field of critical criminology provides an excellent introduction to critical perspectives and their application to an increased understanding of the crime problem in contemporary societies such as Canada and the United States.

McMullin, J. (1992). *Beyond the Law: Corporate Crime and Law and Order*. Halifax: Fernwood.
  Assesses the current state of corporate crime research and provides suggestions as to how this form of illegality might be more effectively addressed in a liberal democracy.

Okihiro, N.R. (1999). *Mounties, Moose, and Moonshine: Patterns and Context of Outport Crime*. Toronto: University of Toronto Press.
  Examines the social implications of the manner in which an increasingly bureaucratized state uses police to wage war on a rural population by criminalizing behaviour that local custom does not regard as crime.

O'Reilly-Fleming, T. (1996). *Post-Critical Criminology*. Toronto: Prentice Hall.
  Collection of largely Canadian readings focusing on the social construction of delinquency and street crime from the vantage points of rights, gender, race, and new critical theories such as left realism.

Taylor, I., P. Walton, and J. Young. (1973). *The New Criminology: For a Social Theory of Deviance*. London: Routledge and Kegan Paul.
  Presents the classic formulation of the critical criminological perspective in its modern form.

CHAPTER 8

NEW DIRECTIONS IN THEORIZING ABOUT DEVIANCE AND CRIME

The aims of this chapter are to familiarize the reader with:

- the meaning of routine activities and the central components of routine activities analysis: motivated offenders, suitable targets, and absence of guardianship
- the organization of routine activities in time and space: periodicity, tempo, and timing
- the left-realist critique of left idealism
- the aims and objectives of the left realist approach
- the fundamentals of feminist theory, especially its analysis of patriarchy
- the similarities and differences among three types of feminist theory: liberal feminism, Marxist feminism, radical feminism
- the contributions of feminist thought to understanding deviance, crime, and social control
- the basic constructs and propositions of power–control theory, especially those of patriarchy, family class structure, and reproduction of gender relations
- the foundations of self-control theory as a general theory of crime
- the central ideas of peacemaking criminology
- the basic arguments of reintegrative shaming
- the emergence of postmodernism as a criminological critique

INTRODUCTION

The previous chapters reviewed the modern sociological theories of deviance and crime and examined their antecedents. The Chicago school and structural functionalism were most influential before 1960. Toward the end of the 1960s, social control theory rose to prominence. During the 1970s, labelling theory became popular and conflict theory firmly took root.

Social theorizing is not a static undertaking. Throughout the 1980s, sociologists and criminologists have continued their efforts to generate logical and empirically supportable explanatory frameworks for improving the understanding of deviance, crime, and social control. Some contemporary approaches blend established theories to form new analytical frameworks, while others represent complete breaks with tradition.

This chapter examines seven comparatively new approaches to the study of deviance and crime. The discussion of routine activities analysis and left realism is followed by an examination of feminist contributions to social theory generally and to sociological theories of deviance and crime in particular. Also included are assessments of power–control and self-control theories as well as of peacemaking criminology and reintegrative shaming.

ROUTINE ACTIVITIES THEORY

The routine activities approach developed by Cohen and Felson (1979) and the **lifestyle–exposure perspective** advanced by Hindelang et al. (1978) explain crime by charting the way in which everyday living creates a structure of opportunity that brings people into direct contact with predatory criminals. In this fashion, **routine activities theory** provides a detailed explanation of a particular type of victimization, one in which a predator definitely and intentionally takes or damages the person or property of another. The intellectual foundations of the lifestyle–exposure approach rest in the pioneering work of the ecological sociologists of the Chicago school.

Cohen and Felson (1979) link fluctuations in crime rates to changes in people's routine activities that create the convergence in space and time of three elements: a **motivated offender**, a suitable target, and the absence of guardianship against predation. (See Figure 8.1.) The convergence or separation in time and space of these three factors, Cohen and Felson maintain, explains increases and decreases in crime rates in the absence of alterations in society's economic and social structure. Structural conditions such as economic recession, racial heterogeneity, rising unemployment, and heightening rates of family dissolution are less relevant as direct explanations of intentional predatory crime than are alterations in space and time of patterns of behaviour that bring together offenders and targets in the absence of

FIGURE 8.1

ROUTINE ACTIVITIES ANALYSIS

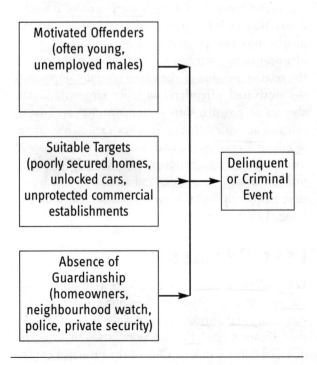

guardianship. Indeed, Cohen and Felson maintain that a target without protection is the key element that produces victimization.

Before examining the central propositions of the theory itself, three important facets of the time dimension should be considered. The first, periodicity, refers to regular cycles of behaviour such as going to work from Monday to Friday, visiting the bars on Friday and Saturday nights, and walking the dog after dinner. The second element, tempo, concerns the number of events in a particular period. The number of visits to bars on Friday night, the number of times church is attended on Sunday mornings, and the number of vacations taken away from home during the winter school break are examples. The final consideration is timing, the co-ordination among different but interdependent activities that comprise the rhythm of life for potential offenders and prospective victims. The meeting in time of victim and offender may well leave the victim feeling that he or she was in the wrong place at the wrong time. The successful offender would respond more positively.

With respect to motivation, routine activities analysis does not try to explain why certain individuals or groups are criminally inclined. The theory treats the motivation of offenders largely as a given. It is the "spatio-temporal" organization of social activities that translates criminal proclivity into action.

Targets suitability varies on a number of important dimensions. First, some targets are more valuable than others, either monetarily or symbolically. To a car thief, a Corvette may be worth more than a Toyota Tercel. Second, some targets are more visible and accessible than others. A case of beer on the passenger seat of an unattended vehicle is more vulnerable than a case hidden in the trunk. Finally, targets vary in terms of their "inertia." By target inertia, Cohen and Felson refer to such considerations as the size and weight of the object to be stolen and to the strength and combat skill of the person to be accosted. In the former case, the large and the heavy are usually less vulnerable than the small and the light. In the latter case, young males may be less at risk than elderly females.

Guardianship refers to the degree to which targets are protected. In routine-activities terms, vulnerability is a function of social organization and technology. The organization of groups and the technology available affect not only access to targets and the ways and means of attack, but also resistance to assailment. In general terms, women's participation in the labour force is a broad change in social organization that has varied over time and across regions. In places and times where most women work at home providing care to young children, burglary rates might be lower than they would be in places and times where most women work outside the home and where children are nonexistent, in day care, or fully grown. Larger numbers of people at home for extended periods of time each day dampens the enthusiasm of all but the most intrepid or stupidest of burglars. Furthermore, the impacts upon target accessibility and target guardianship have changed dramatically over the past 50 years as a result of new technologies. Armoured trucks, automatic weaponry, telephones, closed-circuit televisions, credit cards, time-locked safes, automatic teller machines, and exploding dye bombs have had a considerable impact on both the execution and control of robbery.

Routine activities analysis relates deviant and illegal conduct to other legitimate social behaviours in which people normally engage. Patterns of everyday legitimate activities determine the location, type, and frequency of illegality in a given community or society. Some locations and types of behaviour entail greater risks of victimization than do others (Messner and Blau, 1987). Work and leisure are two spheres of activity that figure prominently in the production of intentional crime because they largely determine the amount of time that people spend in their dwellings. In considering the risk of victimization in relation to recreation, for example, one's lifestyle governs where one is during the day and in the evening, whether one is in the company of friends or strangers, whether or not those in one's immediate environment are the same or different in terms of demographic characteristics, and whether the locations of activity are characterized by the presence or the absence of criminogenic conditions such as alcohol consumption, the availability of weapons, architectural blind spots, and poor lighting.

Routine activities theory posits that social structural variables affect criminal opportunity, which in turn affects the rates of certain types of crime. Structural variables worthy of consideration vis-à-vis their impact on lifestyle include a community's ratio of males to females, its age distribution, its family organization, its affluence, and the nature of its marketplace. Cohen and Felson note that changes in these variables have altered lifestyles from what they were

before World War II. Canadian society in the 1970s, for example, was younger and more affluent than it was in 1935. Changes in the economy and in the labour force reduced the number of women spending their days toiling within the home. Compared with the situation in 1935, the market during the 1970s involved a vastly larger number of valuable, small, and light goods. This trend continues, and Cohen and Felson suggest that increases in rates of theft, shoplifting, burglary, and robbery should not be surprising.

Cohen and Felson argue that motivated offenders in contact with suitable targets without adequate guardianship affect the likelihood of illegal conduct in more than an additive fashion; the effects are multiplicative. Therefore, their convergence results in sharp increases in crime that are relatively immune to control through doctrines and policy initiatives aimed at deterrence. Rather than try to increase the effectiveness of police and court crime-control tactics, routine activities and lifestyle–exposure theorists reason that modest alterations in lifestyle are likely to meet with greater success. Since high material standards of living create opportunities for crime, policy directives based on routine activities analysis stress the importance of controlling victimization through increased guardianship or "target hardening" — steps must be taken to make targets either less suitable or less accessible.

Routine activities theory has received a good deal of support empirically. It has, however, been criticized on several grounds. First, its treatment of offender motivation as both given and constant offers little insight into what propels some but not others, under identical circumstances, to commit crimes. Second, the relative weights of the three central components — motivated offenders, suitable targets, and the absence of guardianship — remain unclear. Finally, routine activities theory ignores expressive crime. While it provides a good account of intentional instrumental illegal conduct, it provides little insight into crimes such as murder and assault, in which passion frequently plays a role (Meithe, Stafford, and Long, 1987).

LEFT REALISM

Left realism is a recent reaction to "traditional" radical theory, which itself was a response to the conservatism of the traditional positivist theories set forth by the Chicago school, the functionalists, and advocates of social control theory. One of the principal contributions of the radical approach was to highlight the roles played in the social construction of crime by economic and political elites. During the 1970s, radical conflict theories focused the attention of the criminological community on a number of inequities associated with deviance, crime, and social control. The creation and application of criminal law, police misconduct and abuse of power, biases inherent in the court's processing of accused persons, high rates of incarceration, and the deplorable living conditions in contemporary prisons came under intense scrutiny. While these contributions were important, radical theorists, particularly instrumentalists, tended to portray the street criminal as a person "more sinned against than sinning." Those accused and convicted of *Criminal Code* offences were romanticized as Robin Hood–like victims of oppression, fighting back however crudely against the authors of their subordination. In the process, it was implied that these socially and economically deprived bandits were merely "redistributing" wealth and exacting a measure of revenge.

During the 1980s, some who identified themselves as radicals became more critical of their own position. This spirit of reflection was spurred largely by feminist work undertaken during the 1970s. Much feminist writing on crime and legal issues during that period focused first on rape and then on violence against women and children generally. Feminist portrayals of male violence, its harm, and its propensity for demoralization shattered the romantic portrait of the aggressive predatory offender and, in so doing, fuelled a rethinking of the "criminal as victim" position (Matthews and Young, 1986).

Adherents of this emerging school of radical thought identify the existing radical approach as "left idealism" and define their new, more refined perspective as "left realism." Left realists argue that their approach is a response to a crisis now occurring in both the conservative mainstream and the radical camps of criminology (Young, 1986). The crisis among conservatives, according to left realists, is that positivism's scientific search for the causes of crime and for the sources of its control has been an abject failure. Having largely abandoned this mission, conservatives have replaced the search for causality with another form of criminological endeavour altogether. The new conservative regimen is an "administrative criminology" based on neoclassical thinking. According to left realists, administrative

criminology emphasizes more punitive correctional measures supported by recent innovations in coercive technologies.

The crisis in left idealism is equally severe; left idealism has overlooked the fact that street crime is a serious social problem, especially for victims, most of whom are from the lower class. The left realist critique of idealism begins by summarizing the radical position that has prevailed to date. First, left idealists view crime among the working class as a function of their poverty. They see the common criminal as possessing the ability to "see through" the inequities in society. The illegal conduct of these insightful rebels is an unsophisticated attempt to balance the ledger. According to the idealist position, to blame the offender who is both poor and oppressed is tantamount to blaming the victim.

Second, left idealists argue that the "real crime" in society stems from the actions of the political and economic ruling classes and from their power over lawmaking, policing, and the dispensation of justice. Idealists compare the high impact of corporate and state wrongdoing with the comparatively low impact of most street crime, which tends to be petty theft and minor violence. The causes of elite deviance, idealists maintain, rests in the single-minded pursuit of profit and power.

Third, left idealists portray criminal law as an expression of ruling-class efforts to protect private and productive property. The police role is essentially political, with constabularies acting more to maintain order in the capitalist interest than to control crime. The media create false impressions of crime by portraying threat and harm as products of lower-class inclinations and behaviours; the role of elites in creating social problems is ignored. These media myths deaden the masses' sense of their plight and inhibit popular support for radical reform (Young, 1986).

Having outlined what they see as the idealist position, left realists criticize it on several grounds. First, left idealism is simplistic; there is more to crime than moral panics and social reaction (DeKeseredy and Schwartz, 1991). Second, idealist portrayals of deviants and criminals as "seeing through" the inequalities that surround them are misguided; the image of the actor is overly rational and that of the offender is unduly romantic. Also, the idealist perspective ignores the fact that many deviant groups are highly disorganized. Third, left idealism overlooks the fact that working-class offenders victimize working-class people more than they victimize capitalists and state officials. Fourth, idealism ignores the question of why people become criminals and focuses exclusively on the ways in which the powerful criminalize the powerless. Structural determinants of crime are ignored or treated as self-evident.

The final criticism levelled at left idealism is that it closely resembles functionalism in its approach. Idealist formulations maintain that the actions of corporate enterprises and state agencies must be linked to the needs of the ruling capitalist class. The function of criminalization is to deflect society's attention from the social problems generated by capitalist enterprise, such as unemployment, inadequate social services, and corporate wrongdoing. The function of social welfare is to placate the masses and to diffuse serious social unrest and open revolt. From the idealist perspective, rising crime rates do not reflect changes in the behaviour of criminals but result from police efforts to maintain order in the capitalist crisis that regularly manifests itself in economic depression and unemployment (Young, 1986).

Left realists argue that their radical position on the crime problem is more realistic than the one put forth by the left idealists. Left realism takes account of data from victimization studies conducted over the past 25 years. This body of research demonstrates that street crime is a serious problem and that it affects society's disadvantaged more so than its privileged. In charting the reality of crime, left realists advocate steering a middle course. Criminals are neither romantic nor pathological. Moreover, left realists would neither minimize nor exaggerate the volume of crime.

Left realists outline several fronts upon which they wish to proceed. First, they would explode the myths about crime and its control that have been created and reinforced by the media. The inaccurate perception of crime risk and victimization as products of exchanges with strangers must also be corrected. Data from victimization studies and from other sources demonstrate that the perpetration and experience of crime are intra-class, intra-race, and intra-familial affairs. Similarly, police work is wrongly presented as glamorous, scientific, and successful. Nothing could be further from the truth; it is routine, straightforward, and boring. When police solve crimes, they do so by accident or because the answers are obvious. Most important, the police are highly dependent on the public to report crime and to co-operate in apprehending and convicting offenders.

Second, left realists advocate the use of a blend of micro and macro thinking about crime and its impact. They desire a theory that elaborates the micro–macro connections among victims, offenders, communities, and the state. Left realists also advocate the combination of qualitative and quantitative research to develop theory and policy. Of special use, they argue, are "local crime surveys" that focus on the neighbourhood or community (DeKeseredy and Schwartz, 1991). Crime-control policies should also be realistic; thus, realist initiatives would not be long-term, revolutionary, and virtually impossible to implement as were the measures of left idealists. Rather, they would be short-term, practical, and achievable (Young, 1986).

Among the strategies for crime control advocated by the left realists are demarginalization, pre-emptive deterrence, the minimization of imprisonment, the democratizing of policing, and the involvement of the community in crime prevention (DeKeseredy, 1988). Demarginalization tactics involve alternatives to incarceration that promote the integration of offenders into the community rather than their separation from it. Suggested courses of action include community service orders and restitution programs. Pre-emptive deterrence involves altering physical environments to make them less crime-prone. This approach also encompasses changing people's day-to-day practices to reduce their vulnerability. Arguing that jails create as much or more criminality than they eradicate, left realists favour restricting imprisonment to serious offenders only. They also advocate making the prison experience more humane. Democratizing the police would transform the constabulary from a force apart from the community to a service within the community. It would also increase police accountability and promote the tolerance of disadvantaged groups (Lea and Young, 1985).

Third, the left realist approach emphasizes the importance first of assessing the risk of street crime and then of deciphering in precise terms its impact on people in certain areas and social groups. Finally, left realists stress the importance of identifying the relationships that connect victims to offenders. They observe that powerless working-class people are not only preyed on by offenders from the same backgrounds but also that these people are disproportionately victimized by the affluent and the powerful. Especially vulnerable are women, the lower class, and visible ethnic minorities.

Although a relatively new approach, left realism is not without its critics. Left realists attack the most extreme position of the left idealists. Much of their criticism appears directed at the early instrumental rather than more recent structural perspectives. In this regard, the realist critique of the radical position closely resembles the barrage fired at instrumental Marxism by traditional positivists in the late 1970s and early 1980s. Some argue that the realist fusillade is directed at an idealist target that has moved on and taken new shape.

The realist criticism of traditional criminology is also somewhat directed at a "straw person." Realists note the rise of administrative criminology out of neoclassical ashes and decry its emphasis on deterrence and its draconian policy suggestions. However, they ignore the fact that other "traditional" criminologies are searching for a better understanding of the causes of deviance and crime. A good deal of causation research continues to be guided by human ecology, strain theory, differential association, and informal social control perspectives as well as by relatively new approaches such as routine activities analysis and power–control theory.

Left realists argue that their perspective provides new focuses. Among other things, they call for the debunking of myths about crime and policing, the integration of theory and method across the macro–micro spectrum, the use of both qualitative and quantitative data, and the choice of pragmatic but humane control initiatives. But many of those who are labelled traditional criminologists by the realists claim that they have been pursuing these objectives for years and making significant strides.

Left realism advocates concentration on the importance of street crime as a social problem. One of the major contributions of radical criminology, however, has been to focus attention on elite deviance.

Finally, critics question whether left realism is as yet actually a theory of crime. Rather than an explanation of illegal conduct, left realism is more a set of philosophical and political statements concerning how society and the criminal justice system ought to function (Akers, 1997).

Left realism is in its formative stages. It is not without promise; if it is able to trace strands of macro-level theories of the state through meso-level community crime and control issues to the micro-level of individuals, left realism will make a significant mark on criminological theory.

FEMINIST THEORY

Noting that women and girls form more than half the population, feminists argue that *all* social experiences are transformed into women's concerns and potentially into women's issues. Moreover, they point out that almost without exception, the social experiences of males dominate in explanations of gender differences. Male perspectives are used to explain gender differences in attitudes, beliefs, and behaviours. Feminists rebuke both sociology and criminology for their blindness to gender concerns, observing that women and their experiences of the world have been almost entirely ignored in the theoretical formulations of social science. In the relatively rare instances where attention has been paid to women in society, females have been superficially "plugged in" to masculine-oriented explanatory frameworks (Chesney-Lind, 1986).

Sociological theories of deviance and crime are "androcentric" — they are heavily governed by male experiences and understandings. Androcentric social theory treats women, where they are included at all, as being the same as men. Feminists maintain that the picture of deviant and criminal women as perpetrators, as victims, as persons accused before the law, and as individuals convicted by the criminal justice system is much more complex than mainstream, or "malestream," social science suggests. With respect to theories of deviance and crime, feminist criminologists note that while the relationships between deviance and crime on the one hand and class, race, and age on the other have received considerable theoretical attention, gender has not. In addition, feminism strongly questions whether general social theory can explain nonconformity and wrongdoing equally well for both males and females (Daly and Chesney-Lind, 1988).

At the foundation of feminist thinking is the notion that gender inequality is the defining feature of society. Women suffer discrimination because of their sex, and as a result, their needs in comparison with those of men are negated and left unsatisfied. The remedy for this inequity involves radical change. In elaborating these basic premises, Daly and Chesney-Lind (1988) summarize five elements of feminist thinking that distinguish it from other forms of social and political thought.

1. Gender is not a natural fact but a complex social, historical, and cultural product; it is related to, but

not simply derived from, biological sex difference and reproductive capacities.

2. Gender and gender relations order social life and social institutions in fundamental ways.

3. Gender relations and constructs of masculinity and femininity are not symmetrical but are based on an organizing principle of men's superiority and social and political–economic dominance over women.

4. Systems of knowledge reflect men's views of the natural and social world; the production of knowledge is gendered.

5. Women should be at the centre of intellectual inquiry, not peripheral, invisible, or appendages to men. (504)

Feminist social theory originated as a response to explanations of sex differences that originated in biology, psychobiology, and conservative sociology. Biological and psychobiological traditions combining anatomy, genetics, and hormonal make-up have presented differences in skill, aptitude, attitude, and temperament between males and females as having "natural" bases. Feminist and nonfeminist scholars alike have widely criticized physiological approaches, pointing out that they do not take account of heavily documented cross-cultural variations in sex differences. More importantly, as feminist theorists emphasize, biological and psychobiological theories cannot explain the unequal social and economic values attached to the traits and roles of men and women in contemporary society (Saunders, 1988).

In the realm of sociology, feminism is a distinct reaction to the conservatism of structural functionalism. Functionalists explain the origins and persistence of sex differences in terms of their contributions to social order and stability. Functional theorists begin their analysis by observing that the division of labour within the modern nuclear family occurs along the lines of sex. This gender-based division ensures role complementarity and interdependence and, in the larger picture, social solidarity. Functionalists argue that men perform instrumental functions outside the family in the workplace, a competitive and public sphere. Husbands work for wages that are then used to support their wives and children. Wives perform domestic chores and orchestrate family activities within the home, a co-operative and private sphere. The family roles performed by women are more expressive than instrumental; they provide emotional,

moral, and domestic support to their husbands and children. From the functional perspective, much of women's effort diffuses the tensions experienced by their children and by their husbands in the public spheres of school and work. According to the functionalist perspective, the family can hold together as an integrative social institution only if the roles performed by men and women do not conflict. Functionalists make no overt claims about the primacy of men's or women's roles; by remaining silent, they portray sex-role differentiation in egalitarian terms (Saunders, 1988).

Feminists disagree with functionalists on many points. They begin by pointing out that the roles of women and men in the private and public spheres are by no means equal. Women suffer discrimination and are systematically excluded from social statuses that are accorded the lion's share of income, prestige, and power in contemporary society. Feminists point out that discrimination against women, like other forms of discrimination, is enveloped in an ideology that justifies unequal treatment. In this case, the ideology suggests that women are incapable of performing certain types of tasks, making decisions and accepting responsibility in the public sphere, and exercising political and economic power (Saunders, 1988).

The key concept in various feminist analyses of gender inequality and gender stratification is **patriarchy** — a hierarchical system in which men in society enjoy more social and economic privilege and more autonomy than do women. The basic premise of this system is male superiority. Various agents of socialization, including the family, the school, organized religion, and the media, transmit and reinforce images that promote different temperaments, aspirations, self-images, and behaviours in males and in females. The ideology of male competence and superiority is a rationale through which men exercise institutional control and exclude women from competing for money, privilege, and power.

Feminism is not a unitary framework; rather, it is a set of perspectives that provides various explanations both for the oppression of women and for its amelioration. The three basic **feminist theories** are **liberal feminism**, socialist or **Marxist feminism**, and **radical feminism**.

Liberal feminism conceives of society as filled with barriers that block women's full participation in public spheres such as education, employment, and politics. Liberal feminists favour changing the system from within by redistributing opportunities as a means of restructuring gender power. They argue that society ought to be transformed into a real meritocracy, in which women's abilities receive full recognition. Merit should form the basis of reward, and women should be given the opportunity to compete on an equal footing with men. Liberal feminists call for initiatives that would change the prevailing sexist ideology by altering the process and content of socialization in the family, in the education system, and in the media. They also advocate legislative changes that would expand opportunities for women and outlaw gender discrimination.

Marxist feminists elevate social class over gender in their understanding of social and economic domination. For them, the control and exploitation of women reflects the larger issue of class oppression and represents the synthesis of class structure and patriarchy. Prominent in this formulation is the argument that women are exploited in two fundamental but related ways. First, husbands who are themselves exploited by capitalists dominate their wives and exploit both their domestic labour and their sexuality. Second, capitalists exploit women directly by using them as a reserve labour army. Women's work power can be used when necessary, often at wages lower than those paid to men, and easily dispensed with during economic contractions.

Marxist feminists draw upon the work of Friedrich Engels, a colleague and collaborator of Marx, to explain the subordination of women in capitalist society. Engels locates the origin of patriarchy in the privatization of property, noting that the development of private property required men to identify their heirs with certainty. This necessity required monogamous sexual relationships. With monogamy, women became increasingly encapsulated in the private sphere of the family. In time, husbands controlled all family property. Not having access to the productive income-generating public sphere of work or any control over property, women became increasingly subordinated to men. In time, subjugated women and children became the property of men. Through this process, the relations of production (work) and of reproduction (childbearing) were profoundly structured by capitalist patriarchy.

Marxist feminist strategies for social change are revolutionary. Only through revolt can capitalism be transformed into a truly democratic socialism free of class and gender stratification. Only through revolutionary means can women be full partners in economic production. Similarly, only through dramatic restructuring can marriage and sexual relations based on notions of private property be abolished and working-class economic subordination eradicated.

Radical feminism differs fundamentally from Marxist feminism in two ways. First, radical feminism sees the basis of gender inequality in the inherent aggression of men toward women and in the inherent needs and desires of men to control women's sexuality and reproductive potential. Women's smaller size and their dependency during childbearing years make them vulnerable to domination and control. Second, radicals maintain that patriarchy predates the rise of private property within capitalism.

According to the radical feminist framework, hierarchical power relations produce a "power psychology" that underlies female subordination. Society socializes both males and females to consider boys and men as superior to girls and women and teaches that males have the right to control females. The power differentials inherent in gender relations are accentuated by male-defined notions of heterosexual sexuality.

Strategies for eliminating the oppression of women hinge on dramatically increasing female autonomy. Modest initiatives for overthrowing patriarchy involve the creation of "women-only" organizations and institutions, while radical measures call for lesbian separatism and for reproductive technologies that would promote women's sexual autonomy (Saunders, 1988; Simpson, 1989).

While feminist scholarship has become firmly established in sociological theory over the past two decades, the same cannot be said for feminist work in the sociology of deviance and in criminology. While feminists have made gains in critiquing existing theories for their inattention to women, feminist explanations of deviance and crime are in the formative stage. The role of female subordination in both creating and responding to female crime has not been developed. Similarly, sociologists are only beginning to examine the impact of existing gender relations on the nonconformity and illegal behaviour of males.

Feminists take several approaches to the study of deviance and crime. They begin by demarcating the central issues and questions that require examination and explanation. Two of the most important theoretical issues about female offending concern generalizability and gender ratio (Daly and Chesney-Lind, 1988). With respect to generalizability, sociologists continue to explore the degree to which existing non-feminist approaches such as strain, social control, differential association, and symbolic interactionism explain deviance and crime equally well for both sexes. The results of these efforts are mixed; some findings indicate similarity in the causal structure of male and female offending, while others explain deviant and illegal conduct much better for males than for females (Harris, 1977; Gomme, 1985a).

In critiquing the "add women" approach to resolving the generalizability issue, feminists make two arguments. First, they point out that using the same old theories "with women added" does not really represent a gender-neutral perspective. After all, the architects of these theories constructed them from "male-stream" conceptualizations of the social world. Second, many of these time-worn theoretical frameworks also fail to provide convincing explanations of male deviance and crime. If they cannot provide good explanations of male offending, their applicability to female offending is questionable (Daly and Chesney-Lind, 1988).

The gender-ratio issue concerns the dramatic gap that separates the frequency and type of male and female offending. In comparison with males, females are infrequent rule violators and rare participants in personal and violent crimes. Feminists question whether male and female offending can have the same causes in light of dramatic gender differences in the incidence and form of male and female deviance. Not surprisingly, they advocate the creation of innovative explanations that take as their starting points three important factors: the power differentials inherent in male–female relationships, the nature and extent of informal and official responses, and the control and commodification of female sexuality (Daly and Chesney-Lind, 1988).

Another issue, and one that has received considerable attention, is the sexism and misogyny that prevailed in social science theory and criminal justice practice before the 1970s. Until then, social scientists either ignored women or explained women's deviance, crime, and criminal justice experiences in stereotypical terms. Feminists have oriented their examination of both individualistic and institutional sexism around three concerns: females as victims, females as offenders, and females caught up in criminal justice processing as defendants, witnesses, victims, or prisoners (Simpson, 1989).

It is in the area of victimization that feminist scholarship has made the greatest contribution. For example, feminists have argued that violence, especially violence directed at women and children, cannot be adequately characterized as the random emotional outbursts of a relatively small number of men. Rather, violence is a form of social domination through which men control "their" women and "their" offspring. This insight has radically transformed the sociology of deviance and crime. Rape is now viewed not as an act of sex but as an act of power and violence. Considerable attention is now being directed toward understanding and controlling pornography, battering, incest, and sexual harassment. Not only are these activities widely considered harmful, but they almost exclusively involve the victimization of females.

As a consequence of feminist scholarship, what were formerly "hidden" crimes and "family secrets" are now in the public domain. Three reasons account for the success of feminism in making victims the top priority. First, these forms of victimization are serious and widespread. Second, the violent victimization of girls and women at the hands of men is an experience cogently accounted for by patriarchal theories. Third, the campaign for remedial action was enthusiastically embraced not only by feminists but also by nonfeminists. It was clear to all that something had to be done quickly to improve the protection of women and children.

Although they do so much less frequently than males, females do engage in deviance and crime. Not only were biology and psychology predominant in early explanations, but much female nonconformity and illegality was interpreted in sexual terms. Depictions of women in conflict with the rules of society portrayed them as morally corrupt, hysterical, manipulative, and devious (Simpson, 1989). Expressing the view that many of these supposedly feminine qualities were manifestations of the female nature, criminological accounts ignored the contributions to female deviance and crime of social and economic factors such as poverty, marginalization, and restricted opportunity (Klein, 1973; Smart, 1976).

During the 1970s, Freda Adler (1975) and Rita Simon (1975) developed explanations of female offending that shunned biological and psychological factors in favour of social circumstances and conditions. Both writers argued that low levels of female crime were linked to women's limited aspirations and restricted opportunities. They claimed that increases were taking place in rates of female crime and that these increases were occurring as a result of women's involvement in the liberation movement. As a result of women's liberation, women's roles changed and became more masculine. Adler and Simon maintained that this role convergence encouraged greater female participation in crime, thereby producing a "new female criminal."

The new female criminal argument was soon criticized on several grounds (Steffensmeier, 1978). First, sociologists pointed out that there had been little real change in the occupational structure. The argument that more women were entering the labour force at higher ranks and taking on the characteristics of similarly positioned men simply was not true. Second, researchers observed that arrested and imprisoned females embrace traditional sexist values. Finally, feminists strongly took issue with the works of Adler and Simon because the writers completely ignored the role of patriarchy in crime and justice. Their formulations paid little attention to the power that males wield over females in the realms of labour and sexuality. Finally, both Adler and Simon ignored women's economic marginality as a major factor in their illegal conduct (Simpson, 1989).

Feminists also argue that sexism manifests itself in the treatment of women by the criminal justice system. Justice is gendered in that an offender's sex affects decision making in the system. The chivalry hypothesis, for example, holds that women, in accordance with their image as powerless and in need of protection, are treated more leniently than men by male-dominated police organizations. It also suggests that the courts may be more lenient to women for offences considered "normal" for females. Where the offences contradict the court's sex-role expectations, the response to females may be harsher than to males committing the same offence under the same circumstances (Simpson, 1989). However, evidence suggests that when all other factors such as offence seriousness and the number of prior convictions are taken into account, women are not penalized more leniently than men (Chesney-Lind, 1986; Johnson, 1986).

Sexism has also been apparent in other criminal justice practices. Female deviance is often subject to "sexualization"; while men are thought to steal because they need money, women — even poor ones — steal because they are sexually frustrated. Also, women who violate rules and break laws are more likely than men to be considered mentally ill. For males who fight, the old adage "boys will be boys" applies, but females who engage in similar forms of violence are thought to need psychiatric treatment.

Relatively little is known about the nature and extent of female deviance, crime, and victimization. The experiences of women as perpetrators, victims, and agents of control have been ignored until the late twentieth century. Theories about the causes and consequences of gender differences in offending and victimization are in their infancy. However, although feminist theorizing about deviance and crime is fairly recent, some noteworthy contributions exist. First, feminist scholars have focused attention on the inadequacies of existing social theories in explaining the deviance, crime, and victimization of both females and males. Second, feminist inquiry has brought to light the extensive, very serious but hitherto hidden victimization of two particularly vulnerable social segments, women and children. It has also focused attention on a particularly dangerous environment, the home. Third, feminism has provided, through the patriarchy construct, a coherent theoretical account of female victimization. Fourth, feminist approaches have emphasized economic necessity over female nature in the production of offences such as shoplifting, cheque forging, and prostitution. Other avenues of thought and other research questions are being explored. The most promising lines of inquiry involve determining the ways in which female deviance and crime are shaped by challenges to patriarchy, discovering the effect on female criminality of the sexism inherent in the social organization of criminal opportunity, and uncovering the ways in which gender relations affect the deviant and illegal conduct of females and males.

POWER-CONTROL THEORY

Power-control theory as it is articulated by John Hagan and his associates at the University of Toronto (1989) is an integrated theoretical perspective that seeks to explain why males, more than females, are involved in juvenile delinquency and crime. In its most basic form, power-control theory presents the following causal sequence. The first construct, family class structure, affects the second, the social reproduction of gender relations. The social reproduction of gender relations subsequently influences the third construct, the propensity for "risk taking." Variations in risk taking produce varying degrees of involvement in delinquent behaviour. Delinquency, in turn, results in official designation as delinquent.

Power-control theory defines delinquency as adolescent rule breaking that is largely fun, liberating, and personally rewarding. In this sense, delinquent acts are attempts by youth to "try out" adult male statuses. Power–control theory maintains that rules are most likely to be broken when the actors are free to deviate from social norms. It hypothesizes that power without control provides such freedom and consequently is the optimal circumstance promoting deviation from normative standards.

It is worthwhile to examine in some detail the first two constructs in the causal sequence that produces delinquency. By family class structure, power–control theory signifies the comparative power wielded by men and women within the family. In patriarchal families men are much more powerful than women, whereas in **egalitarian families** the difference between the sexes is much smaller.

Hagan notes that power for husbands and wives derives from sources not only within the family but also from outside the home. The most important source of the power exercised within the family is involvement in the workforce. Wives who are part of the paid workforce and who earn salaries comparable to their husbands' salaries exercise much more influence on family decision making than do wives who perform solely unpaid domestic tasks in the home. One reason for this difference is that salaried women are much less financially dependent on their husbands than are women without incomes of their own.

The social reproduction of gender relations refers to the process through which gender roles and the character of relationships between males and females are socially created, maintained, and renewed from one generation to the next. Prominent in the cultural transmission of these roles and relationships are the various organizations and institutions charged with the care, protection, custody, and socialization of children.

How do power and control vary by gender, and how does this variation affect risk taking and delinquency? Hagan argues that the concept of patriarchy provides important clues to the ways in which class and family intersect to provide the freedom necessary for adolescent deviation. Power–control theory defines patriarchy as the propensity of males to create hierarchical structures of subordination within which they can dominate females and other males. Within the family, for example, men dominate their wives and children. The world of work is also socially organized around men's domination of male and, in particular, female subordinates.

Power–control theory maintains that the family is the fundamental unit of patriarchy and the central agent that socializes children for adult roles. The theory takes account of the fact that parents informally control children in several ways. Perhaps the most powerful controls within the family are affiliative. These "relational" controls encourage children to conform to parental expectations as a consequence of love and affection. Parents' "instrumental" controls involve supervising and maintaining surveillance over their children's activities. Formal control is also patriarchal because state agencies such as the police and the courts are, like the family, male dominated.

Family experiences, especially those associated with relational and instrumental control, differ for boys and girls. Moreover, these differences are greater in patriarchal than in egalitarian families. In patriarchal families, parents control their sons and daughters in such a way as to differentially deny them access to the opportunity for delinquent behaviour. Opportunities to deviate are more restricted for females than for males.

In patriarchal families, social control is also sexually stratified. Mothers more than fathers socialize and control daughters more than sons. In power–control terms, females are both the objects and the instruments of control through affiliation and subordination. In short, the inclination and opportunity to express freedom through risk taking are freely given to boys but withheld from girls. Boys are encouraged to develop a taste for risk while being subjected to fewer familial controls. In contrast, families socialize girls to risk aversion and passivity and simultaneously subject them to higher levels of informal control. In patriarchal families, boys are likely to be much more delinquent than girls.

Power–control theory draws upon Max Weber's theory of social and economic organization to explain how gender relations are organized and perpetuated from one generation to the next, and in so doing points to the development of capitalism and its impact on the family. Weber argues that the shift to industrial capitalism was accompanied by a new emphasis on economic efficiency and rationality (Weber, 1967). The realization of these two objectives resulted in a hitherto unknown separation of the home and the workplace. Economic production shifted from the home to the factory and the office. The workplace became the productive sphere of labour and was occupied by men doing productive tasks for pay. Conversely, the home became the consumptive sphere and was occupied by women performing unpaid domestic work. This division also represented a sharp separation of the social world into the **private domain** of the family and the **public domain** of employment and politics.

Power–control theory observes that both the private and the public spheres involve the reproduction of gender roles. Just as the family reproduces gender roles, so does the state through its various agencies. The criminal justice system, charged with formally maintaining social control, is one such agency. Power–control theory argues that the exercise of informal controls rooted in the family is inversely related to the exercise of formal controls vested in the state.

Control is sexually stratified. Where family controls are weak, the likelihood increases that adolescents will come into contact with state agencies such as the police. Where family controls are strong, this probability is reduced. Since the patriarchal family informally controls girls more stringently than it does boys, females are less likely than males to come into contact with formal social control agents. In this way, the separation of private and public spheres intensifies the sexual stratification of the reproductive function. Females are disproportionately the instruments and objects of informal social control in the private sphere, while males are disproportionately the instruments and objects of formal social control in the public sphere. In patriarchal families, females are restricted to the home and males are prepared for and sent out into the world to work. Freer from the controlling confines of the home, males are more likely to encounter formal social control beyond its confines.

Power–control theory posits that the gap separating male and female delinquency is widest in the patriarchal family and narrowest in the egalitarian family. It also suggests that this gap is shrinking because of the greater equality between the sexes, which itself stems from the increasing participation of women in the paid labour force. In an egalitarian family, the private sphere of consumption and the public sphere of production are much less clearly divided by gender than they are in the patriarchal family. In the egalitarian family, both husband and wife work outside the home and occupy positions with authority over others. In such families, female as well as male offspring find themselves being socialized for eventual entry into the productive sphere of paid work. Therefore, girls find themselves subjected to the same types and degrees of control to which boys are subject. Power–control theory argues that as mothers gain power in comparison with their husbands, daughters will gain freedom in comparison with sons.

Egalitarian families nurture the taste for risk taking that is essential for success in the public domain of work, and they do so for both sons and daughters. Conversely, patriarchal families encourage males to take risks while strongly discouraging similar action by females. As the egalitarian family type becomes more predominant, power–control theory predicts reduced gender differences with respect to crime.

SELF-CONTROL THEORY AS A GENERAL THEORY OF CRIME

Gottfredson and Hirschi's (1990) general theory of crime is an extension of Hirschi's social control theory. It differs from its predecessor in that it emphasizes only one type of control, self-control, while incorporating such additional components as individual choice, life course events, and psychological constructs. The self-control perspective sets out to explain all individual differences in the propensity to commit crime or to refrain from it. As a general theory, the self-control approach explains all acts of deviance and crime, at all ages, under all circumstances. In so doing, it presents individual differences in criminal propensity as inherently stable. The theory states that individuals with high levels of self-control are less likely, at all periods of life, to engage in criminal acts. Those with low levels of self-control, conversely, are highly likely to commit crimes. Since low self-control can be counteracted by a variety of circumstances, it does not always result in illegal conduct. Circumstances must be right for low self-control to result in a criminal act.

The theory, outlined in Figure 8.2, maintains that low self-control is a product of inadequate socialization, particularly in the family domain. Parents effectively socialize their children when their relationship to their offspring is one of attachment, when they provide close supervision, and when they actively punish rule breaking. Ineffective child-rearing, on the other hand, produces low self-control, which causes people to break laws in a more or less impulsive fashion. People with low self-control engage in crime because it is easy and provides immediate gratification. In contrast, legitimate work involves effort and

FIGURE 8.2

A GENERAL THEORY OF CRIME

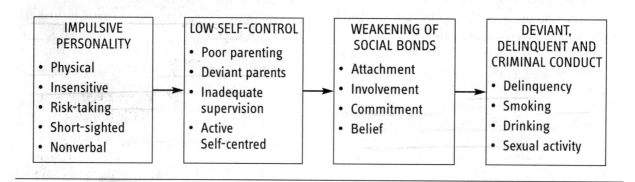

IMPULSIVE PERSONALITY	LOW SELF-CONTROL	WEAKENING OF SOCIAL BONDS	DEVIANT, DELINQUENT AND CRIMINAL CONDUCT
• Physical • Insensitive • Risk-taking • Short-sighted • Nonverbal	• Poor parenting • Deviant parents • Inadequate supervision • Active Self-centred	• Attachment • Involvement • Commitment • Belief	• Delinquency • Smoking • Drinking • Sexual activity

deferred gratification, both of which require high self-control. Work is an unattractive option for those who are drawn to such easy pleasures as smoking, drinking, gambling, and sex and who are captivated by action involving stealth, danger, agility, speed, and power.

The policy implications of self-control theory suggest that official initiatives aimed at deterring crime in adulthood are misplaced and doomed to failure. Preventative policies must be implemented that take effect early in the life course and benefit families.

While self-control theory is logically consistent, parsimonious, broad in scope, and enjoys some empirical support as a general theory of crime, it is new and requires more testing. Because self-control is a psychological variable, its existence and levels are very difficult to measure. A second criticism is that self-control cannot be easily separated from propensities for criminal activity and therefore the theory is tautological or circular in its reasoning. Low and high self-control are labels for differential propensity to commit crime, and measures of low self-control are not clearly separated conceptually from the tendencies to commit crime that low self-control is meant to explain (Akers, 1997).

PEACEMAKING CRIMINOLOGY

Peacemaking criminology emerges from the concern among various critical criminologists that crime engenders real suffering. The theory's authors see the peacemaking tradition as emerging out of religious, humanist, feminist, and conflict approaches to understanding crime and justice (Pepinsky, 1991). Its chief proponents, Harold Pepinsky and Richard Quinney, portray crime and its control as a war, the solution to which involves the negotiation of peace between offenders and victims, police, and the public. Peacemaking criminology involves mediation, conflict resolution, reconciliation, and reintegration of the offender into the community in a dual effort to alleviate suffering and reduce crime. The peacemaking perspective sees the criminal justice system itself as organized around a principle of violence that must be replaced with love and nonviolence if the crime problem is to be effectively resolved (Pepinsky and Quinney, 1991).

Commentators point out that the peacemaking perspective is not a true theory of crime that can be empirically assessed. Rather, it is a philosophy that has at its core a utopian vision of an almost crime-free society with a justice system characterized by nonviolence, the peaceful resolution of conflict, and the restoration of offenders to the community. It does not, however, offer an explanation of why offenders commit crime or why the criminal justice system operates the way it does. Critics also maintain that the policy directives inherent in the peacemaking approach are not new. Both religious and lay organizations working in prisons have for years advocated love and peace in the reformation of offenders and have tried to persuade them of the value of a religious commitment and a lifestyle incompatible with committing crime and causing pain to others.

Some assessments of peacemaking emphasize the internal contradictions that arise from identifying conflict theory and feminist theory as foundations for the perspective. Neither of these origin theories advocates peacemaking. The major recommendation of Marxist theories is to combat power with power, ultimately to overthrow capitalist society. Peacemaking's observation that women support nurturing and caring values seems misplaced, in that feminism tends to portray the caring, loving, and peaceful orientation of women as part of the traditional feminine role. Feminists have rejected such roles as products of patriarchy and its inherent oppression of women.

Finally, peacemakers assert that mainstream criminology has ignored the possibility of achieving peaceful and nonviolent means of addressing the real suffering caused by crime. In response, critics point to the existence of long-standing policies involving non-punitive treatment, mediation, restitution, reintegration, and rehabilitation (Akers, 1997).

REINTEGRATIVE SHAMING

The theory of **reintegrative shaming** is, as its creator points out, not highly original (Makkai and Braithwaite, 1994). The theory attempts to revitalize and provide context for the explanatory power of several existing frameworks that have enjoyed at least modest empirical support over the years. These theoretical traditions include strain, subcultural, differential association, social learning, control, and labelling theories. The reintegrative-shaming framework poses two related questions. First, what are the conditions under which a criminal label is likely to produce a criminal self-concept and future criminal behaviour? Second, what are the conditions under which such a label is likely to have the opposite effect, that is, to prevent crime?

Braithwaite (1989) begins by defining shaming as social disapproval that has the intention or the effect of producing remorse in the person being shamed. Shaming may also involve condemnation by others who become aware of the initial shaming. The central idea of the theory is what Braithwaite refers to as the "partitioning" of shaming into two principal components, each of which forms the opposite pole of a continuum. At one end of the scale is reintegrative shaming, while at the other end is shaming that stigmatizes. When shaming is reintegrative, the explanatory perspective inherent in control theory is mobilized. Shaming operates to reduce crime through informal and formal mechanisms of control. Alternatively, when shaming stigmatizes, the explanatory ideas of labelling and subcultural theory are operative. The stigma associated with shaming provokes and amplifies criminal behaviour.

Reintegrative shaming involves the following components. First, disapproval takes place in a context in which those who disapprove sustain a relationship of respect with those whose acts are rebuked. Second, ceremonies to certify deviance are followed and superceded by ceremonies to decertify it. Third, disapproval of the evil deed occurs without labelling people themselves as evil. Finally, disapprovers make efforts to avoid having deviance become a master status. Shaming through stigmatization, on the other hand, comprises disrespectful disapproval and humiliation. Ceremonies to certify deviance do not culminate in ceremonies designed to decertify it. Not only the act but the person is designated as evil. Finally, deviance is allowed to become a master status.

According to the theory, shaming is likely to be reintegrative and anti-criminogenic under conditions where there is a high level of interdependency between the disapprovers and the disapproved. The theory posits that both individual and structural variables such as sex, age, employment, marital status, and mobility produce varying degrees of interdependence. Characteristics such as being male, young, unemployed, single, and transient combine to reduce the degree of interdependence between the disapprovers and the disapproved. Under such circumstances, shaming is likely to amplify rather than reduce crime, because stigmatization produces reactions comprising anger and vindictive escalation rather than remorse and conciliation (Makkai and Braithwaite, 1994).

While the theory is new and awaits thorough empirical testing (Akers, 1997), there is some evidence to suggest its usefulness in explaining crime. Braithwaite outlines several instances in which crime facts fit the theory. Moreover, a recent study of changes in nursing-home operators' compliance with regulations supports the reintegrative–shaming perspective. Makkai and Braithwaite (1994) found, for example, that the interaction between inspectors' reintegrative ideology and their disapproval of violations produced the desired impact on the operators' subsequent degree of compliance.

POSTMODERNISM

Postmodern criminological thought arose in the late 1980s as the principal successor to more radical forms of critical criminology and from perspectives such as feminism, left realism, and peacemaking. In league with its predecessors, it argues that it is impossible to separate values from the research agenda and that there is a need to advance a progressive agenda favouring disprivileged peoples. Of the various perspectives that make up critical criminology, however, postmodern thought is perhaps the least developed and least understood (Schwartz and Friedrichs, 1994).

Schwartz and Friedrichs (1994) argue that **postmodernism** offers three possibilities for criminology. First, it is a method that can reveal how knowledge is constituted while at the same time uncovering pretensions and contradictions in traditional criminological scholarship. In so doing, postmodernists claim that the theory can provide an alternative to the "linear analysis" of traditional social science. Second, postmodernist theory highlights the significance of language and signs in the domain of crime and criminal justice. Finally, the theory provides a source of metaphors and concepts (e.g., "hyperreality") that capture elements of an emerging reality and the new context and set of conditions in which crime occurs.

Postmodernists emphasize that modernism embraces a naturalistic view of the social world in which science is seen as an objective process aimed at the prediction and control of action and behaviour. They reject the modernist scientific approach by asserting that all thought and knowledge are shaped by language, which itself lacks neutrality. Language, postmodernists claim, always advantages some points of view while disadvantaging others. They argue that modernism particularly privileges "scientific" thinking, according it, in comparison to other modes of thinking, special objectivity and validity. For their part, postmodernists do not grant scientific thinking privileged status, but rather describe it as neither more nor less valid than competing forms of thought. Postmodernism maintains that linear thought processes, statements about cause and effect, syllogistic reasoning, objective analyses, and other standards of scientific thinking are no more valid than other forms of thinking. Postmodernists attempt to "deconstruct" language to identify implicit and unsupported assumptions that buttress the ways in which advantaged points of view are legitimized, while at the same time undermining the validity of alternative perspectives. They also identify disparaged points of view and seek to make them more explicit and rightful in order that different discourses can be simultaneously seen as legitimate and in order that diverse points of view are appreciated without assuming that one perspective is superior to others.

Postmodernism argues that modernism and its emphasis on science has increased oppression rather than bringing about liberation. Modernity has become a force for subjugation, oppression, and repression, extending and intensifying the scope of violence in the world. Even more critical is the fact that the major form of response to this rising violence involves rational organizations, such as those embodied in the criminal justice system, which themselves rely heavily on professional and scientific expertise. Such a response to violence merely reproduces domination in new but no less harmful forms.

Postmodernism seeks to uncover structures of domination in society as a strategy to enable the achievement of greater liberation. Domination occurs, according to postmodernists, through control of language systems because language structures thought. Whether people using those languages know it or not, the languages used to convey meaning are not neutral but rather support dominant world views.

In the pursuit of increased liberation, postmodernists examine relationships between human agency and language in the creation of meaning, identity, truth, justice, power, and knowledge. Their main method of investigating how people construct sense and meaning is called "discourse analysis." Discourse analysis takes account of the social position of those who are speaking or writing in an effort to understand the meaning of what is verbalized or written down. Discourse analysts pay specific attention to the values and assumptions inherent in the language used by a speaker or author. To understand fully what people mean when they speak as actors in specific roles, it is necessary to comprehend much about the roles in question as historically situated and structured positions in society. Examples of such "discursive subject positions" that are interconnected with their own language systems are police, correctional officers, and court workers on the one hand, and drug dealers, armed robbers, and juvenile gang members on the other.

Once people take on "discursive subject positions," the words that they articulate fail to express fully their own realities. Rather, they express, at least partially, the realities of the larger institutions in which they are embedded. With their language at least somewhat removed or disconnected from their own reality, people become "decentred." They are never precisely what their words describe and are continually pressed in the direction of being what their language systems expect or demand (Schwartz and Friedrichs, 1994; Vold, Bernard, and Snipes, 1998).

Vold, Bernard, and Snipes (1998) provide an example to illustrate these points. Victims and defendants must tell their stories to prosecutors and defence attorneys who subsequently reconstruct and reformulate their narratives into the language of the courts. The testimony of victims and defendants cannot deviate from the accepted language system without jeopardizing either the prosecutor's conviction or the defence attorney's acquittal. Even if defendants are convicted, victims may feel that their stories were never fully told, and even if the accused are acquitted, they may believe that their stories, laid out before the court, bore so little resemblance to what actually happened that they too are dissatisfied. Regardless of who prevails, the process has comprised a ritualistic ceremony in which the reality of the courts has dominated the reality of both the victim and the accused. The legalistic language of the court expresses and institutionalizes the domination of the individual by social institutions.

According to postmodernists, the current situation is one in which discourse is either dominant (e.g., legalistic, professional, scientific language) or oppositional (e.g., the language of prison inmates). Their goal is to transform the situation to one in which many different discourses are recognized as legitimate by establishing "replacement discourses." A replacement discourse is a language that helps people to speak with a more authentic voice while remaining continuously aware of the authentic voices of others. The objective is to establish greater inclusivity, more diverse communication, and a pluralistic culture. To do so, postmodernists advocate listening carefully to otherwise excluded perspectives while constituting the meaning of criminal acts. Creating a society in which alternative discourses liberate people from the domination of prevailing speech patterns will also legitimate the role of all citizens in the project of reducing crime and bringing about greater respect for social diversity. Postmodernists believe that the achievement of this objective ultimately will result in less victimization of other people by criminals and less

official punishment of criminals by agents of the state (Vold, Bernard, and Snipes, 1998).

While some criminologists have embraced postmodernism with enthusiasm, many have not. The position of "appreciative relativism" that presents all points of view as equal and treats scientific discourse as having no more validity than any other language exceeds the tolerance of most criminologists who believe in the validity of the scientific process despite some very real, practical limitations.

Critics point out, as well, that postmodernists are infamous for their own use of highly specialized jargon, for inventing and discarding terms, and for "playing" with words. As Schwartz and Friedrichs (1994) observe, this occurrence raises a paradox. While postmodernists insist on not "privileging" the language of the powerful over the language of the powerless, they speak and write in a form and style that is highly inaccessible, not only to the powerless but to most of those in a position to act on their behalf.

Postmodernism provides little practical guidance on policy. Some critics argue that postmodernism is idealistic and completely insensitive to the direct, concrete experiences and needs of victims and survivors of crime. Furthermore, some forms of postmodernist theory echo the romantic early days of radical criminology by regarding violence and insurrection as praiseworthy efforts to deny legitimacy to the state.

While not offering concrete policy suggestions, however, postmodernism does offer a basis for exposing pretences and illusions in the pursuit of a just policy. Postmodernism can be defended as intensely political in that it seeks to obliterate hegemonic discourses, thereby creating opportunities to construct alternative political structures. Postmodernism also promotes empowerment of victims, enabling them to engage more fully in a process of reconstituting the meaning of violence.

Postmodernism may be very useful in the future in developing insights into newly emerging forms of crime. These "information age" illegalities or "techno-crimes" involve computers, telecommunications, the Internet, and other aspects of advanced technology. Postmodern analyses of crimes that take place in a symbolic universe or in the sphere of the "hyperreal" have the potential of enhancing criminological theory in the 21st century (Schwartz and Friedrichs, 1994).

Table 8.1 summarizes the new theories discussed in this chapter.

TABLE 8.1

NEW THEORIES OF DEVIANCE AND CRIME

Theory	Theorist(s)	Central Premise	Key Concepts	Principal Contributions
Routine activities	Lawrence Cohen and Marcus Felson	People's everyday behaviours are linked to a structure of opportunity that renders them vulnerable to intentional property and personal crime. Crime occurs where three essential ingredients – motivated offenders, suitable targets, and the absence of guardianship – converge in space and time. The suitability of target varies in terms of value, accessibility, and inertia. Guardianship also varies on the bases of social organization and technology. The theory considers three dimensions of space and time: periodicity, tempo, and frequency.	Offender; target; guardianship; value; accessibility; inertia; periodicity; tempo; frequency	Highly relevant to the practice of crime prevention in modern society; policy based on the theory is relatively inexpensive, politically palatable, and effective
Left realism	Roger Matthews; Jock Young; Walter DeKeseredy; Martin Schwartz	Left realism examines street crime as a serious problem where left idealism offered only simplistic and romantic images of such offenders. Left realism explores the role of structural conditions in generating criminal activity. The theory seeks to destroy myths surrounding crime and control, integrate micro and macro theories, use qualitative and quantitative data, and generate practical and humane crime control strategies. It advocates demarginalization, pre-emptive deterrence, minimal imprisonment, the democratization of policing, and community involvement in crime prevention.	Left realism; left idealism; demarginalization; pre-emptive deterrence; minimal imprisonment; democratization of policing; crime prevention	A conflict theory that fully addresses issues concerning street crime perpetration and victimization
Feminism	Freda Adler; Carol Smart; Meda Chesney-Lind	Gender inequality is the defining feature of society and is explained in terms of patriarchy, a hierarchical system of power in which males are dominant and females and children are subordinate. Liberal feminism stresses restricted opportunities for women in a public sphere that should be made more meritocratic and less discriminatory.	Gender inequality; patriarchy; liberal feminism; Marxist feminism; radical feminism; power psychology; generalizability; gender ratio	Focuses attention on gender inequality, sexism, the victimization of women and children, and gender discrimination in the criminal justice system

TABLE 8.1

(CONTINUED)

Theory	Theorist(s)	Central Premise	Key Concepts	Principal Contributions
		Marxist feminism emphasizes class and gender exploitation at home and work by the capitalist class that can be overcome only through revolutionary means. Radical feminism stresses a patriarchal power psychology in which male dominance is widely accepted as legitimate. It advocates women-only organizations, lesbian separatism, and women's control of reproductive technologies.		
Power–control theory	John Hagan; John Simpson; A.R. Gillis	Power without control provides males the freedom to deviate. Male and female power in the family is derived from work roles in the public sphere. Boys and girls have different family experiences, especially in patriarchal families where females are both the objects and the instruments of control. Boys, on the other hand, are subjected to less intense informal control and are socialized to take risks. Consequently, they more frequently come into contact with formal control agencies such as the police. In egalitarian families, boys and girls are socialized to risk taking and subjected to informal control in ways that are more similar and therefore the gender gap in delinquency is smaller.	Power; control; patriarchal families; egalitarian families	Integrated theoretical perspective explaining the gender ratio in crime commission
General theory of crime	Travis Hirschi; Michael Gottfredson	Variations in self-control produce variations in the propensity to commit crime. Low self-control is a product of inadequate socialization, primarily in the family context.	Self-control	Refined version of Hirschi's earlier formulation of social control theory. It offers a theory of crime designed to explain all forms of illegal behaviour
Peace-keeping	Harold Pepinsky; Richard Quinney	The criminal justice system is a violent response to crime. Peacekeeping advocates mediation and reintegration as better means of alleviating the suffering caused by crime.	Mediation; integration	Provides an alternative model of criminal justice de-emphasizing violence in favour of restorative justice

continued

TABLE 8.1

(CONTINUED)

Theory	Theorist(s)	Central Premise	Key Concepts	Principal Contributions
Reintegrative shaming	John Braithwaite	Reintegrative shaming specifies conditions under which labelling constitutes a mitigating or aggravating circumstance influencing future criminal behaviour. Shaming that is reintegrative reduces crime, while shaming that is stigmatizing increases crime. Reintegration is likely where disapprovers and the disapproved are interdependent, and stigmatization is likely where they are not.	Partitioning of shaming; reintegrative shaming; stigmatization; certification and decertification of deviance	Blends insights from a variety of earlier theories, especially labelling, to explain criminal involvement and desistance
Postmodernism		Postmodernism reveals the hidden power of language to confer privilege and power on one explanatory perspective as opposed to another. Postmodernists are relativists who seek to avoid "privileging" any mode of thought or language. They challenge the validity and hegemony of modern science's search for testable explanations of crime.	Hyperreality; deconstruction; discourse analysis; discursive subject positions; decentring; replacement discourse; appreciative relativism	Points out contradictions in traditional scholarship. It emphasizes significance of language in spheres of crime and justice

SUMMARY

Routine activities analysis links people's everyday behaviours to a structure of opportunity that renders them vulnerable to intentional property and personal crime. This perspective accounts for crime on the basis of the convergence in space and time of three essential ingredients: motivated offenders, suitable targets, and the absence of guardianship. The theory treats the motivation of offenders as a given. The suitability of targets varies in terms of value, accessibility, and inertia. Guardianship also varies on the bases of social organization and technology. Finally, routine activities theory considers three dimensions of space and time. Periodicity refers to cyclical behaviours, and tempo involves the frequency of certain events in time. Timing refers to the crossover of offenders' and victims' lifestyle patterns. Although the routine activities or lifestyle–exposure perspective enjoys solid empirical support, it is criticized for sidestepping the question of motivation, for being imprecise about the relative criminogenic importance of its central elements, and for ignoring expressive crime.

Radical theory emerged as a response to positivism, while left realism emerged as a response to radical theory and more positivist approaches. Stimulated by feminist insights in the 1970s, left realists criticize their idealist opponents for their "criminal as victim" perspective. Their attack on positivism centres on the rise of administrative criminology, which abandons the search for causality to pursue more coercive formal controls. Realists reject idealism for several reasons. Left idealism overlooks street crime as a serious social problem and focuses on elite deviance. Idealism, according to left realists, is simplistic and romanticizes offenders. It ignores the role of structural conditions in generating criminal activity and borders on functionalism when it suggests that actions of the state exist only to serve the vested interests of capitalists.

Left realism's goals include destroying myths surrounding crime and control, integrating micro and macro theories, using qualitative and quantitative data, and generating practical and humane control strategies. Among its recommended tactics are demarginalization, pre-emptive deterrence, minimal imprisonment, the democratization of policing, and community involvement in crime prevention. Critics of the left realist position point out that it sets up for attack the most extreme versions of radical and conservative approaches, that its insights closely resemble those of existing perspectives that operate outside of the conflict tradition, and that it underemphasizes elite deviance. Left realism, however, is in its formative stages and may well offer valuable insights in the future.

Feminist theorizing begins with the fundamental observation that while women make up at least half of society, their experience of the social world is ignored in social theory. Male experience dominates explanations of social structure and social process. Social science, in short, is "male-stream."

In reacting to biological, psychological, and conservative sociological approaches, feminists maintain that gender inequality is the defining feature of society. They reject the functionalist notion that male and female role complementarity facilitates harmony in the family and promotes social integration in the community. They consider the suggestion that male and female roles are separate but equal to be nonsense.

Feminists document the unequal rewards attached to male and female roles. They explain this inequality in terms of patriarchy, a hierarchical system of power in which males are dominant and females and children are subordinate.

Liberal feminism stresses the gender inequality inherent in a system that restricts opportunities for women in the public sphere. Liberal feminism favours change from within the system to make it more meritocratic. Other recommended changes involve socialization practices and legislation aimed at prohibiting discrimination against women. Marxist feminists emphasize links between class and gender dominance, pointing out how women are exploited by the capitalist class both in the home and in the workplace. The elimination of gender inequality depends on the elimination of class through revolutionary means. Radical feminists argue that society is governed by a patriarchal

power psychology in which men's dominance is widely accepted as legitimate. Radicals advocate changes ranging from the creation of women-only organizations and institutions to lesbian separatism and the control of reproductive technologies.

Feminist theorizing about deviance and crime is in its infancy. Several questions are being debated. First, can "male-stream" theory be generalized to explain female deviance? Second, how can the gender ratio, the gap separating male from female deviance and crime, be accounted for? Third, given the extent of this gap, does it make sense to suggest a general theory of deviance?

Power–control theory sets out a causal chain in its explanation of delinquency that contains the following variables in order of cause and effect: family class structure, the reproduction of gender relations, risk taking, delinquency, and official designation as delinquent. The key factor is power without control, which provides the freedom to deviate. Power for men and women in the private sphere of the family is related to their roles in the public sphere of work. In patriarchal families women are confined to the private sphere, while in egalitarian families they are involved in the public sphere. Family experiences differ for boys and girls, and this difference is greatest in patriarchal families. In patriarchal families, females are both the objects and the instruments of control. Mothers constrain girls more than boys in respect to risk taking. Boys, because they are socialized to take risks and subjected to less intense informal control, more frequently come into contact with formal control agencies such as the police. In the public sphere, males are both the objects and the instruments of control. In egalitarian families, boys and girls are socialized to risk taking and subjected to informal control in ways that are more similar. Therefore, the gender gap in delinquency is smaller for the progeny of egalitarian families than it is for the progeny of patriarchal families.

Self-control, peacekeeping, and reintegrative shaming are three newer perspectives on illegal conduct. The general theory of crime is an extension of social control theory that emphasizes a single causal variable — self-control. Variations in self-control produce variations in the propensity to commit crime. Low self-control is a product of inadequate socialization, primarily in the family context. A major criticism of this approach is that it is tautological. The peacekeeping perspective views the criminal justice system as a violent response to crime and advocates mediation and reintegration as better means of alleviating the suffering caused by crime. Critics of the peacekeeping perspective argue that it is more philosophical than explanatory and that its proposed counter-crime measures are also advocated by more traditional approaches. Finally, reintegrative shaming specifies conditions under which labelling constitutes a mitigating or aggravating circumstance influencing future criminal behaviour. Shaming that is reintegrative reduces crime while shaming that is stigmatizing increases crime. Reintegration is likely where disapprovers and disapproved are interdependent, and stigmatization is likely where they are not. As emergent theories, all three perspectives will benefit from additional empirical testing and logical refinement.

The postmodernist perspective exposes the hidden power of language to confer privilege and power on one theoretical perspective while undercutting the validity of others. Postmodernists are relativists who seek to avoid "privileging" any mode of thought or language. A central part of their mission is to challenge the validity and hegemony of modern science's search for testable explanations of crime.

DISCUSSION QUESTIONS

1. Explain how the organization of routine activities in time and space increases or decreases the risk of victimization.

2. Discuss the aims and objectives of the left realist approach. In what ways is left realism similar to and different from the scientific social science so heavily criticized by conflict theorists?

3. What are the explanations and the policy directives inherent in liberal feminism, Marxist feminism, and radical feminism? Compare the explanations and directives.

4. Demonstrate how self-control theory builds upon Hirschi's original formulation of control theory.

5. Discuss how reintegrative shaming represents a blending of labelling and deterrence traditions.

WEB LINKS

Theoretical Developments in Criminology
http://www.ojp.usdoj.gov/nij/criminal_justice2000/vol1_2000.html
> This issue of *Criminal Justice* contains an article by Charles R. Tittle, in which the author reviews late twentieth century developments in criminology and identifies directions for the future. To view the article, click on the link provided under "Contents." You will need a copy of Acrobat Reader to open it.

John Hagan
http://www.criminology.fsu.edu/crimtheory/hagan.htm
> This paper by Melissa Miguel discusses the power-control theory as it is elaborated by John Hagan.

Critical Criminology – Past, Present, and Future
http://www.soci.niu.edu/~critcrim/CC/cc.html
> This special issue of a newsletter on critical criminology addresses the questions of where critical criminology has been, where it is now, and where it is headed.

Reintegrative Shaming Experiments (RISE)
http://www.aic.gov.au/rjustice/rise/index.html
> Conducted by the Australian Institute of Criminology and the Australian National University, these experiments aim to assess the results of assigning cases to a conference rather than a court hearing.

The Red Feather Journal of Postmodern Criminology
http://www.tryoung.com/journal-pomocrim/pomocrimindex.html
> This peer-reviewed on-line journal contains many articles on recent developments in criminology. Of particular interest for this chapter are Volume 1: Introduction to Postmodern Criminology and Volume 4: Feminist Criminology.

RECOMMENDED READINGS

Braithwaite, J. (1989). *Crime, Shame, and Reintegration*. Cambridge: Cambridge University Press.
  Contains Braithwaite's original formulation of the reintegrative shaming perspective.

Felson, M., and L. Cohen. (1980). "Human Ecology and Crime: A Routine Activities Approach." *Human Ecology* 4:389–406.
  Presents the original articulation of the routine activities or lifestyle exposure approach to the understanding of criminal victimization and crime prevention.

Gottfredson, M.R., and T. Hirschi (1990). *A General Theory of Crime*. Stanford, CA: Stanford University Press.
  Represents an extension and refinement of Hirschi's early theory of informal social control into a general theory applicable to the explanation of all forms of criminality.

Kennedy, L.W. and D.R. Forde. (1999). *When Push Comes to Shove: A Routine Conflict Approach to Violence*. Albany: SUNY Press.
  Uses Canadian survey data to analyze various conflictual situations. Points out the importance of lifestyle, daily routine, and respondent expererience with crime and conflict as important predictive variables. Also includes an analysis of the violent conduct of conflict-prone street youth.

LeBlanc, L. (1999). *Pretty in Punk: Girls' Resistance in a Boy's Subculture*. New Brunswick, NJ: Rutgers University Press.
  Examines the origins and development of punk subculture and investigates the changing roles of women and girls in oppositional subcultures. Analysis is based on field research and interviews with self-identified punk girls in several North American cities including Montreal.

O'Reilly-Flemming, T. (1996). *Post-Critical Criminology*. Scarborough: Prentice-Hall.
  A series of articles outlining recent developments extending from the critical criminological tradition.

Pepinsky, H.E., and R. Quinney. (1991). *Criminology as Peacemaking*. Bloomington, IN: Indiana University Press.
  Sets out the foundations of a peacemaking approach to understanding and coping with crime.

Sommers, E.K. (1995). *Voices from Within: Women Who Have Broken the Law*. Toronto: University of Toronto Press.
  Through intensive interviews with fourteen Canadian women in prison, examines why and how women become involved in crime. Criticizes feminist criminology for overemphasizing and oversimplifying the links between crime and poverty.

Part Three

Measuring Deviance and Crime

CHAPTER 9

MEASURING DEVIANCE AND CRIME

The aims of this chapter are to familiarize the reader with:

- the differences between knowing on the basis of common sense and knowing on the basis of social science
- the uses of data on deviance and crime in society
- official data: the calculation of crime rates, the crime funnel, the reasons for the nonreporting and nonrecording of criminal activity, the weaknesses and strengths of official data
- crime surveys: self-reported deviant and criminal behaviour, self-reported victimization, survey techniques, problems with survey data, the contributions of surveys to estimating the volume of deviant and criminal activity
- participant observation studies: the techniques of participant observation, the problems of participant observation in general, the problems of participant observation in studying nonconforming and illegal conduct in particular
- the relationship between age, sex, ethnicity, and socioeconomic status on the one hand and deviance and crime on the other

INTRODUCTION

Social scientists are first and foremost in our minds people watchers. Their aims are to document and understand people's attitudes and behaviours and to describe and explain the ways in which attitudes and behaviours vary from one individual, group, **aggregate**, or society to the next. Most people, in their everyday lives, seek similar ends. They are constantly trying to comprehend and come to terms with the individuals, groups, circumstances, and events in their social environments. In pursuing a better understanding of the world, however, laypersons do not generally follow specified procedures in the same way that social scientists do.

In making sense of social phenomena people normally rely on their observations, which can be direct — grounded in personal experience — or indirect — based on second-hand information. Indirect observation provides "hearsay evidence" that originates in the interpretations and conclusions drawn by friends, acquaintances, the media, or perhaps all three. In coming to grips with the events that constantly occur around them, human beings digest information and then generalize from their own limited experience. It is from this process of generalization that people form "common-sense" interpretations of the world.

The principal shortcoming of common-sense approaches to "knowing" is that they are highly subjective. Individuals see the world through a relatively narrow window, for it is humanly impossible to directly observe large and disparate groups of individuals carefully. Most direct observations consist of watching and listening to people in the immediate environment. The problem here is that the people with whom one associates tend to resemble oneself. Personal associates and acquaintances usually speak the same language, adhere to the same or similar religions, are similarly educated, and share common values regarding family and work. These commonalities encourage limited and inaccurate perspectives on human experience and on social problems.

Much of what people know about the world comes not from direct personal experience but from media portrayals. However, the entertainment and news media must sell themselves to the public. Because people are often inclined to pay to see and hear what they want to see and hear, the entertainment and news media cater to public tastes. In attracting and holding the attention of their audiences, however, the media offer people a sense of the nature of reality. By creating and reinforcing certain images of social interaction, of social groups, and of social issues and problems, the media make them real in the minds of readers, listeners, and viewers.

The impact of the media is especially significant when the sources claim objectivity (e.g., the news) and when people have little direct experience that challenges the popular portrayals. Because of people's experience of life in the family, in school, and at work, for example, they have at least some opportunity to respond critically to media depictions of these subjects. Few, however, have independent insight into the attitudes and behaviours of social actors whose beliefs and whose actions are highly devalued, hidden from view, and cloaked in secrecy. Most people have little direct access to the world of murderers, professional thieves, and embezzlers. But the indirect and vicarious experiences provided by the media enable people to "know" that prostitutes are major carriers of sexually transmitted diseases and that a court system too soft on offenders cripples police efforts to control crime.

Unlike the mechanics of common-sense knowledge, the techniques of social science are sets of rules governing precisely how sociologists conduct their observations, organize their findings, and draw their conclusions. Through special techniques of research design and **sampling**, sociologists and criminologists seek to reduce as much as possible the distortions inherent in common-sense approaches to deviance and crime. Bias can never be completely eliminated, but it is possible to reduce it and, when interpreting findings, to remain sensitive to its nature and degree. With this objective, research design specifies tactics for making observations, for asking questions, and for using comparison (control) groups. Sampling strategies set out stringent rules governing who and how many are observed or questioned. By using these techniques and by trying to anticipate sources of systematic bias in their investigations, social scientists construct more accurate pictures of deviance and

crime than those created through direct or vicarious personal experience.

The problem with common-sense interpretations is not just that they are so subject to bias. More significant is the fact that few people consider the potential for error in common-sense judgements. Many of their most strongly held beliefs about deviance, crime, and social control are inaccurate. Most are overly simplistic, and many represent only partial truths. Others are patently false.

This chapter begins by documenting the reasons why social scientists gather data on deviance and crime. It then examines the major sources of information on deviant and criminal conduct — **official data**, surveys of offenders and victims, and participant observation studies. Each source's strengths and deficiencies are evaluated. The chapter emphasizes that the shortcomings of each data-collection strategy must be carefully considered in interpreting research findings. It concludes by briefly examining the profiles of deviance and crime generated by these approaches, particularly the ways in which age, sex, ethnicity, and socioeconomic status are related to deviant behaviour and criminal conduct.

THE USES OF DATA ON DEVIANCE AND CRIME

Sociologists construct estimates of the incidence of deviance and crime for several reasons. Compiling these numbers provides an indication of the "communal well-being" of municipalities and regions across Canada. Furthermore, having some idea of the way in which deviance and crime are distributed nationwide makes it possible to compare conditions in Canada with those in other nations (Nettler, 1984). For example, Canadian and American crime rate statistics collected between 1990 and 1999 indicate that, compared with Canada, the United States experiences almost four times as many murders and more than twice as many robberies (Tremblay, 2000; Maguire and Pastore, 2000). On the basis of these figures, the quality of life enjoyed by Canadians is arguably superior to that of Americans.

Collecting information on deviance and crime enables sociologists to identify and classify important characteristics of deviants, criminals, victims, and crime scenes. Crime data sometimes confirm popular perceptions, and sometimes they do not. While it is true, for example, that young males are most likely to commit violent crimes, it is not true that females are more likely to be the direct victims of violent crimes (other than sexual assault). Rather, evidence suggests not only that young males are responsible for most lawbreaking but also that men are the most likely victims of assault and robbery (Johnson, 1996b).

The enumeration of deviance and crime can also be used to assess variations in the risks associated with different locations and different time periods. By compiling and examining data, it is possible to determine whether the risks of being murdered are higher in Toronto than in Twillingate and whether the probability of ending one's life in an unsafely manufactured automobile is lower today than it was in previous decades.

Professionals working in social welfare, health care, and criminal justice frequently use information on the distribution of deviance and crime to plan, implement, and evaluate programs designed to treat patients, rehabilitate inmates, or deter potential lawbreakers. If fewer incidents of self-abuse occur among autistic children after hospital attendants administer shocks from cattle prods, it may confirm that this treatment reduces self-destructive behaviour. This evidence might be used by clinical staff to argue that the practice be continued despite public protests regarding its inhumanity.

Information on incidence, on offender and victim characteristics, and on surrounding circumstances is essential for constructing sociological theories to explain why some people are more deviant and crime-prone than others. In accumulating information on bank crime, for example, criminologists find that bank robbers are disproportionately male, young, unmarried, lower class, and members of disadvantaged ethnic minorities (Gabor et al., 1987; Conklin, 1972). Embezzlers, conversely, share only one of these characteristics: most are male. However, most white-collar criminals are middle aged, married with children, employed in responsible positions, from middle- or upper-middle-class backgrounds, and white (Cressey, 1971). These and related facts can be incorporated into logical explanations. Constructing an adequate theory of robbery or of embezzlement would be impossible if data were not collected on perpetrators and their methods.

OFFICIAL DATA

Until the early 1960s, information on crime in Canada existed only at the municipal and regional levels.

Reports of criminal investigations formed the bases of tallies that were compiled at the local level by police detachments across the country. Two major deficiencies plagued these law-enforcement records. First, since they were collected for police purposes only, they lacked sufficient sociological and criminological detail. Second, the procedures by which crimes were recorded differed substantially among police jurisdictions. Therefore, meaningful comparisons of jurisdictions were difficult, if not impossible.

In 1962, the federal government introduced nation-wide the Canadian **Uniform Crime Report** (UCR) system. The UCR remedied many of the shortcomings of the previous approach. In assembling their crime data, police began using the UCR guidelines' clearly specified set of recording rules. Once the data were compiled, law-enforcement agencies forwarded local crime profiles to Ottawa, where Statistics Canada amassed and published national statistics annually. In 1982, the newly created Centre for Justice Statistics assumed these duties. It now provides sufficiently "uniform" national crime data to make possible meaningful comparisons of Canadian police jurisdictions.

The Canadian UCR, modelled on a similar set of U.S. procedures, is superior to the American system in at least two respects. First, criminal law in Canada is a federal responsibility, whereas in the United States it falls under the jurisdiction of each state. Definitions and classifications of offences do not vary from province to province as they do from state to state in the United States. Second, the crime data gathered by Canadian police are more detailed than those gathered by police in many of the U.S. states.

Uniform Crime Report data are counts of crimes known to the police. These include violations of the *Criminal Code*, the *Narcotics Control Act*, certain provincial statutes, and some municipal by-laws. From these data, crime statisticians calculate both the overall crime rate and rates of specific crimes, such as murder and sexual assault.

Since 1988, the UCR Survey has been expanded to provide more detailed information regarding the characteristics of violent incidents, victims, and offenders. A nonrepresentative sample of 164 police departments in seven provinces covering 46 percent of criminal incidents across the country is currently participating in the Revised UCR Survey (UCRII). While the UCRII provides more detail on a variety of offences, it does not permit generalization of rates of occurrence of police-recorded crimes to the general population because the sample of participating police departments is not nationally representative. Almost three-quarters of all cases in this survey originate in Quebec and Ontario. Coverage will continue to grow, however, as more police agencies convert to the revised instrument (Johnson, 1995; Tremblay, 2000).

Other official agencies also tabulate the incidence of specific types of deviance and crime. The federal Ministry of Consumer and Corporate Affairs collects data on the illegal activities of Canada's corporations, and provincial workers' compensation boards keep track of workers injured on the job. Other quasigovernmental organizations like hospitals and psychiatric institutes monitor cases of mental illness, drug abuse, and alcoholism.

CRIME RATES

Simply counting and reporting the yearly totals for various types of crime is of limited utility because simple counts do not take into consideration differences in population size. Thus, meaningful comparisons, either of one jurisdiction with another or of one time period with another, are impossible. That there were an average of 81 homicides in Toronto between 1989 and 1998 while there were an average of 2 in St. John's (Fedorowycz, 2000) may demonstrate nothing about the relative risks of living in large urban areas. The differences may be due simply to the different population sizes of the two cities. Similarly, the increase from 15 homicides in Toronto in 1900 to 60 in 1994 may be due purely to the population increase in that city over time (Fedorowycz, 2000).

Deviance and **crime rates** are calculated by dividing the number of times a particular event occurs in a certain time period (usually a year) by the population size for a particular geographical area and multiplying this figure by a constant (usually 100 000).

$$\text{Crude crime rate} = \frac{\text{number of events}}{\text{population size}} \times 100\ 000$$

Calculating rates in this fashion permits meaningful comparisons to be drawn among jurisdictions. In 1998, the robbery rate in Canada was 96 per 100 000, while the comparable rate for the United States was 165 per 100 000. The Canadian murder rate per 100 000 in 1975 was 3.1, while in 1999 it was 1.76

(Tremblay, 2000; Maguire and Pastore, 2000). These calculations suggest that the chances of being robbed are greater in the United States than in Canada and that the likelihood of being murdered in Canada decreased substantially between 1975 and 1999.

The Number of Events

The events forming the numerator of the equation for calculating crude crime rates represent the number of occurrences known to those responsible for filling out official reports. For example, police officers complete crime reports, while physicians, counsellors, and psychiatrists document cases of drug and alcohol abuse and mental illness. However, officials cannot know about all acts of deviance and crime. To represent the relationship between recorded events and those that remain hidden, social scientists invoke the image of a "funnel," as illustrated in Figure 9.1. The **crime funnel**, for example, has four basic levels: (1) the number of criminal incidents that actually occur, (2) the number that are detected, (3) the number reported to authorities, and (4) the number that officials record (Silverman, Teevan, and Sacco, 1991). The funnel concept reflects the fact that the numbers of incidents of deviance and crime shrink as one moves from the top to the bottom of the funnel. The recorded numbers of deviant and criminal activities usually drastically underestimate the actual numbers of incidents occurring. The many deviant and criminal acts that remain hidden form what social scientists refer to as the "dark figure" of deviance and crime (Skogan, 1976).

Detected incidents are those that someone, somewhere, observes. Observers may be victims, witnesses, or agents of social control. For the most part, officials can count detected incidents only if civilian observers bring them to their attention. Where citizens take steps to inform authorities, the occurrence descends the funnel into the reported category. Often, however, even when people observe deviant and criminal acts, they do not report them.

There are many reasons why citizens decide not to report crime to the police (CUVS, 1984a; Nettler, 1984). Many people consider some offences, such as breaking highway speed limits, as trivial and tolerable. People are reluctant to inform the police about a crime if they perceive that their reporting will cost them time or money. Even serious crimes such as assault may go unreported if victims feel that the social or economic costs of becoming involved with the police, lawyers, and the courts are not worth the

FIGURE 9.1

THE CRIME FUNNEL

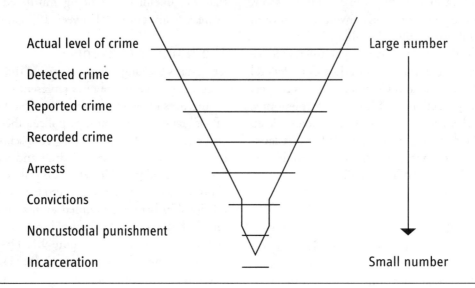

Actual level of crime	Large number
Detected crime	
Reported crime	
Recorded crime	
Arrests	
Convictions	
Noncustodial punishment	
Incarceration	Small number

effort. Still other criminal acts lack a clearly defined victim. The actions of prostitutes, drug dealers, and loan sharks are seldom reported because their "victims" willingly exchange money for the illicit goods and services provided by these outlaw entrepreneurs.

The relationship between the victim and the person observing a criminal offence may also affect reporting. Women may not inform police about assaults by their spouses and boyfriends because they love them. They may also fail to report such incidents to the authorities because their assailants threaten them with violent retaliation. People routinely fail to report sexual assaults because of the shame and the fear of publicity felt by both victims and their families. Reports of crimes such as vandalism or minor theft often do not reach the police because people have little faith in the ability of police to apprehend certain types of criminals. Moreover, some people do not report crime because they fear or distrust law-enforcement agents. This circumstance is true of some ethnic minorities in Canada, especially when the victims are illegal immigrants.

One aspect of crime reporting deserves emphasis. Members of the public play a "gate-keeper" role that significantly affects the numbers of people processed by hospitals, psychiatric institutes, and criminal justice agencies. Most crimes gain the attention of the police through the watchfulness of the public. For this rea-

son, public reporting practices significantly affect, first, the volume of crimes known to the police, and second, as a consequence, crime rates generally. The implications of public reporting are by no means trivial.

North American sexual assault rates increased dramatically during the 1980s, while the rates of other forms of violent crime levelled off or declined. However, changes both in public attitudes and in the law are encouraging more women to report sexual assaults. Intense lobbying by women's groups has strengthened the moral, medical, and legal supports for victims of sexual assault. The gains include better treatment of victims by police, hospitals, and courts and an expansion of a network of rape crisis centres and battered women's shelters. These changes, however, make it difficult to know whether increases in sexual assault rates are due to growth in the actual incidence of this crime or to changes in reporting practices.

Toward the bottom of the crime funnel is recorded crime. For a crime to be officially recorded, the police must first determine that it is a "founded" crime, one that a police officer, upon investigation, is certain actually happened. Even after people report crimes to police and police determine that they are founded, offences are not always recorded. Patrol officers and detectives may have neither the time nor the inclination to complete reports on all offences, especially when the violations are not serious (Nettler, 1984; Silverman, Teevan, and Sacco, 1991).

Complainants may want lawbreakers to be treated leniently. Wives who call police to intervene in family disputes may not want the matter pursued formally. The wishes of complainants or victims are important because if these persons are reluctant to testify, there is little if any chance that a conviction will result.

The demeanour of both victims and perpetrators also influences the responses of law enforcers (Cicourel, 1968). Victims who are belligerent with police officers and offenders who are respectful increase the likelihood that their cases will be dealt with informally and therefore not be recorded. Again, this is especially true for relatively minor offences. Whether offenders and police are acquainted with one another may also influence a police officer's decision about how to deal with a particular offence. If a drunken motorist is well known to them, small-town police may arrange a ride home or time to dry out in jail rather than proceed with a charge of impaired driving (Silverman, Teevan, and Sacco, 1991). Finally, if individual police officers are "on the take" or entire forces are corrupt, offences ranging from parking violations to prostitution, gambling, and narcotics trafficking are unlikely to be recorded even though they have been detected and reported and are known to be founded.

The volume of crime that a police force officially registers is partly a function of its size and the way in which it is organized (MacLean, 1986; Mawby, 1979). While a serious crime like homicide will be carefully investigated regardless of the force's size and type of organization, the same is not true for less serious offences. The latitude granted to officers widens as the seriousness of the illegal act decreases. Moreover, larger numbers of police mean that more crimes of a less serious variety can be investigated and subsequently recorded. Assigning a police officer to every streetcorner or bar in a Canadian city would undoubtedly increase the recorded incidence both of traffic offences and liquor violations, whether or not there were any increases in the actual numbers of these illegalities. Ironically, increasing the size of the police force can increase the crime rate simply because more police are able to investigate, and count, more criminal incidents.

Police forces are organized along different lines. Some represent what criminologists refer to as "professional" models of law enforcement, while others practise a **"watch" style of policing**. The professional force limits discretion and promotes a "by the book" approach to crime control. The watch orientation broadens the base of police decision-making and encourages strategies aimed at "containment." As such, watch-style policing involves informally handling illegal or potentially illegal situations. Officers in a watch-style organization, upon apprehending teenage joy riders, would likely reprimand the lawbreakers and take them home for disciplining by their parents. A professionally oriented force, however, would process the case formally. Thus, professionally oriented forces record more crime, particularly minor crime, than do watch-style detachments (Wilson, 1978).

The nature of police activity and the amount of crime that they record also vary as a result of shifting enforcement priorities. For example, the numbers of recorded minor narcotics offences in Canada stabilized and in some cases declined during the 1980s. According to police at the time, this levelling off occurred because the RCMP were diverting resources away from combatting street-level trafficking and concentrating on the large-scale illegal import and export trade (Barber, 1986).

Law-enforcement priorities are set politically. Interest groups regularly pressure politicians into allocating more resources to the alleviation of specific crime problems. During the late 1970s, for example, three Toronto men sexually assaulted and murdered shoe-shine boy and child prostitute Emanuel Jaques. As a consequence of this killing and as a result of widespread concerns over the degeneration of the Yonge Street "strip," citizens and merchants pressured Toronto police to clean up "unsavoury" establishments and to put out of business the many "seedy" entrepreneurs who were dealing in sex (Fleming, 1983). Amidst such crackdowns, morals offences often increase sharply in number.

As one descends in the funnel from the level of actual crime to the level of recorded crime, a tremendous decline occurs, and continues through subsequent levels of the funnel. Crimes recorded by the police far exceed the number of charges laid. Only a small proportion of charges results in the conviction of an offender. Smaller still is the number of convictions that result in imprisonment.

Even where crime is recorded, our understanding of what recorded crime means is not complete. The UCR figures from 1962 to 1992 — when important changes were introduced — demonstrate additional idiosyncrasies that make them difficult to work with. Police count crimes against the person and crimes against property differently. The rule for crimes against the person is generally one victim, one crime. For crimes against property, the unit of count becomes not the victim but the occurrence. If a woman in a bar punches three other patrons, three assaults have taken place. If a man sneaks into the locker room of a health spa and removes wallets from three adjacent lockers, police will likely record only one theft. The different counting practices make the comparison of violent crime rates and property crime rates problematic (Silverman, Teevan, and Sacco, 1991).

Usually, police do not distinguish attempted crimes from completed crimes, except for attempted murder, which is enumerated in a separate category. Theft and attempted theft are counted as the same offence. The distinction is important because, although attempted and completed offences are counted as the same thing, the courts tend to treat them differently. Attempted crimes often result in lighter sentences than those meted out for completed offences. Lumping together attempted and completed offences obscures this fact, making it appear that courts are sometimes soft on offenders.

When one criminal incident involves a series of offences, police frequently record only the most serious of the crimes (Silverman, Teevan, and Sacco, 1991). If a man breaks into a dwelling, takes some jewellery, smashes some glassware, kills the owner of the house, and escapes in a stolen car, only the most serious of his crimes would likely become official statistics.

Recording only the most serious crimes in a series has several impacts on crime estimates. It deflates the overall crime count and overstates the proportion of serious to minor crimes, because only serious crimes are counted. Also, enumerators decide which crime in a series is the most serious on the basis of the maximum penalty allowed under the *Criminal Code*. Police then count the offence with the most severe sanction while ignoring others. Occasionally, however, authorities count crimes that the public considers comparatively trivial while omitting crimes that the public generally believes more serious. Criminologists have criticized this criterion for deciding seriousness for its lack of sophistication (Akman and Normandeau, 1967).

The figures for overall crime rates are often misleading. Statisticians calculate these rates by counting many offences that few people would consider real crime. Not only do they include *Criminal Code* offences in their calculations, they also include violations of some provincial statutes and municipal bylaws. Many such illegalities are minor offences and traffic violations. Sociologist Lynn McDonald has argued that over 90 percent of the increase in overall crime rates since 1900 is due to the invention of the automobile and to laws regulating its use (McDonald, 1979).

Legislators' ability to eliminate, modify, and create entire offence categories makes comparisons of changes in rates over time difficult if not impossible. In 1983, Parliament eliminated rape as a crime and replaced rape laws with legislation framed in terms of sexual assault. Since sexual assault encompasses a wider range of victim types and illegal acts, it becomes extremely difficult to ascertain whether "rape" is increasing, decreasing, or occurring with the same frequency after 1983 as it did before 1983.

Police may manipulate information to serve their own ends. By misclassifying, downgrading, or failing to record certain offences, they may create evidence attesting to their effectiveness in controlling certain types of criminal activity. Inaccuracies are more likely to occur, however, by different forces' use of different rules of thumb for coding information from investigation reports onto the standardized UCR forms. Interpretations of how to classify the descriptions of certain offences vary among both individual officers and detachments. Whether a purse-snatching is theft or robbery is a judgement call. As a result of this latitude, identical acts may be recorded differently by various jurisdictions (Farrington and Dowds, 1985).

Marked differences in crime rates occur in different locations as a result of these variations in recording rules. Canadian criminologist Robert Silverman, noting that Edmonton's crime rates far exceeded Calgary's despite considerable similarities in the two cities' demographic characteristics, accounted for the differences by citing the different recording practices of the Calgary and Edmonton forces (Silverman, 1980).

Social scientists use recorded crime data to explore suspected causes of crime and to test their theories. One of the major difficulties in using official data for this purpose is that police need not gather and enter into the record much information related to the incident. It is difficult to convince officials to collect data that they do not see as directly relevant to their own needs. Thus, police records rarely contain much information on many theoretically interesting socioeconomic and demographic variables.

Population Size

Several problems involving the denominator in the equation for calculating crude crime rates — the population size — also require discussion. Statisticians must use base population figures from the **census** (Nettler, 1984). This number is insensitive to changes in population size between each census. If crime rates are computed in 2004 by using population counts derived from the 2001 census, incalculable inaccuracies can result. If the population in 2004 is larger than in 2001 and the actual number of crimes is the same, crime rate estimates will be artificially low. If the population size in 2004 is smaller than it was in 2001 and the number of crimes is the same, crime rate estimates will be artificially high.

Using **gross population counts** to calculate crime rates does not take into account shifts in population composition, which can affect the likelihood both of committing crime and of becoming a victim. For example, consider two hypothetical communities with populations of identical size, one of which is a retirement town in the American sunbelt, while the other is a booming oil town in northern Alberta. The residents of Suncity tend to be affluent, married, and older. There are very few children and youth in the community, females outnumber males, and most people have lived there for several years or more. Oiltown is different. Its residents are relatively uneducated and unskilled migrants looking for work on the nearby rigs. Most are young males, and many are single or have younger, growing families. Males outnumber females. Many have been in Oiltown for only a few weeks. If one were to speculate about which city would have the higher rate of delinquency or crime, Oiltown would get the nod on both counts. While this hypothetical example is an extreme case, it is easy to see how population composition can affect crime rates.

Rapid increases or decreases in birth rates alter the proportions of young and old in a population. Younger populations are more crime-prone than older populations. Rates of some violent crimes in Canada and the United States declined at various times in the past decade partly because baby boomers began to "age out" of violent behaviour. The average age of the Canadian population has now increased beyond the average age of offenders involved in violent crimes.

Shifts in a society's age composition are quite important in accounting for variations in crime over time.

When evaluating changes in certain crime rates, it is also useful to consider what criminologists refer to as the "**unit at risk**" (Nettler, 1984). Increases in both the number and portability of consumer goods have increased rates of theft. Stealing a radio 60 years ago would have required three strong people and a moving van. A modern radio can be carried off by a child. Similarly, a society of two-car families like Canada is likely to have higher rates of auto theft than one like China, where automobiles are extremely scarce.

To reduce distortion and to make the calculation of official rates of deviance and crime more meaningful, Canadian social scientists have long advocated certain refinements to the computation procedure. Age- and sex-specific crime rates could be worked out by taking into account the numbers in the population most at risk of becoming either perpetrators or victims. For example, rates of violent crime would concentrate on the most violence-prone age and sex groups — males in their twenties. Similarly, sexual assault rates would take into account the numbers of females in a population. Another refinement would be to exclude children under the age of 12 from base counts. Young children are technically ineligible for designation as criminal.

The Canadian Centre for Justice Statistics has developed a new system of gathering official crime data. This new computer-driven system has been implemented by police departments across the country and became operational in 1992. The revised data-collection methods generate more information about crime and provide a focus on individual criminal incidents (Silverman, Teevan, and Sacco, 1991). These innovations not only make it possible to better document crime trends, they also offer the opportunity to test theory because the new system collects information on the demographic traits of victims and accused persons, the levels of personal and property victimization, and the characteristics of criminal events (e.g., weapons, time, location, presence of drugs and alcohol). The new system also improves on the old by eliminating differences in counting techniques for personal and property crimes, by making possible the computation of age- and sex-specific crime rates, and by including information on the less serious offences in multiple-offence incidents.

Although basing estimates of deviance and crime on official records involves significant problems, these data are still useful. The idiosyncrasies from one jurisdiction to the next that arise from differences such as police force strength, law-enforcement strategies, and record-keeping practices probably cancel each other out when criminologists consider the entire nation. Moreover, since official rates for a variety of crimes are consistently similar over time, some stability in estimates exists at the national level. The proportion of violent to property crimes, for example, tends to be very similar from one city to another. While it may be difficult to know precisely how much crime is occurring, criminologists have some confidence, given the stability of these rates, that they know the relative proportions of the total represented by various subtypes.

Official data provide better estimates of the volume of violent and property crimes as the seriousness of the offence increases. Police estimates of murder are much more accurate than their estimates of assault because murder is much more difficult to conceal. Since people consider this crime extremely serious, they almost always report it. Similarly, since automobiles cost so much and insurance claims require police reports, car thefts are almost always brought to the attention of law enforcers.

A final reason for using official data on deviance and crime is straightforward. Uniform Crime Report data remain the only statistics on crime that are collected nationally and compiled annually. Despite their many deficiencies, official statistics reduce pure speculation and allow researchers to make more informed estimates (Silverman, Teevan, and Sacco, 1991). Nonetheless, everyone, whether a government policy analyst or a viewer of television news, must interpret official crime data with considerable caution.

UCR CRIME TRENDS, 1999

Excluding traffic and drug incidents, Canadian police agencies recorded 2.36 million *Criminal Code* offences in 1999. Violent crimes comprised 12 percent of offences while 55 percent were property crimes and 33 percent were "other" *Criminal Code* violations, such as prostitution, arson, and disturbing the peace. The proportion of offences classified as property-related has declined continuously since 1971, when property crime represented 69 percent of all illegalities. In addition, police recorded approximately 137 000 *Criminal Code* traffic incidents of which about 60 percent involved impaired driving.

Drug crimes numbered about 80 000, while violations of the Excise, Immigration, and Shipping Acts accounted for 39 000 other federal statute incidents.

After reaching its peak in the early 1990s, Canada's crime rate has been steadily declining. (See Figure 9.2.) In 1999, the official crime rate — 7733 incidents per 100 000 population — fell for the eighth year in a row (an average of 4 percent per year). The length of this decline has been unprecedented since the UCR survey was first established in 1962 and has resulted in the 1999 rate being the lowest since 1979. The major offence category that contradicts this trend is drug enforcement. Drug offences, which are heavily influenced by patterns of police activity, have risen in recent years.

As Figure 9.3 illustrates, crime rates vary considerably by region with rates in eastern Canada (Atlantic provinces, Quebec and Ontario) generally being lower than those in the west. Exceptions to this trend are Nova Scotia and Alberta, with Nova Scotia's being higher and Alberta's lower than adjacent provinces. Both Nova Scotia and Alberta currently have crime rates that approximate the national average. In 1999, Newfoundland's total crime rate was the lowest at 5921 incidents per 100 000 population, while Saskatchewan's was the highest at 12 155. All three territories had offence rates substantially higher than any of the other provinces, ranging from 18 074 to 24 040.

Only in Atlantic Canada and the Yukon did crime rates increase in 1999. The Yukon and Prince Edward Island rates increased 10 percent while gains were more modest in Nova Scotia (+2 percent), Newfoundland (+2 percent) and New Brunswick (+1 percent). In Quebec, Ontario and British Columbia, which contain three-quarters of the Canadian population, officially recorded crime declined 8 percent, 7 percent, and 5 percent, respectively. Overall, the national decline was 5 percent.

Canada is by no means alone in registering declines in recorded crime in recent years. The Federal Bureau of Investigation reports that index crimes in the United States fell for the eighth consecutive year. Crime is down 3 percent overall and down 5 percent for violent crime and 2 percent for property crime. All index crimes in America fell in 1999, including murder (–7 percent), robbery (–5 percent), burglary (–5 percent), and motor vehicle theft (–4 percent). Crime is also down in England and Wales (–1 percent) where it has fallen every year since 1992. Violent crime

FIGURE 9.2

CRIME RATES, BY TYPE OF OFFENCE, CANADA, 1962–1999

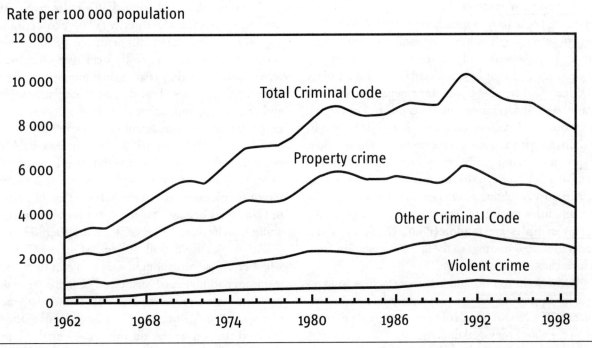

Rate per 100 000 population

Source: S. Tremblay. (2000). Canadian Crime Statistics, 1999. *Juristat Service Bulletin* 20(5). Ottawa: Canadian Centre for Justice Statistics, Statistics Canada, Cat. No. 85-002.

declined 6 percent while property crime showed a 1 percent decrease. Australia, Germany and Spain have also recorded falling crime rates since 1995 (Tremblay, 2000).

CRIME SURVEYS

Two types of survey are used by social scientists to study deviance and crime. **Victimization surveys**

FIGURE 9.3

PROVINCIAL AND TERRITORIAL CRIME RATES

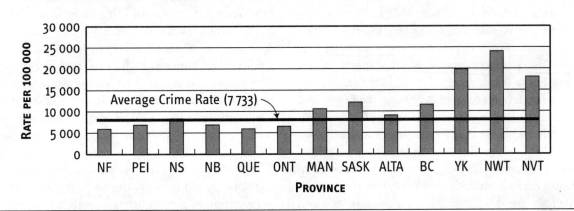

Source: Based on *Juristat Service Bulletin* 20(5). Ottawa: Canadian Centre for Justice Statistics, Statistics Canada, p. 17, Cat. No. 85-0002.

gather information from victims, while **self-report crime surveys** ask members of the public about the extent to which they have committed certain deviant and illegal acts.

Surveys involve several basic steps. Since surveying an entire population is usually impractical, social scientists select small subsets, or samples, from these larger populations and question people over the phone, in person, or by questionnaire about a variety of crimes and crime-related phenomena. Surveys typically seek information on perceptions, opinions, intentions, behaviours, experiences, and demographics. Investigators usually take steps to ensure their respondents' anonymity or to keep their identities confidential. Survey data are usually but not always quantitative, enabling researchers to use many descriptive and inferential statistics to present findings. When survey **samples** are **randomly** chosen, analysts can generalize their findings to the larger population from which the sample was drawn.

Both victimization and self-report crime surveys usually inquire about people's crime-related experiences over a certain length of time, usually six months or a year. Since they deal directly with the experiences of respondents, surveys avoid the "filtering out" problem that plagues official measures. With survey techniques, events are not weeded out either by public decisions not to report or by police decisions not to record. Therefore, survey research on victimization, deviance, and crime sheds a good deal of light on the size of the "dark figure." Both victimization and self-report crime surveys count events at a higher level in the funnel than is possible with official data-collection techniques. Self-report crime studies collect data closer to the level of actual crime, while victimization studies gather information at the level of detected crime — at least insofar as victims are aware of their victimization (Gomme, 1986a; 1988).

There are two basic types of victimization: direct and indirect. Direct victims are those who suffer economic loss, property damage, physical injury, or loss of life at the hands of another. Indirect victims are those who develop fears of becoming the target of a criminal act. People experience anxiety about becoming a crime victim at different levels of intensity. For many, the fear is sufficient to undermine a full enjoyment of life. It usually originates in three ways: from personal contact with others who have been crime victims, from personally witnessing a criminal act, and from viewing portrayals of criminality presented by the news and entertainment media. In a much smaller number of cases, people develop intense fears of crime because of personal victimization.

The number of persons in Canada indirectly victimized through fear of crime dramatically exceeds the number of persons who directly fall prey to a criminal act. Fear of crime frequently results in persons taking concrete and sometimes costly steps to protect themselves. Indirect victims restrict their movements to certain places and times of the day, purchase alarm systems and watchdogs, and, particularly in the United States, keep weapons on their premises (Gomme, 1986b).

Between 1991 and 1998, the crime rate fell 22 percent, making the 1998 rate the lowest since 1979. Despite this lengthy period of decline, however, recent public opinion surveys indicate that 75 percent of Canadians believe that the crime problem is worsening (Environics, 1998; CCJS, 2000 Factfinder).

An Angus Reid poll conducted in 1997 asked whether Canadians thought that crime in their communities had increased, decreased or remained stable over the past five years. The poll found that most Canadians, and especially those in western Canada, believed that crime was on the rise. Overall, 59 percent thought that crime had increased, down from 68 percent in 1994, but on the same plane as perceptions in 1990 (57 percent). When asked about becoming a victim of crime in their communities, 21 percent were fearful, compared to 19 percent in 1990. The poll also revealed that persons aged 55 and over were more likely than younger people to believe that crime had risen (Janhevich, 1998b).

Surveys consistently show that women, much more than men, report higher levels of fear and concern for personal safety regardless of their ages, places of residence, victimization experiences, or other personal characteristics. Women, for example, are much more fearful than men of being alone in their homes in the evening or at night. A recent survey shows that 37 percent of women are very or somewhat worried, a figure three times as high as for men (12 percent). The proportion was highest among women aged 15 to 24 (42 percent). Levels of fear were also elevated by Canadians' previous victimization experiences with sexual assault, robbery, or break and enter (Sacco, 1995; Janhevich, 1998b).

Self-report crime surveys ask people to report, for a specific period of time, the frequency of their own perpetration of certain behaviours that, if brought to the attention of the authorities, could result in negative sanction at the hands of the criminal justice system. Among prohibited behaviours commonly contained in self-report crime instruments are major and minor theft, drug and alcohol violations, vandalism, and common assault (Linden and Fillmore, 1981).

Victim surveys ask respondents if they have been the victims of a range of specific crimes during a particular span of time. From those answering yes, the surveys gather information about the circumstances surrounding the crime and the physical, economic, and emotional results of the victimization. Researchers also ask victims to reveal whether and why they did or did not report the crime to police. If they did make a report, they are asked to describe the police response. Often the researchers also gather information about fear of crime and about the respondents' perceptions of and attitudes toward criminal law and criminal justice. The questions may concern the severity of legal sanctions and the operation of the police, the courts, and the prison system (Nettler, 1984).

Victimization and self-report crime surveys are less frequent in Canada than in the United States. In 1981, the federal Ministry of the Solicitor General conducted the first major survey of victims in this country — the Canadian Urban Victimization Survey (CUVS). Government researchers interviewed residents (aged 16 and older) by phone in seven cities across the country: St. John's, Halifax, Montreal, Toronto, Winnipeg, Edmonton, and Vancouver. The eight categories of victimization included sexual assault, robbery, assault, break and enter, motor vehicle theft, house theft, personal theft, and vandalism. Only a handful of small-scale investigations, many of them pilots for the 1981 survey, predate this larger study (CUVS, 1983).

More recently, the Canadian government sponsored two additional surveys, the General Social Survey (Statistics Canada, 1999) and the Violence Against Women Survey (Statistics Canada, 1993). The GSS is a multi-cycle survey designed to measure the social conditions of Canadians (health, family, work and leisure, and crime and accidents). Each cycle runs once every five years, and the 1999 GSS represented the third running of the crime and accident survey. Researchers conducted telephone interviews with approximately 26 000 Canadians aged 15 and older. The sample covered the non-institutionalized population of the ten provinces and was selected using random-digit dialling techniques. Interviewers asked respondents about their experiences with crime

and the criminal justice system over the previous twelve-month period. Analysts then constructed estimates of the incidence of three violent and five property crimes among the general population aged 15 and older (Besserer and Trainor, 2000).

For the VAWS, funded by Health Canada, a sample of women were interviewed by telephone about their experiences with sexual and physical violence since age 16, about their experiences with the criminal justice system, and about their fear of violence. The sample of 12 300 women, which was selected using random-digit dialling techniques, allows generalizations to be made to the non-institutionalized female population aged 18 years or over living in the ten Canadian provinces.

Self-report delinquency and crime surveys in Canada are rare. Edmund Vaz, a criminologist at the University of Waterloo, was among the first to use the method in this country during the 1960s (Vaz, 1965). Since then, sociologists in Canada have undertaken only a handful of self-report studies of delinquency (Vaz, 1965; LeBlanc, 1975; Hagan, Gillis, and Chan, 1980; Gomme, Morton, and West, 1984). Self-report studies of adult crime are virtually nonexistent.

Self-report delinquency inventories tap both criminal and **status offences**. Crimes routinely included in self-report delinquency instruments are vandalism, theft, motor vehicle theft or joy riding, burglary, and minor assault. Status offences are offences solely because the person committing them occupies a particular status, in this case age. Until the replacement of the *Juvenile Delinquents Act* with the *Young Offenders Act* in 1984, behaviours such as being absent from home without parental permission were against the law for those under a certain legal age, which, incidentally, varied both by offence and by province (West, 1984). The *Young Offenders Act* eliminated many status offences. One prominent status offence still in force is the prohibition against alcohol consumption by the young.

While surveys provide improved estimates of the **"dark figure" of crime**, they are not without their shortcomings (Box, 1981; Brantingham and Brantingham, 1984). Victimization studies depend on victims' knowing that they have been preyed upon. Those who are cheated, swindled, or physically harmed by others through fraud, price fixing, or land, water, and air pollution are often unaware that they have been victimized. Even less artful crimes such as theft may go unnoticed. Often victims erroneously

Box 9.1
EXAMPLE OF A SELF-REPORT DELINQUENCY STUDY

In their study, Keane, Gillis, and Hagan (1989) use a complex statistical technique to test the impact of police contact on delinquency. The authors begin by noting that deterrence theory and social reaction theory offer different and mutually exclusive predictions about the impact of police contact on the delinquent behaviour of juveniles. Deterrence theory hypothesizes that being picked up by the police will discourage future illegal conduct, while social reaction theory suggests that such formal processing will only amplify subsequent deviance by increasing the exposure of youth to deviant subcultures. These deviant subcultures in turn facilitate socialization to an ever-more-intensive nonconformity.

Keane, Gillis, and Hagan suggest that both deterrence and amplification processes may operate to produce delinquency but that these processes may vary in their explanatory power along gender lines. They seek to explore this possibility by examining the reciprocal relationship between police contact and a particular form of delinquency, marijuana use, first for males and then for females. Their selection of marijuana use as a measure of delinquency is not accidental. Cognizant of the comparative lack of involvement of females in most forms of illegal conduct, they chose a form of delinquent behaviour in which large numbers of females do participate.

The authors hypothesize that teenagers who enjoy taking risks will be more likely to resist the forces of control represented by their families and the authorities, and as a result will be more likely to engage in such delinquencies as marijuana smoking. Furthermore, they contend that, because females demonstrate more aversion to risk taking than males do, females are more susceptible to deterrence. Males, alternatively, are more oriented to risk taking. They are also more likely to view a run-in with the law as a challenge to their autonomy than an inducement to desist.

Keane, Gillis, and Hagan selected four secondary schools in Metropolitan Toronto. Seeking to maximize variation on class-related variables, they chose schools situated in upper-middle-class, middle-class, and working-class neighbourhoods. School-board rosters provided the list of students from which a random sample was drawn. With 835 respondents, the sample reflected a response rate (those present and agreeing to participate) of 83.5 percent. A researcher administered the questions at the end of the school day to groups of students in various classrooms by reading the items aloud and having the students follow along and fill out their individual forms. This procedure was followed to increase students' comprehension of the questions. When teenagers who left out information on relevant questions were statistically removed from the sample, the researchers were left with 360 male cases and 305 female cases upon which to base their statistical analysis.

To estimate the frequency of marijuana use, Keane, Gillis, and Hagan asked how often a respondent had used cannabis during the previous year. The question, "Have you ever been picked up by the police?" provided the measure of police contact. To assess orientation to risk taking, the researchers asked students to indicate agreement, from "strongly agree" to "strongly disagree," with the statement "I like to take chances." Differential association (involvement in a delinquent peer group) was measured by asking the adolescents in the sample whether or not any of their close friends had been picked up by the police. The scale for this item ranged from "none" at one end of the continuum to "most close friends" at the other.

Using a multivariate statistical technique known as LISREL, the authors tested these and other hypotheses. The findings support their contentions. Being more risk averse, females' contacts with the police led to reduced marijuana use. Being more risk oriented, males' police contacts appear to have stimulated marijuana use among them. Keane, Gillis, and Hagan concluded that the reason for these gender effects is orientation to risk. Males are more likely to take risks while females tend to be risk averse. Because of this, females are more likely to be deterred from delinquency as a result of police contact while male delinquent behaviour is likely to be amplified.

These findings support both deterrence and amplification arguments in explaining the presence of adolescent deviance, and highlight the importance of specifying the scope of theories. That is, deterrence theory and amplification theory are both useful in explaining deviant behaviour; what is necessary is to specify the conditions under which each will apply. This research points to orientation to risk as the key scope restriction.

Discussion Questions

Discuss the adequacy of the following self-report delinquency measures. Marijuana use – "How often have you used cannabis during the previous year?" Police contact – "Have you ever been picked up by the police?" Orientation to risk taking – "Indicate your agreement, from 'strongly agree' to 'strongly disagree,' with the statement 'I like to take chances.'" Differential association – "Have any of your close friends been picked up by the police – none to most." How might these questions be improved?

Source: C. Keane, A.R. Gillis, and J. Hagan. (1989). "Deterrence and Amplification of Juvenile Delinquency by Police Contact: The Importance of Gender and Risk Orientation." *British Journal of Criminology* 29:336–52.

believe that what has in fact been stolen has only been temporarily misplaced or lost. Self-report crime surveys, alternatively, present less of a problem in this respect. Usually, if questions are worded carefully, respondents know that they have behaved in certain ways even if they themselves do not recognize their actions as violations of the law. A youth of 14, for example, might self-report smoking cigarettes without actually realizing that this action was against the law.

In conducting surveys, social scientists employ sampling techniques designed to include people from the diversity of cultural and socioeconomic groups that comprise the community, the region, or the country from which the sample was drawn. Researchers standardize survey questionnaires and interview schedules and attempt to ask all respondents the same questions in the same way. Consequently, these instruments can sometimes be insensitive to cultural factors that influence the way in which people interpret certain items (Babbie, 1973). In the case of child abuse, for example, the understanding of what this offence is may vary among subcultures. Questions concerning "hitting" or being "hit" may be interpreted differently in different cultures. For some, paddling a child's bottom is both necessary and in the child's best interest; spanking is not encompassed by the term "hit." For others, both actions represent violence.

One of the major problems with surveys concerns the honesty of respondents (Babbie, 1973). Lack of truthfulness may occur for a variety of reasons. Some respondents may lie to researchers out of pure deviltry. Others are simply reluctant to confess either having done bad things or having experienced them. Many people also hesitate to admit being the victims of certain types of crime, especially when such admissions are embarrassing (Sanders, 1980). Many incest and sexual assault victims are loath to admit victim-

ization because they are ashamed or fear that their tormentors will find out about their confessions and seek revenge (CUVS, 1984a). Similarly, persons asked to self-report their perpetration of violent crimes may hold back because they fear that a researcher will subsequently inform police.

While dishonesty usually results in the underenumeration of crime, a lack of truthfulness can have the opposite effect. For some, there is glory in being an outlaw. Fighting, drunk driving, smoking dope, guzzling booze, and having kinky sex can be construed as glamorous and prestigious. Consequently, some respondents may admit to committing certain offences to cast themselves in what they consider a favourable light (Nettler, 1984).

Even if most people are forthright in their responses, the accuracy of survey data can suffer by virtue of the faulty memories of respondents (Babbie, 1973). Victimization surveys, in particular, require the recollection of events that may have faded in the victim's mind over time (Skogan, 1975). The flawed memory of respondents poses another problem, namely, "telescoping," or compressing events in time. Although surveys seek to collect information for events occurring over a specified period, some people compress previous events into this time frame. As a result, poor memories inflate the overall count of crime.

Social characteristics such as education affect a person's power of recall. Educated people are more likely to recollect events and are better able to describe them articulately (Babbie, 1973), whereas lower-class persons and disadvantaged members of certain ethnic groups may provide artificially low estimates of both their criminal involvements and their victimization experiences. This fact introduces a class bias into survey results.

Inquiring about only some offences limits the accuracy of overall estimates of crime based on

Box 9.2
EXAMPLE OF A CANADIAN VICTIMIZATION SURVEY

In 1999, as part of its General Social Survey program, Statistics Canada conducted a survey on victimization and public perceptions of crime and the justice system. It was the third time that the General Social Survey (GSS) had examined victimization – previous surveys were conducted in 1993 and 1988.

For the 1999 survey, interviews were conducted by telephone with approximately 26 000 people, aged 15 and older, living in the 10 provinces.[1] Respondents were asked for their opinions concerning the level of crime in their neighbourhood, their fear of crime and their views concerning the performance of the justice system. They were also asked about their experiences with criminal victimization. Those respondents who had been victims of a crime in the previous 12 months were asked for detailed information on each incident, including when and where it occurred; whether the incident was reported to the police; and how they were affected by the experience.

This *Juristat* will present an overview of the findings of the 1999 General Social Survey and, where possible, make comparisons to results from 1993 and 1988. Survey results pertaining to the issue of spousal violence are examined in the year 2000 edition of the report *Family Violence in Canada: A Statistical Profile*.[2] Other reports analyzing results from the 1999 GSS will be released over the next few months. A future edition of *Juristat* will provide an analysis of the 1999 GSS data on public perceptions of crime and the justice system, while a second report will provide a more in-depth profile of victimization in Canada.

Offence types

The 1999 GSS measured the incidence of victimization for eight offence types, based on the *Criminal Code* definitions for these crimes. Sexual assault, robbery, and assault are classified as violent crimes. These three offences combined with theft of personal property form the personal crime category. The remaining four offences are considered household crimes. For personal crimes, it is an individual who is victimized, while for household crimes, it is typically all the members of the household. Rates of personal offences are therefore calculated per 1,000 persons

aged 15 and older, while rates of household offences are expressed per 1,000 households.

Incidents involving more than one type of offence, for example a robbery and an assault, are classified according to the most serious offence. The rank of offences from most to least serious is: sexual assault, robbery, assault, break and enter, motor vehicle/parts theft, theft of personal property, theft of household property and vandalism. Incidents are classified based on the respondent's answers to a series of questions. For example, did anyone threaten you with physical harm in any way? How were you threatened?

Highlights

- Canada's victimization rate was virtually unchanged in 1999. According to the 1999 General Social Survey (GSS) conducted by Statistics Canada, 25% of Canadians aged 15 and older were victims of at least one crime in the previous year, compared to a figure of 23% in 1993, when the victimization survey was last conducted. Of the eight crimes measured by the GSS, the rates for sexual assault, robbery, assault, break and enter, motor vehicle/parts theft and vandalism did not change significantly between 1993 and 1999. However, increased rates were observed for theft of personal property and theft of household property.

- Reporting to the police declined in 1999. For the eight GSS crime types, fewer than 4 in 10 incidents (37%) were reported to the police. This was down from 42% in 1993. The main reason that victims cited in 1999 for not reporting their incident was because it was "not important enough" (36% of unreported incidents). This same reason was given for 25% of unreported incidents in 1993.

- In all, 8.3 million victimization incidents were reported to the GSS in 1999. About one-half of these incidents involved a personal crime (sexual assault, robbery, assault or theft of personal property), while about one-third involved a household crime (break and enter, motor vehicle/parts theft, theft of household property or vandalism). The remaining 15% of incidents could not be classified into one of these eight crime types.

1. See Methodology section for more details.
2. See Statistics Canada Catalogue no. 85-224-XIE.

Crime category	Offence	Description
Personal crimes	Theft of personal property	Theft or attempted theft of personal property such as money, credit cards, clothing, jewellery, a purse or a wallet. (Unlike robbery, the perpetrator does not confront the victim.)
	Violent crimes	
	Sexual assault	Forced sexual activity, an attempt at forced sexual activity, or unwanted sexual touching, grabbing, kissing or fondling.
	Robbery	Theft or attempted theft in which the perpetrator had a weapon or there was violence or the threat of violence against the victim.
	Assault	An attack (victim hit, slapped, grabbed, knocked down, or beaten), a face-to-face threat of physical harm, or an incident with a weapon present.
Household crimes	Break and enter	Illegal entry or attempted entry into a residence or other building on the victim's property.
	Motor vehicle/ parts theft	Theft or attempted theft of a car, truck, van, motorcycle, moped or other vehicle or part of a motor vehicle.
	Theft of household property	Theft or attempted theft of household property such as liquor, bicycles, electronic equipment, tools or appliances.
	Vandalism	Willful damage of personal or household property.

- Overall, for the four personal crimes that were examined, the rates for men and women were very similar. Higher rates of victimization were reported by young people (15 to 24 years), urban dwellers, and those with household incomes under $15,000.

- For the four household crimes, the rate of victimization was once again higher for urban residents. However, households with higher income ($60,000+) had a higher rate than households with lower incomes. As well, the rate of household crime was highest for people living in a semi-detached, row house or duplex compared with an apartment or single home. Rates were higher for those who rented rather than owned their home.

- Victimization rates tended to be higher in western Canada. Among the ten provinces, British Columbia had the highest rates of both personal and household victimization in 1999, due partly to higher rates for theft of personal and household property. Newfoundland, New Brunswick and Nova Scotia had the lowest rates of personal victimization, while Prince Edward Island, Newfoundland and New Brunswick had the lowest household victimization rates.

- The majority of Canadians believe that crime levels are stable. In 1999, 54% of the population believed that crime in their neighbourhood had stayed the same in the last five years. This was up considerably from the figure of 43% recorded by the 1993 GSS.

- The GSS results indicate that a large proportion of the population is satisfied with their personal safety and that this percentage is growing. In particular, 91% of Canadians reported being very or somewhat satisfied with their personal safety in 1999, an improvement from 86% in 1993. Additionally, people felt safer in a variety of situations, such as when home alone, walking alone or using public transportation alone after dark.

- Canadians are quite satisfied with the job being done by their local police. They are far less satisfied with the performance of the criminal courts, the prison and the parole systems.

Discussion Question

To what degree do the images of crime presented in this victimization survey report coincide with those presented in official data?

Source: S. Besserer and C. Trainor. (2000). Criminal Victimization in Canada, 1999. *Juristat Service Bulletin* 20(10). Ottawa: Canadian Centre for Justice Statistics, Statistics Canada, Cat. No. 85-002.

victimization and self-reported crime surveys (Box, 1981). With the exception of a few American studies of delinquency (Elliot and Ageton, 1980), self-report surveys enumerate mostly trivial offences. Victimization surveys do not ask questions about respondents' experiences with consensual vice crimes. Involvement in "victimless" crimes such as drug use, gambling, and prostitution remain unmeasured. Other crimes regularly omitted from victimization studies include disturbing the peace and public drunkenness. Furthermore, since victimization studies confine themselves to individuals as respondents, they provide no estimates of crimes, such as vandalism and arson, that are most often suffered by organizations (Nettler, 1984).

Neither type of survey investigates murder. Asking someone to report his or her experience as a direct victim of murder is impossible; requesting someone to confess to a homicide on a self-report crime survey invokes a myriad of ethical and legal problems. These concerns aside, murder is such a rare event that it is very unlikely that samples of the sizes currently used would include a murderer. Even if criminologists included questions on homicide, few would confess to committing it. Finally, there is no need to collect survey data on homicides because official statistics reflect its incidence with considerable accuracy.

The way in which survey researchers select respondents for inclusion in their samples also causes problems. Canadian self-report crime studies tend to use **nonrandom samples**. Moreover, because adolescent samples are most easily derived from student rosters, they exclude school dropouts and street youth. These omissions are very significant because it is precisely these types of youth who are most likely to commit serious delinquent acts (Empey, 1982).

While the CUVS in 1981 collected data from Canadians living in large cities, the victimization experiences of residents of small towns and rural areas remain unexplored. Whether or not urban and rural Canadians have similar experiences with property and violent crime cannot be assessed from CUVS data. The GSS (1993; 1999) is more representative but the information gathered is not as detailed. The VAWS (1993) focuses exclusively on violence and female victims. Also, because all three samples were based on households, researchers were unable to document the victimization experiences of transients.

Criminal acts, particularly serious crimes, are comparatively rare events. Their rarity poses problems because researchers must draw enormously large samples to capture the entire range of relevant offences. The CUVS sample size, for example, exceeded 61 000 Canadians. Interviewing a group of this size, even by phone, is extremely costly. Because of the great expense, the Canadian government has not repeated the CUVS (except once in one city) and its future remains uncertain. By comparison, the United States government conducts its National Crime Survey yearly (Waldron, 1989).

Compared with the samples drawn for the CUVS, the sizes of self-report delinquency samples in Canada tend to be small. They are also small in comparison with similar studies in the United States. The largest American investigation to date employed a national sample of several thousand youth (Elliott and Ageton, 1980), who were asked about their involvement in a variety of forms of illegal conduct, both trivial and serious. This study was longitudinal; separate face-to-face interviews were conducted with respondents at regular points in time over several years. For studies of delinquency in Canada, the emphasis on trivial offences, the relatively small sizes of the samples, and the selection of samples from student populations combine to obscure the extent of serious offending. Hardcore career criminality perpetrated by Canadian youth remains almost entirely uninvestigated.

While victimization and self-report crime surveys are by no means perfect, they do offer certain advantages. First, both approaches probably provide reasonably valid estimates of the illegal behaviours they are designed to measure. Second, rather than having to rely on data gathered by the police for law-enforcement purposes, survey researchers gather data directly to meet their own particular needs. Consequently, social scientists regularly include theoretically relevant questions in interview schedules and questionnaires. The acquisition of information on respondents' demographic characteristics, social psychological traits, and personal experiences make possible the testing of various competing theories that cite, as causes of deviance and crime, factors such as weak social controls, involvement in deviant subcultures, and poverty. From the point of view of victimization, theories that suggest that becoming a crime victim is related to one's age, sex, the routine activities comprising one's lifestyle, and so forth may be assessed. Researchers use data collected in surveys to confirm or reject existing theoretical formulations and to develop new ones.

The images of deviance and crime provided by data from official sources and surveys of victims and criminals can be likened to aerial photographs. While such snapshots offer, from distant vantage points, informative glimpses of broad and general patterns, they unavoidably leave obscure much of the finer detail regarding the nature and processes of involvement in deviant and criminal lifestyles. The precise dynamics of interaction that enable experienced prostitutes to encourage neophytes to join their ranks cannot be captured in official data on prostitution. Likewise, insights into the process of developing a positive self-concept in the context of homosexuality cannot be gleaned from survey data on gay men and women.

PARTICIPANT OBSERVATION

Participant observation is a nonquantitative approach that offers techniques for examining how individuals normally think and act in their natural habitats (Strauss, 1987). Sociologists of deviance and crime have carried out research in such natural environments as streets (Visano, 1987), street corners (Leibow, 1967), video arcades (Ellis and Choi, 1984), pool halls (Polsky, 1969), brothels and gay baths and bars in both "shady" and exclusive hotels (Prus and Irini, 1988), public restrooms (Humphreys, 1970), and even the territory of an organized crime family (Ianni, 1972).

Participant observation differs from official records and surveys because it requires researchers to encounter subjects directly on their own turf in real-life situations. By watching, listening, and asking questions, the participant observer attempts to understand particular social worlds as they are understood by their inhabitants. Careful documentation of the ways in which people in their own milieu behave and interact with one another, define their situations, and interpret events forms the core of participant observation. A major advantage of this technique is that it allows the researcher to enter the field without preconceived ideas. The subjects themselves dictate what factors are most relevant and what processes and issues deserve detailed description and explanation.

In participant observation, the emphasis placed on participation varies from one study to the next. Clearly, full participation in some forms of deviant and criminal activity could be ethically unacceptable, inordinately dangerous, or both. Most often, sociologists participate in only some of the group's activities. By participating at least partially, they are better able to fit into the group being investigated and to establish and build rapport with its members. As pseudo-members of these groups, investigators are able to elicit a broad range of information through direct observation of group interaction, by listening to the discussions of group members, and through informal unstructured interviews.

Some participant observers participate in some minor way in the deviant activity under examination, while others associate with subjects only when they are not actively violating rules. In his study of homosexual exchanges in public restrooms in an American state, Laud Humphreys (1970) performed the relatively minor role of "watch-queen." While the central participants, the "insertor" and the "insertee," engaged in oral sex in the "tea room," Humphreys kept watch to guard against interruption by police, "gay-bashing" youths, or unsuspecting members of the public.

Participant observation studies vary in the degree to which the researcher is integrated into the group's activities. In his study of an outlaw motorcycle gang in Western Canada, Wolf (1991) partook fully of club activities. Prus and Sharper (1977), in their examination of Canadian road hustlers, operated at close quarters with a confidence gang. More typical, however, are researchers who associate with their subjects in their law-abiding activities but do not participate at all in the group's deviant or criminal activities. Three Canadian examples of this approach are West's (1983) investigation of serious thieves, Prus and Irini's (1988) study of hotel prostitutes, and Visano's (1987) examination of young male prostitutes.

At the opposite end of the participation scale is Desroches's (1990) study of sexual exchanges in men's restrooms in several Canadian communities. In seeking to replicate Humphreys's work in this area, Desroches conducted lengthy interviews with police officers who had conducted investigations and laid charges in a variety of cases. Unknown to the participants in these particular tea-room exchanges, the police had installed video cameras in strategic locations. Their taped exploits formed the basis for Desroches's analysis.

Participant observers enter the field in a variety of ways. They may frequent establishments like arcades or pool halls or haunt strategic areas like street corners and bars. While participating in normal activities and conversing with people of particular interest, they develop initial contacts. It is common for these initial key informants later to serve as intermediaries and

Box 9.3
AN EXAMPLE OF CANADIAN RESEARCH
USING PARTICIPANT OBSERVATION

In gathering data for his analysis of the social organization of serious thieving, West (1979) used participant observation techniques. While access to a delinquent population is often problematic, West was able to make connections through his earlier work with youth. He had been employed as a camp counsellor, boys' club organizer, and youth worker between 1963 and 1969 and had some contact with between 200 and 300 working-class boys. He began his formal research in 1971.

Since the lack of a clearly defined population of serious thieves made random sampling impossible, he used purposive sampling with key informants. In classic participant observation fashion, West actually lived in his subjects' neighbourhood for twelve months. In beginning his work, he traded on his personal relationships with some of the boys and, by so doing, gained multiple entry into six delinquent groups.

He began collecting data by casually associating with the two groups that were crime-prone. He observed and recorded his accounts of family exchanges, "work" activities, and leisure pursuits on 143 days over thirteen months. After being in the field for about a quarter of this time, West undertook formal, structured, in-depth interviews with 40 of the serious thieves, two of their non-thieving peers, two professional thieves, and four "fences." Most of his subjects were interviewed more than once in sessions ranging from 90 to 120 minutes.

West recorded his observations immediately after his excursions into the field. To test the accuracy of his recall, he taped two interviews while making his notes as usual (without the assistance of the electronic recording). Later, to check validity, he compared the taped interviews with the information recorded in his notes. Finding that his recall was better than 90 percent, he carried on without the tape recorder, the use of which might have interfered with the rapport he had built with his delinquent subjects.

West's work is a good example of grounded theory. When he first entered the field, he was interested in exploring some aspect of delinquency in the context of adolescent peer groups. After a few interviews, he learned that many of his subjects were heavily involved in theft to generate income, so West drew upon sociological literature in the fields of work and occupations as well as deviance to form and refine his research questions. His subsequent field research pointed to secrecy and trust as key processes and conceptual constructs organizing the social world of the serious thief.

After each interview in the field, West expanded his analysis of the role of secrecy and trust in the lives of his acquisitive delinquents. When new data confirmed his working hypotheses, he elaborated his framework. When they did not, he generated revised accounts with modified postulates. Through this process, West constructed an account of the conditions under which trust is established in solving the problems that are integral to clandestine criminal enterprise.

To further validate his impressions of the social organization of the world of serious thieves, West used another means common to participant observation work. He asked seven of his informants to read drafts of his reports and to make suggestions for modifications. Through this strategy, he encouraged several of his subjects to offer some entirely new insights that further enriched his understanding of their subculture.

West also highlights a major problem associated with using participant observation to study those who routinely break the law. He was inadvertently involved at the scene of several thefts and, by his own admission, he could have been held accountable as an accomplice before and after the fact. His presence while thefts were occurring and goods were being fenced was not without ethical ramifications.

West's research revealed much of the world of serious thieves that was hitherto unknown. Among his findings: serious thieves do not possess specialized criminal skills, are nonmigratory, and are seldom able to "fix" cases that come to the attention of the police. Their earnings run in the hundreds, not thousands, of dollars. Among other things, West notes that serious thieves define their work with an ethical code that exempts from victimization the old and the very young, the helpless, and the impoverished. Subcultural values and norms also militate against the use of unnecessary violence. As with other organized criminal groups, secrecy and loyalty are paramount and take precedence over moral evaluations and self-interested action.

Discussion Questions

What ethical issues arise for the participant observer of criminal groups? Should social scientists be exempt from criminal charges for not reporting the crimes they observe?

Source: W.G. West. (1979). "Trust Among Serious Thieves." *Crime and/et Justice* 7/8:239–46. Copyright University of Ottawa Press, 1979.

sponsors who can introduce researchers to other group members and who can vouch for their integrity.

Whether participant observers should reveal their identities as social researchers to their subjects is a matter of some controversy. If subjects know they are being studied, this awareness may cause them to alter their behaviours or exclude observers altogether. One view holds that it is unnecessary to obtain the informed consent of subjects so long as they are not exploited, exposed to the scrutiny of the public or the police, or harmed in any other way. The opposing argument maintains that all people have rights to privacy and autonomy and that they should decide whether they wish to be involved in a study.

In his exploration of homosexual exchanges in public washrooms, Humphreys did not inform his subjects of his identity as a sociologist. When his research was published, his "deception in the name of science" caused considerable controversy. One of Humphreys's interests was to document the tea-room participants' backgrounds. His strategy for acquiring this information involved jotting down his subjects' automobile licence plate numbers as they left the location, tracing the plate numbers, donning a suit, and visiting the subjects' homes in the guise of someone doing a social health survey. After performing a bogus interview, he was able to construct background sketches of many of the men. Humphreys discovered, using what many have argued were highly unethical tactics, that many of the participants in impersonal homosexual exchanges were married and had children.

Participant observation studies employ nonrandom and judgemental samples (Lofland, 1984). Researchers usually include subjects in the sample on the basis of the nature and quality of their knowledge of the group or the phenomenon under examination. Samples selected in this fashion are called "purposive" samples because researchers select subjects with a spe-

cific purpose in mind. Social scientists interested in studying bar prostitutes might begin by talking to taxi drivers, who might be asked questions about the "action" in particular hotels, about the sort of clientele who frequent the various establishments, and about the management of the various operations. Researchers might then try to discover the names of well-known bartenders, bouncers, and prostitutes, contact the most promising of them, informally interview them, and, after building rapport, observe them over a period of time in at least some of their daily activities. This particular way of selecting subjects and gradually increasing the size of a purposive sample is known as "snowballing." Since purposive samples are nonrandom, however, findings cannot be generalized to larger populations in any straightforward way. In the above example, it might be found that pimps play no role in the lives of bar prostitutes in a particular city. Because the sample is nonrandom, it could not be inferred from this finding that Canadian pimps exert no control over bar prostitutes.

Participant observers usually derive their data from some combination of unstructured interviewing and direct observation. Unstructured interviews resemble inquisitive conversations. Researchers do not construct standardized questions in advance, as they do for surveys. Rather, they decide "on the spot" what the most fruitful lines of inquiry will be. Since these interviews are unstructured, they are much more relaxed and natural and usually do not seem to the informants to be interviews.

While researchers sometimes take notes during these "guided conversations," they often rely on their memories. Observers record the information as soon as an opportunity to slip away for this purpose presents itself. In their records, they carefully describe the behaviours, interaction sequences, and norms guiding action in the setting. They also document the informants' attitudes, values, and beliefs. Finally, separate from the description and the documentation, researchers note their preliminary analyses of data for careful consideration at a later stage (Lofland, 1984).

Unlike survey respondents, subjects in a participant observation study cannot be granted anonymity because the observer cannot help but know who they are. Researchers normally assure subjects that their identities will remain confidential and that findings will be reported so as to make it impossible for readers to link certain information to specific respondents. To ensure that identities are protected, for example, it is common for researchers to use pseudonyms when making references in published accounts to subjects, establishments, institutions, and even cities.

Many problems confront the sociologist wishing to use participant observation to study deviance or crime (Schatzman and Strauss, 1973). Both accessibility to informants and the forthrightness of their responses can be problematic when the activity being investigated is socially devalued and prone to negative social or legal sanction. Deviants and criminals are often a secretive lot because they clearly have something to lose if incriminating information falls into the wrong hands. Consequently, people may disguise or completely alter certain aspects of their behaviour or refuse to participate because they fear being informed on or are ashamed of what they do. In short, the presence of an observer may significantly change important aspects of what is being observed.

Participant observation is demanding for the researcher. These studies are very time consuming; gaining access to informants, building rapport, staying on the scene long enough to make enough observations, constantly having to think on one's feet, and having to analyze data continuously make this form of research more than challenging. There are also long periods of boredom in which little of consequence occurs.

The success of participant observation depends a good deal on observers' patience, flexibility, and willingness to withstand demands made on their home lives. For example, as Visano (1987) notes, street kids associate with dangerous people and are sometimes dangerous themselves. Moreover, they are young, active at all hours, sleep on sidewalks, smoke heavily, and survive on junk food and coffee. Fitting in with a group like this is difficult for many sociologists.

Maintaining the correct distance between themselves and their subjects is often tricky for participant observers. Remaining aloof or becoming identified with particular individuals or segments in a group can potentially alienate at least some of its members. On the other hand, becoming overly involved and sharing first-hand the experiences of group members can result in researchers' losing their objectivity (Lofland, 1984).

Participant observation can be particularly troublesome when researchers become witnesses or unknowing accessories to crimes. If they report a crime, observers destroy their rapport, sacrifice their projects, and run the risk of retaliation. If they try to stop a crime, their interference in natural group activity inevitably changes the nature and dynamic of the group. If they do nothing, someone may suffer a loss or an injury and the researchers may be charged with an offence. There are no easy answers for social scientists in these situations.

Despite the drawbacks of participant observation, the method often provides the only way to study little-understood groups and their illicit activities. Its major strengths are the detail of description and depth of understanding it provides, which can be gained only from a careful study of groups in their own milieu.

Data on deviance and crime enable researchers to describe the distribution of these phenomena in society and to identify some of the conditions associated with their various forms. The substantive chapters that follow examine in some detail particular types of deviance and crime. They rely on data generated by official agencies, surveys, and participant observation studies. To introduce these chapters, the general profile of deviance and crime contained in data from these sources should be investigated. First, the distribution of deviance and crime by age, sex, ethnicity, and social class is examined. Second, the ways in which social scientists use theory to explain the links between these social traits and nonconforming conduct are explored.

AGE

THE DATA

Official data indicate that most who break criminal laws in Canada are young. This finding holds true for both violent and property offences, although those committing violent offences tend to be slightly older.

Figure 9.4 displays the results of an analysis for 1999 of the relationship between age and violent and property crime. Those 14 to 19 are at considerable

FIGURE 9.4

AGE SPECIFIC RATES OF PERSONS ACCUSED OF VIOLENT AND PROPERTY CRIME, DATA FROM 164 POLICE AGENCIES, 1999

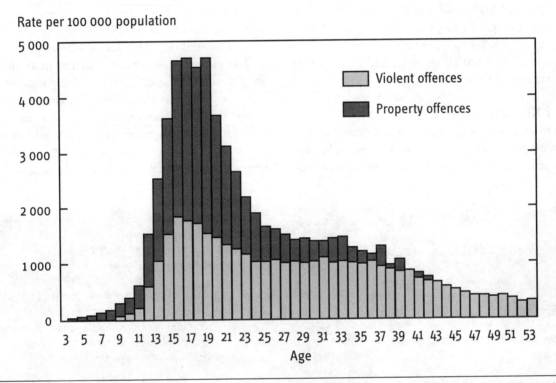

Source: S. Tremblay. (2000). Canadian Crime Statistics, 1999. *Juristat Service Bulletin* 20(5). Ottawa: Canadian Centre for Justice Statistics, Statistics Canada, Cat. No. 85-002.

risk of committing both property and violent offences. It should be noted, however, that people in this age group perpetrate a third of all property crimes but only a fifth of all violent crime. This difference in volume means that the median age for persons accused of property crimes (23 years old) is lower than for those accused of violent crimes (29 years) (Tremblay, 2000).

This pattern holds remarkably constant across nations and over time. Official data for 1994 indicate that Canadian youth are charged with criminal offences more frequently than would be expected given their proportions in the general population. While young people aged 12 to 17 represent 10 percent of the population aged 12 and over, they account for 22 percent of crimes for which an offender was identified. An examination of conviction rates for indictable offences by age group for 1973 (the last year in which such data were collected in Canada)

reveals a similar pattern for the age–crime relationship (Hartnagel, 1987). The peak age for criminal involvement in Canada (except Quebec and Alberta) was 18 to 19. The conviction rate per 100 000 for that age group was 2119.7. For those aged 16 to 17, the comparable rate was 1650. For those a few years older, in the 20 to 24 and 25 to 29 age groups, the rates fell to 1322.2 and 716.5, respectively. Rates for those over 30 years of age were even lower.

Survey data confirm the image apparent in official statistics. Self-reports of respondents aged 18 and over in three Canadian cities indicate that adults under the age of 30 reported committing offences far more frequently than did the middle-aged and the elderly (Gomme, 1986b). In some victimization studies, victims of personal crime have been asked to provide information on offenders. Where they have been able to do so, respondents confirm that most of their attackers are young (Johnson, 1986).

The picture presented for victims in survey data is similar to that for perpetrators. The 1999 GSS indicates that victimization is highest among young adults and declines steadily with age. Young people aged 15 to 24 report the highest rates of personal victimization at 405 per 1000. The rates for the groups aged 25 to 34, 35 to 44, and 45 to 54 are 262, 170, and 128. Those aged 55 to 64 and those 65 and older have the lowest rates of victimization at 64 and 27 per 1000 (Besserer and Trainor, 2000).

THE EXPLANATION

The association of youthfulness and crime is one of the most persistent in criminological research. Two important considerations are warranted, however.

First, there are exceptions to the rule. Certain types of deviance and crime, such as homosexuality, gambling, and some mental illnesses are more evenly distributed across the age spectrum. Second, investigations routinely exclude certain forms of nonconforming and illegal conduct. Many white-collar and corporate crimes are carried out by middle-aged executives, and many leaders of the Mafia are middle-aged or elderly.

The young, however, commit the lion's share of deviant acts and street crimes. Many reasons have been put forward to account for this. One explanation is that the young possess the physical strength and agility required to commit many personal and property crimes. Another is that young people are over-represented in official statistics, partly because police

---

BOX 9.4
CHANGING DEMOGRAPHICS AND THE CRIME RATE

The decline in crime rates since the early 1900s has coincided with the decreasing proportion of persons aged 15 to 24 during this time period. This group is recognized as those who commit a large number of criminal offences as well as being victims of crime. In 1999, persons aged 15–24 years represented 15% of the total population while accounting for 43% of those charged with property crimes and 30% of persons charged with violent crimes.

The figure shows the trend in overall crime and in the number of 15 to 24 year-olds as rates per 100,000 population. Between 1962 and 1978, both lines show a constant increase: the crime rate climbed 158%, while the rate of 15 to 24 year-olds increased by 34%. However, while crime continued to increased until peaking in 1991, the rate of 15 to 24 year-olds declined. Since 1991, both measures have decreased: the crime rate by 25% and the population 15 to 24 by 6%. In summary, variations in the size of the high-risk offender age group have had some effect on the crime rate, but the amount of this influence is not clear, and other factors have also influenced the crime rate trend.

The third line on the graph represents the important growing segment of the population aged 55 and over. In 1999, this age group represented 21% of the population. Contrary to the 15–24 age group, the 55+ age group is characterized by very low involvement in crime, both as accused and as victims, yet is most fearful of being a crime victim. This group is increas-

ing by an average of 2.5% each year, and is projected to grow continuously from now until 2020. The growth of this segment of the population will certainly have an influence on criminality as well as police practices over the years to come.

CRIME RATE AND DEMOGRAPHICS, CANADA, 1962–1999

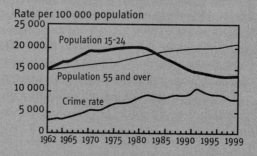

Source: S. Tremblay. (2000). *Canadian Crime Statistics, 1999. Juristat Service Bulletin* 20(5). Ottawa: Canadian Centre for Justice Statistics, Statistics Canada, Cat. No. 85-002.

Discussion Question

Crime rates are at least partially associated with changes in society's age structure. Given that the number of Canadians aged 15 to 24 is expected to grow in the first decade of this century, what impacts might be anticipated for Canadian crime rates?

and court officials expect trouble from this age group and react swiftly to the trouble they do find with formal controls. Yet another account is that young people lack the experience and finesse that enable experienced criminals to avoid detection and apprehension (Nettler, 1984).

A more elaborate theory of the age–crime association is developed by David Greenberg (1980), who cites the social location of the young in contemporary urban industrial society as the key to understanding their involvement in crime. He argues that the young in Western society experience a role ambiguity that generates stresses and strains that in turn are resolved by committing deviant and criminal acts. Specifically, Greenberg argues that in modern industrial societies, adolescence is an age of transformation. While adolescent boys and girls are freed from many of the constraints placed upon them in childhood, they are denied status as full-fledged adults. Advertising, peer pressure, and parental encouragement converge to pressure those aged 16 to 19, in particular, to behave as mature and responsible grown-ups. At the same time, however, they are excluded from many of the rewards of adulthood. The way in which Canadian society is structured cuts young people off from jobs, incomes, and full-fledged intimate relationships. At the same time, society severely constrains their participation in leisure activities. Earning and spending money, having sex, and drinking beer to unwind are restricted both socially and legally.

In an **age-segregated society** like Canada, the young are cut off from the world of adults. Without the countervailing influences of grown-ups, adolescents form a youth culture with its own norms, values, and beliefs. Life in this subculture involves strong peer pressures aimed at social and material conformity. Cigarettes, make-up, DVDs, MP3 players, clothes, and automobiles not only offer pleasure and escape, they also confer status. Possessing and consuming these essentials requires a good deal of money. Since teenagers' major source of income is their parents and since allowances are rarely sufficient to meet their needs, youth experience a good deal of strain. The need for money, the exclusion from the labour market, and the intense peer pressure combine to propel the young toward illegal strategies aimed at satisfying their material needs.

Besides these strains and the ambiguities, youth face other conditions that promote deviance. Adolescents are heavily dependent on and controlled by their parents at home and by their teachers at school.

Dependency and control breed rebellion. Rebellion itself may be construed as deviant, or it may produce a short-term involvement in crime.

Hirschi and Gottfredson (1983) present a detailed critique of the age–crime explanations examined thus far. They point out that the age–crime association persists even among young people possessing traits that the above explanations suggest should militate against nonconformity and illegal conduct. Even within low-risk categories (those who have jobs, who have a lot of money to spend, who are out of school, who are married, and who are independent), the young are more involved in deviance and crime than are older people with comparable traits. Hirschi and Gottfredson also point out that the relationship between age and participation in rule breaking has persisted throughout history and in different types of societies. According to Hirschi and Gottfredson, increasing pressures upon youth in modern urban industrialized capitalist societies inadequately explain the age–crime relationship. They point out that in both previous feudal societies and current socialist societies, the young continue to be over-represented among deviants and criminals. Nonetheless, some analysts take issue with Hirschi and Gottfredson's position, citing evidence suggesting that aging out of crime is hastened by finishing school, getting married, and having children, and is retarded by exposure to deviant peers (Rand, 1987; Warr, 1993).

SEX

THE DATA

Regardless of the data-collection method, males dominate among deviants and criminals. Official data indicate that police charged men with 82 percent of criminal offences in 1999. (See Figure 9.5.) Although charged with only 18 percent of offences overall, women accounted for 53 percent of prostitution offences, 30 percent of thefts $5000 and under (mostly shoplifting), 29 percent of frauds, and 40 percent of abductions (Tremblay, 2000). (See Figure 9.6.) Data also show that while men and women are equally likely to be the victims of officially recorded violent crime, women made up the majority of sexual assault victims (85 percent) and slightly over half of level I assault victims (53 percent). Men were over-represented as victims of robbery (61 percent) and more serious level II and III assaults (65 percent and 79 percent, respectively) (Hendrick, 1996).

FIGURE 9.5

CRIMINAL CODE OFFENCES

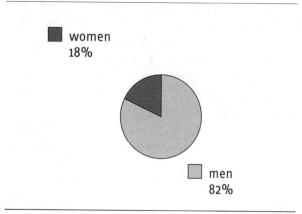

Source: *Juristat Service Bulletin* 20(5). Ottawa: Canadian Centre for Justice Statistics, Statistics Canada, p. 20, Cat. No. 85-002.

Survey data present a similar profile. Victims who observe the person offending against them usually report that these offenders are male. Self-report surveys also show that males outnumber females in committing deviant and criminal acts. As in the official data, the gap separating male and female self-reported deviance and crime is especially large for incidents involving violence and aggression (Gomme, Morton, and West, 1984).

The 1999 GSS indicates that violent victimizations are very similar for men and women (112 per 1000 and 109 per 1000, respectively). Women represent the majority of sexual assault victims with a rate of 33 per 1000 (compared to men at 8 per 1000). Men are more likely than women to be victims of both assault (92 compared to 70 per 1000) and robbery (12 compared to 7 per 1000) (Besserer and Trainor, 2000).

THE EXPLANATION

Sociologists explain the under-representation of females among deviants and criminals in three related ways: sex role socialization, differential social control, and variations in opportunity. In Canada and the United States, females learn from an early age to be compliant, deferential, and nonaggressive. Males are expected to be more defiant of authority, more assertive, more willing to take risks, and more aggressive. Furthermore, they are rewarded for displaying these traits. Sociologists suggest that these fundamentally different patterns of socialization encourage conformity among females while discouraging it among males.

FIGURE 9.6

SEX AND SELECTED OFFENCES

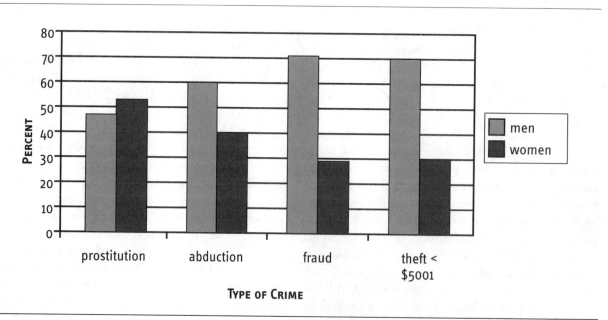

Source: *Juristat Service Bulletin* 20(5). Ottawa: Canadian Centre for Justice Statistics, Statistics Canada, p. 20, Cat. No. 85-002.

Box 9.5
STATS SHOW CRIME IS DOWN — SO WHY DON'T WE BELIEVE THEM?

The common wisdom on crime isn't common sense.

The average citizen — influenced by politicians and the media — is convinced our young people are dangerous, our streets are filled with gunfire and our backyards are haunted by murderers and rapists.

Yet the numbers say otherwise. Statistics Canada's annual crime report this week revealed that the crime rate in every kind of offence — with the exception of marijuana possession — has gone down relentlessly for eight years.

Consider the following:

- A growing number of women report carrying a weapon, taking self-defence courses and staying home at night to protect themselves from strangers. But it's people they know who present the greater threat. Women are almost five times more likely to be killed by a spouse than a stranger.

- Premier Mike Harris has announced two more boot camps for young offenders and a strict code of conduct in schools, yet the youth crime rate dropped 7 per cent last year. That includes a 5 per cent drop in violent crime and an 11 per cent decrease in property crime.

- Violent crime fell 2.4 per cent last year across Canada, the seventh straight decline.

- Parents are taking all kinds of measures to protect their children from strangers, yet abductions account for only 0.2 per cent of all violent crime, and six in 10 abducted children are taken by a parent.

- The highest murder rate for any age group is among babies younger than one year — and 21 of the 23 victims last year were killed by a parent.

The list goes on. But perceptions won't budge.

"The data overwhelmingly shows that women should hang out with strangers and yet we have this image of the streets being fearful places," says demographer David Baxter.

Claire Sinclair, for example. When she moved into her Eglinton Ave. and Allen Expressway apartment in 1969 she never locked her door.

"Now I lock and deadbolt it, and I even have a security system," says the 68-year-old tour guide.

REALITY CHECK

The majority of Canadians think that crime is increasing when in reality, it's going down.

	Perception % who think crime is on the rise	Reality % change in crime rate '98-'99
Fraud	71%	−5.2%
Property crime	62%	−6.4%
Violent crime	59%	−2.4%
Family violence	60%	−2%*

* change '95-'98

Source: Ekos Research, Statistics Canada

Sinclair dreads returning to her building's underground parking lot alone.

"It's worrying, waiting in the basement for that elevator, day or night," she says. "I won't go out alone at night, because I've got this to deal with when I get home."

A survey by Ekos Research in December found that six in 10 Canadians believe violent crimes, family violence and property crimes are increasing, although all are falling.

"In recent years, an increasing number of non-news television shows such as COPS, its Canadian equivalent To Serve and Protect, America's Most Wanted and American Justice have been created to meet North Americans' seemingly insatiable appetite for 'real life' stories of crime," an Ekos analysis said.

"It is not surprising therefore to find that most Canadians perceive that crime is on the increase, in spite of the reality that most types of crime are actually decreasing."

But it's not all television's fault. The day Statistics Canada released its crime figures, Mayor Mel Lastman announced that a cornerstone of his re-election campaign will be ending lawlessness on Toronto streets.

"I want to bring back the idea you can walk the streets at night," he told reporters.

Yet violent crimes in Greater Toronto fell by 3.9 per cent last year from the year before, and property crimes fell by 6.5 per cent. Toronto has the third lowest crime rate of any city in Canada – and the nation's lowest break-in rate.

"If you're going to have a law-and-order government, you have to create a crisis so you can solve it," says Vince Carlin, chair of journalism at Ryerson Polytechnic University.

"We have a provincial government that used an attack on squeegee kids as the centerpiece of its re-election campaign, when I've never seen an illegal act performed by one."

Carlin says that when he came to Canada from the States 30 years ago, Canadian television news focused on issues and events. Viewers flipped to the Buffalo channels to catch the latest crime news.

"But all that has eroded," he says. "Our media are dominated by crime and violence. You can easily come away from every evening's television news with the belief we live in a crime-ridden society."

U.S. politicians began in the mid-'90s to take credit for dropping crime rates. Finally, the public began to buy it.

It was a hard battle to convince Americans that crime is down, says David Murray of the Washington-based Statistical Assessment Service, who marvels that Canadians believe they live in unsafe times. Part of the problem is we're getting less tolerant of crime.

"You've got an unusually swollen baby boom cohort in their 40s and 50s who think about this stuff more than they did in their 20s and 30s," says Frank Graves, president of Ekos Research.

"News accounts provide this constant evidence of grisly violence," he says. "People don't read the social indicators and crime statistics. They draw their images from what they see on the suppertime news hour and read in the paper, reinforced by popular culture."

Lydia Miljan of the Vancouver-based Fraser Institute analyzed CTV and CBC television coverage of murder over 10 years. She found that even as

the murder rate fell dramatically in the mid-'90s, coverage of murder stories soared.

"The story that gets all the attention is a young woman abducted by a stranger," she says. "It makes for a more frightened society, because you think it can happen to anyone. But it's very difficult to get murdered in this country."

University of Toronto criminologist Tony Doob says the claim that crime is on the rise often goes unchallenged.

"I hear people start sentences all the time with 'because crime is a growing problem in our society.' Why shouldn't people think it's much worse?

"Just try to get Mel Lastman or Mike Harris to say, 'Crime is down, so let's do everything we can to keep it down,'" he said.

Television coverage

The number of news stories about murder on national television networks in Canada peaked in 1994, well after Canada's murder rate began to drop

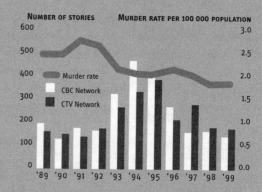

Source: The National Media Archive (Toronto Star graphic)

Discussion Questions

Given the ideas presented in this article, how socially responsible are Canada's media? Why does·the claim of rising crime rates so often go unchallenged?

Source: Elaine Carey, *Toronto Star*, July 23, 2000, p. A1 and A11. Reprinted with permission from The Toronto Star Syndicate.

Besides being socialized differently, males and females are socially controlled to different extents (Hagan, Simpson, and Gillis, 1979). Females, particularly when young, are subjected to many informal social restrictions. Parents supervise their daughters more closely than they do their sons. Later, boyfriends and husbands continue what parents began. On the other hand, young males enjoy more freedom from supervision, which places them in contexts where deviant and criminal activity is more probable. Young males are more likely than young females to be out on the street at all hours and to associate with people who are also inclined to break rules.

Women are also more restricted in their opportunities to commit certain types of crime. Since there are few women among the corporate elite in Canada and most powerful executive and professional positions belong to males, women have fewer opportunities for business crime. They are also under-represented in higher-status white-collar positions. Furthermore, women are also denied influential positions in criminal organizations. The Mafia, for example, is not an equal-opportunity employer.

While male dominance in deviance and crime is undisputed, females may have been catching up in certain areas in recent years. Some sociologists support the "**role convergence** hypothesis," arguing that increased equality between the sexes in legitimate spheres is spilling over into the realm of deviance and crime (Simon, 1975). The increased labour-force participation of women provides them with more opportunities for committing offences. First, they are less confined to the home and more likely to be independent of the informal social controls placed on them by fathers, boyfriends, and husbands. Second, they have more opportunity to carry out employment-related crimes such as employee theft, forgery, fraud, and embezzlement. Finally, as a result of their increased participation in the labour force they are experiencing the criminogenic stresses formerly experienced only by men.

The convergence hypothesis has its critics (Steffensmeier, 1980). Crimes for which a narrowing gap between female and male participation is most evident include minor property crimes, such as shoplifting, which have always been heavily engaged in by women. Offences of this type are more associated with women's traditional roles. Women steal on the job (shopping) in the same way that men do; it is merely that traditional jobs for men are different. Similarly, critics point out that where women commit fraud, forgery, and embezzlement, their crimes involve smaller sums than do the same crimes committed by males. Furthermore, many such offences involve welfare fraud or forging personal cheques. Where women embezzle, the offence is of the type performed by bank tellers or other low-level bank employees, many of whom are female. Finally, despite changes in sex roles, the evidence indicates that the gap separating male and female participation in violent offences like assault and murder remains virtually unchanged.

Where the gap between male and female offending has narrowed, several sociologists point out that it is difficult to determine whether it is due to changes in women's behaviour or changes in police reaction to female offenders. Police may be more willing to pursue cases against females as a result of broader changes in the perception of the role of women in society. From this perspective, the actual criminal behaviour of women may be virtually unchanged but the police may now be less likely to divert women out of the criminal justice net.

ETHNICITY

THE DATA

Unlike their American counterparts, Canadian police do not systematically tabulate information about the ethnicity of lawbreakers. In the United States, certain groups — particularly blacks and Hispanics — are significantly over-represented in crime statistics (Waldron, 1989). U.S. data for 1992 indicate that African Americans in that country represent about 12 percent of the population but about 45 percent of those arrested for violent offences and 32 percent of those arrested for property crimes (Tonry, 1995).

In Canada, most of the attention paid to this issue has been directed toward the treatment of Native people by the criminal justice system (Griffiths and Verdun-Jones, 1989).

Of Canada's many ethnic and racial groups, Native people are the most over-represented in Canadian jails. While the 1991 census estimates the number of Native Canadians at 2 percent of the population, data indicate that this group represents 24 percent of those in custody for criminal offences (Brantingham, Mu, and Verma, 1995). Recent investigations of crime committed by Native persons in Saskatoon, Regina, Calgary, and Vancouver highlight their over-representation among those accused of violent and property crime (Trevethan, 1993; Griffiths, Wood, Zellerer, and Simon 1994). Table 9.1 shows that Natives are five to nine times as likely as non-Natives to be accused of violent crimes, four to eight times as likely to be accused of property crimes, and three to six times as likely to be victims of violence. Table 9.2 focuses specifically on homicide and demonstrates that rates of perpetration and victimization are also considerably higher for Natives compared to non-Natives (Wood and Griffiths, 2000). In his analysis of federal homicide data for 1999, Fedorowycz (2000) points out that while Natives now account for about 3 percent of the Canadian population, they comprise

TABLE 9.1

PATTERNS OF CRIME AND VICTIMIZATION IN FOUR WESTERN CITIES, 1990 AND 1992

City	% Population That Is Aboriginal	% Aboriginal of Accused of Violent Offences	% Aboriginal of Accused of Property Offences	% Aboriginal of Victims of Violent Offences
Saskatoon	6	36	29	(Not Reported)
Regina	5	47	42	31
Calgary	2	10	8	6
Vancouver	3	17	15	10

Source: D. Wood and C.T. Griffiths. (2000). "Patterns of Aboriginal Crime." In R.A. Silverman, J.J. Teevan, and V.F. Sacco (eds)., *Crime in Canadian Society*. Toronto: Harcourt Brace.

TABLE 9.2

NON-ABORIGINAL AND ABORIGINAL HOMICIDE, SUSPECT AND VICTIM RATES (PER 100 000 POPULATION), BY SELECTED CITIES, 1980–1989

City	Non-Aboriginal Suspects	Aboriginal Suspects	Non-Aboriginal Victims	Aboriginal Victims
Halifax	3.4	0.0	2.9	0.0
Montreal	2.5	0.4	4.3	0.8
Ottawa	1.7	3.8	1.8	0.0
Toronto	2.1	7.5	2.3	4.8
Thunder Bay	1.3	17.4	1.5	15.3
Winnipeg	2.1	25.7	1.6	19.1
Saskatoon	1.1	19.9	1.0	12.9
Regina	0.9	76.6	1.2	45.3
Edmonton	2.6	27.9	2.7	21.1
Calgary	1.7	19.7	1.8	12.5
Vancouver	3.9	15.3	5.5	14.4

Source: D. Wood and C.T. Griffiths. (2000). "Patterns of Aboriginal Crime." In R.A. Silverman, J.J. Teevan, and V.F. Sacco (eds)., *Crime in Canadian Society*. Toronto: Harcourt Brace.

at least 19 percent of homicide suspects and 14 percent of victims.

An earlier study conducted by the Ministry of Indian Affairs and Northern Development (1980) estimated that Natives represented 9 percent of those incarcerated in federal penitentiaries and 40 percent of those behind bars in provincial prisons and local jails.

In Ontario, historically, the rate of Native crime has been 4.5 times that for all other ethnic groups combined. For offences involving Ontario liquor violations, the rate was sixteen times greater for Native than for non-Native groups.

Most of the Native people incarcerated in Canada's jails and provincial institutions have been convicted of relatively minor illegalities such as liquor and motor vehicle offences and failing to pay fines.

THE EXPLANATION

Social scientists explain the over-representation of Native people in lawbreaking by citing a combination of culture conflict, economic inequality, and discrimination. The culture conflict explanation argues that members of the dominant culture consider Native culture objectionable and criminalize certain behaviours of Native people. Shortly after their arrival in Newfoundland, Europeans clashed with the indigenous people. The conflict stemmed in large part from the Beothuk practice of "borrowing" the property of the European fishermen. The more powerful whites responded by initiating the extermination of the "thieves." Canadian law also considered as homicide the Inuit custom of casting out the elderly to die alone in the snows of frigid Arctic winters (Hagan, 1991). The Inuit, however, knew that the drain on scarce food supplies by its unproductive members would threaten the group's survival.

Sociologists also argue that the severely deprived position of Native people in the Canadian class structure and their extreme economic dependency on government propel them into various forms of deviance and crime. Many Native groups across Canada experience acutely the pains engendered by low levels of education, high unemployment, abject poverty, and social isolation, all of which encourage alcohol abuse (Depew, 1986). When a large proportion of a highly visible and impoverished minority drinks to excess, alcoholism and vagrancy are difficult to hide from a disapproving middle class and the police.

Not only are laws regulating alcohol consumption routinely broken by Native people, but excessive alcohol use is also a factor in the commission of other crimes (Gerson and Preston, 1979). Many violent acts involve liquor consumption by either the perpetrator, the victim, or both. Native people also commit many minor alcohol, motor vehicle, and property crimes for which the customary penalty is a fine. The impoverishment of many Native groups, however, routinely makes the payment of fines difficult if not impossible. It is not unusual for failure to pay a fine to result in arrest and incarceration (Moyer, Kopelman, LaPrairie, and Billingsley, 1985).

Discrimination by criminal justice agents and the public also contributes to the over-representation of Native people in crime statistics. A dishevelled appearance, frequent inebriation, and a high visibility in towns near reservations and on big-city skid rows combine to bring Native people to the attention of authorities. Some police officers may reveal their personal prejudices by officially processing "drunken Indians" more frequently than they would "intoxicated" non-Natives. Furthermore, it is more likely that members of the non-Native public will insist to the police that something be done about the "Indian problem."

Finally, Native groups have higher crime rates in part because their members are, on average, younger than their non-Native counterparts. Compared to non-Natives, there is a larger percentage of Native people in the more crime prone 15- to 34-year-old-age bracket (Trevethan, 1993). In a similar vein, Fedorowycz (2000) points out that the high risk age group for committing homicide and other violent crimes is comprised of those between 15 and 34 years of age. While 36 percent of Natives were in this age bracket in 1999, only 28 percent of the rest of the population were in this group.

SOCIOECONOMIC STATUS

THE DATA

According to analyses of official data, there is a significant association between involvement in crime and the combination of low income, lack of education, and lower occupational status. Whether this is due to high rates of offending by the lower classes or to discrimination against the lower classes by the criminal justice system has been a matter of vociferous debate. During the 1960s and the 1970s, several self-report delinquency studies added fuel to this fire by demonstrating that, when the criminal justice filtering process was bypassed by asking respondents

Box 9.6
ABORIGINALS IN CUSTODY — A CAUSE FOR CONCERN

Consistent Aboriginal over-representation has been the focus of much concern, both within the Aboriginal community and the justice system. Aboriginal people represent 2% of the adult population, but accounted for 17% of the admissions to provincial/territorial custody in 1998–99, and the same proportion to federal custody. At the provincial/territorial level, this represents a slight increase (2%) in the proportion of Aboriginal admissions over 1997–98, while the representation of Aboriginal persons as a proportion of federal custodial admissions remained relatively stable.

However, as [the figure in this box] shows, there is considerable variation across the country with respect to the presence of Aboriginal people in the general adult and adult inmate populations. The Western provinces and the territories are home to the largest proportions of Aboriginal persons in the general adult population, as well as the greatest disproportionate representation of adult admissions to custody. For example, in 1998–99 the proportion of Aboriginal persons admitted to adult provincial facilities in Saskatchewan (76%) was almost ten times that of their proportion in the provincial adult population (8%). In Manitoba 59% of admissions to provincial custody were Aboriginal (compared to 9% in the provincial adult population) and in Alberta, 38% of admissions to provincial facilities were Aboriginal persons (compared to 4% in the provincial adult population). In other jurisdictions, the proportion of Aboriginal admissions ranged from twice to ten times their proportion in the provincial/territorial population.

Data from the One-Day Snapshot showed that on Snapshot day, Aboriginal inmates were incarcerated for crimes against the person more often than non-Aboriginal inmates, and had lower levels of education. In addition, a larger proportion of Aboriginal than non-Aboriginal inmates was unemployed at the time of admission. The Snapshot also revealed that a larger proportion of Aboriginal than non-Aboriginal inmates

were classified as a high risk to re-offend, and scored higher in all areas of a general needs assessment, particularly in the area of substance abuse.

Traditional Aboriginal justice practices have generally taken a restorative approach, emphasizing healing and the importance of community involvement in the justice process. When a restorative approach is not used, it is important that programs that are responsive to Aboriginal needs, values and traditions be made available.

REPRESENTATION OF ABORIGINAL ADMISSIONS TO CUSTODY AND IN THE GENERAL CANADIAN ADULT POPULATION, 1998–99

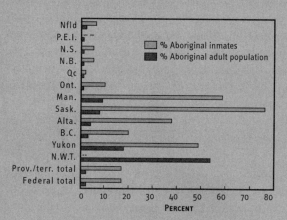

--amount too small to be expressed.
.. figures not available.

Source: Adult Correctional Services Survey, Canadian Centre for Justice Statistics, Statistic Canada, 1996 Census of the Population, 20% Sample, Statistics Canada.

Discussion Question

To what degree do the data and arguments presented in this box support the idea that Canadian society and its criminal justice system are racist?

Source: J. Thomas. (2000). Adult Correctional Services in Canada, 1998–1999. *Juristat Service Bulletin* 20(3). Ottawa: Canadian Centre for Justice Statistics, Statistics Canada, Cat. No. 85-002.

directly about their involvement in delinquency, the association between delinquency and lower-class status disappeared (West, 1984).

Critics of these early self-report delinquency studies pointed out that the items comprising the delinquency scales were restricted in terms of both the seriousness of the delinquent acts and the number of events a respondent could report. Self-report inventories rarely included serious violent offences such as armed robbery, assault with a weapon, and rape. Furthermore, the response categories for delinquency scales in these initial studies were typically "1. never, 2. once or twice, 3. three or four times, 4. five or more times." Therefore, offenders who had committed 100 thefts of under $50 in the past year had the same score as offenders who had stolen one package of cigarettes on five occasions. In short, the activities of high-frequency offenders and of those committing serious crime are inadequately captured by this type of scale. The failure to find a relationship between membership in the lower class and criminal involvement, critics maintained, occurred largely because of the inadequacies inherent in the delinquency scales.

More recent investigations conducted in the United States support these criticisms. In their national longitudinal study of delinquency, Elliott and Ageton (1980) included questions about serious offences and asked respondents to report the actual number of illegal acts that they had committed. Elliott and Ageton found that lower-class youth were four times more likely than middle-class youth to report committing serious predatory offences such as assault and robbery. The class–crime association was weaker for status and minor criminal offences, and stronger for high frequency, more serious offending and for male offenders (Elliott and Huizinga, 1983). Similar patterns have been found in Britain (West, 1982).

One very important consideration to keep in mind when reviewing these findings is that official statistics and survey data usually produce estimates of the volume of street crime, not white-collar and corporate crime. Consequently, what may vary by class is not the frequency but the form of criminal activity. Lower-class people may break, enter, steal, and murder, while higher-class people may defraud, fix prices, and cause death by failing to institute legislated safety regulations in the workplace. Some criminologists speculate that the association between social class and crime is curvilinear (Tittle, Villemez, and Smith, 1978). People who are lowest and highest on the socioeconomic continuum commit the most crime, while those in the middle commit the least. These criminologists also point out, however, that harmful acts committed by the socially advantaged are far more devastating than those committed by the socially disadvantaged. A single incident of corporate wrongdoing, for example, may result in financial loss, injury, or even death for many workers, consumers, or members of the public.

THE EXPLANATION

The explanation of the **social class**–crime relationship has occupied sociologists for some time. Sociologists of the Chicago school stress the disorganization or differential social organization of urban slums by pointing to the socialization processes of the subcultures in these neighbourhoods. Through social learning in these settings, individuals acquire the skills and rationalizations necessary for deviance. Strain theories take a different approach by arguing that blocked legitimate opportunities, combined with access to illegitimate strategies, produce nonconformity and illegal conduct. Lower-class people are denied the education necessary to acquire the jobs that will permit them to accumulate material wealth. Having a desire for financial well-being but denied legal access to it, they adopt illegal means to achieve their ends.

Conflict theories take two approaches in explaining the class–crime correlation. The first is that lower-class people engage in deviance and commit crime as a consequence of the pains of the impoverishment they endure in capitalist society. They drink to drown their sorrows, sell drugs and steal to survive, and become violent out of frustration and the desire to rebel against oppression. The second proposition is that the middle and upper classes create and apply laws that criminalize marginalized lower-class groups. From this perspective, criminal law is a tool that the powerful apply to force compliance from society's disadvantaged and to preserve social order even during social and economic crises. At the same time, the harmful activities of the affluent are unconstrained by the law.

SUMMARY

Social scientists estimate the volume and calculate the rates of various forms of deviance and crime for several reasons. This information permits comparisons of community well-being by geographical areas and over time. It also enables sociologists and criminologists to identify the characteristics of deviants, criminals, victims, and crime scenes and to assess the risks of victimization and perpetration associated with certain settings and situations. Data on deviance and crime are very useful in evaluating crime control, rehabilitation, and treatment policies and programs. Finally, social scientific information provides the opportunity to construct and test social theories of deviant behaviour, criminal offending, personal and property victimization, societal reaction, and social control. The principal data sources are official records, surveys of victims and perpetrators, and participant observation studies.

Official statistics on crime represent crimes that are known by the police to be founded. Before 1962, law-enforcement records were deficient because police created them solely for their own purposes and because different recording techniques were used by various jurisdictions. In 1962, police adopted a standardized Uniform Crime Reporting (UCR) system. The results of UCR reports were compiled by Statistics Canada and published yearly. In 1982, the Centre for Justice Statistics took over this task.

The base of the UCR system is crimes known to the police. From crimes known to the police, law-enforcement agencies calculate crime rates. Calculating rates is important because it enables analysts to study the impact of changes in population on volume of crime. To depict case attrition in the estimation of crime, criminologists use the image of a funnel, in which criminal incidents decline from the top of the funnel (actual crime) through the centre (detected and reported crime) to the bottom (recorded crime).

Many factors affect case attrition in the funnel. Much crime remains undetected. Moreover, many detected crimes never come to the attention of authorities because they are not reported. People choose not to report a crime because they may consider it trivial or tolerable, they may be concerned about their costs in time and effort, or they may be willing participants in victimless vice offences. Others do not report a crime because of their attachment to or fear of the offender, because of the shame and embarrassment that might ensue, or because they either fear or have little faith in the police. Since police must enforce the law selectively, and since most police activity is initiated in response to citizens' reports, the public plays an important gate-keeper role in invoking the machinery of justice and, in the process, counting crime. The volume and rates of crime vary with the reporting practices of the citizenry.

Even when the public reports crime, police do not always record it, especially if it is not serious. Factors affecting police recording include the amount of paperwork involved, the volume of incidents being processed at the time of the report, the wishes of complainants, the demeanour of suspects and victims, the degree of police corruption, the size and organization of the force, and the nature of politically defined enforcement priorities. Some difficulties with the UCR system that have been addressed in the latest procedural modifications include the use of different procedures to count personal and property crime, the lumping together of attempted and completed offences, the enumeration of only the most serious of multiple offences, the insensitivity of the rate formula to population composition and to units at risk, and the failure to collect detailed offence-related information. Distorting influences that are more difficult to deal with include changes in legal categories and counting procedures over time, jurisdictional variations in recording, the inclusion of nonserious offences in overall crime rates, and the use of the census to estimate the base population.

Despite deficiencies, official data are and should be widely used to increase the understanding of crime and to orient policy and program implementation. It is likely that biases resulting from differences in the size and organization of police forces and from variations in recording techniques cancel each other out. The proportions of various types of crime appear constant from one jurisdiction to another. Finally, in Canada at least, official data are the only data collected systematically and annually. While they should be used with caution, they are far better than no data at all. Official data should be even more useful as the new UCR system is fully implemented.

Two types of survey are commonly employed in research on crime and deviance. Using a particular time frame, victimization surveys collect information on people's experiences as direct and indirect victims of crime, while self-report surveys ask people about their involvement in deviant and criminal activities. Both types of survey usually make use of samples, ask questions through interviews or questionnaires, generate quantifiable statistical data, and permit generalizations to be made about the wider populations from which samples are drawn. In Canada there has been only one major study devoted exclusively to victimization, only a handful of self-report delinquency studies, and only one self-report crime study involving adult respondents.

Among the problems plaguing surveys are sampling bias, item wording, the confusion of lay and legal definitions, and varying degrees of respondent honesty and recall. Another drawback of surveys is their almost exclusive concentration on street crime. Furthermore, they omit questions about crimes lacking clearly defined victims and about crimes that target organizations.

Properly executed, surveys provide more accurate estimations of the volume of some forms of crime. Moreover, survey data frequently contain a wealth of information on demographic and situational crime correlates that is highly relevant to both theory construction and policy implementation.

Participant observation is a qualitative data-collection strategy that permits researchers to investigate how people act and think in their natural settings. Depending upon the context, researchers participate in or simply observe the operation of the group and its members. By watching, listening, and asking questions, participant observers investigate their subjects' social worlds and the behaviours, interactions, norms, meanings, and processes embedded in these environments. Because of legal and ethical considerations, social scientists studying deviance and crime participate only partially in the activities of the group under study. The problems of participant observation include gaining access to subjects in sensitive contexts, altering subjects' behaviour with the presence of observers, investing the large amounts of time required for such studies, and enduring the sometimes uncomfortable if not hazardous conditions presented by on-site field work.

Regardless of the type of data-collection strategy employed, the demographic profiles of deviants and criminals are consistent. With very few exceptions, they tend to be young, male, and members of disadvantaged socioeconomic and ethnic groups. Reasons given for the strong age–crime relationship include physical prowess, police reactions, social control, and the patterns of role strain inherent in the experience of the young. Criminologists account for differences in the illegal conduct of men and women in three basic ways: different patterns of socialization, varying means of social control, and differing opportunity structures. Explanations of the over-representation in crime data of members of disadvantaged class and ethnic groups include culture conflict, economic inequality, and discrimination.

In the 1960s, the results of self-report delinquency studies challenged the validity of the strong correlation between socioeconomic status and crime that has traditionally been observed in official data. Recent self-report applications using new instruments have enabled social scientists to find a correlation between these sets of variables. The main reason for the "re-emergence" of this relationship is that contemporary self-report crime instruments contain items that tap serious offences and measurement scales that permit more accurate frequency counts.

Most investigations linking socioeconomic status to crime focus on street crime and ignore business deviance. In light of this observation, some criminologists speculate that the relationship between class and crime is curvilinear, that those at the very bottom and very top of the status hierarchy are the most criminal. Those between the poles, the middle class, are least so.

DISCUSSION QUESTIONS

1. How are crime rates calculated? How useful are they in determining the nature and extent of "the crime problem"? Why must crime rates be interpreted with caution?

2. Discuss the advantages of crime survey statistics in comparison with official data.

3. How and why are age, sex, ethnicity, and socioeconomic status related to deviance and criminality? How does the strength of the relationship between these demographic variables and deviant and criminal activity vary by data-collection method?

4. Discuss the relationship between social class and illegal conduct. How does one's social status affect both the frequency and the nature of his or her participation in deviant and criminal actions?

5. To what extent is the image of the form and extent of Canada's "crime problem" a product of the vested interests of state agencies of social control?

WEB LINKS

Justice and Crime Statistics
http://www.statcan.ca/english/Pgdb/State/justic.htm

This section of the Statistics Canada Web site contains recent statistics on crimes, victims, suspects, criminals, police, and courts for Canada, its regions, provinces, and territories.

Community Profiles
http://www.csc-scc.gc.ca/text/rsrch/community/commun_e.shtml

This section of the Correctional Service of Canada Web site provides access to recent demographic, social, economic, crime, court, and correctional information for 27 Canadian cities. You will need a copy of Acrobat Reader to open these reports.

Male Young Offenders in Canada
http://www.csc-scc.gc.ca/text/rsrch/reports/r78/r78e.shtml

Female Young Offenders in Canada
http://www.csc-scc.gc.ca/text/rsrch/reports/r80/r80e.shtml

These two reports from the Correctional Service of Canada provide information on recent trends with regard to young offenders in Canada.

Adult Male Offenders in Canada: Recent Trends
http://www.csc-scc.gc.ca/text/rsrch/reports/r79/r79e.shtml

Adult Female Offenders in Canada: Recent Trends
http://www.csc-scc.gc.ca/text/rsrch/briefs/b21/b21e.shtml

These two reports available on the Correctional Service of Canada site use data from the Uniform Crime Report Survey and the Adult Criminal Court Survey.

Uniform Crime Reports
http://www.fbi.gov/ucr/ucr.htm

Recent statistics on crime in the United States, from the Federal Bureau of Investigation.

RECOMMENDED READINGS

Babbie, E. and M. Maxfield. (2001). *Research Methods for Criminal Justice and Criminology*. Belmont, CA: Wadsworth.
Presents a very thorough overview of research methods and provides detailed examples from the domains of criminology and criminal justice.

Braithwaite, J. (1981). "The Myth of Social Class and Criminality Reconsidered." *American Sociological Review* 46: 36–57.
Reviews evidence of the class–crime relationship and refutes the argument that this long-observed correlation is a myth.

Farrington, D.P. (1986). "Age and Crime." In M. Tonry and N. Morris (eds.) *Crime and Justice* (pp. 189–250). Chicago: University of Chicago Press.
Investigates various aspects of the correlation between age and crime and examines principal explanations.

Kennedy, L.W. and D. Veitch. (1997). "Why Are Crime Rates Going Down?: A Case Study in Edmonton." *Canadian Journal of Criminology* 39: 51–69.
Examines and seeks to explain the dramatic decline in crime rates in Edmonton in the closing years of the 1990s. Emphasizes the importance of changes in crime reporting, policing strategies, and crime prevention.

Nettler, G. (1984). *Explaining Crime* (3rd ed.). New York: McGraw Hill.
A text that is particularly strong on its presentation of the logic of social scientific investigation and the methodological basics of designing criminological research and interpreting data.

Ouimet, M. (1999). "Crime in Canada and the United States: A Comparative Analysis." *Canadian Review of Sociology and Anthropology* 36: 389–408.
Presents a comparative analysis of Canadian and American crime rates that questions whether they are as different as commonly portrayed.

Statistics Canada. *Juristat.*
Series of short reports, about 20 per year, on various aspects of crime and justice in Canada. Of particular relevance is the issue documenting crime statistics for the previous year. Canadian Crime Statistics, 1999 is the most recent such issue.

Part Four

The Practice of Deviance and Crime

CHAPTER 10

HOMICIDE

The aims of this chapter are to familiarize the reader with:

- legal definitions of homicide in Canada and the categorization of its different forms
- the extent of homicide
- characteristics of offenders, victims, and situations
- characteristics of specific types of homicide: upper-class homicide, serial killing and mass murder, and terrorism
- selected theories of murder: symbolic interactionism, subculture of violence, and deterrence
- issues surrounding the control of murder in Canada: the capital-punishment controversy

INTRODUCTION

Violent crime, especially homicide, has long been the object of public fascination. Romantic stories of masked marauders, gunslinging outlaws, and "trigger-happy" gangsters have captivated many novelists, movie directors, and television newscasters. The mystery novel, the crime drama, and the evening news have popularized violence and, in the process, have distorted its reality. One of the most dramatic misrepresentations is that strangers and psychopaths perpetrate most violent crime. Another inaccurate perception is that violent crime, particularly murder, is routinely puzzling and mysterious — without meticulous investigation by police, private eyes, coroners, and investigative reporters, the search for cunning killers might end in failure. Except in the rarest of instances, however, Canadians are most at risk of being injured or killed by relatives, friends, and acquaintances. Most homicides are easily solved because most involve clear motives, no planning, nondisposable bodies, witnesses, and incriminating weapons.

Violent crime that ends in severe injury or death is extremely serious. Damages to victims are incalculable; unlike the aftermath of most crime, the suffering experienced by homicide victims and their relatives and friends is monumental and beyond compensation.

Media portrayals of homicide produce fears of falling prey to violence that are quite unrealistic. Many people believe that homicide routinely accompanies robbery, burglary, and theft. In fact, crime of any type is relatively rare and violent crime is even rarer. In 1999, only about 12 percent of *Criminal Code* offences involved violence, and in only a few of these incidents did people suffer serious injuries. Homicide represented only 0.02 percent of crimes reported to the police in 1999 and only 0.2 percent of all violent incidents (Tremblay, 2000).

This chapter begins by examining the various forms of **homicide** and their incidence in Canada. First, it focuses on "typical" homicides and the characteristics of "routine" offenders, victims, and homicide situations. Later, it explores several types of homicide that are very uncommon in Canada: upper-class homicide, serial and mass murder, and terrorism. The discussion concludes by examining several sociological theories of homicide drawn from the interactionist, subcultural, and deterrence traditions and then by discussing the legal control of homicide in Canada.

Box 10.1
HOW THE INNOCENT END UP BEHIND BARS

The Supreme Court of Canada has reviewed the case of David Milgaard, who claims to be innocent of a crime for which he has spent the last 22 years in prison. The Milgaard case raises the issue of the ultimate nightmare for the criminal justice system: false convictions.

How often do these travesties occur, what factors are responsible, and, as importantly, are they likely to occur more often at a time of growing public fear of crime?

No form of human judgment is perfect. Criminal proceedings run the risk of making two kinds of errors: they can exonerate the guilty or convict the innocent. While both are judicial miscarriages, the legal system, in keeping with the presumption of innocence principle, has sought to avoid false convictions even if this has meant that some criminals go free.

The prospect of jailing an innocent person for someone else's crime has been considered more abhorrent to our sense of justice than a guilty person evading punishment. The Crown must prove its case beyond a reasonable doubt. This means that if the evidence points strongly toward guilt – but some reasonable doubt remains – then the accused is to be found not guilty.

Despite such safeguards, false convictions are not new. This century has witnessed many famous cases.

In the Evans-Christie case in Great Britain, for example, a man was executed for murders committed by another. That same country has recently seen a series of wrongful convictions for terrorist crimes. These cases (including the so-called "Birmingham Six," the "Guildford Four" and the Maguires) provoked the creation of a royal commission to study the criminal justice system that permitted such injustices to occur.

In the United States, there have been numerous cases where innocent people have spent many years in prison.

The case of Donald Marshall, who spent 11 years in prison for a murder he did not commit, focused attention on our system and raised, for many Canadians, a discomforting question: Are the false convictions of which we are aware exceptional, or are they the tip of the iceberg? Was the Marshall case without precedent, or are there still inmates in Canada's prisons serving time for other peoples' crimes?

Some cases of wrongful conviction are never uncovered. There are few incentives for those aware of the error to come forward. The real perpetrator has nothing to gain (other than a clear conscience) and possibly much to lose. A witness recanting his or her testimony admits to perjury.

U.S. research on this issue suggests that, in about 5 per cent of cases, there was compelling evidence to suggest the wrong person was convicted. Of course, the presence of the death penalty in the U.S. raises the stakes considerably. Last year, there were almost 2,500 inmates awaiting execution in America.

False convictions can occur for a variety of reasons: (1) Errors by eyewitnesses in identification; (2) perjury; (3) incompetent legal defences; (4) false confessions by the mentally ill or feebleminded (this was a cause of the false conviction in the Christie/Evans case); (5) excessive zeal on the part of police or prosecutors; (6) community pressure; (7) plea bargaining; and (8) errors by medical examiners or forensic experts.

U.S. researchers have shown that, among these factors, overzealousness by the police may be the most important. On some occasions, the police form a hypothesis about an individual and then, convinced that the right man has been found, tend to ignore evidence pointing in other directions.

Misidentifications of suspects can also be due to stereotypes, rather than incompetence or negligence on the part of police or the Crown. Increasingly in Canada, public statements are being made attributing certain types of crime to particular racial, ethnic, or national groups.

Research on human perception shows that victims or witnesses associating crime with a certain social group may mistakenly identify a suspect as the perpetrator if the individual fits their stereotype of a criminal.

It is no coincidence that the individuals wrongfully convicted of IRA attacks in Britain were Irish. One reason for their original arrest was that they fitted the police stereotype of a terrorist, i.e., young, male laborers heading back to Northern Ireland shortly after a terrorist attack in England.

A growing fear of crime in Canada, too, may make wrongful conviction more prevalent in the future. As public fears mount, there are growing pressures on the police and justice system to convict accused persons, especially in notorious cases. Polls tell us that people consistently feel that criminals are dealt with too leniently. Such a shift in the public mood will not be lost on those administering the system.

The increasing levels of fear, exasperation with the justice system, and frequent demands for a "quick fix" to the problem of crime increase the danger that we will become more intolerant of the presumption of innocence and of erroneous acquittals.

Where undue pressure is placed on the system to make an arrest and achieve a guilty verdict, wrongful convictions are sure to follow.

Discussion Questions

Which is the greater evil — freeing a certain number of guilty people by adhering to strict rules of due process, or executing a small number of innocent people by relaxing due-process provisions in the interests of stronger crime control? Is it possible to avoid both problems at the same time? In light of the reasons given for false convictions, what steps would you advocate to achieve a reduction? How many wrongful convictions out of 100 should Canadians be prepared to tolerate?

Source: T. Gabor and J. Roberts, *Toronto Star*, February 12, 1992, p. A21. Reprinted with permission from the authors.

DEFINITIONS OF HOMICIDE

Homicide requires two primary criteria (CCJS, 1989): first, the death of a human being must occur; and second, someone other than the victim must have caused that death. Homicides include the *Criminal Code* offences of murder, manslaughter, and infanticide. The line between homicide and assault, particularly aggravated assault, is very thin. If the loser in an altercation dies, the charge is homicide. If the loser in the altercation suffers serious injury but lives, the offence is aggravated assault. If the offender meant only to injure but killed instead, the crime is not assault; the doctrine of general intent requires the incident to be charged as homicide.

Murder is a matter of degree — first and second, to be precise. At least one of three conditions is required to classify a murder as first degree: (1) planned and deliberate murder, (2) the murder of police officers, custodians, or prison personnel while they are on duty, or (3) murder committed during certain other criminal acts (e.g., hijacking, kidnapping and forcible confinement, or sexual assault). Murders not meeting these requirements are second degree (Fedorowycz, 2000). The line separating first- from second-degree murder is often obscure (Boyd, 1988b). Usually at issue is how planned and deliberate the killing was. Only about 5 percent of Canadians charged with homicide are convicted of **first-degree murder**; about 30 percent are found guilty of **second-degree murder** (Boyd, 1988b).

Manslaughter, another form of homicide, is a "culpable homicide that would otherwise be murder" except that "the person who committed it did so in the heat of passion caused by sudden provocation." The *Criminal Code* states that "a wrongful act or insult that is of such nature as to be sufficient to deprive an ordinary person of the power of self-control is provocation enough." However, the accused must have acted immediately and before there was time for passion to subside. Manslaughter represents over 60 percent of convictions for homicide.

The remaining form of homicide under the *Criminal Code* is **infanticide**, which occurs when a female, by wilful act or omission, causes the death of her newly born child. The child must be under one year of age and the mother must not have fully recovered from the effects of childbirth (CCJS, 1989).

DATA ON HOMICIDE

The Canadian government devotes considerable resources to collecting and disseminating information about homicide. Homicide data are by far the most accurate official crime data for two reasons. First, people report virtually all homicides. Second, unlike other reported crimes, police investigate homicide with extreme thoroughness and prepare records with painstaking detail.

Before the 1960s, Canadian crime statistics were neither standardized nor collected on a national basis. Data on crime were contained in local police records, collected strictly for police purposes, and organized differently in each locality. Although these circumstances make it difficult to assess changes in homicide rates over long periods of time, it is possible to make some tentative comparisons. The rate in 1930 was 2.14 homicides per 100 000 Canadians and in 1986 had risen only slightly, to 2.19 per 100 000. Since Confederation, Canadian homicide rates have fluctuated between 1 and 3 per 100 000 (Boyd, 1988b).

Boyd notes that throughout the late 1920s and the early 1930s the annual homicide rate approximated 2 deaths per 100 000. The next 30 years were marked by a gradual decline to a rate of about 1.2 per 100 000. Indeed, the 1940s and 1950s were a period of relative decline for interpersonal violence.

Changes in health-care technology, transportation, and communication have likely affected Canadian homicide rates in the past century just as they have affected U.S. rates. The U.S. homicide rate also dropped substantially in the late 1940s and the 1950s. The proliferation of ambulance services, the improvement of emergency medical care and facilities, better roads and highways, and faster communication combined to reduce the likelihood that aggravated assault victims would die of their wounds (Hagan, 1986). Since 1961, homicide trends in Canada have followed two distinct trends. As Figure 10.1 shows, several years of stability were followed by a period of steady increase from 1.25 per 100 000 in 1966 to 3.03 per 100 000 in 1975. This growth represents an increase of 142 percent. From 1975 to 1999, despite some fluctuation

from year to year, the homicide rate gradually declined to 1.76 in 1999, a decrease of 42 percent.

INCIDENCE OF HOMICIDE

Violent crime, particularly homicide, is rare in most countries, and Canada is no exception. Furthermore, despite popular perception, the homicide rate has been declining since the mid-1970s. In 1999, 536 Canadians were victims of homicide. This number is 22 fewer than in 1998 and fell well below the average of 639 for the previous decade. The comparable figure for the United States was about 16 000. Between 1991 and 1999, the Canadian homicide rate declined steadily, by 35 percent, to 1.76 per 100 000 — the lowest recorded since 1967. In the United States, the rate was more than three times higher in 1999 — 5.8 per 100 000. In some large American cities, homicides occur at over 30 times the Canadian rate (Fedorowycz, 1996; 2000).

The reasons cited for these differences include the emphasis on individualism in the United States, the

FIGURE 10.1

HOMICIDE RATE, 1961–1999

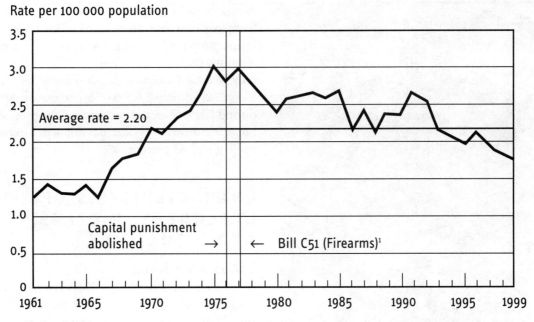

Rate per 100 000 population

Average rate = 2.20

Capital punishment abolished →   ← Bill C51 (Firearms)[1]

[1]*Firearm Acquisition Certificate required.*

Source: O. Fedorowycz. (2000). Homicide in Canada–1999. *Juristat Service Bulletin* 20(9). Ottawa: Canadian Centre for Justice Statistics, Statistics Canada, p. 5, Cat. No. 85-002.

revolutionary spirit in which that country was born, the massive economic gaps separating classes and races there, and the American romance with firearms (Lenton, 1989). Table 10.1 shows that, in comparison with Canada, countries such as Germany, England and Wales, Switzerland, and France had slightly lower rates per 100 000: 1.24, 1.25, 1.26, and 1.62, respectively (Fedorowycz, 2000).

As Figure 10.2 demonstrates, homicide in Canada generally increases from east to west. In 1999, the rates per 100 000 in Newfoundland and Prince Edward Island were 0.37 and 0.72, respectively, while for Alberta and British Columbia they were 2.06 and 2.73. Cities with populations of half a million or more averaged rates of 1.84. The rate of 1.76 in localities with populations under 100 000 was not, as one might expect, the lowest among all municipalities. Instead, urban areas with populations of 100 000 to 249 999 had the lowest rate (1.28), while cities of 250 000 to 499 999 showed a rate of 1.57. Among Canada's largest cities, Vancouver recorded the highest rate (2.83), followed by Hamilton (2.41), and Winnipeg (2.21). Police recorded the lowest rates in Toronto (1.28) and Calgary (1.39). For smaller cities, Thunder Bay and Sudbury had the highest rates, 3.16 and 2.49 per 100 000 respectively. At the other end of the scale, Trois Rivières and St. John's recorded no homicides. According to police reports for 1999, 51 percent of homicides were first degree, 39 percent were second degree, and 11 percent were manslaughter. No infanticides were recorded in 1999 (Fedorowycz, 2000).

The Canadian homicide rate grew from 1.4 per 100 000 in 1962 to its peak of 3.1 in 1975. From the late 1970s to the mid-1980s, rates declined slightly, to an average of about 2.8. In the United States, however, the homicide rate in 1962, 4.5 per 100 000, grew steadily to 10.2 in 1980. By 1999, as noted earlier, the rates in both countries had declined to 1.8 and 5.8, respectively (Fedorowycz, 2000).

Canada's homicide rate is low in comparison with that of the United States, average in comparison with those of many other developed nations, and incredibly lower than those of many underdeveloped Third World countries. The relationship between economic underdevelopment, material deprivation, and homicide rates is not entirely clear. Some countries, such as Spain and Haiti, have much lower homicide rates than the United States. In others, such as some Latin American nations, a masculine-oriented culture of violence may contribute to high rates. There, virtually any insult, particularly among young males, is considered a serious challenge to manliness. These disputes can only be settled violently (Clinard and Abbot, 1973).

Canadian police solved 75 percent of homicides during 1999. Over the past decade, the proportion of homicide cleared by police has fluctuated between 75 percent and 85 percent.

CHARACTERISTICS OF OFFENDERS, VICTIMS, AND SITUATIONS

CLASS AND RACE

One important deficiency in Canadian homicide data is the lack of information about the socioeconomic and ethnic characteristics of offenders and victims. This omission is significant because evidence from other countries, like the United States, indicates that homicide is primarily a lower-class phenomenon.

TABLE 10.1

HOMICIDE RATES FOR SELECTED COUNTRIES, 1999

Country	Homicide rate per 100 000 population	% Change 1998-1999
Germany	1.24	+5%
England & Wales	1.25	–5%
Switzerland	1.26	+19%
France	1.62	–1%
Canada	**1.76**	**–4%**
Hungary	2.48	–12%
United States	5.80	–8%

Source: O. Fedorowycz. (2000). Homicide in Canada–1999. *Juristat Service Bulletin* 20(9). Ottawa: Canadian Centre for Justice Statistics, Statistics Canada, p. 3, Cat. No. 85-002.

FIGURE 10.2

HOMICIDE RATES BY PROVINCE, 1999

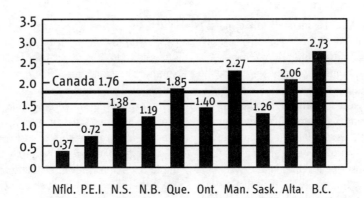

Source: O. Fedorowycz. (2000). Homicide in Canada—1999. *Juristat Service Bulletin* 20(9). Ottawa: Canadian Centre for Justice Statistics, Statistics Canada, p. 3, Cat. No. 85-002.

Major American studies by Wolfgang (1958) and Swigert and Farrell (1976) suggest that somewhere between 90 and 95 percent of killers are near the bottom of the socioeconomic hierarchy. Most American killers are semi-skilled, unskilled, or unemployed. Similarly, Boyd's (1988b) analysis of Canadian homicide files showed that about 66 percent of the Canadian murderers he studied were unemployed. For the half of their subjects for whom data on education were available, Silverman and Kennedy (1993) report that 43 percent had Grade 8 or less and 30 percent had Grade 9 or 10. They also report that, of the two-thirds of their sample for whom occupational status was known, one-third were labourers. The implication of these findings is that patterns apparent in official data are patterns of lower-class homicide. There are important differences between the majority of homicides, committed by lower-class people, and the few committed by higher-class people.

Canadian UCR data are equally silent about the relationship between race or ethnicity and homicide. Some of Boyd's findings, however, are suggestive: while Native people represent only 2 percent of the Canadian population, they make up 13 percent of its homicide victims and 18 percent of its homicide suspects. Silverman and Kennedy (1993) note that the Native rate has been as high as ten times that of the rest of the population.

American studies show that blacks are disproportionately involved in murder. While blacks represent only about 12 percent of the American population, they are involved in the commission of just over half of all killings. U.S. investigations also reveal that murder is an intra-racial affair. Killers and their victims tend to share the same racial and ethnic characteristics (McCaghy and Capron, 1997). Boyd's research suggests that the Canadian picture is similar — most homicide involving Native people is also an intra-racial phenomenon.

SEX, AGE, AND MARITAL STATUS

Male killers outnumber their female counterparts by a ratio of about 9 to 1. In 1999, 90 percent of suspects were male and 10 percent were female. The gender breakdown of homicide victims, however, is different; males outnumbered females as victims by a margin of only 2 to 1; two-thirds of victims were male and one-third were female. (Fedorowycz, 2000; Tremblay, 2000).

Homicide victims and offenders tend to be young adults. The median age for male victims in 1999 was 35 and for females, it was 36. The most common single age for a homicide perpetrator was 24 years while for a victim it was 30. Sixty percent of those accused of homicide were aged 15 to 32, even though that age bracket represents only 25 percent of the Canadian population. The propensity to be either a perpetrator or a victim declines with age. The size of the 15 to 32 age group, as a proportion of the total population, reached its smallest size in 2000 and is expected to rise

Box 10.2
MORE EQUALITY, GREATER RISKS

On Dec. 6, 1989, when Marc Lépine stalked the halls of the engineering building at the University of Montreal with his .223-calibre Sturm, Ruger semi-automatic rifle, he was hunting women. He spared the men in his path – then screamed "You're all a bunch of feminists" before he gunned down the 14 females who died during his murderous rampage. Across Canada, women reacted with bitter outrage, some claiming that the carnage was part of a deadly backlash by men against the advances made by women in recent years. But according to Statistics Canada, the rate of female murders in Canada has remained remarkably constant – at around 0.8 per 100,000 people – for almost 20 years. And, the experts add, while troubled individuals such as Lépine strike fear into the hearts of women, they remain an aberration. Said University of Alberta sociologist Robert Silverman, a leading authority on murder: "If you were doing a trend line on female murder, it would be a flat line. Marc Lépine was not a trend."

Still, some experts say that the statistics hide some subtle changes. University of Victoria sociologist William McCarthy, who in association with University of Toronto sociologist Rosemary Gartner earlier this year published a major study on female homicide in Vancouver and Toronto, noted that 62 per cent of female murder victims are killed in their homes by their husbands or other men that they know intimately – a figure that has remained consistent over the years. But while the female murder rate has not changed dramatically, the actual number of women killed has risen in accordance with increases in the Canadian population, to 234 in 1990 from 172 in 1971. And within that increase, said McCarthy, are greater numbers of younger, single women who are being murdered by strangers.

The explanation, according to McCarthy, is that over the past two decades, younger women have come to enjoy a measure of social equality with men. As a result, they have increasingly become vulnerable to the same types of incidents that put men at risk of being murdered, such as being assaulted in an underground parking lot after work or late in the evening at a bar. Said McCarthy: "In the same way that males leading these types of lifestyles have greater homicide risks, females who lead these lifestyles also have greater homicide risks."

Another study done by Gartner last year appears to support that contention. Examining the rate of female murder in 18 countries, she discovered that in societies where women play a subservient role to men, female murder rates are low. But in Western societies where women have achieved a greater degree of independence, the rates are higher. It is a chilling prospect: greater equality brings greater risks.

Discussion Question

Can you identify other circumstances associated with equality between the sexes that might contribute to a greater likelihood of women becoming the victims of violent and property crimes?

Source: Tom Fennell, *Maclean's*, November 11, 1991, p. 30. Reprinted with permission from *Maclean's*.

over the next decade. It would not be surprising, therefore, if homicide rates were to rise accordingly in the next few years (Fedorowycz, 2000).

An earlier analysis of homicide data suggests that the largest concentration of male and female homicide victims (about half) is in the group aged 20 to 39. Again, the very young (15 and younger) and the elderly (60 and older) account for rather small proportions of total homicide victims (about 10 percent each). For both males and females, the highest numbers of victims are between 20 and 29 years of age and the lowest are between 7 and 10 (Wright, 1991).

While the most common age for a victim in 1999 was 30, it has not been uncommon in recent years for infants to be at greatest risk (Fedorowycz, 2000).

OFFENDER-VICTIM RELATIONSHIPS

Most people fear death at the hands of a cold-blooded stranger, most likely in the dead of night, on some remote, dimly lit street. Victims, however, are typically killed by spouses, lovers, friends, and acquaintances. Furthermore, the most dangerous locations are those with which people are most familiar and in which they feel safe.

Silverman and Kennedy's analysis of Canadian homicides between 1961 and 1990 showed that almost half occurred within the family and that an additional third involved friends and acquaintances. The perpetrators were strangers in less than 10 percent of cases. For solved homicides in 1999, 35 percent of victims were killed by a spouse or other family member and 49 percent were killed by an acquaintance. Only 15 percent were dispatched by persons unknown to them. The percentage killed by strangers remained fairly constant between 1989 and 1998, ranging from 12 percent to 16 percent. Victims of strangers tend to be male; 19 percent of male victims are killed by strangers, compared with only 7 percent of females. Women are six times more likely to be killed by a spouse than by a stranger. A little more than half (56 percent) of homicides perpetrated by strangers involved the commission of another criminal offence, usually a robbery. Of all spousal homicides in 1999, 6 in 10 involved a history of domestic violence that was known to the police (Fedorowycz, 2000). Where women commit homicide, victims are family members in about 60 percent of cases. By comparison, men's homicide victims are family members in about 30 percent of cases (Fedorowycz, 1996).

Figure 10.3 illustrates the relationship of sex and homicide victimization by type of relationship for the years 1979–1998. During this period, female victims outnumbered male victims by a considerable margin for homicides occurring within the family. In all other types of homicides, such as those involving acquaintances and strangers, males predominated as victims.

Most people are killed by someone they know, and often victims are dispatched by those with whom they are intimately involved. Those to whom one is emotionally attached are most capable of stirring passions ranging from joy to hatred. Upset and agitated people are most likely to strike out at those who are close; these homicides occur in the heat of the moment. Whether the victim actively incurs the wrath of the attacker is not always relevant. The fact that people share large amounts of time together is often sufficient to make them targets of aggression. This is particularly true for women and children, who are frequently abused by husbands, lovers, or fathers (Chalmers and Smith, 1988).

Homicide victims may escalate the violence preceding their death by starting a disagreement or becoming angered themselves. "Victim-precipitated" homicides are those in which the victim plays a sig-

FIGURE 10.3

HOMICIDES BY TYPE OF RELATIONSHIP, CANADA, 1979-1998[1]

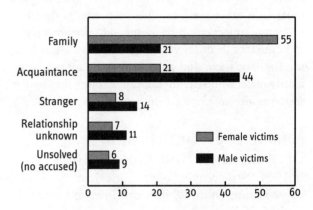

Figures may not add up to 100% due to rounding.
[1] Includes only those cases in which the sex of the victim is known.

Source: CCJS. (2000). Justice Factfinder, 1998. *Juristat Service Bulletin* 20(4). Ottawa: Canadian Centre for Justice Statistics, Statistics Canada, p. 7, Cat. No. 85-002.

nificant part in initiating or escalating the violence. American social scientists Marvin Wolfgang (1958) and David Luckenbill (1977) provide varying estimates of the percentages of victims who precipitate their own deaths. Luckenbill's study of homicide suggests that as many as 65 percent of victims play either an initiating or an escalating role. Wolfgang, counting only incidents in which victims had initiated the altercation, found only 25 percent to be **victim-precipitated homicides**. In his analysis, Wolfgang speculated that these people may secretly have wanted to die.

HOMICIDE COMMITTED IN THE CONTEXT OF ANOTHER CRIME

In their study of homicide between 1961 and 1990, Silverman and Kennedy (1993) classify 14 percent of killings as occurring in the context of another crime. They indicate that homicide in conjunction with thefts and robberies was lowest in 1965 (6 percent) and highest in 1988 (14 percent). Homicide in the course of sexual assault incidents was lowest in 1961 (1 percent) and highest in 1981 (7 percent). They note, as well, that while the number of killings occurring in the context of other crimes is low, there is some indication that it is rising. Official data for 1999 support this observation. One-third of homicide incidents for 1999 involved the commission of other crimes. Almost 70 percent of these were violent offences, such as assault (38 percent), robbery (18 percent), sexual assault (9 percent), kidnapping (2 percent), and other violent crimes (4 percent). Arson, a property crime, accounted for an additional 6 percent of homicides (Fedorowycz, 2000). Victims killed during robbery, theft, and break and enter are predominantly male, while victims killed in conjunction with a sexual assault are predominantly female (CCJS, 1987).

NUMBERS OF VICTIMS AND OFFENCERS IN HOMICIDE INCIDENTS

In 1999, 94 percent of homicide incidents involved a single victim. Of the 29 incidents involving multiple victims, 26 involved two victims, two involved three victims, and one incident involved four victims. Incidents involving five or more victims are quite rare in Canada; notable examples are the Air India bombing that resulted in the deaths of 329 people over the North Atlantic (1985), the killing of 14 women by Marc Lépine in Montreal (1989), the murders of 11 children and youth by Clifford Olson (1981–82) and the deaths, at the hands of persons unknown, of at least 8 infants at the Hospital for Sick Children in Toronto (1980–81). Other incidents in the "five and over" homicide category frequently involve arson.

Most homicides (85 percent) involve offenders acting alone; in only about 15 percent of incidents is there more than one suspect.

MOTIVATIONS FOR HOMICIDE

Police report that the most common motive for homicide in 1999 was an argument, quarrel or incident inciting a vengeful or jealous reaction or an act of despair (57 percent of all homicides). Financial gain or a settling of accounts motivated another 20 percent. Only 6 percent of homicides had no apparent motive and in the remainder of cases, the motive was unknown. There were only three "random" killings in 1999. While there were no hate-motivated homicides in 1999, between 1991 and 1998, there were thirteen such killings for an average of less than two per year.

METHODS OF COMMITTING HOMICIDE

The weapons employed to kill others are rarely exotic; usually they are one's hands or a conveniently accessible object. The more efficient the weaponry, however, the more likely it is that the incident will be a homicide rather than an assault. Fists and blunt objects more often result in injury than in death. Knife attacks, while more lethal than assaults with hands and clubs, often end only in charges of aggravated assault or attempted murder. The use of firearms, however, is deadly. The gun is the most common murder weapon in the United States and, by a very small margin over stabbing, in Canada.

One of the major reasons why Canada has a much lower homicide rate than the United States is because access to firearms (particularly handguns) is much more restricted in this country (Sproule and Kennett, 1988; 1989). The American constitution entrenches the right to bear arms. It is a strongly guarded privilege; the United States boasts the most heavily armed civilian population in the world (Hagan, 1986). Given the easy access to guns of all kinds, it is not surprising that the United States has the highest homicide rate of any developed nation. More Americans have been killed on their own soil by guns during this century than have been killed in all wars in which their country has been involved, from the American Revolution to the Gulf War. During the Vietnam war, fewer Americans were killed in the war than were killed at home by guns. In 1999, handguns killed 8829 people (52 percent of all homicides) in the United States. By comparison, only 89 Canadians (17 percent) were murdered by this means (Fedorowycz, 2000).

Silverman and Kennedy's research (1993) indicates that guns were used in 38 percent of homicides between 1961 and 1990, while 25 percent involved stabbing as the cause of death. Another 16 percent involved such means as strangulation, drowning, and arson. Of homicides involving guns over that period, about two-thirds involved long guns such as rifles and shotguns. Figure 10.4 shows that, in 1999, slightly more homicides were committed by shooting (30 percent) than by stabbing (27 percent). Other methods used during that year included beating (23 percent), strangulation (10 percent), fire (2 percent), and poisoning (1 percent). Shaken Baby Syndrome accounted for an additional 1 percent (Fedorowycz, 2000).

Fedorowycz (1996) observes that since 1979 firearms have been employed in approximately one-third of all homicides each year. Indeed, with the exception of the years 1990, 1995, and 1998, shooting has been the most common means of homicide since 1961. In 1999, shootings made up 31 percent of all homicides,

FIGURE 10.4

METHODS USED TO COMMIT HOMICIDE, 1999

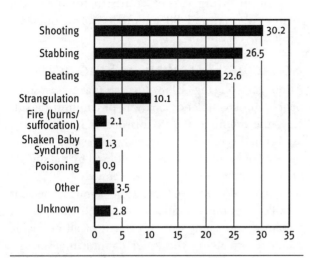

Source: O. Fedorowycz. (2000). Homicide in Canada–1999. *Juristat Service Bulletin* 20(9). Ottawa: Canadian Centre for Justice Statistics, Statistics Canada, p. 7, Cat. No. 85-002.

a figure slightly lower than average. Eighty-nine homicides involved handguns and 58 involved long guns. Sawed-off rifles, shotguns, and fully automatic weapons accounted for twelve killings.

Between 1975 and 1990, 10 percent of homicides involved handguns. In 1999, that percentage rose to almost 17 percent. The use of long guns declined steadily from 26 percent in 1975 to 20 percent in 1989, and then to 11 percent in 1999. Homicides with handguns increased from 70 in 1998 to 89 in 1999 (Fedorowycz, 1996; 2000).

There are some interesting differences in the methods used in homicides that occur in connection with another criminal act. Firearms figure prominently in homicides committed during robbery, theft, and break and enter. The predominant murder technique in cases of rape and sexual assault is strangulation. In homicides involving arson, the most frequent cause of death is suffocation as a result of asphyxiation caused by smoke inhalation.

Three methods account for the largest proportion of male and female homicide: stabbing, shooting, and beating. While males have always outnumbered females in these categories, women are more likely than men to die from strangulation, suffocation, and drowning. Female victims also outnumber

male victims in bombings and axe swinging incidents (CCJS, 1987).

LOCATIONS OF HOMICIDES

Canadian data indicate that there are three locations in which the risk of homicide is particularly high. The victim's residence, frequently shared with the offender, is the most common locale in which people kill one another. The next most common location is a public place. Other private places (the residence of an acquaintance, a friend, or a relative) and the workplace run a distant third. In 1999, locations were known for 498 homicides. Sixty percent occurred in private residences, usually that of the victim. (Fedorowycz, 2000). These percentages are broadly consistent with the findings of Silverman and Kennedy (1993) for the period 1961–90, in which these locales figured prominently in almost three-quarters of homicides. Other locations for homicides in 1999 were open areas such as streets, parking lots and fields (24 percent), commercial areas such as bars, restaurants, and banks (10 percent), private vehicles (5 percent), and public institutions such as prisons, hospitals, and schools (3 percent).

Private residences are more likely to be the place of death for females (76 percent) than for males (56 percent). Contributing to this pattern is the fact that females are killed by spouses and other family members in greater proportions than are males (60 percent versus 24 percent) and that domestic homicide involves a private residence 87 percent of the time (Fedorowycz, 1996). American data suggest that, for homicides occurring in the home, men are more likely to die in the kitchen, while women are more likely to die in the bedroom (Wolfgang, 1958).

Even homicides that take place in public places (often bars) involve persons who know one another. However, strangers are involved in killings in these locations in greater proportions than they are in homicides that occur in the home. Homicides occurring in the victim's residence seldom involve strangers (CCJS, 1987).

Homicide data for Canada show no discernible monthly patterns, and there is little consistency from year to year in the numbers of homicides committed each month (CCJS, 1987). A stronger pattern is apparent in the United States, where homicides occur more frequently in the summer months. During June, July, and August, the hot southern sun may fuel the heat of passion. Christmas, gatherings of family and friends, and the consumption of large quantities of alcohol combine to make December the most dangerous of the winter months in America. Murder in the United States also appears to be a weekend pastime, particularly on Saturday evenings. Again, weekends are times when people come together and more alcohol is consumed (Wolfgang, 1958; Messner and Tardiff, 1985).

THE ROLE OF ALCOHOL AND DRUGS IN HOMICIDES

Alcohol consumption by either the victim or the suspect plays a greater role in Canadian homicide offences than does drug consumption. Police classify as alcohol-related offences those in which either the victim or the suspect consumes alcohol before the killing. Drug offences are those in which either perpetrator or victim consumes substances such as hashish, cocaine, or heroin before the crime. While acknowledging some problems in arriving at firm estimates, Silverman and Kennedy (1993) report that the police recorded alcohol involvement in 30 percent of cases and drug involvement in 33 percent of cases between 1961 and 1990. In the rest, it was unknown whether alcohol or drugs were involved. In 1999, police reported that 38 percent of victims had used alcohol, drugs, or both. Male victims were almost twice as likely as female victims to have used them, even though for accused killers the proportions were almost the same for males and females. Consistent with previous years, police reported that half (50 percent) of accused persons had consumed alcohol, drugs, or both (Fedorowycz, 2000). In the United States, the proportion of homicides involving alcohol may be higher than in Canada. Some U.S. data suggest that alcohol plays a role in homicide in about half of all cases (McCaghy and Capron, 1997).

Criminologists hypothesize that alcohol and drugs are prominent in precipitating assault and homicide for two reasons. First, these substances reduce one's ability to maintain emotional control, and second, they render prospective assailants (and victims) less aware of the consequences of their actions.

PRIOR CRIMINAL HISTORY

In 1999, 64 percent of those accused of homicide had a criminal record, and the majority of these (57 percent) were for violent crimes: 7 for homicide, 44 for robbery and 121 for other violent offences. Six of the seven accused persons with a previous homicide conviction killed again in a correctional facility. Similarly, 41 percent of victims had a criminal record, with half of these involving violent crimes: 3 for homicide, 24 for robbery, and 88 for other violent offences. (Fedorowycz, 2000).

HOMICIDE FOLLOWED BY SUICIDE

Although Wolfgang (1958) suggests that at least some people initiate violence as a way of committing suicide, the extent to which this occurs is difficult to ascertain. There is little mystery, however, about the number of homicides that are followed by the suicide of the offender. Silverman and Kennedy (1993) estimate that, between 1961 and 1990, about 10 percent of killers committed suicide. In 1999, this pattern remained consistent with 8 percent of all homicide incidents involving the killer committing suicide. Forty murder–suicide incidents produced a total of 52 victims. Perpetrators were predominantly male (93 percent) and almost 90 percent of incidents were family-related, a proportion which has been relatively constant over the past twenty years. Twenty-five percent of murder–suicides involved more than one victim and in every case the perpetrator was male. Men killed their spouses in half (48 percent) and their children in 15 percent of all murder–suicides. They killed both their spouse and their children in 13 percent of cases. (Fedorowycz, 2000).

In their study of murder–suicide in Ontario, Greenland and Rosenblatt (1975) discuss why killers take their own lives. They maintain that some killers commit suicide either because they wish to escape punishment or because they experience intense remorse at having caused the death of another. Others commit homicide before committing suicide for altruistic reasons: they feel that those who would be left behind — children or an ailing spouse perhaps — would be better off dead than left to fend for themselves. Finally, a few killers commit suicide in order to reunite immediately with their victims in the afterlife or to avoid having to go on living without their victims. Spouses who kill their disabled or terminally ill loved ones as acts of mercy are examples of this form of murder–suicide.

Most murder–suicides involve spouses or children as victims. More than half of the murder–suicides that Greenland and Rosenblatt studied occurred in the home of either the victim or the offender, and a third took place in a bedroom. Guns were used in over two-thirds of cases, and alcohol played a role in

Box 10.3
DNA TESTING TRANSFORMING SCIENCE

With yesterday's announcement that DNA testing vouched for his innocence on rape and murder charges, David Milgaard becomes part of a revolution that in a little more than 10 years has changed the face not only of forensic science, but of science in general.

Variants of the technique commonly called DNA fingerprinting have shown during the past decade that:

- Bones found in the Ural Mountains were indeed those of the Russian royal family, and Anna Anderson, who claimed she was the Princess Anastasia, was in fact a fraud.

- The body of a man buried in Brazil was that of Nazi doctor Josef Mengele.

- Englishman Adrian Targett had a genetic kinship with the oldest known complete skeleton found in that country, the 9,000-year-old Cheddar Man.

- A 30,000-year-old Neanderthal belonged to a different species from modern humans.

- Argentine military officers and others had stolen, and claimed as their own children, the offspring of political dissidents killed during the country's military rule.

- The likely progenitors of the cabernet sauvignon grape are the cabernet franc and the sauvignon blanc, with odds that two other randomly chosen varieties are not the cabernet sauvignon's forebears in the order of trillions to one.

- Dogs either separated genetically four times from wolves, or separated once and were cross-bred back three times. Among the oldest dog species: The greyhound.

- Many species of supposedly monogamous birds are in fact not monogamous.

However, Mr. Milgaard most directly can trace his exoneration by DNA to the saga of Richard John Buckland, Ian Kelly and Colin Pitchfork. These three were players in the 1980s British case known as the Narborough Murders – the first time DNA cleared one defendant and pointed its accusatory genetic fingers at another.

A DNA test developed by Leicester University geneticist Alec Jeffreys, now Sir Alec, showed that Mr. Buckland, then 17, was not guilty of the rape and murder of two teen-aged girls near the village of Narborough. This was the case even though police had extracted a confession to one of the murders from Mr. Buckland. DNA sampling of more than 5,000 men living in the area came up empty until Mr. Kelly revealed in a bar conversation that he had taken the test for Mr. Pitchfork. The DNA evidence subsequently led to Mr. Pitchfork's conviction.

DNA fingerprinting relies on the fact that certain sections of DNA – the two-metre-long strands of genetic material found in the cells of all living creatures – are highly variable. While the genetic variance between humans averages only 0.1 percent, Prof. Jeffreys observed in 1984 that in certain sections – generally those not containing genes – there are multiple copies of the four basic chemicals (base pairs) that create DNA.

The sequences may be from about three to 30 base pairs long, and depending on the individual, will repeat themselves 20 to 100 times. In the general population there can be between tens and hundreds of fragments of different lengths residing in the same area of DNA.

DNA fingerprint analysis compares the lengths of variable DNA fragments found in these areas – areas technically known as loci. The basic principle of DNA testing is to compare these variable, repeatable sections between people or other creatures being studied.

The more fragment lengths two samples share, the greater the likelihood that the DNA comes from the same person. Positive identification is not absolute, because there might be rare instances in which two people shared all the DNA fragment lengths tested for, but would show up as different if other areas in the DNA were looked at.

However, if two samples do not have the same DNA fragment lengths, they did not come from the same person. This is the reason why negative DNA results are absolute. The sampling begins by removing the DNA from cells found in saliva, sperm, hair, blood, skin, or, in a startling recent development, fingerprints. It is then purified. Enzymes – sort of chemical scissors – then cut the genetic material into fragments. If the DNA is old and possibly degraded, as in the Milgaard case, naturally fragmented pieces of interest can be selectively multiplied by a technique known as polymerase chain reaction, or PCR.

This process can also tag the fragments under study with fluorescent markers.

In the Milgaard case, short fragments – 200 to 400 base pairs long – were analyzed using a technique known as "short tandem repeat" analysis. Although it was not used in the Guy Paul Morin or O.J. Simpson cases, STR is often the technique of choice where the DNA may be old and degraded, or could be contaminated with other material. STR is relied on because more of the short fragments it studies are likely to be preserved intact in degraded material.

Once it is labelled and divided into fragments, the DNA is passed through a special gel to which an electric current has been applied. The negatively charged fragments move at different rates through the gel, with the smaller pieces moving more quickly. Within a few hours they sort themselves according to length. In the Milgaard case, an automated detection technology was able to sort the DNA lengths by activating the fluorescent tags with a laser, and then counting the amount of time the various fragments took to pass by.

It probably took less than 48 hours, and cost the British laboratory around $4,000, to show that Mr. Milgaard did not rape and murder a young nurse's aide in Saskatoon 28 years ago.

Discussion Question

Discuss the impact of DNA technology on law enforcement and criminal justice processing. Can you see any problems associated with its use – particularly in the area of civil liberty legislation? What effects on the justice system are likely to be felt as DNA evidence in Canada and the United States continues to exonerate people convicted of serious crimes?

Source: Stephen Strauss, *Globe and Mail*, July 19, 1997, p. A6. Reprinted with permission from the *Globe and Mail*.

more than a quarter of the incidents. Some form of family disturbance usually preceded the event. Such disruptions included the breakup of an intimate romantic relationship or marriage, marital infidelity, the loss of a job, or a serious financial crisis (Greenland and Rosenblatt, 1975).

One final category of murder–suicides deserves mention — those in which suicidal people, intent on leaving their families financially secure and free from the stigma of having a suicide in the family, risk the lives of others along with their own in order to disguise their actions as accidents. Indeed, this is one of the most convincing ways of making a suicide appear to be an accident. Many fatal car accidents and plane crashes are thought to be driver or pilot suicides in which others are also killed, intentionally or through gross negligence (Phillips, 1980).

HOMICIDE IN THE UPPER CLASS

The major factor distinguishing the typical lower-class killing from homicide among the members of the upper class is the degree of premeditation (Green and Wakefield, 1979). Upper-class killings are less likely to occur on the spur of the moment; rather, the affluent often carefully plan their homicides, and their motives are frequently more utilitarian. The privi-leged kill with calculation for money, for freedom from an unhappy marriage, and for revenge. Since they are well planned, upper-class homicides are often more difficult to solve, and the guilt of accused persons more difficult to prove. These factors, combined with the higher profile of the well-to-do, make for sensational murder investigations and spectacular trials that the media delight in reporting. As a result of such intensive coverage, it is not surprising that the public believes that extensive premeditation and malice characterize most homicides.

Two much-celebrated homicide investigations involving members of Canada's upper classes occurred during the 1980s. Both cases received extensive media coverage and were the subject of several books (Bird, 1985; Bissland, 1986). On January 23, 1983, 43-year-old JoAnn Wilson was found in the garage of her Regina home, bludgeoned with a meat cleaver and shot through the head with a high-calibre handgun. Her body was discovered by her second husband. Her first husband, Colin Thatcher, was later charged with murder and convicted. On July 5, 1984, Hanna Buxbaum and her husband, Helmuth, stopped by the side of a highway west of London, Ontario, to assist stranded motorists whose car appeared to have broken down. Hanna was dragged from the Buxbaum car by one of the occupants of the disabled vehicle and shot several times in the head. Soon after, police charged

Box 10.4
DECONSTRUCTING DOMESTIC VIOLENCE

The recent spate of domestic homicides has produced a predictable series of questions. Are these kinds of killings increasing in Canada? Is there more or less homicide in our country today than a decade ago, or a generation ago? And are men largely to blame for the violence?

The answers to the first two questions are relatively simple. Domestic homicides are not increasing; the rate of killing among intimates has actually declined since 1975. Similarly, Canada's homicide rate is about 60% lower today than it was 25 years ago.

Many Canadians will be reluctant to accept these figures. What of Paul Bernardo, Karla Homolka, the killing of Reena Virk, and more recently, the family massacre perpetrated by Bill Luft in Kitchener, Ont.? It is easy for any of us to point to relatively recent instances of horrific violence.

But lost in the extensive coverage of these terrible cases is the fact that they are not typical of violence in Canada; this is precisely why such events become front-page news. When one alcoholic stabs another to death in a Vancouver rooming house at 3 a.m., the press pay little attention. And counting the annual tally of death from culpable homicide is even less interesting or exciting. But this is what the Canadian Centre for Justice Statistics asks police forces to do every year. And police tell us that homicides are decreasing.

The question of whether men are mostly to blame for domestic homicide is more complex. In every country in the world and in every era in global history men have been almost 10 times as likely as women to kill. But this portrait changes when we look at domestic homicides. In this context men are only three to four times more likely to kill than women. And when we consider the killing of children in Canada we must acknowledge that almost half these crimes are committed by women.

It is, accordingly, critical that we do not subscribe to a mythology of female innocence. Karla Homolka was no victim; neither was Kelly Ellard, the young woman who killed Reena Virk. But the myth of innocence persists, largely driven by professional victims, therapists, and some feminists. We've all heard the mantras; Women never lie; men are oppressors; women are victims. These slogans have given us "battered women's syndrome" and "repressed memory." Karla Homolka was not a murderer; she was a victim of male oppression.

But having said all this about women and their moral culpability, let's not pretend that male and female violence are equivalent. Women kill their intimates when their backs are against the wall, often after suffering years of physical and emotional abuse. Women also kill their intimates when they are out of control with alcohol and other drugs – and they kill their children, almost as often as men do.

But men perpetrate family massacres. They hunt down their entire families and kill their wives and children. Women virtually never hunt down their husbands and children and murder the entire family. Men will also subject their wives to abuse for years and then kill them; women do not behave in a similar manner. Men commit sexual assault-homicide; women virtually never do. The killing of strangers is almost exclusively the province of men. Indeed, the most horrific of crimes are committed by men – acts of terrorism, mass murder and serial murder are almost always male.

Why is it that men are almost 10 times more likely to kill than women? The best answers to this question are found in the realm of biology. First, men are faster, stronger and larger than women. Women may hit men as often in domestic conflicts, but the difference is in the consequences – women are more likely to be seriously injured or killed in such struggles.

Second, boys and girls and adult men and women play differently, for reasons that appear to relate to the male hormone testosterone and to difference brain structures. Boys are more physical and aggressive than girls, not because they have been given trucks and baseball bats, but because they have experienced a testosterone bath in the womb, for which there is no female equivalent.

This notion that biology is a critical feature of male violence is often met with fierce resistance. Many social workers, sociologists and criminologists have claimed that all behaviour is socially conditioned; anyone who says biology is a variable of relevance is necessarily a social Darwinist or a believer in biological determinism. But both biology and environment are critical to an understanding of male violence.

As we embark on this new millennium, we need a much more nuanced view of male (and female) violence. Child abuse and neglect are major risk factors for future violence, but so is being born with testicles and a penis. We males may be biologically predisposed to violence in a way women are not, but at the end of the day this is no excuse. Violence need not and should not be our destiny.

Discussion Questions

Is biology as significant in explaining male versus female violence as Professor Boyd suggests? Why or why not?

Source: Neil Boyd, *National Post*, July 21, 2000, p. A14. Reprinted with permission from the author.

her husband with murder. He was subsequently convicted of hiring killers to do the job.

Both Thatcher and Buxbaum were millionaires. The former was a wealthy rancher and, until a few days before the murder of his ex-wife, held a cabinet portfolio in the Saskatchewan government. He was also the son of a former Saskatchewan premier, Ross Thatcher. Buxbaum, a prominent businessman in southwestern Ontario, owned a lucrative chain of nursing homes.

Thatcher and Wilson separated in 1979 and divorced in 1980 after seventeen years of marriage. The divorce settlement was first set at $819 648. It was, at the time, the largest property settlement in the history of divorce in Canada. Along with the property settlement came a long and bitter battle for custody of the couple's children. The courts gave responsibility for the care of the two younger children to JoAnn Wilson, while the oldest son went to live with his father. About nine months later, Wilson was shot and wounded while standing in front of her kitchen window. Police failed to apprehend her assailant. Several weeks later, she gave up her battle for custody of the children, stating that she feared for her life. She reported that her tires had been slashed, that sugar had been put in her gas tank, and that she had received a series of threatening phone calls (Bird, 1985).

Widely considered a pillar of his community, Helmuth Buxbaum was a man with a hidden passion for cocaine and prostitutes. Several months before his wife's murder, he purchased a $1 million insurance policy on her life (Bissland, 1986).

In the Thatcher and Buxbaum trials, witnesses testified that both men had attempted to hire killers to dispatch their wives for them. A key informant in the Thatcher case testified that Colin had offered to pay $50 000 to have his wife killed. The witness also

stated that he had supplied Thatcher with a .303 rifle and a rental car before Wilson was shot and wounded in her kitchen. The witness also claimed that he had supplied Thatcher with a .357 magnum pistol and another rental car just before JoAnn Wilson was finally murdered in her garage. Witnesses in the Buxbaum trial, who were parties to the roadside killing, stated that Helmuth Buxbaum had paid them to murder his wife. Both Thatcher and Buxbaum are currently serving life sentences.

HUNTING HUMANS*

Serial killing and mass murder are rare but dramatic forms of violent crime. The serial killer murders individuals in a series of homicides spanning weeks, months, or years. Mass murder refers to a homicide incident in which a killer intentionally kills several people at about the same time (Jenkins, 1988).

SERIAL KILLING

Serial killers are usually strangers to their victims. Since few of these predators have a direct connection to their prey, it is very difficult for police to apprehend them. Serial murderers are as often caught through luck as through the investigative efforts of law-enforcement agencies (McKay, 1985). The U.S. Department of Justice has estimated that the number of victims murdered yearly by serial killers runs into the thousands. American authorities believe that there are between 35 and 100 serial killers at large and operating in any given year (Hickey, 1991). For serial killers, these killings, like the hunting of wild game, are recreational pursuits (Leyton, 1986).

One of the most notorious serial killers in Canadian history is Clifford Olson. In a murder spree spanning nine months (1980–81), Olson, aged 41 at

Hunting Humans: The Rise of the Modern Multiple Murder is the title of a best-selling book on serial killing and mass murder written by Elliott Leyton, an anthropologist at Memorial University, and published by McClelland and Stewart in 1986.

the time, killed at least eleven children and teenagers in lower mainland British Columbia. The victims ranged in age from 9 to 18 and were of both sexes. In the end, to find the bodies of the victims, authorities paid Olson about $100 000.

Olson's hunt was planned, and as a result there were no witnesses and little physical evidence — most victims disappeared without a trace. There was no link either between the offender and his victims or among the victims themselves. The communication between police detachments was normal — not particularly well co-ordinated. Olson eluded capture for quite some time. Once he was apprehended, the evidence against him was not particularly strong.

On November 17, 1980, a 12-year-old girl became Olson's first victim. Her nude body, stabbed repeatedly, was found by the bank of the Fraser River. Olson did not strike again until April 16, 1981, when he abducted a 13-year-old girl using a strategy to which he routinely resorted. Once in his car, Olson offered the teenager a Coke laced with chloral hydrate, ostensibly to pep her up. Chloral hydrate, however, is a sedative. Olson took her to a forested area, where he raped and beat her to death with a hammer. Five days later, on April 21, Olson abducted and bludgeoned to death a 16-year-old boy.

On May 15, Olson married Joan Hale. In April, they had become the parents of a baby boy. Four days after the wedding, he clubbed to death a 16-year-old girl. On June 20, he strangled a 13-year-old girl; on July 2, he strangled a 9-year-old boy; and on July 13, he stabbed to death another young girl. Olson bludgeoned his next victim, a 15-year-old boy, on July 23. Two days later, he struck again, clubbing to death an 18-year-old woman. Olson picked up his next victim on July 27, gave her a Coke laced with choral hydrate, then abducted and strangled her.

Olson, who had been one of three suspects in the first murder, fell under considerable police suspicion at this point. Nonetheless, on July 30, he was able to pick up, drug, and bludgeon to death his final victim, a 17-year-old girl.

By this time, the public pressure on the police to get results in their investigation of the disappearances and murders of the British Columbia children had reached a fever pitch. On July 31, Olson appeared in court on indecent assault charges. He then left town, before police could assign officers to follow him. When he reappeared on August 6, police placed him under 24-hour surveillance.

On August 7, police observed Olson rob a pensioner. On August 11, they watched as he broke into two residences. On August 12, they saw him pick up two women on Vancouver Island. Although police did not have a strong case, they had solid evidence of the minor crimes that they had just witnessed Olson commit. In addition, they had one woman's accusation of indecent assault and a tenuous link between Olson and one of the murder victims. This evidence, however, was not strong enough for a first-degree-murder conviction.

Police followed Olson and his two female passengers across Vancouver Island to the west coast. Just south of Tofino, Olson left the main highway and drove up an old logging road. Police officers trailed him through the forest on foot. When Olson ordered one of the women out of the car, they moved in and made their arrest. They initially charged Olson with impaired driving and break and enter (Ferry and Inwood, 1982).

The only pieces of proof the police had were a victim's name in Olson's address book and a witness who could place Olson and that victim together on the night she was killed. Authorities believed the best they might do with this evidence was get a conviction on a single second-degree-murder charge. At this time, only four bodies had been recovered.

Confronted with the killing of the person named in his address book, Olson began on August 18 to talk about striking a bargain with police in return for a guarantee of favourable conditions in prison. On August 20, he proposed the $100 000 payment, telling police that he would provide information on each murder that only the killer could know. Olson was paid in cash by the end of that month. According to Ferry and Inwood, the RCMP justified the deal by arguing that the crime was without precedent in Canadian history and that they could later recover the cash payments either through a seizure or through a civil suit. The RCMP noted as secondary considerations the peace of mind that could be achieved for the grieving parents by determining what had happened to all the victims. They also believed that a fearful and panic-stricken community would be calmed by the knowledge that the killer had been apprehended and put behind bars (Ferry and Inwood, 1982).

Between 1987 and 1990, Paul Bernardo carried out at knife point at least eighteen violent sexual assaults in Toronto's east end. Composite sketches of the Scarborough rapist turned up Bernardo, who was interviewed by police in November 1990. At that time, he co-operated fully, providing the requested saliva, blood, and hair samples. On December 24 of that year, Bernardo and his girlfriend, Karla Homolka, drugged and raped Karla's 15-year-old sister, Tammy. Tammy died later that evening, having choked on her own vomit. Autopsy results at that time failed to indicate foul play, and neither Bernardo nor Homolka was charged.

With assistance from Homolka, Bernardo abducted, sexually assaulted, and finally strangled 14-year-old Leslie Mahaffy. In June 1991, her body was found in a reservoir near St. Catharines, dismembered and encased in pieces of cement. Bernardo and Homolka were married that same month.

On April 16, 1992, the couple abducted Kristen French, aged 15, while she was walking home from a St. Catharines high school. Over the next thirteen days, French was repeatedly sexually assaulted. After strangling her with an electrical cord, Bernardo and Homolka dumped French's body in a Burlington ditch.

The Green Ribbon Task Force, the police unit set up to investigate the crimes, experienced little success until, in January 1993, Bernardo beat Homolka viciously with a flashlight. The couple separated thereafter. When Homolka subsequently met with police, she agreed to testify against Bernardo as part of a negotiated plea for charges of manslaughter and concurrent sentences of twelve years. The DNA collected from Bernardo in 1990 was finally tested in January 1993. He was convicted in 1995 of the first-degree murders of Mahaffy and French as well as of other charges including kidnapping, forcible confinement, aggravated sexual assault, and committing an indignity to a human body. Subsequently declared a dangerous offender, Bernardo will almost certainly never emerge from prison (Jenish, 1993; 1994; 1995; 1996).

Murders performed by predatory killers like Clifford Olson and Paul Bernardo differ considerably from the typical homicide. First, the serial killer demonstrates no link with the victim. Police usually solve the standard homicide precisely because such a connection exists. Second, serial killers do not kill on the spur of the moment as most killers do. Rather, they carefully plan their homicides to conceal their own identities. They cunningly stalk, abduct, and dispatch their victims in the absence of witnesses. Moreover, they go to great lengths to destroy traces of murder weapons and other pieces of material evidence. Olson, for example, followed many victims, attracted them with promises of high-paying part-time jobs, drugged them in his rental cars, killed them in remote areas, carefully buried the bodies, and thoroughly cleaned the rental vehicles before returning them.

Not only did Olson diverge from the patterns usually demonstrated in a murder, he also deviated from the "normal" method of serial killers. Most killers of this type follow a pattern with respect to their victims' ages and sex and with regard to the method of killing (Jenkins, 1989). Olson, however, both selected his victims and chose his methods indiscriminately. He killed both boys and girls, his victims varied in age, and there was no single homicide method.

In December of 1999, police arrested William Patrick Fyfe for homicide. He was subsequently charged with the commission of five murders of middle-aged women in the Montreal area. Four of the victims, linked by Fyfe's DNA, were killed in 1999. One was murdered in 1981. When the 1999 arrests were publicized, the son of the 1981 murder victim contacted police to report that he had become acquainted with the accused around the time of his mother's death. DNA tests subsequently linked this first victim with Fyfe. Police are conducting an investigation into unsolved homicides between 1981 and 1999 in an effort to determine whether William Patrick Fyfe might have been a more prolific serial killer (Anderssen, 2000).

Since the United States experiences the lion's share of multiple murder, it is not surprising that American criminologists have developed typologies of serial killing and mass murder in an effort to increase our understanding of the motivations and circumstances underlying these forms of homicide.

Criminologists classify serial killers on several different dimensions: geographical mobility, degree of organization, and motivation (Hickey, 1997; Egger, 1998). In terms of geographical mobility, researchers categorize killers in one of three ways. *Place-specific* serial killers murder their victims in the same place each time. During the 1970s, John Wayne Gacy killed 33 young men and boys mostly in his own home in Des Plaines, Illinois, near Chicago. Serial killers classified as *local* confine their murderous activity to cities and surrounding areas or to specific regions. David Berkowitz, known as the Son of Sam or the .44 Calibre Killer, committed seven murders in the streets of New York City in the summer of 1977. The unsolved Green River killings involved the murder of at least 50 Seattle-area prostitutes in the early 1980s. Finally, *mobile* serial killers cover enormous geographical areas in their search for victims. During the 1970s, Theodore Bundy was responsible for the deaths of between 20 and 30 young women and girls in at least five states from Washington in the Pacific Northwest to Florida in the southeastern United States.

In their efforts to develop psychological profiles of serial killers, the FBI classifies these murders on a continuum, ranging from highly organized on the one hand to severely disorganized on the other. Profilers determine the degree of the killer's psychological organization from characteristics of the crime scene and provide investigators with tentative profiles of the killer's personality traits and personal habits. Organized killers are intelligent, charismatic, and socially and sexually adept, while disorganized killers exhibit below average intelligence and are immature and withdrawn. Organized serialists are better educated, more likely to hold jobs, and to be married. Being single, living alone, and holding low-skilled jobs or being unemployed are likely to be traits possessed by disorganized killers. Organized murderers are more in control of their emotions and are more interested in media attention than are their disorganized counterparts. Where organized killers come and go by day and tend to be more mobile, disorganized killers are nocturnal and live and work near the scenes of their crimes (Hickey, 1997).

Criminologists have also developed a scheme to classify serial killers on the basis of motivation. The principal motivational types are visionary, mission, hedonistic, power–control, comfort, and disciple. *Visionary* killers are usually mentally ill. They hear voices and see images that encourage them to kill again and again. The occurrence of this type is very rare. The motivation of the *mission-oriented* killer is to eliminate certain groups in order to make society a better place to live. Unabomber Theodore Kaczynski, for example, targeted individuals associated with the science and technology that he believed was destroying the world. His career as a serial bomber spanned the years 1978 to 1995, when he was finally apprehended. His bombs killed three people in sixteen attacks. Many more victims were seriously injured. Kaczynski pled guilty and is serving a life sentence in a maximum security prison in Colorado (Holmes and Holmes, 1998).

Hedonistic serial murder takes two forms — lust and thrill — that are difficult to separate in practice. Lustful sexual desire and the thrill of terrorizing vic-tims have served as intoxicants to a long list of killers, such as Kenneth Bianchi and Angelo Buono (the Hillside Strangler) and Leonard Lake and Charles Ng. In the Los Angeles area between 1977 and 1979, Bianchi and Buono kidnapped, raped, and murdered a dozen young women. They subsequently dumped their victims on area hillsides. Both are serving life sentences for their crimes.

Another hedonistic killing team, Leonard Lake and Charles Ng, were responsible for a series of brutal murders in the mid-1980s on a ranch in Calaveras County, California. Lake and Ng used Lake's house and an adjacent bunker to rape, torture, and murder numerous female victims they had abducted. They videotaped many of these events. Caught shoplifting in June 1985, Lake was apprehended, while Ng escaped. Later, under questioning, Lake committed suicide. Ng fled to Canada, where police apprehended him in Calgary a month later. Ng was eventually extradited to the United States in 1991. He was tried, convicted on twelve counts of murder, and sentenced to death in June 1999 (Newton, 2000).

For the *power–control* killer, the desire to exert total control over the life and death of victims is a strong motivator, one that compelled nurse Donald Harvey to kill at least 37 of his patients over fifteen years during the 1970s and 1980s. Harvey, who is currently serving a life sentence for his crimes, may be the most prolific serial killer in America during the twentieth century (Newton, 2000).

Comfort killers murder for material reasons. Into this group fall professional killers and others whose goal it is to meet the financial needs required for a comfortable existence. During the 1970s and 1980s, Richard Kulinski worked as a freelance killer and hitman for a New Jersey organized crime syndicate. Known as the "Ice Man," he admitted to the murders of approximately 100 people. Having made a good living at his trade for a considerable period of time, he was apprehended by undercover police and is now serving several life sentences (Bruno, 1993). Dorothy Puenta is a comfort killer of a different sort. In 1988, California officials charged Puente with nine counts of murder in the deaths of boarders at her rooming house in Sacramento. Puente murdered her tenants, buried several in the backyard, and fraudulently cashed their Social Security cheques (Holmes and Holmes, 1998).

Disciple killers follow charismatic individuals who operate in a leadership role or represent someone with whom they are deeply in love. During the late 1970s, for example, Charlene Gallego played a crucial supportive role in her husband's murderous undertakings. Accepting and embracing Gerald's bizarre sexual fantasies, Charlene assisted in the abduction, sexual assault, and brutal murder of nine women. When a former boyfriend became suspicious of her husband, Charlene actively participated in his death. For their crimes, Gerald was sentenced to death and Charlene is serving life in prison. Investigators believe that Carol Bundy performed a similar supporting role in Doug Clark's killing of seven women in Hollywood in 1980. Some observers also believe that Caril Ann Fugate actively aided Charles Starkweather in a week-long murder spree that resulted in eleven deaths in Nebraska and Wyoming in 1957 (Newton, 2000).

MASS MURDER

Mass murder, like serial killing, is an extremely rare form of homicide. The worst such incidents to occur in North America have taken place in the United States. In 1995, Timothy McVeigh set off a bomb that killed 168 people in Oklahoma City. In 1991, George Hennard drove through the front window of a diner in Killeen, Texas. He emerged from his vehicle and murdered 22 people before taking his own life. In 1984, James Huberty entered a McDonald's restaurant in San Ysidro, California, and shot to death 21 people, some of them children. In 1966, Charles Whitman climbed the tower at the University of Texas in Austin and began firing at people around the campus, killing 16 people. More recently, in 1987, Ronald Gene Simmons also shot and killed 16 in a murder spree in Arkansas. In terms of loss of life, the next most serious of these events have involved death tolls of 14. One of these incidents occurred in Canada in 1989; with the exception of the Air India bombing, the "Montreal massacre" was the worst mass murder in the country's history (Came, 1989).

At 5:10 p.m. on December 6, 1989, 25-year-old Marc Lépine entered the six-storey engineering building on the campus of the University of Montreal. He carried a green garbage bag containing a .223 calibre Sturm Ruger semi-automatic rifle weighing 3 kilograms and capable of firing 50 rounds in rapid succession. The versatility of the weapon, the devastating "knockdown" power of its bullets, its light weight, and its deadly accuracy have made it a popular choice with police SWAT teams and military units around the world.

After shooting and killing his first victim, a young secretary, in a hall on the second floor, Lépine entered a classroom that contained 60 students. Interrupting the lecture, he ordered the men to leave the class. When no one moved, Lépine fired two shots into the ceiling. With the full attention of his audience, he said, "You are all a bunch of feminists and I hate feminists." The male students and their professor complied with his request at this point, leaving behind the ten women in the class. As one of these young women attempted to reason with him, Lépine opened fire. When he left the room, six lay dead.

Descending to the first floor, Lépine continued his rampage, shooting sporadically at fleeing students. He entered a cafeteria, where he eventually murdered three more women before walking up to the third floor, where he entered another classroom, this time containing only 26 students and two professors. After ordering the men to leave, Lépine once again opened fire, leaping up on desks and shooting at women who ducked for cover. After killing four more women, he ended his murder spree by turning the rifle on himself. In less than half an hour, in four locations on three different floors, Lépine had shot and killed fourteen women and wounded another thirteen people, most of whom were also women. In the suicide note he left behind, he blamed feminists for ruining his life (Wallace, 1989).

The "Montreal massacre" raised a number of issues beyond the loss of life and injuries sustained by the victims. Two were specifically related to the crime. A coroner's report criticized police and other emergency workers for their very slow response to this emergency. The report pointed out that, had Lépine not decided to end his life when he did, the number of dead and wounded could have been much higher. Another concern was the need for stricter controls on the availability of semi-automatic rifles of the type used by Lépine. Most semi-automatics can be easily converted to fully automatic weapons. At the time, Canadian gun merchants were legally selling about two thousand .223 calibre rifles annually (Kaihla, 1989).

The Montreal massacre highlighted the fact that violence against women is widespread in Canada. Some researchers estimate that as many as a million Canadian women may be abused by husbands and live-in partners each year. Many social scientists view the high rates of violence against women as an outcome of men's growing feelings of inferiority and inadequacy in the face of women's increasing demonstrations of competence, intelligence, and talent. Presenting the greatest threat to men are the increasing numbers of women entering professions formerly dominated by men. Engineering, it has been pointed out, is but a case in point.

Of perhaps the greatest concern were some of the statements following the massacre, many of which supported Lépine's position on women. Across Canada, media talk shows and letters to the editor indicated that some Canadians believed that the dead and wounded women in Montreal, and feminists generally, deserved such a fate; women were urged to know their "rightful place" in Canadian society (Bergman, 1989).

Criminologists have developed a typology of the mass murderer that includes the following analytic categories: the family annihilator, the pseudo-commando, the disgruntled employee, the disciple, and the set-and-run killer (Deitz, 1986; Holmes and Holmes, 1994).

The most common type of mass murder is *family annihilation*. In such cases, family members comprise both the victims and the perpetrators. Usually, the killers are husbands and fathers and the victims are wives and children. It is not unusual for family annihilation incidents to end with the perpetrator's suicide. The most sensational case of family annihilation in recent decades involved Ronald Gene Simmons who, in Arkansas in 1987, wiped out over a dozen family members spanning three generations. His murder spree also resulted in the deaths of several others outside the family. Forgoing his rights of appeal, Simmons hastened his own execution, which took place on June 25, 1990 (Fox and Levin, 1994).

Canada is not without its fair share of such incidents. On July 6, 2000, in Kitchener, Ontario, William Luft stabbed his wife to death and shot his four children, aged three months to seven years, with a .22 calibre rifle. The chronically unemployed and financially distressed mechanic subsequently used the rifle to take his own life (Freeze, 2000). In 1996, Mark Chahal of Vernon, B.C., used two handguns to kill his wife, eight relatives, and then himself.

Pseudo-commando killers display two principal characteristics — a fascination with firearms and a penchant for planning. Several spectacular U.S. cases exemplify this type of killer. In August 1966, former marine Charles Whitman climbed the tower at the University of Texas in Austin carrying with him a trunk-load of high-powered rifles and other weapons.

He began sniping just before noon. By the time he was shot and killed by police less than two hours later, the death toll had mounted to sixteen (Lane and Gregg, 1994). More recently, in 1999, teenagers Dylan Klebold and Eric Harris launched an intricately planned, two-man assault on a high school in a suburb of Denver, Colorado. They killed eleven classmates and a teacher and wounded many others. Their suicides terminated the event.

Disgruntled-employee murderers are workers who feel egregiously wronged in the workplace and seek revenge on their presumed persecutors. Several such incidents in the United States in recent years have involved postal workers who have resorted to very violent means to express their displeasure with the perceived affronts of supervisors and co-workers. The concentration of such highly publicized cases involving U.S. postal employees has introduced into vernacular the term "going postal." The most serious of these incidents involved Patrick Henry Sherrill, a postal worker in Edmond, Oklahoma. After being reprimanded for inferior performance, Sherrill returned on the morning of August 20, 1986. Dressed in his blue postal uniform and carrying a mail bag filled with weapons and ammunition, he entered his former workplace and began shooting. Before eventually taking his own life, he killed fourteen and wounded six (Fox and Levin, 1994).

While work-related mass murders are extremely rare in Canada, they have occurred. Valery Fabrikant was a gifted engineer and researcher who migrated to Canada in 1979 and was hired as a researcher at Concordia University. Because of an enduring series of conflicts with colleagues and administrators, Fabrikant's department recommended, in the fall of 1991, that he be dismissed. Although a faculty committee reversed the original decision, Fabrikant was not satisfied. Beginning in the spring of 1992, he sent electronic mail to faculty members at universities throughout Canada and the United States accusing Concordia engineering professors of engaging in academic fraud and claiming that his proposed dismissal was an effort to silence him before he could expose their malfeasance. Concordia University fired Fabrikant. In August 1992, the former employee entered the Henry Hall Building on Concordia's campus in Montreal wearing a dark suit, a white shirt, and sunglasses and carrying three pistols. Fabrikant took escalators to the ninth floor where he began his search for his former colleagues. In all, Fabrikant killed four and wounded one before being captured by police at the scene (Fox and Levin, 1994). Another example is Pierre Lebrun, who in 1999 shot six co-workers at an Ottawa-Carleton transit company, killing four and injuring two before killing himself.

Mass murderers of the *disciple* type are followers of a charismatic leader. Perhaps the most infamous example is the "family" led by Charles Manson. On August 9, 1969, Manson family members Charles "Tex" Watson, Patricia Krenwinkel, Linda Kasabian, and Susan Atkins scaled the fence surrounding the estate of film director Roman Polanski and his wife, actress Sharon Tate. On the grounds and in the house, they brutally murdered the pregnant Tate and four visitors. Several days later, members of the family broke into the house of Leno and Rosemary LaBianca and killed them with particular viciousness. While Manson was present at neither location when the murders were committed, authorities held him responsible for the homicides and convicted him along with the rest. Manson family members and other witnesses attributed the homicidal acts of Watson, Krenwinkle, Kasabian, and Atkins to the extremely powerful control that Charles Manson exerted over them. All are serving life sentences (Lane and Gregg, 1994).

The *set-and-run mass murderer* sets murder in motion but is absent from the scene when the death occurs. Typical devices for this form of killing include bombs, incendiary devices, and poison. Because of the absence of the perpetrator and the careful planning of these incidents, culprits are often very difficult to apprehend. Many terrorist acts are examples of set-and-run mass murders. In April of 1995, former soldier Timothy McVeigh parked a Ryder truck packed with explosives adjacent to the Murrah Building in Oklahoma City. The resulting blast killed 168 and wounded many others. The U.S. Federal courts subsequently convicted McVeigh and sentenced him to death. A Canadian example of this type of mass murder took place in 1992 and involved the deaths of nine replacement mine workers. Miner Roger Warren was convicted of nine counts of second-degree murder for planting a bomb, which exploded at the Giant gold mine in Yellowknife, N.W.T.

TERRORISM

Terrorism involves the calculated stimulation of fear through the threat or actual use of cruelty, killing, or both. Terrorists actively disseminate fear through a population to obtain or maintain power. Whether particular acts are defined as terrorist varies considerably with moral assessments of the justice of the cause for which the acts are carried out. One person's terrorist is another's martyr, hero, or heroine (Nettler, 1982; Vetter and Perlstein, 1991).

Terrorists can be individuals, independent organizations, or agents of recognized state governments. The underlying rationale for most terrorist acts is the amelioration of economic or social conditions that terrorists or their sponsors find unacceptable. Insurgent efforts to change the world result in all types of acts. Nettler (1982) cites, in this regard, the extremist views of French philosopher Maurice Merleau-Ponty, who argued that idealistic killing is not murder. When killers experience neither personal gain nor pleasure and risk their own lives in their deeds, the acts cannot, according to Merleau-Ponty, be defined as murder. Terrorists see themselves as governed by a higher morality, under which "righteous homicide justifies killing innocents."

The amount of support terrorists receive from recognized world governments varies. The sponsorship of terrorism is not confined to Libya, Syria, Iraq, Iran, and Cuba. Both democratic and communist governments, including the United States and the former U.S.S.R., have been accused of complicity in the training, funding, planning, and execution of terrorist acts. Not only do some governments terrorize others, they terrorize their own citizens to maintain control and remain in power (Vetter and Perlstein, 1991).

The terrorist incidents receiving the widest attention in the media are those that ostensibly are carried out against a government by individuals or small bands of rebels. This is the situation that characterizes terrorism in Canada.

The goals of terrorist activities are varied. Some groups seek support for worldwide revolution against the "forces of oppression." The Red Army of Japan, the Red Brigade of Italy, and the Baader Meinhof gang of the former West Germany have championed such causes. Other revolutionaries advocate sovereignty for the groups they claim to represent. Campaigns to overthrow dominant governments, create independent states, or accomplish first one and then the other are common. Infamous examples of groups with these goals in mind are the Palestine Liberation Organization (PLO) and the Irish Republican Army (IRA) (Nettler, 1982). A militant cell of Canada's Front de libération du Québec (FLQ) was a terrorist organization of this type. The FLQ's goal was to create an independent Quebec. Examples of groups with similar aims that are currently active in Canada include Armenian and Sikh nationalists fighting for the creation of homelands in other parts of the world.

Terrorists turn a blind eye to conventional rules of premeditated violence. They consider no one off limits as a potential target; their victims are frequently women and children. Often, victims have no link whatsoever with the problem for which the terrorists seek redress. Sometimes terrorists select victims for shock value (e.g., innocent children), while at other times victims are chosen at random. It is also not uncommon for terrorists to increase the impact of their acts by striking the largest number of victims possible.

Terrorists rationalize the killing of innocents on two grounds. First, they argue that the righteousness of the cause justifies the destruction of any life and property. Second, they maintain that there are no truly innocent victims. In the eyes of terrorists, people who are otherwise innocent assume guilt for their complicity in maintaining the status quo opposed by the insurgents.

Efficient terrorism necessitates a certain economy of action and impact. The goal is to produce the greatest possible shock and indignation with a deed of limited scope. To meet these objectives, terrorists must hold captive, injure, or kill a few in a way that will strike terror in the hearts of many. The media play a major role in this amplification process. Indeed, the electronic media in particular often shape the focus of such terrorist activity, ensuring that for every individual victimized, perhaps millions are intimidated. Through the media and their ability to amplify impact, terrorists exert leverage well beyond their actual means and strength. With a massive media audience, terrorist groups can draw attention to their causes, present political justifications for their actions, and cultivate sympathy for their plights (Rubin and Friedland, 1986; Vetter and Perlstein, 1991).

One of the great fears regarding terrorism involves the acquisition and application of nuclear technology. Billed by some as the crime of the twenty-first century, nuclear terrorism would involve gangs stealing the essential materials and manufacturing small nuclear devices. The bomb might then be hidden somewhere in a large city and its inhabitants held for ransom. Weapons-grade nuclear material is often found missing from nuclear reactors; it appears likely that much of this material is being stolen (Vetter and Perlstein, 1991).

Although much more common in European and Central and South American countries, terrorist activity has been and is practised in North America. In Canada, terrorism involves both members of long-established collectivities and recent immigrant groups. In 1970, the FLQ initiated terrorist activity in pursuit of an independent Quebec. On October 5, a small militant cell of the FLQ kidnapped British trade commissioner James Cross. In a note found in a University of Montreal locker, the cell demanded three things in exchange for Cross's safe return. First, FLQ members insisted that 23 "political prisoners" be released by Canadian authorities. Second, they demanded $500 000 in gold. Finally, they insisted on safe passage from Canada to Cuba. The government of Canada rejected all but the last of these conditions.

Forty minutes after the government announced its decision not to comply with all three demands, the FLQ kidnapped Quebec's minister of labour, Pierre Laporte. On Friday, October 16, after receiving formal requests from the city of Montreal and the province of Quebec, Prime Minister Pierre Trudeau introduced in Parliament the *War Measures Act*, which gave sweeping powers to the police to search, seize, and lay arrests without warrants and to detain individuals without trial. On October 18, police discovered the body of Pierre Laporte in the trunk of a car near Montreal. Within hours, Parliament passed the *War Measures Act*.

In short order, police made about 450 arrests, most of them in Montreal. Many who were jailed had only the vaguest connections with the Quebec liberation movement. The government moved significant numbers of armed soldiers into the streets of Ottawa, Quebec City, and Montreal and placed the RCMP on full alert across the nation.

On November 6, police raided a Montreal apartment in search of James Cross. FLQ members Jacques and Paul Rose, hiding behind a false wall in a closet, eluded apprehension. On December 3, Montreal police and the army surrounded the building in north Montreal where Cross was being held captive. The captors agreed to free Cross in return for safe passage to Cuba. On December 28, police traced the killers of Pierre Laporte to a farmhouse outside of Montreal. They were captured, tried, and subsequently convicted of kidnapping and murder.

Terrorist acts in Canada have had as their goal the instigation of political change and the creation of independent states in foreign countries. During the early 1900s, Turks slaughtered such enormous numbers of Armenians living in Turkey that a United Nations report referred to these killings as the first case of genocide in this century. As a result of the persecution of Armenians by past Turkish governments, radical Armenian groups around the world have championed a cause that has two key demands: an official recognition of the incident and a formal apology. More importantly, they are also insisting on the creation of a separate Armenian state on land now under Turkish rule.

To realize these ends, some Armenians have engaged in acts of terrorism in Canada and other countries. In the early 1980s, Armenians seriously wounded a commercial counsellor for the Turkish government. In another incident in Ottawa, Armenian terrorists killed a Turkish attaché in his car at a traffic light. In May 1985, three Armenian nationalists attacked the Turkish embassy in Ottawa. A Pinkerton guard who fired on the terrorists was killed, and the Turkish ambassador was seriously injured. The three took eleven hostages and held them for four hours before their release was negotiated (Clugston, 1985). There are other examples. In May 1989, a man hijacked a Greyhound bus headed from Montreal to New York City and forced the driver to take him and the loaded bus to Parliament Hill in Ottawa. The hijacker demanded the withdrawal of Syrian troops from Lebanon. He eventually surrendered and no one was injured. In another incident, on April 20, 1995, a pipe bomb exploded outside the Prince Edward Island legislature, injuring one man (*Toronto Star*, 1995).

One of the bloodiest acts of terrorism in modern history took place in Canadian jurisdiction on June 22, 1985, when a bomb planted in Toronto exploded an Air India jet bound from Toronto to Bombay. The jet went down off the coast of Ireland, killing all 329 people aboard. Most passengers were Canadian women and children of Indian origin. Militant Sikhs are believed responsible for the action.

On the afternoon of June 23, a CP Air jumbo jet out of Vancouver landed at Tokyo's Narita airport about fourteen minutes ahead of schedule. Shortly afterward, an explosion killed two baggage handlers and seriously injured four others who were unloading luggage from the jet. CP Flight 003 from Vancouver was a connecting flight for Air India Flight 301 to Bangkok. Investigators believe that terrorists intended the bomb to explode on that Air India flight — a second attack on Air India in as many days — but timed the bomb incorrectly.

The cause championed with an all-consuming passion by Sikh extremists around the world is the establishment of Khalistan, an independent Sikh homeland in India's Punjab state. Radical Sikhs see this homeland as vital to their political autonomy and cultural and religious identity.

The incident that provoked violence between Sikhs and other Indians was an attack ordered by Indian Prime Minister Indira Gandhi against a group of Sikhs who had occupied the Golden Temple, a Sikh shrine. Largely in retaliation for this attack, Ghandi was herself assassinated by her Sikh bodyguards on October 31, 1984 (Barber, 1985; Posner, 1985).

Commentators have offered several accounts of why Sikh extremism is so deeply rooted in Canada. First, a relatively large number of Sikhs live in this country. Second, many Sikh immigrants are young, have no jobs, have little education, and are easily impressed by radicals in their midst. Third, ethnic passions have become powerful incentives for terrorist activity in democratic countries like Canada and the United States. Lengthy borders, numerous ports of entry, technological sophistication, affluence, and proximity to the United States make Canada a relatively attractive target for international terrorists (CSIS, 1995). Nonetheless, as of 1998, the government cut its funding for the Canadian Security Intelligence Service to $155 million from $244 million in 1993 (*Toronto Star*, 1997).

After the largest and most expensive homicide investigations in Canadian history, two men were charged in October 2000 with eight counts of murder, attempted murder, and conspiracy to bomb aircraft including the Air India and Narita incidents. While the investigation continues, the government has assigned over a dozen prosecutors to what is expected to be a lengthy, complicated, and expensive trial. One man was previously convicted of manslaughter for the Narita incident. The suspected mastermind of the Air India bombing was killed by Indian police in 1992 (Mickleburgh, 2000).

THE THEORETICAL EXPLANATION OF HOMICIDE

THE INTERACTIONIST INTERPRETATION OF THE TYPICAL HOMICIDE SITUATION

Regardless of the identities of the participants, the relationship between them, and the location of the occurrence, the progression of events in the typical violent interchange reveals a remarkably consistent pattern. In his research on the sequential process of events in assault and homicide, Luckenbill (1977) outlines a series of stages through which offenders and victims usually proceed. The first event in a violent altercation is typically a gesture or statement that one of the parties interprets as offensive. The second stage involves the decision that must be made by the affronted party. Insulted persons have three choices: they may excuse the insult by judging that the offending persons are crazy or drunk or that they meant the insult as a joke; they may simply agree to lose face and decide to back down; or they may retaliate verbally, physically, or both.

The third stage is contingent on a decision to retaliate. At the beginning of this stage in the interpersonal dispute, with the initial offence reacted to combatively, the instigator must decide whether to end the exchange or escalate hostilities. If he or she decides to counterattack rather than capitulate, the altercation moves to the fourth stage.

At this point, people usually resort to weapons. One or both participants may simply transform a readily available object into a fighting implement. Alternatively, they may leave in search of a weapon. Then, either one person immediately overcomes the other or the battle continues until one person gets the upper hand and lays low the opponent. If the loser lives, the crime is assault, aggravated assault, assault with a weapon, or attempted murder. If the loser dies, the crime is homicide.

Onlookers play important roles throughout this interaction sequence that depend on their definition of the situation. They may intervene to de-escalate hostility, they may remain neutral throughout, or they may incite the participants to even more aggression and violence.

After the loser has been downed, both the winner and the audience have some choices to make. These decisions become particularly important if the loser is dead. In such circumstances, the killer must decide whether to remain at the scene or flee. Where intimates are victims, assailants usually remain voluntarily; it is not uncommon for them to call the police. The audience can either encourage the offender to run or restrain the culprit from leaving the scene of the crime.

THE SUBCULTURE OF VIOLENCE

To account for variations in murder rates among different regions and different groups, Wolfgang and Ferracuti (1967) formulated a theory of homicide based on the sociological concept of subculture. Sociologists refer to a subculture as an identifiable segment of the broader societal culture that differs from the larger culture in terms of certain distinctive values and norms. These unique values and norms adhered to by members of the subculture are passed on from one generation to the next through socialization. Wolfgang and Ferracuti argue that the lower classes and some ethnic groups possess values and live by rules that differ from those that orient and govern the actions of people in the middle and upper classes and other ethnic collectivities. Members of these violence-prone subcultures hold different conceptions of the meaning and importance of honour and status, place less emphasis on the value of human life, and view the world as an inhospitable jungle.

Specifically, Wolfgang and Ferracuti argue that lower-class people and people who are black or Latino have different orientations to violence. They are socialized from an early age to view physical aggression as an acceptable, expected, and occasionally necessary response to a challenge to their masculinity. For lower-class males whose status has been threatened, responding with aggression is a culturally mandated way of expressing courage and defending against a loss of dignity. Violence is viewed as neither wrong nor antisocial but rather as the normal way to resolve interpersonal conflict. Those who employ violent tactics experience neither guilt nor disapproval from their peers. When two or more people who are strongly integrated into the violent subculture come into conflict, chance events, the respective strength of the opponents, and the presence or absence of weapons decide the outcome of the altercation.

Using their "**subculture of violence**" perspective, Wolfgang and Ferracuti provide an account of higher rates of violence in the southern United States, in black urban ghettos, and in Latin American nations. They explain the high homicide rates among lower-class blacks in urban slums and in the American south generally by pointing to prevailing subcultural values and norms that promote the settling of disputes through physical means. In another application of their theory, Wolfgang and Ferracuti explain the astronomically high numbers of homicides in Colombia during the *violencia Colombia* of the 1950s. During that decade, nearly one in every 50 Colombians was killed by a countryman. Wolfgang and Ferracuti cite the Latino subcultural emphasis on "machismo" as the primary explanation.

The subculture of violence perspective has been criticized on several grounds. First, some studies suggest that there are no differences between the lower and the middle classes in terms of their enthusiasm for violence as a means of conflict resolution. Second, some of the research through which the subculture of violence hypotheses have been tested is tautological; that is, the subculture of violence is identified by high murder rates, the very phenomenon it is supposed to cause. Cause and effect, in short, are the same.

THE THEORY OF DETERRENCE AND THE USE OF CAPITAL PUNISHMENT

Since Confederation, Canada has executed 706 convicted murderers — 693 men and 13 women — all by hanging (Boyd, 1988b). The most recent execution took place at Toronto's Don Jail in 1962, when two convicted murderers were hanged. Parliament declared a moratorium on the death penalty in 1968, and in 1976 it abolished **capital punishment** in a free vote in the House of Commons (130 to 124). On June 30, 1987, Parliament voted on this issue again; the results were 148 to 127 in favour of continued abolition (MacKenzie, 1987).

Although Canada abolished capital punishment for all intents and purposes in the 1960s, widespread support for it continues. According to a 1995 Angus Reid survey, 69 percent of Canadians favour capital punishment. In 1992, a Gallup poll estimated that 60 percent felt this way (Western Report, 1995).

Canadians have supported a return to capital punishment for a number of reasons. First, certain types of murder receive much publicity, particularly when police officers are killed by armed assailants. The Canadian Association of Chiefs of Police has consistently lobbied for the reinstitution of capital punishment. The extensive coverage given to the funerals of officers killed in the line of duty (nine in 1984) does much to raise public sympathy (Hackler and Janssen, 1985). It is not unusual for thousands of delegates to attend these ceremonies.

A tremendous amount of publicity surrounded the cases of serial killers Clifford Olson and, more recently, Paul Bernardo. The events of the case fuelled the public's demand for protection from such "crazed homicidal maniacs." The celebrated trials of Peter Demeter in the 1970s and of Helmuth Buxbaum and Colin Thatcher in the 1980s have also focused Canadian attention on the issues of murder and its control. The

media routinely report the fine details of many violent crimes, creating the mistaken perception among Canadians that violent crime is rising rapidly, that it is reaching epidemic proportions, and that controlling this "critical" problem requires drastic action.

Polls have consistently indicated that a majority of Canadians believe that a large portion of all crime is violent. In fact, fewer than 10 percent of *Criminal Code* offences are violent, and in only a fraction of these incidents is anyone seriously injured. Sixty-five percent of Canadians believe that the murder rate in Canada has increased since the abolition of capital punishment. In fact, it has declined. In addition, many Canadians feel that the legal system is not tough enough on criminals perpetrating serious crimes. For example, 87 percent of Canadians believe that convicted murderers are allowed back into society too soon. The public perception is that a life sentence in reality means release after a few years behind bars (Nichols, 1987).

Capital punishment is believed to serve three separate functions. First, the death penalty permanently incapacitates the offender and precludes the possibility of a convicted person committing the offence again. Second, it represents retribution; it satisfies the public's call for "an eye for an eye." Finally, many Canadians firmly believe that capital punishment is the strongest possible deterrent to those who might consider taking the life of another human being. It is the issue of deterrence around which the debate is most heated. Because it seems more civilized, deterrence is favoured over retribution as the rationale for capital punishment. Many proponents of capital punishment believe what deterrence theory proclaims but cannot empirically substantiate. According to the popular deterrence doctrine, severe sanctions such as capital punishment will deter more effectively than punishments such as life in prison, which are presumably less dire.

Critics dispute, on both logical and empirical grounds, the ability of severe punishment to dissuade people from murderous action. As deterrence theory points out, the only crimes subject to deterrence are those in which offenders contemplate the implications of their acts. Crimes in which people do not calmly weigh the potential costs against the potential benefits cannot be deterred. But people seldom rationally consider the implications of their homicidal actions. Rather, murders are usually crimes of passion, which are bereft of reason and, as such, immune

Box 10.5
OTTAWA AIMS TO UNCOVER WRONGFUL CONVICTIONS

Ottawa will give itself wider powers to uncover wrongful convictions such as those pronounced on Donald Marshall, Guy Paul Morin and David Milgaard.

Government officials confirmed yesterday that Justice Minister Anne McLellan will unveil the law today as part of a multifaceted bill, another part of which would force judges to consider tougher sentences on those convicted of so-called home-invasion robberies.

Sources said that the minister intends to strengthen the powers of justice officials when investigating a case under Section 690, also known as the "mercy clause." Under 690, a convicted individual can apply for a review of his or her case if he or she feels wrongfully convicted. The law has come under criticism because it is not transparent enough and because the process is viewed as too closed.

Under the changes, the Justice Department will begin hiring investigators to look into the controversial cases. The department would be given the power to compel the production of all documents and the appearance of all witness relevant to a particular case.

"The unit will actually be expanded to actually include investigators to assist counsel in reviewing cases," the source said. "Right now, we don't have that."

Under Section 690, people who claim they were wrongfully convicted can apply to the Justice Department for a review, provided that they have exhausted all other avenues of appeal. However, only a handful of the hundreds of applications made over the years have been successful, and legal groups such as the Association in Defence of the Wrongfully Convicted have argued that the clause is too defensive of the status quo and premised on the assumption of guilt.

Other changes in the law would compel the minister to produce an annual report for Parliament.

Sources said the government wants to widen access to the process, and plans to advertise the mechanism on the Internet.

Discussion Questions

Why is the government of Canada considering this initiative at this time? Is the measure a case of too little, too late?

Source: Brian Laghi, *Globe and Mail*, June 8, 2000, pp. A1 and A8. Reprinted with permission from the *Globe and Mail*.

to deterrence. Not only are crimes of passion "undeterrable," the deprivations faced by disadvantaged class, ethnic, and racial groups, within which murder is concentrated, may well be too severe to be affected even by a punitive deterrent as dire as death.

There is much empirical support for these contentions. Many studies of deterrence conducted in the United States, for example, show little difference in homicide rates between states with the death penalty and those without the death penalty. Rather, they suggest that many states with capital punishment have higher homicide rates than those without. Similar findings are evident for states that have abolished capital punishment. Comparisons of murder rates before and after abolition show no significant differences. Moreover, when states that had abolished capital punishment in the 1970s re-instituted it in the 1980s, no significant decline occurred in the murder rate (Archer and Gartner, 1984; Bowers, 1984).

Canadian evidence also calls into question the deterrent value of capital punishment. The death penalty appears to be no more of a deterrent than is a sentence of life imprisonment. First, when Parliament abolished capital punishment in 1976 the homicide rate declined rather than rose. Second, the numbers of police killed in the decade before abolition and in the decade after abolition are virtually identical — 38 and 37, respectively. This is particularly significant because the number of Canadian police officers from 1976 to 1985 was nearly double the number from 1966 to 1975 (Hackler and Janssen, 1985).

Other critics of the death penalty argue that rehabilitation is a more desirable and civilized response to homicide than is execution. Some assert that the taking of a human life by other human beings, regardless of the circumstances, is immoral. Still others cite evidence, largely from the United States, suggesting that capital punishment is applied unequally; there, blacks continue to be dramatically over-represented on death row. Boyd (1988b) reports similar findings for his study of murder in Canada. In the cases analyzed for his study, all other things being equal, convicted murderers of Native and French descent were more likely to be sent to the gallows than were English Canadians. With respect to the commuting of death sentences by Parliament, Boyd notes,

> Cabinet clemency decisions seem in retrospect to have been something of a macabre lottery, subtly influenced by considerations of race, religion, and sexual orientation, among other things. Natives, French Canadians, Jews, and homosexuals were, at least occasionally, at greater risk of dying for their crimes. (Boyd, 1988b:62)

One of the main criticisms of the death penalty is that the legal system is not infallible; it makes mistakes. The possibility of sending innocent people to their deaths is sufficient, in the minds of many, to make execution unacceptable. As Edward Greenspan, a prominent Canadian criminal lawyer, expresses it,

> There is the possibility of a mistake. In our legal system human error is inevitable. Usually, a mistake in sentencing can be revoked either completely or in part. This is not possible after an innocent man has been executed. Capital punishment is essentially different from all other penalties because it is ultimate, final, and irrevocable. (Maclean's, March 16, 1987:10)

Could an innocent person be convicted of murder in Canada? The answer is unequivocally affirmative, as the cases of Donald Marshall, Guy Paul Morin, David Milgaard, and Thomas Sophonow attest. Largely on the basis of the testimony of three key witnesses, the court convicted Donald Marshall of stabbing a young man to death in a Sydney park on the night of May 28, 1971. Police found no weapon, took no crime scene photos, and performed no autopsy. Marshall was sentenced to life behind bars. A subsequent inquiry has shown that Sydney police intimidated witnesses and manipulated evidence to implicate Marshall. An RCMP investigation eventually exonerated him and he was released from prison on March 30, 1982. Another man was convicted of manslaughter in the incident (Harris, 1986). For the eleven years he spent behind bars, authorities initially awarded Marshall $270 000; a total of $100 000 of this sum went to cover his legal costs. An inquiry into this case held the justice system, and the police in particular, responsible for a miscarriage of justice (Harris, 1986). On review, Marshall's compensation was increased. He was awarded a lump-sum payment of $200 000 and is to receive a yearly income of approximately $20 000 for the rest of his life (Spears, 1990).

Guy Paul Morin's neighbour, nine-year-old Christine Jessop, was last seen alive on October 3, 1984. On New Year's eve, her remains were found in a farmer's field 50 kilometres east of her Queensville home. The investigation revealed that she was nude and that she had been sexually assaulted, stabbed, and bludgeoned. Police charged Morin in the slaying on April 22, 1985. In the subsequent trial in 1986, a jury acquitted him. Upon appeal by the Crown, the appellate court ordered a new trial and, in 1992, Morin was convicted of first-degree murder. The case against him was based on circumstantial evidence, incriminating fibre and hair samples, and reports of Morin's jailhouse confessions to other inmates of questionable credibility. Efforts at DNA testing in 1988 and 1992 proved inconclusive. With improvements in DNA technology, scientists retested the genetic material from the crime scene and proved conclusively in January 1995 that Morin was innocent. The Ontario government has compensated Morin with $1.25 million. The resultant inquiry has suggested that police manipulated evidence and that the inmates who served as witnesses lied in order to gain favourable treatment (Canadian Press Newswire, 1997; Jenish, 1997).

By the time the Supreme Court recommended a new trial in 1992, David Milgaard had served 22 years for the 1969 rape and murder of Saskatoon nursing assistant Gail Miller. For many years, another man, a convicted serial rapist, was suspected by some of being the real killer. The Saskatchewan Attorney General declined prosecution in 1992, thereby denying Milgaard the opportunity to have his name cleared. Refined DNA testing in 1997 indicated conclusively that the semen on Miller's clothing did not belong to Milgaard (Hawaleshka, 1997). The other suspect in the case, whose DNA reportedly matched that of the killer, was charged with Miller's murder in July 1997. On the basis of DNA evidence, Larry Fisher was convicted in November 1999 of the Gail Miller murder. For his years in prison, David Milgaard was awarded $10 million and an apology from the government of Saskatchewan (Nadeau, 2000).

Box 10.6
POLICE "TUNNEL VISION" GIVES NO JUSTICE

In the circles of the wrongfully convicted, it is referred to as "tunnel vision."

Scratch any number of cases — involving David Milgaard, Guy Paul Morin or the scores of other exonerations in Commonwealth jurisdictions — and one is likely to find at least a subconscious effort by police to fashion the case to fit the suspect.

"Once the police come to believe a person is guilty—for whatever spurious or nonsensical reason—they develop a blind focus," said Rev. James McCloskey, whose U.S. organization has helped exonerate 18 innocent men serving life sentences, including Mr. Milgaard.

"They get a suspect," Mr. McCloskey, founder of Centurion Ministries, said. "Then the pressure is on to close the case. There is a need to satisfy their bosses and the public. They disregard, ignore or suppress any information they come across that might point in a different direction. The human mind has an infinite capacity to justify what it wants to believe."

In the wake of the recent exonerations of Mr. Milgaard and Mr. Morin, the questions arises: How many other miscarriages of justice lie undetected? The prevalence of wrongful convictions in recent years supplies a discomfiting clue.

"The system has been shaken recently in England, Canada, Australia and the US," said Dianne Martin, a law professor at York University's Osgoode Hall law school in Toronto. "The wrongful conviction problem is staggering, and we are all facing it."

Approximately 50 serious wrongful convictions have come to light in Britain in the past couple of decades alone, half of them involving suspected Irish Republican Army terrorists.

The Australian justice system is staggering from the exposure of a series of wrongful convictions brought about through deliberate fabrication of evidence by a clutch of rogue police officers.

The situation is worst in the United States. For every five inmates executed during the past 25 years — a total of about 325 individuals — one is exonerated before the scheduled execution.

And those are only the most serious cases, Mr. McCloskey said. Wrongful convictions are almost certainly more plentiful for lesser offences. "In America, an innocent person is as rare as a pigeon in a park," he said.

Besides the Milgaard, Morin and Donald Marshall cases, Canada has had several lesser-known wrongful convictions. They include Richard Norris, who spent two years in an Ontario jail on a rape conviction before he was freed because of DNA evidence, and Wilson Nepoose, who served five years of a sexual-assault sentence in Alberta before a key witness admitted to having lied.

Mr. McCloskey said that when it comes to wrongful convictions, the impulses that drive U.S. and Canadian authorities are the same. Each case tends to feature many of the following elements:

- Suspects who are indigents or ne'er-do-wells. Not only do they closely conform to public and police stereotypes of wrong-doers, but they are least able to secure competent lawyers to represent them;

- A greater willingness to cut corners in the super-heated atmosphere of a high-profile crime. "You usually find a recklessness," said James Lockyer, a lawyer representing Mr. Morin and Mr. Milgaard. "They think it's the right guy, and they go crazy to get him";

- Suppression of evidence that the defence would have wanted to use at trial to enhance an alibi or blunt the credibility of a prosecution witness;

- An ignoring or suppression of the existence of other strong suspects;

- Construction of the case by inept investigators, particularly when a small force is involved;

- A pro-prosecution judge who undercut the defence.

Many wrongful convictions also feature evidence of a so-called jailhouse confession supplied by unsavoury and unreliable prison denizens who trade their testimony for favours. In a minority of cases, investigators overtly framed suspects using duress to extract a false confession or threatened witnesses to get them to provide false evidence.

However, the U.S. Department of Justice concluded recently that the No. 1 cause of miscarriages of justice is bad eyewitness identifications. The finding backs up a study several years ago in which professors Michael Radelet, William Lofquist, and Hugo Adam

Bedau found that mistaken eyewitness testimony lay at the heart of 209 of the approximately 350 U.S. wrongful convictions they studied.

Quite unwittingly, civilian and expert witnesses can fall prey to the urge to provide the police with what they plainly hope to hear, Prof. Martin said.

"I think it is almost a Stockholm Syndrome," she said. "The witness wants to be part of the team, part of the solution. They internalize this pressure and produce the testimony the team needs."

This urge is most pronounced with victim-witnesses, Prof. Martin said. "Their unspoken question to the police is: 'Which way do you want me to go?' Very little needs to be said by police officers before evidence starts changing like crazy."

Meanwhile, the police believe they alone understand the true rules and realities of their insular world, Prof. Martin said. The ends of convicting bad guys quickly justify the questionable means.

"Many police officers are afraid the justice system won't get it right," she said. "So they gild the lily. They leave things out. They try to give the courts what they think they want. You add in pressure from the community to solve a crime, and I sometimes think it is amazing we get it right as often as we do."

Experts in wrongful convictions believe that although prosecutors are much less likely than police to cut corners recklessly, they nonetheless may have trouble at times standing up to investigators.

"They have to work with them, so they won't always ask the hard questions," Mr. McCloskey said. "They just take it and run with it."

In its recent study, the U.S. Justice Department concluded that poor forensic work was the second-most-prevalent problem in wrongful convictions.

Joe Bellows, a senior Vancouver prosecutor, said in an interview that most prosecutors are just as shocked as the public when a wrongful conviction comes to light.

"These cases are absolutely dreadful when you see them," Mr. Bellows said. "It can shake you." He said he doesn't think he and his colleagues need a reminder, but the situation certainly underlines the need for prosecutors to maintain a fair and impartial role in presenting evidence before the court.

According to the Radelet-Lofquist-Bedau study, the average wrongful conviction takes seven years to correct. They estimated that 23 men were executed in the United States before their innocence was proved. Eight died in prison.

Mr. McCloskey said the greatest misconception in the field of wrongful convictions is that the exonera-

tion of a wrongfully convicted person is proof that the system has worked.

"In the Milgaard case, the system did everything it could to hide the truth and keep it from coming forward," he said. "The system was eventually unable to resist the force of truth. We kept coming back and coming back – for 23 years."

The reality is that police and prosecutors invariably fight such a process tooth and nail, he said, and rarely end up accepting even the most clear-cut exoneration.

"They are afraid of being embarrassed, humiliating their predecessor, or bringing the justice system into disrepute," he said. "It takes a lot of dedicated people to bring forward devastating new evidence for year after year in order to break down the walls."

Among the small band listening for cries of innocence are Centurion Ministries and the Innocence Project, a U.S. group that works exclusively on exonerations by DNA testing.

In Canada, the Association in Defence of the Wrongfully Convicted, or AIDWYC, will be joined by a new partner this fall – a York University group modelled on the Innocence Project. The centre, of which Prof. Martin will be co-director, will delve into cases referred to AIDWYC.

Mr. Lockyer, a director of AIDWYC, estimates there are three or four dozen innocent people in Canadian prisons waiting to be freed from life sentences. Mr. McCloskey believes the problem is proportionately even more profound than that.

"Since 1992, we have had 4,666 requests for help," he said of his group. "I feel safe in saying that anywhere from 50 to 70 percent of these are exactly what they say they are. We have only seen the tip of the iceberg."

The public and the justice system have learned "absolutely zero" from the slew of miscarriages of justice exposed to date, Mr. McCloskey added. He said the response instead has been a wave of dissatisfaction over the right of prisoners to appeal their convictions.

Prof. Martin is more hopeful. Ten or 15 years ago, allegations of police lying were viewed with great skepticism, and even the commissioners of the Marshall inquiry needed to be persuaded to consider systemic flaws reflected through the case.

Now, she said, it is not uncommon for a judge to reject a police witness. And the commissioner of the Morin inquiry – Fred Kaufman – automatically scheduled a phase of the probe to search for flaws in the justice system.

Discussion Questions

This box and Box 10.1 highlight a number of reasons why miscarriages of justice occur. Which of these factors do you consider most significant? Which segments of society are most likely to bear the brunt of wrongful convictions? Why is this the case? What measures need to be undertaken to correct the tunnel vision not only of the police but of other criminal justice officials? From your reading of these two boxes, identify potential sources of resistance to reforming Canada's criminal justice system and making it more accountable.

Source: Kirk Makin, *Globe and Mail*, July 22, 1997, pp. A1 and A5. Reprinted with permission from the *Globe and Mail*.

Box 10.7
LENIENCY URGED IN SOME MURDER CASES

The judge reviewing the sentences of abused female killers says Canada's murder laws are sometimes too harsh and should allow for leniency in "exceptional circumstances."

Judge Lynn Ratushny of Ontario Court (provincial division) was appointed by the federal government to examine the cases of women who claim they killed abusive men in self-defence but were still convicted of murder or manslaughter.

In her final report, obtained by Southam News, Ratushny said she is very concerned that some people accused of murder – especially women – face "irresistible" pressure to plead guilty to the lesser charge of manslaughter even though they have legitimate defences that could acquit them.

She blames this on the "relatively severe" penalties for second-degree murder – an automatic life sentence, with no eligibility for parole for between 10 and 25 years.

By contrast, there is no set penalty for manslaughter and sentences average three to eight years, with parole eligibility after one-third of the sentence.

Rather than risk a self-defence claim which if not believed will result in an automatic life sentence, Ratushny says some women opt to plead guilty under "duress" to the lesser charge – even though they may be legally innocent because they acted in self-defence.

This is a "very serious" problem, the Ottawa judge warns, adding: "Miscarriages of justice may be occuring as a result of systemic forces."

Ratushny's report was submitted last month but has not been made public.

The judge says the "extraordinary" pressure to plead guilty may be even greater on women who are charged with killing abusive partners, because they often have young families to care for and may be reluctant to testify in public about the abuse they have suffered.

Under her "modest" proposal, juries would be allowed to recommend that a person convicted of second-degree murder be considered for a more lenient sentence because of the "exceptional circumstances" in which the killing occured. The judge would then be able to impose any sentence up to life imprisonment.

In all other cases, the automatic life sentence would remain.

Ratushny said judges in other places – England, Australia, New Zealand, and some American states – have discretion to consider mitigating circumstances in sentencing people convicted of murder.

Although she reviewed 98 self-defence claims, Ratushny only recommended the federal government reopen the cases of seven women.

She said four women should be given complete freedom, one should have her sentence reduced, one should be pardoned and another should be given a new hearing before an appeal court to determine whether she was guilty of a lesser crime than first-degree murder.

Discussion Question

Do you agree that leniency in such cases is warranted and that judges should be given this discretion? What opposition might be faced by those favouring reforms along these lines?

Source: Stephen Bindman, *Toronto Star*, July 25, 1997, p. A11. Reprinted with permission from Southam News Services.

The most recent case involves Thomas Sophonow who was finally absolved in June 2000 of responsibility for the strangling death of a sixteen-year-old waitress in a Winnipeg doughnut shop in 1981. Sophonow's first murder trial in 1982 ended with a hung jury. In 1983, he was convicted in a second trial, but the verdict was overturned on appeal. Convicted in the third trial, Sophonow was once again set free by the Manitoba Court of Appeal in 1985. Sophonow was released largely because the court felt that it would be unfair to try him again. Manitoba's attempt at a fourth trial was rejected by the Supreme Court of Canada. Sophonow suffered through three trials, two convictions, two appeals, and 45 months behind bars. He spent eighteen years in an effort to clear his name. The evidence against him involved both eyewitness testimony and the words of a jailhouse informant. His evidence of an alibi was ignored. The Winnipeg police have apologized and an inquiry and compensation have been recommended (Tyler and Levy, 2000; Roberts and Ubha, 2000).

On the danger of executing the innocent, some research involving meticulous analysis of police and court records of murder cases has produced some rather unsettling results. Boyd (1988b) carefully studied 96 murder cases that ended in execution. In four of these cases, Boyd believes that an innocent person died on Canadian gallows.

Those favouring the continued abolition of capital punishment argue that other strategies are more likely to have an impact on reducing homicide rates in Canada. They note that guns, alcohol, and family violence figure prominently in murder. Stricter gun control, programs designed to control alcohol abuse, and better social policies aimed at combatting family violence and wife battering, they maintain, are more likely than capital punishment to reduce the numbers of deaths attributable to violent crime. Criminologists also point out that some countries have much less severe penalties for murder and yet produce the same results. Japan, for example, imposes sentences for murder that average about five years (Boyd, 1988b). They also note that sentences of 25 years or more leave convicted murderers with little or no hope and little left to lose. The practice may contribute to prison violence. Finally, criminologists point out that most people convicted of homicide are eventually released. When they are set free, fewer than 1 percent reoffend (Boyd, 1988b).

SUMMARY

Assault and homicide differ largely in terms of whether or not someone dies in a violent exchange. Under the law, there are several different types of homicide. These types vary according to the degree of premeditation, the context, the status of the offender, and, in some cases, the identity of the victims. Each type of homicide has punishments attached to it that vary in severity according to the nature of the offence.

Only a small proportion of *Criminal Code* offences are violent. Of violent crime, assault is the most common, while homicide is the least common. Homicide rates have levelled off in recent years and are now in decline. Rates of violent crime in general, and homicide in particular, are relatively low in Canada compared with those of the United States and, especially, Latin America.

Homicides usually occur without careful and lengthy premeditation and are most often committed by young adult males of lower-class origins. While males are also over-represented as victims, substantial numbers of females are victims. Females, however, are rarely the perpetrators of violent attacks. Most homicide victims are either acquainted with their assailants or know them well. Shooting is now the most popular method by which Canadian offenders kill their victims. The home is the location in which Canadians are at greatest risk of being injured or killed in a violent attack. Alcohol consumption is often associated with violence. A small number of killers commit suicide after a murder; they are usually emotionally attached to the victim and either overwrought with guilt and sorrow or attempting to escape punishment.

Homicides, most of which occur in the heat of the moment, are unusual in comparison with violent crimes in general. Rarer still in Canada are homicides that are meticulously planned. Even so, upper-class homicides, serial killings, mass murders, and terrorist acts, many of which are carefully planned, are each represented in the annals of Canadian crime. Serial homicides, mass murders, and acts of terrorism are further differentiated from most other types of homicide by virtue of the fact that there are often no personal connections tying victims to offenders. In the case of serial killing particularly, this makes apprehension and conviction extremely difficult.

Criminologists classify serial killers in terms of geography (place-specific, local, and mobile), psychology (organized and disorganized), and motivation (visionary, hedonistic, power–control, comfort, and disciple). Analytic categories for mass murderers are the family annihilator, the pseudo-commando, the disgruntled-employee, the disciple, and the set-and-run killer.

Symbolic interactionists point out that, while violence usually occurs spontaneously, it nonetheless follows a clearly defined sequence. The stages involve the actions, interpretations, and reactions of participants through which an escalation of aggression occurs. If someone is injured, the nature of the violent exchange is assault. If someone dies, the act is homicide. "Subculture of violence" explanations of homicide, on the other hand, stress that certain social segments have sets of values, beliefs, and norms that promote violent behaviour as a solution to problems. Values favouring violent responses are passed from one generation to the next through the process of socialization. The subculture of violence perspective, while not without its deficiencies, provides an account of regional, international, and group variations in murder rates.

The use of capital punishment as a sanction is rooted in premises derived from deterrence theory. The debate over the deterrent value of capital punishment continues in Canada, despite a recent parliamentary vote in support of continued abolition of the death penalty. Both logic and data suggest that capital punishment is unlikely to reduce homicide rates significantly. Most murders occur in the heat of passion. Most killers do not carefully contemplate the punitive costs of apprehension and conviction. Furthermore, even when murder is carefully planned, most killers believe that they will be able to elude the long arm of the law. Comparing jurisdictions that employ capital punishment with those that do not shows no meaningful differences in homicide rates. Evidence that the state has wrongly convicted accused persons and, in some instances, has executed the innocent, continues to mount.

DISCUSSION QUESTIONS

1. Discuss the similarities and differences between serial killing and mass murder.

2. Explain what makes serial killing an especially difficult crime for police to solve.

3. How do symbolic interactionism, the subculture of violence perspective, and deterrence theory explain murder? Which of these theories is the most convincing? Why?

4. What are the prospects for reducing the homicide rate in Canada?

5. Opponents of gun control are fond of claiming that it is not guns that kill people, but rather people who kill people. Assess the validity of this argument. To what extent does variation in gun-control legislation in Canada and the United States explain the sharp differences in homicide rates between the two countries?

WEB LINKS

Colin Thatcher Time Line and News Stories
http://cbc.ca/news/indepth/facts/thatcher_colin.html
A time line of events in the Colin Thatcher case, with news clips and stories from the CBC.

Researching Serial Murder: Methodological and Definitional Problems
http://www.sociology.org/content/vol003.002/hinch.html
In this paper from the *Electronic Journal of Sociology*, Ronald Hinch and Crysal Hepburn examine issues related to the definition and study of serial murder.

The Montreal Massacre
http://www.chebucto.ns.ca/CommunitySupport/Men4Change/montreal.html
This page, from a Nova Scotia organization called Men for Change, provides details of the Montreal Massacre of December 6, 1989.

Trends in Terrorism
http://www.csis-scrs.gc.ca/eng/miscdocs/200001_e.html
   This report from the Canadian Security Intelligence Service examines recent trends in international terrorism and their impact on Canada.

Air India Bombing Disaster
http://www.airindia.istar.ca/
   This Web site, produced by the RCMP, provides details of the history and investigation into the Air India Flight 182 crash.

RECOMMENDED READINGS

Boyd, N. (1988). *The Last Dance: Murder in Canada*. Scarborough: Prentice-Hall.
   An engagingly written account of homicide in Canada and the criminal justice response.

Egger, S.A. (1998). *The Killers Among Us: An Examination of Serial Murder and Its Investigation*. Upper Saddle River, NJ: Prentice-Hall.
   Contemporary analysis of various approaches to the study of serial killers using particular cases as examples. Cases include Ted Bundy, Jeffery Dahmer, John Gacy and Kenneth Bianci.

Fox J.A., and J. Levin. (2001). *The Will to Kill: Making Sense of Senseless Murder*. Needham Heights: Allyn and Bacon.
   Provides a detailed introduction to criminal homicide and its various forms as it occurs in the United States.

Harris, M. (1986). *Justice Denied: The Law versus Donald Marshall*. Toronto: Totem Books.
   Presents an articulate account of the Donald Marshall case and its aftermath.

Hickey, E.W. (1997). *Serial Murderers and Their Victims* (2nd ed.). Belmont, CA: Wadsworth.
   Reports the findings of a sociological study of contemporary serial killers.

Holmes, R.M., and S.T. Holmes. (2000). *Murder in America*. Thousand Oaks, CA: Sage.
   Discusses various types of murder in America and provides an account of why homicide rates in that country are higher than in other developed nations.

Makin, K. (1992). *Redrum: The Innocent*. Toronto: Penguin.
   Examines the case of Guy Paul Morin and his subsequent acquittal on homicide charges.

Silverman, R.A., and L. Kennedy. (1993). *Deadly Deeds: Murder in Canada*. Scarborough: Nelson.
   Provides a solid introduction to the study of murder in Canada and presents the authors' analysis of criminal homicide over the years from 1961 to 1990.

Vallee, B. (1986). *Life with Billy*. Toronto: Seal Books.
   Presents the case of Jane Hurshman who killed her spouse Billy Stafford with a shotgun blast as he dozed at the wheel of his truck in the couple's laneway. Discusses details of the case that gave rise to the battered woman defence in Canada.

White, J.R. (1998). *Terrorism: An Introduction*. Belmont, CA: Wadsworth.
   Introduces the concept and explanations of terrorism and provides a comprehensive overview of domestic and foreign terrorist activity in North America and abroad.

Williams, S. (1997). *Invisible Darkness: The Strange Case of Paul Bernardo and Karla Homolka*. Toronto: Little Brown.
   Provides a detailed discussion of the murders of Kristen French, Leslie Mahaffy, and Tammy Homolka by Paul Bernardo and Karla Homolka.

CHAPTER 11

SEXUAL ASSAULT

The aims of this chapter are to familiarize the reader with:

- the differences between rape laws and sexual assault laws
- the extent of sexual assault
- characteristics of victims, assailants, the offence, and its effects
- the concept of double rape and its implication for rape reform
- the way in which a culture encourages sexual assault
- the similarities and differences between sexual assaults against adults and children
- the sexual assault of children in institutional settings
- feminist perspectives on sexual assault
- issues surrounding the control of sexual assault: the intent and effects of legal reform

INTRODUCTION

Canadians have traditionally viewed **rape**, indecent assault, and child molestation as heinous crimes committed by dangerous psychopathic strangers. Widely recommended self-defence measures reflect this stereotype. To protect themselves from attack by presumably deranged predators, women are advised by crime-prevention experts to check their car's rear seats for potential attackers before getting into their automobiles and to lock their doors while driving. They routinely caution women against walking alone, especially at night, and to be wary of men they do not know. Similarly, adults warn children about talking to

or accepting gifts or rides from strangers. The implication is that precautions like these can be effective in significantly reducing **sexual assault**.

In the past thirty years, the **women's movement** has considerably heightened public awareness of sexual assault. Feminist groups have focused a great deal of attention on the plight of women and children who are its principal victims. Not only have they prompted intense debate about the adequacy of the responses by medical, social service, and criminal justice agencies, they have challenged the fairness and integrity of Canadian sexual assault legislation.

Contemporary studies have demonstrated that sexual assault is pervasive, that most of its perpetrators are not "abnormal," and that many aggressors are known by their victims before the attack. Furthermore, research has demonstrated that many victims of sexual assault suffer greatly and for a long time, both physically and emotionally. It has also made the public aware that medical and law-enforcement personnel, especially before the reforms implemented in 1983, tended to treat adult female victims with indifference or suspicion and to put the victims themselves on trial in the courts. Changes in Canada's criminal law have encouraged police departments, lawyers, and doctors to change their procedures to better serve justice and protect complainants.

This chapter begins by discussing the definition of sexual assault. It examines the incidence of sexual assault and rape and outlines the principal traits of victims and assailants. Then, it investigates the motivations of offenders and the nature of the offence. Describing the typical experience of a rape victim before major alterations to the law in 1983, it discusses the idea of "the victim as defendant," whereby the victim, after an assault, is subjected to a second victimization by hospital personnel, the police, and the courts. The 1983 reforms in rape legislation are explained as a response to this "**double rape**" of victims. Drawing on feminist theory, this chapter explains the victimization experience of women and children and documents how sexual assault is supported by mainstream culture. The chapter concludes with a description and evaluation of Canada's current sexual assault legislation.

DEFINING SEXUAL ASSAULT

In January 1983, Parliament enacted a new law replacing the offences of rape and indecent assault with the current offences of sexual assault, sexual assault with a weapon, and aggravated sexual assault. As a result of the reforms, significant differences exist for the periods before and after January 1983, not only in the definitions of the crime but also in the procedures used to investigate and try it, the penalties on conviction, and the enumeration of its incidence.

Canadian research on sexual assault conducted before 1983 focuses on rape. Similarly, many of the major studies of sexual assault in the United States have also concentrated on various aspects of forcible rape. Indeed, the intent of much research on rape has been to point out the serious deficiencies in the old rape laws and then to build a case for the reforms contained in the new sexual assault legislation.

In general, rape is a man's carnal knowledge of a woman who is not his wife and who has not given lawful consent. Sexual assault is the threat or use of force by one person on another in the execution of a sexual act. In the *Criminal Code* of Canada, sexual assault includes the pre-1983 crimes of rape, attempted rape, and indecent assault on a male or female. The new law specifies three levels of sexual assault offences. Sexual assault and aggravated sexual assault differ in terms of the seriousness of the harm done to the victim. When attackers use potentially lethal weapons, the crime becomes sexual assault with a weapon. The maximum sentences for sexual assault (level I), sexual assault with a weapon (level II), and aggravated sexual assault (level III) are, respectively, 10 years, 14 years, and life.

In 1988, Canada created legislation covering the sexual abuse of children. "Sexual interference" involves sexual touching of a child under the age of 14. "Invitation to sexual touching" prohibits adults from inviting children under 14 to touch them sexually. Maximum sentences for these provisions are 10 years. "Sexual exploitation" prohibits a person in a position of trust or authority over a youth aged 14 to 18 or upon whom the youth is dependent from sexually interfering with or inviting touching from that youth. Incest is also prohibited under this statute. Maximum penalties for exploitation and incest are 5 and 14 years, respectively.

Victims of the former crime of rape could only be women. Now, the victims of sexual assault can be women or men. Perpetration is also gender neutral. In addition, husbands can now be charged for sexually assaulting their wives. Most importantly, there is a considerable difference in the legal rules and regulations pertaining to rape and to sexual assault as it is now defined. Since most victims of sexual assault are female and virtually all attackers are male, these gender categories will be assumed in the following discussion.

THE INCIDENCE OF SEXUAL ASSAULT INVOLVING ADULT VICTIMS

Sexual assaults recorded by the police numbered 23 872 in 1999 and accounted for less than 10 percent of all officially recorded violent crime in Canada. The rate for 1999 was 78 per 100 000. As Figure 11.1 shows, the vast majority of sexual assaults (85 percent) were level I. The rate of total sexual assaults fell for a

FIGURE 11.1

DISTRIBUTION OF SEXUAL ASSAULTS REPORTED TO POLICE, 1999

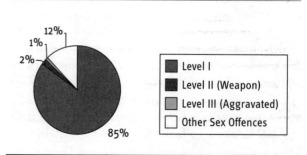

12%
1%
2%
85%

Level I
Level II (Weapon)
Level III (Aggravated)
Other Sex Offences

Source: S. Tremblay. (2000). Canadian Crime Statistics, 1999. *Juristat Service Bulletin* 20(5). Ottawa: Canadian Centre for Justice Statistics, Statistics Canada, p. 16, Table 2.

sixth consecutive year with 7 percent drops recorded in both 1998 and 1999. Compared to the previous year, all three levels of sexual assault were down in 1999. Less serious sexual assault, aggravated sexual assault, and sexual assault with a weapon declined by 7 percent, 4 percent, and 14 percent, respectively (Tremblay, 2000).

The national rate per 100 000 of sexual assault peaked in 1992 at 124. This rate represents a 10 percent increase over 1991 and a 12 percent average annual increase over the previous ten years. There was a 164 percent increase in the rate of sexual assaults between 1983, when the sexual assault legislation was passed, and 1992. The major increase came in the first few years after this legislation was implemented (Roberts, 1994).

In 1983, the first year under the new legislation, police classified 88 percent of sexual assaults at the lowest level of seriousness. The percentage of incidents classified as level I increased steadily after 1983. By 1989, police classified 96 percent of all sexual assaults as level I offences (Roberts, 1994). In 1999, the figure was comparable, at 97 percent (Tremblay, 2000). Level I sexual assault accounts for the most victims overall. Children and youth are more likely to be victims of sexual assault level I while adults are more likely to be victims of sexual assault levels II and III. In particular, UCR data for 1997 indicate that adults comprised only 41 percent of level I sexual assault victims. Conversely, adults comprised 69 percent of level II and 56 percent of level III sexual assault victims (CCJS, 1999).

Police records are not the sole source of information on sexual assault in Canada. The violence against women survey (1993) and the earlier Canadian urban victimization survey of 1982 generated considerable data on sexual assault in this country. Small-scale regional surveys and rape crisis centres across Canada have also provided information, primarily on rape. These nongovernmental sources paint a picture of the frequency of sexual assault that differs dramatically from the one provided by police records.

According to the VAWS, 39 percent of Canadian women aged 18 or over have experienced at least one incident of sexual assault in their adult lifetimes. Almost 60 percent of those reporting sexual assaults were victimized more than once. Twenty-six percent have been sexually assaulted four or more times. Considering their numbers in the Canadian population, this means that more than four million women in this country have been sexually assaulted, many of them more than once. Moreover, 5 percent of women, representing 572 000 Canadian women, experienced at least one incident of sexual assault in the year preceding the survey. The VAWS indicates that only 6 percent of sexual assaults were reported to police (11 percent of attacks and 4 percent of unwanted touching incidents). Only 6 percent of victims consulted a physician or social service agency. Women were more likely to talk to friends (51 percent) or other family members (38 percent) (Johnson, 1996a). Similarly, the 1993 General Social Survey estimated that 90 percent of sexual assaults in Canada go unreported (Johnson, 1996b). The CUVS indicates that the rate of sexual assault in the seven Canadian cities studied in 1982 was 350 per 100 000. About 50 percent of these offences were molestation, 25 percent were rape, and 25 percent were attempted rape. A total of 15 100 women in the seven cities reported being victimized, and 6 percent were sexually assaulted more than once in the year covered by the survey. Victims refrained from reporting 62 percent of these sexual assaults to authorities (CUVS, 1984a; 1985a).

On the basis of a study undertaken in Winnipeg in 1980, Brickman (1980) estimates that one woman in seventeen is raped at some point in her life and that one in five women experiences some form of sexual assault. Based on a review of sexual assault research conducted for the Canadian Advisory Council for the Status of Women, Kinnon (1981) argues that the official figures on sexual assault represent only about 10 percent of the incidents actually occurring. Consequently, she argues that figures based on reports to the police must be multiplied by ten for a realistic estimate of occurrence.

Criminologists explain the discrepancies between official and unofficial estimates of sexual assault by pointing out that this crime has one of the lowest reporting rates of any type of crime. Victims of sexual assault, almost all of whom are women, are reluctant to report it for several reasons. Many feel embarrassed by the thought of recounting to police the minute details of an attack. Furthermore, having relatives and friends made aware of the incident and having the details of the event publicized by the media greatly disturb many victims. Some victims do not report the offences because they know their attackers well and do not wish to cause them any harm. Others keep quiet because they fear retaliation by their assailants. Many decide not to report sexual assaults

Box 11.1
ACCOUNT OF A SEXUAL ASSAULT

Karen lived in a small town in southern Ontario. She was sexually assaulted the summer she was twelve.

One day, Karen, a girlfriend of the same age, her sister and her cousin were playing and swimming at Karen's family pool.

While they were on the front lawn, a boy Karen knew from the local skating club pulled up in his car. They all chatted and fooled around and the boy, Terry, asked them if they wanted to go in his car to the Dairy Queen. Karen went into the house to ask her mother if it was alright.

"If it would have been anyone else, she would have said no," says Karen in telling her story now, five years later. "Terry had a good reputation in the town, he taught figure skating, played on various school teams, was a 'good Samaritan' in the community. He was well known and well liked."

Karen's mother said it would be fine for them to go to the Dairy Queen, and to invite Terry back for a swim afterwards.

The trip to the Dairy Queen was uneventful except for a few remarks that Terry made that struck Karen as a little strange. When one of the younger girls spilt ice cream on her leg, Terry asked if he could lick it off. It was said jokingly and everyone laughed.

On the way back they stopped at Terry's house to pick up his swimsuit. He asked all the girls to come into the house to say hello to his mom. They went inside but his mother wasn't there; Terry said she must have gone out. He then asked if they wanted to see a trophy he had just won which was up in his bedroom. They all went up to his room and admired the trophy.

The younger girls began looking through a stack of Playboy magazines in the room, giggling and laughing. Karen and her friend didn't look at the magazines and decided it was time to leave. At that point Terry shut the bedroom door and started to take his clothes off.

"It was when I saw that he had an erection that I really got scared. I decided we all needed to get out of there. But I still had no idea what was to come."

When Karen's friend tried to get out the door, Terry grabbed her and threw her across the room onto the bed. He wasn't fooling around anymore.

Karen feels she played the "mother" role, trying to get the younger ones out of the room. After trying vainly to hide them all in a closet, she fought with Terry while the other three made it out the door.

He pushed her down on the bed and began taking off her T-shirt and bathing suit. During this time he was pleading with her not to fight. When she continued to struggle, he told her not to move or he would kill her.

"It wasn't Terry. He was completely changed, not the person I had known. I don't remember what I felt at that time, it all happened very fast. I don't know what was happening to me, and I didn't know what would happen next. I just knew I was in trouble."

She was kicking and screaming and trying to get away. At one point she tried to grab a lamp to hit him. He pinned her hands above her head, and raped her.

Immediately after, he ran downstairs because Karen's girlfriend was trying to phone for help. Terry ripped the phone out of the wall before they could get through, but the girls managed to run out the front door before he could catch them.

Karen ran into the bathroom, locked the door and screamed out the window. She remembers putting her hand through the glass as the bathroom door crashed in. The next thing she remembers is lying naked on the living room floor. Terry was gone.

"I went outside, clutching my T-shirt to my front, and saw my cousin standing there. My friend and sister had run off to get help and she didn't know her way around so all she could do was wait. I looked around and didn't know where I was. Nothing looked familiar though I had lived in that town all my life. I couldn't run, I could hardly move."

Terry was driving away in his car when he saw Karen standing there. He came toward her, fell on his knees and said over and over "Please don't tell."

Karen's sister had got word to her family and Karen's father drove up in his car and took her home. Both Karen's and her friend's mother were there – both were hysterical and everyone asked a lot of questions, which Karen answered briefly and quietly. Her father tried to find a doctor who would come to the house, but none would unless the police were called. Karen remembers her parents arguing and finally deciding to call. Both a doctor and a police officer arrived at the house.

"I felt removed from the situation at that time. The room was full of people being upset. I was worried about my mother who was hysterical and sick in the bathroom. I just sat in a chair staring at the wall. I still didn't understand what had happened, except that it was bad. My mother had told me about sex but I knew it wasn't supposed to be like that. I was very confused."

After a statement was taken from Karen and her father, she was taken to a hospital to be examined.

She received immediate attention. First, a nurse took each article of clothing she was wearing and put it in a separate bag. The nurse didn't say anything to Karen except to ask for the clothes. There were three nurses, a doctor and the policeman there for the pelvic examination. Her mother was at first refused permission to be there as well, but she insisted and was allowed to be in the room. The doctor began by telling Karen he "didn't like to do this sort of thing but he had to." Karen feels he may have been trying to reassure her but the feeling she got was that the procedure was distasteful to him. A nurse read from a textbook while the doctor performed the required tests.

Karen's over-riding memory of the period following the rape, in her own words, is that she was made to feel like "baggage." They seemed to be trying to hide her as she went into the hospital; there was something furtive in their manner. People didn't speak directly to her, explain things to her or try to comfort her. Although she repeatedly told people she had to go to the bathroom, she was not allowed to, or told why until after the examination.

The hospital visit took about an hour altogether and she has no memory of the trip home.

The court experience several months later was also accompanied by a sense of being only an accessory, almost an onlooker. Although Karen went to the courthouse three times, she was not required to testify at the preliminary hearing or the trial. She did finally appear before the grand jury on one occasion. Karen had wanted very badly to testify.

"I wanted people to know it happened. I wanted to say in court that he did it. It made me feel the whole thing had nothing to do with me. It wasn't the Queen who got raped. It was me. But it was totally out of my hands."

Only afterwards did Karen learn that the prosecuting attorney had sought to keep her off the stand, had in fact plea bargained and so allowed the case to be tried as attempted rape. Karen feels she had a right to know what was happening and to have some input into the decision to testify or not.

Terry pleaded guilty to attempted rape, was found guilty and given a suspended sentence with psychiatric care recommended. No appropriate psychiatric service was available in or near the town so he never did receive treatment.

In the immediate weeks after the assault, Karen thought about the incident every day, trying to understand what had happened and why. The night following the rape she had a dream in which Terry came toward her in a white robe. She never slept in that room again.

"I felt someone had stolen something from me and my family. I was still really concerned about how much my mom had been hurt. I changed that summer. I became tough. Until then I was a prim and proper little girl, after the assault I didn't want anyone to cross me."

Because they both still lived in the same town, Karen continued to see Terry. He would smile and say hello to her in the street. When she was fourteen she attempted to beat him up and was charged with assault. After that they were both ordered by the court to keep the peace: neither could frequent the skating club in the town, which had been a focal point in Karen's life.

Karen was ostracized by her friends whose mothers "didn't want them hanging around with a rape victim." Her closest friend who had been involved in the assault incident was forbidden to see Karen.

Shortly afterwards the family moved, and Karen's parents subsequently divorced. She can't separate cause and effect but knows the sequence of events had a large impact on her teenage years.

Her contact with Rape Crisis counsellors then and now is helping her to understand what happened, and to work through some of her anger and other feelings.

"I'm a very possessive person, of things and people, I think because I had so much taken away from me during those years. I also have a lot of trouble relaxing sexually, I get stiff and tense and I want to get over that. I've had a lot of support from my family and current friends but I remember how people treated me then. I was definitely blamed by some people."

Discussion Question

How does this case fit the notion of the "victim as defendant"?

Source: D. Kinnon, *Report on Sexual Assault in Canada* (Ottawa: Canadian Advisory Council on the Status of Women, 1981). Reproduced with the permission of the Minister of Public Works and Government Services Canada, 2001.

because they anticipate callous treatment by medical personnel, the police, and the courts. Finally, many female victims assume responsibility for their own victimization. They hold themselves responsible for the attack, believing that they have been careless or gullible in talking to a stranger, accepting a ride, or inviting someone in for a drink (Schur, 1984). The VAWS indicates that women chose not to report sexual assault for a variety of reasons. Some believed that the incident (especially unwanted touching) was too minor to report (44 percent) or that police were powerless to do anything about it (12 percent). Others wanted to keep the incident private (12 percent) or to deal with it in some other fashion (12 percent). More often than victims of unwanted sexual touching, victims of sexual attack cited shame or embarrassment (15 percent) and a desire to avoid the justice system (12 percent) as reasons for not reporting the incident (Roberts, 1994). According to CUVS (1984a) data, of those who did not report their experiences of sexual assault, 43 percent cited as the major reason trepidation about their treatment by the police and the courts, while an additional 33 percent cited fear of revenge from their attackers.

Clark and Lewis (1977), in their study of rapes recorded in the files of the Toronto police for 1970, uncovered yet another source of the underestimation of sexual assaults in official data: the police "unfounded" 64 percent of the cases reported to them. Their own detailed analysis of police reports led Clark and Lewis to conclude that only 10 percent (not 64 percent) of these reported rapes were unequivocally false accusations by complainants.

The extent to which the increasing numbers of sexual assaults in Canada and the United States are more apparent than real is uncertain because of possible changes in the reporting practices of the victims. Changing social attitudes toward women and sexual assault, the development of specialized health care and police sexual assault units and procedures, the establishment of rape crisis centres and other victim assistance programs, and recent reforms to the rape law may have combined to make victims more willing to report sexual assaults now than they have been in the past (Sanders, 1980).

An examination of U.S. data casts some light on this issue. American Uniform Crime Reports (UCR) and national victimization survey data can be compared over time. Official U.S. crime records show sharply rising rape rates, while victimization surveys reveal much greater stability in the incidence of this crime (Hagan, 1986). If the situation in Canada is similar to that in the United States, much of the recent increase in official sexual assault rates may be explained by changes in the reporting practices of women.

VICTIM CHARACTERISTICS

SEX

Official and survey data indicate that sexual assault victims are overwhelmingly female. According to the UCR, about 85 percent of victims are women or girls (CCJS, 2000). Similarly, 90 percent of the 17300 sexual assault incidents reported in the CUVS (1985a) involved female victims. Women were found to be about seven times as likely as men to be sexually assaulted.

Kinnon's analysis of cases from Ontario rape crisis centres (March 1979–February 1980) presents a similar picture. Ninety-six percent of victims in her study were female, and only 4 percent were male. Despite the considerable disparity in the victimization of males and females, male victims are no less likely to be severely traumatized by the experience of sexual assault. Indeed, the stigma attached to male victims of sexual assault may be even greater than it is for female victims. As a result, males may be even less likely than females to report it (Kinnon, 1981).

AGE

Data from the UCR indicate that sexual assault victims of are quite young, with almost 60 percent of victims being under 18 years of age. (CCJS, 2000). The VAWS (1993) indicates that young women aged 18 to 24 were by far the most likely to have experienced sexual violence in the year preceding the survey. Where the national rate was 5 percent for women generally, for this group it was more than three times that — 18 percent. The percentages decline sharply for older women. Among those aged 25 to 34, 8 percent reported a sexual assault in the previous year. For those aged 35 to 44 and 45 and older, the percentages were 5 and 1, respectively (Johnson, 1996a). CUVS (1985a) data reveal that 68 percent of female sexual assault victims were under 25 years of age. Since respondents for both the VAWS and CUVS were all 16 years of age or older, the inclusion of persons under the age of 16 would probably inflate this figure. The pattern apparent in the data from the study of Ontario rape crisis centres is similar, with 53 percent of victims under the age of 20 and 32 percent in the 15- to 19-year-old age bracket. Only 14 percent of victims were 30 years of age or older (Kinnon,

1981). Clark and Lewis (1977) report that 58 percent of the victims in their study were between 14 and 24 years of age and that 29 percent were over 30. The CUVS reports (1985c) show few sexual assaults for those aged 60 and older.

MARITAL STATUS

The probability of being the victim of a sexual assault, according to the CUVS (1985a), is highest for unmarried women, and again the data from the research of Kinnon (1981) and Clark and Lewis (1977) support this finding. Canadian studies report that between 53 and 78 percent of sexual assault victims are single. The authors of the CUVS reason that this relationship between victimization and being single may exist because single people are more often involved in more evening activities outside the home. Kinnon qualifies this somewhat by pointing out that many of the victims in her study were married or living common-law and that many of the assaulted singles were dependent on and living with other people, such as parents, guardians, or friends. Her point is that even those living in "protected" environments are at risk. Clark and Lewis point out that finding so many victims to be single is hardly surprising, given the youthfulness of most victims of sexual attack; many are assaulted before they reach marriageable age.

SOCIOECONOMIC STATUS

According to the CUVS (1983), sexual assault victims tend to have low incomes or come from lower-income families. This finding corresponds with the finding that most victims are young females — a generally low-income group. In Kinnon's study, 63 percent of those who were sexually assaulted were students. Other victims in her study were evenly distributed across the occupational spectrum, although professionals were under-represented, perhaps because they sought assistance from agencies other than rape crisis centres. The lack of association between sexual assault victimization and occupational status is commonly reported in the research literature, indicating that women in all occupations are at risk of sexual assault.

ASSAILANT CHARACTERISTICS

SEX, AGE, AND MARITAL STATUS

According to UCR data for 1997, 98 percent of accused sex offenders were male. This percentage was considerably higher than the overall figure for violent offences (85 percent). Eighty-one percent of perpetrators were adults aged 18 or older, a percentage slightly higher than the representation of adults in the population as a whole (76 percent). Overall, 37 percent of accused persons were between the ages of 18 and 34, 21 percent were between 35 and 44, and 23 percent were 45 or older. The median age of accused sex offenders was 32 compared to 29 for violent offenders more generally (CCJS, 1999). In Kinnon's study (1981), 99 percent of offenders were men and, where the ages of offenders were known, 53 percent were under 25 years of age, 32 percent were between 25 and 40, and only 15 percent were 40 or older. The trends revealed by these studies are apparent in many others as well (Amir, 1971; Russell, 1984). Most assailants are young males a little older than their victims. Where the assaults involve incest and molestation, the age gap increases because many victims are quite young. In terms of marital status, Kinnon reports that, for those occurrences for which information was available, about half (48 percent) of assailants were single, while just under half (44 percent) were married or living in a common-law relationship. The remaining 8 percent were separated, divorced, or widowed.

MOTIVATIONS OF ATTACKERS

Sexual assaulters can be classified on the basis of their motivations. In their assessment of rape offenders in the United States, Groth and Birnbaum (1979) outline the characteristics of three types of assailants: those who rape out of anger, those who rape to assert power over women, and those who rape to experience sadistic pleasure. According to psychiatric evaluations conducted by Groth and his associates, about 65 percent of rapes are **power rapes**, 29 percent are **anger rapes**, and 6 percent are **sadistic rapes**.

The "anger rape," according to Groth and Birnbaum, involves assailants who are filled with hate and frustration. They direct their vengeance toward women in general, toward a particular female, or perhaps even toward the entire world. The outlet for rage is a rape in which the attacker humiliates his victim. Anger rapes tend to be more brutal and to consist of acts specifically designed to demean the victim. Sexual gratification is not a motive in these incidents.

The "power rape" is an attempt by an attacker to possess his victim rather than to humiliate her. The object of the attack is sexual conquest expressed in the pursuit, capture, and control of the woman. In this

Box 11.2
A CASE OF SEXUAL MISCONDUCT

In Barrington Passage, N.S., the love affair between the doctor and the artist is the talk of the town. Everyone knows that, last summer, Hunter Blair (married) took up with his former patient, Joanna Hyde (ditto, mother of two). And they are, in a word, scandalized.

"It's just devastating," says Ruby May, 68, who, like most people in this hard-working fishing town, is a God-fearing Baptist. She called a town meeting last night to see what can be done.

"This isn't the right thing to do to a small community," says Leigh Stoddard, mayor of next-door Clark's Harbour.

"Totally unethical!" snaps Ian Cree, a surgeon in nearby Shelburne.

The citizens are mad as hornets. But they're not mad at the wayward lovers. They're mad at the College of Physicians and Surgeons, which last week found the 60-year-old doctor guilty of sexual misconduct and suspended his licence for the next year. His last day of practice is tomorrow.

"Oh, my land, people were on his side and still are," says Mrs. May, who got up a petition begging for a reprieve for the popular doctor. Four thousand people signed it.

But rules are rules, says the college. And sex between doctors and their patients (or even ex-patients) is one of the biggest no-nos of the medical profession. Doctors have been kicked out forever for that.

What makes this case unusual is that the woman herself never complained. On the contrary, Ms. Hyde, 39, is outraged that the doctor has been penalized. She says the affair was completely consensual, that they ended the professional relationship before they began the personal one, and that their romance is none of the disciplinary body's business. She begged them to cease and desist (as did Dr. Blair's wife). Instead, they violated her privacy, pried into her medical records and, as she told the CBC, "tried to insinuate that I am some kind of a psychotic dimwit victim who doesn't even know she's a victim."

Dr. Blair, who worked out a plea bargain, isn't talking. "He's a little mixed up right now," says the mayor.

Ms. Hyde first went to see Dr. Blair at the end of 1996 to seek help for a lingering depression over the death of her mother. "Don't give up," he would encourage her. His diagnosis was bipolar depression,

and twice he had her check into a psychiatric hospital. According to the college, Dr. Blair knew another doctor had once dropped her as a patient because of romantic infatuation; according to her, neither she nor Dr. Blair were ever informed of that. In any event, one day last June, she says, they both realized they were in love, and decided he could no longer be her doctor. "He never touched me. We never even held hands," she told a reporter. "So we thought that's the dividing line, and if you can sever the doctor-patient relationship before there's any physical contact whatsoever, let alone sexual intercourse, then everything should be okay."

Not so.

Ms. Hyde and Dr. Blair gave their spouses the bad news, and started their affair in August. Then Dr. Blair's partner, new in town, blew the whistle. "I have reason to believe Dr. W. Hunter Blair may be guilty of sexual misconduct with a patient, or former patient," he wrote in a brief note. "Given the reporting obligation of the College of Physicians and Surgeons, I am accordingly notifying the college." In September, Dr. Blair learned the college had launched an investigation. The romance has been on and off ever since.

So what's the problem? It's this: In the eyes of the disciplinary body, sex with an ex-patient, especially one who's received psychological counseling, adds up to exploitation. It doesn't matter what the ex-patient thinks about the whole thing.

"There is always a risk of an abuse of power on the part of the physician since, consciously or not, he/she may use or exploit the trust, the confidential information, the emotions ... created by the professional relationship," said the college.

"Nonsense," declares Dr. Cree. "They're using the ancient Freudian theory of transference, which holds that the patient is largely deprived of the capacity to determine what her true feelings are. They believe a physician and a patient can never be in love. One or the other must be deluded and, if they manifest such a horrible emotion, then one or the other must be punished very severely."

Family doctor Leo Wisniowski observes that this case is bad news for the rural doctor shortage. "If you're practising in a small town, everyone is your patient, your ex-patient or potentially your patient. So, essentially, it's a lifetime ban on any relationship with anyone."

Ruby May sees the practical side, too. Dr. Blair is one of only three doctors serving a population of 10,000. He makes house calls, and he's available around the clock. The old folks adore him because of his old-fashioned ways. "We believe in the Lord," Mrs. May says, "and we're prayin' that the Lord will help us out."

Source: Margaret Wente, *The Globe and Mail*, July 6, 2000, p. A15. Reprinted with permission from the *Globe and Mail*.

Discussion Questions

Ms. Hyde suggests that her relationship with Dr. Blair "is none of the disciplinary body's business." Is she right? What are the dangers of permitting such relationships?

form of rape, the assailant frequently views the attack as a seduction. The power rapist believes that the sexual dominance of females by males is expected and socially acceptable and that the needs and rights of females are subordinate to those of men.

Both **marital rape** and **date rape** are frequently of the power type. Marital rape occurs when a husband or common-law cohabitant sexually assaults his spousal partner. Date rape occurs when a man forces sex on a woman with whom he is out on a date (Kinnon, 1981). In cases where women are legally married to their attackers, their personal autonomy is often nonexistent; men often justify marital rape by citing their "conjugal rights" to sex on demand.

Some date rapes occur when men mistakenly interpret a woman's provocative clothing, sensual way of walking, conversation in a bar, or acceptance of a ride as invitations to sexual activity (Schur, 1984). Sexual assault on a date does not necessarily involve full intercourse. Necking, fondling, and petting that occur despite the woman's objections are sexual assaults. Many men consider a firm "no," even when accompanied by other signs of resistance, as a subtle invitation to sex. They consider resistance the initial stage of an eventual submission. Furthermore, where the relationship has involved consensual sexual relations at some point in the past, many men consider forfeit the woman's right to refuse on any subsequent occasion. Research indicates that virtually all women have unwanted sexual attention forced upon them at some time, if not early, in their lives.

Groth and Birnbaum's third category, the "sadistic rape," is the least common type. Here, rapists subject their victims to bizarre, violent acts specifically to cause pain and to disfigure and mutilate sex organs. These incidents are the ones that most often culminate in the murder of the victim and promote the stereotype of the rapist as the pathological, knife-wielding night-stalker bent upon torturing and killing his victim. Silverman and Kennedy (1993) report that, between 1961 and 1990, 525 murders in Canada (about 4 percent of all murders) were sex-related. Evidence suggests that strangers committed most of these murders and that most of the killers were young (53 percent under 26 years of age) and single (63 percent).

OFFENCE CHARACTERISTICS

PREMEDITATION

Unlike violent offences such as assault and murder, sexual assault usually is premeditated. Isolating a vulnerable person, selecting a suitable location for the attack, and developing appropriate strategies of approach and execution each require some planning.

VICTIM RESISTANCE

Because they fear for their lives, many sexual assault victims do not resist their attackers. The image of the rapist as a Jack the Ripper type of madman militates against any resistance. At most, the opposition may consist largely of pleading, shoving, and pushing (Sanders, 1980).

In addition to the victim's obvious concern for her personal survival, another factor reduces opposition in a sexual assault. Society's socialization to the female role renders women more vulnerable to sexual attack. They learn to be passive and submissive to men rather than aggressive and assertive. For example, women are socialized to be tolerant of offensive sexual remarks and gestures. Being "ladylike" precludes loud and aggressive responses to acts of sexual harassment. Verbal sexual harassment often represents the initial stage of physical sexual assault. Moreover, socialization fails to provide women with the combat skills to defend against attack. Even the clothing that women wear to fit the ideal of femininity makes evasive tactics difficult. High heels make running almost impossible, and most skirts make vigorous kicking difficult (Griffin, 1971).

In reality, few rapists are mad slashers and, as Sanders (1980) and Kleck and Sayles (1990) show in their studies of rapes in the United States, when resistance takes the form of an all-out fight, the rape is frequently not completed. Assailants simply do not anticipate an encounter with a hitting, kicking, biting, and screaming female. When the victim's reaction is vigorous and combative, the attacker may well retreat.

THE RELATIONSHIP OF THE VICTIM AND THE OFFENDER

The experience of sexual assault varies by the age of the victim and by the relationship between the victim and the offender. Older people are more likely to suffer rape and attempted rape while younger persons are more often subject to molestation and incest. Victims of sexual offences usually know the perpetrator. According to UCR data for 1997, friends and acquaintances represented the largest category of offenders in cases involving both male and female vic-

tims and both child and adult victims. In 50 percent of cases, the accused was a friend or acquaintance. In 28 percent of cases, the perpetrator was a family member. The offender was more likely to be a family member when the victims were children and youths (34 percent victimized by a family member) than when the victims were adults (19 percent victimized by a family member). In only 23 percent of cases were victims and offenders strangers to one another. (CCJS, 1999).

According to the VAWS (1993), most victims know their assailants. Kinnon (1981) reports "stranger" rapes at about 27 percent. Acquaintances perpetrated about 36 percent of the rapes in her study, and boyfriends, family friends, or family members, 28 percent.

Victims report sexual assaults committed by strangers much more often than they do those carried out by someone whom they know. When attackers are friends, acquaintances, or relatives of the victim, the probability that the victim will be viewed with suspicion and suspected of complicity increases dramatically. Moreover, when the assailant is a relative, victims feel a heightened sense of guilt and shame. Also, when the assailant and victim are related, offenders can retaliate more easily. Guilt, shame, and

---

BOX 11.3
LONDON POLICE WARN OF DATE-RAPE DRUGS

Women in the city are being warned to watch their drinks at local bars after a second woman was drugged with GHB, a drug linked to date rapes.

A 35-year-old London [Ontario] woman was taken to hospital by friends Sunday morning after fainting repeatedly at a local drinking spot, police said Monday.

Tests showed the woman had drunk a combination of pharmaceuticals including GHB and Rohypnol, a drug that can cause drowsiness, confusion and amnesia.

The woman, who had not been assaulted, was treated and released from hospital the same day, police said.

They said it's likely the drug was slipped into her drink at the bar.

"She'd been to another place, but she was at (a second bar) for a period of time before she started feeling the effects of it," said Det. Sgt. Rick Harriss.

Bar staff could not be reached for comment.

The incident is not the first time a woman has been drugged with GHB in London.

Last January, bodybuilder Christopher Humphrey was convicted of sexual assault and sentenced to 30 months in prison after giving a woman a drink laced with the drug.

GHB is a clear liquid that can create euphoria and sexual arousal. Vials sell for $20 to $50. Rohypnol, or "roofies," is legally available in some countries and sells for about $5 a pill.

Discussion Questions

Is the use of drugs to subdue a victim in sexual assault an aggravating factor? How should the use of such drugs affect penalties, if at all? What measures would you advocate to counter this predatory strategy?

Source: *The Toronto Star*, August 2, 2000, p. A4. Reprinted with permission – The Canadian Press.

fear reduce the victim's enthusiasm for going public about a sexual assault (Schur, 1984).

THE RACE OF VICTIMS AND OFFENDERS

Data on the racial or ethnic characteristics of the victims and offenders in sexual assaults in Canada are not available. American criminologists, however, have studied extensively the impact of race on rape in the United States. Amir's investigation of several hundred Philadelphia rape cases suggests that sexual assault is an "intra-racial" crime; perpetrators and their victims tend to be members of the same ethnic or racial group (Amir, 1971), probably because women of certain ethnic backgrounds are simply more available to men from the same ethnic groups. In the United States, blacks are disproportionately involved in rape, both as offenders and as victims.

LOCATION AND TIME

According to UCR data, the private home is the location where most sexual assaults occur. In 1997, 67 percent of victims were assaulted in a domicile. The other common locations were public areas (17 percent) and commercial/public institutions (16 percent). When violent offences overall are considered, victims were less likely than sexual assault victims to have been attacked in a home (47 percent), but more likely to have been attacked in a public area (26 percent) or commercial/public institution (27 percent) (CCJS, 1999).

The VAWS also shows that a common location for sexual assault is a private home. Altogether, 35 percent of sexual assaults happened in the home of the victim (15 percent), her attacker (11 percent), or someone else (9 percent). Approximately 10 percent of occurrences took place in a car and about 10 percent happened at the victim's place of work. About 40 percent involved public locations such as bars, streets, and public buildings (Johnson, 1996a). CUVS (1985a) data indicate that 21 percent of attacks took place in the victim's home, while an additional 11 percent occurred in the home of an acquaintance or a friend or in the victim's neighbourhood. According to Kinnon (1981), 72 percent of incidents occur in or near the victim's residence.

Studies reviewed by Katz and Mazur (1979) echo these findings; they note that estimates of the percentages of attacks occurring in a domicile range from about 50 to 70 percent, depending on the study. Where strangers enter victims' homes, several common patterns emerge: the interloper may be a bona fide service or sales man, an imposter allowed in on business, or an illegal entrant such as a burglar.

According to their examination of official rape reports for Winnipeg (1966–75), Gibson, Linden, and Johnson (1980) conclude that 80 percent of rapes occur between 8 P.M. and 8 A.M. Many rapes were associated with the victims' acceptance of rides home or hitchhiking; some victims appeared to have been followed home after a late night out.

THE COMMISSION OF OTHER OFFENCES AND WEAPON USE

Although sexual assaults do occur during other offences such as burglary and robbery, these incidents are comparatively infrequent. Sexual assaults culminating in the murder of the victim are extremely rare. Of the 656 homicides in Canada in 1990, for example, only 35 involved sexual assault (Wright, 1991). CUVS data show that 12 percent of sexual assaults occurred in conjunction with break and enter. They also indicate that offenders use weapons in about 25 percent of attacks and that weapon use is more common when the assailants are young (CUVS, 1984a, 1985a).

Roberts's analysis of UCR data suggests that attackers use firearms in less than 1 percent of cases and other weapons in 18 percent of cases. More frequent was threatening or using physical force (61 percent of cases) (Roberts, 1994).

Similarly, the VAWS found that sexual predators rarely used weapons. In only 3 percent of sexual assault incidents was a weapon present. Almost half of the latter assaults were carried out by strangers. Johnson (1996a) notes that this fact helps to explain the higher rate of injury in attacks by strangers. Knives and other sharp instruments were the type of weapons most frequently used (half of all incidents with weapons) (Johnson, 1996a).

THE NUMBERS OF ASSAILANTS

Empirical investigations have presented an inconsistent picture of the number of assailants involved in a single sexual assault. CUVS data suggest that 85 percent of sexual assaults are carried out by a lone offender. This coincides with Kinnon's finding, in her survey of rape crisis centre cases (1981), that 15 percent of all incidents involved more than one assailant. These data differ from those of several other studies indicating higher proportions of multiple-offender incidents. Amir (1971), in his investigation of rape in Philadelphia, reported that 43 percent of rapes involved multiple offenders and that group rapes involved more planning and violence than rapes carried out by lone assailants.

ALCOHOL

According to the VAWS (1993), 43 percent of sexual assaults involved a man who, in the opinion of the victim, had been drinking at the time of the occurrence. Alcohol was more likely to have been detected by victims of the more serious sexual attacks (47 percent) than by victims of unwanted sexual touching (39 percent). Most likely to occur within the context of drinking were sexual attacks by dates and boyfriends (50 percent) (Johnson, 1996a).

Using Winnipeg police data, Johnson, Gibson, and Linden (1980) examined the relationship between alcohol and rape and compared their findings with Amir's for Philadelphia. In the Winnipeg study, alcohol was consumed in 72 percent of the rape cases, while in the Philadelphia investigation the figure was 34 percent. In the Winnipeg and Philadelphia studies, respectively, alcohol was consumed by both victim and offender in 39 percent and 21 percent of the cases, by only the offender in 24 percent and 3 percent of the cases, and by only the victim in 9 percent and 10 percent of the cases. Moreover, the consumption of alcohol appeared to be associated with a greater use of force by the offender.

Criminologists account for alcohol's contribution to sexual assault in several ways. When women are out alone at night and drinking in a bar, some men view them as legitimate targets of sexual aggression. Moreover, when drinking, women are more likely to be physically and mentally vulnerable to approach and attack. Also, some researchers have argued that alcohol triggers aggressiveness in those drinking to excess. Finally, after an evening of drinking, males may have expectations regarding sex that are quite different from those of their female counterparts. Johnson, Gibson, and Linden (1980) cite as evidence for this last point the fact that alcohol use was more prevalent in cases of spontaneous rapes (83 percent) than in rapes that were carefully planned (55 percent).

VICTIM PRECIPITATION

Victim-precipitated crime occurs when victims play a role in initiating and escalating the offences in which they are victimized. Rape is considered victim precipitated if the victim consents to some form of sexual

exchange and later reneges on the agreement. Frequently, however, the agreement exists only in the mind of the rapist. Many men interpret dressing provocatively, agreeing to have a drink, accepting a ride home, or simply being out alone at night as indicating a willingness to engage in sex. Furthermore, many believe that a woman's failure to resist to the death the sexual advances of a potential attacker constitutes evidence of her "hidden" desire for this type of attention.

From his analysis of rape cases in Philadelphia, Amir concluded that about 20 percent were victim precipitated. Critics respond with two points, however. First, what constitutes the precipitation of rape is heavily laden with a male bias about the sorts of words and gestures that imply a sexual invitation. Second, the concept of victim precipitation allocates responsibility for the assault to the victim and implies that she loses her right to refuse to participate in sex at some stage in the exchange (Russell, 1984).

THE IMPACT ON THE VICTIM

Although the impact of sexual attack on a few victims may be so minimal as to cause little concern, for many others the shock is devastating. According to the VAWS, 11 percent of sexually assaulted women were physically injured. The percentage was much higher in attack incidents (22 percent) than in cases of unwanted sexual touching (4 percent). Attacks by strangers were the most likely to result in injury (27 percent). Most cases involved injuries described as bruises (82 percent), internal injuries (13 percent), or cuts, scratches, or burns (27 percent). In about 20 percent of cases, injuries were sufficiently serious to require medical assistance (Johnson, 1996a). The experience had a negative emotional effect on the women in 85 percent of sexual assaults. The most commonly reported impacts were anger (31 percent), becoming more cautious and less trusting (31 percent), becoming more fearful (22 percent), shame or guilt (11 percent), and problems relating to men (10 percent) (Roberts, 1994). CUVS data also provide some information on injuries suffered by victims. In 65 percent of the incidents, victims experienced some physical harm or financial loss. Material losses usually occurred as a result of the simultaneous commission of another crime such as robbery or burglary.

Kinnon's study (1981) provides more detail on the harms inflicted on victims. In addition to committing sexual assault, many attackers inflicted another type of abuse. Of the instances reported by 200 victims of sexual assault, 177 involved rape. Twenty-eight of these rapes involved repeated vaginal penetration. In 36 cases, offenders verbally abused victims, and in 60 instances, they fondled, humiliated, and forced the victim to perform sexual acts other than intercourse. There were 48 occurrences of beating and choking, 10 of tying, blindfolding, or drugging, and 40 of other forms of physical abuse. One case involved a shooting and a stabbing. Kinnon found, in addition, that in over half of the incidents for which information was available, the victim's captivity and subjection to physical and verbal abuse extended beyond 30 minutes. By way of comparison, Amir (1971) reported that in 27 percent of rape incidents in Philadelphia, there was additional sexual abuse, including fellatio, cunnilingus, sodomy, and repeated intercourse. One in four Philadelphia victims was beaten, and one in five of these was beaten severely.

Some of the rape incident reports studied by Kinnon contained information about the extent of the physical injuries sustained by victims during the sexual assault. Forty-one percent suffered little or no physical impairment, while 59 percent experienced some form of bodily harm. Among the traumatized, there were 15 whose injuries resulted from severe beatings and 51 who were burned, choked, or punched. Twelve victims were left with internal damage, bruises, and lacerations of the vagina or anus. Twenty suffered other miscellaneous injuries, and three victims had to cope with serious long-term physical debilitation.

In addition to suffering physical abuse, victims of sexual attack also undergo emotional trauma. During the assault, victims fall completely under the control of their assailants. Most often, victims know neither the sequence of acts they will be forced to perform nor the outcome of the attack. How soon the assault will end and how seriously they will be hurt are also unknown. Becoming pregnant, being injured, becoming infected with a venereal disease, contracting the virus that causes AIDS, or being murdered are truly terrifying possibilities. Holmstrom and Burgess (1983) have found that, after an attack, many victims develop phobic reactions directly related to the location and precise circumstances of their victimization. Depending on the scene and the circumstances of the sexual assault, the objects of a victim's fears may include the indoors or the outdoors, being alone or being in a crowd. Victims are often fearful of someone walking behind them.

The general betrayal of trust felt by victims frequently produces a cynical outlook. Their perception of themselves as foolish and gullible often leaves victims with depreciated self-concepts. Since many view those who are sexually attacked not only as responsible for their own victimization but also as undeserving of sympathy, it is not surprising that victims blame themselves and that they experience shame and guilt. Indeed, compassion is assured only for those who are very young or very old, who are attacked by a gang of men, or who have experienced considerable physical injury. Sexual assault often causes victims to suffer from anxiety, depression, sleep disorders, uncontrollable crying, and difficulties in concentration (Brickman, 1980).

Many victims of sexual assault also report less interest in and satisfaction with normal sexual activities. Often these disruptions strain the victim's relationships with her intimates. Some evidence suggests that the intensity of the trauma of rape is most acute when the victim is young and sexually inexperienced and when the attacker is a stranger who uses physical force (Ruch, Chandler, and Harter, 1980).

THE SEXUAL ASSAULT OF CHILDREN

INCIDENCE

Estimates of the incidence of child sexual abuse in Canada are imprecise. The victim counts most widely cited by law-enforcement personnel, social and health services, and the media are one in five girls and one in ten boys. However, as the Badgley Committee on Sexual Offences Against Children and Youths (CSOACY, 1984) notes, these figures are often derived from unreliable sources.

Growing public awareness, the creation and improvement of reporting procedures, and the increased numbers of protection services designed to identify and assist abused children have facilitated the reporting of incidents in recent years. Before 1977, there were few references in the reports of provincial child-protection services to cases involving the sexual abuse of children. In 1977, however, 300 cases were identified. By 1980, when 1593 cases were reported, the volume of incidents known to these public agencies had increased by 431 percent. In 1981, the Canadian government appointed the Badgley Committee to undertake an extensive investigation of this problem in

Box 11.4
FORMER PRIEST HELD LIABLE FOR ASSAULTS ON ALTAR BOYS

St. John's, Nfld. A supreme Court judge has found a former Roman Catholic priest liable for sexual assaults on dozens of young altar boys.

A high-ranking church official and the Episcopal Corporation of St. George's were found liable for the priest's conduct in a decision by Justice Robert Wells of the Newfoundland Supreme Court.

Judge Wells found former priest Kevin Bennett liable for the sexual assaults on altar boys in his parish during the 1960s and 1970s.

"[Mr. Bennett] dominated the parish and its communities. He recruited and directed altar boys, who quickly became his victims," Judge Wells wrote in his 65-page decision. "The awe in which Father Bennett was held by the community at large contributed to his ability to control his victims and thus to satisfy a prodigious appetite for constant sexual gratification."

Judge Wells also found Archbishop Alphonsus Penney, the former archbishop of the archdiocese of St. John's and metropolitan of the province, liable for negligence toward the boys assaulted by Mr. Bennett after 1979, the year that Archbishop Penney was informed of the assaults.

Mr. Bennett, who had been with St. Bernard's 10 years, remained at the parish for another six months. The sexual assaults on boys aged 10 to 16 continued.

"Archbishop Penney failed to take the steps which were his duty to take under canon law and as a senior prelate of the church and metropolitan. Thus, he failed in his duty of care to those plaintiffs who continued to be sexually assaulted," Judge Wells wrote.

Judge Wells ordered the Roman Catholic Episcopal Corporation of St. George's, as well as Raymond Lahey, the current Bishop, to pay damages.

The much-publicized civil case was launched by 36 men who were victims of abuse in the isolated communities.

Mr. Bennett, a 67-year-old native of St. George's, pleaded guilty in 1990 to more than 30 counts of sex-related offences. He was sentenced to four years in prison.

In a move that may have a serious impact on the financial compensation to the victims, Judge Wells cleared the Episcopal Corporation of St. John's, among the wealthiest of its kind in Newfoundland, or responsibility.

Compensation amounts have not been decided.

Discussion Questions

If the Archbishop was negligent, why would criminal liability be confined to the Episcopal Corporation of St. George's? Why would the Catholic Church more generally not be held accountable?

Source: Christina Frangou, *The National Post*, July 6, 2000, p. A7. Reprinted with permission of the *St. John's Telegram*.

Canada. Since this committee's report is the most detailed Canadian investigation into sexual offences against children and youth, its findings will be reviewed in detail. First, however, it is worthwhile to examine some recent findings of a project analyzing data gathered by the new Uniform Crime Report system. These data, gathered between January 1988 and September 1990, come from the records of seven police forces using the new system. Of the approximately one thousand cases included in the study, two-thirds involved female victims and one-third involved males (Wright and Leroux, 1991). This finding closely resembles that of the Badgley investigation.

In 98 percent of the sexual assaults, the perpetrator was male. In 81 percent of the cases, the attacker was known to the victim. Of those committing sexual assaults, 24 percent were parents of the victim, 17 percent were other family members, and 40 percent were acquaintances. In 11 percent of cases, attackers were strangers. More girls (48 percent) than boys (33 percent) were victimized by parents and family members. Conversely, more boys (45 percent) than girls (35 percent) were sexually assaulted by acquaintances. Almost twice as many boys (14 percent) as girls (8 percent) fell prey to strangers. Finally, 75 percent of girls, compared with 63 percent of boys, were accosted in a home setting. Conversely, more boys (27 percent) than girls (17 percent) became victims in public places. Firearms were used to subdue 12 percent of all victims (Wright and Leroux, 1991).

Four surveys formed the basis of the Badgley Committee's research findings (CSOACY, 1984). The National Population Survey gathered information from a sample of 2008 adults about their sexual victimization as children. The remaining surveys collected data from samples of police forces, child-protection agencies, and hospitals across the country. Unlike the National Population Survey, the latter three surveys tapped reported cases only. Hence, estimates of incidence based on data from police, social service agencies, and hospitals are conservative.

On the basis of the results obtained by the National Population Survey, the Badgley Committee reports that about one in every two females and one in every three males in Canada have been victims of some form of sexual offence. Most respondents indicated that they were children or teenagers when they were first sexually victimized. About four in five of the victims were under age 21 when they suffered their first sexual assault. On the basis of offences reported by adults of all ages, however, it appears that there has not been a sharp increase in recent years in the incidence of sexual offences against children. Finally, the survey revealed that most sexually abused victims sought the assistance of neither public services nor the police.

Sexual assaults against children, like those against women, are dramatically under-reported for several reasons. Due to their immaturity and inexperience, children are frequently unaware that a crime has actually been committed against them. If they are sufficiently mature to comprehend their victimization, children and youth often feel shame and embarrassment. Informing others about their experience frequently requires the disclosure of intimate and discomforting details. Fear that such revelations will result in their being stigmatized deters many young people from informing the authorities. Some fear reprisals at the hands of their molesters. In addition, it is common for victims to be unsure to whom they should report an assault. Even when they do seek help, many children are not believed and are discouraged from seeking assistance. Confronted by these barriers, young victims are often left feeling helpless, devalued, and rejected (Russell, 1984).

THE VICTIMS AND THE OFFENCE

Sizable numbers of Canadian female, and to a lesser extent, male children receive unwanted sexual advances. Many sexually abused children are accosted at a relatively early age. According to the Badgley Committee report, almost 40 percent of child victims were under the age of 12 when they were first victimized.

The unwanted sexual acts forced on children encompass a broader range of sexual behaviours than one might think. Tactics range from touching, fondling, and kissing parts of the body to oral, anal, and vaginal penetration by a penis, finger, or other object. The most common form of assault on children is the touching and fondling of genital areas, breasts, and buttocks. About 16 percent of males and 47 percent of females surveyed experienced this sort of molestation. The unwanted licking or sucking of a vagina, penis, or anus occurred at least once to 2 percent of females and 3 percent of males.

The National Population Survey discovered that about 4 percent of females had been raped at least once before they were 16 years old. About 2 percent of persons of both sexes experienced an unwanted anal penetration with a penis, a finger, or an object at least once. Most of the unwanted sexual acts were not reported to family members or friends, and in only a few cases were public services notified.

Overall, the results of the three national surveys indicate that a sizable number of sexually assaulted children had been threatened or physically assaulted during or before these incidents. Only about 7 percent of victims voluntarily agreed or consented to the sexual acts. In the remainder of the incidents, attackers persuaded, bribed, or seduced the children. On the basis of these estimates, Badgley claims that few assaults against the young involve only casual or relatively harmless contacts. Most, he emphasizes, were carried out against the child's will.

Of female victims, 20 percent were physically injured and 24 percent were emotionally harmed. Substantially fewer male than female victims reported injuries; only 4 percent suffered a physical injury, usually an irritated or infected penis or anus. Seven percent of males were emotionally traumatized (CSOACY, 1984).

According to police data, sexual offences against children usually occur during daylight hours in the spring and summer months. Longer days, clement weather, and holidays from school combine to increase vulnerability — children tend to be outside and away from the direct supervision of parents, teachers, and other adults. Fifty-six percent of children who were assaulted, according to police data, were accosted in private homes and in most cases, the home was their own. The next most common

Box 11.5
FORMER USHER JAILED INDEFINITELY

John Paul Roby, the former Maple Leaf Gardens usher whose sexual abuse of young hockey fans blighted dozens of lives, was jailed indefinitely yesterday after a judge declared him a dangerous offender.

Mr. Justice Victor Paisley, who sighed frequently and took many large swallows of water as he read a damning, two-hour litany of the damage inflicted by Mr. Roby, said the 57-year-old man is an incurable pedophile who is virtually certain to continue molesting children if ever freed from jail.

He rejected the defence argument that Mr. Roby poses little threat because of his age and serious heart condition.

"Pedophilia is a lifelong preference," Judge Paisley said. "Mr. Roby does not need physical strength [to practise it.] All he needs is a can of Coke or a bottle of beer, and access to children."

Mr. Roby rocked gently and mumbled to himself throughout the grim proceeding; the energy that fuelled histrionic courtroom outbursts that became his trademark seemed to have ebbed away.

The man who has cursed his victims in public tirades stood meekly and let police officers lead him away while a scattering of his now-adult victims watched in silence.

Only a couple were willing to talk to reporters, and their comments expressed a mixture of sad emotions.

"Testifying was the hardest thing I've ever had to do," said a 44-year-old former Little League player who struggled with alcohol abuse and an ability to keep a job after Mr. Roby lured him as a teenager into games of strip poker that ended with Mr. Roby masturbating naked in front of him.

"None of the victims were allowed to talk to each other and I sometimes wondered if I was crazy," the man added. "It's unfortunate that everyone had to go through what they did. But I'm happy at what's happened today, and I will move on with my life."

Mr. Roby was convicted a year ago of 35 counts of sexual molestation involving 26 victims, all but one of them boys, between 1967 and 1983.

He lured them into sexual acts by approaching them at Gardens events and offering them refreshments, hockey memorabilia or free tickets to games.

He was the third man in a sex scandal that rocked the hockey shrine when charges were laid four years ago.

George Hannah, an equipment manager with the Toronto Marlboroughs, died before charges were laid.

Gordon Stuckless, a former equipment manager at the Gardens, pleaded guilty to 24 sex-related charges in October of 1997, and was sentenced to two years less a day. Two weeks later, one of Mr. Stuckless's victims – Martin Kruze, 34 – jumped to his death from the Bloor Street viaduct.

Mr. Stuckless's sentence was increased to five years by the Ontario Court of Appeal.

Judge Paisley yesterday drew a sharp distinction between Mr. Roby's and Mr. Stuckless's cases.

Mr. Stuckless expressed remorse, began work on his rehabilitation while in custody before sentencing, and pleaded guilty, the judge said.

Mr. Roby, on the other hand, continues to protest his innocence on every single charge, calls his victims liars and denies ever having had sex, or even a sex drive.

Furthermore, his long, angry outbursts in courts as well as the numerous physical tantrums he has thrown in custody, show he lacks impulse control and any willingness to control his behaviour, the judge said.

He rejected the opinion of defence psychiatrist John Bradford that Mr. Roby can be rendered harmless by a combination of group therapy and drugs to kill his sex drive.

"It is not reasonable to believe he would follow chemical castration treatment," Judge Paisley said. "Mr. Roby has not burned out his sexual interest.... He has caused severe psychological damage to his victims and, if given the opportunity, would do so again."

The decision to declare Mr. Roby a dangerous offender who will probably spend the rest of his life in jail was based on 19 "index offences" – sex crimes committed after 1977 when the dangerous-offender designation was added to the Criminal Code.

Judge Paisley read out brief overviews of the facts of each case, along with short victim-impact statements.

Over and over again, Mr. Roby tricked boys as young as 10 or as old as 15 into thinking he was a kind friend who would give them treats. If that didn't work, he followed them into a Gardens washroom. Only a few of the cases involved intrusive touching of the boys' genitals. Usually, Mr. Roby was content to masturbate in front of them and encouraged them to do the same.

But despite the absence of literal violence, each boy suffered the permanent damage of humiliation, shame and fears about intimacy, Judge Paisley said.

Many did not tell anyone what had happened to them, but buried the memory, only to have it burst to the surface when Mr. Roby was arrested in 1997.

In their statements, the victims spoke of wrecked marriages, alcohol and drug abuse and intractable self-esteem problems.

Discussion Questions

Does Mr. Roby deserve a life sentence for his crimes? Why or why not? Are the alternatives suggested by the defence viable in this case?

Source: Jane Gadd, *Globe and Mail*, June 7, 2000, p. A19. Reprinted with permission from the *Globe and Mail*.

location, where 14 percent of children were victimized, was "open spaces" like parks, woods, and vacant lots. Ten percent of children were sexually molested on streets, 10 percent in buildings other than private homes, 5 percent in motor vehicles, and 4 percent in a variety of other places, such as beaches, hospitals, and summer camps (CSOACY, 1984).

The Offenders

Ninety-nine percent of suspected offenders were males and 1 percent were females. Predictably, males committed virtually all of the sexual offences (99 percent) perpetrated against female victims. Although the proportion of female assailants was higher when boys (3 percent) rather than girls (0.8 percent) were victims, most of the boys and male youths were sexually assaulted by males as well.

According to respondents who were assaulted as children and youth, the vast majority knew their assailants before the incident took place. Twenty-four percent were accosted by family members, 48 percent by family friends and acquaintances, 9 percent by other persons known to them, and 1 percent by persons in positions of trust. Strangers victimized only 18 percent. These findings indicate that children primarily need protection from persons whom they already know and trust.

In the national surveys of cases reported to police, social services, and hospitals, 343 incidents involved children who were sexually assaulted by two or more persons. Girls were victims in 90 percent of group attacks. Of all types of sexual assaults committed against girls, 9 percent involved two or more assailants. While there were only 36 instances of boys being sexually assaulted by two or more assailants, the findings confirm that these acts do occur. Boys were victims in 10 percent of the sexual assaults perpetrated by groups. Of all sexual assaults committed against boys, about 5 percent involved two or more attackers (CSOACY, 1984).

The Sexual Assault of Native Children in Residential Schools

For more than a century, over 100 000 Aboriginal children attended Native residential schools operated jointly by the federal government and four Canadian churches. In total, around 20 percent of Canadian Aboriginals attended these facilities. The principal objective of the schools was assimilation which, particularly at this time, meant stripping Native children of their language and their culture.

In 1879, the government of Sir John A. Macdonald established church-operated boarding schools. The schools removed Native children from their homes and the influences of their parents thereby facilitating efforts to assimilate them into mainstream white culture. Acceding to pressure from church officials, in 1894, the federal government passed a compulsory attendance amendment to the *Indian Act*, forcing even greater involvement of Native children in the system. It was not until 1947 that the United Church became the first to declare a desire for residential schools to be closed and replaced by non-denominational day schools. The church cited as its reason the harm to children brought on by separation from their families. Over the next two decades, many schools were phased out. In 1969, the Canadian government assumed full responsibility for the management of the 60 remaining residential schools. In 1973, a new federal policy surrendered control of Native education to the tribal bands and councils.

Throughout its history, the drastically underfunded system subjected its young charges to emotional,

Box 11.6
HOW DO THE CHURCHES ATONE?

The ghosts of Canada's Indian residential schools continue to haunt not only their former residents, but the Anglican, Presbyterian, Roman Catholic and United Churches that ran the schools, and the federal government that asked them to. Is there a way to resolve the misery short of forcing the Anglican Church in particular into partial bankruptcy?

The residential schools were created a few years before Confederation, when the government sought to assimilate Indian children into the broader society by removing them from their parents and sending them to schools where they were forbidden to speak their mother tongue and to honour their parents' traditions. As the General Council of the United Church wrote in a 1986 apology to native congregations, "We tried to make you like us and in doing so we helped to destroy the vision that made you what you were."

The 100 or so schools operated for more than a century. About 60 of them were run by the Catholics, 26 by the Anglicans and 13 by the United Church and (before union in 1925) its Methodist and Presbyterian predecessors. Beyond the monstrous crimes revealed in recent years – the physical and sexual abuse by some teachers and principals of the youngsters entrusted to their care – some schools subjected their charges to beatings and near-starvation. Even when the officials' intentions were good, the effects could be monstrous; with only the principals' consent, federal doctors stopped cleaning the teeth of children in eight schools in the 1940s and 1950s as part of an experiment to improve their nutrition.

The experience of the schools ripped apart the native communities and contributed to the high rates of violence, alcohol abuse and high suicide rates on and off the reserves.

After the Royal Commission on Aboriginal Peoples called in 1996 for a public inquiry, Jane Stewart, then federal minister of Indian Affairs, responded in 1998 that the Canadian government was "deeply sorry" for those who "suffered the tragedy of the residential schools." She announced a $350-million healing fund to help pay for treatment and counselling for abuse victims, but neither accepted blame for the schools nor precluded individual lawsuits against the government.

Phil Fontaine, grand chief of the Assembly of First Nations, accepted the apology. A number of other Indian leaders did not. And the number of individual lawsuits against the government – and against the churches – increased.

An estimated 5,800 claims have been filed against the two groups, not counting four class-action suits. In a pastoral letter issued last week, Archbishop Michael Peers, primate of the Anglican Church of Canada, said that more than 1,600 claims have been brought against the church's (national) General Synod. "About 100 cases involve the proven abuse of children, and the perpetrators are in prison. The costs of litigation and settlements for these alone [are] sufficient to exhaust all the assets of the General Synod and of some dioceses involved."

The four national churches run their affairs differently enough that some face greater risks from successful lawsuits than others. For instance, the United Church, which is more centralized than the Anglican Church (with its dioceses) and the Roman Catholic Church (which ran the schools through separately incorporated orders such as the Oblates), said on May 5 that "it would not be responsible for the United Church" to talk of imminent bankruptcy as the decentralized Anglican Church is doing.

Even if the churches can successfully ward off the lawsuits, the legal expenses may be crippling. Some cases have been settled out of court, but the cost ranges from $15,000 to $100,000. The churches, which not surprisingly have been comparing notes, are negotiating with Ottawa to find an alternative to litigation.

The world does not lack for models of reconciliation between those who have suffered and those who imposed the suffering. South Africa reasoned that it had two choices after the collapse of apartheid: endure decades of bitter, violent recrimination or relieve its pain by forgiving those who confessed to their crimes and sought forgiveness. It took the second path through its Truth and Reconciliation Commission.

Something similar might work in Canada's case, at least as a parallel track to the arrest and conviction of those who committed specific crimes against the boarding-school children. Speaking in February,

Jim Boyles, general secretary of the Anglican Church of Canada, said, "I don't believe the Canadian public wants to see churches forced into bankruptcy." Justice may well be served by a less drastic, but no less satisfying way of atoning for the wrong done.

Discussion Questions

Are those who were victimized entitled to compensation? Who is most liable: church or state? Must church bankruptcy be avoided? What solutions would you propose to remedy this problem?

Source: *Globe and Mail*, June 5, 2000, p. A14. Reprinted with permission from the *Globe and Mail*.

physical, and sexual abuse. In 1986, the United Church became the first church to apologize to its Native congregations for these transgressions. Many victims began demanding compensation for their painful experiences and the first residential school lawsuit was filed in British Columbia in 1989. The following year, Phil Fontaine, former Grand Chief of the Assembly of First Nations and, at the time, leader of the Assembly of Manitoba Chiefs, stated publicly that he had been sexually and physically abused at the residential school in Fort Alexander, Manitoba, during the 1950s.

In 1996, former students of the Mount Cashel Orphanage in Newfoundland, operated by the Christian Brothers, settled sexual abuse claims with the provincial government for approximately $11 million. This settlement bolstered the momentum for Natives to press for damages. The $58-million Royal Commission on Aboriginal Peoples issued a report strongly criticizing Native residential schools. The last residential school in Canada, on the Gordon reserve 100 km north of Regina, Saskatchewan, closed in 1996.

Taken over from the Anglicans in 1969, the Gordon reserve's residential school was the first such institution for which the federal government settled a large number of claims out of court. Approximately 230 plaintiffs, from both on and off the reserve, received between $25 000 and $150 000 each in compensation for past sexual abuse at the school.

The school's administrator, William Starr, directed the Gordon residential school from 1968 to 1984. There, he engaged in a long series of sexual assaults extending over sixteen years. In 1993, Starr pleaded guilty to sexually assaulting ten students and was sentenced to over four years. Those convictions aside, of the 230 Gordon school plaintiffs who received a federal settlement, all claimed to have been abused by Starr (O'Hara, 2000a).

In 1998, Indian Affairs Minister Jane Stewart offered an apology to Natives for the residential school experience. At that time, she announced a $350-million "healing fund." By 2000, the number of people involved in residential school lawsuits against the federal government and, in many cases, the Roman Catholic, United, Anglican, and Presbyterian churches, reached 6324. Representatives of the federal government believe this figure could double in the near future. In response to this litigation, the churches began to voice concerns that the legal process and eventual settlements would bankrupt them.

Potential payouts in the billions of dollars notwithstanding, legal fees alone could well bankrupt some religious organizations. In 1999 alone, the United Church spent $2.3 million in legal fees and only one case had made its way into court. That trial involved the sexual abuse of 30 students at the Port Alberni Indian Residential School on Vancouver Island (O'Hara, 2000b).

In the late 1960s, the churches began to withdraw from administering the schools. After the federal government subsequently assumed sole responsibility, Natives themselves took on important roles in running the institutions. Many worked as dormitory supervisors, child-care workers, and sports coaches. Some of them, victims allege, either facilitated or participated in the abuse. Since Native abusers were themselves often products of the abusive residential system for which they worked, the residential schools fuelled a vicious cycle wherein the recipients of abuse became abusers themselves (O'Hara, 2000a).

THE ADULT FEMALE VICTIM AS DEFENDANT

Many victims of rape have suffered considerably in the reporting and the official processing of their cases. The phrase "victim as defendant" captures the essence of this experience (Landau, 1974), especially as it occurred under Canadian law before 1983 and as it continues to occur in jurisdictions that still operate under similar legislation. While the introduction of legal reforms in 1983 was intended to solve the problem of double rape, it appears doubtful that the new law has entirely accomplished this goal.

Immediately following a rape, the victim had to make several crucial decisions: whether to solicit help immediately, whether to seek medical attention, and whether to report the offence to the police. If she did decide to report the attack and if the police deemed it worthy of further investigation, the rape victim had to decide whether to co-operate in the police inquiry and whether to participate in the court proceedings if the case progressed to trial.

The stigma attached to victims of sexual assault was considerable, so many chose not to report the offence. One-quarter of sexual assault victims in the VAWS had told no one at all about the experience before the interview (Johnson, 1996a). In her study of rape in Winnipeg, Brickman (1980) found that about 50 percent of rape victims and 94 percent of the victims of other sexual assaults did not report the incident to any professional outsider. Indeed, 12 percent of rape victims and 18 percent of the victims of other forms of sexual assault informed no one about the attack. Only about 12 percent of rape victims in Brickman's study went to a hospital for treatment.

The Hospital Experience

When victims did enter a hospital, they did so for two reasons — to seek medical assistance for injuries sustained in the attack or to guard against venereal disease (Kinnon, 1981). Many were tested for pregnancy and, if they tested positive, many had abortions. When the victim had become pregnant, having an abortion frequently caused additional emotional upset for several reasons. Many rape victims had to confess their situations to hospital abortion committees. Many had to endure the financial burden of travelling to a centre where such services were available. Some victims had to leave their home provinces altogether to get abortions. In places without hospitals, in isolated communities, and in cases where the victim did not immediately report the assault, the hardships of getting an abortion were formidable.

The second reason for entering the hospital was to undergo a forensic examination, in which doctors gathered evidence of the assault.

Research indicates that hospitals processed sexual assault victims in various ways. Often, victims entered emergency wards, where they were given low priority unless they had severe physical injuries. Many hospitals did not provide qualified gynecologists for the victim's medical examination. Rather, they delegated this task to inexperienced interns and junior residents. Many physicians balked at examining sexual assault victims because, if the case proceeded to court, they might have been called away from their practices to testify. Since trials were often scheduled at inconvenient times and could take several weeks, many physicians were extremely reluctant to participate in the evidence-gathering process (Clark and Lewis, 1977).

The Police Experience

If the assault was reported to the police, officers questioned the victim and assessed the likelihood of the case holding up in court. To screen out false reports and shaky evidence, the police required the victim to recount, in minute detail, the exact characteristics of the assailant, the specific actions performed during the incident by both the assailant and the victim, and the precise sequence of events in the attack. It was not uncommon for a sexually assaulted person to tell her story repeatedly to a variety of men, not only immediately following the incident but for months afterward.

Even if a case was reported to the police, it might not have been pursued. Clark and Lewis report that police determined 64 percent of incidents to be unfounded and halted their inquiries.

Based on their own independent analysis of police records, Clark and Lewis suggest that in only 10 percent of cases (rather than the 64 percent reported by police) could it be concluded that a rape had not actually occurred. Police "unfounded" many incidents not because they were necessarily convinced that a rape had not occurred but rather because they felt that the crown would not be able to obtain a conviction from a jury.

Clark and Lewis cite several conditions that, alone or in combination, regularly led police to classify incidents as unfounded. If the victim violated established norms of respectable female behaviour — perhaps by being promiscuous, drinking heavily, or living on welfare — police tended not to consider her a credible witness. Also, police officers believed that the absence of powerful corroborating evidence, such as severe injuries, strongly undermined the likelihood of conviction. The inability of the victim to name and provide a detailed description of her assailant also substantially weakened a case. Finally, Clark and Lewis cite cases where the victim herself had simply become very reluctant to participate in the trial as the primary witness for the Crown. Fear of reprisals and concerns over the publicity of a rape trial were prominent reasons for becoming an uncooperative or, in legal terms, "hostile" witness.

Burgess and Holmstrom (1974) describe an "ideal" founded incident. Police were most likely to consider the rape founded when the information was verifiable, when witnesses existed, when the victim could provide a detailed description of her assailant, when supporting medical evidence such as sperm or injury was present, and when the details of the victim's story remained consistent in several interrogations over a long time. Chances of cases being investigated and convictions subsequently obtained were also increased if the victim was a virgin at the time of the attack, was sober, was minding her own business, was physically coerced by an assailant with a long list of prior charges for sexual assault, and was visibly distraught following the incident. Very few cases, however, fit all these criteria.

In many cases, police officers believed the victim but unfounded the case because of their perceptions of a jury's reaction to the "facts." There were, however, many instances of police officers making negative moral judgements about victims on the basis of their own prejudices. Requiring victims to take lie detector tests and laying charges of public mischief against sexual assault complainants who are not believed, Kinnon (1981) maintains, borders on police harassment. She also describes a rape crisis centre case in which police badly treated a sexually assaulted man.

A young man was sexually assaulted in a parking lot by two men; he was forced to perform anal and oral sex with each of them. After he escaped from his assailants, he began to walk toward the police station. He encountered a police cruiser on the way and reported the assault to them. He was laughed at and asked, "What do you want us to do about it? We're busy." The man continued walking and arrived at the police station, by this time hysterical. His story there was received with: "Why are you trying to cause trouble?" He was made to wait one and a half hours before a statement was taken. In the opinion of the Rape Crisis counsellor, "the officers couldn't accept the concept of a man being sexually assaulted." (p. 31)

THE RAPE LAW AND THE EXPERIENCE IN COURT

Laws prohibiting rape were introduced at a time when women were considered to be the property of men (Clark and Lewis, 1977). Indeed, the original meaning of "rape" was to steal or carry off the belongings of another. Before their daughters' marriages, fathers owned them. Upon marriage, fathers relinquished that ownership to husbands in exchange for a payment known as a bride price. Since the most prized traits of young females were virginity and chastity, fathers could levy the highest charges for these qualities. Once married, women became the exclusive property of their husbands.

To ensure that they could pass on land and wealth to their own male heirs, men required that they alone could make sexual use of their wives. For married women, extramarital sex, involuntary or otherwise, cast in doubt the precise parentage of their offspring. To protect themselves as the owners of sexual and reproductive property, men created rape laws to punish those responsible for defiling and rendering worthless previously chaste or faithful women (Clark and Lewis, 1977).

The direct ancestor of twentieth-century Canadian and American rape legislation was the British Statute of Westminster, drafted in 1275 (Kinnon, 1981). This statute set out rules regarding sexual assault and laid down several important foundations of contemporary rape legislation. Rather than treat rape as a crime against a particular person to whom compensation for damages would be owed, the Statute of Westminster formalized rape as a crime against the state. It also ensured that the sanctions for raping a virgin and for raping a married woman would be equally severe. **Statutory rape**, defined as sexual intercourse with a child with or without her consent, was also made illegal at this time. Moreover, this document included sections that made any woman who did not vociferously resist attack partially responsible for her own fate. The statute proclaimed, as well, that there could be no rape of a wife by a husband, since a wife's consent to her husband's sexual advances was permanently entrenched in her marriage vows and could not be withdrawn.

The rules laid out in the Statute of Westminster of 1275 were reflected with remarkable clarity in the

Canadian rape legislation that remained in force until 1983 (Boyle, 1984). The *Criminal Code* defined rape as a sexual act committed by a male against a female outside of marriage. Rape occurred if there was penetration, however slight, of a vagina by a penis without the woman's consent. If consent was given, the act could not be considered rape. Implicit in this law was the necessity that the victim be able to prove that she withheld consent and that she resisted attack. Evidence of force or of threats to inflict bodily harm were necessary to corroborate a victim's claim that she had been raped. A man could also be convicted of rape for impersonating a woman's husband during intercourse or for misrepresenting the sex act as something else, such as physical or psychological therapy. Until 1954, conviction for rape was punishable by death. From 1954 until 1983, the maximum punishment for rape was life imprisonment (Boyle, 1984).

The law contained three provisions designed to reduce the risk of women falsely accusing men. Two of these rules governed the introduction into evidence of "recent complaints" and of information on the victim's past sexual history. The third rule required judges to issue a mandatory warning regarding juries' acceptances of uncorroborated evidence (Clark and Lewis, 1977).

As a general rule in criminal proceedings, information about the time that elapses between a person's becoming the victim of a crime and the reporting of that crime to authorities cannot be introduced into evidence to determine whether the crime took place. The fact that someone waited several hours before reporting a robbery cannot be introduced as testimony that the complaint was a fabrication. However, contrary to this general rule, the recency of complaint was admissible in rape cases. The **recent-complaint rule** required victims to report the offence or "complain" at the first reasonable opportunity. The court equated a lack of immediacy in reporting with a lack of urgency that lent credibility to defence claims that a rape had not taken place. When delays occurred, the defence could challenge the victim's credibility by arguing that, after the fact and on taking time to think things over, she was fabricating the incident. Defence lawyers routinely contended that the victim desired revenge on a former lover, perhaps for having jilted her, or that she had willingly slept with the defendant and later accused him of rape to save face with her family or boyfriend.

Before 1976, when Canadian legislators first modified the law, defence lawyers could freely introduce into evidence, as another challenge to her credibility, the victim's past sexual history. Implicit in this rule were two notions: being unchaste or promiscuous was directly linked with a propensity to lie; and consenting to sex in the past increased the probability that the victim had consented to sex on the occasion under investigation.

After 1976, the law limited somewhat the admissibility of the victim's past sexual conduct. While there were still no restrictions placed on discussions of the victim's prior sexual experiences with the suspected rapist, her sexual interchanges with persons other than the accused could not be raised in court without prior notice in writing and without arguments being presented to the judge that such information was "necessary for the just determination of the case." Critics pointed out that the law continued to allow discussion of prior sexual relationships between the victim and the accused. They also argued that the judge (usually male) was given discretion regarding the relevance to the case of the past sexual relationships between the victim and persons other than the defendant. Despite the revisions, little had changed.

It is not uncommon for judges to warn juries of the dangers of convicting persons on the basis of uncorroborated evidence. These dangers are presumably greatest when guilt or innocence must be decided solely on the basis of the word of the complainant against the word of the accused. Since rape was most often carried out in the absence of witnesses and since the victim's compliance with her attacker's wishes was often attained without her becoming visibly injured, corroborating evidence in rape cases was often lacking. Still, only in rape cases did the judge have no choice but to administer this caution. The mandatory warning regarding corroboration, the admission of evidence about the victim's past sexual behaviour, and the recent-complaint rule permitted the accused rapist protection against false accusations not available to people accused of other types of crime. Furthermore, each of these provisions implied that female rape victims, especially those with certain contentious traits, could not be readily believed (Clark and Lewis, 1977).

To obtain a conviction in a Canadian court, the guilt of an accused person must be proved beyond a reasonable doubt. In a rape trial, it was necessary for

Box 11.7
LESSONS OF SEXUAL DANGER

The whole scene takes no more than 30 seconds.

A six-pack of teenage boys in sneakers and shorts, with baseball caps turned front and back, hanging out on a steamy summer night.

Two girls – 14 or 15, no older – in halters and shorts, walk down the street, their sandals slapping the concrete.

The boys check them out, who's hot, who's not. They close ranks, narrow the sidewalk, so the girls must pass single file.

It's then that I see the girls' antennae go up, notice the way they speed-read the scene, the boys, and the single file between play and danger. The taller girl strikes a pose as a good sport but not a willing player. The smaller takes on a role neither offended nor interested.

The boys stare; the girls smile slightly but make no eye contact. The oldest and boldest of the pack pretends to untie one girl's halter top as she goes by. The girlfriends reach the corner and break into nervous giggles.

Thirty seconds and the boys, like sidewalk hall monitors, have let them pass. It's over.

For once, I don't take this scene for granted. I'm struck tonight by how carefully, precisely, the girls read these boys. How they calibrate both the danger and their own reaction.

How much time and energy went into acquiring these street smarts? Where did they learn? Did their parents teach them to be sexually literate? For their own safety?

Safe sex – no, safe sexuality – is on my mind. In the weeks since I wrote about the Central Park assaults on some 50 women in broad daylight, my mail has been filled with people, many sharing my dismay. But in the mix, there were questions: Didn't I see how some women were playing along? Didn't I see what some women were wearing?

One man described women on the infamous videotapes who would "giggle and laugh as the guys doused them with water. Only when they felt things were getting 'out of hand' did they complain... . They got exactly what was coming to them."

Another man wrote about female "exhibitionists" who send the "wrong message" to men: "It's akin to dangling a pork chop over a pack of starving wolves."

A woman wrote of "skin" fashions, of women with expressions that said "Hi Sailor, want to have some fun? All sailors want to have fun."

And still another reader forwarded a newspaper column on the Central Park assaults by Stanley Crouch that detoured onto "scantily clad young women" and told approvingly of a father admonishing his teenage daughter, "You are not leaving this house looking like a prostitute."

I won't revisit the argument that safety can be found in a dress code. If that were true, rape would have been much rarer among our crinoline-covered foremothers. Such a belief leads backward to the sad, distorted thought of a Bangladeshi woman. Brutally disfigured by acid, she proclaimed herself a convert to purdah: "If I had been kept under the veil, Rakim (her assailant) would not have seen me or been able to talk to me."

But I am struck by the difficulty our daughters still have being safe and sexual. They are supposed to calibrate the continuum from horseplay to harassment to assault. The culture expects them to be sexy but not "pork chops," to attract men and beware of them. And to manoeuvre carefully through this terrain, single file.

Remember the sexual assaults at Atlanta's Freaknik celebration, the rapes at Woodstock? Some women were labelled "fair game." In Central Park, "good sports" who laughed as their T-shirts were sprayed with water were less credible "victims" when those T-shirts were torn off.

Boys – and men – are also subject to double messages. They're surrounded by R-rated images of playgirls who just wanna have fun, and lectured on sexual harassment. They know girls who want to be seen but not stared at.

But girls are the more endangered of our species. So even those who want our daughters to be comfortable in their own skins, to feel powerful in their own bodies, and to be sexually at ease, end up teaching them to be wary.

Girls learn to read boys. They learn that they have to manoeuvre single file – to be safe. They learn who owns the street and the park. These lessons of sexual danger sometimes linger even in relationships with men they love.

There are times when I'm convinced we've updated the book on men and women. But until we teach our sons their own set of reading lessons, this piece of the story will remain the same.

Discussion Questions

What are the lessons of sexual danger? How are they taught? What is the role of culture in this process? Where does the author suggest that responsibility lies for sexual victimization?

Source: Ellen Goodman, *The National Post*, July 14, 2000, p. A12. Copyright 2000, The *Boston Globe* Newspaper Co./*Washington Post* Writers' Group. Reprinted with permission.

the crown to prove beyond a reasonable doubt that the accused's penis had penetrated the victim's vagina and that she had not consented to this penetration. A jury had no choice but to return a verdict of not guilty where reasonable doubt could be raised about whether penetration had in fact taken place. In cases where the accused admitted to penetration, a not-guilty verdict hinged upon the defence's establishing reasonable doubt about whether the victim had withheld consent. The defence lawyer's strategy was clear. By questioning the crown's principal and perhaps only witness — the victim — the defence lawyer tried to foster in the jury uncertainty about the victim's truthfulness on either of these counts.

Unrepresented by council, the victim had to take the stand and recount the assault in considerable detail in front of strangers, most of whom were men. She also had to give her evidence in close physical proximity to her alleged attacker. Since, in the absence of witnesses, the issue of consent was often a question of the victim's credibility, the defence lawyer, as a matter of course, attempted to discredit the witness's honesty and sexual morality. Defence cross-examinations were particularly gruelling.

As researchers have pointed out, the typical penalties meted out for rape by the courts hardly approached the maximums possible under the law. For example, of 103 rape convictions registered during 1973 in British Columbia, the following dispositions were recorded. The courts suspended without probation the sentences of 2 accused, suspended with probation the sentences of 34 accused, and fined 9 accused. Twenty-one were jailed for a year, and 19 for between 1 and 2 years. Eleven received prison sentences between 2 and 5 years, 7 between 5 and 10 years, and 1 between 10 and 14 years. The average sentence for a rape conviction in Canada was between 2 and 3 years (Kinnon, 1981). In their research, Clark

and Lewis (1977) note that sentences for rape averaged from 5 to 7 years, but that when remission for parole is considered, they ranged from 18 to 24 months.

FEMINIST THEORY ON THE SEXUAL ASSAULT OF WOMEN AND CHILDREN

The sexual assault of females is not a result of the psychological abberations of offenders. Beliefs about, attitudes toward, and expectations of women in Canada support this form of violence. The propensity for high rates of sexual assault is imbedded in the social roles of men and women, in the differing nature of power resources attached to these roles, and in the conception of women as objects and possessions to be used by men for their own pleasure (Russell, 1984; Sanders, 1980). In the overwhelming majority of sexual assault cases, males are the perpetrators and females are the victims. From the feminist perspective, sexual assault, like other forms of violence against females, is another expression of sexual inequality and male dominance. By means of such violence, men create in women a fear of sexual victimization that further promotes and reinforces their subjugation.

People expect males to be strong, independent, and dominant and to exercise power over others in general and over females in particular. Conversely, people expect women to be vulnerable, dependent on males, and deferential to male authority. Society rewards males and females for performances approximating these expectations.

Males who successfully compete with other males in the pursuit of higher status reap commensurate social rewards. One of the activities that grants males higher esteem is the "acquisition" of desirable females. Women, on the other hand, learn to see their own status as a reflection of the status of the males who are attracted to them and to whom they are able to attach themselves. They learn at an early age to use their sexuality to attract worthy mates and to bargain for the economic and emotional security that coupling is thought to provide. In this exchange, women offer their good looks and sex appeal, expressed through physical appearance, fashionable clothing, and seductive gestures. The more sexually desirable a woman is, the greater her bargaining power.

Males enhance their masculine status and self-esteem when they sexually conquer beautiful women in large numbers. The media emphasize the importance to a positive male self-image of possessing and enjoying highly desirable females. The acquisition and control of valued females is portrayed as a large part of success and "the good life." Men come to think of and to treat women as commodities that confer status rather than as complete human beings. References to women as "pieces of tail," "meat," and "cunts" betray and reinforce the view that they are objects to be possessed and used in the gratification of male desires.

If male self-esteem depends on attracting and seducing women, rebuffs become direct threats to masculine self-concepts. Rejections produce frustration and anger. When men have few assets to trade in the pursuit of sexual conquests and when as a result they feel both powerless and inadequate, their aggravation and irritation at being denied may be acute. Rejection is even more cutting when sexual permissiveness is the norm. Under sexually restrictive conditions, unsuccessful men can more easily deflect blame to a rigid moral structure in which religious and family values inhibit the free expression of sexuality. But where most males appear to be enjoying sex, the aggravation of failure is heightened (Chappell, Geis, Schafer, and Siegal, 1971).

What men cannot attain through influence and persuasion, they take by force. Sexual assault, then, is a violent behaviour supported by cultural roles and the competition for status. Society socializes its members to a variety of attitudes and beliefs broadly supportive of sexual assault. First, men learn to see women as their property. Second, men view women as objects to be acquired and used for their pleasure and the enhancement of their status. Finally, in a wide variety of circumstances it is considered legitimate to acquire women through force if persuasive bargaining fails.

Many cultural myths support men's use of force in their sexual conquests of women (Hills, 1980). While these beliefs have no basis in fact, men commonly employ them to rationalize their use of coercion in obtaining sex. There is a widespread presumption, for example, that women prefer the use of a certain amount of force in sexual relations and that many fantasize about being raped. Media representations reinforce this conception of the initially resistant female being overpowered by a tall, dark, and handsome stranger into whose arms she eventually melts. Reports of rape victims indicate that many rapists envisage themselves as providing sexual satisfaction to their unwilling partners. Questions from the rapist concerning whether the victim is enjoying herself, whether she has had an orgasm, and whether she considers the rapist a good lover are not uncommon.

Another cultural myth about sexual assault concerns a popular belief that women strongly desire sex but ask for it through subtle means. To satisfy their lust, the thinking goes, women have an intense desire to engage in sex with "forbidden" persons, who may be casual friends, acquaintances, or strangers. Later, they cry rape to save face. Closely tied to this idea is the notion that women who sincerely wish to avoid being sexually attacked will do so — if a woman is not looking for a sexual liaison, she will avoid situations in which one might occur. If she truly has no interest in a sexual tryst, she will dress conservatively, stay out of bars, be accompanied everywhere by an escort, avoid hitchhiking, and so on. Furthermore, the saying that "moving needles cannot be threaded" embodies another folk belief about rape: if a woman really resists forced intercourse, it cannot occur (Russell, 1975).

Many people erroneously believe that some types of women deserve to be the targets of unwanted sexual attention. Among these deserving candidates are the "temptress," the "loose woman," and the "worldly" female. The temptress is a "cock teaser": she excites in "normal" men a masculine sex force that, once unleashed, cannot be controlled. According to this idea, females who tempt men must accept the blame for whatever befalls them. Many believe that loose women, those with reputations for promiscuity, have nothing left to lose. As a result of their sleeping around, these women forfeit forever their right to say no. Finally, some believe that women who have lost sight of their "proper place" are acceptable targets of sexual aggression. Many men see women who have become confident, independent, self-assured, and upwardly mobile as needing a not-so-subtle reminder of their true worth and proper function. Sexual assault is seen as a means of re-establishing their sub-servience to men (Brownmiller, 1975).

Male dominance and sex role socialization to a view of females as sexual commodities are powerful predispositions conducive to the sexual abuse of children, especially female children, by adult males. Finkelhor (1981) points out that society ineffectively socializes men to distinguish between sexual and non-sexual forms of affection. Men then learn to become easily aroused by sexual activities and sexual fantasies that are divorced from the content of the relationships in which they occur. As a consequence of the "attraction gradient," men are attracted to sex partners who are smaller, younger, and less powerful than themselves. In short, men are socialized to desire sexual partners who are more childlike (Russell, 1984).

Changes in the perceived power differences between the sexes may also focus the sexual interest of men on children. Particularly when men are insecure and feel relatively powerless, they may feel especially threatened by females. Some feminists suggest that some men desire young girls as sexual partners because they can no longer easily dominate mature women.

Children who are socially isolated are more vulnerable than are those who are tightly integrated into family and friendship networks. Since molested children often know and trust their attackers, it is ironic that many adults deliver strong warnings against the potential sexual advances of strangers. Thus, children are ill-prepared to protect themselves.

Children who are relatively unsupervised by fathers or mothers are more vulnerable to attack from those both outside and inside the family. Incest, for example, frequently occurs when mothers are sick, drunk, absent, or powerless and therefore unable to protect their daughters adequately (Russell, 1984).

THE 1983 REFORM OF THE LAW ON SEXUAL ASSAULT

A multitude of criticisms of the *Criminal Code* sections governing sexual assault were raised during the 1970s and the early 1980s. Commentators pointed out that the rape law focused more on the sexual act than on the violence of the assault. In addition, the rape laws were rebuked for their inherent gender discrimination. In the first place, only males could be attackers and only females could be victims, and in the second place, a man could not be charged with rape when the victim was his wife (Boyle, 1984).

Critics, many of them members of the women's movement, argued that the overriding concern of the law before 1983 was to protect men as the rightful owners of women. They pointed out that the law did not recognize women's rights to sexual autonomy and failed to safeguard women. According to feminists, the misplaced legal emphases on the protection of men had two sources. First, almost all lawmakers have been and continue to be male. Second, because they were male, lawmakers were unable to place themselves in the position of a female rape victim. Rather, the architects of the rape law were only able to identify with the relative or friend of a victim or with a falsely accused man. Unlike any other criminal legislation, the rape law incorporated special rules to guard against false accusation. These concerns for protecting accused men resulted in a rape law that shielded only women who managed to reflect an entirely unblemished image (Clark and Lewis, 1977).

The calls for reform spearheaded by the women's movement were aimed at making it less onerous for women to report their sexual victimization and more straightforward for the courts to charge and convict offenders (Hinch, 1988a). Accomplishing these goals hinged on three points: recognizing rape as an assault rather than viewing it as a sexual offence, ensuring that the sexual discrimination inherent in the law was eliminated, and ensuring that maximum penalties were more realistic and more rigorously enforced (Boyle, 1984). On the first point, rape legislation highlighted the sexual nature of the attack (e.g., penetration, previous sexual experiences). This emphasis paved the way for defence lawyers to claim that the victim was responsible for her assault because of the sexual provocation inherent in her appearance or her actions. Taken to its extreme, any woman conforming to any standard of sexual attractiveness or behaviour that could be construed as seductive could be held at least partially responsible for the unwanted advances of a man. Conversely, where the law focuses not on sex but on the force and violence integral to a sexual assault, blame is shifted away from the victim onto the assailant, where it belongs. Regardless of the victim's attractiveness or behaviour, "no" means no. If a man uses threats or force to shift refusal to compliance, then an assault has occurred and the attacker is solely responsible for his actions.

In 1981, Parliament introduced a bill containing amendments to the *Criminal Code* that transferred sexual assault from the sections dealing with sexual offences to the sections dealing with offences against the person (Hinch, 1988b). These amendments emphasized the assaultive nature of sexual attacks and classified offences by the degree of violence and risk experienced by the victim. The bill specified two types of crime: sexual assault included actions ranging from unwanted touching to forced intercourse, while the more serious offence of aggravated sexual assault included incidents in which greater harm was experienced by the victim or in which the assailant used a weapon. These sections of the *Criminal Code* closely paralleled the sections for assault and assault causing bodily harm. Because of the added sexual component of the attack, the bill made the penalties for sexual assault offences more severe than for nonsexual assault. Bill C-53 passed as the *Criminal Law Amendment Act* in January 1983 (Boyle, 1984).

The new legislation replaced the crimes of rape, attempted rape, having sexual relations with a feeble-minded person, indecent assault on a female, and indecent assault on a male with those of sexual assault, sexual assault with a weapon, and aggravated sexual assault. Since the degree of penetration in a sexual assault was no longer relevant, extensive questioning on this point was no longer required. Moreover, the *Criminal Code* sections on sexual assault — the rape shield provisions — stated that evidence of sexual reputation for the purpose of challenging the credibility of the victim could only be admitted under very limited circumstances. The intent of these measures was to ensure that the trial experience was more humane for sexual assault victims.

The new law contained a neutral expression of gender. Both males and females could be either the perpetrators or the victims in sexual assaults. Moreover, the law subjected those convicted of sexually assaulting either women or men to the same penalties. The reformed law eliminated spousal immunity from prosecution, and the trial judge was no longer required to instruct the jury that it was dangerous to find the accused guilty in the absence of corroboration (Boyle, 1984).

Rape shield provisions were designed to protect a sexual assault victim from interrogation by a defence lawyer about her past sexual activity with anyone other than the accused. In a 7-to-2 decision on August 22, 1991, the Supreme Court of Canada ruled that this legal provision was unconstitutional. The court's opinion was that the rape shield section in the *Criminal Code* could result in the exclusion of relevant evidence and thereby interfere with an accused's right to a fair trail.

This ruling had two basic implications. First, the absence of a **rape shield law** might reduce the willingness of victims to report sexual assaults to the authorities. Second, the lack of rape shield provisions considerably increased judicial discretion regarding the admission of sexual history evidence. On this point, critics pointed out that one of the reasons for the 1983 rape shield statute was that judges themselves could not be trusted to make just decisions about the admissibility of sexual history evidence in an area so heavily imbued with cultural myth and social stereotype.

In 1992, Parliament set out judicial guidelines governing the admissibility of evidence concerning past sexual conduct. These directives defined consent and placed restrictions on the introduction of mistaken belief as a defence. The legislature indicated that consent is not given when a victim is incapacitated by intoxication or some other means. Consent is also absent when it is induced by abusing a position of trust, power, or authority, if the victim indicates by word or conduct that it is withheld, or if the victim indicates by word or conduct that it is withdrawn. By specifying word or conduct in these latter provisions, lawmakers take account of the vulnerability of women with disabilities that preclude verbally denying consent. This legislation effectively shifts the focus from the use of force and the cause of injury to the granting or withholding of consent (Johnson, 1996a).

An accused who uses the defence of mistaken belief in a sexual assault case must prove that he honestly believed that the victim had given consent. The 1992 legislation restricted the use of this defence, stating that it could not be applied if the belief stemmed from the accused's drunkenness, recklessness, willful blindness, or neglect in taking precautions to ensure that consent was in truth being granted. Despite these provisions, however, in 1994 the Supreme Court allowed the defence of severe drunkenness as it reversed the conviction of a man found guilty of sexually assaulting an elderly woman. In 1995, Parliament amended the *Criminal Code* to disallow drunkenness as a defence in violent offences such as sexual assault that require proof of general intent (Johnson, 1996a).

In 1995, a Supreme Court of Canada decision required that victims' counselling and other personal records be made available to accused persons under certain specified conditions. Critics of this decision charged that these guidelines were overly lenient and that neither the privacy and nor the equality rights of victims were being protected. Parliament subsequently passed a bill in 1997 that restricts access to victims' medical and other personal records and provides clearer guidelines for determining how and under what circumstances defence attorneys can examine these documents (CCJS, 1999).

THE EFFECTIVENESS OF THE NEW SEXUAL ASSAULT LEGISLATION

The new law downplayed the sexual nature of sexual assault and emphasized its assaultive quality. Its intent was to encourage victims to report sexual attacks to the police by improving police and court processing of these crimes, reducing the trauma to victims, and increasing the number of convictions (Roberts and Gebotys, 1992). The broadened scope of the new law permitted charges to be laid in cases of sexual assault involving spouses. It also made the law gender-neutral with respect to both victims and perpetrators.

Although the rate of sexual assaults reported to the police from the time the new legislation was introduced in 1983 to 1992 increased 164 percent, the proportion of cleared sexual assault incidents resulting in charges against the suspect increased only slightly, from 69 percent in 1983 to 72 percent in 1994. Johnson (1996a) outlines three reasons why increased reporting may have occurred. First, changing the law may indeed have had the desired effect of increasing reporting and improving the rate of criminal justice processing. Second, the new law extended the range of assaultive behaviours (unwanted touching), potential perpetrators (husbands), and potential victims (men) beyond those contained in the previous rape legislation. Finally, two-thirds of the sexual assaults reported to the police between 1983 and 1992 involved persons under the age of 18. The dramatic increase in reported incidents might therefore reflect increases during this period in sexual assaults against children.

An evaluation of the sexual assault law carried out by the department of justice suggests that the changes in the law may not have been sufficient to engender so sharp an increase in reported cases. This research demonstrated that incidents recorded as sexual assaults since the introduction of the new law have not differed significantly from the kinds of incidents formerly recorded as rape or indecent assault. The number of cases in which the suspect was the spouse of the victim or in which the victim was male has remained small (5 percent or less in both cases). The increase in the number of child victims has also been relatively small and therefore cannot explain the dramatic increase in overall reports of sexual assault (Department of Justice, 1985; Johnson, 1996a).

Clark and Hepworth's analysis of the impact of the new sexual assault legislation in six Canadian cities — Vancouver, Lethbridge, Winnipeg, Hamilton, Montreal, and Fredericton — suggests minimal change. They found that there was little overall change in rates of founded crime, of crimes cleared by charge, or of convictions (Clark and Hepworth, 1994). In their assessment of the new law's impact on case processing in Winnipeg, Gunn and Linden (1997) found that conviction rates did not increase and that the character of the victim continued to have an effect on the likelihood of laying charges and gaining convictions.

Gunn and Linden suggest several reasons why the change in sexual assault legislation may not have produced all of its intended outcomes. First, criminal justice officials may have resisted implementing the changes. Second, the new initiatives are aimed at the trial stage. It is entirely possible that they would exert little effect on the informal discretion exercised by police and prosecutors. Finally, sexual assault is a difficult crime to prosecute because it typically occurs in private and without witnesses other than the victim and the accused. Where cases revolve around one person's word against another, the defence's establishment of the reasonable doubt necessary for an acquittal is facilitated.

A number of important historical and social factors must be considered in estimating the impact of the reform legislation. Johnson (1996b) points out that the 1970s and 1980s saw significant changes in the social and economic status of women, in the media attention accorded to crime victims (particularly female victims), in the training provided to police officers and hospital staff, in the expansion of sexual assault support centres, and in the growth of the women's movement (Clark and Hepworth, 1994). There has also been a growing tendency for adults to disclose sexual assaults that took place in their distant past, often when they were children. All of these factors, Johnson argues, may have influenced victims' willingness to report sexual victimization even in the

Box 11.8
COURTS ARE LENIENT IN SEX ASSAULT

Canada's courts are handing out "discount" sentences to sex offenders, particularly when their victims are children, says a researcher who has extensively studied sexual assault cases.

Edward Renner, a professor at Carleton University in Ottawa, said a perfect example is the case of a Winnipeg man spared jail, despite having sex with his children's babysitter when she was 12 or 13 and he was in his 20s.

Dean James Bauder was originally sentenced to nine months in jail. But the Manitoba Court of Appeal reduced the term to community service, saying the girl willingly participated in sex.

"It's not surprising that women's groups have been outraged," said Renner, whose research appears in this month's issue of Canadian Psychology.

"Everybody says 'Oh, that's just an exception or that's just a bad judge,' That's not an isolated case. That is the rule about what's taking place."

Renner studied more than 1,000 cases in the Halifax area for his research.

He found just one in five people convicted of sexual assault got more than two years in prison while one of every two people convicted of robbery was sentenced to more than two years.

The victim was a woman or girl in 87 percent of sexual assault cases, compared with in 34 percent of robberies.

Renner also found adults who have sex with children get off more lightly than those who victimize adults. Only 13 percent of child sex offenders he studied received a sentence of two years or more, compared with 30 percent of those who assaulted adult women.

Violence does tend to be more common in adult sex assaults, occuring in about 80 percent of such cases and in about 20 percent of offences against children.

In the Winnipeg case, Justice Kerr Twaddle of the Manitoba Court of Appeal has been criticized for saying the girl was "willing," although he noted consent cannot legally be given by a child.

"This judge made explicit with his statement what you see all the time going on in the courtroom," said Renner.

He said judges routinely let defence lawyers ask children what kind of clothes they were wearing or whether they accompanied their assailants willingly, as if they could be held responsible for luring their attackers into the assault.

"Most judges don't put their foot in their mouth ... but they do the same thing by essentially allowing all that kind of questioning."

The result is that the courts in general treat sexual offenders quite leniently, imposing more severe sentences only in cases where violence or personal injury is involved, said Renner.

"If they can't see a broken bone, if there's no blood, if there's no physical exhibits, if there's no medical testimony, then no harm took place, which we know is foolish from other kinds of research."

Discussion Question

How can the situation outlined in this article be reconciled with the purposes of the new sexual assault laws?

Source: Scott Edmonds, *Toronto Star*, June 9, 1997, p. A2. Reprinted with permission from Canadian Press.

---

absence of law reform. Johnson (1996a) notes that the women's movement mobilized public opinion to shape legal reform not only by emphasizing the breadth of the problem but by focusing attention on the treatment of women by the courts, by pointing out the lack of appropriate sexual assault support services, and by lobbying for social change (Roberts, 1994; Johnson, 1996a).

Finally, one indicator of the 1983 sexual assault law's effectiveness is the severity of punishments meted out. One recent investigation reveals that convicted sex offenders received harsher sentences from Canada's courts than other violent offenders. In 1997–98, 57 percent of adult sex offenders received prison sentences compared to 38 percent of offenders convicted of other violent offences. In only 39 percent of sexual assaults was the sentence probation, while for other violent offences 51 percent of offenders received probation.

Not only were sex offenders more likely than other violent offenders to receive prison terms, but they were also more likely to be incarcerated for longer

Box 11.9
CONVICTED, JAILED, RELEASED – AND HOUNDED

The vicious beating here last week – in broad daylight and in full view of a newspaper reporter and photographer – of a convicted pedophile by a man who didn't want him living in the neighbourhood is the brutal, but inevitable, result of one of the most misguided policies concocted by police departments across the country in the name of the so-called public interest.

Yes, the man had been jailed for sex crimes involving children. Yes, such crimes are repulsive. Yes, children must be protected from sexual predators. But he had been released from prison after serving his full sentence. He had duly paid his debt to society and had a right to expect to be left in peace.

Instead, the police, in their unerring wisdom, designated him a danger to the community and "outed" him to the media, which promptly publicized his whereabouts. Forced to flee from one home, he was "outed" again last week to his new neighbours by a reporter and photographer from *The Ottawa Sun*. Photos of the subsequent beating were published in glorious colour on the front page of the newspaper the next day.

This is but the latest in a long list of similar "outings" by police and media across Canada and elsewhere, sometimes with even more frightening results. In England, an elderly man was beaten up by a bunch of punks who mistook him for a child molester who had been "outed" by the police.

Such "outings" amount to harassment as public policy and are largely the result of an unholy alliance of police, who claim they are protecting the public, governments, which refuse to outlaw the practice, and much of the media, which gleefully lap up what the police throw their way with apparently nary a thought for the consequences.

The reason given is protection of society, especially children. That's a commendable goal. But examined in the harsh light of reason, such "outings" amount to little more than state-sanctioned revenge upon what many consider the lowest form of humanity. Normally reasonable people turn into vigilantes; it is an updated version of the lynch mob.

But however heinous their crimes might have been, and however despised they may be, these offenders too have rights. The cornerstone of our justice system is rehabilitation; it is, after all, Corrections Canada, not Vengeance Canada. All offenders, even child molesters, should expect to be able to rejoin society as productive members of that society.

Instead, they are hounded, harassed and driven from community to community by the hysteria whipped up by the police and the media. What chance have they of finding and keeping a job when their pictures and crimes are plastered all over the newspaper and television screen? What chance, then, of rehabilitation? The end result is this: The cry that the system doesn't work, that rehabilitation is a sham, becomes a self-fulfilling prophecy.

The "outing" of such offenders amounts to a kind of double jeopardy. Having served their sentences and been released, they are condemned by police and media to a life sentence of harassment and abuse. This abuse of their civil rights encourages lawlessness; it should come as no great surprise that the Ottawa man's attacker had, as of yesterday, not been charged. After all, he is a hero who, according to one neighbour, deserves a medal. The man he attacked, on the other hand, is again in hiding – a modern-day leper.

And while "outing" is justified as a protection of child-abuse victims, what about the other class of victims it creates – people who are innocent bystanders, but often just as deeply affected? We forget that offenders also have families who end up being stigmatized, traumatized and sometimes ostracized. Often they are children too. What about their rights?

Child abusers need help, not persecution. Canada needs privacy laws to end this scurrilous practice before someone is seriously injured, or worse.

Discussion Questions

Do those who have been released after having served their sentences for sexual assault against children have any rights? What rights should they have? Is "outing" a reasonable practice for ensuring the safety of children in Canadian communities?

Source: Klaus Pohle, *Globe and Mail*, May 23, 1997, p. A25. Reprinted with permission from the author.

TABLE 11.1

PRISON TERMS FOR ADULT SEXUAL OFFENDERS, 1997-98

Offence	1 month or less	More than 1 to 6 months	More than 6 to 12 months	More than 1 to less than 2 years	2 years and over	Total
			% of prison terms			
Total Sexual Offences	10	35	18	17	19	100
Sexual assault	10	33	18	18	21	100
"Other" sexual offences	9	40	18	17	16	100
Total Violent Offences	33	43	9	6	8	100

Note: Figures may not add due to rounding.

Source: CCJS (1999). Sex Offenders. *Juristat Service Bulletin* 19(3). Ottawa: Canadian Centre for Justice Statistics, Statistics Canada, p. 8, Cat No. 85-002.

terms. As Table 11.1 indicates for 1997–98, of the 1533 sexual offence cases resulting in a prison sentence, 45 percent of the terms were for six months or less, while 36 percent were for more than one year. The comparable percentage for violent offence cases were 76 percent (six months or less) and 14 percent (more than one year). The median prison term for violent offence cases was three months compared to ten months for sexual assault cases.

Probation terms were lengthier for sex offenders than for violent offenders more generally. For sex offenders who received probation in 1997–98, 72 percent of terms were longer than one year and 29 percent extended beyond two years. For violent offenders, only 47 percent of probation terms were longer than one year and only 9 percent extended beyond two years (CCJS, 1999).

SUMMARY

Victim surveys demonstrate that sexual assault occurs more frequently than is indicated by studies of official records, because official data depend on victims reporting offences to health-care, social service, and law-enforcement agencies. Victims do not report offences for a variety of reasons, including embarrass-ment, fear, and self-blame. The process, initiated by police, of "unfounding" rapes is another source of the underestimation of official rates of sexual assault. Unfounding often occurs because the victim displays characteristics that undermine her credibility as a witness. Either police do not believe her or, if they do, they feel there is little chance that the case will result in conviction.

Victims of sexual assault tend to be female, young, unmarried, and from the lower class. Assailants are male and also young. Both married and unmarried men commit sexual assaults against women, in roughly equal proportions. Assailants are motivated by the desire to humiliate their victim (anger), possess her (need for power), or physically injure her (sadism). Power rapes seem most common, while sadistic rapes are comparatively rare. Sexual assaults tend to be premeditated, and victims, because of their intense fear of injury or death, frequently do not resist attack vigorously. Many victims know their assailants. Sexual assault is most often an intra-racial event, tends to occur in or around the victim's residence, and happens most frequently during the evening hours. Few sexual assaults in Canada occur as part of another offence, and few involve lethal weapons. There is some disparity in the Canadian research on the numbers of offenders involved in any given incident. Depending on the study, from 50 to 85 percent of attacks are perpetrated by lone attackers. Alcohol appears to play a role in many sexual attacks; its consumption may increase male aggressiveness, decrease a woman's defensive capacities, and contribute to men's misinterpretation of signals.

Victim precipitation is a concept that implies that the victim has behaved in a way that invites attack. With regard to sexual assault, this idea has been criticized as being male-biased. Victim-precipitated rape assumes that many neutral behaviours (e.g., being alone in a bar, having a drink with a man) are in fact risk-taking because they invite sexual advances.

Sexual assaults can involve verbal and physical abuse (e.g., beating, burning, choking) as well as forced sex. Victims experience both physical and emotional traumas, which may endure long after the assault.

Double rape refers to the legal practice of trying the victim and defending the accused. After the assault, rape victims faced a trial by ordeal at the hands of health-care personnel, social service workers, and police officers. Before reform of the legislation in 1983, court proceedings reflected a concern for false accusation that was unique to rape and, in so doing, facilitated acquittals. Special rules governed the admission into evidence of the recency of the complaint and evidence about the victim's past sexual history. Rules also required judicial warnings about uncorroborated evidence. Even in the rare instances when convictions were attained, punishment for rape in Canada, despite maximum penalties of life imprisonment, was slight.

The sexual abuse of children is, like the sexual assault of women, frequent but under-reported. Victims are primarily female, and molesters are primarily male. Perpetrators force a broad range of unwanted acts on children, but most common are touching and fondling. Private homes are the most frequent location for sexual molestation, and summer holidays, when children are least supervised, is the time of greatest risk. Most victims know their assailants.

Children are also subject to sexual assault in institutional settings. The cases most recently receiving attention involve Aboriginal persons who were victimized as children in residential schools sponsored by the federal government and operated by Canada's churches.

Feminist social theory presents the argument that gender-based power differences, dominant cultural values, male and female sex roles, and the conception of women as objects combine to encourage the sexual victimization of females. Moreover, several prevalent myths support and justify sexual assault: women enjoy forced sex; they secretly desire sex despite their protests; unwilling women cannot be raped; and women with certain characteristics are legitimate targets for sexual aggression. Cultural factors, such as male sex role socialization and the conception of females and children as male property, combined with variable opportunity structures, are important facilitators of child sexual abuse.

Revisions to the rape law that took effect in 1983 shifted the emphasis from the sexual to the violent nature of sexual assault and eliminated rules offering undue protection to accused persons. They also removed sex discrimination from the law. These initiatives were undertaken to make the law more just and thereby to increase rates of reporting and conviction to the levels of similar crimes, like ordinary assault. While the extent to which these goals have been met has been evaluated only tentatively, there is some indication that they are not being fully realized.

DISCUSSION QUESTIONS

1. Why is it more difficult to win a conviction for sexual assault than to win a conviction for common (nonsexual) assault?

2. What measures will have to be undertaken if sexual assault and violence against women and children are to be more effectively controlled?

3. What is the relationship between sexual harassment and sexual assault? More specifically, how is sexual harassment related to acquaintance or date rape?

4. How should rape shield protections be properly balanced against an accused's right to a fair trial?

5. What rights to compensation are possessed by the victims of the Native residential schools? Who bears greater responsibility for the damage done to them: church or state?

WEB LINKS

Sexual Assault: Dispelling the Myths

http://www.womanabuseprevention.com/html/sexual_assault.html
> This fact sheet prepared by Ontario Women's Directorate dispels common myths about sexual assault.

Survey of Sexual Assault Survivors

http://canada.justice.gc.ca/en/ps/rs/rep/rr00-4-a-e.html
> This report, prepared by Tina Hattem, contains the findings of a national survey of sexual assault survivors conducted by the Department of Justice in collaboration with Canadian Association of Sexual Assault Centres and its members.

Male Sexual Victimization

http://www.victimsofviolence.on.ca/malesex.htm
> An overview of male sexual victimization in Canada, including information on sexual assault laws, myths surrounding male sexual assault, effects of victimization, and offenders.

National Clearinghouse on Family Violence

http://www.hc-sc.gc.ca/hppb/familyviolence/
> This Web site includes information on sexual abuse of children and on wife abuse.

Institutional Child Abuse

http://www.cdc.gc.ca/en/themes/mr/ica/2000/index.html
> This site contains the full text of "Restoring Dignity: Responding to Child Abuse in Canadian Institutions," a report prepared by the Law Commission of Canada, as well as information and links related to the abuse of children in institutional settings.

RECOMMENDED READINGS

Amir, M. (1971). *Patterns of Forcible Rape.* Chicago: University of Chicago Press.
> This work is a classic in its field. Many of the patterns uncovered in Amir's analysis are replicated in more recent studies of rape and sexual assault.

Benedict, J.R. (1998). *Athletes and Acquaintance Rape.* Thousand Oaks: Sage.
> Explores three high-profile cases to determine why the culture of professional athletics supports sexual assault. Discusses celebrity, athleticism, groupies, and the roles of defence attorneys in court.

Boritch, H. (1997). *Fallen Women: Female Crime and Justice in Canada.* Toronto: Nelson.
> Contains a coherent overview of issues surrounding the sexual assault of women in Canada, as well as a good review of the literature more generally. See especially Chapter 7, pp. 210–253.

Boyle, C.L.M. (1984). *Sexual Assault.* Toronto: Carswell.
> Presents a very detailed feminist review of the reasons underlying the introduction of Canada's sexual assault legislation in 1983.

Cruise, D., and A. Griffiths. (1997). *On South Mountain: The Dark Side of the Goler Clan.* Toronto: Viking.
> Discusses a recent case involving the widespread sexual assault of children in a rural area of an eastern Canadian province. Emphasizes the role of subculture in supporting and concealing sexual victimization.

Harris, M. (1990). *Unholy Orders: Tragedy at Mount Cashel.* Toronto: Penguin.
> Presents the facts surrounding the sexual assaults of boys at the Mount Cashel orphanage in St. John's, Newfoundland. Harris explores how these events could have happened and details the impact of these events on the church and the community.

Russell, D.H. (1998). *Dangerous Relationships: Pornography, Misogyny, and Rape.* Thousand Oakes: Sage.
> Examines the connection between rape and pornography. Provides a coherent summary of literature on pornography and male sexual aggression.

CHAPTER 12

PROSTITUTION

The aims of this chapter are to familiarize the reader with:

- the complexities of defining prostitution
- the legal status of prostitution in Canada
- popular misconceptions about prostitution
- the extent of prostitution
- types of prostitutes and their background traits
- how people become part of the subculture of prostitution
- the roles related to prostitution: madam, pimp, and customer
- the prostitutes' rights movement
- selected theories of prostitution: functionalism and feminism
- issues surrounding the control of prostitution

INTRODUCTION

While it is unlikely that prostitution is Canada's oldest profession, it has been in evidence for a considerable length of time. Prostitution in Canada dates back at least to the time when Europeans began to settle here and, depending on one's definition of the practice, to even earlier periods, when the Native people were the country's sole inhabitants. After colonization began, houses of ill-repute became common near military establishments, fishing and trading ports, and other commercial centres (SCPP, 1985).

Sex solely for the sake of pleasure flies in the face of traditional moral values and religious beliefs. The free expression of sexuality and the immediate gratification of sensual desires are often regarded as sins of the flesh. Because prostitution is a commercialized form of sex practised solely for the enjoyment of recipients and the profit of providers, Canadians historically have disapproved of it and rebuked its participants. Rough traders, working girls, and children of the night have met with disapproval from citizens and legal sanctions from the criminal justice system. Despite the condemnation, there has been and always will be a commercial demand for illicit sex.

Contrary to popular conception, prostitution has never been illegal in Canada, although it is illegal in parts of the United States (Sansfacon, 1985). Rather than make prostitution itself illegal, the *Criminal Code* of Canada in 1972 prohibited solicitation for the purposes of prostitution. In 1985, the solicitation law was changed, and communication for the purpose of prostitution became illegal. The Code also bans a number of other related activities, such as operating a common bawdy house, living off the avails of prostitution, and procuring. Similarly some U.S. states do not prohibit prostitution per se but rather forbid the solicitation of clients for sexual purposes.

Legal bans on prostitution and solicitation are by no means universal. Prostitution is legal in the Netherlands and Germany. A few counties in the state of Nevada are the only areas in the United States where prostitution and many of its adjunct activities are lawful. Under a system of legalized prostitution, governments control and regulate the enterprise through licensing and inspection. State regulations give prostitutes and their clients legal protection, require prostitutes to undergo regular medical checkups for sexually transmitted diseases, and impose taxes on sales of sexual services (Sansfacon, 1985).

The word "hooker" conjures familiar images that fascinate and intrigue — painted ladies, dimly lit street corners, seedy hotels, and rundown bars. These well-worn images provide people with their common-sense understandings of this illicit profession. However, like many deviant vocations, prostitution is romanticized, misunderstood, and stereotyped.

This chapter begins by examining some issues associated with defining prostitution and by questioning several popular misconceptions about prostitution. The focus shifts to ascertaining the extent of prostitution in Canada, describing its various types, and showing how people enter the profession. The chapter then investigates the ancillary roles associated with prostitution. Two theoretical approaches — a pioneering functionalist interpretation and a recent feminist explication — are examined. The chapter concludes by assessing the prospects for effectively controlling prostitution in Canada.

DEFINING PROSTITUTION

Little empirical research had been done on prostitution in Canada until the 1980s, when two federally mandated committees' investigations generated considerable data. The Committee on Sexual Offences Against Children and Youth (CSOACY), headed by Robin Badgley, investigated prostitution among children and youth, while the Special Committee on Pornography and Prostitution (SCPP), headed by Paul Fraser, examined the illegal sex trade among adults.

Prostitution is not easily defined. Most Canadians (90 percent) conceive of it as a simple exchange of sexual services for money (SCPP, 1985). According to this perspective, people who have sex and accept money in return are prostituting themselves. But what about people who accept as remuneration for sex other material goods or benefits in lieu of cash? Are these people also prostitutes? Over half of Canadians (57 percent) would agree. Does this mean that those who, on occasion, engage in sexual relations in return for a night on the town, a "line of coke," a place to "crash," or a week in Jamaica are prostitutes? What about people who engage in relationships or marry for financial security? To what extent are they prostituting themselves? Where does one draw the line?

For most Canadians, the exchange of sex solely for material gain fails to meet their moral standards — 62 percent feel that exchanging sex for money is inde-cent, improper, and worthy of disapproval. Fewer (53 percent) believe that sex in return for material goods other than money is also wrong (SCPP, 1985). Clearly, Canadians disagree both on what constitutes prostitution and on how objectionable the practice is.

Although a consensus on a definition of prostitution is probably impossible, most sociologists of deviance agree on several points. First, it is sexual in nature, and the reward for performing the sexual act is either money or other material goods exchanged at or near the time of the act. Second, the relationship between the provider and the recipient of sexual services involves neither love nor affection. Finally, because there is an exchange of material reward for a service, prostitution is a full- or part-time vocation (Benjamin and Masters, 1964). Furthermore, prostitutes are not necessarily female (Visano, 1987) and not necessarily adults (Weisberg, 1985). Male and female prostitutes of various ages provide sexual services for both the opposite and the same sex.

MISCONCEPTIONS ABOUT PROSTITUTION

Prostitution has always been a subject of both curiosity and controversy. Inaccurate depictions in both the news and the entertainment media encourage popular misconceptions about the sex trade. Many people believe that pimps force large numbers of women into prostitution through a combination of threats, violence, and drugs. Canadian research, however, suggests that this is relatively rare; about half of all prostitutes enter "the life" without any outside encouragement, let alone coercion (SCPP, 1985).

Force seems to play a role in the recruitment of teenage runaways. Still, while more young persons than adults may be coerced into prostitution, this means of entry is uncommon even for them. The rarity of forced teenage participation in prostitution is underscored by the Badgley Committee's report (1984), which stated that 50 percent of young prostitutes interviewed could not identify a key person who got them into the trade. Moreover, of those who could name such a person, only 1 percent of males and 10 percent of females identified the person as a pimp. Since not all pimps are violent, physical coercion into prostitution in Canada appears uncommon.

Sixty percent of the Canadians surveyed by the Fraser Committee in its national opinion poll believed that most prostitutes work for pimps. However, many

Box 12.1
POLICE CHARGE 80 IN STRIP CLUB RAIDS

Hundreds of police officers descended on three strip clubs in the Toronto area last night, in a large-scale raid to shut down the trafficking and exploitation of foreign exotic dancers.

An estimated 300 Toronto law enforcement officers participated in the operation, the largest police raid of its type in recent history, at clubs in Mississauga and Brampton. One hundred and fifty prostitution and related charges were laid against 80 club owners, managers, women and customers. Those charged included bartenders, DJs, doormen and dancers.

Police vehicles surrounded the clubs, blocking off traffic and turning back patrons as men and women were led out of the buildings in handcuffs. Many of the women were sobbing as they were led into police vans.

Police, including members of the tactical squad, burst into the clubs and told customers and dancers to remain seated with their hands on the table.

The raid on the strip clubs, in suburbs west of Toronto, was part of a special joint task force, Project Almonzo, set up to combat organized prostitution and the international recruitment of sex slaves into Canada, police said.

After weeks of undercover work and police intelligence, officers uncovered evidence for the first time that an organized criminal group from Romania was trafficking women from Eastern Europe to Toronto, and forcing them to work in clubs such as the Million Dollar and Second Locomotion in Mississauga, and Cannonball in Brampton.

"This raid is the biggest of this project so far," said Superintendent Ron Taverner, of the Toronto police Special Investigations Unit. "We're targeting the trafficking of women from Third World countries. This is a problem we continue to face when dealing with these types of establishments."

The women arrested in the clubs came from Romania, Hungary, Thailand and Latin America.

Some were Canadian. Officers working on the case said they have been shocked at the extent of illegal activity in the strip clubs.

Geoff Ramdowar, a social worker with Toronto's Streetlight Support Services, was on the scene with translators to assist the women. "Some will be charged with regard to immigration matters, some will be released," said Inspector John Nielsen, a Peel region officer who was part of the raid.

Since its inception 13 months ago, officers with Project Almonzo have conducted raids of more than 16 establishments in an attempt to curb the vast underground network of strip club owners and managers, who police say recruit and then exploit foreign dancers.

Police have laid more than 650 criminal charges against 200 club owners and 100 foreign strippers – although the goal of the project is not to do a "hooker sweep" but to attack organizations involved in the trafficking of women for a sexual purpose.

Project Almonzo includes officers from the RCMP, the federal Immigration department, Peel, Durham and York regional police, Ontario Provincial Police, Ontario's Alcohol and Gaming Commission and the Toronto police morality squad.

The extensive police investigation has already closed down some clubs. For example, the liquor licence of the Fairbank Hotel was revoked after the owners acknowledged dancers performed sexual acts on customers in exchange for money. The former manager pleaded guilty to two prostitution offences and received a $10,000 fine.

Discussion Questions

How great a problem is posed in North America by the trafficking and sexual exploitation of foreign women? Why does the problem exist? Is law enforcement its solution? Are there alternative measures that might be undertaken?

Source: Marina Jiménez and Stewart Bell, *National Post*, June 16, 2000, p. A23. Reprinted with permission from the *National Post*.

prostitutes report that they are self-employed. Again, 60 percent of Canadians believe that organized crime controls much of Canada's sex trade. Empirical research also disputes this, finding few links between prostitution and Canadian organized crime.

The widespread belief that many people take up prostitution to support their addiction to drugs is another misconception. Canadian prostitutes do make use of drugs, but the extent of their addictions and drug trafficking does not appear to be great.

Although most prostitutes do have criminal records, the offences for which they have been convicted tend to be relatively minor crimes, such as petty theft and shoplifting. Not surprisingly, many prostitutes also have previous convictions for soliciting and other crimes directly related to prostitution (Sansfacon, 1985).

Many Canadians (69 percent) believe that prostitution is prominent in the spread of sexually transmitted diseases (SCPP, 1985). Common-sense notions of how prostitutes perform sexual acts and of how people spread sexually transmitted diseases are at the root of these beliefs.

The extent to which prostitution contributes to the spread of sexually transmitted diseases seems to be exaggerated. Prostitutes in Canada and the United States likely transmit sexual diseases no more, and perhaps less, than other sexually active people who have many partners. Since the introduction of the birth control pill in the early 1960s, the number of people engaging in sexual activity with more than one partner has increased dramatically. More important than the popularity of promiscuous sexual activity, however, is the fact that most female prostitutes insist on using a condom when performing vaginal, anal, and oral sex acts. Recent Canadian research shows that over 90 percent of adult female prostitutes use condoms extensively; the same is true for 30 to 40 percent of male hustlers (SCPP, 1985). The recent publicity regarding HIV transmission among homosexual males and the public campaign for safer sexual practices make it likely that condom use among male prostitutes will increase.

Many people think that prostitution is extremely distasteful and unpleasant work and that prostitutes are miserable, guilt ridden, and dislike their clients. Because of the severely limited number of legitimate jobs available to many of those who enter the trade, prostitution presents itself as a relatively forthright way to earn a living. Little formal education, inadequate vocational training, and a lack of experience in the labour force routinely translate into extremely low-status, part-time, low-paying menial work, if not unemployment. This situation is particularly common for many young women during economic recessions.

The emotional and psychological costs of prostitution are not as great as many commonly assume. Like others who provide services to customers, prostitutes find some customers likable, some objectionable, and most nondescript. The image of female prostitutes as man-haters or lesbians is incorrect. Most male and female prostitutes are heterosexual and many have enjoyable sex lives with those whom they love (Carman and Moody, 1985).

THE EXTENT OF PROSTITUTION

Determining the extent of prostitution in Canada is difficult. Using official crime data to count the number of prostitutes is virtually impossible, for a variety of reasons. A prostitute may be arrested once, occasionally, or frequently; thus the number of charges for communicating for the purposes of prostitution (or, before 1985, soliciting charges) does not indicate the number of prostitutes. Moreover, prostitutes may be arrested for offences other than communicating or soliciting, such as vagrancy and public indecency. In these cases, officials underestimate both the incidence of prostitution and the number of prostitutes. Also, because higher-class prostitutes do not work the street and hence are far less likely to be arrested, their numbers remain largely unknown. Since prostitution is an illicit activity without an angry victim, it is less likely to be reported to or recorded by the police. Finally, prostitution routinely generates police crackdowns, which result in many charges being laid in short periods of time. While these brief escalations in charging appear to show an increase in the number of prostitutes, the growth in numbers is artificial. It is more a reflection of police activity than of an influx of prostitutes (Clinard and Meier, 1989).

Only somewhat more accurate than official records are the estimates of the numbers of prostitutes made by the police. In several Canadian cities, as part of the research for the Fraser Committee's report, police officers were asked to estimate the numbers of working prostitutes in their cities. Many factors, particularly transience, contaminate estimates of this type. While some researchers argue that these data are among the best available, the counts they produce are highly speculative. These estimates are the educated guesses made by police officers, and it is not surprising that the appraisals of police officers in the same cities vary considerably.

According to Fraser Committee's police data, eastern Canada in the 1980s had relatively few prostitutes. In the more populous cities of the region, such as St. John's, Halifax, Saint John, and Moncton, there were very modest levels of prostitution while in the smaller eastern cities, such as Gander, Dartmouth, Charlottetown, and Summerside, commercial sex was virtually nonexistent (Crook, 1984). Quebec City police estimated their population of prostitutes at about 400 prostitutes, most of whom worked either out of clubs (35 percent) and agencies (28 percent) or from advertisements (25 percent). Street prostitution in Quebec City was practically nonexistent (Gemme et al., 1984).

Not surprisingly, the Committee determined that Canada's largest cities had higher numbers of prostitutes. Police in Montreal, Toronto, and Vancouver reported that between 500 and 600 prostitutes were plying their trade in each of these cities. The inclusion of temporary and occasional prostitutes increased those numbers from two to six times. As might be expected, mid-sized cities such as Ottawa, Winnipeg, Saskatoon, and Calgary had fewer prostitutes (100 to 400) while smaller municipalities such as Windsor, St. Catherines, and Niagara Falls had the least (20 to 100) (Fleischman, 1984; Lautt, 1984; Lowman, 1984).

TYPES OF PROSTITUTES

Like any other occupation, prostitution is diversified and each of its several types has different status characteristics and modes of operation. Ranging from low to high on the status continuum are prostitutes who ply their trade in the streets, in bars, in brothels and massage parlours, and in the employ of escort services. At the very top of the status hierarchy are call girls and call boys. Upward mobility through these ranks is extremely unlikely; street prostitutes, for example, rarely become call persons (Sansfacon, 1985).

The prostitute's position in this status hierarchy is reflected in the amount of money made, the means of operation, the type of clientele, and the degree of safety on the job. Lower-status prostitutes make less money, hand over a larger proportion of it to pimps, and exercise less choice regarding whom they service. They must process more customers more quickly to earn an acceptable income. Lower-class prostitutes must solicit clients in public places and as a consequence are more subject to public haranguing and police harassment. They are also more likely to be the victims of violence, drug abuse, and exploitation by pimps and procurers. Finally, streetwalkers are more likely than call persons to have criminal records, although they usually involve minor crime.

STREETWALKERS

Because of the high visibility of prostitutes on the streets, on TV, and in the movies, most people think of the prostitute in terms of the "lady of the evening." While "painted ladies" make up the largest number of prostitutes, they are by no means all ladies; young male hustlers also work the sex trade. A major difference between male and female prostitution is that pimps are rare in male prostitution (Sansfacon, 1985); pimps are most actively involved in the street prostitution of young females.

Streetwalkers acquire clients mainly through public solicitation. While some prostitutes hit the street around 11 A.M. to service the "lunch-time quickie crowd," most ply their trade from late afternoon until midnight. A few work into the early hours of the morning. Prostitutes conduct most business from Wednesday through Saturday; business is briskest during the warmer months of the year (SCPP, 1985).

Transactions occurring on the street between prostitute and customer generally involve neither persistence nor pressure on the part of either party. Typically, prostitutes advertise their services through their provocative attire and the location in which they stand. Ideal worksites are either commercial districts or nearby locations that ensure customers easy access by car. Commercial sectors provide reasonably large numbers of prospective clients and provide anonymity to customers.

Most incidents of commercial sex begin with the customer approaching the streetwalker. For very good reasons, prostitutes encourage customers to take the initiative. Having the "john" make the opening move serves as a first line of defence against entrapment by plainclothes police officers (CSOACY, 1984; SCPP, 1985). Once they agree upon a price, the prostitute and the client retreat to a private place such as an alleyway, a deserted park, an automobile, or a hotel room. Only after the money has changed hands does the prostitute perform the sexual service.

Since streetwalkers are large in number and work in public places, they are highly visible to clients, to members of the public, to neighbourhood merchants and businesspersons, and of course, to police. Area residents and pedestrians frequently view solicitation as a nuisance, and for this reason the arrest and detainment of streetwalkers is common.

Many streetwalkers and gay hustlers ply their trade in certain clearly demarcated urban neighbourhoods known as "red light districts." Well known to city residents, Davie Street in Vancouver, "the track" in Toronto, "the main" in Montreal, "the triangle" in Halifax, and "the hill" in Winnipeg have each become local landmarks. Male and female prostitutes tend not to work the same area. In Halifax, for example, male prostitutes work the Citadel Hill area, while Gottingen and Barrington streets are the exclusive domains of female prostitutes (Crook, 1984). In some cities, the locations worked by street prostitutes are direct reflections of their statuses. Vancouver, for example, can be divided into higher- and lower-status street prostitution by area. West Georgia is a higher-class location, while the West End, Granville Street, and the East End are the lower end of the scale (Lowman, 1984).

Street prostitution, although at the bottom of the status continuum, has its own status structure. According to Lautt (1984), "high-class pros" have seniority over other streetwalkers and are more able to set their own prices. Also, they are more likely to have a stable clientele of regulars. High-class streetwalkers also tend to be well known to the police and to have better relations with them.

Lower on the ladder are the "tough broads," who display less sophistication in talk and dress and are more often involved in violence. Lower still in status, and smaller in number, are the "drunks" and "druggies," who are dependent on alcohol and drugs and hence are very susceptible to violent abuse, for two reasons. First, since they must acquire these addictive substances at all costs, they are forced to take risks. Second, since their sensibilities may be dull, even while on the job, they are more easily robbed and assaulted.

At the absolute bottom of the streetwalker hierarchy are the "chippies," who offer their services at bargain prices. Chippies are frequently very young and engage in prostitution as a result of a temporary need for cash. Since they undercut the prices of established prostitutes, they are not popular among their colleagues on the street (Lautt, 1984).

BAR PROSTITUTES

Bar prostitutes, most of whom are female, operate out of a variety of public drinking establishments, ranging from seedy taverns in rundown areas to cocktail lounges in luxurious hotels. In the lower-class bar, part-time prostitutes often supplement their incomes from legitimate jobs as bar maids. Prostitutes working cocktail lounges are frequently better educated, better dressed, and more refined in the social graces. Because the setting is more private, police interfere with bar prostitutes less frequently than they do with streetwalkers, particularly if the establishments' own-

ers condone the sale of illicit sex on their premises. Bartenders and managers often serve as procurers by referring patrons to particular prostitutes (Prus and Vassilakopoulos, 1979). Managers also instruct bar prostitutes regarding the rules for recruiting clients in the lounge.

> Maggie was discussing an interview that she had prior to starting at Main. She said that the interview ran about an hour and that the manager told her a set of rules that she was to follow. Such things as not being too obvious on the job and buying drinks, not beer, and also to take people upstairs rather than to a hotel on the outside. (Prus and Irini, 1988:7)

The approach to customers employed by the bar prostitute depends on the nature of the drinking establishment. In lower-class bars, the overture may be more direct and resemble street soliciting. In higher-class lounges, the prostitute positions herself strategically at a table until approached by a prospective customer. The client sits down, engages the prostitute in conversation, and perhaps buys her a drink. The exchange between the two resembles flirtation, as discretion is of the utmost importance both to the operators of the establishment and to the potential customer. After an arrangement has been tactfully agreed upon, the prostitute and client leave the lounge and proceed to the client's room, where the transaction takes place (Prus and Vassilakopoulos, 1979).

HOUSE PROSTITUTES

Although houses of prostitution are more common where neither prostitution nor related activities are illegal, some of these establishments exist in Canada (SCPP, 1985). Managed by experienced prostitutes called "madams," they operate illegally and on a small scale. Madams generally recruit and train the house prostitute. To ensure constant variety for regular customers, the turnover of prostitutes in these houses is high. Customers enter the establishment and select a prostitute; then client and prostitute retire to a room where they discuss the sexual activities to be performed. After they reach an agreement on fee for service, the customer makes a payment and the house prostitute performs the negotiated sexual act (Winick and Kinsie, 1971).

Where houses of prostitution are legal and operate on a large scale, state agencies regularly check prostitutes for sexually transmitted diseases and tax their proceeds. Where houses of prostitution are illegal, their operation is fraught with problems. To remain in business, managers of unlawful bawdy houses employ several protective strategies. They schedule hours of business during the day, when vice squads are least active, and shift locations regularly. The most effective means of staying in business is to bribe police to ignore the house and its clandestine business (Winick and Kinsie, 1971).

MASSAGE-PARLOUR PROSTITUTES

While many massage parlours and their masseuses are legitimate, a growing number of prostitutes now find employment in body-rub parlours in Canada and the United States. In Canada, virtually all massage-parlour prostitutes are female. Male masseurs catering to the sexual desires of male customers became extremely rare after police crackdowns on gay bath houses in Montreal, Toronto, and Vancouver in the mid-1970s (Sansfacon, 1985). Advertisements for massage parlours are widespread; some are more explicit than others in referring to massage and "hotel" services and employing suggestive pitches such as "all muscles massaged."

Whether or not customers are interested in sexual services, they must pay a basic fee in the reception area of the massage parlour. After showering, patrons are ushered by their attendants into the privacy of a small room. Here the masseuse usually begins to provide a "straight," a massage devoid of an act of sex. If customers desire a "local," they must ask the masseuse for a "complete massage" and negotiate the price. A complete massage involves a body rub that includes the client's genitals. For a few extra dollars, the masseuse may agree to perform the service topless or completely naked. The performance of other sexual acts such as fellatio or coitus is not customarily part of the masseuses' repertoire of services. Clients tend to be middle-class men, many of whom work in white-collar jobs (Rasmussen and Kuhn, 1976).

A recent development on the Canadian massage-parlour scene has been the use of closed-circuit video equipment by proprietors to protect the masseuse against a customer's violent attack. This practice has raised concerns that these films might be edited into pornographic movies or used to blackmail customers, many of whom hold respectable positions in the community (Sansfacon, 1985).

Since the clients of these establishments must request being masturbated by the body-rub prosti-

tute, massage parlours have had a ready defence against police charges of solicitation and keeping a common bawdy house. Nonetheless, these defences have not always been successful in Canadian courts (Sansfacon, 1985).

THE CALL PERSON AND ESCORT-SERVICE PROSTITUTE

The highest-ranked prostitutes are those who are self-employed or who work for escort services. These prostitutes, commonly referred to as call girls (or call boys), tend to be better educated and more sophisticated than their lower-status counterparts. Dressing tastefully, these individuals service a more elite clientele and often command impressive fees. They do not solicit but rather acquire new clients through the recommendations of their customers and referrals from other call girls or procurers.

Higher-status female prostitutes are referred to as call girls because they initiate most of their contacts over the phone. Clients call either the call girl herself or her answering service. Through discussions on the phone, they make arrangements to go out on a "date," which usually involves dinner and an evening out at some social function. The occasion usually culminates in sexual activity. High-class prostitutes are careful to minimize the commercial aspects of these transactions (Greenwald, 1971).

Clients interested in hiring escorts for dates in which sexual services will be provided must first select an escort agency. The selection is usually done on the basis of the agency's reputation or on the basis of advertisements placed in newspapers, magazines, and the yellow pages of telephone books. Ads vary in their explicitness; some picture couples in passionate embrace, and others prominently display suggestive phone numbers (e.g., 969-6969).

When clients phone an escort service, a receptionist assesses their credibility. The receptionist and the potential customer discuss in veiled terms the range of services for hire. If the callers seem credible (not vice squad officers), agency personnel invite them to visit the office, where they are screened once again. Clients are shown photographs or video tapes of a variety of "escorts," make their choice, and pay the fees, often with a charge card. They leave the premises and are joined by their escorts at locations distant from the agency offices. Insisting that the customer and the escort meet away from their offices helps escort services to avoid charges of keeping common

Box 12.2
TOURIST TRADE IN CHILDREN

San Jose, Costa Rica. At a beach resort in Costa Rica's lush Pacific region, sex tourists who whisper a special code phrase are served up teenagers from the old banana-exporting town of Quepos.

Guests uttering the words, "I want a tiny tasty," are taken to family homes in the nearby countryside, where, for an undisclosed sum, they have sex with young girls, said Bruce Harris, executive director of the Latin American branch of Casa Alianza (Convenant House), a non-governmental organization that works with street children.

Last month, Mr. Harris told Costa Rican authorities of this pedophile operation, which is based in a hotel owned by a Canadian. His complaint is one of 194 similar cases of sexual exploitation of minors now being considered by Lilliam Gomez, the country's special prosecutor for sex crimes. Five of them involve Canadian expatriates.

The international sex trade has caught officials here off guard. As authorities in Thailand and the Philippines crack down on sex tourism, Costa Rica is emerging as a "sexual Disneyland for the American, white male."

According to a U.S. State Department report, as many as 3,000 children in this Central American country work as prostitutes, although Costa Rican officials say this number is greatly exaggerated.

Last year, the number of tourists who visit the country surpassed one million for the first time. Experts believe they included sex tourists looking for teenage prostitutes who charge as little as US$16 an encounter.

Desperately trying to restore its image as a destination for ecologically conscious families and white-water rafters, the Tourism Ministry has launched a nationwide "Save Our Children" television campaign. The government is also distributing colourful brochures at airports, highways and ports, warning visitors: "It is a crime to facilitate the corruption and prostitution of an underaged child ... All hotels and bars are under surveillance to avoid this."

"The problem of sexual exploitation of minors gives our country a bad name," concedes Walter Neahaus, the Tourism Minister. "We are very respectful of human rights and concerned about our children and about family values."

The government introduced new legislation last year, making sexual acts with minors and production of child pornography illegal. It also eliminated an article in the criminal code that said male rapists could not be convicted if they agreed to marry their victims.

Ms. Gomez has charged 22 people so far — including five North Americans — with sex crimes involving minors; five have been convicted. "It is a serious offence. It's like killing children, killing their innocence," she says.

To enforce the new anti-prostitution laws, police patrol San Jose's brothels and bars, some of which are owned by Canadians and Americans.

Rogelio Ramos, the Security Minister, regularly joins the midnight raids, flanked by a team of legal advisors and police officers on motorcycles.

"We've picked up that girl 20 times," he said on a recent sortie, pointing to a 16-year-old on a street corner.

As he patrolled the downtown streets, ragged adolescents took refuge in the trees.

The police brigade searched for underaged prostitutes in Key Largo, an elegant colonial home that is now the city's most infamous brothel, stocked with women and girls from Cuba and the Dominican Republic.

"We have had complaints about minors, but whenever we go in there, there are never any," said Rodolfo Vicente Salazar, a lawyer with the government's National Institute for Children.

"There is a ring operating. The owner of the club gives a ticket to the underaged girls on the street and foreigners get assigned a number. But getting the proof of this is difficult."

Most young prostitutes work in private brothels or as independents on busy downtown intersections.

Business is brisk a few blocks from Key Largo. A silver Mercedes-Benz four-by-four with a Beverley Hills licence plate screeches to a halt in front of a burned brick building. Andrea and Carla climb out of the back seat, collapsing into giggles on the pavement.

Andrea, 13, dressed in a cotton jumper, plastic thongs and a blue striped top, says she just performed oral sex on an older European man for $20. She is saving her virginity for the customer with the fattest wallet.

"I want $700 for it," she shouts boisterously, sucking her thumb. "There's a man who will pay that much for it."

She arrived here 11 months ago from Guanacaste, a province in the northwest interior, after running away from her mother. She says she smokes crack occasionally and lives in a cheap hotel. "My parents don't know I'm here," she says.

Carla, a 15-year-old with greasy hair and heels, says she sells her body to earn money to look after her eight-month-old baby.

She stamps her feet on the sidewalk in excitement and claps her hands as a red Mercedes pulls up.

"Wait, here comes a regular," she cries. "Oooo, it's an American, a gringo, he's my client."

The girls are suspicious of the government campaign to "protect them," saying the police officers frequently abuse them, especially when the security minister does not accompany the street patrols.

The offices do not always take them to overnight shelters, they say. Instead, they sometimes drive the girls to Zurqui, a suburb 20 kilometres outside the city, and dump them in a field after robbing and raping them.

But Ms. Gomez she has not received complaints about police abuse from teenage prostitutes.

Although the exploitation of Costa Rica's children is receiving international attention this year — CNN, ABC and other U.S. networks have all reported on U.S. sex tourists and their underaged victims — the problem is as old as the profession.

Two British sociologists from the University of Leicester who studied the issue in Costa Rica concluded: "Many of the male tourists who are ostensibly drawn to Costa Rica for ... surfing, water sports, eco-tourism ... also sexually exploit local women and children during the course of their stay."

Sex tourists often return to the country to open bars, hotels and restaurants in San Jose, and on the Caribbean and Pacific coasts, which enables them to become involved in adult and child prostitution, adds their report, which was presented at the 1995 World Congress Against the Commercial Sexual Exploitation of Children, in Stockholm.

The authors anonymously quote a 52-year-old French-Canadian expatriate with a taste for teenage girls who used to own a bar in Cahuita. The man bragged he could "get a little girl if he offered her mother 5,000 colones [$16].... Here, 13-year-old girls smile at me ... I mean smile in that 'come-on' way."

Mr. Harris says part of the problem is cultural: Adult prostitution is legal in Costa Rica, and children grow up thinking this is normal.

"There is an acceptance of prostitution and the image that everything in Costa Rica is *pura vida* — everything is wonderful," he says.

In addition, Costa Rican men consider 14-year-olds "ready for sex," he says. Twenty-five per cent of Costa Rican mothers have their first child between the ages of 15 and 18 and 41% of births are to single mothers.

Mr. Harris applauds the government's efforts to stamp out pedophiles, but believes the country is still in denial about the extent of the sexual exploitation.

Last month, he launched a complaint with the Inter-American Commission on Human Rights in Washington, D.C., saying Costa Rica has failed to live up to its obligations to protect children from sexual abuse, and calling on the commission's special rapporteur on children to evaluate the problem.

When the young sex workers are asked what the government should do to eradicate the abuse of minors, Andrea takes a clump of hair out of her mouth and says: "I'd like the government to give me clothes, perfume, chocolate, food and ice cream."

Carla adds: "The government always says the same thing and then never does anything. We are nobody's children."

Discussion Questions

Discuss the social, economic, and cultural forces contributing to the maintenance of an international sex trade involving children. Is law enforcement the answer? What other measures might be effective in reducing this problem?

Source: Marina Jiménez, *National Post*, June 5, 2000, p. A13. Reprinted with permission from the *National Post*.

bawdy houses (Sansfacon, 1985). Call girls and escort-service prostitutes experience comparatively little interference from the police, partly because of the privacy of the transactions and partly because of the relatively high social standings of many of their clients.

PROFILE OF CANADIAN PROSTITUTES

Canadian prostitutes surveyed by the Badgley (1984) and Fraser (1985) committees range in age from 14 to 56 years. Most are between the ages of 22 and 25, although the majority began their careers while they were still in their teens. Since the prostitute's earning power is directly related to physical attractiveness, most careers last less than 10 years. On average, Canadian prostitutes enter the occupation around age 16 and retire around age 26. Prostitutes working off the street tend to be older than those working on the street, partly because laws restrict access to bars and lounges on the basis of age. For similar reasons, the young are ineligible for employment by escort agencies. Consequently, off-the-street prostitution is the exclusive domain of adults.

For males, the prostitution career is shorter than for females because they tend to lose their youthful appearance earlier. Most males exit the ranks around the age of 21, while many females remain in the trade until the age of 30. As women age, they lose their competitive edge and become downwardly mobile. Prostitutes visibly beyond their physical prime are forced to work in less desirable locations, both on the street and in bars. They also find that they must increasingly offer their services for lower prices.

Survey data collected for the two committees suggest that the ratio of female to male prostitutes is about 4 to 1. Most, especially males, are single, but 20 percent of females are married. A minority of prostitutes support and care for dependent children. In terms of family backgrounds, Badgley (1984) reports that 49 percent of child and teenage prostitutes come from broken homes. Similarly, 43 percent of the adult prostitutes surveyed by Crook (1984) in selected cities in Atlantic Canada and 56 percent of the Vancouver prostitutes surveyed by Lowman (1984) came from disrupted families.

Both the Fraser and the Badgley reports indicate that the socioeconomic backgrounds of Canadian prostitutes vary widely. Most come from lower-middle or middle-class backgrounds, while a few come from more affluent families. Most prostitutes, particularly those working the street, are poorly educated. In Vancouver, 70 percent had not completed high school. For the Prairies, Quebec, and the Maritimes, the comparable figures were 77 percent, 68 percent, and 84 percent, respectively. In the Ontario report on prostitution, Fleischman (1984) attempted to ascertain the education levels of prostitutes according to the type of prostitution in which they were engaged. Fleischman reports, for street prostitution, that females tend to have completed only the early years of high school, while males are more likely either to

have completed higher grades or to have graduated. Not surprisingly, call girls report higher levels of education; most had at least a postsecondary education of some sort.

Another background trait commonly reported by prostitutes is childhood abuse at the hands of a male. Twenty-five percent of boys and 33 percent of girls interviewed for the Badgley Committee had suffered physical assault. Seven percent of the boys and 21 percent of the girls reported being victims of some form of sexual assault. Among Vancouver prostitutes, Lowman found that 67 percent were physically assaulted and 33 percent were sexually assaulted in the family context. Seventy-two percent had been attacked in settings outside the family. Similarly, Crook reports that 40 percent and 28 percent of her sample of prostitutes in Atlantic Canada had suffered physical and sexual assault, respectively. In Quebec, 44 percent of prostitutes questioned had been sexually assaulted by some member of the family and 33 percent had been raped (Gemme et al., 1984).

The backgrounds of many Canadian prostitutes appear to be a combination of humble origins and physical and sexual abuse. Although these findings are generally consistent with those of investigations of prostitution in other countries, one must be cautious in assuming that these traits are precipitators of prostitution. The studies from which these findings were taken necessarily focused on the lower echelons of prostitution. Streetwalkers do tend to have lower-class backgrounds, but so do automobile assembly line workers and secretaries. In contrast, call girls, like female teachers and bank managers, tend to come from middle-class backgrounds.

To establish a link between abuse and entry into prostitution, it would have to be demonstrated that far more streetwalkers were physically and sexually attacked during childhood than were other persons who are not prostitutes but who have the same social and economic backgrounds. Thus, although many street prostitutes report being physically and sexually abused during childhood, information is scant on how many lower-class children in general suffer such abuse. Furthermore, prostitutes may exaggerate the extent of their victimization to portray themselves as innocent victims not entirely responsible for their vocation. In reference to the impact of prior abuse, Badgley goes so far as to conclude that children and youth who become prostitutes are no more likely to have been abused than those children and youth who

Box 12.3
PROSTITUTION: TWO PROFILES

Charles

Charles is a 19-year-old street prostitute, born in New Brunswick and now living in Dartmouth, N.S. He is single and describes himself as bisexual. He does part-time body-work in a garage and lives with his mother, who pays the rent.

His childhood was spent in Dartmouth. He was the second in a family of three children. His father was a vending machine repair man and his mother worked on a fish and chip truck. When he was seven his parents separated and he stayed with his mother.

His strongest childhood memories are of hating school and of his father hitting him with a belt. He ran away from home once but soon returned home again. His first sexual experience was oral sex with a girl at school. He was 13 at the time.

His introduction to prostitution was through a friend who was also a "hustler" on the street. Charles was 18 and made $80 from his first transaction.

Some of the hazards he describes on the street are: "fag beaters," loud prostitutes and rude comments by detectives. He would prefer the privacy and convenience of the telephone/escort system of prostitution but says no such service for males exists at this time.

He works two to three hours a night and sees about two customers. He estimates their average age as 35 and that most of them are professionals. Though they are married, he feels that they are "closet" homosexuals. Oral sex performed on him by the customer is the most requested act. He will give anal sex but will not receive it. He has also performed unusual requests, such as ejaculating in the customer's face and allowing his body to be squirted with lotions while the customer masturbates.

Charles has been physically assaulted by customers who do not want to pay for extra services, but he himself has admitted to stealing money and drugs from customers. He does not drink while working, in order to be in control. However, he does take drugs after working, saying, "I'd live on acid if I could."

He finds the work enjoyable "when the customer is good-looking." He goes to Dartmouth General Hospital for check-ups every two months.

He charges $30 for oral sex and $50 for anal sex on the customer. A good night's financial intake would be $70 which he spends on food, clothing and V.C.R.'s.

He has no criminal record. His contact with the police is limited to rude comments on their part and their telling him to "move on."

Laura

Laura is a 19-year-old ex-prostitute. She worked the streets for seven months, but is now attending the Dartmouth Work Activity Program through Probation services, where she is upgrading her clerical skills in order to get a job. She is separated, has no children and lives by herself in a rooming house.

Born in Halifax, her early childhood was spent in a rural setting. From the time she was 8 years old she lived in Halifax and Dartmouth, spending the summers in the country. During this period she was adopted, for reasons unknown to her, into a very large family, where the father was a building superintendent. The mother, who was an invalid, was described by Laura as "her best friend." She recalls arguments between her adoptive parents, at which time she would physically defend her mother against her father. She also remembers being sexually abused at the age of 10 when her mother's 18-year-old nephew threatened to beat her up if she did not have intercourse with him. This was her first sexual experience. Her adoptive mother was supportive by banishing the nephew following the sexual assault. However, Laura felt that both parents were very restrictive and this is the reason she gave for constantly running away.

It was during one of these escapades that she met Pimp No. 1 on Gottingen Street (the pimp numbers refer to case studies elsewhere in the Report). "He knew I was scared and had no place to go. He asked if I was hungry and if I needed a place to sleep. So I said O.K." She lived at his girlfriend's house and was forced to earn her keep by prostituting. Pimp No. 1 initiated and then encouraged her dependency on drugs to keep her working for him. She was 14 when she turned her first trick.

Laura worked on the street with all the hazards inherent to that type of prostitution. She remembers being "hassled" by several pimps, being physically abused by a customer who wanted more than he had paid for, and having treatment for gonorrhea at a community clinic.

She would work for an average of five hours a night. During this time she would see six or seven customers who were predominantly "white collar" workers and whose average age she estimated at fifty years. At one point she had ten or twelve regular customers. The act that was most requested of her was oral sex. On occasion she was called upon to perform unusual acts, for example, spatting (defecating on the customer) and various S & M acts. She had also posed nude for photographs for a customer for $150.00. Laura did not like her work; she was continuously stoned on speed, mescaline or cocaine in order to forget what she was doing.

She was expected to make at least $150.00 per night for Pimp No. 1. She turned it over nightly. In return for money she was given cigarettes and drugs.

After some time on the street, Pimp No. 1 sold Laura to Pimp No. 4. Despite this, she "... fell in love with him." One night, when she held back some of the money from Pimp No. 4, she was locked in the living room, beaten and given no food for a long period of time.

Laura commented about Pimp No. 4 who was in jail at the time of the interview, "I was scared to death of him and his violence. If he comes back to Halifax, he's coming for me."

Laura has a criminal record for such offences as shoplifting, disturbing the peace and impeding other persons.

After a severe beating when Pimp No. 4 broke her nose and ribs and "drove a bullet in the wall above her head," she decided (with encouragement from another prostitute) to charge and testify against him. She remembers the Halifax morality officers as being very supportive. The support she received from the other prostitute and the police enabled her to leave prostitution.

Discussion Questions

Compare the experiences of prostitutes Charles and Laura. To what extent do they typify the experience and background of male and female prostitutes in Canada?

Source: Special Committee on Pornography and Prostitution, *Pornography and Prostitution* (Ottawa: Department of Justice, 1985), vol. 2, pp. 371–72, 375–76. Reproduced with the permission of the Minister of Public Works and Government Services Canada, 2001.

do not (CSOACY, 1984). Lowman (1995) argues, however, that closer examination of the committee's data suggests that juvenile prostitutes are twice as likely as non-prostitutes to have been the victim of sexual assault involving threats or actual force.

ENTRY INTO PROSTITUTION

In her investigation of prostitution in the Prairie provinces, Lautt (1984) documents three entry processes: exploitation, recruitment by the big-sister figure, and the independent pragmatic decision. Exploitation appears most frequently in the recruitment of girls aged 12 to 16. In search of young female candidates, street pimps patrol bus depots, train stations, airports, and other points of entry to the city. When they spot suitable prospects, the pimps follow them until dusk. At nightfall, pimps approach the young girls and engage them in conversation. Afterwards, they buy the young girls refreshments and offer them places to stay. After a short time, when financial and emotional dependencies have been created, pimps ask their new-found friends to engage in commercial sex. If the girls resist manipulation, pimps occasionally use more coercive tactics, including threats and assaults.

According to Lautt, the influence of a "big sister" is a very important means of occupational recruitment. In this process, older, experienced female prostitutes influence novices aged 15 to 19 to take up prostitution. Davis (1978) details this process in her American research. First, sexually active girls are attracted to companions with similar values and predispositions. The promiscuous girls offer each other support in their search for adventure and excitement. The second step, receiving occasional remuneration for partying, is a short one. What begins as sex for fun becomes sex for profit. Those in the group already accepting money for sex convince novices to redefine the meaning of their sexual activity. Davis suggests that the transformation to professional prostitute is complete when girls begin to view the selection of their sexual partners predominantly in monetary terms.

The third entry process observed by Lautt involves the more mature individuals aged 18 to 24. These young women usually base their independent pragmatic decision to enter the occupation on economic necessity. Usually having little formal education, these women simply decide that they can make more money through prostitution than by pursuing the limited alternatives available to them in legitimate careers. The words of several prostitutes illustrate this rational decision making:

> The same night, after I lost my job, I thought about the advantages and the disadvantages of it and to me it seemed very rational in my mind ... Like most of the books I have read, the prostitute is a sweet innocent little girl at first and she knows nothing about nothing and she gets talked into or tricked into it by the pimp, that is sort of the common stereotype. You know, the girl comes to the big city and she doesn't know what all is happening. Whereas with me, I sort of looked at it and said, "Well, I am not sweet and innocent. I know about the whole thing." I knew there was good money in it and I knew it was easy work, so to me it made sense at that time. (Prus and Irini, 1988:54–55)

> I got to Canada and couldn't find a job. I needed money to live, so I became a prostitute. (SCPP, 1985:376)

> I was in a locked setting for youths. Some of the girls there were involved in prostitution. They told me about it, so I went out and did it. I was on the run and needed the money to eat. (SCPP, 1985: 376)

Some people take up prostitution because they are emotionally attached to someone, a friend or a lover, who encourages them to enter the trade. Fraser (SCPP, 1985) reports that 50 to 60 percent of prostitutes in Canada indicate that another person played some role in their recruitment. Similarly, Badgley (CSOACY, 1984) found that about half of young prostitutes were enlisted by others. These entry factors, according to Canadian research, are much the same for males and females.

Once entered, a career as a prostitute is difficult to leave behind. After several years in prostitution, individuals have acquired no legitimate marketable skills. Moreover, they cannot claim experience on their work records. Offering a prospective employer a satisfactory explanation for several years of inexperience and a complete lack of references is no easy matter. As one prostitute explains,

> Most of the girls I know are 26 or 28 and have been in the business for 10 years and they don't see an end to it. They say they'd all like to get out, that they're going to leave, but if they've been doing that since they were 16, what else are they going to do?

> Like, I've worked in an office and I know I couldn't go back to that. I could if I had to, but I wouldn't want to. And most of them haven't even had that experience. So what are they going to do, go out with no experience? So they just stick with it. It's the only way they know how to make money. They know what they're doing and their friends are there. (Prus and Irini, 1988:48)

LEARNING THE SUBCULTURE OF PROSTITUTION

An apprenticeship period normally follows the decision to enter "the life." While training varies by the type of prostitution, certain aspects are common. Novice prostitutes learn the trade from trainers — pimps, madams, or, more often, experienced prostitutes. Trainers may or may not receive a fee; some experienced prostitutes instruct without charge novices who are friends. Pimps and madams who teach neophytes the tricks of the trade are often recompensed later, when the trainees go to work for them. Aspiring call girls are usually taught by their more experienced colleagues, who receive a fee for their instructional services. For each trick turned by the novice call girl during training, the instructor receives 40 to 50 percent of the fee charged to the client.

The training period for most prostitutes other than call girls is quite short — usually only a few days. The major reason for the call girl's lengthier training period is that it involves not only the acquisition of skills and occupational values, it also involves the development of a client list for later use. Customers recruited at this stage return again and again after the apprenticeship. Moreover, clients acquired in this way usually refer new customers to the beginner. Training ends when apprentices feel that they have a long enough list of clients to keep them busy (Bryan, 1965). The importance of the "good book" is evident in the words of one prostitute interviewed by Prus and Irini (1988:70):

> If a call girl has a good book and clients that have money, then she has a good set up. But if she has a little book, like thirty or forty names in it, then she is probably not going to make that much money. Some girls try to work off a book that is very small but it is just not possible. You have to have a big number of customers, you have to have that volume, just to keep you going ... Some girls don't keep that much information on their clients so that it isn't

much help to them when they are working on the phone calling the clients. Even things like favourite drinks and what the guys like, it really helps.

The skills associated with prostitution involve locating and initiating contact with clients, negotiating the type of service and the fee, shielding oneself from disease, and protecting oneself from the hazards presented by customers, pimps, irate citizens, and the police. Streetwalkers determine the best locations in which to display their wares. They learn quickly that areas on the street are distributed on the basis of seniority and power. Encroaching on other prostitutes' territories may well result in retaliation from those threatened prostitutes or from their pimps.

Mastering solicitation is particularly important. To avoid interference from citizens and police, streetwalkers learn to advertise their services without being unduly pressing. In their opening lines, prostitutes mention neither sex nor money (Sansfacon, 1985). Rather, they use phrases such as "show you a good time" or "have some fun." Higher-status prostitutes frequently "confess" to their customers that they need the "date" money for rent or doctor's bills. Last but not least, trainers instruct their higher-status protégés in the proper use of the telephone. Novices learn how to introduce themselves, what to say, what tone of voice to use, and the importance of personalizing calls by mentioning things particular to the client (Bryan, 1965).

Street and bar prostitutes make the least money per client and must therefore work to increase their number of clients. Being able to induce orgasms in customers quickly is a useful talent. Having learned that they must be paid before the service is rendered, prostitutes refine tactics that induce customers to "come" early, during the inspection and washing of their genitals. One prostitute interviewed by Prus and Irini (1988:46) explains:

So you not only check him for VD, but what you are up there for is to get him to come, and if he comes while you're checking him out, great, you can leave! Sometimes they really get mad in that situation, but that was the deal, until they come. That is something you learn over time, and you find the less you get the guy inside of you, the less likely you are to have any problems or get sore, or whatever. So you try to do as much as you can by hand. Then if he has a hard on and gets on top of you, he comes very shortly, to where he is not doing very much to you. And that is good too.

Prepayment discourages customers from withholding the fee, and rapid service enables prostitutes to search for more clients. The time spent with a customer from the very beginning of a transaction until the return to the street or the bar is usually less than half an hour. Most prostitutes feel that processing three or four customers represents a good day. One or no customers is a bad day, while anything over half a dozen is exceptional for most (SCPP, 1985).

Prostitutes' fee structures in given locations are remarkably consistent, and the perils of charging bargain prices are considerable. Undercutting brings potentially violent retaliation from competitors, as a bar prostitute points out:

The standard minimum fees at Central are $40. You try to get as much as you can. You don't go for less than that. Any girl who does will get into trouble with the other girls if she undercuts their fees. (Prus and Irini, 1988:42)

Of great importance to prostitutes' livelihoods is avoiding customers who have sexually transmitted diseases. Should an individual or an area become associated with the transmission of "social diseases," business can suffer dramatically. These concerns lead prostitutes to demand that customers wear condoms during most sexual activity. To gain compliance from customers, prostitutes learn to warn them about infecting girlfriends or wives if they "pick up something." In the words of a street prostitute:

All of my dates have to wear safes. Also, I do not let them kiss me or go down on me. If a safe breaks, I don't do anything with anyone until I know I'm all right. Some of the girls out there aren't that careful, though ... I go for regular check ups with my own doctor, but if I just want to check for something specific I will go to the clinic. They are really polite there and don't make any comments about what I do. If a date doesn't want to use a safe I just explain to him what could happen — taking something home to his wife. (SCPP, 1985:384)

The person who poses the greatest threat to most prostitutes is the customer. Danger is particularly acute for streetwalkers whose work frequently isolates them from assistance. To protect themselves from abuse or injury by clients, prostitutes employ several techniques. Streetwalkers avoid customers who are known to be violent, who behave suspiciously, or who appear to be carrying weapons. Many prostitutes carry a weapon, usually a knife, for protection. Occasionally, they work together as a safety measure. One streetwalker will record the customer's licence number, while the other goes off to service the trick. The "watch" informs police if the colleague is overdue in returning. Other precautions include not providing services in the isolation of a customer's van, not performing alone for more than one client at a time, and not engaging in transactions at a client's residence (Sansfacon, 1985).

Prostitutes do not, as a rule, use alcohol or drugs on the job. They reserve these substances for use after a hard evening's work, to cope with the stresses and strains of the job. Prostitutes know that being drunk or high in the company of potentially dangerous strangers can be fatal. Those engaging in coitus learn to keep one arm across their chests as a means of leverage should they suddenly need to ward off blows. When prostitutes do agree to work under hazardous conditions, they usually demand a higher fee (SCPP, 1985).

Acquiring job skills is only part of successful performance in the role of prostitute. Prostitutes must also master the proper social values and occupational ideologies. As in other fields of work, their values perform vital functions. They affect self-concept and guide relations with others in or near the occupation. Prostitutes learn not to undercut one another and not to leak information about the identities and activities of pimps and colleagues. They also learn that clients are to be "tricked" and exploited and that authorities cannot be trusted.

Prostitutes are highly devalued in our society. Learning to cope with stigma and to justify disreputable activities is an important part of becoming a member of this deviant enterprise. Many prostitutes maintain that they perform vital functions for society. They meet people's needs for a variety of sexual experiences that many spouses, girlfriends, or boyfriends find distasteful. Moreover, they claim that much of their work consists of "counselling" clients about personal and family problems.

Prostitutes often present themselves as ministering to the sexual needs of a variety of social outcasts, including the unattractive, the deformed, the physically disabled, and those with psychological or emotional deficiencies. Given their rendering of unique sexual services and psychological counselling, prostitutes argue that they contribute to the maintenance of family accord. After all, their services spare their clients' spouses undue pressures to perform acts or discuss sensitive topics that they might prefer to avoid. The same line of reasoning is used to argue that the availability of their services reduces both sexual assaults and other sexually oriented crimes. In either case, prostitutes see themselves as safety valves through which the sexually frustrated can let off steam (Bryan, 1965).

In order to view themselves in a favourable moral light, many prostitutes believe that they are little different from men and women who, to attain material security, marry or become involved in long-term relationships. Thus, prostitutes claim that they are more honest and more straightforward about the real motivations underlying sexual relationships. Along similar lines, prostitutes contrast their honesty to their customers' hypocrisy. They point to the irony of clients' using their services while decrying the existence of commercial sex.

Although rationalizations of functional contribution and moral superiority form the core of prostitution's occupational ideology, the extent to which prostitutes actually embrace this philosophy is not entirely clear. Just as many members of legitimate occupational and professional groups demonstrate various degrees of commitment to their occupation's ideological framework, many prostitutes appear uncommitted to the value system associated with their deviant profession.

Most prostitutes perform a limited range of sexual acts for which they receive virtually no training. Most frequent activities for both male and female prostitutes are manual and oral sex, known in the trade as "locals" and "blow jobs," respectively. About 60 percent of all requests by clients of Canadian prostitutes are for oral sex. For female prostitutes, the next most frequently requested act is coitus, which on the street is termed a "straight lay." Some customers ask male prostitutes to engage in anal intercourse (Gemme et al., 1984; Fleischman, 1984). Research does not substantiate the notion that prostitutes will perform any act with anyone, providing that the price is met. More exotic specialty services such as spatting (being defecated upon), golden showers (being urinated upon), and various forms of sadomasochism are rare. As one prostitute explained to Prus and Irini (1988:24):

Another problem with the tricks is that some of them think that all the girls are the same, that all the girls will do everything, and that they are all into Greek or S & M. And it's just not the case, but they all have their own ideas, and so when they get a girl in the room, they figure that she should go along with whatever it is that they want. Now if they would explain things to you at the table, it would be different, because you could tell them who is into this or that, but they often don't do that. They just expect that when they get there, they will get what they want.

The Fraser and Badgly Committees' estimates of prostitutes' incomes in the 1980s vary widely. Female street prostitutes in eastern Canada reportedly earned, without any deductions for expenses, about $28 000 working alone and about $8000 working for a pimp (Crook, 1984). Committee researchers estimated that males made more than females; gross incomes for males averaged approximately $31 000. For Montreal street prostitutes, Gemme et al. (1984) suggested that incomes of $1000 for a five- or six-day working week were the norm. Badgley (1984) reported that male and female juvenile prostitutes earned about $140 and $215, respectively, per day. Lowman (1984), after deducting projected overhead costs, calculated that the incomes of Vancouver prostitutes ranged from nothing at all to around $22 000. At the other end of the scale, income levels of escort-service prostitutes and call girls were reportedly as high as $144 000 (Crook, 1984). While the accuracy of the various estimates is difficult to assess, some trends are clearly discernible. On the whole, males earn more than females and, in particular, more than females managed by pimps. Street prostitutes earn less than those working off the street, and juveniles earn less than adults.

ROLES RELATED TO PROSTITUTION

Several ancillary roles surround prostitution. Central among them are the madam, the pimp, and the customer.

THE MADAM

Large-scale brothels do not appear to be common in Canada, and hence madams, although they exist, are not prominent in Canadian prostitution (SCPP, 1985). Madams are typically experienced prostitutes who are past the point where their physical attractiveness will ensure a high income. Where prostitu-

tion is legal, madams perform normal management duties. Where maintaining a house of ill-repute is against the law, however, they assume the additional duties associated with running an illegal operation. In all cases, the madam's responsibilities involve recruiting, training, organizing, and supervising house personnel. Bawdy-house staff include domestic helpers, bartenders, barmaids, bouncers, and, of course, prostitutes themselves.

The madam's obligations also involve recruiting customers and keeping them happy. Advertisement is usually by word of mouth, although, where houses of prostitution are legal, madams place ads in local papers and trade magazines. Finally, the madam must negotiate suitable "live and let live" arrangements with the police. For these managerial activities, madams receive about half the fees that house prostitutes charge to customers (Heyl, 1979a). This income may be considerable; the money earned by one madam in the Maritime provinces reputedly approached $400 000 (Crook, 1984).

To meet the need for fresh faces and new bodies, madams often communicate with one another and exchange prostitutes within and across city jurisdictions. Consequently, many young house prostitutes travel a circuit, moving every few months from one brothel to another. Madams ensure that their workers function effectively by settling any disputes and by enforcing house rules to the letter. Disturbances of any kind are bad for business.

When a client enters the establishment, the madam greets him in her role as hostess. She encourages the customer to visit the bar, where he is introduced to a selection of prostitutes from whom he makes his choice. As in any hospitality industry, the madam's principal concern is to ensure the satisfaction and repeated visits of her customers (Heyl, 1979a).

The madam must also negotiate a viable working relationship with police. A positive rapport with police is particularly essential if the house of prostitution is illegal. Occasionally, the madam will attempt to secure police co-operation by bribing them but more often she will attempt to reach some form of mutual agreement. In the absence of widespread public outcry, police often ignore the existence of brothels. Madams increase the likelihood that police will tolerate their activities by making certain that their establishments are free of illicit drugs, simple assaults, and minor thefts and ensuring that they bar minors from their premises (Winick and Kinsie, 1971).

PIMPS AND PROCURERS

Most people believe that a **pimp** is someone who exploits and controls a prostitute and who lives off the avails of prostitution. The issue of what constitutes pimping can be complex, however. Is anyone who lives with or is married to a prostitute and who is at least partially supported by the funds acquired through prostitution a pimp? Many working and unemployed males live to some extent off the money earned by prostitutes. In return, they provide their companions with love and moral support. These men offer comfort and assurance in much the same way that conventional spouses and partners do. Coercion and exploitation are, in other words, not routinely characteristic of the relationship between prostitutes and their male partners. The following two quotations are illustrative:

They're there for that every third night, somebody to sleep with and somebody to be there in the morning, and somebody to call every night when you come home, because most of these girls live alone. And maybe fun to plan for every third Sunday, you know. But, a lot of these guys are rough. Pimps aren't like the image people have of them, beating girls up usually, or even saying "You'd better have $200 or else!" There are some like that. They're a little harder to work for, because that's what they really are like. But most of the guys aren't. You may have the occasional fight, but you don't really get beaten up or that often. But that's life in general. (Prus and Irini, 1988:33)

In any situation that you are involved with a person, on the personal level you are going to share things and they're going to share what they have; it's just a give and take type of thing, sometimes they might not have something and you help them or they help you when they have it and you don't, and they look after you when you are sick and keep you company. (SCPP, 1985:379)

Pimps are supposed to perform a number of tasks for the prostitute, including providing necessary training, supplying protection from unruly customers and other prostitutes, making certain that the prostitute receives legal assistance when required, recruiting customers, and providing a residence, a car, expensive gifts, clothes, and jewellery. In reality, most pimps offer none of these services. Training usually consists of being told to hit the street and to return with money. Pimps rarely provide protection, either from customers or from the law. Indeed, streetwalkers are sometimes beaten or injured by their own pimps. Finally, few pimps recruit customers for their prostitutes (CSOACY, 1984; Lowman, 1984).

A procurer is a person who, for a fee, refers potential customers to prostitutes. For people in legitimate occupations (e.g., bartender, taxi driver, or hotel clerk) procuring supplements their income, while for others (e.g., escort-service receptionist, massage-parlour manager) it is a full-time occupation (Sansfacon, 1985). In Halifax, a taxi company, through an arrangement with a prominent madam, held a virtual monopoly on referrals and transportation to prostitution services in that city (SCPP, 1985). The fee charged by part-time procurers typically ranges from 5 to 20 percent of the charges levied against the customer by the prostitute. The fee is usually paid to the procurer by the prostitute, and only occasionally by the customer. However, it is not uncommon for full-time procurers to receive anywhere from 40 to 60 percent of a prostitute's fee. Full-time procurers working for escort services command higher commissions because they provide more services: care, protection, and recruitment of clients (Gemme et al., 1984; Crook, 1984).

Pimping and procuring differ in that the business arrangement between prostitute and procurer is often voluntary, while the relationship between a prostitute and pimp is less often so. Pimps are more likely than procurers to exploit their prostitutes. Also, procuring is against the law in Canada but pimping is not (Sansfacon, 1985).

The Fraser Committee found that pimps were most prominent in prostitution in Winnipeg and Halifax. Most female street prostitutes in Winnipeg were of Native origin and were managed by Native men. In Halifax, researchers estimated that pimps controlled from 75 to 100 percent of street prostitution. According to Sansfacon (1985), pimps did not appear to play a large part in prostitution in Canada's three largest cities. They were rare in Vancouver and Montreal and present only in some parts of Toronto. For the west coast and Quebec, Lowman (1984) and Gemme et at. (1984) reported that the traditional notion of the pimp as coercive exploiter applied only in about 20 percent of the cases studied.

In her research on prostitution in the Prairie provinces, Lautt (1984) describes three types of pimps: the name, the loser, and the bodyguard. "Names" are well known and maintain their "girls" in very com-

Box 12.4
LAWYER-TURNED-PIMP JAILED FOR SEVEN YEARS

A Toronto lawyer who led a double life as a sadistic pimp received a seven-year prison sentence yesterday for kidnapping a 19-year-old woman and forcing her to work as a street prostitute.

Mr. Justice Lee Ferrier referred to Gabriel Patterson, 36, as a "parasite" whose actions must be "firmly denounced." During the sentencing address, Judge Ferrier also spoke about the damage to society caused by pimps.

The judge conceded that he received a "brief of impressive letters" in support of Patterson. However, Judge Ferrier said the fact that Patterson was a "sophisticated lawyer" and the victim was poorly educated and naïve was an aggravating factor.

Wearing an elegant navy blue suit, Patterson did not show any emotion when the sentence was pronounced. Judge Ferrier declined to ask Patterson and his two co-defendants if they had anything to say on their behalf.

A jury convicted Patterson on 10 charges last month, including kidnapping, obstruction of justice and living off the avails of prostitution. Royce Briscoe, 37, and Penny Roberts, 34, were convicted of six pimping-related offences. Briscoe received a four-year sentence. Roberts, who the court was told is two months pregnant and expecting her fourth child, received a 3½-year sentence.

During the trial, the court heard that the defendants arranged to meet the victim in August, 1997, at a restaurant in the Eaton Centre. The young woman, whose identity is protected by a publication ban, was employed at an escort agency. She testified that Patterson said he now owned her life, and ordered her not to testify against another pimp in an upcoming trial.

The woman said she was made to work as a street prostitute in the Jarvis Street area. A week later, she said Patterson forced her to strip and kneel in front of him. He threatened to cut off her arms and legs and burn them if she did not do what he said. The woman managed to escape later that night.

The jury was not told that Patterson is wanted by Las Vegas police on charges of pandering and battery. He is also awaiting trial in Toronto on a separate series of pimping-related charges.

In asking for a sentence of between four and six years, Patterson's lawyer said, "there are redeeming qualities to his character." Michelle Fuerst detailed his community work, which included a term on the board of a foundation that provides scholarships to minority students.

Patterson, who is black and of aboriginal descent, graduated from Osgoode Hall law school in 1988. He articled briefly at the Department of Justice and is qualified to practise law in Ontario and the state of New York.

In her submission, Mary Humphrey, the Crown attorney, described Patterson as "the ultimate predator."

"One cannot image a worse offender than a lawyer who kidnaps and controls a young woman to obstruct justice," she said.

Discussion Question

How is Gabriel Patterson similar to and different from the "typical" pimp working in Canadian prostitution?

Source: Shannon Kari, *National Post*, June 22, 2000, p. A22. Reprinted with permission from the author.

fortable lifestyles. Women working for these pimps are well dressed and well cared for. In return for this care and protection, the name takes from 30 to 100 percent of the prostitute's income. Names resort to violence only to maintain discipline among their working girls. Lautt points out that since they are high-class pimps, names tend to associate with the middle and upper classes. Consequently, they have an advantage in negotiating working arrangements with the police. Names often engage in other criminal activities beyond prostitution, including gambling and the drug trade.

Losers are very exploitative in that they use violence against prostitutes more frequently. Their provision of "protection" merely signifies that they agree not to harm the prostitutes under their control. Unlike the "name," the loser earns his income solely from prostitution. Lautt's third and perhaps the most common type of pimp — the bodyguard — falls somewhere between the name and the loser. The bodyguard is neither as exploitative nor as violent as the loser, and prostitution is not his sole source of revenue.

Pimps generally make an effort to control their prostitutes by creating in them material or psychological needs for which prostitution offers a simple solution. Creating a dependence on drugs or a strong need for emotional support, for example, is an effective way of influencing prostitutes to continue working. When manipulative strategies are unsuccessful, violence is an option. Much of the physical brutality that does occur is concentrated in the lower levels of the occupation. Consequently, socioeconomically disadvantaged women experience more violence. The pimp's aggression toward the lower-class prostitute probably differs little from the aggression directed by lower-class men toward their girlfriends and spouses.

The Fraser Committee found that pimps' incomes in the 1980s were usually based on a fixed levy applied against each prostitute in the "stable." These set amounts, which the prostitute was required to turn over after each day or night of work, typically ranged from $100 to $200. The size of a stable was generally small (one or two prostitutes), but in some cases ranged to seven or eight. Thus, a pimp might have expected to gross from $100 to $1600 on a good day (CSOACY, 1984; Crook, 1984; Gemme et al., 1984).

CUSTOMERS

The customers of prostitutes have received almost no attention in sociological research, probably because they are of little concern to law enforcement. Police have tended not to view the customer as being nearly as responsible for the existence of prostitution as pimps, procurers, organized crime figures, and prostitutes themselves. Indeed, the attitude toward customers reflected by the law borders on indifference, so long as the prostitute involved is not a minor.

About 4 percent of the Fraser commission's national population survey respondents (all of whom were men) reported hiring a prostitute at some point in their lives. Prostitutes' customers come from all walks of life and vary widely in terms of their educational and occupational backgrounds. Many, although not all, are married or involved in a continuing relationship with someone. While virtually all clients are male, there are exceptions. Small numbers of females avail themselves of male escort services, and a few proposition child prostitutes. Badgley (1984) reports, for example, that half of the juvenile prostitutes studied for his committee's report were approached for their services at least once by a female.

There are several reasons why men desire the services of prostitutes (CSOACY, 1984; Gemme et al., 1984). Some men want quick and easy sex. Turning a date into a sexual exchange can tax both a man's mind and his ego. Moreover, seducing women can be expensive. Obtaining sex from a prostitute does not require much conversation or companionship. Prostitution also provides a sexual outlet for the emotionally troubled, the physically disabled, the very old, and the unattractive, who might feel unable to compete with attractive and socially desirable men. Furthermore, many men wish to satisfy their sexual needs without making the emotional and financial commitments inevitable in serious dating relationships and marriage. They wish to avoid the turmoil associated with interpersonal conflicts and accidental pregnancies.

Finally, many men, even those involved in physical relationships with others, crave variety. Some clients simply find their partners boring. They desire new bodies with "which" to experience sex. In some cases, they may want to perform acts that their spouses or partners find offensive. These activities range from oral and anal intercourse to more exotic activities such as sadism, masochism, bondage, and three-way sex. Customers wishing to conceal their homosexual interests use male prostitutes to satisfy these sexual needs. As one customer interviewed by Prus and Irini (1988:25) explains:

> Before, I used to come down just now and then, but now, I'm making better money and I can treat myself more often. I haven't found a (straight) girl that I really love, and this way, I get to try out a lot of different girls. If she treats me well, I might go back to her, if she doesn't, then I'll try somebody else. … I tried two black girls. I wanted to see what they were like. They weren't bad, they weren't good. … Carol over there, I've tried her three times. The first time, she was just super. I could not believe how good she was! The second time and the third time she didn't seem as satisfying to me, so after the third date, I let her go.

Customers, often referred to as "**johns,**" can be categorized into three types: occasional, habitual, and compulsive (Greenwald, 1970). The central characteristic of the occasional john is mobility. He may be a sailor, a travelling salesman, or a conventioneer. Many occasional johns are married and only infrequently use the services of a prostitute. Occasionals often seek out prostitutes in the company of friends and associates, thus turning the search into a group activity. By comparison, the habitual john wants to make friends with a particular prostitute and to become one of her regular customers. The relationship between habituals and prostitutes tends to involve greater degrees of affection, more frequent and detailed "conversations," and perhaps gifts purchased by the john for his "lover." Habituals form a part of the clientele of a large proportion of prostitutes across Canada. Finally, compulsive johns are a rare breed. They tend to be psychological misfits who are entirely dependent on prostitutes for sexual gratification.

Customers usually initiate negotiations over fees and services. This is particularly true for exchanges involving higher-status prostitutes. Only in the rare cases where prostitutes are competing with each other are they likely to pester potential customers for their business.

Canadian prostitutes report that many johns are under the influence of alcohol or drugs during their sexual exchanges. Most clients behave reasonably well during their transactions with prostitutes, although violence is not rare. In his Vancouver study, Lowman (1984) found that 38 percent of female prostitutes had been physically assaulted and 21 percent had been raped by customers. Similarly, Gemme et al. (1984) report that 35 percent of the Quebec female prostitutes surveyed were physically assaulted and 36 percent raped by clients. A prostitute interviewed by Prus and Irini (1988:22) provides more than a hint that, from her perspective, at least some of the violence experienced by prostitutes is victim precipitated:

> They don't want to be reminded that they're paying you, and a lot of these girls do remind them. And they remind them by saying, "Don't touch me," when the guy would go and touch them, their breast or something and they'd say, "Don't touch me! I don't want anyone to touch my breast. Hurry up. What's taking you so long? Your time is running out." They do that. They don't worry about it taking longer, they say, "Look I've been here a half hour, I'm sorry. I've done my best." They figure, "Well, I've been paid for a half hour," and they just get up and leave. A lot of men say, "Hey, wait a minute!" Like to a prostitute $40 is not a lot of money, that's the lowest, except for the girls who go for less. But for a guy, $40, especially if he's only

making $200 a week, and maybe he has to explain to his wife why he's $40 short, is a lot of money plus the hotel, plus he hasn't even gotten off. They're not going to just say, "Well, sure."

Sixty-three prostitutes were murdered between 1991 and 1995. Customers caused 80 percent of these deaths, while 13 percent were perpetrated by pimps or were the result of a drug-related incident. The remaining deaths occurred at the hands of intimates — husbands and boyfriends. Almost all of the victims (95 percent) were women. Seven juveniles, all female, were among the dead. Prostitutes accounted for 5 percent of all female homicides during this period (Duchesne, 1997). In 1999, there were three known prostitutes murdered in the course of their work, down from seven in 1998 and four in 1997 (Fedorowycz, 1999; 2000).

Evidence suggests that prostitution is also a risky business for customers, pimps, and others dealing with prostitutes. Between 1991 and 1995, police implicated eighteen prostitutes in the deaths of sixteen people — ten customers, one pimp, and five others. Virtually all of the victims (94 percent) were male, while most of the killers (83 percent) were female (Duchesne, 1997).

Male hustlers are rarely assaulted by bona fide customers, but they do risk beatings by "queer bashers" posing as prospective clients. Male prostitutes are sometimes lured into situations where they are severely beaten by groups of young men espousing hatred for homosexuals (Lautt, 1984).

THE PROSTITUTES' RIGHTS MOVEMENT

The belief that laws against prostitution have generally discriminated against women fuels the sex-workers' argument that women should be able to engage legally in sexual intercourse for material gain if they wish to do so. In the name of this cause, female prostitutes in the United States formed an organization called COYOTE (Call Off Your Old Tired Ethics) in San Francisco in 1973. The principal objectives of this organization are to **decriminalize** prostitution and change public attitudes toward sex for hire. The organization publishes a newsletter called *COYOTE Howls* in which it regularly calls upon the states to repeal laws against prostitution. COYOTE also maintains that laws prohibiting pimping (living off the earnings of a prostitute) and pandering (encouraging someone to work as a prostitute) should be repealed and replaced with labour laws that address adverse working conditions in prostitution businesses owned and managed by persons other than prostitutes themselves. It also takes the position that commissions comprised mostly of prostitutes or former prostitutes who have worked on the street, in massage parlours and brothels, and for escort services, should develop guidelines for the operation of sex trade businesses. COYOTE maintains that these guidelines should address various aspects of concern to sex workers, including health and safety and employer–employee relations.

COYOTE works diligently to separate prostitution from its traditional connections to sinfulness and criminality and to develop an image of prostitution as work deserving civil rights protection (Jenness, 1993). By encouraging the repeal of existing laws and engaging politicians and community leaders in debate over questionable law enforcement practices, COYOTE attempts to transform prostitution from a problem of crime to nothing more than an occupational choice that some people find desirable. COYOTE emphasizes that prostitution is by no means always forced on its practitioners and that it represents a service occupation in the community. Members maintain that prostitution actually benefits communities by providing outlets for the male sex drive. Finally, COYOTE makes the case that denying people the choice to engage in commercial sex violates their civil rights to work as they choose (Clinard and Meier, 1998).

In addition to offering public education and lobbying for changes in the law, COYOTE provides crisis counselling, support groups, and legal and social service referrals to prostitutes, most of whom are women. Its members testify at government hearings, serve as expert witnesses, and assist law enforcement agencies with investigations of crimes where prostitutes are the victims. The organization also provides sensitivity training to government and private nonprofit agencies that provide services to prostitutes (COYOTE Web site, n.d.).

Canada also has a number of prostitutes' rights groups based on the COYOTE model. La Coalition pour les droites des travailleuses et travailleurs du sexe (Coalition for the Rights of Sex Workers) is a sex workers' group in Montreal that lobbies for the legal recognition of various forms of sex work. A similar organization, the Canadian Organization for the

Rights of Prostitutes (CORP) was founded in 1983 in Toronto. Prostitutes have formed Sex Workers' Alliance groups in a variety of cities across the country including Halifax (SWAH founded in 1995), Toronto (SWAT founded in 1992), Niagara Falls (SWAN founded in 1997), and Vancouver (SWAV founded in 1994) (Commercial Sex Information Service Web site, 1999).

The Sex Workers' Alliance of Vancouver originated in response to a "Shame the Johns" campaign in that city. Like other such Canadian organizations, SWAV's objectives include establishing sex workers' rights to fair wages and to working conditions that are safe, clean, and healthy. SWAV opposes any law that criminalizes sex work, pointing out that

> Everyone has rights, regardless of what they do for a living. When prostitution is made a crime, sex workers are prevented from working together for greater security, organizing to improve working conditions, getting health and dental plans, and sharing and investing earnings. Laws prohibiting sex work force sex workers into an environment of crime where their rights are not protected. Factors that keep sex workers from getting help when they have been victimized are fear of being busted, outstanding warrants and the likelihood of being treated as unreliable witnesses with no credibility. Decriminalization would provide sex workers with real protection from people who rob, rape, assault, and harass them (SWAV Web site, 2000).

SWAV distributes information on a variety of sex work issues concerning laws, sexual health, commerce, and culture. The organization publishes a *Bad Calls List*, a database of descriptions of violent men who rob or assault prostitutes. It also provides health and legal information and free condoms, and sponsors the *Commercial Sex Information Service* Web site. SWAV members make themselves available to support others working in the sex trade and to educate service providers and policy makers about the needs of sex workers.

Membership in SWAV is open to anyone who works or has worked in the sex trade, including prostitutes, exotic dancers, and pornographic performers. The organization is affiliated with other sex worker groups in Canada. It is also a member of the International Network of Sex Work Projects and the North American Task Force on Prostitution (NTFP) (SWAV Web site, 2000).

Despite the arguments made by prostitutes' rights groups in the United States, Canada, and other countries around the world, efforts to repeal laws against prostitution have not been successful.

TWO THEORIES OF PROSTITUTION

FUNCTIONALISM

Prostitution is something of a social institution. It has endured despite ridicule, strong opposition, and concerted attempts to eradicate it. Cognizant of prostitution's longevity and stability, functionalist Kingsley Davis (1937) developed a sociological theory of prostitution to explain how such a devalued social practice could contribute to order, stability, and the maintenance of society. Davis began by noting the existence of a value system that condemns sex outside of the family for purposes other than the expression of love or the procreation of children. Moral values extol the virtues both of premarital chastity and of marital fidelity.

While society condemns promiscuity and adultery, males experience a powerful sex drive, more intense than that of females. They must either sublimate their sex drives or seek release. When sublimation of the sex drive is not possible, males are forced to look beyond the legitimate outlets for their passions — their wives — to women who are unmarried or, worse, married to someone else. Since promiscuous and adulterous activities cause social conflict, prostitution enables the powerful sex drives of many men to be dissipated by a relatively small number of women. Prostitution is a safety valve because men can satisfy their need for sex without creating social disruption. Men who are serviced by prostitutes can avoid extramarital romantic entanglements that might undermine the security of their family and work lives.

Davis's theory also explains why the customers of prostitutes are seldom criminalized. Being male, they are integrated into the labour force and their services are needed by society's economic institutions. Jailing workers would disrupt economic productivity. But society can express its denigration of prostitution by locking up its female practitioners. They, after all, are less integral to the economy. Finally, from the functionalist perspective, prostitution contributes to social solidarity through the general societal condemnation of exchanging sex for money. Those whose sexual practices conform to society's moral standards can feel virtuous while heaping ridicule on their tainted targets, prostitutes.

FEMINISM

Feminists have rejected the functionalist theory of prostitution on two fundamental counts. First, they argue that Davis roots his perspective in a faulty biological premise, the overwhelming sex drive of males. Second, the functionalist approach overlooks the role of sexual inequality in creating and perpetuating prostitution. Feminists point out that money, prestige, and power are stratified on the basis of sex. In patriarchal societies, males command higher incomes, are accorded more prestige, and wield more power than women do. In stratified societies, those with power dominate while those without it serve. In a sexually stratified society, males are dominant and females are devalued, oppressed, sexually objectified, and exploited. As sex objects, women and girls become commodities to be purchased and sold at the will of men.

Women can be either exclusive or common property. Females are the exclusive property of males within the framework of the family. Marriage contracts dictate that husbands will provide economic security while wives provide domestic and sexual services. Failure of wives to do so has traditionally justified discipline or dissolution of the arrangement. Daughters also are exclusive property insofar as they are under the control of their fathers until they marry.

Women can also be common property. Promiscuous females meet this definition, and women whose promiscuity generates income are at the extreme end of an exploitative sexual stratification system (Heyl, 1979b). Thus, prostitution represents the ultimate commodification and exploitation of females as sex objects because prostitutes are the most dominated of a dominated social segment, women. First, prostitutes must minister to the desires of their male clients. Second, they must satisfy the dictates of their male pimps. Third, they must endure harassment and arrest by male police officers while these officers largely ignore the illegal conduct of male clientele. Customers, feminist theory asserts, avoid legal sanction not because of their functional necessity to the economy but rather because of their position of power and privilege as males in a sexually stratified society. Fourth, prostitutes must suffer the consequences of their chosen vocation as male judges fine them and lock them up. Finally,

Box 12.5
FEMINIST PERSPECTIVES ON LEGALIZATION AND DECRIMINALIZATION

Prostitution is a problematic and divisive issue for feminists. Indeed, more than any other issue, prostitution has provoked a sharp split in feminist writing and theorizing. In the most general sense, feminists see the practice of prostitution as wrong since it epitomizes male dominance and is the most glaring example of how capitalism and patriarchy permit women to be viewed as sexual objects and commodities to be bought and sold. At the same time, most feminists, along with prostitute groups and advocates for prostitute rights, take the position that prostitution should be decriminalized. Legalization is rejected as a policy option because it would involve the state taking on the function of a pimp, and systems of licensing would continue to stigmatize prostitutes (Faith, 1993:80; Lowman, 1991:127).

Beyond this, there is an obvious uncertainty in feminist writing as to the nature, meaning, and value of prostitution and, consequently, how to develop a framework for addressing the problem. Philosophical and political differences are apparent not only among feminist writers but also between feminists and women who work (or have worked) in the sex-trade industry. The different strands of feminist theorizing on prostitution can be broadly classified as either radical-feminist or liberal-feminist in origin (Shaver, 1993:166–67). The fundamental point of divergence between the two perspectives is the traditional feminist conviction that prostitution is degrading and oppressive to women and the equally fundamental and widely shared belief in a woman's right to control her own body (Lowman, 1991:130; McConnell, 1991; Overall, 1992; Shaver, 1988, 1993; Sumner, 1981).

Radical feminists argue that all prostitution involves coercion and reinforces the subordinate status of women in society. From this perspective, prostitution is an institution of male supremacy in the same way that slavery was vis-à-vis its exploitation and degradation of women. Moreover, prostitution exemplifies virtually every form of inequality in society – it is a classist, ageist, racist, and sexist industry (Overall, 1992:717). It is classist because it uses the sex labour of disadvantaged women for the service of those who are more advantaged. It is ageist because it tends to be dominated by young women (often children) who are discarded when they are no longer considered sexually attractive. It is racist because it victimizes blacks, Asians, and Aboriginal women who serve the sex needs of white males. And it is sexist because it is primarily women who are exploited for the purposes of serving men. From this perspective, in the short term, feminists should support decriminalization as a means of improving the working conditions of prostitutes, but the long-term goal is the eventual elimination of prostitution.

Liberal feminists argue that it is not so much prostitution in and of itself that is undesirable, but rather the broader socioeconomic conditions that support and maintain it in its present form (Shaver, 1988:87; 1993). From this perspective, there needs to be a recognition that some women enter prostitution by choice rather than as a last resort, and that noncoercive prostitution is no more exploitive or degrading than many other forms of female labour in society – besides which a woman's right to control her body includes the right to sell sexual services if she so chooses. Finally, most of the negative effects of prostitution and the dangers to prostitutes stem from prostitution's illegality and, as such, would be minimized were it to be decriminalized.

Many liberal feminists came to this position as the result of their discussions over the years with prostitutes and prostitute advocate groups. They had been uncomfortable with the traditional uncompromising feminist stance toward prostitution, which had served to alienate prostitutes from feminism, as exemplified by the following statement from the Second World Whores' Congress (1986): "Due to feminist hesitation or refusal to accept prostitution as legitimate work and to accept prostitutes as working women, the majority of prostitutes have not identified [themselves] as feminists" (Overall, 1992:707). According to many sex-trade workers, feminism is hypocritical in that, while it purports to support all women, its traditional expressions, no less than patriarchal ideology, have served to condemn, reject, and stigmatize prostitutes. Prostitutes resent the assumption that their work is demeaning and never freely chosen. They do not want to be the objects of pity or rescue work, or to be seen as symbols of oppression. Instead, they defend their right to work as prostitutes free from criminalization and stigmatization.

While liberal feminists like Shaver (1988) argue that feminist support of prostitution should go beyond support of prostitutes' rights to include an endorsement of the profession itself, many other feminists remain reluctant to actively condone prostitution. As Overall (1992:722–24) suggests, they take the position that it makes sense to defend the right of prostitutes to do their work, but not to defend prostitution itself as an institution. While some prostitutes may view their work as no different from any other form of labour, prostitution as an institution nevertheless serves to reinforce patriarchal ideology and women's social subordination. Moreover, prostitution is not exactly comparable with other feminist issues concerning a women's right to control her body (e.g., abortion/reproductive rights), since the work of prostitutes cannot be separated from the industry of prostitution. For these reasons, while it is important in the short term to address the stigmatization, criminalization, and dangers associated with prostitution, a long-term strategy must address its eventual elimination.

Discussion Questions

What difficulties has feminism encountered in theorizing about prostitution? What are some of the problems feminist theory faces when it comes to formulating policy for addressing prostitution in Canadian society?

Source: Helen Boritch, *Fallen Women: Female Crime and Criminal Justice in Canada* (Toronto: Nelson, 1997), 127–29. Reprinted with permission of the author.

prostitutes are subjected to the scorn and derision that society heaps upon its "scarlet women."

Feminists advocate two responses to prostitution. First, prostitution needs to be decriminalized to reduce or eliminate the victimization of its female practitioners by the criminal justice system. Second, and more difficult to achieve, feminists call for the eradication of the system of gender stratification that promotes the sexual objectification and commodification of women and largely creates the demand for illicit commercial sex.

THE CONTROL OF PROSTITUTION

There are three basic approaches to the control of prostitution: prohibition, regulation, and abolition (Sansfacon, 1985; SCPP, 1985). Under the prohibition model, criminal law strictly prohibits any exchange of sexual services for remuneration. The prohibition approach to the control of prostitution is prevalent in 38 of the U.S. states and in most eastern European nations.

Regulation involves the state administering prostitution as a legal, although perhaps restricted, enterprise. In jurisdictions such as Mexico, Panama, Germany, and the state of Nevada, governments ensure that the provision of prostitution services meets legal requirements in terms of customer relations, hours of operation, disease control, and the reporting of income for taxation purposes.

Abolition does not make prostitution itself an offence but rather designates as illegal a number of closely related activities, including communicating for the purposes of prostitution, soliciting, keeping a common bawdy house, procuring, and living off the avails of prostitution. Canada, the United Kingdom, and a minority of the U.S. states have adopted the abolition strategy. The United Nations also officially endorses this approach.

From 1892, when Canada enacted its first *Criminal Code*, until 1972, the government controlled prostitution largely by enforcing vagrancy laws. As a result of difficulties associated with gathering evidence and gaining convictions and because the existing legislation discriminated against women, Parliament repealed the relevant sections of the *Criminal Code* in 1972 and replaced them with laws designed to suppress soliciting in public places (SCPP, 1985).

Not long after the enactment of this new anti-solicitation law, however, the question arose in the courts as to whether or not certain actions by prostitutes actually constituted soliciting. In a controversial decision in 1978, a Canadian judge ruled that the propositioning of potential customers had to be both pressing and persistent for a soliciting charge to hold up in court (SCPP, 1985). The main impact of what became known as the "Hutt decision" was to make the anti-solicitation law toothless. Since customers usually play a large part in initiating transactions with prostitutes, police found it almost impossible to prove that the solicitation in question was both pressing and persistent. As a result, public officials in many Canadian communities and the police themselves were not pleased with this ruling.

The intensity of police efforts to enforce laws intended to curb prostitution varies considerably across the country (SCPP, 1985). The extent of enforcement depends upon the resources available to the police, the visibility of the prostitutes and their actions, the ardour of local public opinion, and the general political climate. Also significant are police officers' predictions of court decisions in prostitution cases. Police are most likely to step up law enforcement when the sex trade is obvious enough to produce negative public opinion and mobilize citizens. Moreover, when police think that a conviction is at least possible, they have been more prone to lay charges. Where the likelihood of a conviction for soliciting is faint, they have tended to lay charges on morality offences instead. Regardless of all other factors, however, police vigorously enforce anti-prostitution laws when the prostitutes are children or teenagers.

Prostitution is less likely to become a salient issue as long as it remains hidden from the view of potentially disapproving citizens. It confronts few concerned citizens in the established red-light districts of Canadian cities. Sometimes, operators of commercial establishments actually welcome the revenue generated by the use of their facilities (e.g., restaurants, hotel rooms, and bars) by prostitutes and their customers. The expansion of the sex trade into residential areas, however, increases the likelihood of public outcry. Residents complain about the provocative attire of prostitutes, the exposure of children to unsavoury individuals, and the increases in traffic congestion. Another problem is the harassment of residents with sales pitches from prostitutes and with misguided overtures from prospective customers. Many citizens also believe that prostitution results in significant increases in drug dealing, robbery, and assault (Sansfacon, 1985).

When prostitution encroaches into neighbourhoods, people frequently mobilize in opposition. For example, the practice of soliciting along sections of Toronto's Queen Street West, Montreal's St. Louis Square, and Halifax's Barrington Street led property owners and renters in these areas to lobby city councillors and police for a clean-up of the streets. Residents of Vancouver's West End launched a widely publicized reaction. They traded abuse, insults, and projectiles with local streetwalkers. In addition, they formed an organization to combat prostitution and began a controversial "shame the johns" campaign.

Despite widespread and sometimes vociferous public outcries, police action against prostitution has usually been ineffective. The legal precedent set by the Hutt decision in 1978 made it virtually impossible for the police to gain convictions on charges of solicitation because prostitutes generally do not persist when prospective clients demonstrate little interest. Given the constraints imposed by the Hutt decision, police either ignored prostitution or resorted to other means of control. One tactic involved charging both prostitutes and their customers with other violations, such as disrupting the flow of traffic, jaywalking, littering, loitering, or conducting sales without a city permit. The fact that police enforced such laws selectively against those whom they felt were members of a class of undesirables was not without its problems.

Sometimes police bent on deterring customers have adopted informal strategies of dubious legality (SCPP, 1985). One police initiative involved stopping clients, asking for identification, and threatening to inform the customers' family members and employers. Police also forewarned customers that they would receive additional surveillance if they approached a prostitute in that location again. Law-enforcement officers explain their tactics as follows:

> We don't as often search the girls. Sometimes we take them in and search them. It takes them (the women) off the street and interrupts their business flow. If we see a guy talking to a prostitute, we'll stop and converse with them. They usually get nervous and drive away when we pull up. If we see them in a parking lot with a guy, we may approach and talk to them. Run the client's name for warrants. Maybe give them a parking violation. A lot of them know we can't do much, but the average person gets embarrassed and leaves. If they get offensive, we try to embarrass them and dissuade them from returning. We make it clear to some people that we don't want them back. We tell them they'll get in trouble from prostitutes or us. We say "who knows what will happen in a dark alley," and let them draw their inferences from that. If they do come back, nothing happens. Sometimes it works. Sometimes it doesn't. (SCPP, 1985:391)

> We spot check clients. We ask for two things, a driver's licence and hospitalization card. That way we can tell if he has a wife and kids. If he does, we tell him if we see him down there one more time, his

wife will be getting an anonymous phone call telling her where her husband is. We do this if we see the guy enough. These guys backtrack like you wouldn't believe, even don't take the girl back to where they pick her up, to miss us. The department [police] would rake us over the coals if they ever found out we did this. (SCPP, 1985:391)

The basic intention of these formal and informal control strategies is to reduce prostitutes' turnover of customers and thereby to reduce income.

In the early 1980s, since none of these approaches had proved particularly effective, several municipalities, including Montreal, Vancouver, and Niagara Falls, introduced municipal by-laws prohibiting solicitation for the purpose of prostitution. Not surprisingly, prostitutes fought the charges and appealed their convictions. The courts ruled that municipal bylaws prohibiting prostitution were unconstitutional because neither municipal nor provincial governments have jurisdiction to create criminal law.

In response, Vancouver officials issued injunctions against individual prostitutes that barred them from certain parts of the city. Other Canadian municipalities quickly followed suit. The principal outcome of this tactic was to initiate a cycle of "displacement" — barred from pursuing their vocation in one area of a city, prostitutes simply moved to a new area and set up business as usual. As a result of mounting public complaint and increased police frustration, changes were made to the *Criminal Code* that made it unnecessary to prove that solicitation was both pressing and persistent. In December 1985, "communicating" for the purpose of engaging in prostitution or of obtaining the services of a prostitute was outlawed. The new legislation specifically targets both the providers and the consumers of illicit sex.

Lowering the numbers of prostitutes and reducing their visibility, targeting the consumers as well as the providers of illicit sex, and making it easier for police and the courts to lay charges and obtain convictions were among the principal goals of the communicating legislation (Moyer and Carrington, 1989). It is ironic that Parliament introduced this law at the same time that the Fraser Committee released its recommendations favouring some combination of decriminalization and legalization as the official response to prostitution (Boritch, 1997). Among its recommendations, for example, were changing bawdy-house laws to allow one or two prostitutes to work out of a

private residence, empowering provincial governments to license small-scale prostitution establishments, and revising the "living on the avails" law to apply only to coercive behaviour (Lowman, 1991).

The communicating law increased substantially the charges laid in an effort to control prostitution. In 1985, police laid only 129 charges for soliciting. The next year, after the communicating law was introduced, they laid 5868 charges (Boritch, 1997). By 1995, that number had grown modestly, to 6710. Over half (55 percent) of those charged with communicating for the purposes of prostitution were female. Since December 1985, there has been a shift toward charging more males. Males accounted for 36 percent of soliciting charges between 1977 and 1985; by comparison, 47 percent of those charged with communicating between 1986 and 1995 were male (Duchesne, 1997). The percentage of males charged in 1999 remains at 47 percent (Tremblay, 2000).

Although more men are being charged under the communicating law, a number of researchers point out that men remain under-represented among the ranks of those officially processed. First, female prostitutes outnumber males in the trade by about 4 to 1. Second, the clients of both male and female prostitutes are overwhelmingly male. Third, females service twice as many male clients as male sex workers do. From this perspective, simple math suggests that only about 4 percent of those involved in the selling and purchasing of sexual services are female (Shaver, 1993). Research in several Canadian cities provides evidence that police charge more prostitutes (predominantly female) than clients (predominantly male) and fewer male than female prostitutes. An investigation of charging practices involving prostitutes and clients in ten Canadian cities in 1986–87 showed that police lay the lion's share of charges, 70 percent on average, against the sellers as opposed to the purchasers of sex. Percentages of charges against prostitutes as opposed to customers ranged from a low of 55 percent in Calgary to a high of 83 percent in Toronto. Compared to customers, prostitutes were more likely to be detained overnight, found guilty, and confined (Lowman, 1990; Shaver, 1993).

In another piece of research, head counts in Calgary, Toronto, and Halifax estimated the percentages of prostitutes who are male at 18 percent, 25 percent, and 33 percent, respectively. Corresponding percentages for charges laid were 12 percent, 5 percent, and 11 percent. Montreal was an exception,

BOX 12.6
ALBERTA LAW ON CHILD PROSTITUTION STRUCK DOWN

In a decision that will be scrutinized across the country, a judge struck down Alberta's landmark child-prostitution law yesterday, saying it was "Draconian" in its lack of protection for individual rights.

The legislation, thought to be the first of its kind in the world, allowed police and social workers to apprehend suspected sex-trade workers who are under 18 years old and lock them in safe houses for up to three days without search warrants or court orders. The goal was to provide counselling and a haven from predatory pimps.

Yesterday, Provincial Court Judge Karen Jordan ruled that the 18-month-old law violates the Constitution because of an alarming lack of "procedural safeguards," such as a requirement that a judge approve the seizure and confinement of each child.

She noted that the legislation gave young prostitutes, who are defined in the law as victims of sexual abuse, less protection that accused criminals.

"... We should acknowledge and protect their rights even before we do so for an accused in a criminal proceeding. That is the moral standard to apply. The legal standard is equally clear," she wrote.

In court yesterday, Judge Jordan rejected a request by government lawyer Margaret Unsworth to stay the ruling so that the legislation, whish is not schedule to sit until at least the fall, could consider and possibly amend the law. The judge noted that the government has the option of convening an emergency sitting.

Children's Services Minister Iris Evans said after the decision that officials need time to comb through the 24-page ruling.

This is necessary, she said, in order to determine whether the province will appeal the decision or amend the law.

"Clearly this is a mountain we're going to have to climb," Ms. Evans said, adding that the government is solidly committed to the principles behind the legislation.

Ms. Evans said the decision is "disappointing" because it means police can no longer immediately seize young prostitutes.

"It's a black day because the protection that we've had isn't there," she said.

The Protection of Children Involved in Prostitution Act had been celebrated as an effective tool by police officers and groups that work with child prostitutes.

Earlier this month, the British Columbia government passed a similar law, and other provinces are considering enacting their own legislation.

The "secure care" legislation in British Columbia goes even further than the controversial law in Alberta, giving authorities the right to scoop juveniles off the street and detain them for 72 hours, not merely for prostitution but for drug abuse as well.

After a review, the youngsters could be forced into secure treatment facilities for up to 30 days.

Jerry Adams, executive director of Urban Native Youth in Vancouver, welcomed the Alberta court's decision. He said his group is planning a similar challenge in B.C. "Aboriginal youth are the most at-risk population and the most likely to be affected by this act."

The Alberta constitutional-court challenge was spearheaded by two Calgary lawyers, Bina Border and Harry Van Harten, acting on behalf of two 17-year-old girls who were seized under the law last September at a home police consider a "trick pad," where children are locked up to have sex with men.

One of the girls has since got her life in order, and the other has disappeared. The lawyers say they fear she has gone to work as a prostitute in another province.

Ms. Border said yesterday's decision, which will be considered "persuasive" for other courts in the province and which resulted in the government's vow to stop apprehending children under the law, was a huge victory for all children's rights.

"It's very important ... the judge was very clear in her ruling that the violations are huge," Ms. Border said.

Aside from stepping on individual rights and locking up victims, Ms. Border said the law served to further drive child prostitution underground. As well, young girls who were apprehended reported that their pimps beat them once they were released and made them work harder to recoup lost earnings.

Judge Jordan struck down the law, which she acknowledged was well-intentioned, because it violates three sections of the Charter of Rights.

Children cannot answer to the allegations against them, they are apprehended in warrantless searches that are not subject to judicial review and they are seized and detained without the ability to have the action judicially reviewed.

Discussion Question

Should this law have been struck down? Explain your position.

Source: Jill Mahoney, *Globe and Mail*, July 29, 2000, pp. A1 and A8. Reprinted with permission from the *Globe and Mail*.

with male prostitutes representing 20 percent of the total but 27 percent of charges laid (Shaver, 1993). Despite the increases in charging and the tendency to charge more men than was the case under the previous legislation, the focus of criminal justice initiatives remains firmly fixed on female sex workers and on street prostitution. Moreover, while arrests have increased sharply under the new law, it does not appear that the prevalence of street prostitution has been reduced but rather that it has simply been displaced to other locations (Boritch, 1997).

Police have found it equally troublesome to control the activities of those involved in roles related to prostitution. Pimping is not against the law in Canada, although procuring is. Part-time procurers who also work in legitimate jobs are difficult to catch in the act of receiving kickbacks from prostitutes. Police have also found it arduous to convict full-time procurers, such as those operating in the context of escort services. Not only is the procuring law ambiguous, but the individuals and the organizations charged often have considerable resources with which to fight their cases in court. Legal proceedings have been time consuming, costly, and of uncertain outcome. For example, Lowman (1984) cites a Vancouver case where the costs of closing two establishments against which charges of procuring had been laid reached $1 million. In one of the cases, the appeal court overturned the conviction of the accused, and in the other, the establishment, a nightclub, burned to the ground before the police could complete their investigation.

SUMMARY

Most sociologists agree that prostitution essentially involves the exchange, without affection, of sexual services for material gain. While almost all customers are men, prostitutes may be male, female, or transsexual. Prostitution has a lengthy history in Canada, dating back to the period before European colonization.

In more recent times, two contradictory themes in contemporary North American society have significantly influenced prostitution and social reaction to it: cultural values emphasize the free expression of sexuality, while long-standing religious and moral beliefs discourage sex purely for the sake of enjoyment.

The legality of prostitution varies by geographical area. In some places it is illegal, and in some it is not. In Canada, prostitution itself is not against the law but related offences such as communicating for the purposes of prostitution, procuring, and keeping a common bawdy house are. Research on prostitution and its control in Canada is not extensive, although the investigations for the Badgley and Fraser committees have provided some empirical data.

The Canadian public has many misconceptions about prostitution. Canadians believe that people are forced into prostitution and that the vast majority of prostitutes work for pimps. That organized crime runs prostitution, that prostitutes are likely to be drug addicts, and that prostitutes are involved in serious crime in addition to prostitution are other common misconceptions. Many Canadians also wrongly believe that prostitutes figure prominently in the spread of sexually transmitted diseases. Finally, the public mistakenly thinks that prostitutes are psychologically distressed persons who are guilt-ridden and who dislike men intensely.

The extent of prostitution varies from city to city across the country. Using police estimates, the numbers of prostitutes range from several hundred in larger urban centres to less than a dozen in smaller municipalities. Street prostitutes, because they are far more visible, are more easily enumerated than those who work off the street in more private settings.

There are several different types of prostitutes; they vary in terms of income, means and location of operation, type of clientele, and general working conditions. In ascending order of status are the streetwalker, the bar prostitute, the house and the massage-parlour prostitute, the escort-service prostitute, and the call person. Despite their different types, prostitutes share certain characteristics. They tend to be young and single, although some are or have been married and a few support children. Canadian prostitutes come from both lower- and middle-class backgrounds and are relatively uneducated. While many have histories of family disruption and abuse, the extent to which these factors actually predispose individuals to become paid participants in the sex trade is not clear.

Entry into prostitution in Canada is much more a consequence of economic deprivation than of coercion. Nonetheless, some prostitutes are recruited and trained by those already in the occupation. The novice must learn the skills and rationalizations of the subculture of prostitution, usually through an apprenticeship. Vital skills include locating customers, negotiating transactions, avoiding dangers, and eluding police. Rationalizations include the beliefs that prostitutes contribute to family stability, provide for the needs of social outcasts, and reduce the incidence of sexual assault. Prostitutes' ideology also suggests that their notions about the connection between sex and money are less hypocritical than those held by most conventional people.

The madam, the pimp, and the procurer are the principal supporting characters who earn their livings wholly or in part from prostitution. In return for fees, they provide varying degrees of support in the form of training, referrals, and protection. Three different types of pimps are the name, the loser, and the bodyguard. Customers, commonly called johns, also vary by type: occasional, habitual, or compulsive. Clients come from all walks of life and seek the services of prostitutes for quick and varied sex free of entanglements.

Beginning with COYOTE, various prostitutes' rights groups have sprung up around the world. Their objectives are to decriminalize prostitution and to educate the public about sex work. They also provide other services to prostitutes, such as crisis counselling, support groups, and legal and social service referrals. Sex Workers' Alliance groups now exist in many Canadian cities.

Functionalist theory provides an account of the way in which prostitution contributes to the maintenance of the social order by serving as a safety valve for men's sexual release. Feminist theory explains the persistence of prostitution and its impacts in terms of deeply rooted sexual inequality. Feminism stresses the treatment of women as men's property and emphasizes the importance of understanding both the objectification of women and the commodification of sex. Feminism advocates the decriminalization of prostitution and the amelioration of sexual stratification.

The three basic approaches to the control of prostitution are prohibition, regulation, and abolition, the last of which characterizes Canada. Under the abolition model, endorsed by the United Nations, activities associated with prostitution (e.g., soliciting, communicating, etc.), rather than prostitution itself, are designated illegal. Until 1972, authorities typically used vagrancy laws to control prostitution in Canada. That year, Parliament passed legislation making public solicitation an offence. The Hutt decision in 1978 set a precedent, making it necessary for the propositioning of customers by prostitutes to be both pressing and persistent. Subsequently, convictions on soliciting charges became so difficult to attain that some municipalities initiated alternative steps to control prostitution. These initiatives included bylaws (later ruled unconstitutional) and court injunctions banning certain prostitutes from specified city sectors. None of these efforts proved particularly effective, and consequently, in 1985, legislators changed the law, banning communication for the purpose of prostitution, in an effort to make it easier for police to gain convictions. As with other crimes involving the enthusiastic public consumption of an illicit service, control measures aimed at curbing prostitution are likely to have limited success.

DISCUSSION QUESTIONS

1. What are some of the more popular misconceptions about prostitution and prostitutes? What implications do these misconceptions have for the control of the sex trade in Canada and for the achievement of the goals of prostitutes' rights groups?

2. The social world of prostitution consists of the interrelation of several social roles (madam, pimp, procurer, customer, police officer, prostitute). To what extent are these roles integrated and mutually interdependent?

3. Why has prostitution flourished throughout the ages despite concerted efforts to stamp it out?

4. Laws controlling prostitution represent the state's effort to legislate morality. What are the benefits and liabilities of these initiatives?

5. Of the three strategies for controlling prostitution (prohibition, regulation, and abolition), which one would you advocate? Why?

WEB LINKS

Prostitution Law Reform in Canada
http://mypage.uniserve.ca/~lowman/ProLaw/prolawcan.htm
> In this paper, John Lowman considers the effects that several laws enacted in the 1980s have had on prostitution in Canada.

Prostitution: A Review
http://www.acjnet.org/cgi-bin/legal/legal.pl?lkey=no&ckey=prostjhs&tkey=docs
> This report, published by the John Howard Society of Alberta, succinctly discusses factors that cause entry into prostitution, problems associated with street prostitution, and legislative options available in Canada.

The Desired Object: Prostitution in Canada, United States, and Australia
http://www.aic.gov.au/publications/proceedings/14/index.html#hatty
> In this comparative study, Suzanne E. Hatty outlines the different conceptualizations of prostitution by prostitution advocacy groups, research on the experience of prostitution, and legal regulation concerning prostitution in Canada, United States, and Australia. You will need a copy of Acrobat Reader to open this file. The page on which this link is located contains links to many other fascinating papers on the sex industry.

Working Group on Prostitution Report
http://www.canada.justice.gc.ca/en/news/nr/1998/toc.html
> Full text of the 1998 "Report and Recommendations in Respect of Legislation, Policy and Practices Concerning Prostitution-Related Activities" by Federal/Provincial/Territorial Working Group on Prostitution.

Commercial Sex Information Service
http://www.walnet.org/csis/
> The Commercial Sex Information Service (CSIS) site contains many useful background resources on prostitution, such as research papers, links to prostitutes' rights organizations and to court records, news clippings, and bibliographies. Note the warning stating that this site contains explicit sexual information.

RECOMMENDED READINGS

Aggleton, P. (1999). *Men Who Sell Sex: Interntational Perspectives on Male Prostitution and HIV/AIDS*. Philadelphia: Temple University Press.
> International collection of articles uses ethnographic data to examine lives of male sex workers in developed and developing countries.

Boritch, H. (1997). *Fallen Women: Female Crime and Justice in Canada*. Toronto: Nelson.
> Presents a coherent overview of issues concerning prostitution in Canada and the response of the Canadian criminal justice system. See especially Chapter 4, pp. 89–132.

Brock, D.H. (1998). *Making Work, Making Trouble: Prostitution as a Social Problem*. Toronto: University of Toronto Press.
> Traces changes in urban prostitution and changes in efforts to control commercial sex in the closing decades of the twentieth century.

Committee on Sexual Offences Against Children and Youths. (1984). *Sexual Offences Against Children: Report of the Committee on Sexual Offences Against Children and Youths*. Ottawa: Minister of Supply and Services. See pp. 945–1076.
> Outlines dimensions of child prostitution in Canada during the 1980s and provides guidance regarding measures aimed at effective control.

Elias, J.E., V.L. Bullough, V. Elias, and G. Brewer. (1998). *Prostitution: On Whores, Hustlers, and Johns.* Amherst, NY: Prometheus Books.
> Presents a good overview of the field. Sections are written by both academics and sex workers. Adopts the perspective that sex work is valid and should be decriminalized.

Greenwald, H. (1970). *The Elegant Prostitute.* New York: Walker.
> This is a classic study of professional call girls. Many of its insights are relevant to contemporary higher-status sex work.

Highcrest, A. (1997). *At Home on the Stroll: My Twenty Years as a Prostitute in Canada.* Toronto: Knopf.
> Observations on a career in prostitution by an experienced member of this occupational group. Addresses several myths surrounding prostitution. Highcrest's contribution is not without humour.

McNamara, R.P. (1995). *The Times Square Hustler: Male Prostitution in New York.* Westport, CT: Praeger.
> Offers an interesting discussion of hustling in a major American city.

Prus, R., and S. Irini. (1988). *Hookers, Rounders and Desk Clerks.* Salem: Sheffield.
> A detailed and highly readable study of Canadian prostitution that involves sex workers who work off the street. Numerous quotes tell prostitutes' stories in their own words.

Shaver, F. (1996). "Prostitution: On the Dark Side of the Service Industry." In T. O'Reilly-Fleming (ed.), *Post-Critical Criminology.* Toronto: Prentice-Hall.
> Presents a discussion of sex work in Montreal from data gathered from approximately 100 prostitutes in the early 1990s. The analysis concentrates on issues of occupational health and safety.

Special Committee on Pornography and Prostitution. (1985). *Pornography and Prostitution: Report of the Special Committee on Pornography and Prostitution.* Vol. 2. Ottawa: Minister of Supply and Services.
> Contains the results of a massive study of prostitution as it existed across Canada in the 1980s.

Visano, L. (1987). *This Idle Trade: The Occupational Patterns of Male Prostitution.* Toronto: VitaSana Books.
> Reports the findings of qualitative research on a group of male prostitutes in a large Canadian city.

Weisberg, D.K. (1985). *Children of the Night: A Study of Adolescent Prostitution.* Lexington, KY: D.C. Heath.
> Presents a detailed assessment of the involvement of children and youth in American prostitution.

CHAPTER 13

DRUG ABUSE

The aims of this chapter are to familiarize the reader with:

- the complexities of defining drug abuse
- misconceptions about drug abuse
- sources of data on drug dependency and addiction
- the personal and societal costs of drug problems
- the dynamics of drug use
- types of drugs: stimulants, depressants, and hallucinogens
- becoming a drug user
- the history of drug legislation in Canada
- the key explanatory mechanisms in positivist theories of illegal substance use
- a Marxist theory of the creation of Canadian drug legislation
- issues surrounding the control of the drug problem through supply-side strategies and demand-side strategies

INTRODUCTION

Politicians, police, and media commentators appear virtually unanimous in their observations that North America has a serious drug problem. Large numbers of people consider the illegal use of mind-altering drugs to be one of the world's most serious social crises and many advocate a total war on drugs (Blackwell and Erickson, 1988; Trebach, 1987). Suggestions for controlling the drug problem range from education and mandatory drug testing in the workplace through intensified law enforcement to monetary and military intervention in drug-producing countries.

The dynamics and ramifications of the drug problem are complex. The substances about which most Canadians express the greatest concern are "**psychoactive**" **drugs** capable of altering the functioning of the brain and the central nervous system. They can affect perceptions, attention span, memory, psychomotor dexterity, cardiovascular and respiratory functioning, and hormonal balance. Although psychoactive substances affect emotions and behaviours, the user's personality, the circumstances prompting the drugs' use, and the values and beliefs of the surrounding culture mediate their effects (Fehr, 1988a; 1988b).

This chapter begins by discussing the difficulties of developing an adequate definition of drug abuse. Popular misconceptions about drug and alcohol consumption are examined and sources of information on substance abuse are outlined. The chapter investigates the social and economic costs generated by addiction and dependency and explores the dynamics of drug and alcohol use and the effects of different classes of psychoactive substances. After describing the process of becoming a drug user, the chapter examines the development of Canadian drug and alcohol legislation. It concludes with discussions of how sociological theory explains substance abuse and drug crime and of why solving Canada's drug and alcohol problems is so difficult.

DEFINING DRUG ABUSE

The meaning of "drug abuse" is ambiguous (Blackwell, 1988c). Does it mean overuse, physical addiction, psychological dependence, use of a dangerous or illegal substance, or some combination of these elements? Consider the smoker who regularly consumes three packs of cigarettes a day. Is this abuse, even though tobacco is legal? Overuse, addiction, dependence, and the dangerousness of the drug used (nicotine) might qualify it as abuse. On the other hand, consider the person who occasionally smokes a marijuana joint. Most medical experts agree that the occasional joint is unlikely to be harmful to health. Is this smoker an abuser of drugs, even though he or she uses the substance rarely? In other words, does any degree of marijuana use qualify as abuse simply because the drug is illegal?

The use of some psychoactive drugs, such as crack, marijuana, LSD, and heroin, is against the law. Some psychoactive substances, however, are legal if prescribed by a physician but illegal if they are used under other circumstances. Prescription drugs such as tranquillizers and antidepressants fall into this category. The possession and use of other psychoactive drugs such as alcohol, caffeine, and nicotine are perfectly legal. The nonmedical use of certain over-the-counter drugs, such as Nytol or Contac-C, while not illegal, is still considered abuse.

People use legal psychoactive drugs much more often than they do those that are illegal. The nonmedical use of over-the-counter and prescription drugs, alcohol, and nicotine is much greater than the use of heroin, cocaine, LSD, and marijuana, and mortality statistics reflect this fact. Annually there are about 40 000 deaths attributable to the abuse of legal and illegal drugs in Canada. Over 33 000 of these deaths are due to tobacco use while about 6700 are due to alcohol consumption. Use of illegal drugs produces about 750 deaths annually (Single et al., 1997).

Compared with the havoc wrought by nicotine and alcohol, the total number of deaths due to illegal drugs was quite modest — 732 in 1992. Forty-two percent of these deaths involved suicide. Only 168 involved opiate and cocaine poisoning. Abuse of illegal substances resulted in 7095 hospitalizations and 58571 hospital days (Single et al., 1997).

Both public concern about the drug problem and the legality of the drugs are cyclical (Fehr, 1988a). The hysteria of the 1960s over marijuana gave way in the 1970s to fears concerning the hallucinogenic drug PCP. During the 1980s, concern shifted first to cocaine and subsequently to an inexpensive form of coke called crack. The legality of certain drugs also varies over time. In the early years of this century, cocaine was an ingredient in a wide variety of patent medicines and in the soft drink Coca-Cola. Smoking opium was lawful, and heroin was a cough remedy. However, narcotics are now illegal except when prescribed. Another example of shifting legal status involves the manufacture, sale, and consumption of alcohol. Brewing, selling, and drinking booze were against the law at various times during the 1920s and 1930s in both Canada and the United States. Before and after these periods of prohibition, however, one could legally drink to one's heart's content (Smart and Ogborne, 1986).

Although public concerns and the legality of various substances differ with time and place, virtually everyone uses or condones the use of at least some drugs. Canadians use them to cure or to kill the pains of common ailments such as aching heads, stuffed and runny noses, clogged bowels, and flagging appetites. Drugs keep us awake. Drugs put us to sleep. Drugs calm us down. In addition to their medicinal uses, drugs play important roles in the rituals and religious ceremonies of many groups. The consumption of at least small amounts of some psychoactive substance often occurs during weddings, wakes, rock concerts, dances, dinner parties, and baptisms. Moreover, depending upon the society, many people consider as acceptable drug use that enhances moods, pleasure, sexual performance, and personal growth (Fehr, 1988a; 1988b).

MISCONCEPTIONS ABOUT DRUG ABUSE

A number of popular misconceptions exist about the abuse of drugs and alcohol. Canadians believe that drug use is not only widespread but skyrocketing. The evidence, however, simply does not support this fear. Through the 1980s, the overall trend in the use of illegal drugs, with the exception of cocaine, was stabilization. The use of cocaine was, however, nowhere near the rates suggested in many law-enforcement and media reports (Blackwell, 1988b). Evidence suggests that between 1989 and 1993, Canadians' overall use of amphetamines (speed), heroin, and LSD remained stable, while cocaine and cannabis use declined (McKenzie and Williams, 1997). The trend toward overall stability or decline has persisted in recent years, although there are some indications of increased use in certain drugs, especially among adolescents (Canadian Profile, 1999; CAMH, 2000).

Many Canadians think that some drugs are so powerful that a user can be overwhelmed and permanently addicted after only one or two doses. Scientific evidence supporting the "**enslavement**" **hypothesis** is extremely shaky (Blackwell and Erickson, 1988). Moreover, the assumption that any drug has an invariable chemical effect on anyone who takes it is false. The attitudes, motivations, and expectations of users affect the manner in which the drug experience evolves. Moreover, the setting in which a user partakes of a substance has important impacts (Fehr, 1988a, 1988b). For example, alcohol consumed at a party may stimulate the drinker to be talkative and boisterous. For the same person, a stiff drink before going to bed may be an effective sedative.

Another popular but erroneous conception is that some chemical ingredient in soft drugs like marijuana and hashish compels consumers to escalate their drug use to include more potent substances like cocaine and heroin. Again, evidence fails to support this assertion (Blackwell and Erickson, 1988). The "**gateway**" **hypothesis** rests on the observation that heroin addicts usually report having consumed alcohol and marijuana before using narcotics. The difficulty with this line of reasoning is that many Canadians have used marijuana but very few use heroin. If marijuana smoking were a physiological cause of heroin use, many more Canadians would be using it.

Law-enforcement agents and the media frequently cite drug use as a major cause of property crime, implying that people steal and rob to finance their addictions. Research suggests that the relationship between acquisitive crime and drug abuse is dramatically overstated and that many users of illegal substances who also steal and rob did these things before they became involved with drugs. Substance abuse perpetuates predatory crime rather than creates it (Blackwell and Erickson, 1988).

Many Canadians subscribe to the image of evil pushers lurking on street corners and in bars, pool halls, and video arcades. Worst of all are those who haunt school yards and playgrounds, luring children into lives of addiction. But this perception is highly questionable. Most invitations to try drugs in the first place are issued by a first-time user's friends (Blackwell and Erickson, 1988).

Much of Canadians' "knowledge" about drugs comes from biased samples, from sources with axes to grind, and from unbalanced media reports. Certain types of drug and alcohol users are more likely to receive publicity as a result of the activities of police, social welfare agencies, and the media. Those who are arrested, who die of overdoses, whose addiction is visible, and who engage in crime and drug use concomitantly represent a subset of all substance users. As Blackwell and Erickson (1988:132) point out, we often draw our general conclusions from our knowledge of the worst cases:

> A school principal or child psychologist may encounter many young cannabis users whose grades are falling, who are in trouble with their teachers and parents, or who have drawn attention to themselves because of other problem behaviour. The well-behaved cannabis users, by virtue of the fact that they can use drugs while continuing to be successful in the other areas of their lives, may go about their business unobserved. Similarly, if all the heroin or cocaine users seen by professionals are hopelessly enmeshed in a life of crime, addiction, or both, it is tempting to conclude that this is the inevitable result of using the drug.

DATA ON DRUG USE

There are several sources of official information about the extent and location of drug use in Canada. They include the Uniform Crime Reports, the records kept by poison-control centres and hospitals, public inquiries into drug use (the Le Dain Commission), various opinion polls (Gallup), and the research undertakings of universities and of organizations such as the Addiction Research Foundation and the Canadian Centre for Substance Abuse. Information on drug use also comes from interviews with key informants, from studies employing participant observation techniques, and from surveys of school populations and university students (Rootman, 1988).

THE PERSONAL AND SOCIETAL COSTS OF DRUG ABUSE

The economic and social costs of drug and alcohol abuse are staggering. Drugs and alcohol are prime causes of accidental death and injury in the home, on the street, and on the job. Alcohol dependence in particular is a major factor in family disruption, marital dissolution, and violence against women and children. Alcohol also plays a large role in assaults, homicides, and work-related accidents. People who make

Box 13.1
TOBACCO FIRMS FORGED JOINT STRATEGY IN 1970s

Anti-smoking activists and Health Minister Allan Rock have gained valuable ammunition in their battles with the tobacco industry.

Newly unearthed documents show industry giants secretly plotted a global strategy to combat cancer fears and block efforts to reduce smoking.

The meeting in Britain in 1977 resulted in a clandestine agreement for the industry to deny "with one voice" around the world that smoking causes cancer and other diseases.

Despite government warnings in the U.S. and Canada linking smoking and cancer, the tobacco executives agreed that "we do not accept as proven that there is a causal relationship between smoking and various diseases," according to a position paper after the conference.

They also agreed to shun advertising saying one cigarette brand was "healthier or less harmful" than others and to influence medical and official opinion to avoid "unnecessary" smoking restrictions. They also decided to "strenuously resist" government-mandated warnings on cigarette packages.

The revelations are likely to feature prominently in the ongoing political and legal struggles pitting governments, private citizens and anti-smoking groups against tobacco producers.

"These documents are certainly going to be cited by plaintiffs suing the tobacco industry, whether they are provincial governments or individual or class action cases," said Rob Cunningham, a senior policy analyst at the Canadian Cancer Society.

"Here you have the heads of the world's largest tobacco companies getting together at a secret meeting and the result was an agreement, a conspiracy, to deny smoking caused disease, oppose governments from placing warnings on packages and generally engage in activities that would respond to the anxiety that smokers were sensing," he said.

The governments of Ontario and British Columbia are trying to sue large tobacco firms over public addiction and health problems arising from smoking. Quebec and Newfoundland may take similar steps.

Rock is also clashing with the industry over his efforts to force producers to put large, graphic health warnings on cigarette packs. On Thursday, three large tobacco companies – Imperial Tobacco Canada Ltd., JTI-Macdonald Corp. and Rothmans, Benson and Hedges Inc. – went to court to block the new rules.

Rock was unavailable for comment, but a Health Canada spokesperson said Ottawa would use the documents "to further develop our regulatory process and policies."

Rothmans spokesperson John McDonald said he hasn't seen the documents, but questioned their value.

"The anti-tobacco lobby continually rehashes documents from many years ago," McDonald said. "I think the real test will come when, and if, they are ever produced in a court of law and people get an opportunity to put them into some context."

The documents are part of millions of internal tobacco industry documents from Britain, produced by the firms as a result of a deal struck with U.S. states to stave off never-ending legal suits.

Discussion Question

Mr. McDonald argues that the tobacco industry documents need to be viewed in context. Is there any context that would cast the tobacco firms' joint strategy in a more favourable light?

Source: Les Whittington, *Toronto Star*, July 8, 2000, p. A13. Reprinted with permission – The Toronto Star Syndicate.

excessive use of alcohol are absent from work more often and, while at work, are more likely to be inefficient and lower economic productivity.

The 1993 General Social Survey (GSS) indicates that nearly 10 percent of Canadian adults reported drinking problems. The most common difficulties that people reported were harm to physical health (5.1 percent) and material well-being (4.7 percent).

Also, 44 percent indicated that they had experienced problems as a result of other people's drinking, including being disturbed by loud parties (23.8 percent), being insulted or humiliated (20.9 percent), and having serious arguments (15.6 percent).

Alcohol consumption killed about 6500 Canadians in 1995. It also caused almost 81 000 hospital admissions in 1995–96. Motor vehicle accidents, cirrhosis of the liver, and suicide produced the largest number of alcohol-related deaths while falls, alcohol addiction, and car accidents generated the largest number of alcohol-related hospitalizations. Of all driving fatalities in 1996, 42 percent of the drivers had at least some alcohol in their blood and 35 percent were legally impaired (.08 percent blood–alcohol concentration).

In 1995–96, 17 pregnant women were treated in hospitals for fetal problems believed to result from the women's heavy drinking. Hospitals cared for 58 infants suffering from toxins transmitted by the placenta or breast milk. In 1995–96, hospitals treated 254 pregnant women for drug dependence, a problem contributing significantly to the illness of newborn infants (Canadian Profile, 1999).

Of the 581 homicides that took place in Canada during 1997, one-third of victims and one-half of accused had consumed alcohol and/or drugs at the time of the crime. Male victims were one-and-a-half times more likely than female victims to have used psychoactive substances. According to police, 12 percent of homicide incidents with a known motive were drug-related. (Tremblay, 1999).

Smoking causes one in six deaths in Canada. In 1995, the mortality count was 34 728 deaths, a figure that represents 500 345 years of life lost. In addition, tobacco accounted for 191 922 hospital admissions in 1995–96 or 7.6 percent of the total number of hospitalizations in this country.

In 1995, illegal drugs caused 804 deaths in Canada for a total of 33 669 years of life lost. Suicides (329 deaths) and opiate poisoning (160 deaths) produced almost two-thirds of all deaths related to illegal drugs. In 1995–96, use of illicit drugs resulted in 6947 hospital admissions.

Between 1977 and 1997, more than 40 000 Canadians tested positive for HIV. More than 15 500 have contracted AIDS. Injection drug users are at an especially high risk of HIV infection and AIDS. Needle use as a cause of AIDS is a problem that continues to grow in Canada and it is one that is currently cited as the primary risk factor in about 15 percent of AIDS cases. Researchers conservatively estimate that about 20 percent of AIDS cases are in some way related to injecting drugs. Furthermore, needle use has played a very significant role in spreading AIDS to the heterosexual population. Estimates of the numbers of intravenous drug users vary from 50 000 to 100 000, with high numbers in Montreal, Toronto and Vancouver. Indications are that the seroprevalence rate among injection drug users continues to rise, particularly in Canada's largest cities (Canadian Profile, 1999).

Governments spend billions of dollars on law-enforcement, education, and treatment programs. Estimates suggest that substance abuse in Canada annually costs about $18.5 billion or almost 3 percent of the Gross Domestic Product. Alcohol consumption costs $7.5 billion or 41 percent of the total costs of substance abuse. The most significant economic costs of alcohol involve about $4 billion for lost productivity due to illness and early death and over $2.5 billion for law enforcement and health care. Tobacco use costs almost $10 billion annually or over half (52 percent) of Canada's total pricetag for substance abuse. Lost productivity due to illness and early death generates more than $6.8 billion of tobacco-related expenses, while the costs of health care amount to over $2.6 billion. By comparison, the economic costs of illegal drugs are less than $1.5 billion. The largest expense for illicit drugs (approximately $823 million) is the result of lost productivity due to illness and early death. Health-care costs associated with illicit drugs are about $88 million annually. Not surprisingly, a substantial proportion of the economic costs associated with illicit drug use involves funding for law enforcement (Single et al., 1997).

People convicted of drug and alcohol offences are fined and imprisoned. They also face the disadvantages of having a criminal record, including social stigma, job loss, employer discrimination, and passport restrictions. On the other hand, governments that control substance abuse through punitive means face the ugly realities of expensive prison expansion programs or of prisons bursting at the seams, or both (Solomon, Single, and Erickson, 1988; Inciardi, 1986).

For many, the poor in particular, money spent on drugs and alcohol is money not spent on goods or services necessary for a sound quality of life. The addiction of parents frequently exacts a significant toll on the well-being of their children.

Because the law prohibits the use of many psychoactive substances, the black market for illicit drugs is both expansive and lucrative. The immense profits entice organized crime groups to manufacture, import, and distribute illegal drugs. The enormous black market proceeds ensure the continuation of the drug trade not only through illegal and violent tactics but also through widespread graft and corruption. Law-enforcement officers, court officials, and politicians are prime targets. In recent years, because of the enormity of drug profits, political movements all over the world are purchasing weapons with money generated by the drug trade. Arms purchased with drug money have supported terrorist activity and have caused political instability and military destabilization in many countries around the world.

THE DYNAMICS OF DRUG TAKING

Drugs may be ingested into the body in several ways. When taken orally, absorption is relatively slow, usually taking between 30 and 60 minutes. Both inhalation and injection result in much quicker absorption times, ranging from a few minutes to a few seconds. Sniffing, snorting, and smoking result in the chemical entering the bloodstream through the linings of the nose or the lungs and can provide pleasurable sensations in 10 seconds.

There are three main ways of injecting drugs. Intravenous injections produce the fastest results. Users inject the substances directly into the blood through a vein and experience a "rush" very quickly, perhaps in 15 seconds. Subcutaneous injection, or "skin popping," is another popular technique. Injecting the drug just under the skin, the user gets the desired results in 5 to 10 minutes. Skin popping is a common technique among long-term needle users whose veins have become so severely scarred that intravenous injections are impossible. Intramuscular injections are unpopular because the 10-to-15-minute absorption time is too long (Fehr, 1988b).

Taking drugs by needle on the street is hazardous. Foreign particles or air bubbles can easily be injected and are quite deadly. The chances of overdose are high because absorption is so rapid. Moreover, users frequently know neither the chemical content nor the degree of purity of substances acquired on the black market. Finally, users often share needles, increasing substantially the risks of infection with hepatitis or the virus that causes AIDS (Fehr, 1988b).

In addition to the level of the dosage, the purity of the chemical being taken, the degree of tolerance built up in the user, and the method used to get the substance into the body, other factors cause the effects of psychoactive drugs to vary widely among drug takers. Some people intensify their reactions to a particular drug by combining it with some other substance. One common mix is the "speedball," a combination

of heroin and cocaine, which caused the death of American comedian John Belushi. Other popular mixes are "killer weed," a blend of PCP and marijuana; "T's and Blues" a combination of pentazocine and tripelennamine; and "T's and R's," a mix of pentazocine and methylphenidate (Fehr, 1988a, 1988b).

There are two types of toxic reactions to drugs: acute and chronic. Acute reactions, which result in injury or death after a single dose, usually involve either an overdose or some deadly contaminant in the psychoactive substance. Chronic toxic reactions, which follow prolonged periods of use, include cirrhosis of the liver, which usually occurs after years of excessive alcohol consumption, and lung cancer or emphysema, both of which develop after decades of cigarette smoking (Fehr, 1988b).

Uncontrollable desires for psychoactive drugs can take two forms: physical addiction and psychological dependence. Physical addiction occurs when the user develops a physiological need for a mind-altering substance. When a potentially addictive drug reaches the brain, natural chemicals in brain cells adapt to its presence to compensate for its impact and maintain some physiological and biochemical normalcy. Withholding the addicting drug after its prolonged use, however, causes the brain cells to produce unpleasant reactions as the brain continues to counter a psychoactive chemical no longer present in the body. The result of this deprivation is known as withdrawal. Withdrawal can be quite traumatic for the physiologically addicted drug user; symptoms may include profuse sweating, uncontrollable shakes and shivers, nausea and vomiting, diarrhea, fever, insomnia, hypertension, extreme lethargy, and general feelings of ill health. Alcohol, nicotine, caffeine, and heroin can produce physiological dependence and withdrawal (Fehr, 1988b).

Not all psychoactive drugs induce physiological dependence, however. There are substances upon which people become dependent but which result in no physical disturbance when they are withheld. This type of dependency is psychological. Users strongly desire to repeat the pleasurable feelings associated with taking the drug. The chemistry of the drug is of secondary importance; it is the user's psychological reaction to the drug rather than the physiological action of the substance that produces the dependency (Inciardi, 1986).

Users often develop a physical tolerance to certain drugs over time. Tolerance involves the gradual loss of

Box 13.2
DO JUSTICE TO CANADA'S COURTS

An American court has just dismissed Ottawa's billion-dollar lawsuit against the tobacco industry on the issue of alleged smuggling. The court was right to do so: Ottawa's decision to use U.S. courts in its fight with Big Tobacco is a slap in the face to the Canadian justice system. The fact that Ottawa did not choose the Canadian courts is also an indictment of our legal system, which makes it virtually impossible for a citizen to take on a giant corporation or industry.

This week a Miami jury was asked to make tobacco companies award punitive damages of more than $196-billion (U.S.) to 700,000 sick smokers. Such a case would never make it so far in Canada.

When Justice Minister Anne McLellan announced Ottawa's smuggling suit in December, 1999, she gave two reasons for going to the American courts. First, she said that most of the documents and witnesses were located there. She also said that it would be possible earn a higher damage award.

Neither argument holds water. The majority of the documents and witnesses are in this country. The damages, if any, have been suffered here. The defendants, RJR-Macdonald Inc. and the Canadian Tobacco Manufacturers' Council, are based here. The alleged smuggling occurred along our border.

And the possibility of higher damages from a U.S. court is unlikely. The so-called "revenue rule" that U.S. District Court Judge Thomas McAvoy used to strike down the case is only one obstacle. That rule refers to the legal principle that one government should not try to collect another government's taxes. Even if Ottawa is ultimately successful on appeal, and manages to convince a U.S. appeals court to overturn the "revenue rule," its suit against Big Tobacco faces more difficulties.

Besides, our southern neighbours may like us, but no U.S. jury will look favourably on a foreign government's attempt to take advantage of the American legal system. If Ottawa's case ever gets to trial, the jury is going to ask why Canada couldn't use its own justice system to deal with this dispute. And Ottawa doesn't have a solid answer.

On the face of it, there seems to be no reason why Ottawa could not use our own legal system to pursue this case. Canada has courts – and lawyers too, who will surely work for less than the $5-million (Canadian) that Ottawa has already paid to the Chicago-based firm of Bartlit, Beck.

If Ottawa thinks that the U.S. concept of triple damages for certain acts of fraud, known as treble damages, is a great idea, then it should pass legislation akin to the Racketeering Influenced Corrupt Organizations (RICO) statute, which it sought to take advantage of in its suit – not download the responsibility on a foreign court.

Perhaps Ottawa's attraction to American lawyers is understandable. No doubt, Department of Justice officials watched the Oscar-nominated movie *The Insider*, and saw what a great job U.S. lawyers did in taking on the tobacco industry. Ottawa's not alone: Last year the Ontario government retained the South Carolina firm Ness Motley to recover the province's smoking-related health-care costs. Had Queen's Park set out to create the appearance of taking action without having to fight, it couldn't have found a better way. It's only a question of time before this action also faces a successful jurisdictional challenge.

By going the U.S. route, however, both Ottawa and Ontario have turned their backs on the Canadian justice system, and on the Canadian public. The tobacco industry sells a product that kills 45,000 Canadians a year, but it has never been called to account for those deaths. In contrast, before Big Tobacco finally raised the white flag in 1997, the U.S. legal system attacked the industry in dozens of trials. (Indeed, virtually all of the once-secret tobacco industry documents that Ottawa and Ontario now rely upon for their suits were uncovered by the hard work of U.S. lawyers.)

The truth is, our legal system makes it nearly impossible for the average person to sue a big corporation. Ordinary Canadians cannot afford to hire lawyers in this country. Rules against contingency fees, caps on general and punitive damage awards and the threat of paying a corporate defendant's legal costs all serve to deny access to justice for average Canadians. No wonder there have been virtually no legal actions brought in Canada against any manufacturer of dangerous products, from automobiles to asbestos.

Before Ottawa goes racing off to hire American lawyers again, it needs to meet with the provinces to discuss how to make our civil justice system more accessible to all Canadians. And if it wants to go after Big Tobacco, it should bring its suit in Canada. A lawsuit should not be motivated by money alone. It should be about justice for families who have lost loved ones to tobacco. And it might uncover the truth about alleged tobacco-industry wrongdoing. A trial in a foreign country can never accomplish those goals.

Discussion Questions

Is this case an indictment of Canada's legal system? Do Canadian rules deny access to justice for average Canadians? Are there disadvantages to the American system – apparently the world's most litigious system?

Source: Joel Rochon and Douglas Lennox, *Globe and Mail*, July 13, 2000, p. A17. Reprinted with permission of the authors.

the sensation originally produced by the drug. Users who develop tolerance must increase the dosage to achieve the same effect as was achieved earlier with smaller amounts of the substance. Tolerance is common to a variety of drugs, including both alcohol and heroin (Fehr, 1988b).

The Stages of Drug Use

In its investigation of drug using, the United States National Commission on Marijuana and Drug Abuse (1973) outlines five types of drug user or, viewed differently, five stages of drug abuse, shown in Figure 13.1. Thought of as stages, the typology can be used to describe the career of seriously dependent substance abusers who have progressed through several or all of the steps.

The "experimental" user tries a drug out of curiosity. Drug taking is occasional and occurs over a short period of time. After a few experiences, the experimental user abandons the drug. The "recreational" user takes psychoactive substances with friends, usually in the context of a social gathering. The social drinker and the person who smokes joints at parties from time to time are recreational consumers because their experience is social and because they increase neither the frequency of use nor the amount consumed. "Situational" users take drugs to cope with

certain problems. An executive hitting the bars after a stressful day at work, a trucker popping pills to stay awake behind the wheel, and a shift worker taking sleeping pills to get to sleep during the day are situational users. "Intensified" users take drugs daily to cope with life in general. Finally, "compulsive" users are those for whom drug taking is a dominant activity. They have become at least psychologically if not physiologically dependent. For some, substance use must continue if the unpleasantness of withdrawal is to be avoided. Smoking two packs a day, downing a bottle of scotch between sunrise and sunset, and chain-smoking crack cocaine represent compulsive drug use.

Drug Types

Three broad classes of psychoactive substances affect the central nervous system: stimulants, depressants, and hallucinogens (Fehr, 1988a). These categories are not entirely mutually exclusive; marijuana, for example, is a "crossover" drug because its effects on the central nervous system can resemble those of a stimulant or a depressant. It may also induce the sensory distortion characteristic of hallucinogens.

Stimulants, or "uppers," keep users alert, excited, and able to resist fatigue. As the name suggests, they

Figure 13.1

Stages of Drug Abuse

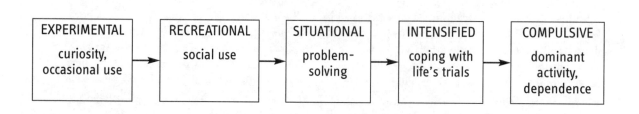

also elevate the user's mood. Stimulants can be either natural or synthetic. Natural stimulants are extracted from plants, while synthetic stimulants are made in laboratories. Caffeine, nicotine, cocaine, and crack come from natural compounds, while amphetamines are synthesized. Stimulants also vary in terms of their potency; amphetamines and cocaine have a much greater impact on the central nervous system than do caffeine and nicotine.

Depressants, or "downers," slow the functioning of the central nervous system. They induce sleep, alleviate pain, relax muscles, reduce anxiety and inhibition, and produce a sense of euphoria. Natural depressants include alcohol and the opium derivatives heroin and morphine. Barbiturates, antihistamines, PCP, and many aerosol sprays are synthetic depressants.

Hallucinogens produce perceptual distortion and hallucinations. Many users report "out-of-body" experiences, see sounds, and hear colours. Hallucinogens also exaggerate the appearance of objects and produce a sense of timelessness. These "psychedelic" drugs are derived both naturally and synthetically. Peyote, mescaline, and marijuana are natural hallucinogens, while LSD and PCP are manufactured.

STIMULANTS

Nicotine

Nicotine is a natural stimulant found only in tobacco. Almost 29 percent of Canadians aged 15 years or older in 1996–97 smoked cigarettes. Use was highest among the group aged 20 to 24 (35.1 percent) and lowest among those over 74 (11.2 percent). In 1997, tobacco sales in Canada fell by almost 6 percent from 1996. In 1997, consumption was 2144 cigarettes per person aged 15 or older. In 1994 and in 1993, the comparable rates were 2315 and 2103, respectively. Current smokers consume an average of 10.6 cigarettes per day (Canadian Profile, 1999; Van Truong et al., 1997).

Almost 30 percent of Ontario students reported smoking more than one cigarette in the past year and 22.6 percent admitted smoking daily. One-third (31 percent) of student smokers (8.5 percent of all students or 78 500 students) reported dependence on cigarettes, as indicated by lighting up within 30 minutes of rising in the morning. While student smoking rates have remained stable since 1995, the 1999 rate of 28.3 percent is considerably higher than the rates in 1993 (23.8 percent) and 1991 (21.7 percent). In 1999, 15.7 percent of students under the legal age of 18 were successful in buying cigarettes during the last month. Moreover, 63 percent of underage smokers were not asked for photo identification when buying cigarettes. Research suggests that this level of access for underage smokers has remained relatively stable since 1995 (CAMH, 2000).

As a drug habit, nicotine has several advantages over other drugs. Nicotine is legal, widely available, and does not normally impair psychomotor or cognitive activity. Smokers can, for example, legally operate a motor vehicle on Canadian highways while smoking a cigarette. Moreover, cigarettes are relatively inexpensive and have been, until quite recently, viewed as acceptable by those otherwise opposed to habitual drug use (Lung Association, 1987a).

Tobacco is promoted by billions of dollars' worth of corporate advertising that links its consumption to the experience of the good things in life. But for many Canadians nicotine dependence is less than resplendent. Cigarettes kill and maim both directly and indirectly. Approximately 35 000 Canadians each year die prematurely, and countless others find themselves disabled with diseases produced by tobacco products — lung cancer, heart disease, emphysema, and chronic bronchitis (Lung Association, 1987a). Lung cancer is the leading cause of death from cancer among men in Canada. Medical experts note that it has recently displaced breast cancer as the leading cause of death from cancer among women. The chances of beating lung cancer once it is diagnosed are only about 5 percent. Medical experts point out, however, that 85 percent of lung cancer is avoidable if a person refrains from smoking (Lung Association, 1986). Needless to say, the costs of treating diseases caused by smoking are enormous. Canadian taxpayers underwrite most of these costs.

Tobacco smoke also kills and injures indirectly, through "involuntary consumption." Nicotine users exhale over two-thirds of their effluent. This "side-stream smoke" contains 50 times the carcinogens absorbed by the user (Lung Association, 1987a). Medical researchers estimate that second-hand tobacco smoke accounts for 3 percent of all lung cancer deaths in Canada (Lung Association, 1987b). The U.S. Environmental Protection Agency reports that, in that country, side-stream smoke accounts for 5000 lung cancer deaths annually among nonsmokers (Lung Association, 1987a).

Nicotine is highly addictive, both physiologically and psychologically, and is the most widespread

Box 13.3
CANDY CIGARETTES USED TO LURE CHILDREN TO THE REAL THING

New documents show the tobacco industry has given its tacit support to the makers of candy cigarettes for more than 60 years to encourage children to smoke.

A study of the documents, published today in the *British Medical Journal*, shows tobacco firms gave confectioners permission to copy their packaging and brands.

It also alleges one U.S. candy maker hid its own research that suggested children who eat candy cigarettes were more likely to become smokers.

"Candy cigarettes are kind of like smoking toys," says co-author Dr. Jonathan Klein, associate professor of pediatrics at the University of Rochester School of Medicine in New York.

"They allow children to respond to tobacco advertising and allow children to practise the behaviours involved in smoking."

Candy cigarettes have been available in North American since at least 1915, when Victoria Sweets pronounced itself "the home of chocolate cigarettes." By 1939, tobacco companies recognized the potential of the goodies for future sales.

In 1990, Dr. Klein presented research that showed sixth graders who used candy cigarettes were twice as likely to also have smoked real cigarettes. And five- to 11-year-olds in focus groups called them "smoking toys" and different from other types of candy.

In response, the candy industry paid for a study of its own. Conducted by Dr. Howard Kassinove, a psychologist at Hofstra University in New York, the study found adult smokers and non-smokers both used candy cigarettes.

But when Dr. Klein and his colleagues began examining papers filed by tobacco firms as part of the massive 1998 settlement with U.S. attorney-general, they found 153 documents about candy cigarettes, which led them to question Dr. Kassinove about his study.

Dr. Kassinove told them his original study – which the candy companies asked him to revise from 76 to 31 pages – included a session with 31 young children, who considered the candies to be "cigarettes" based on the size, shape and colour of the packaging.

The original study concluded there was "little doubt that some of the children were pretending to be smoking as they held the candy cigarettes in their hands, and some of them will likely begin to smoke when they are older."

World Candies, which commissioned the Kassinove report, denied it hid anything. The company refused to comment on today's *British Medical Journal* study.

Discussion Questions

Is there a double entendre in "smoking toys"? Should candy cigarettes be banned?

Source: Brad Evenson, *National Post*, August 2, 2000, p. A2. Reprinted with permission from the *National Post*.

drug-dependency problem in Canada. Low doses of nicotine provide the user with a pleasurable sensation almost immediately. Within 7 seconds of inhalation, 25 percent of the nicotine ingested has reached the brain. In the time it takes to smoke the cigarette, the concentration of nicotine peaks. Within about 30 minutes, smokers feel the desire for another "fix" (NIDA, 2001).

Smokers build up tolerance to the effect of nicotine, which results in their smoking more cigarettes and inhaling more deeply to achieve satisfactory stimulation. Along with ingesting nicotine, tobacco smokers inhale approximately 4000 harmful chemicals, among them carbon monoxide, nitrites, ammonia, hydrogen cyanide, sulphur, vinyl chloride, hydrocarbon, urethane, formaldehyde, and hydrazine. Unfortunately for smokers, their lungs retain at dangerous levels from 85 to 99 percent of the compounds inhaled (Lung Association, 1987a).

Smokers also experience withdrawal symptoms when nicotine is absent from their bodies for prolonged periods of time. Once dependent, most smokers require at least ten cigarettes daily. Many heroin addicts find it easier to give up heroin than to quit smoking (Lung Association, 1988; Gorman, 1988). The relapse rate for those attempting to give up either of these drugs is similar. About 70 percent of those attempting to quit either heroin or nicotine return to the drug within 3 months (Lung Association, 1987a; 1988).

Amphetamines

Although amphetamine, or "speed," enhances a person's mood, it also possesses a high potential for both dependence and toxic reaction. The medical use of amphetamines in Canada has consequently been very limited since 1972. The proportion of Canadians who used amphetamines remains stable, with 2 percent reporting use over their lifetimes (McKenzie and Williams, 1997). Despite this general stability, however, between 1993 and 1995, the Canadian Community Epidemiology Network on Drug Use (CCENDU) (1997) found that the use of amphetamines among Metropolitan Toronto students had increased significantly, from 0.6 percent to 2.5 percent. Use of methamphetamine increased again in 1999 to 7 percent, for the highest estimate during the study period (Bernstein, Adlaf, and Paglia, 2000).

Amphetamines make their way onto the street either through theft from pharmacies or through manufacture in illegal underground laboratories (Fehr, 1988a).

Particularly when taken intravenously, amphetamines produce a "rush." Users high on this drug experience a rapid flow of ideas, feelings of strength, and increased powers of concentration. The drug also reduces fatigue and delays the onset of sleepiness. Taking amphetamines often involves a "run," followed by a "crash." During a run, the user injects the drug repeatedly over several days. As the run progresses, feelings of euphoria disappear and the user is beset by feelings of paranoia. Usually but not always, the user recognizes these feelings as effects of the drug. The crash occurs when the user stops administering the amphetamine. Crashes are followed by fatigue, hunger, irritability, and depression (Fehr, 1988a). Speed is a hazardous drug, and its dangers are widely acknowledged on the street. Its checkered reputation appears to have limited its use. There are far fewer "speed freaks" now than there were in the early 1970s, before the perils of this substance became so widely known.

Cocaine

Cocaine, also known as "coke" or "snow," provides users with feelings of euphoria, self-confidence, and energy. Many users consider it an attractive choice for several reasons (Erickson et al., 1987). Cocaine use does not lead to lung cancer, nor does it leave the user with a hangover. Since needles need not be used, there is little danger of contracting diseases associated with sharing syringes. Furthermore, many experts claim that cocaine is not physically addictive (Inciardi, 1986). It can, however, produce psychological dependence because the low following the dissipation of the drug is as intense as the high brought on by taking it. To avoid plumbing the depths when the drug is not in the body, some users take larger doses of the drug more often over longer periods of time, until taking the drug becomes an obsession. This fate, however, befalls only a few (Inciardi, 1986).

Three percent, or 640 000 Canadians, admit that they have used cocaine or crack at some point in their lives (McKenzie and Williams, 1997). Surveys continue to show low levels of past-year cocaine use in the general population. Among Toronto adults, reported rates in 1998 remained stable at about 1 percent. Among Toronto students in 1999, however, 6 percent reported using cocaine. Less than 1 percent of adults and about 2 percent of students use crack cocaine (Bernstein, Adlaf and Paglia, 2000).

The principal methods of ingestion include snorting, smoking, and injection. Users snorting cocaine draw the white powder into their noses, where it is quickly absorbed into the bloodstream (Blackwell, 1988b). Cocaine can also be distilled into a smokable distillate by "freebasing," which involves purifying the cocaine by heating a mixture that contains highly flammable ether (Inciardi, 1986; Fehr, 1988a). Crack, the newer, less expensive, and more potent form of cocaine that hit the streets in the late 1980s, is processed by combining cocaine with baking soda and water and heating the mixture in a container. The dried residue remaining after the liquid evaporates forms pellets or "rocks," which are then smoked in a heated glass pipe. Since the effects of crack are very powerful, with rushes coming on and dissipating rapidly, it is even more dependency-producing than ordinary cocaine. Moreover, because of its low price, the drug has grown in popularity among both the young and the lower classes (Fehr, 1988a).

Cocaine has recently become extremely popular and is now second only to marijuana as an illegal drug of choice in the United States and Canada. Its increased popularity is due to a combination of two factors. First, other stimulants, such as amphetamines, have acquired

Box 13.4
'SAFER' CRACK PIPES DISTRIBUTED BY GROUP

A group of illegal drug users says it will hand out 1,500 "safer" crack cocaine pipe kits to protect addicts from unsafe use.

The Drug Users' Union of Toronto announced yesterday it would begin distributing the "safer crack pipe kits" last night.

Over the next two to three weeks, volunteers will be giving out the "Crack-Me-Up Kit" – they say is the first program of its kind in the world.

The kit includes a safety-tested pipe with stainless steel bowl and screens that won't emit toxic fumes, plus a stem of chrome-plated copper that won't heat up.

Crack pipes made of plastic water bottles, pens or lipstick tubes emit toxic fumes that cause respiratory problems, Cheryl White, a Drug Users' Union member, told a news conference at All Saints Church, at Dundas and Sherbourne Sts.

As well, glass or metal pipes get very hot, burning and cracking users' lips.

Kits also include condoms to reduce sexually transmitted diseases: moisturizer for cracked lips; a postcard with instructions on safer sex and crack cocaine use, and telephone numbers of health promotion and harm reduction centres.

There is nothing illegal about handing out the kits, police spokesperson, Constable Devin Kealey said yesterday.

"It doesn't become drug paraphernalia until it becomes contaminated with a drug," he said.

He said police would prefer the users' group directed its energies at getting people off drugs.

White, a former heroin user now on methadone, said, "People are going to do drugs and you can shout at them and tell them to stop all you want. They're just going to turn away."

Dr. Joyce Bernstein, an epidemiologist with Toronto Public Health, said her department is ambivalent about programs like the crack kit.

"We've been discussing this for over two years, but we haven't been able to come to an agreement," she told the Toronto Board of Health Substance Abuse Sub-Committee yesterday.

But Lee Zaslofsky, a citizen member of the board of health, thinks the kits are a great idea. He said he was discouraged the drug users' union doesn't receive any public funding for the project. He says the union's approach fits perfectly with the policies of Toronto Public Health.

Dr. Peggy Millson, an assistant professor with the HIV, social, behavioural and epidemiological studies unit at the University of Toronto's department of public health, attended the group's news conference in support. She said U.S. studies show crack use increases the transmission of hepatitis C and HIV from contaminated pipes and cut lips.

The 1,500 pipes cost $14,000 alone, White said. She wouldn't say which organizations provided the money.

Charmaine North, a member of the users' group, who has used crack cocaine for 15 years, said the kits would have helped her.

The 33-member union includes illegal drugs users, methadone users and supporters.

Discussion Questions

How does this initiative fit into a strategy of "harm reduction"? Should such programs be supported with public funds? What are the benefits and pitfalls that surround this strategy? What, if any, are the parallels between the Drug Users' Union of Toronto and the Sex Workers' Alliance of Toronto?

Source: Peter Small, *Toronto Star*, July 8, 2000, p. A10. Reprinted with permission – The Toronto Star Syndicate.

---

bad reputations and have become more difficult to obtain. Second, the World Bank recently funded the construction of a roadway into the remote jungle regions of coca-growing areas in Peru. Cocaine originates from the leaves of coca plants, most of which grow in Peru and Bolivia. The leaves are ground into paste and then processed into a powder in Colombia. From Colombia, smugglers transport powdered cocaine into Europe, the United States, and Canada by air and sea routes known collectively as the "cocaine highway." Thanks to the efforts of the World Bank, it has become much easier to transport coca leaves out of the jungle, thereby increasing availability and lowering the price of manufactured cocaine (Inciardi, 1986).

DEPRESSANTS

Alcohol

Although not commonly thought of as a mind-altering drug, alcohol is just that. Like nicotine, it is legal, addictive, and can be deadly. Also, like tobacco, alcohol is heavily advertised. Alcohol depresses the functioning of the central nervous system. In moderation, it can leave drinkers feeling relaxed and at ease. Alcohol consumed in any amount also affects mental judgement and psychomotor functioning. For this reason, drinking and driving a motor vehicle is against the law. The acceptable blood–alcohol reading in Canada is 0.08, a level that, depending upon certain factors such as body weight and amount of food in the stomach, may be reached with as few as two drinks in an hour.

Alcohol consumption has continued to decline. Seventy-two percent of Canadians reported drinking in 1994, compared with 79 percent in 1990. The average adult consumed the equivalent of about 7.5 litres of absolute alcohol in 1992–93, a decline of 5 percent from 1991–92. Young adults, males, and those with higher incomes consume more alcohol than other Canadians (McKenzie and Single, 1997).

Patterns of alcohol use vary along demographic lines. While Canadian surveys indicate that 85 percent of males and 75 percent of females drink, they also show that this gender gap is narrowing. The highest proportion of heavy consumers were males aged 20 to 24.

In 1999, two-thirds of Ontario students reported drinking during the previous twelve months. Over 7 out of 10 reported drinking at some point during their lifetimes. The percentage of drinkers rose significantly from 59.6 percent to 65.7 percent between 1997 and 1999. In 1999, about 20 percent of drinkers consumed alcohol weekly. This figure represents a significant increase from 17.1 percent in 1997 and 14.4 percent in 1993. Also, more drinkers in 1999 indicated involvement in episodes of heavy drinking. Since 1993, the percentage of students reporting consumption of five or more drinks at a single sitting rose from 30.5 percent to 42.4 percent. Furthermore, 7.1 percent of drinkers in 1999 indicated having consumed five or more drinks on a single occasion five or more times during the previous month. This percentage is significantly higher than the 5 percent reported in 1997 and the 4.2 percent reported in 1993 (CAMH, 2000).

Most regular drinkers are male (63 percent of men versus 43 percent of women) and young (aged 20 to 24 years) (68 percent). Also, more than one-third (36 percent) of this age group reported regularly drinking to excess, consuming five or more glasses at a single sitting and doing so a dozen times or more during the previous year. The next heaviest drinkers were even younger (34 percent of persons aged 18 to 19 years (Sauvé, 1999).

People from some ethnic groups, such as Chinese, Jews, and Italians, are under-represented among drinkers (Smart and Ogborne, 1986; Trainor, 1984). For these groups, drinking is either ceremonial or takes place only at meals. The most over-represented ethnic groups in terms of alcohol consumption in Canada are the Native peoples. Explanations of their excessive drinking usually stress the historical absence of role models for proper drinking. Of considerable importance in understanding alcohol dependency among Native people is their experience of extreme social and economic deprivations (Smart and Ogborne, 1986).

The reasons for drinking beer, wine, and spirits vary widely. Many consume alcohol to facilitate social interaction and promote the social cohesion of their informal groups. Many users of this type are "social drinkers" who consume only on occasion. For others, like university students, social drinking is much more regularized. Some people drink to excess in order to acquire status; in some groups, being able to "hold your liquor" is a sign of maturity or manhood. Some people consume alcohol to reduce their anxieties and inhibitions, to escape from trying circumstances, and to reduce stress. A few people drink in the name of maintaining good health. Some recent medical research has suggested that small amounts of alcohol may be beneficial to the body in various ways, such as aiding in blood circulation. Physicians hasten to point out, however, that the health risks of alcohol consumption dramatically outweigh any benefits to be gained from anything more than very light consumption (Smart and Ogborne, 1986).

Acute overindulgence often results in the legendary "hangover." Chronic overindulgence has a variety of deleterious effects, including brain damage, cancers of the mouth, throat, and pancreas, malnutrition, and cirrhosis of the liver. Indeed, cirrhosis is the fourth-leading cause of death from disease among Canadians aged 45 to 64 (Statistics Canada, 1996).

Experts cannot agree on the precise meaning of "alcoholism" and "problem drinking." Some speak of

Box 13.5
ALCOHOL A FACTOR IN SUICIDES: RCMP

Nain, Nfld. (CP) – The number of suicides continues to climb in Labrador's largest Inuit community, a remote town racked by widespread alcoholism.

In the past six months, six people have committed suicide in the coastal community of 1,300.

And RCMP officials say alcohol was a factor in almost every case.

The latest suicide was reported yesterday when police reported the discovery of a body in a home.

Sources in the community said the 34-year-old man hanged himself Wednesday after his common-law wife failed to return home after a drinking binge.

Premier Brian Tobin said any solution to Nain's problems has to come from the community itself. However, he said if he was living in Nain, he would push for a ban on alcohol sales.

"I would certainly be part of a group that would be working to put a moratorium in place – absolutely," Tobin said.

The president of the Labrador Inuit Association, William Barbour, said "a fairly large portion" of the community supports such a ban, but more work needs to be done before such a drastic step is taken.

"Everyone wants us to take giant steps," said Barbour, who has previously admitted to having a drinking problem. "This process requires little steps. This is a long process and we have a long way to go."

RCMP Sergeant Kevin Baillie, who was posted in Nain just seven months ago, said the latest death has mobilized some residents to act.

"There seems to be a strong will among a growing group of people to get out and be heard in regards to the sale of beer," he said. "If there was ever a time when a protest could have an effect, now is the time."

Earlier this week, a cargo vessel carrying 134,000 cans of beer was met by a small group of protestors when it arrived at the town wharf.

And about 20 demonstrators carrying placards gathered Wednesday outside the Puff & Snack convenience store, which is the only retail outlet that sells beer in Nain.

The store ran out of beer in February and a fresh supply couldn't be brought in until after the sea ice had broken up.

Residents were limited to buying one case of 24 beers per day, a measure introduced a few years ago to prevent hoarding.

But the store owner, feeling the heat from the protestors, now says the limit will be cut to 12 beers per day.

The only bar in town, at the Atsanik Lodge, also ran out of beer during the winter, although it continued to sell hard liquor.

The bar was the fourth-largest buyer of liquor among all licensed establishments in the province last year.

It came ahead of 1,164 other bars and restaurants, though the owner insists the numbers were skewed by the lack of beer, which is cheaper.

"I think you're going to see more protests," said Baillie. "We had a busy night with about 10 complaints, all alcohol-related."

The officer said the community needs more health-care workers to help alcoholics deal with their addictions.

"The Labrador Inuit Health Commission is already overworked," he said.

In a bid to solve some of Nain's social problems, a group of volunteers recently drafted a report based on discussions with residents.

Discussion Questions

Can the solution to this problem come from the community itself? What might such a home-grown remedy be like? Would a ban on alcohol attack the cause of the problem or its symptoms? Would such a ban work?

Source: *Toronto Star*, July 14, 2000, p. A7. Reprinted with permission – Canadian Press.

---

alcoholism as an addiction, noting that people build a tolerance to this drug and experience withdrawal when it is withheld. Alcohol withdrawal is referred to as "delirium tremens" or, more popularly, the "DTs," and its symptoms include shaking and hallucinations

(Smart and Ogborne, 1986). Other experts prefer to define alcohol abuse as problem drinking and to measure problem drinking in terms of the amount a person consumes on a regular basis. According to this line of thinking, a problem drinker is a person who consumes more than four drinks at one sitting or more than fourteen drinks in a week (*National Drug Test*, 1988).

Because they build a tolerance to alcohol, those using it to escape pressure must escalate its use. As drinking continues, the signs of problems begin to appear. Alcoholics not only consume large quantities of the drug, but they begin to do so alone and from morning to night. The loss of control over when and where to drink and the inability to function normally at home, at work, and in social settings are key signs of "problem drinking" (McCord and McCord, 1960). Other more serious signs of alcoholism include encounters with law-enforcement and social service agencies and the experience of withdrawal (Smart and Ogborne, 1986).

Researchers estimate the number of alcohol abusers in Canada at about 500 000. The notion that most alcoholics are "skid-row bums" is patently false. Only about 3 percent of problem drinkers conform to this stereotype (*National Drug Test*, 1988). The image of the "true" alcoholic as a skid-row derelict has developed because the intoxication of the impoverished and the destitute is much more visible. People who are very poor must drink in public places because they lack the resources with which to possess private space. In reality, most alcohol-dependent people work for a living and have families. They have much greater privacy in their homes and offices, where excessive drinking as well as other forms of deviance may be more effectively hidden from the public and the authorities (Blackwell, 1988c).

Sedatives

People usually obtain both hypnotic and anti-anxiety sedatives by medical prescription. Hypnotic sedatives are sleeping pills, many of which originate from the barbiturate family and include such brand names as Seconal and Amytal. Anti-anxiety sedatives or tranquillizers induce calm without sleep. Valium and Librium are widely used examples. Over 2 million Canadians use tranquillizers; most are older and female (McKenzie and Williams, 1997).

Users' tolerance to barbiturates builds over time, inducing them to mix this drug with another to increase the pleasurable sensation. Since barbiturates cause drowsiness, some enthusiasts develop a pattern of taking "downers" to sleep and "uppers" (stimulants) to wake up. Barbiturate use, especially in combination with alcohol, caused many deaths in the 1970s, so

physicians prescribe the drug less frequently now. Withdrawal from addiction to barbiturates can be intense (Fehr, 1988a).

Whether they are depressants (sedatives) or stimulants (amphetamines), two basic sources provide the prescription drugs destined for nonmedical use: medical organizations and illegal manufacturers. Users obtain these substances from physicians and pharmacists by means of corrupt practices, theft, robbery, or — as is usually the case — outright fraud. Their deception may be as simple as lying to an unsuspecting doctor or it may involve forging prescriptions. "**Double doctoring**" is a manoeuvre that involves consulting a number of physicians for relief from a particular malady and obtaining a prescription for the same drug from each one (Solomon, 1988a).

In 1992, there were 1321 reported thefts and other losses involving narcotics and other controlled drugs. Over half of these thefts were from pharmacies, almost one-third were from hospitals, and about one-tenth were from licensed dealers. Canadian officials detected 2170 prescription forgeries over the same year — 2018 for narcotic drugs and 152 for controlled drugs (McKenzie and Williams, 1997).

Prescription drugs destined for nonmedical use can also be purchased on the street. Some of them are initially stolen from legitimate manufacturers and distributors and later sold by the thieves or their "middlemen." Some clandestine laboratories manufacture various types of these drugs specifically for illegal street sales.

Heroin

Traditionally, the words "heroin" and "drug problem" have been virtually synonymous. Although there are more heroin users in Canada now than in the past, researchers do not consider heroin addiction a rapidly growing menace. Heroin use in Canada peaked in 1970 and then went into decline; in the 1980s, the number of addicted users remained stable at approximately 3000 (Blackwell, 1988b). The proportion of Canadians using heroin remains stable, with less than 1 percent reporting having ever used this drug (McKenzie and Williams, 1997).

A variety of means is available for taking heroin, including "popping," shooting the drug into a muscle, or "mainlining," injecting heroin directly into a vein. Users can also sniff the drug or take it orally, although these means are less appealing because they markedly diminish the "rush." Once it is in the user's

Box 13.6
B.C. CASE PUTS COMPANY SMOKING POLICIES IN SPOTLIGHT

Talk to committed smokers, and they may tell you that the severe symptoms of nicotine withdrawal amount to a disability.

But many non-smokers see smoking as a personal choice or a weakness that can be overcome with willpower.

A recent B.C. legal case dealt with the disability issue, and it may change how we look at smoking in the workplace.

The case arose in the unionized workplace of Cominco Inc. in Trail, B.C. The employer had an extremely broad smoking policy: It prohibited the use and personal possession of tobacco in any form, anywhere on company property, inside and outside company buildings.

Employees were unable to smoke for their entire shift, because the size of Cominco property made it impossible to leave during breaks or lunch periods.

The union argued the policy was unreasonable because it was overly expansive in restricting smoking in outside areas. It said withdrawal symptoms caused by abstaining from smoking for a full shift constituted a disability, which required Cominco to provide "reasonable accommodation."

The dispute was referred to an arbitrator, who concluded that while employees do not have an inherent right to smoke, nicotine addiction constituted a disability. People addicted to nicotine, he said, experience uncomfortable withdrawal symptoms akin to suffering from a physical or mental disability.

The arbitrator relied on evidence that nicotine was just as addictive, if not more so, than cocaine or heroin. He reasoned that in the chronic stages, when people experience withdrawal symptoms, they should be considered in the same class as suffers from a disability.

The finding may seem shocking to some. But the decision is based on an interpretation of human rights legislation, which is designed to promote equality and respect and provide for equal rights and opportunities.

Typically, the legislation is interpreted liberally to advance its objectives. The words will be stretched to reach an interpretation most consistent with the purposes of the law.

Alcohol and drug dependency also has been found to be a disability under human rights legislation. Not everyone who abuses alcohol or drugs will be considered to be suffering from a disability – it generally has to reach a point where severe abuse leads to significant impairment.

For example, it would have to be shown that the substance abuse prevented an employee from fulfilling work obligations, or that the addicted worker suffered major health or behavioural problems as a result.

Perhaps the same analysis could be applied to nicotine addiction. A casual smoker would not be considered "disabled" compared with someone smoking 50 or more cigarettes a day. It depends on the level of addition and the adverse effects.

In a society plagued by addictions – to gambling, sex or overeating, for example – it's important that human rights legislation be given the widest interpretation where addiction has had severe personal consequences.

As the arbitrator concluded, it is the state of disablement that is protected by the legislation, not the behaviour that may have led to the addiction.

If we accept as a society that addictive behaviour may constitute a disability in certain circumstances, employers need to determine what constitutes "reasonable accommodation."

It is well recognized that employers have an obligation to accommodate a person with a disability up to the point of "undue hardship." But it's generally difficult for companies to prove what constitutes undue hardship.

The employer must accept at least some degree of hardship, and its obligations must be tailored to meet the disabled person's requirements. The employee must co-operate in these efforts.

The employer must also recognize that what it does will vary according to the nature of the disability and the person's needs.

For example, it's long been accepted that an employer may have to allow a worker with a substance abuse problem to take a leave of absence to attend a treatment program. In dealing with a nicotine addiction that is accepted as a disability, the company may have to provide the employee with a stop-smoking program.

The company may also have to allow the worker to smoke during breaks or lunch periods, outside the workplace or in a designated smoking area. In some cases, it may be inappropriate to discipline a nicotine-addicted employee in the absence of these measures.

Companies should review their smoking policy in the wake of the B.C. case. If the policy provides a designated smoking area or permits employees to smoke outside on company property during breaks or lunch periods, it will likely be considered reasonable in the circumstances.

Discussion Questions

Do you agree that nicotine addiction constitutes a disability? Why or why not? What reasonable accommodations should employers provide in such cases?

Source: Malcolm MacKillop, *Globe and Mail*, June 5, 2000, p. M1. Reprinted with permission of the author.

---

system, heroin causes euphoria while reducing anxiety and killing pain.

Although heroin is physically addictive, many users are not addicts. Furthermore, even after heavy use for prolonged periods of time, users show few if any signs of physiological damage to tissues and organs (Inciardi, 1986). The same cannot be said for alcohol and nicotine, which eventually devastate the body.

Heroin users build up a tolerance to the drug, which necessitates heavier and heavier doses to achieve the high experienced after initial use. For regular users who are also addicted, cessation of the drug causes withdrawal, the symptoms of which are sweating, a runny nose, watering eyes, chills, cramps, nausea, and diarrhea.

Although not particularly harmful physically, heroin addiction poses unique problems for many users. Because heroin is illegal, dealers charge high prices, and street addicts must spend considerable time and effort securing funds for purchases. Money intended for food and shelter buys drugs, and users must cope with poor nutrition, inadequate clothing, and substandard or no housing. Moreover, some "junkies" commit acquisitive crimes to support their habits. Lack of access to the drug, to the necessities of life, and to the funds to make purchases, of course, are not problems faced by more advantaged heroin addicts, such as those found among the ranks of physicians and other medical personnel.

Users purchasing heroin from street dealers face two other serious problems. First, street users are often ignorant of the purity of the heroin they buy. Misjudgements about the strength of a dose are often deadly. Second, because heroin is injected and syringes are in scarce supply, street users share needles, which, particularly in the United States, has rapidly spread HIV and hepatitis C infections among impoverished addicts, many of whom may have passed these viruses on to their sexual partners (Inciardi, 1986).

HALLUCINOGENS

LSD

In 1938, European scientists developed a synthetic compound, lysergic acid diethylamide. First used in the study of psychosis, the drug gained attention in the 1960s, when it became popular for its "mind-expanding" properties. Its popularity declined toward the end of the 1970s, and its use levelled off. The proportion of Canadians who use LSD continues to remain stable, with about 3 percent reporting its use at some point during their lives (McKenzie and Williams, 1997). Survey data show that Toronto students' past-year LSD use rose slightly to 6 percent in 1999, compared to 3 percent in 1997. The percentage of students indicating use of other hallucinogens such as mescaline reached about 13 percent in 1999, an all-time high (Bernstein, Adlaf and Paglia, 2000).

LSD is a colourless and odourless liquid that is taken orally in very small doses. The drug produces effects in about 15 to 45 minutes. Intoxication usually peaks between 1 and 2 hours after it has been swallowed. The disorientation of audio-visual stimuli that it produces may last over 12 hours. LSD is non-addictive physically, and rarely produces psychological dependence. Because total tolerance builds within 3 or 4 days, daily use is rare. (Fehr, 1988a).

LSD use has two unique drawbacks. One is the "bad trip," an unpleasant and perhaps even terrifying experience. Some users have died as a result of trying to fly off high buildings to escape pursuing monsters. Also, some LSD users experience "flashbacks" — days, weeks, and even months after they last took the drug, they relive its effects. Why flashbacks occur in some users and not in others remains a mystery (Fehr, 1988a).

PCP

Also known as "angel dust," phencylidine reached the height of its popularity in the 1970s. Originally an anaesthetic used on large animals, the drug can be taken orally, smoked, or injected. In its powder form, PCP is frequently taken by sprinkling it on a cigarette or a joint. The drug is not physically addictive and produces psychological dependence in only a few users. PCP in small doses produces sensations of weightlessness and euphoria. As the dosage increases, users become disoriented and may experience hallucinations or paranoia and, in rare cases, may become violent. Because of its painkilling properties, the very few PCP users who do become violent are difficult to control (Fehr, 1988a).

PCP's decline in popularity may be a result of widely circulated horror stories about its effects and its relationship to violent behaviour. As Fehr (1988a) points out, however, the terrifying reputation of PCP may actually make it a drug of choice in the future. In some groups, taking a psychoactive drug widely considered to be extremely dangerous is a way of gaining status.

Cannabis

More commonly known as "weed," "grass," "pot," and "hash," both marijuana and hashish originate in the Indian hemp plant. Marijuana comes from the leaves of the entire plant, while the more potent

---

Box 13.7
MARIJUANA AS MEDICINE

The Ontario Court of Appeal has decided that Terrance Parker can be both a legal pot grower and a legal pot user – he, and everyone like him who requires the drug for medical purposes.

The court reasoned on Monday that, since the federal law on marijuana possession and cultivation doesn't recognize the paramount nature of Mr. Parker's need to use the drug to control the epileptic seizures that have afflicted him for almost 40 years, it is "forcing Parker to choose between his health and imprisonment." This does not accord with "principles of fundamental justice," and therefore the law should be struck down.

The effect of the judgment on everyone but Mr. Parker is stayed for a year to give Ottawa an opportunity to redraft the law to include a medical marijuana exemption. While the government has recently started to grant selected people the right to obtain marijuana to ease symptoms associated with various medical conditions, the court pointed out that there is no clear rationale for what and who qualifies. Being dependent on the "unfettered and unstructured discretion of the Minister of Health is not consistent with the principles of fundamental justice," it concluded.

The judgment is right both in legal reasoning and in matters of the human spirit. It is madness for every sick person to have to appeal to the federal Health Minister to get his or her drug. (An estimated 150,000 people in Ontario alone might benefit from marijuana's ability to ease the effects of AIDS, glaucoma, cancer and epilepsy.) It is also madness that, once the exemption has been granted, there is no safe and legal supply of the drug for those entitled to have it.

The present ministerial exemption system seems designed not to speed delivery of medical marijuana to the sick people who would benefit from it, but to employ all the sticky slowness of a bureaucracy to limit medical marijuana's use.

More than Kafkaesque, this approach ignores obvious parallels in the rest of the medical system. Other drugs, notably opiates, have two regimes applied to them. While their recreational use is illegal, their medical use isn't. The decision about when it is appropriate to prescribe them isn't a whim of bureaucracy; it is soberly arrived at by a doctor and patient.

There is nothing about marijuana that says it should be treated any differently from other drugs, and a lot (its physical effects and addictive characteristics are relatively benign) to say it is ultimately safer than many other drugs.

In the interest of both the sick people of Canada and natural justice, the federal government should bow to the wisdom of the courts and get on with providing a cheap and easy way for sick people to get their medication.

The clear reason this hasn't already happened is the oft-stated fear that the medical use of marijuana is simply a stalking horse for total legalization.

While nowhere in the Western world is smoking the drug entirely legal, there have been various efforts at what is sometimes termed decriminalization. In the Netherlands, licensed "coffee shops" selling the drug openly must adhere to strict rules, including not selling more than 30 grams at a time and being responsible for public disturbances caused by high clients. In those rare instances when people are charged with possession, the penalty is confiscation, not a jail term. The Swiss have recently proposed a similar law.

In many other European countries – and indeed in many jurisdictions in Canada – possession of a small amount of marijuana is simply ignored by the police.

So why not go all the way and make marijuana legal? Some worry about the social side effects: the marijuana-high equivalent of drunk driving, or marijuana as a gateway to harder drugs.

The case for these concerns is not strong. What studies there are suggest that while there may be some loss of control, marijuana users become more cautious drivers when they get high. The most likely outcome of marijuana smoking seems to be more marijuana smoking.

What is clear is that outright legalization would cause serious trouble with the United States, where prohibiting the substance is part of a national drug war.

Therefore, Canada should follow its historical nature and take a middle path first proposed in 1973 by the LeDain Commission of Inquiry into the Non-Medical Use of Drugs. Decriminalize marijuana. Make using it illegal in name but regulated and legal in practice.

Discussion Questions

Which road should Canada take in its response to marijuana: prohibit it entirely as is now the case, permit its use for medicinal purposes, or legalize it? Should Canadian drug policy be affected by drug policy in the United States? What do you think about the Le Dain Commission's recommendations of 1973? Are they still relevant?

Source: Editorial, *Globe and Mail*, August 2, 2000, p. A16. Reprinted with permission from the *Globe and Mail*.

hashish comes from the resin extracted from the upper leaves, buds, and flowers. Hashish is more potent than marijuana because it contains more of the psychoactive substance THC. While cannabis can be grown all over the world, certain locations are more favourable than others. Mexico, Asia, Colombia, and Jamaica produce a plant that contains THC in greater concentrations (Inciardi, 1986). Traditionally, cannabis grown in Canada has been less desirable because the THC levels are too low. Hydroponic technology, however, is making it possible to produce a better-quality product in Canada (Boyd, 1991).

Cannabis is the most widely used illicit drug in Canada, with 20 percent of Canadians reporting its use at some point in their lives. While current national data are not available, the Canadian Centre on Substance Abuse reports that past-year cannabis use grew from 4.2 percent in 1993 to 7.4 percent in 1994. (Canadian Profile, 1999). A local population survey for Toronto shows that past-year cannabis use among the city's adult population remained comparatively stable in 1999, at about 10 percent. Among Toronto students, however, past-year use doubled

from 9 percent in 1993 to 18 percent in 1995, and was up to 19 percent in 1997. In 1999, the percentage of students admitting past-year cannabis use rose to 26 percent of junior high and high school students, the highest rate since the survey was begun in 1974 (Bernstein, Adlaf, and Paglia, 2000). In 1999, about 29 percent of Ontario students used cannabis during the previous year and about 35 percent reported using it in their lifetimes (CAMH, 2000).

In the 1960s and 1970s, cannabis above all other drugs, became a symbol of the youth protest movement of the turbulent 1960s. Marijuana and hashish came to represent youthful defiance of authority and broader social upheaval, which helps to explain the heated opposition to its use that persists to this day (Blackwell, 1988b).

Cannabis users consume the substance in a variety of ways, of which smoking is the most popular. It can be smoked in home-made cigarettes known as "joints," "reefers," or "spliffs" (hash mixed with tobacco), or in a pipe. A few enthusiasts consume the drug orally, in such concoctions as "hash brownies" (Fehr, 1988a).

The effects of cannabis vary with a person's expectations and moods, the potency and dosage of the drug, and the technique used to take it. Usually, people smoke cannabis by inhaling deeply, holding the smoke in the lungs, and exhaling slowly. The high involves relaxation, euphoria, and sometimes mild visual distortion. The THC in cannabis impairs both judgement and psychomotor control.

While it is not entirely without danger, the perils of this drug have been overstated. Cannabis is not physically addictive, although some users do become psychologically dependent. Only a few become compulsive users. The major dangers are the noncannabinoid constituents of the smoke and the risks of operating automobiles, airplanes, or machinery while physically and mentally impaired (Fehr, 1988a).

BECOMING A DRUG USER

Most drug use, at least initially, is social. People are introduced to psychoactive substances by their friends, not by entrepreneurial strangers who deal drugs. Whether one takes up smoking tobacco, drinking beer, snorting cocaine, or shooting heroin, the begin-

---

Box 13.8
COURT WRESTLES WITH FETAL RIGHTS

The Supreme Court of Canada struggled yesterday with the murky question of where to draw the line when it comes to forcing a pregnant woman to look out for the interests of her unborn child.

The landmark case involves a pregnant Winnipeg woman whom child welfare authorities tried last year to force into a treatment program for a solvent-sniffing addiction.

The woman, known only as Ms. G., had her baby about six months ago and it appears to be healthy, so the case doesn't directly affect her anymore.

She's now 23, pregnant again, and her lawyers say she has kicked her habit of sniffing solvents such as nail polish remover.

But more than a dozen lawyers gathered in Ottawa to intervene in the matter that has become a legal and ethical test of the limits of state intervention in pregnancy.

More than half of the nine justices expressed reservations over what, if any, limits the courts can force on pregnant women without violating their rights under the Charter of Rights.

If limits on freedom can be imposed for sniffing glue, can they also be imposed for smoking or drinking? And how much would warrant intervention?

"Can a pregnant woman work in a place where there's a lot of smoke?" asked Chief Justice Antonio Lamer, who said he was worried about the potential "slippery slope" of the court stepping in.

"Isn't there another way?" implored Justice Claire L'Heureux-Dubé.

Parliament and most provincial governments have stayed away from the issue of whether lawmakers can step in to protect an unborn child. Only New Brunswick and the Yukon allow court orders to force pregnant women into treatment.

Last summer, when Ms. G. was five months pregnant with her fourth child, she was forced into treatment by Winnipeg Child and Family Services. She had already surrendered her three other children to government care. Two are mentally and physically handicapped as a result of her drug abuse.

A lower court upheld the move, but the treatment order was overturned by an appeal court that ruled it's up to politicians, not the court, to act on the issue.

The family services agency then took the case to Canada's high court.

Heather Leonoff, the lawyer representing the agency, asked the court to come up with a golden rule for when the state can intervene.

She suggested the bar be set at behaviour that could cause "great irreparable harm" to an unborn child.

Although abortion is not illegal in Canada, the Charter of Rights provides for the protection of a baby injured while in the womb.

Discussion Questions

Should governments be able to force pregnant women into treatment to protect their unborn children? Whose rights should assume primacy? Where might the "slippery slope" lead in such cases?

Source: *Toronto Star*, June 19, 1997, p. A13. Reprinted with permission from Canadian Press.

ner's friends and their drug-using behaviour patterns are critical elements in the novice's introduction to psychoactive substances. Friends teach the prospective user the attitudes and techniques of drug use, provide support and protection, and connect neophytes to networks of dealers (Blackwell and Erickson, 1988).

There are several distinct phases in becoming a drug user. One must first learn the techniques for taking the selected substance and then learn to recognize the drug's effects and interpret its mind-altering impacts as pleasurable. To smoke marijuana properly, for example, novices must learn how to roll and consume a joint. They learn to inhale deeply, to hold the smoke in their lungs, and then to exhale slowly. Next, they must learn to recognize the effects of the drug and to define them as enjoyable. Users must be taught to watch for certain cannabis-induced reactions, such as a dry throat, hunger, disequilibrium, temporal disorientation, and perhaps a hallucination. Once experienced, initiates learn to interpret these sensations as enjoyable rather than frightening (Becker, 1963).

Research on heroin use shows a similar pattern. The initial use of the drug occurs in a social context where the novice obtains access to the drug and learns both the correct technique of injection and the proper dosage. Once these techniques have been learned, veterans train novices to recognize and enjoy heroin's effects and to rationalize its prolonged use.

Many drug users, at some point, also learn to stop taking their drugs. Some quit on their own, while others use drug-rehabilitation agencies. Of those who stop on their own, many simply "age out." Drug use, like other forms of deviance and crime, is negatively correlated with age. Others, regardless of age, decide to discontinue their consumption perhaps because they find that certain negative aspects of the drug make its continued use undesirable. Drug use can become inordinately expensive, and the risks of developing health problems or running afoul of the law can simply become too great. (See Table 13.1.) Some people give up drugs because they believe that continued use is too detrimental to their personal relationships. Finally, some

TABLE 13.1

CANADA'S DRUG TAKERS: USERS, COSTS, AND ATTRIBUTABLE DEATHS

	Annual Number of Users	Cost per Week for Average User	Possibility of Overdose Death	Drug Related Deaths per Year
Alcohol	16 000 000	$10 – $100	YES	3000 – 15 000
Amphetamines	<100 000	$100 – $500	YES	<100
Cocaine	300 000 – 500 000	$10 – $5000	YES	<100
Heroin	<100 000	$50 – $5000	YES	<100
LSD	<100 000	<$20	NO	<10
Marijuana	1 500 000 – 2 500 000	$10 – $100	NO	<10
Tobacco	6 000 000 – 8 000 000	$30 – $100	NO	35 000
Tranquillizers	1 500 000 – 2 500 000	$0 – $20	NO	<10

Source: N. Boyd, *High Society: Legal and Illegal Drugs in Canada.* (Toronto: Key Porter Books, 1991). Appendix, p. 224. Reprinted with permission from the publisher.

people stop because the use of their favourite drug is too objectionable socially (Blackwell and Erickson, 1988). Tobacco smokers often quit smoking for this reason.

THE HISTORY OF DRUG AND ALCOHOL LEGISLATION IN CANADA

DRUG LEGISLATION

During the nineteenth century, the Canadian government placed few restrictions on the manufacture, sale, or use of psychoactive substances. It was only toward the end of the century that authorities became concerned about the use of drugs among certain segments of the population, specifically, Asians on the West Coast. Until the 1880s, Canadian immigration policy had encouraged the importation of cheap labour from China. Chinese labourers earned modest wages for building the Canadian Pacific Railway through the Rocky Mountains and mining British Columbia's precious minerals. By 1885, however, the railway was complete and the mining boom had tapered off. The downturn in employment meant a restricted, more competitive labour market, and the Chinese labourers entered into direct competition with whites for jobs. Because they worked cheaply, they undercut the position of white labourers and their unions. In response to the mounting "Asian problem," the Canadian government, in the *Chinese Immigration Act* of 1885, restricted Chinese immigration, denied Chinese the right to vote, made it difficult for them to own land or businesses, and imposed on them an annual immigrant tax.

Racial unrest in British Columbia culminated in a riot in 1907, and the federal government dispatched a young troubleshooter, Mackenzie King, to arrange compensation for Asians whose businesses had been damaged or destroyed in the 1907 melee. Much to his dismay, King discovered a large opium industry that involved the importation of tonnes of the narcotic into Canada. The opium in question was, of course, destined for consumption primarily by the Chinese. King recommended strict controls on the opium trade, and in 1908 the Canadian government enacted the *Opium Act*, which made the Chinese custom of smoking opium illegal. This had the effect of increasing illicit trade in the newly prohibited substance while driving up its price.

Before Parliament introduced the *Opium Act*, the consumption of opium by any means caused little concern and was perfectly legal. Not only had the Chinese imported the substance in great quantities for sale in their opium shops, but opium was also widely available in a variety of other forms. Medicine shows, patent-medicine companies, and general stores all legally distributed concoctions containing this narcotic. It is of some significance that these enterprises did not market their product to the Chinese and did not, at this time, become subject to the restrictive legislation. It is also worthwhile to note that reformers had failed miserably in their efforts to limit the use of other products, like alcohol and tobacco, which were widely held to undermine Christian ideals. In contrast, the initiatives against opium were enormously successful largely because they singled out for persecution a strongly disliked and powerless racial minority (Solomon and Green, 1988).

In 1911, Parliament passed a newly created *Opium and Drug Act*. This legislation expanded the list of prohibited substances to include morphine and cocaine. Later, in 1922, Canadian magistrate Emily Murphy wrote an influential book entitled *The Black Candle*, in which she claimed that drug use was running rampant in some sectors of the country and that it was linked to moral turpitude, spiritual depravity, crime, and insanity. Filled with racial biases and replete with moralistic overtones, *The Black Candle* led its readers to believe that vile and corrupt Asian and black addicts and drug dealers were preying on innocent whites and, in particular, spreading addiction among innocent white women.

The *Opium and Narcotic Drug Act* of 1929 added cannabis to the list of prohibited substances as well as adding a provision for the deportation of aliens convicted of certain drug offences. This Act also introduced the infamous "writ of assistance" that gave specified RCMP officers the power to search for drugs anywhere and at any time. The writs, which even permitted breaking and entering, were valid for the officer's entire career with the force. Writs of assistance remained in effect until as recently as 1985. From 1930 to 1950, the Canadian government continued to expand both the numbers of prohibited drugs and the range of drug offences punishable by law (Solomon, 1988b).

The 1950s marked a shift away from a purely control orientation to reflect a growing concern for treatment. It was during this period that drug dependence gradually started to become less of a crime and more of a social and medical problem. At the same time, nonetheless, Parliament created a new offence, namely "possession for the purposes of trafficking," because most trafficking charges were winding up as convictions for simple possession, even when the amount of drugs involved was substantial. The new law required anyone found with drugs in their possession to prove that those drugs were for their own use exclusively and not intended for sale to others. The law effectively shifted the burden of proof in this instance from the Crown to the accused, making it relatively straightforward for prosecutors to obtain convictions for this more serious possession offence.

In 1961, the federal government enacted the *Narcotics Control Act*, which increased the severity of sentences. Life in prison became the maximum sentence for several types of drug convictions: possession for the purposes of trafficking, trafficking, and importing or exporting narcotics. This Act also imposed a minimum sentence of seven years for the importing or exporting offence. Only murder and treason had more severe minimum sentences (Solomon and Green, 1988).

The numbers of convictions for cannabis offences rose markedly during the 1960s. The trend continued during the 1970s, until marijuana and hashish offences represented 90 percent of all drug convictions. During the same period, heroin use increased modestly, while the use of hallucinogens rose sharply. Because many of those found guilty on cannabis charges during this period were young, middle class, and had no prior records, the penalties actually meted out by the courts became less severe than they had been in the past (Boyd, 1988a).

Before 1997, two separate federal Acts governed illegal drug use. The *Narcotics Control Act* covered illegal drugs such as cannabis, cocaine, and heroin and the *Food and Drugs Act* covered controlled and restricted drugs such as amphetamines, LSD, and anabolic steroids. In May 1997, the federal government implemented new legislation to replace the two existing acts. The *Controlled Drugs and Substances Act* incorporates certain sections of the two previous Acts in an effort to modernize and improve Canada's drug control and abuse policies. Furthermore, the Act aims to meet Canada's obligations under a number of international drug protocols. (Tremblay, 1999).

As under previous legislation, official data on drug crimes are strongly associated with the intensity of police drug-enforcement efforts. As in the past, investigations leading to the seizure of illicit drugs routinely result in the arrest of suspects. Although the official drug-crime rate increased by 6 percent in the late 1990s, the rate of persons charged fell by 7 percent. The rate of incidents "cleared otherwise" grew by 12 percent over the same period in most provinces. This trend is partially explained by the introduction of alternative measures for adults that came into effect in 1997. These measures permit police to use discretion in referring adult suspects, who could otherwise have been charged, to a diversion program of the type already in place for young offenders. (Tremblay, 1999).

On August 1, 2000, the Ontario Court of Appeal struck down as unconstitutional the federal law prohibiting possession of marijuana. This decision effectively invalidated sections of the *Controlled Drugs and Substances Act*. The existing law remains in force for twelve months to provide the federal government with sufficient time to rewrite the law. Other options include appealing the decision to the Supreme Court of Canada or allowing the law to remain struck down by failing to take any action. Were the latter option chosen, marijuana use would be decriminalized. In reaching its decision, the court ruled that marijuana as a medicine should not be denied to those who could benefit from its effects. Among such beneficiaries are those needing treatment for a variety of maladies including glaucoma, multiple sclerosis, migraines, epileptic seizures, AIDS, chronic pain, and chemotherapy side-effects. It is estimated that about 150 000 people in Ontario alone need marijuana for medical reasons.

In its ruling, the court argued that the origin of the existing prohibition lacked sufficient foundation and was based on misinformation and racism. Unconstitutionality, according to the court, does not apply to recreational use of marijuana. The *Canadian Charter of Rights and Freedoms* can only overturn laws that threaten significant domains, such as a citizen's life, liberty, and security. Recreational use does not meet this standard. Currently, there are about 600 000 Canadians with criminal records for marijuana offences (Johnson, 2000; Gadd, 2000).

ALCOHOL LEGISLATION

A group of well-educated women began the Women's Christian Temperance Union (WCTU) in New York State in 1874. The same year, a group of Ontario women opened a Canadian chapter of the movement. By 1885, the WCTU had spread to all the Canadian provinces. The primary goal of the organization was to

Box 13.9
HUGE JUMP REPORTED IN USE OF ECSTASY BY ONTARIO STUDENTS

Use of ecstasy among Ontario students has jumped eightfold since 1993, and the use of hallucinogens in general is now greater than at the height of hippie culture.

Almost 5 per cent of students in Grade 7 to 13 now report that they have used the drug in the previous year, according to a new study. And one in five adolescents, even in the younger age group, say they have been to a rave, where use of ecstasy is fashionable, in that same time period. (Ecstasy is an amphetamine-based hallucinogen.)

"In general, the use of hallucinogens has skyrocketed," Angela Paglia, a research associate at the Centre for Addiction and Mental Health said yesterday in an interview. "The levels of hallucinogen consumption have matched or surpassed those of the 70s, when many of these kids' parents were teenagers," she said.

The research is featured in today's edition of the Canadian Medical Association Journal, which has published a special issue on substance abuse.

It reveals that 13.6 per cent of junior high and high school students use the hallucinogenic drugs mescaline or psilocybin (magic mushrooms), up from 3.1 per cent in 1993. Use of LSD has remained steady at 6.5 per cent.

Ms. Paglia said there appear to be three principal reasons why drug use is on the rise among young people: a decreased perception of risk, decreased moral disapproval and increased availability.

She added that the numbers indicate that education strategies are failing.

"Kids today are really media savvy. Pop culture has a pretty strong hold on them and they don't seem to believe the messages they are hearing elsewhere," she said. "They also notice the hypocrisy surrounding drug use, particularly when it comes to smoking and alcohol."

In fact, Ms. Paglia said that while the rate of illicit-drug use is rising rapidly, one cannot lose sight of the fact that the "vast majority of kids, 60 or 70 per cent, don't use illicit drugs at all."

The same is not true of legalized drugs like tobacco and alcohol. The abstention rate is 26.8 per cent among students.

Two-thirds of teenagers surveyed said that they had taken a drink in the past year, a rate that is up 19

DRUG USE

Percentage of Grade 7 to Grade 13 Ontario students reporting non-medical use of drugs in 1993 and 1999.

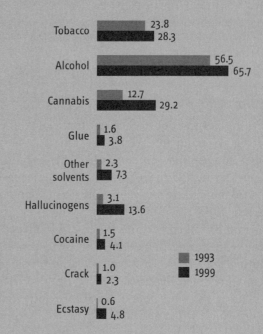

Source: *Canadian Medical Association Journal*, The Globe and Mail.

per cent since 1993. Further, the research shows that binge drinking is up considerably, with 7 per cent of junior high and high school students saying they have five or more drinks in a sitting.

Similarly, despite widespread public health campaigns, teenage smoking is up 16 per cent in the 1990s, with 28.3 per cent of those surveyed saying they smoke.

The good news, from a public health perspective, is that school children appear to be delaying the age of experimentation with drugs. For example, 5 per cent of students said they began smoking in Grade 4 (about age 9), down from 7 per cent in the 1997 survey, and 16 per cent in 1981. Similarly, only 2 per cent of students said they began smoking cannabis by Grade 6 (about age 11), down from 5 per cent in 1997 and 8 per cent in 1981.

The numbers are derived from a study that has been going on since 1977, the most in-depth health research on adolescents ever conducted in Canada. The Ontario student-drug-use survey sends questionnaires to students in Grades 7, 9, 11 and 13.

Discussion Questions

Is there any suggestion here that the use of a particular drug and the concern it raises is cyclical? Could ecstasy be today's drug of concern in the same way as crack and marijuana have been in the past?

Source: André Picard, *Globe and Mail*, June 13, 2000, p. A6. Reprinted with permission from the *Globe and Mail*.

eliminate the production and consumption of alcohol through Prohibition legislation. The group took the position that the true victims of excessive drinking were the scores of women and children who suffered various forms of abuse at the hands of their drunken husbands and fathers. The spokeswomen for the group also argued vehemently that alcohol was the root cause of virtually all social ills, including poverty, disease, crime, prostitution, and divorce. Alcohol, they claimed, reduced Canada's economic productivity and competitive position in the world marketplace.

The WCTU was a broadly based organization admitting representatives of all ethnic and class segments. Men could join but were not accorded voting privileges. By the 1890s, the temperance movement had successfully lobbied to have "temperance" taught as a subject in the public school system. At the time, heavy drinking was customary at various social functions, ranging from barn-building bees to community dances. While the WCTU successfully reduced excessive consumption at these events, the movement was not without strong opposition. Drinkers, farmers who sold grain to liquor manufacturers, people who worked in breweries, distilleries, taverns, and inns, and newspapers that sold liquor advertising put up considerable resistance to the group's Prohibition efforts. Even some churches opposed Prohibition, arguing that nothing in the Bible forbade moderate consumption. For the time, liquor represented one of the government's few sources of tax revenue. Consequently, politicians were not entirely enthusiastic about the WCTU's anti-alcohol campaign.

In 1898, the WCTU finally succeeded in forcing the government to hold a Canada-wide plebiscite on the question. Prohibition proponents won, with 52.5 percent of the vote. Unfortunately for them, however, only 44 percent of eligible Canadians had cast a ballot. Prime Minister Wilfrid Laurier, arguing that Prohibition was favoured by only a fifth of Canadians,

refused to implement the legislation. Not until World War I did Parliament institute Prohibition. When it did so, it justified the anti-drinking law in the name of economic productivity and the war effort. Between 1915 and 1917, all provinces approved Prohibition Acts, which remained in place until 1919, when the federal government terminated the *War Measures Act*. Referenda on the continuation of anti-alcohol laws ushered in the 1920s. Most provinces repealed their Prohibition Acts during that decade. In Prince Edward Island, however, Prohibition remained in force until 1948.

After the war, national Prohibition grew increasingly distasteful and eventually failed for a variety of reasons. Anti-drinking laws were unpopular with the public and difficult to enforce. They invited bootlegging and police corruption. Moreover, numerous loopholes in the legislation allowed people to legally consume "near beer" (2.5 percent alcohol content) and permitted "patients" to consume alcohol prescribed by a physician. Demographic shifts also eroded the position of the temperance movement. The numbers of keenly supportive Methodists and Baptists were declining while the numbers of those most inclined to drink — urban dwellers, immigrants, and the working class — were rising. Finally, despite Prohibition, the social maladies attributed to alcohol abuse endured. The persistence of social problems despite forced abstention fuelled doubts in the minds of many Canadians about the effectiveness of these drastic measures.

With the failure of Prohibition, the WCTU lost much of its power. The Moderate Leagues replaced the WCTU and advocated watered-down restrictions. Governments abandoned outright Prohibition as a control strategy and passed a series of statutes that limited consumption rather than banning it. First, governments made themselves the sole distributor of alcoholic beverages. Second, they enacted laws placing restrictions on who could drink, what could be drunk, and when and where people could consume alcohol. Under the "local option" clauses of the *Canadian Temperance Act*, municipalities could decide on the basis of a vote whether to be "wet" or "dry." By the 1950s, most areas permitted the sale of alcoholic beverages (Smart and Ogborne, 1986).

Federal and provincial governments share responsibility for laws regulating the manufacture, distribution, advertising, possession, and consumption of alcoholic beverages. Provincial Liquor Licence Acts regulate marketing and consumption. In Ontario, for example, laws prohibit anyone under age 19 from purchasing, possessing, or consuming alcohol. It is also illegal to sell or supply alcohol to people under the legal drinking age. Additionally, it is a violation to sell or supply alcohol to persons who are already intoxicated. Furthermore, anyone who sells or supplies alcohol to others, whether they are patrons of a tavern or restaurant or guests at a private home, may be held liable in civil court if intoxicated patrons or guests injure or kill themselves or others.

Drinking and driving offences are covered under federal legislation. Criminal law prohibits the operation of a motor vehicle, boat, or aircraft while under the influence of alcohol or other drugs. It is a criminal offence to drive with a blood–alcohol concentration (BAC) over .08 percent (more than 80 mg of alcohol in each 100 mL of blood in one's bloodstream). The *Criminal Code* also authorizes police to obtain breath samples or, in limited circumstances, blood samples, from drivers suspected of drinking. Refusal to comply can result in conviction unless drivers can provide a reasonable excuse. In Ontario, the *Highway Traffic Act* accords police the power to issue a twelve-hour licence suspension for a BAC above .05 percent (more than 50 mg of alcohol per 100 mL of blood).

Drinking and driving is by far the largest criminal cause of injury and death in Canada. In 1999, police charged 73 148 people with impaired driving. This figure represents a very slight increase from 1998 (+0.3 percent) after years of decline (Tremblay, 2000). Several factors account for this overall decrease. First, more severe penalties and higher insurance rates are now attached to convictions for drinking and driving. Second, police now issue roadside suspensions rather than charging drivers with BACs only slightly over the legal limit. Third, agencies have created numerous programs to sensitize drivers to the dangers of drinking and driving and to change their attitudes. Finally, the public has become increasingly intolerant of impaired driving (Tremblay, 2000).

THEORIES OF DRUG ABUSE AND CRIMINALIZATION

Sociological theory provides two types of explanations of drug abuse. One explains why people become drug users. Strain theory accounts for substance abuse by stressing the disjunction between ends and means in contemporary society. Merton (1938) argues that people who reject both the social goal of material well-being and the legitimate means of its attainment are retreatists. They withdraw into the world of drugs. Merton's theory also permits another interpretation of drug abuse. Athletes who use illegal drugs to enhance their competitive performances are innovators who fully embrace the objective of winning but abandon the rules of the game to triumph at all costs. Cloward and Ohlin (1960) introduce into their version of the strain explanation the notion of legitimate and illegitimate opportunity, maintaining that when a person is denied both types of opportunity and lacks prowess as a fighter, he or she will join a retreatist rather than a criminal or conflict subculture. The retreatist, in Cloward's and Ohlin's terms, is a double failure who finds solace in a chemically induced, mind-altered world.

Proponents of the differential association perspective view drug taking as a result of the development, in the peer-group context, of pro-use as opposed to anti-use definitions. People who fall into the company of those already involved in heavy drug use learn the skills and motivations necessary to use a drug and to feel good about it. Finally, control theorists account for involvement in drug use in the same way that they explain other forms of deviance — inadequate social controls or weakened social bonds.

The other approach to theorizing about drugs, and the one that is emphasized in this discussion, explains why the use of certain psychoactive substances is against the law. In this vein, Canadian sociologist Elizabeth Comack (1985) has constructed a Marxist interpretation of the development of Canadian anti-opium legislation.

Comack begins her analysis by noting that one of the state's primary roles is to mediate conflicts between social classes, specifically between capitalists and workers. In capitalist societies, the state has two functions in creating conditions favourable to economic prosperity. First, the state must facilitate "accumulation," the production of profit by the capitalist class. Second, it must ensure that social harmony is maintained through a process Marxists call "legitimation." It is not unusual for the state's two goals to conflict; the balance between facilitating capitalist accumulation and ensuring legitimation is a delicate one.

As capitalism has developed historically, industry has sought to substitute machines for people and to reduce production to its constituent parts. Mechanization and assembly-line piecework have made possible the widespread use of a labour force that is lacking in skill and, as a consequence, is relatively inexpensive. Especially where it is abundant, unskilled labour offers two advantages to capitalists. First, its "reserve army" capacity increases flexibility. Workers can be hired when times are good, fired when times are bad, and re-hired when the economy improves. Second, an oversupply of labour facilitates strike breaking.

Abundant cheap labour is particularly advantageous in resource industries such as logging and mining because these sectors of the economy are labour intensive. Workers' wages are responsible for most of the costs associated with production. The Chinese on the West Coast were a blessing for the capitalist owners of industry because they worked for low wages and were available in endless numbers through immigration. According to Comack, the federal government promoted Chinese immigration, especially during the building of the Canadian Pacific Railway. When the need for inexpensive unskilled labour is high, concern for the immigrant group's moral habits — opium smoking, in this case — is low. While their willingness to work for less and their seemingly infinite numbers were a boon to capitalists, these qualities were a curse for white workers and skilled labour groups. Anti-Asiatic sentiments began to intensify among the latter.

The late nineteenth century was a time when Canadian labour in the West was unionizing in increasing numbers. The unions took anti-Chinese stances partly because their members were racist, but more because they opposed the practice of permitting large numbers of unskilled workers to enter the country from abroad. By the turn of the century, as Comack points out, the situation reached crisis proportions. Militant and increasingly radicalized unions began staging strikes that disrupted the accumulation of capital by industry. Worse still, some of the more radical unions began to espouse socialist platforms.

The British Columbia unions of the time were split into two fundamental groups. While conservative unions opposed the importation of inexpensive and unskilled labour from Asia, the socialist unions were more radical. The more radical elements tended to see the "real problem" not in terms of Chinese immigration but in terms of capitalist exploitation. While they were certainly seeking a better deal from industry, the conservatives were inclined to be more co-operative with their capitalist employers in the long run. As a consequence of their stance, radical socialists became a threat to political and economic stability. Having successfully facilitated capitalist accumulation, the Canadian state was now called upon both to support capitalist interests and to restore social harmony through a process of legitimation.

Comack argues that the opium law was a strategy employed by the state to contain and channel class conflict. With the railway near completion and Chinese labour less essential from the government's point of view, Parliament organized the Royal Commission on Chinese Immigration. About the same time, the conservative unions formed the Asiatic Exclusion League. The league was instrumental in an ensuing riot in 1907. The government defined the riot, in which much Asian property was destroyed, as labour unrest and sent its emissary Mackenzie King to investigate. Faced with a "crisis of legitimacy," wherein social order was threatened, Canadian government officials managed the conflict in such a way as to deflect attention away from the issue of capital–labour conflict. First, they defined the riot as the result of the work of "foreign agitators." Second, they attributed the labour unrest to racial conflict brought about by extensive Asiatic immigration. Third, they cast the Asiatic problem in moral terms by concentrating efforts on the criminalization of opium. By creating anti-opium legislation, the government manufactured a social problem that it subsequently solved by restricting Asiatic immigration.

According to Comack's analysis, the new law deflected attention from the problem of class relations by defining British Columbia's troubles in racist and moral terms. The solution called for strategies of control aimed squarely at Asians. The state's initiative had three effects. First, it undermined the competing and more radical view that the problem lay in class exploitation. The socialist position was delegitimized. Second, the new law limiting Asiatic immigration was a concession to the conservative labour faction, which was most likely to co-operate with the capitalist class in the economic sphere. Third, the government's undertaking nurtured a split, albeit small, between conservative and radical elements of the union movement; union solidarity is never in the best interests of the capitalist class.

THE CONTROL OF DRUGS IN CANADA

Controlling substance abuse is not easy. One strategy is to eliminate the sources of supply; another is to reduce demand. Attacks on the supply side range from legislation and law enforcement through military intervention in drug-producing countries. Demand-reduction initiatives include treatment, counselling, and drug education (Blackwell and Erickson, 1988).

CONTROLLING SUPPLY

Estimates of drug-trade profits are difficult to calculate and subject to exaggeration. Nonetheless, there is little doubt that profits are enormous. The Canadian government estimates the value of the illegal drug market in Canada at between $7 to $10 billion annually (Porteous, 1998; Tremblay, 1999). These figures make it easy to understand how drug barons in Bolivia could become partners with the military in running that country. The revolutionary event precipitating this unique partnership aptly became known as the "cocaine coup." Neither is it surprising that drug kingpins in Colombia once offered to pay off their country's national debt ($13 billion U.S.) in return for immunity from prosecution and from extradition to the United States (Blackwell, 1988a).

Mark-ups on drugs from processing to marketing in the West are dramatic. In 1988, 10 kg of opium in Asia sold for about $1500. Refined into 1 kg of heroin, its value increased to $11 500. Smuggled into Canada, the funds generated by its sale to distributors totalled about $225 000. Cut and sold on the street, the value of the heroin eventually rose as high as $15 million (Francis, 1988b).

Ill-gotten gains as monumental as these make it virtually impossible to control the drug trade. Not only do the enormous profits provide huge incentive, they make it child's play for international and domestic drug dealers to bribe police, customs officers, and government officials.

The Golden Triangle (Myanmar, Thailand, and Laos) provides two-thirds of Canada's illicit heroin. Most of the remainder originates in the Golden Crescent (Iran, Afghanistan, and Pakistan). The Bekaa Valley in Lebanon supplies a significant proportion of Canada's hashish. Much of the cannabis and cocaine making its way into this country comes from remote and inaccessible regions of Latin America (Blackwell, 1988a). These regions figure prominently in drug production because the climatic and growing conditions are ideal and because the economic conditions are near perfect (Blackwell, 1988a). Processing the poppy plant into opium, for example, is a labour-intensive process requiring about 650 hours of work per kilogram. For this kind of production, the optimal economic conditions include an underutilized labour force, low per capita income, and a government lacking the resources to destroy or damage the manufacturing operation. For many source countries, massive poverty and astronomical levels of unemployment make drug-related agriculture both an economic mainstay and a necessity for survival. Agricultural production of this nature is absolutely vital to many Third World economies, and they are unlikely to be enthusiastic about losing it.

The cultivation techniques associated with drug production have become more sophisticated. Harvesting the plants from which illegal drugs are manufactured now involves factory-farming techniques, the use of fertilizer and insecticides, and "double cropping," which involves cultivating two crops yearly — for example, the opium poppy in the spring and hashish in the fall. Another agricultural innovation making its appearance in North America is hydroponics, a combination of chemical and greenhouse techniques that simulates ideal tropical growing conditions (Blackwell, 1988a). As a result of more sophisticated cultivation techniques and technologies, Canadian traffickers can now produce large quantities of high-quality cannabis. This product currently accounts for at least 50 percent of the total Canadian market supply compared to 10 percent in 1985 (Porteous, 1998; Tremblay, 1999).

It is virtually impossible to police drug production at its source in underdeveloped nations, and it is equally challenging to halt its importation into affluent consuming nations. Canada is an immensely large country with a relatively small population, thousands of miles of unguarded border, and an uninhabited coastline. About 36 million foreign visitors enter and leave this country per year. In addition, Canadians make approximately 40 million border crossings each year (Blackwell, 1988a). Although smugglers bring large quantities of illegal drugs into Canada from the

Box 13.10
DRUG-TESTING PLAN VIOLATES RIGHTS, PROVINCE WARNED

The Ontario government's controversial plan to impose mandatory drug testing on welfare recipients is sitting in limbo because the government has been warned it would break the province's Human Rights Code.

Human Rights Commission Keith Norton has advised the government that drug users cannot be denied welfare benefits because an addiction to drugs or alcohol is "a handicap."

In a confidential letter obtained by The Globe and Mail, Mr. Norton said, "Individuals with handicaps or perceived handicaps have a right to equal treatment in services."

And the Ontario Court of Appeal, the province's highest court, has provided muscle to Mr. Norton's argument by ruling late last week that "Substance abusers are handicapped and entitled to the protection of the [Human Rights] Code."

A spokesman for Social Services Minister John Baird indicated that the government has not found a way to get around the Human Rights Code to impose mandatory testing on welfare recipients.

"This is very much a policy in development," Dan Miles said.

But he stressed that the government has not abandoned its intention to test welfare recipients. "The minister has made it perfectly clear the policy will be introduced over the course of the [government's] mandate," which runs for another four years.

He said ministry officials developing the policy on drug testing "will look at" the Appeal Court's ruling and "will take into consideration" Mr. Norton's warning.

But Paul Cavalluzzo, a lawyer who successfully argued before the Appeal Court that drug testing violates the Human Rights Code, said it would be very difficult for the government to impose drug testing contrary to the views of the court and Mr. Norton.

"The highest court in the province has now said that dependence, drug dependence or alcohol dependence, is a handicap and that denying people

the kind of services provided in the [welfare] legislation on the basis of that is discriminatory," Mr. Cavalluzzo said.

One option would be for the government to amend the code. But Mr. Cavalluzzo said this would be unlikely.

The pledge to test welfare recipients was one of several popular promises dealing with welfare in the Progressive Conservative Party's Blueprint book of campaign promises last year.

"You can't get off welfare and hold a job if you're addicted to drugs. That's why we'll provide mandatory treatment for welfare recipients who use drugs.... Those who refuse treatment or who won't take tests on request will lose their benefits," said the pledge, which was enthusiastically promoted by Premier Mike Harris.

This pledge led Mr. Norton to write to Mr. Baird on July 27 last year. He said the pledge "appears to create a requirement that may discriminate against persons with disabilities."

Mr. Baird replied with a letter on Nov. 15. He defended the pledge, arguing: "People with addictions need treatment to give them a chance at dignity, hope and the opportunity of a job. Accordingly, participation in a substance abuse recovery program is considered to meet the participation requirements of Ontario Works [the province's work-for-welfare program]."

But while the government was holding to its pledge on drug testing, the Appeal Court in January heard the case of Entrop v. Imperial Oil. The decision stressed that drug and alcohol abusers cannot be discriminated against.

Discussion Questions

Is addiction a handicap? Should Ontario welfare recipients be tested for drug use and be cut off from benefits if they test positive? Is it true, as the Ontario government suggests, that "you can't get off welfare and hold a job if you're addicted to drugs"?

Source: Richard Mackie, *Globe and Mail*, July 26, 2000, p. A19. Reprinted with permission from the *Globe and Mail*.

United States, many shipments enter Canada directly from other countries. Most of these nations are located in the Middle East and in the Third World. While some illegal drugs are destined for Canadian consumption, Canada also serves as a major trans-

shipment point for the huge market offered by its neighbour to the south (Solomon and Green, 1988).

While most drugs illegally crossing Canadian borders are concealed in the tonnes of imports shipped into this country each year, some substances enter

Box 13.11
SHOULD DRUGS BE LEGALIZED IN CANADA?

This fall [1989], U.S. President George Bush declared a war on illegal drugs. Although the United States has consistently increased its anti-drug spending, Bush's solution was to continue to beef up law enforcement – more police, more jails, stiffer penalties – at a cost of $7.9 billion.

Two years ago Prime Minister Brian Mulroney claimed that we, too, suffer from a "drug epidemic." He offered a five-year program and $210 million to fight the war on drugs.

But at a recent meeting of 39 Canadian mayors and police chiefs, the call was for harsher measures.

Increasingly, some people argue that these kinds of solutions are short-sighted, and only serve to exacerbate a worsening situation. They claim that drugs don't cause the problems; their illegal status does.

"Crime, overdosing, murder, all the tragic effects we hear about, are not because of the drugs," says Walter Block, senior research fellow at the Fraser Institute, a conservative think-tank, "but because of their prohibition.

"In fact, prohibition creates worse dangers than the medical and social ones it is supposedly intended to avert."

The dangers include:

- The creation of a multi-billion-dollar illicit market (a $500 billion industry worldwide).

- High prices, which push users to commit crimes to maintain their habit.

- Impurities in the drugs, which can cause illness and even death.

- A dependence by users on criminals in order to get their drugs.

- Increasing the spread of AIDS through infected needles (about 25 per cent of all AIDS cases in the U.S. and Europe come from illegal intravenous drug use).

- Inhibiting addicts from seeking treatment because they fear reprisals.

- Diverting scarce tax money into increased law enforcement, leaving considerably fewer resources to fight other forms of crime. (In 1986, Ontario spent $263 million on law enforcement fighting illegal drugs. The U.S. equivalent is $8 billion a year.)

- The very real possibility that law enforcement officers will fall prey to graft and corruption.

- Criminalizing users and increasing their disrespect for the law. (In the U.S., illegal drugs are responsible for between 50 per cent and 75 per cent of crime in the cities.)

But advocates make it clear that promoting the idea of legalizing drugs is not the same as condoning their usage.

"I don't approve of drugs; I've never taken drugs or tried any," says American economist Milton Friedman. "But I think they should be legalized because the harm being done by the prohibitionists is vastly greater than the harm being done by users."

Opponents of legalization are quick to point out that legalization is also a dangerous route. Risks include:

- Skyrocketing usage.

- Greater social costs (higher health bills, destruction of families and property damage).

- An undermining of the preventive education message.

- The diversion of organized crime to another destructive business.

"No one in their right mind would suggest that an individual zonked out completely on legally purchased drugs will be a citizen of some respect and put away a propensity to commit crime," says Metro Police Chief Bill McCormack.

"The idea of legalizing drugs is absolutely abhorrent to me. I have never felt so strongly about anything." ...

"Prohibition creates terrific pressure to increase police powers at the expense of fundamental freedoms in society," says Alan Borovoy, general counsel for the association. "It allows police to take shortcuts with our freedoms."

But that's not the only reason why the organization is seriously examining the idea of legalization.

There's also the issue of how coercively paternalistic a democratic state should be. Should the government have the right to invade our medicine cabinets?

And, says Borovoy, "There's the issue of the risks to our civil liberties when you make war on, what has to be, a not insignificant element of the population. After all, making war on drugs is also making war on those who crave them. To what extent does a democracy want to criminalize its own people?"

Legalization advocates point out that ours is a drug-using society. Whether it's prescription drugs, tobacco, alcohol, illegal drugs — even tea and coffee — most people use some kind of stimulant.

And it's clear that denying access simply doesn't work. At least that's what the Americans learned when they tried to prohibit alcohol in the '20s. People still sought it but paid more for it.

And they wanted more bang for their buck — hard liquor, instead of beer or wine. Needless to say, this was also to the advantage of the Mafia-controlled black marketers.

"To me," says Block, "it's much better not to have competition behind the point of a gun. We want peaceful, commercial operations. Alcohol distillers, after all, are now law-abiding, tax-paying citizens."

A key word here is "taxes." If drugs were legal, they could be taxed. And we're not talking peanuts. According to Superintendent Neil Pouliot, drug enforcement director of the RCMP, "the value of black market drugs is a multi-billion dollar business per year. We can't place an exact dollar value on it."

The taxes on a multibillion-dollar product could be used for better education and rehabilitation services.

Yet, in 1986–87, Ontario spent $1.17 billion on excess health care for illegal drug problems, and $472 million for lost labor productivity as a result of illegal drug usage.

Would the money gained from taxing those drugs simply be shifted into coping with the problems of increased usage? Today, in a time of illicit usage, there are 20,000 known heroin addicts in Canada, more than 1 million cocaine users, and an incalculable number of users of marijuana and other drugs.

With legalization, those numbers are bound to increase. The question is, by how much?

"Legalization suggests a transient increase in the use of illegal drugs," says Howard Cappell, director of the social and biological studies division of the Addiction Research Foundation. "But as with the introduction of any forbidden fruit, you usually see an increase, then a decline and a levelling off."

That theory has been borne out in Holland. Holland decriminalized drugs in 1976. (Decriminalization means users don't get a criminal penalty. But large traffickers and people selling to minors can be charged. Legalization, on the other hand, eliminates criminal sanctions on both the use and sale of drugs.)

In Holland, marijuana can be bought in cafes with a cup of coffee. Yet marijuana use by teenagers has dropped from 12 per cent 10 years ago to just 1 per cent today.

And a 1987 household survey in Holland showed that only one-sixth of all residents used marijuana, less than 1 per cent used cocaine and slightly more than 1 per cent used heroin.

Alcohol, however, continued to be the drug of choice: 74 per cent used it.

Canada has considered decriminalization. Sixteen years ago, Gerald Le Dain handed in his report on the non-medical use of drugs. Le Dain recommended that "the sale and use of cannabis (be) placed under controls similar to those governing the sale and use of alcohol, including legal prohibition of unauthorized distribution and analogous age restrictions. ...

This is the crucial question: How much does society pay because the drugs are illegal, and how much does it pay because the drugs themselves are harmful?

"Sure cocaine and crack are harmful," says Aline Akeson, a community worker in Ottawa's inner-city trenches for the past 30 years. "But we have to ask ourselves why people get stoned and drugged."

Working on a daily basis with people mired in poverty, desperate for affordable housing and dependent on food banks to feed their children, Akeson feels she knows some of the answers.

"Pushing drugs is a way of making money for the disenfranchised," she says. "We need to legalize drugs in order to bust the drug industry. Then we need to examine why we're so drugged." ...

More serious questions revolve around such issues as: Which narcotic and psychotropic drugs would be legalized? Who would administer the doses — the state or the individual? Would addicts be allowed as much as they need or only enough to tease? Would we create our own internal sources? Who would set the price?

But even if logic favors legalization, political cowardice knows few boundaries, and informed public opinion is often outweighed by political inaction.

Friedman points out that it's difficult to inform the public when the news media consistently insist on reporting this issue from the perspective of politicians and police.

Discussion Questions

Who are the stakeholders in this debate, and how are they likely to influence a move toward decriminalization? What stand do you take on this issue, and why? Are there any problems with your own position?

Source: Lois Sweet, *Toronto Star*, November 4, 1989, pp. D1 and D6. Reprinted with permission — The Toronto Star Syndicate.

Canada on the persons of travellers. These couriers use methods that reflect varying degrees of ingenuity. Enterprising smugglers have stuffed Jamaican coconuts with contraband substances and hidden drugs in the belongings of innocent tourists. International drug traffickers have also recruited the services of needy welfare recipients, tempting them with a little extra cash for acting as "mules." Some drug importers have even drafted senior citizens as smugglers, assuming that the authorities will neither suspect nor search the elderly (Corelli, 1986).

"Swallowing" is a common way to conceal contraband substances. The "swallower" downs one or more condoms packed with drugs, crosses the border, and then waits for a bowel movement. Afterward, the swallower retrieves the condoms, empties them out, and turns their contents over to distributors. Swallowing is not without its risks, however. If the condom breaks somewhere in the smuggler's digestive tract, the unwanted high is quick, intense, and usually fatal (Barber, 1986).

Limiting the supply of drugs entering Canada is a challenging task. The RCMP drug force contains over a thousand officers. Provincial and municipal forces deploy about the same number of agents in their drug squads (Francis, 1988b). Canada Customs, which captures about 80 percent of the drugs seized in this country, saw the value of confiscated cannabis, heroin, and cocaine rise from $100 million in 1984 to $387 million in 1988 (Dolphin, 1989). In 1999, Customs officials seized $165 million worth of drugs at a single Canadian airport — Pearson International in Toronto. In 1992, Canadian authorities seized 115 081 kg of cannabis, 5285 kg of cocaine, and 85 kg of heroin (McKenzie and Williams, 1997). Advances in international co-operation and inter-agency co-ordination, the acquisition of better equipment, the recruitment of more officers, and the growth in the volume of drugs have combined to account for these increases.

Since the costs incurred by law-enforcement agencies in the fight to limit the supply of drugs have risen enormously, governments in Canada, Australia, and the United States have enacted legislation enabling authorities to appropriate from convicted drug dealers the proceeds of their crimes. From 1983 to 1985, the RCMP's Anti-Drug Profit Program netted over $20 million in cash and assets (Blackwell, 1988a). These sorts of confiscations have led analysts to observe that the trade in illegal drugs is now lucrative enough to finance both sides in the war on drugs.

Organizations illegally importing and distributing drugs are not only affluent, they are adaptable. They quickly replace captured leaders, and when authorities sever international trade routes, drug importers and exporters quickly create new ones. When law-enforcement agents discover one smuggling method, international drug traffickers invent another. If one source of illegal drugs is shut down, drug entrepreneurs develop and tap alternative ones. The immense profits also permit big-time drug smugglers to purchase sophisticated technologies (e.g., airplanes, boats, guns, listening devices) to thwart law enforcement. One of the ironies of successful enforcement is that when supplies are reduced, drugs become more expensive. This rise in price puts some addicts in a tight spot. In some cases, they must commit acquisitive crime more frequently to secure the funds to make purchases. It is more than a little ironic that as prices and profits increase, there is added incentive for more dealers to become involved in the drug trade (Blackwell, 1988a).

Laws to control drug abuse vary around the world. A drug conviction in Malaysia can result in death. In Canada and the United States, fines and imprisonment are the usual punishments. While less draconian, North American legal responses to the drug problem are nonetheless inequitable. Sociologists point out that many control measures, both historically and in current times, have singled out segments of the population that are relatively powerless — certain ethnic groups and the lower classes. Narcotics control in both Canada and the United States began as an effort to contain the Chinese on the western coasts of both countries. Marijuana and cocaine legislation in the United States initially targeted Hispanics and blacks. Recently, American social scientists have argued that the effort to stamp out the current crack "epidemic" is a campaign disproportionately directed against blacks and the poor. The "crack attack," they maintain, is for all intents and purposes a "black attack."

In addition to fortifying interdiction efforts, the Canadian government is amending drug legislation to expand the arsenal of laws available to enforcement agents. One new initiative aims at prohibiting drug dealers from circulating profits through legitimate businesses. These money-laundering endeavours involve between two and four billion dollars yearly in Canada. Recent laws also make it possible for police to freeze bank accounts and to seize vehicles and other assets suspected of having been bought with proceeds from drug sales. Moreover, financial institutions can now legally require clients to identify the sources of large cash deposits, and they are free to provide the RCMP with this information. Formerly, Canadian laws did not permit the seizure of profits already deposited in a bank. Even Switzerland, once the paragon of bank secrecy, is co-operating in the monitoring of drug profits by law-enforcement agencies around the globe (Wood, 1989; Chisholm, 1988).

The United States, as an unwilling and unhappy drug consumer, has vigorously pressured the cultivating countries in the Third World to increase their domestic efforts to eradicate production. The sentiment in many Third World nations, however, is that the drug problem is a crisis for the consuming nations to deal with within their own borders. In past years, major consuming countries have threatened to reduce investment and foreign aid to nations not wholeheartedly joining in the global war on substance abuse. Another strategy of consuming nations, primarily the United States, has been to provide funding and military support to Third World nations like Colombia so that they may more effectively carry out their own attacks on the drug cartels.

Military undertakings have been numerous. Attack helicopters have been used in missions to destroy agricultural and manufacturing operations in several South American countries, including Bolivia and Colombia (Inciardi, 1986). The United States has used surveillance planes and satellites to detect airborne smuggling operations and to estimate the size of drug crops. Acting on the basis of military reconnaissance, foreign governments have implemented battle plans ranging from setting fires to using defoliants. Closer to home, technology is also being used to curb various forms of drug abuse. In Saskatchewan, for example, the province's pharmacies are tracking prescriptions by computer to reduce "double doctoring" (Dolphin, 1989).

Linked to the law-enforcement approach is the introduction of mandatory drug testing (Ellis, 1988). Despite the fact that this strategy is advocated by some interest groups and governments alike, drug testing is unlikely to gain widespread acceptance, for several reasons. First, testing programs are expensive. They may cost between $35 and $250. Regardless of the monetary factor, however, civil libertarians express great concern over the invasion of privacy represented by mandatory testing. Finally, some experts contest the reliability of drug tests, pointing out that errors occur as frequently as half the time. For example, poppy-seed cake and some common-cold capsules can cause people to test positive for heroin and speed, respectively. Similarly, inhaling second-hand marijuana smoke can result in an innocent bystander's testing positive for cannabis (Barber, 1986).

CONTROLLING DEMAND

Curbing drug abuse by attempting to limit the supply of drugs is unlikely to be successful because of the enormous demand for prohibited substances. Reducing demand requires education programs to discourage experimentation with drugs, and treatment and counselling programs to get abusers off substances upon which they are dependent.

In much of their campaign against substance abuse, educators have focused on the perils of taking drugs. Scare tactics have been combined with moralizing to dissuade potential users from partaking of psychoactive substances. Seldom, however, has fantasy been divorced from fact, and the fact is that many drugs can be used sensibly without causing great harm to oneself or to others. Scare tactics have failed because many drug users have seen that predictions of disaster routinely fail to materialize. While more balanced presentations may deter drug use, the utility of education in reducing consumption is unclear. What is certain is that, compared with their support of law-enforcement initiatives, Canadian and American governments have consistently underfunded drug and alcohol education programs.

Drug treatment programs involving both maintenance and aversion have curbed addiction and dependency for some people. In England, until recently, authorities viewed heroin addiction more as a medical than a legal problem (Giffen and Lambert, 1988). Treating addicts on an out-patient basis in heroin maintenance programs, physicians administer just enough of the drug to stave off withdrawal symptoms. This approach enables addicts to avoid involvement in drug cultures and eliminates needle sharing, which in turn limits the spread of HIV. On the other hand, drug maintenance allows drug dependence to continue (Agar and Stephens, 1975).

Another drug maintenance program substitutes methadone for heroin. Methadone has several advantages over heroin. It not only relieves the heroin withdrawal symptoms, but its effects last longer, making it possible for addicts to reduce their overall drug

Box 13.12
SHOULD POLICE TEACH ABOUT DRUGS?

In the turbulent '60s, educators posed the question, Who Educates? This query addresses the heart of the quality and content of the curricula that our school system delivers to our children. Today, the question may be rephrased with some urgency, Who Educates About Drugs?

Increasingly, the answer appears to be the police.

The police are already a presence in our schools, and the Canadian Association of Chiefs of Police plans to raise $14 million to implement an educational program in schools. In the understandable urge to counteract drug misuse, education is often viewed as an important preventive strategy. But is it appropriate that the police should be the educators? There are several reasons why this may not be appropriate.

First, the ability of the police to design and deliver effective drug education may be questionable. Boards of education and police departments in many jurisdictions have traditionally co-operated in efforts to deliver road safety instruction. To teach traffic safety and rules of the road to budding cyclists in order to prevent or reduce accidents is a fairly straightforward and laudable objective.

To my knowledge, police effectiveness as educators in this and other areas has not been evaluated. The automatic extension of police involvement into other areas that are much more difficult and complex may therefore not be warranted. For instance, the Lewis Task Force recently raised doubts about the ability of the police to conduct suitable instruction on race relations for its own members.

Current knowledge regarding drugs arises from a variety of highly specialized disciplines. In most of these areas the "facts" are, in fact, unclear but require expert interpretation.

Second, the police do not normally assume a mandate for education regarding all activities that are subject to criminal sanctions or prohibition. Such knowledge about law-abiding behavior is usually acquired by children at various stages, from a variety of sources including parents, other family, teachers, peers and others. The police are only one of the possible influences.

A third concern is the inherent conflict between the primary role of the police as law enforcers and any role they might play in education about illicit drugs.

Police have the power to arrest and to use force if necessary. This clearly sets police apart. Even in situations of conflict or disruption in the community which do not result in the laying of charges, it is often the implicit authority of the police presence which restores order. How then can the police reasonably be expected to deliver any message about drug use other than "thou shalt not"?

No matter how skilled the presentation, the ultimate delivery implies "and if you do, you will be punished." The police have a vital role in society, to maintain order. Is it wise to confuse this with other roles that are already occupied by social workers, teachers, psychologists, pharmacologists, physicians, or others?

We do not encourage the police to lecture children about the risks of alcohol and tobacco. We would be skeptical about permitting the tobacco and alcohol industries to fund educational programs for the schools. We would also likely hesitate to assign the role of creators or deliverers of such programs to representatives of these legal drug industries.

Yet the police establishment does have a vested interest in the continuation of anti-drug distribution activities. Their traditional role in the drug area has been on the side of supply reduction. If the preventive strategies like education – regardless of who conducts it – were totally successful in eliminating demand, what would it mean for the police bureaucracies devoted to supply enforcement? Would they disappear?

At the national level, the RCMP and other forces continue to receive substantial monies to improve interdiction efforts. In Metro, police arguments for more resources needed for street level enforcement were successful in obtaining 97 new officers. To recognize the sincerity of individual officers who are concerned with the adverse effects of drug misuse on young persons does not deny a real and fundamental conflict of interest at the institutional level.

Just as important as who delivers drug education are the objectives of the drug education program. These must be clear and achievable, and be capable of evaluation. Is the goal to be the prevention of all illicit drug experimentation, to delay it, to teach responsible use, or to minimize harmful use by those already using?

Clearly, there may be considerable disagreement about these goals. Also, the target groups for education must be determined. Various types of programs would be required according to the age, experience and other characteristics of the children.

Who will determine the objectives and principles of police drug education programs, and are police educators willing to commit the resources required for such a complex educational pursuit?

What we do know is there are three possible outcomes of any kind of program: improvement, no change or harm.

Reviews of existing programs have indicated that it is possible to make things worse; in other words, drug use has shown an increase after some programs, possibly by glamorizing the risks or simply provoking curiosity. If programs have no effect, this may mean that scarce resources have been wasted. Even if the programs are beneficial, without proper evaluation, it will not be possible to know why and thus duplicate the effort elsewhere. Thus, no matter who designs and implements the programs, it is vital that careful screening and thorough assessment of their impacts be conducted.

Many of these concerns could also be raised about various private sector groups which are competing for drug education dollars. It is also clear that education aimed at preventing drug misuse is potentially an important component of any overall strategy to reduce drug problems in Canadian society.

Education carries a tacit recognition that the reality of drug use must be addressed. The sole reliance on prohibition and the coercive threats and penalties that accompany it are not enough. Educational approaches recognize the need to discuss, to persuade, to consider alternative styles of coping with stress and boredom, and to practice ways to "say no."

Since most students do not even try illicit drugs, and fewer still go on to become regular users, it is also important that available resources are used wisely where they are needed most. The challenge is to determine not just "what works?", but why it is effective, and for whom, in what situations, and whether it can be made more effective. There are many concerned and creative educators at work on this issue in our communities. The police can provide important input, but is it their role to be contributors or determiners of drug education?

Discussion Questions

Should police teach the public about drugs? If not, who should do the job? What problems might arise from giving this responsibility to teachers in elementary and secondary schools?

Source: P.G. Erickson, *Toronto Star*, May 7, 1989, p. C3. Reprinted with permission from the author.

intake. Methadone also has a "blockading" effect, in that it blocks the heroin high, and it can be taken orally, thus circumventing the need for injection. Finally, methadone treatment does not require hospitalization (Stephens, 1987). In the early years of methadone's use, physicians thought that addicts could be more easily weaned away from methadone than from heroin. They now realize that methadone may be as addictive, if not more addictive, than heroin. Like heroin maintenance, methadone substitution does little to eliminate addiction. Furthermore, some methadone makes its way onto the black market for sale to addicts on the street (Agar and Stephens, 1975).

In aversion treatments, health-care workers use "behaviour modification" techniques that expose drug dependents to some unpleasant experience. The association of a drug with a discomforting reaction is intended to deter its use. Physicians, for example, administer chemicals to alcoholics that have the effect of inducing nausea when alcohol is ingested. The success of aversion programs in the long term remains uncertain.

Counselling and psychotherapy are major non-chemical strategies for drug and alcohol treatment. Therapeutic sessions involve groups of individuals with a similar drug dependency. Some counselling efforts include not only drug-dependent persons but their families as well. It is becoming more common for employers to offer these counselling services to employees who are problem drinkers or drug abusers.

One of the most popular and most effective approaches to curbing substance abuse is the self-help organization. Among the better known are Alcoholics Anonymous (AA), Alanon, and Narcanon. The objective of self-help strategies is for recovering addicts and alcoholics to provide one another with the extensive social supports necessary to encourage abstention from drugs and alcohol (Maxwell, 1984; Tournier, 1979; Yablonski, 1965). Veterans of the group encourage neophytes to develop attitudes and norms that deter substance abuse. Group members make themselves available to provide support to compatriots who are in danger of "falling off the wagon." For long-term group members in leadership and training roles, "retroflexive reformation" bolsters the conversion from a life of substance abuse to a life free of dependency. For example, veteran alcoholics who instruct recent AA recruits must internalize AA's anti-drinking norms before they can pass them on to others. Retroflexive reformation also provides the reformed with added resistance to a backward slide (Cressey, 1955).

Self-help groups seem to be effective in achieving their goals. However, those who join and remain in these networks are usually very determined to succeed before they become group members. Self-help-group supports may be much less effective for those whose commitment to a drug-free life is less intense (Ohlin, 1980).

A final response to the problems posed by illegal drugs deserves mention. Most of the drug-control efforts by Canada and the United States have involved some form of police action to limit supply. However, the massive public demand for illegal psychoactive substances has rendered these crime-control measures less than successful. In the face of continual failure, some experts and laypersons argue for the decriminalization of at least some illegal drugs (Solomon, Single, and Erickson, 1988). In the United States, for example, some states have legalized the possession of small amounts of marijuana.

Advocates of decriminalization maintain that it would have several positive effects. It would shrink the black market, reduce the power of organized crime, cut the costs of crime control, limit the corruption of criminal justice officials, reduce the number of people in jails, and lower the number of people with criminal records. It would also increase public faith in the law and in the criminal justice system by eliminating some unenforceable laws around which there is little consensus. Moreover, decriminalization would permit the police to concentrate on catching truly dangerous criminals. Finally, it would increase tax revenues because drugs could be taxed by governments in the same way that alcohol and cigarettes are now taxed.

Opponents of decriminalization counter these arguments by pointing out that the legal but addictive drugs alcohol and nicotine wreak the greatest havoc in society. The legalization of other substances like pot and coke would only escalate the devastation

wrought by these drugs to levels now registered by alcohol and tobacco (Blackwell and Erickson, 1988).

The furor over the drug problem makes it unlikely that significant decriminalization will occur, and it is equally unlikely that limiting supply or reducing demand will stem the use of psychoactive substances (Inciardi, 1986). The most sensible policy may be to develop ways of living with drugs that minimize serious harm to both users and those around them.

SUMMARY

A widespread perception exists among Canadians that the drug problem is a constantly escalating crisis that warrants counteraction on a scale approaching all-out war. At issue is the abuse of psychoactive substances that affect the functioning of the brain and central nervous system. The reality of the drug scene is not what it appears. Concern over the misuse of psychoactive drugs is cyclical — rising to fever pitch on some occasions, and at other times taking a back seat to pressing social problems.

The term "abuse," while widely used, is not simply defined and varies tremendously in meaning. It can refer to both legal and prohibited substances and can mean overuse, nonmedical use, physical addiction, psychological dependence, or some combination of all these conditions. It can also signify the peril associated with the use of a particular substance, or it can identify the taking of a drug prohibited by law. Regardless of terminology, however, the damage wrought upon humanity by illegal drugs such as heroin and cocaine pales in comparison with that done by legal substances such as alcohol and nicotine.

A number of misconceptions distort the image of the drug problem. These include the belief that certain drugs quickly enslave first-time users, that certain drugs operate as a gateway to the use of more addictive substances, that other forms of crime are heavily fuelled by the acquisitive needs of addicts, and that evil-hearted pushers bear considerable responsibility for any increases in the numbers of users. While these claims are greatly exaggerated, this does not mean that drug abuse is without negative consequences. Indeed, the misuse of legal and illegal psychoactive substances is costly to Canadians in many ways. Drug abuse in Canada is linked to people's experiences of violent crime, accident, drug-induced disease, fetal addiction, the spread of AIDS, and death. Drug abuse brings about losses in economic productivity and results in enormous financial consequences because governments must pay the costs of law enforcement, prison expansion, and health care. The black market created by the demand for prohibited drugs is a major source of income for organized crime.

There are several different types of drug user, exemplified by a sequence of stages through which people pass on their way to compulsive drug use. Experimental users take drugs only occasionally. Recreational users employ psychoactive substances as a part of their social interactions on special occasions. Situational users take drugs to help them cope with the trying circumstances of life that arise from time to time. Intensified users are situational users for whom drugs are a routine way of dealing with problems. For compulsive users, drugs are the dominant force in their social worlds.

Drugs can be classified into three fundamental groups. Stimulants such as nicotine, amphetamine, and cocaine make people alert, while depressants such as alcohol and heroin leave users feeling relaxed. Both produce feelings of euphoria. Hallucinogens such as LSD and PCP produce distortions in sensory perception. Cannabis highlights the variation of the social experience of drug taking; it can produce the symptoms of a stimulant, a depressant, or a hallucinogen.

There are two basic approaches to the sociological explanation of drug abuse. In the first, sociologists account for why some people become dependent or addicted while others do not. On this theme, several positivist theories of deviance and crime were discussed. For anomie theory, the process involves retreat. For differential association, the key variables are peer involvements and the development of pro-deviance definitions of the situation. For social control theory, people become involved in drug abuse because they are insufficiently bonded to society or because they are not deterred by the potential penalties of this form of lawbreaking.

The other approach is to explain why some drugs are prohibited by law while others are not. An example of this perspective is a Marxist theory of the criminalization of narcotics use in Canada. This analysis argues that what was essentially a class-based conflict in British Columbia around the turn of the century was transformed and responded to as a problem of race and morality. Through these means, the government preserved order and accommodated capitalist accumulative interests.

Two fundamental strategies exist for limiting drug abuse: controlling supply and controlling demand. Supply is difficult to control because demand is intense and the value of the illicit market is monumental. Moreover, dollars from the drug trade play an important role in the economies of producing countries in the Third World. Criminal organizations marketing banned substances are well equipped, innovative, and very adaptable. Moreover, they use modern agricultural technology and growing techniques to cultivate drug crops, making production both efficient and hard to eliminate.

The main strategies for reducing the public's demand for drugs are education and treatment. Education programs, especially in the past, have tended to be moralistic and have been guilty of presenting inaccurate information. Education programs, both past and present, are dramatically underfunded in comparison with programs aimed at reducing supply through crime control. Treatment programs are of two types — chemical and counselling. Some chemical strategies involve drug maintenance, while others involve behaviour modification based upon drug-aversion techniques. Treatment through counselling usually takes the form of either advice and direction from helping professions, such as social work, psychology, or psychiatry, or membership in a supportive peer group like Alcoholics Anonymous.

Another more radical approach to the problems posed by drug abuse involves the decriminalization of many if not all drug offences. Proponents point to failed but costly crime-control initiatives, the solid entrenchment of organized crime in the illegal drug trade, and growing prison populations as evidence for their position. Decriminalization would free up more funds for much-needed and more appropriate education and treatment programs. Critics respond to the decriminalization movement by noting that society's major problems involve legal drugs and argue that legalizing more drugs is not the answer to effective control.

DISCUSSION QUESTIONS

1. Discuss the personal and societal costs of the "drug problem." Which of these costs are the most damaging?

2. How rational is Canada's current drug policy? What changes in policy would you advocate, and why?

3. The government of Canada, following the lead of the United States, launched a "war" on drugs. The term "war" evokes powerful imagery. Can such a war be won? Are the costs of such a war justified? Support your arguments.

4. What strategies could be developed to control the use of each of the following drugs: alcohol, cocaine, tobacco, marijuana? Why and how would the chosen strategies resemble or differ from one another?

5. How is the drug problem related to other forms of criminal activity? Consider both the law-enforcement perspective and the insights into the creation and application of law that are provided by conflict theories.

WEB LINKS

Canada's Drug Strategy
http://www.hc-sc.gc.ca/hppb/cds-sca/cds/index.html
This Web site, maintained by Health Canada, contains papers and reports, fact sheets, statistics, and surveys on many topics, as well as links to other organizations.

Canadian Centre on Substance Abuse
http://www.ccsa.ca
CCSA is a non-profit organization working to minimize the harm associated with the use of alcohol, tobacco, and other drugs. The Web site offers access to hundreds of reports, articles, statistics, and more. For a discussion of costs of substance abuse in Canada, go to http://www.ccsa.ca/costhigh.htm.

Canadian Foundation for Drug Policy
http://www.cfdp.ca
CFDP's site includes news updates, articles on drug policy and drug use, and information on Canada's past and present drug laws.

Addiction and Mental Health
http://www.camh.net
The Centre for Addiction and Mental Health in Toronto offers resources related to mental health and addiction, including drug and alcohol abuse.

RCMP's Drug Awareness Service
http://www.rcmp-grc.gc.ca/das/default_e.htm
This site contains information on the drug abuse prevention programs of the Royal Canadian Mounted Police, including a brief section on the role of police in preventing abuse.

RECOMMENDED READINGS

Adler, P. (1985). *Wheeling and Dealing: An Ethnography of an Upper-Level Dealing and Smuggling Community*. New York: Columbia University Press.
An interesting account of drug use and dealing in the upper echelons of American society.

Alexander, B. (1990). *Peaceful Measures: Canada's Way Out of the "War on Drugs."* Toronto: University of Toronto Press.
Examines drug policy in Canada and suggests alternatives to courses of action emphasizing law enforcement.

Blackwell, J.C., and Patricia G. Erickson. (1988). *Illicit Drugs in Canada: A Risky Business*. Scarborough: Nelson.
Contains readings on a variety of aspects of illicit drugs, treatment, and control in Canada.

Boyd, N. (1991). *High Society: Legal and Illegal Drugs in Canada*. Toronto: Key Porter.
A highly engaging analysis of drugs in Canadian society.

Currie, E. (1993). *Reckoning: Drugs, the Cities, and the American Future*. New York: Hill and Wang.
Discussion of the impacts of the drug trade and its criminalization on urban America and its minority residents.

Ericson, P.G., D.M. Riley, I.W. Chung, P.O. Hare. (1997). *Harm Reduction: A New Direction for Drug Policies and Programs*. Toronto: University of Toronto Press.
Delineates the collateral harm generated by current efforts to prohibit drug abuse. Discusses means by which substance-related harm might be reduced or minimized without necessarily requiring complete abstinence.

Inciardi, J.A. (1991). *The Drug Legislation Debate*. Newbury Park, CA: Sage.
Provides a coherent discussion of arguments for and against the legalization of drugs in America.

Jensen, E.L. and J. Gerber. (1998). *The New War on Drugs: Symbolic Politics and Criminal Justice Policy*. Cincinnati, OH: Anderson.
Presents a sociological critique of drug control policy with emphasis on social constructionism, the role of the media, and political opportunism. Examines control efforts in several countries and explores the prospects for "harm reduction" as an emerging strategy.

Saggers, S. and D. Gray. (nd) *Dealing with Alcohol: Indigenous Usage in Australia, New Zealand, and Canada*. Melbourne: Cambridge University Press.
Discusses deleterious effects of excessive alcohol consumption by indigenous peoples primarily in Australia but also in Canada and New Zealand. Focuses on the roles of colonialism and capitalism in which indigenous and non-indigenous relationships are formed. Provides suggestions for the development of effective policy.

Taylor, A. (1993). *Women Drug Users: An Ethnography of a Female Injecting Community*. New York: Clarendon Press.
Examines women's involvement in illicit drug use in America.

CHAPTER 14

ORGANIZED CRIME

The aims of this chapter are to familiarize the reader with:

- stereotypes of organized crime
- problems in defining organized crime
- the social and economic costs of organized crime
- sources of information on underworld activity in Canada
- two views of organized crime: the syndicate and the confederation
- the historical development of organized crime in Canada
- organized crime groups: Italian, Asian, Colombian, and outlaw motorcycle gangs
- organized crime activities: strategic crime, illegal business, and legal business
- the "queer ladder of mobility" and ethnic succession as a theory of organized crime
- issues surrounding the control of organized crime

INTRODUCTION

For years, organized crime has fuelled an industry of novels, movies, and television shows. It has sold countless newspapers, magazines, and biographies, and has drawn large audiences for investigative news reports and documentaries. Widely publicized police reports and the occasional public inquiry have also embellished popular images of organized crime. Blazing machine guns hastily drawn from violin cases and gangsters with heavy Italian accents are two prevalent stereotypes.

Most Canadians think of organized crime as an underworld monopoly controlled by a powerful group

of Italians through a national syndicate with international connections. According to popular belief, this sinister organization, called the Mafia or La Cosa Nostra, first rose to prominence during the Prohibition era in the United States, later spread to Canada, and now controls many illegal operations within this country's borders. The very word "Mafia" brings to mind the wholesale use of violence to monopolize gambling, prostitution, pornography, and the drug trade. Finally, there is widespread belief that organized crime touches only a few Canadians who live in the poorer districts of the country's large cities.

This chapter begins by assessing the validity of popular images of organized crime. It examines the controversies surrounding what "organized" crime means and explores the social and economic costs of underworld activity. The adequacy of information about criminal organizations is evaluated, and two competing views about the nature of their organization are outlined. The chapter discusses the development of organized crime in North America, the nature of the groups involved, and the range of illegal businesses in which they engage. The theory of ethnic succession is outlined, and its roots to anomie theory are traced. The chapter concludes by examining the problems associated with controlling organized crime in Canada.

STEREOTYPES OF ORGANIZED CRIME

Many social scientists contend that popular images of organized crime are inaccurate. First, rather than being an alien conspiracy, contemporary organized crime is largely a product of North American society and its capitalistic, profit-oriented economy. Many of the founders of now-respected North American families initially established their fortunes through devious, unethical, and at times illegal means, and many of North America's commercial empires rest on these foundations (Tyler, 1981; Bell, 1962). Second, criminologists dispute the notion that organized criminal actions are orchestrated by a national or international syndicate. They claim that while organized crime itself is real, the syndicate is a fiction promoted by police forces and the courts to garner public support for the expansion of criminal law and the escalation of crime-control initiatives (Rhodes, 1984).

Third, far from involving only disreputable people, organized crime adversely affects almost everyone. Some of its activities are illegal, but many are not. On one hand, the enormous success of criminal organizations is rooted in the extensive demand from virtually all segments of society for some illegal goods and services, such as gambling, illicit sex, and drugs. On the other hand, much of the commerce of organized crime is perfectly legal. It includes restaurants, garbage-disposal companies, legal gambling casinos, stocks and bonds, trucking firms, and hotel chains. The line differentiating legitimate businesses from those run by organized crime groups is becoming increasingly difficult to decipher (Rhodes, 1984).

DEFINING ORGANIZED CRIME

Organized crime is vaguely conceived in Canadian criminal law, and simply being a member of a criminal organization is not illegal in this country. Canadian police officially state that organized crime occurs where two or more persons consort together on a continuing basis to participate in illegal activities, either directly or indirectly, for gain (Dubro, 1985). This statement begs a question. Does any profit-oriented crime or series of crimes perpetrated through the co-ordinated activities of members of a group represent organized criminal activity? If this is the case, could one not classify as an organized crime group a crew of pickpockets, the Hells Angels, the T. Eaton Company, Shell Canada, and the Montreal-based Cotroni family with its supposed connections to the Mafia in the United States? All of these organizations have been convicted of offences under Canadian law.

The difficulties of developing an adequate definition stem from two sources. First, the groups involved display tremendous diversity. Second, criminal organizations engage in many commercial activities, not all of which are against the law. Only slightly more refined is the definition developed by the Bureau of Alcohol, Tobacco, and Firearms in the United States. The Bureau says that organized crime is composed of self-perpetuating, structured, and disciplined associations of individuals or groups that combine together for the purpose of obtaining monetary or commercial gains or profits, wholly or partly by illegal means. Central to this definition is the observation that criminal organizations protect their activities through graft and corruption (Stamler, 1987). References to graft and corruption, at least insofar as they refer to the bribing of law-enforcement officials, might exclude some the groups mentioned above.

At the other end of the continuum are the less formal and more encompassing definitions offered by organized crime figures themselves. Vincent Teresa, for example, offered the following observations to interviewers during the CBC documentary series "Connections," first broadcast in 1977. Referring to the nature of organized crime, Teresa claimed "It is just a bunch of people getting together to take all the money they can from all the suckers they can" (Dubro, 1985:4).

Rather than attempt a precise definition, some criminologists have opted for describing the major traits of organized crime groups and their activities (Abadinsky, 1985). Organized crime groups display a hierarchical division of labour differentiated in terms of authority and expertise. Some positions in the structure command more power than others, and some posts are defined exclusively by their specialized tasks. These specialties include enforcing the rules, fixing bribes, and moving money. The organizational structure of crime groups is often complex. Strict codes of behaviour govern conduct and insulate the leadership from apprehension and prosecution. Unlike bureaucracies involved in legitimate business, communication among members of organized crime groups is almost always by word of mouth and is rarely documented.

The actions of organized crime groups are conspiratorial and shrouded in secrecy. These criminal organizations are self-perpetuating; when members leave as a result of retirement, imprisonment, or death, organizations quickly replace them and business continues. Criminal organizations routinely restrict membership in at least two ways. First, organized criminals are virtually all male, and second, criminal groups recruit on the bases of kinship, ethnicity, or possession of a criminal record. The admission of initiates to the inner circles, when it occurs, normally involves a trial period of apprenticeship under the direction of a sponsor who is also a group member in good standing. Criminal organizations usually hold the sponsor responsible for the actions of the recruit.

The business activities of organized crime involve the rational pursuit of economic goals. Crime groups provide illegal and legal goods and services to meet public demand. As with legitimate commercial enterprises, criminal organizations expend considerable energy in developing monopolies to augment their already considerable profits. Criminal monopolies are based on either geographic or sector dominance. In the former case, a single group in one region controls all organized crime businesses, ranging from pornography to "numbers" games. In the case of sector dominance, rather than control all business in a particular location, a single group holds a geographically widespread monopoly over a specific illegal activity, such as the manufacture and distribution of prohibited synthetic drugs.

Organized crime uses two illegal strategies to develop, maintain, and expand markets and to protect them from the incursion of law-enforcement agencies: extortion (the threat and application of violence) and corruption. Criminal organizations use violence to acquire customers and eliminate informers, witnesses, and troublesome police officers. Through corrupt practices, crime groups entice corporations and labour unions to do business while persuading police officers, judges, and politicians to look the other way.

THE COSTS OF ORGANIZED CRIME

Organized crime has many victims, including governments, legitimate businesses and industries, consumers, workers, and citizens in general. Not only are these victims numerous, but the harm inflicted on them physically, economically, psychically, and morally is monumental. Organized crime deprives governments of billions of dollars in lost taxes, in the costs of law enforcement and criminal prosecution, and in the price of treating and rehabilitating those addicted to illegal drugs. One government study released in 1983 estimated the costs of Canadian organized crime conservatively at $10 billion annually (Beare, 1996). Governments also suffer because citizens lose faith in

political systems that create unenforceable morality laws and subsequently become riddled with corruption (Abadinsky, 1985; Reuter, 1984).

Organized crime, because it enjoys an unfair competitive edge in many markets, routinely drives legitimate industries out of business. Resources available to organized crime that are not available to legitimate businesses include the use of untaxed capital, the employment of labour at illegally low wages, the sale of stolen merchandise at bargain prices, and the ability to use extortion against workers and customers. Moreover, organized criminals routinely dupe legitimate companies into extending long lines of credit to crime-controlled establishments. These legitimate businesses suffer enormous losses through planned bankruptcy and stock fraud. Criminal organizations regularly cost insurance companies enormous sums of money through arson, large-scale merchandise thefts, and hijacking. Furthermore, the mob victimizes workers when corrupted union leaders knowingly negotiate disadvantageous labour contracts or facilitate the theft of union pension funds (Abadinsky, 1985; Rhodes, 1984).

The illegal practices of organized crime also harm Canadians in less visible ways. Citizens pay higher taxes as "sales tariffs" on the inflated values of many goods and services. They also pay higher property and income taxes to support law-enforcement efforts aimed at criminal organizations. Also deleterious to the Canadian public is the potential for the erosion of their own civil liberties. The introduction of intrusive laws intended to apprehend organized criminals is risky because these laws may be used against any suspected lawbreaker. Finally, the initiatives of organized crime can be deadly. Every year in North America, crime groups directly and indirectly injure and kill a large number of people, some of whom are innocent bystanders. Some are the targets of assassinations, some die by accident in shootouts, some overdose on drugs, and some burn to death in deliberately set fires. The lives of future generations are also at risk, as organized crime branches out into schemes such as the unsafe but inexpensive disposal of hazardous toxic wastes (Block and Scarpitti, 1985).

SOURCES OF INFORMATION ON ORGANIZED CRIME IN CANADA

For the business of criminal organizations to operate efficiently, it must be carried on unobtrusively and in

Box 14.1
CANADA A 'WELCOME WAGON' FOR CRIME

Canada has become one of the world's most important hubs for global crime syndicates, an acclaimed authority on organized crime warned a summit of senior police and government officials yesterday.

"Law enforcement officials everywhere agree that Canada is ... the hub of international drug trafficking, organized fraud and corresponding money-laundering operations by many crime syndicates," said Antonio Nicaso, a lecturer in organized crime and author of nine books on criminal gangs.

"Canada has always been a welcome wagon for organized crime; a revolving door that lets everyone in regardless of their criminal past, he said. "As other countries begin cracking down on organized crime figures, Canada is quickly becoming an easy mark for criminals; a key entry point for Asian heroin and Colombian cocaine headed for the North American market."

As anecdotal evidence, Mr. Nicaso read the transcript of a conversation, recorded by police, between Alfonso Caruana, a powerful Mafia boss serving a 14-year prison term in Canada, and a drug trafficker: "Canada, for wanted people, is the safer place to live," Caruana said. "Here there is much lower risk of detention and prosecution than in the United States or Europe."

The annual take from organized crime in Canada is in the hundreds of millions of dollars, Mr. Nicaso said, and the country is widely considered a source country for marijuana, speed and designer drugs, largely controlled by organized crime. He said there are 18 criminal organizations with international links working in Canada.

Mr. Nicaso was invited to speak at the summit, organized by the government of Ontario and attended by the attorneys-general of Ontario, P.E.I. and New Brunswick, as well as senior policy-makers and police officials from several countries, to help law enforcement agencies better combat organized crime.

Mr. Nicaso is a consultant on organized crime for the FBI, the RCMP and Italian police. He sits on the advisory board of the Nathanson Centre for the Study of Organized Crime and Corruption at York University in Toronto, and on the governing council of the Alliance Against Contraband in Geneva, Switzerland.

He attacked the federal government's anti-gang legislation, Bill C-95, as ineffectual. The bill defines organized crime as a group of five or more criminals acting together.

"If four Hells Angels work together in a drug trafficking ring, does the absence of the fifth member mean it is not a criminal organization?" he asked.

The bill's landmark test case, against members of a native street gang in Winnipeg, spent more than a year in court.

"Rather than dealing with organized criminal activity it merely shows the government's ineffectiveness and ignorance. The act, passed in 1997, has yet to score a single big hit and, in my personal opinion, is doomed to failure."

After Mr. Nicaso's comments left the audience in awkward silence, Giuliano Zaccardelli, Deputy Commissioner of the RCMP, defended the federal record.

"I just want to remind everyone that Canada is a very safe place to live and, with all due respect to our guests, is the best country in the world to live. The threat is very real but we have done very well up to now," he said.

However, Deputy Commissioner Zaccardelli agreed that significant changes are needed to meet the challenges of organized crime.

"Unless we are able to create a seamless body of police forces across the world, working with one another, we are not going to succeed, because the enemy has already done this," he said. "We've been given a lot of tools. But [Bill] C-95 is not the answer to everything."

James Flaherty, Attorney-General of Ontario, said he is drafting legislation for presentation this fall that will allow the use of civil law to pursue assets before a criminal conviction is registered.

"We intend to be the first jurisdiction in Canada to use civil law to take the profit out of unlawful enterprises," said Mr. Flaherty.

"We want to say to organized crime that if you have gained property in Ontario through the proceeds of crime, you don't own it, have no ownership rights to it. It belongs to the people of Ontario."

He said the current Criminal Code provisions for seizing the proceeds of crime after a successful prosecution "hasn't done very well in terms of discouraging organized crime in Canada."

Asset forfeiture occurs so many years after charges are laid that it is "a meaningless deterrent," Mr. Flaherty said.

He also promised to fund special forces of police officers, forensic accountants and special prosecutors to attack the growing organized crime problem in Ontario.

Mr. Nicaso had several suggestions for the policy-makers, including:

- Creating a national, integrated policing strategy that sees all related agencies working as one to attack gangsters;

- Enacting a broad law, similar to the U.S. Racketeering Influenced and Corrupt Organizations (RICO) statute, that helps government agencies dismantle an entire criminal enterprise;

- Directing the courts to pay special attention to mobsters, including additional sentences for criminal association and eliminating parole for drug traffickers;

- Entrenching a better definition of organized crime in federal law;

- Vigorously seizing criminal assets and giving the money to police to fund the fight against organized crime.

Discussion Questions

Mr. Nicaso makes several recommendations for improving the effectiveness of the fight against organized crime. How valid are the measures he advocates? Are they likely to function as intended? At what cost?

Source: Adrian Humphreys and Chris Eby, *National Post*, August 3, 2000, pp. A1 and A6. Reprinted with permission from the *National Post*.

secret. As a result, much of the literature on organized crime is unsystematic and incomplete. Much of the data comes from law-enforcement investigations, from journalists relying on small pools of informants, and from the biographers of organized crime figures. The principal problem with the latter two sources of data is that many reported facts cannot be independently substantiated. Empirical research on organized crime carefully executed by trained social scientists is rare on the whole, and virtually nonexistent in Canadian criminology.

Perhaps the most complete sources of data about organized crime in Canada are the reports of several commissions investigating mob activity in Ontario and Quebec. They were generated by the Roach Commission on gambling in Ontario during the early 1960s, the Waisberg Commission on the Ontario construction industry in the early 1970s, and the Quebec Commission on Organized Crime in the late 1970s.

Other sources of information include the many smaller-scale police investigations that have been carried out in Canada over the years. One such case involved a listening device planted behind a milk cooler in a dairy operated by Montreal crime figure Paolo Violi. Facts acquired from this bug confirmed the existence of connections between a Quebec Mafia organization, the Cotroni family, and one of the major New York crime families, headed by Joseph Bonanno. The device also provided the police with intimate details concerning mob leadership disputes, robberies, and murders (Dubro, 1985). Another famous police investigation, this time in Ontario during the early 1970s, resulted in the arrest of Francesco Caccamo on a firearms charge. In a search of Caccamo's residence, police discovered a 27-page document that was an authentic description of an ancient ritual practised by a secret Italian criminal organization. Popularly known as the "Caccamo papers," these documents provided conclusive evidence, in the eyes of law-enforcement officials at least, of the existence in Canada of the "Honoured Society," otherwise known as the "Sidernese Mafia" (Dubro, 1985).

Journalistic efforts have played a large part in developing the picture of organized crime in Canada. In the late 1970s, the documentary "Connections," aired on CBC, described Canadian Mafia groups and provided considerable detail on their connections, their activities, and the potential for mob conflict. A hooded figure named "Lou," who worked for Toronto crime boss Paul Volpe, explained the sources of strain at the time among competing segments of the Mafia:

The old group (headed by Paul Volpe) never believes in bombing bakeries or blowing up cars, but these new Italian immigrants coming to Canada, they came here and they brought along with them traces of narcotics, whereas the old group never got involved in narcotics. This new group, we've learned that they are smuggling narcotics into Canada. There have been many arrests if you look in the papers. You see these Italian names and it is none of the old group. The old group are still trying to control Toronto and it is very difficult with the new group sabotaging out at the west end, and the old group does not do that kind of work (Dubro, 1985:113).

The tensions described by Lou later erupted into open gang warfare in southern Ontario.

Perhaps the most famous informant in the history of organized crime in Canada is Cecil Kirby. Kirby, who initially worked as an enforcer and hit man for the Commisso family of Toronto, eventually became a key prosecution witness in the Crown's case against that group. His testimony resulted in the convictions of the three Commisso brothers (Kirby and Renner, 1986).

Since police forces have their vested interests in how organized crime is perceived, since informants may know less than they let on, and since journalists may emphasize evidence that they consider most newsworthy and of greatest interest, much of the information about the origins, structure, and activities of organized crime in Canada is tentative, uncertain, and insufficiently documented. The picture is only partial.

TWO VIEWS OF ORGANIZED CRIME

Researchers disagree about the extent of organization exhibited by groups involved in underworld activities. One view contends that organized crime is a highly co-ordinated and systematic national syndicate. The competing perspective maintains that organized crime consists of a variety of small rival groups that often compete with one another but co-operate when circumstances warrant a partnership.

The official or law-enforcement perspective claims that a syndicate does indeed exist (Cressey, 1969). Police maintain that the Mafia, the mob, La Cosa Nostra, or simply "the syndicate" is a tightly knit group of Italian immigrants and their descendants, many of whom trace their ancestry to Sicily. According to the official view, the Mafia is bound together not only by ethnicity but also by family bonds. The families are thought to have both national and international connections to one another. In the

United States, for example, police report that there are 24 different families, some of which have ties to Canada. A southern Ontario family based in Hamilton and headed by Pops Papalia before his death in 1997 has been linked to the Magaddino family operating across the border in nearby Buffalo. In Quebec, the activities of the Cotroni family of Montreal were overseen for a time by Carmen Gelente, an underboss in the New York–based organization run by Joseph Bonanno. Moreover, police believe that Canadian and American mafiosi maintain strong connections with and are heavily influenced by their relatives in Sicily.

The official approach claims that crime families are connected by a "commission" or council of high-ranking representatives from each member organization. This commission has two basic functions: it co-ordinates inter-family joint operations and, in the event of territorial or market conflicts, serves as an appeal court for settling disputes (Cressey, 1969).

The law-enforcement perspective maintains that each family has a hierarchical authority structure and a complex division of labour. The most powerful figure is the don, or boss, while the underboss is next in the chain of command. Beneath these figures are several *consiglieres* (councillors) and *caporegimes* (captains). The *soldati* (soldiers) are the lowest ranking and most numerous members. In addition to the family-based hierarchical authority structure, the division of labour in mob organizations is also affected, albeit to a lesser extent, by certain highly specialized roles, some criminal and some legal. The Mafia, for example, employs persons who specialize in execution, extortion, and bribery. It also routinely retains the services of highly educated professionals, including criminal and corporate lawyers, accountants, and computer analysts (Cressey, 1969).

Soldiers oversee the organized crime initiatives planned or approved by their superiors. Often, employees of the mob who are not Mafia members carry out the illegal activities at the street level. Typical employees include non-Italian street gangs and renegade motorcycle bands. Money from criminal enterprises is passed from mob employees upward through the Mafia hierarchy, with persons in each rank pocketing their agreed-upon share (Cressey, 1969).

According to the police, the Mafia or La Cosa Nostra operates by an unwritten code of conduct designed to protect its members in general and its leadership in particular. The code originated in the

Sicilian notion of **omerta**, which loosely translated means "manliness." Historically, Sicilian peasants were both suspicious and resentful of the Italian government and its elected representatives. In time, they grew to distrust all figures of authority and to abhor any form of co-operation with government officials.

Under the *omerta* code that emerged from this tradition of distrust and noncompliance, Italian men learn to exhibit great self-control and resilience in the face of adversity. They place a high value on the sanctity of the family and accord great respect to women and the aged. Moreover, the code dictates that loyalty to family members will be demonstrated at all costs, regardless of the circumstances (Cressey, 1969).

The preservation of the honour of family members and friends is a cornerstone of the *omerta* rules. A classic case of revenge for the preservation of honour took place in Toronto on a July night in 1971. Domenic Racco was the son of Mike Racco, an underworld kingpin in Toronto until his death of cancer in 1980. Domenic, known to be "quick on the draw," had been bothered in a bar by several young men, one of whom had called Domenic's Sidernese colleague a "wop." Journalist James Dubro (1985: 124) provides this account:

> Even more than the Sicilian Mafia, the Calabrian Mafia have a complex and rigorous code which considers such an insult a "debt of honour" that must be severely punished. … The incident at the Newtonbrook Plaza was a classic case of an insult demanding a dramatic response from the man of honour. Domenic Racco, armed with a gun, returned to the plaza the following night with two Sidernese soldiers. He found some friends of the youths who had made the original insult and simply shot them. As Siderno family member "Joe" later told it on the Connections program of March 27, 1979, "Domenic goes by the 1920's style. He'll just drive by, roll down the window, and shoot you. That's his style. And there are people who like that style…. He shot three people just for the respect of his friend."

In August, Domenic Racco fled Toronto and Canada.

The defence of honour, based on old-country traditions, is frequently expressed through the "vendetta," wherein the offended party seeks violent redress for past insults. Dubro (1985:178) describes one such vendetta, involving the Commisso brothers of Toronto:

Remo Commisso has a memory like an elephant. Nothing is ever forgotten, especially if it has to do with revenge or the honour of the family. He is rather Jacobean in his thirst for revenge. Although his father Girolomo Commisso was killed in the late 1940's, it was only recently, in 1982, that Remo arranged his final acts of revenge in a little town in Calabria when he had the sons of his father's 1940's rival murdered. Remo has that long a reach and memory. A breach of honour or respect, even if it happened thirty-five years ago, must be avenged.

In addition to demanding loyalty and the vigorous defence of honour, the Mafia code also emphasizes rational behaviour and silence. Members of the mob must avoid business-related conflicts with each other, maintain low profiles, and minimize their use of violent tactics. Of paramount importance is the successful pursuit and realization of profit in the family business. Also, *omerta* rules reflect the premium that family members place on silence. Indeed, the consequences of violating this pivotal expectation are immediate and severe (Cressey, 1969).

The alternative view of organized crime maintains that the existence of a single powerful syndicate that co-ordinates illegal enterprises and imposes dispute settlements on member groups is at best a grave oversimplification and at worst a falsehood (Clark, 1971; Chambliss, 1978). The "confederation" perspective asserts that organized crime consists of an informally linked collection of diverse groups occupying different territories. Some of these groups are Italian, and some are not. They represent a system of gangs governed by similar rules, all of which are designed to foil law enforcement through secrecy. Alliances between groups are seen as occasional and specific to particular criminal enterprises. When it is in their best interests, crime groups collaborate. Much of the time, however, criminal organizations are dissociated from one another or directly competing for larger shares of illicit markets.

The confederation approach suggests that criminal groups are best understood by using the notions of client and patron (Albini, 1971). Clients ask for considerations, and patrons deliver favours. The successful pursuit of profit through organized crime depends largely on the individual's ability to cultivate favourable working relationships with people in strategic positions. Generally, the consideration of a client by a patron involves providing access to capital or to specialized personnel. Making use of a system of contacts, the patron acts in the best interests of the

Box 14.2
HIGH-TECH PHONES DODGE EARS, EYES OF POLICE AND CSIS

Ottawa. Government memos say Canada's police and spy agencies risk losing their ability to probe "the most serious crimes" as the rapid growth of global satellite-based communication erodes their efforts to tap phone calls.

Briefing notes prepared by the Solicitor-General's Department say new legislation or treaties might be required to ensure authorities can continue to intercept the phone calls and e-mail messages of organized criminals and terrorists.

One option under consideration is to encourage countries to make court-approved wiretap authorizations valid in each other's jurisdictions in light of the global reach of new phone systems.

"This is a serious issue. For federal and non-federal law enforcement agencies, interception is an essential investigative technique used to detect, investigate and prevent the most serious crimes when other means have been tried or failed, or are unlikely to succeed," one memo says.

For spy agencies, tapping into conversations is often the only feasible tactic, given the challenges of the alternative – having sources infiltrate rogue organizations. Only 3% of all federal criminal cases involve wiretapping. However, these cases consume 80% of Justice Department resources and make up 49% of major cases, the notes say.

The records, prepared last year, were released to Southam News under the Access to Information Act. They underscore the fears voiced by police and intelligence officials in recent years that international criminals are gaining the upper hand in the adoption of new technologies.

Officials believe the issue will become more pressing as some 40 satellite companies offering a range of global communication services plan to be up and running by 2004.

Federal laws enable agencies, including the RCMP and CSIS, to apply to a judge for authorization to eavesdrop on a suspected criminal's calls through access to a telephone company's switching network. However, interception of satellite-based calls requires switching activity at a ground station, or gateway, in order to route targeted calls to a facility where an interception warrant can be executed.

Often only one gateway is required to offer phone service to an entire continent, meaning a switching system may not be present in every country where the service is offered. For instance, a gateway in the United States could serve all of North and Central America.

This creates a dilemma since a Canadian wiretap warrant is not valid outside the country.

The notes say Solicitor-General officials have been working with several other ministries and foreign governments to develop solutions. Companies are equally anxious as some foreign governments have threatened to deny necessary spectrum licences if their national security requirements are not met.

Last year, the FBI balked at allowing Ottawa's TMI Communications, which is owned by BCE and Telesat Canada, to offer satellite-based telecommunication service in the United States. The parties arrived at a compromise in September.

Although the company's ground station will be in Canada, a special digital switch in the United States will give the FBI and other U.S. security agencies access to calls. The federal memos raise other thorny issues. Some foreign governments are concerned that a gateway located in another jurisdiction would allow that country to see a complete listing of their surveillance efforts, including spy operations.

Foreign-located switches might also make it easier for agencies to illegally spy on citizens.

In addition, some countries are concerned about their ability to take control of foreign networks if needed in response to a natural disaster or terrorist incident.

At the same time, civil libertarians worry the efforts to keep pace with criminals will interfere with the privacy of ordinary citizens. Proposals in Britain and the United States to enhance authorities' access to e-mail traffic have raised concerns about needless invasion of privacy.

Discussion Questions

Why are organized crime groups now gaining the upper hand in the adoption of new technologies? How might this trend be reversed? How real is the concern over the invasion of law-abiding citizens' rights to privacy?

Source: Jim Bronskill, *National Post*, July 31, 2000, p. A7. Reprinted with permission from Southam News.

client by asking favours of certain persons who are in a position to fulfil the client's request. For example, patrons may put clients in touch with forgers, arsonists, fences, loan sharks, enforcers, or corrupt law-enforcement officials.

In the patron–client relationship, roles may switch as favours are passed back and forth over time. Moreover, the bond of trust between the patron and the client may be based on kinship ties, friendship, or simply mutual respect. When the participants in the patron–client interaction are Italian, kinship seems to play an important role in establishing mutually beneficial working relationships. Even when the criminal organizations are Italian, however, proponents of the confederation perspective maintain that co-operation is neither highly regimented nor stringently orchestrated. Finally, the confederation view disputes the claim that the Mafia has a monopoly on organized criminal ventures in North America (Clark, 1971; Albini, 1971).

A compromise point of view, falling somewhere between "Mafia as syndicate" and "Mafia as confederation," may best capture the nature of organized crime in North America. Some criminal groups are well organized and stable, while others are haphazard transient unions. Criminal organizations vary in terms of power, and Italian Mafia families continue to be dominant. It seems likely that more potent groups are able to influence the actions of their less powerful counterparts. Certain groups sometimes collaborate with others or pool resources to facilitate work on some projects. Of organized crime in Canada, Charbonneau (1976:49) points out:

> The underworld is not an organization but an environment, a "milieu" of crooks, bandits, dealers, outlaws of all description. Within the milieu a multitude of gangs, clans or organizations exist or co-exist. Some are powerful, well organized and stable; others are loose, haphazard and even temporary coalitions of odd-job criminals and journeyman crooks. The Mafia, as such, is a collection of gangs or families and feudal chiefs of Italian origin united by cultural, family and ethnic links, as well as by mutual interest. For various historical and cultural reasons the Italian clans of the Mafia have long been a dominating influence in the North American underworld. But they have no monopoly on criminality.

More recently, Dubro (1985:287) echoes Charbonneau's assessment. He suggests that

the mob in Canada is not as highly structured and organized as most of us think it is. Many different groups operate simultaneously in many different areas and many individuals within crime groups operate simultaneously in other criminal enterprises. The bottom line for all criminal operations is taking advantage of an opportunity when it comes along and using "connections" to further the scheme or bring it to fruition.

The official law-enforcement view of organized crime has enjoyed prominence until recently. Its acceptance has been encouraged by the remarkable prosperity of criminal groups in North America. How else could the Mafia persist so successfully, if not through a carefully co-ordinated national and international conspiracy? In providing an alternative answer to this question, opponents of the official perspective point out that organized crime groups are supplying goods and services that are in heavy demand and enormously profitable. Consumers are willing to purchase these prohibited goods and services at virtually any price. The profits are so large that the success of criminal organizations is simply not that dependent on high levels of inter-group co-ordination (Hills, 1980).

The official view of organized crime has considerable appeal because it permits citizens, law-enforcement personnel, and politicians to conveniently identify the causes of widespread illegal acts such as gambling, prostitution, and drug trafficking. With a clearly visible target, public attention is diverted from other social problems such as inflation and unemployment. To combat the alien menace, calls abound for expanding the scope of criminal law, for increasing the sizes of police forces, and for new and expensive technologies that can be applied to the war on crime. The official view justifies hiring and equipping more and more police on the one hand and relaxing legal due-process provisions on the other. These factors, critics maintain, contribute to empire-building by law-enforcement agencies (Reuter, 1984).

THE DEVELOPMENT OF ORGANIZED CRIME IN NORTH AMERICA

Organized crime became firmly entrenched earlier and on a larger scale in the United States than it did in Canada. The origins of organized crime in the two countries, however, are similar. Perhaps the first organized criminals in North America were the sea pirates who plundered off the coasts of Canada and the United States and in the Caribbean Sea. During the rapid expansion of European civilization across North America, two other groups became prominent predecessors of organized crime. The more visible of these groups, the desperadoes of the American wild west, appeared after the U.S. Civil War.

Less notorious, but nonetheless highly organized, were early industrialists and land owners in the United States and Canada. These English, Scottish, and German immigrants used ruthless business practices and routinely resorted to violence to secure land, eliminate competition, obtain investment capital, and gain political power. These "robber barons" denied settlers the right to acquire land or drove them off property that was rightfully theirs. They had disgruntled workers beaten into submission and thrown in jail by police. They also undermined their employees' bargaining positions by regularly recruiting strikebreakers. The early industrialists decimated the Native people and forced them onto reserves so that their lands could be confiscated. These are the origins of many North American industrial, manufacturing, and commercial elites (Tyler, 1981; Bell, 1962).

The end of the nineteenth century and the beginning of the twentieth were marked by the massive influxes of impoverished European ethnic groups, first to the United States and later to Canada. Many immigrants had very limited opportunities for advancement. Some lacked the necessary skills, and others were discriminated against by those who had already established themselves. Many encountered both obstacles. Faced with few if any avenues for legitimate advancement, members of impoverished and ghettoized ethnic groups turned to crime as a means of survival and betterment. Some members of disadvantaged groups formed urban gangs and began extorting money from their law-abiding ethnic comrades.

As the years passed, many disadvantaged immigrants became wealthy as a result of their criminal enterprises. Upwardly mobile, many gradually abandoned crime and found more law-abiding ways of making a living. This process, called "ethnic succession," provides a historical account of ethnic involvement in the North American underworld. The Irish, who were prominent in organized crime in the United States during the first two decades of this century, gradually assumed ownership of legitimate construc-tion firms and public utilities. Similarly, the Jews, who rose to prominence in American organized crime during the 1920s, later invested in legal businesses and industries and joined the professions (Bell, 1962).

The transition from illegal to law-abiding means of earning a living did not occur in the same way for the Italians as it had for their predecessors, the Irish and the Jews. Italians rose to prominence during the American Prohibition era of the 1920s and 1930s and have yet to relinquish their control over the lion's share of organized criminal enterprise. While new disadvantaged groups, including Chinese, Vietnamese, Russian, and black immigrants, continue to become involved in organized crime, they do so in the shadow of the Italian Mafia. Ethnic succession has been impeded by Italian dominance, but it has not been halted entirely.

During the late nineteenth and early twentieth centuries, large numbers of poverty-stricken Italians migrated to the United States and Canada to carve out better lives for themselves and their children. They arrived over several decades from a variety of areas in Italy, mainly Sicily, Calabria, and the region immediately adjacent to Naples. Each locality produced its own distinct organized crime group. From Sicily came the Mafia, from Calabria came the Ndrangheta or Honoured Society, and from Naples came the Camorra (Hills, 1980).

The Mafia, the Ndrangheta, and the Camorra are tightly knit organizational structures based on family recruitment. They emphasize bravery, loyalty, anti-authoritarianism, and, above all, secrecy. Despite their common national origin and their sharing of similar norms and values, however, the North American descendants of these old-world criminal organizations have not always gotten along harmoniously. Indeed, conflicts over territories and markets have occasionally erupted into violence.

Known at first as the "Black Hand," Italian organized crime was initially confined to robbery, hired assassination, and extortion. Most of the victims of these crimes were recent Italian immigrants, who were generally law-abiding, industrious, and frugal. Because they were not yet integrated into North American society and still shared the peasant mistrust of the authorities, the new arrivals were reluctant to approach police for assistance. Furthermore, recent Italian immigrants made the most appropriate victims because they understood the significance of Black Hand threats.

Black Hand activities first surfaced in Canada in Hamilton (Dubro, 1985). In 1909, the trial of five Black Handers in that city became headline news. The extortion technique was simple. The Black Hand selected a victim of some financial means and sent him a note, written in a Sicilian dialect and signed "Mano Nera." The threatening letter warned of impending injury or death to the victim or to members of his family. Sometimes, the note threatened to bomb or set fire to a person's property. To insure the victim against "misfortune," the Black Hand demanded payment. Recalcitrant victims were sent a series of notes, the last of which bore the insignia of a black hand. If the deadline for payment was not met, the threat was carried out. Dubro (1985:36) cites the example of Monaco Natale, who was contacted by the Black Hand in Hamilton in March 1921:

> Monaco Natale received a letter demanding a thousand dollars. The stationery depicted a black hand and was marked with a cross. Natale was instructed to take the money to the GTR bridge on John Street in Hamilton where he would be met by a Black Hander who would accept the extortion payment. Natale failed to comply. Two and a half months later, at one o'clock in the morning, a bomb rocked Natale's house at 7G Sheaffe Street. The windows were blown out and the glass was driven deep inside the bedroom but miraculously no one was injured. The explosion was of such force that it was heard in remote parts of the city of Hamilton.

Robbery, extortion, and murder were not the only opportunities created for the Black Hand by the large-scale Italian migration to North America. These new immigrants also brought with them a demand for certain restricted or forbidden services. Consequently, the Black Hand diversified to deliver gambling, usurious loans, and prostitution first to Italian immigrants and later to any interested customers.

The tight, family-based organization is only one reason why Italians have dominated North American organized crime for such a long time. The impact of an important historical development is also critical. In 1919, the U.S. government passed the *Volstead Act*, which made the manufacture, distribution, sale, and consumption of alcohol illegal in that country (Smart and Ogborne, 1986). Despite the law, neither the public thirst nor the supply of liquor faded. Risks to suppliers, however, increased substantially. The result was the creation of monopoly conditions that bene-fited those willing to take the necessary risks in violating the new law. Supplying liquor to millions of thirsty consumers became an extremely lucrative business (Abadinsky, 1985).

Prohibition in the United States had a number of far-reaching effects on organized crime and its control both in that country and in Canada. First, it dramatically increased the scale of organized criminal enterprises. Before Prohibition, organized crime was essentially a neighbourhood or, at most, city-wide operation. The vast market created by the ban on alcohol generated connections between criminal organizations. Organized crime families forged links between cities, between regions of the United States, and, facilitated by the open U.S.–Canada border, between countries. The passing of the *Volstead Act*, by dramatically expanding an illegal industry, contributed immeasurably to making the enterprise of organized crime much more rational and more businesslike than it had been in the past (Homer, 1974).

Second, Prohibition dramatically broadened the scale of corruption in North American politics and law enforcement. The intense demand for alcoholic beverages existed among all classes. As a result, organized crime figures were able to develop close associations with influential businessmen, industrialists, professionals, and politicians. Criminals and their enterprises enjoyed legitimacy; Al Capone, for example, socialized regularly not only with the mayor of Chicago but with state and federal politicians as well. These highly visible associations between underworld figures and prominent social leaders encouraged public complicity in organized criminal activity. The public construed violating Prohibition laws as neither real crime nor serious wrongdoing. Many police officers and judges did not balk at accepting hefty bribes to ignore or treat very leniently violations of the *Volstead Act* (Hills, 1980).

Prohibition had another deleterious effect on crime control in the United States. The anti-alcohol law was able to gain neither the support nor the acquiescence of the American people; it was extremely unpopular and vehemently resisted. As a result, it was virtually unenforceable. A law that many feel justified in breaking undermines respect not only for that law but also, through "negative contagion," for law in general (Packer, 1968).

During the 1920s, some provinces, such as Ontario, passed Temperance Acts. While they limited the availability of alcohol across Canada, these statutes did not provide the major incentive to expand illegal alcohol sales. The pressure came from the *Volstead Act* south of the border. Liquor control in the United States was a federal responsibility, so Prohibition was universal in that country. The complete ban on alcohol and the long and largely unsupervised Canada–U.S. border created an enormous opportunity for Canadian suppliers. Canadian liquor sales skyrocketed as people like Al Capone established smuggling connections in towns just north of the U.S. border.

At that time, Canadian exporters of alcoholic beverages required only minimal credentials. The federal government permitted virtually anyone to purchase merchandise from a Canadian distillery, providing that the distilled products were destined for an offshore locality in which no Prohibition laws were in force. Among the destinations approved by Canadian officials were Cuba and the West Indies. With payment of the excise tax to the Canadian government, liquor shipments to destinations as far away as the Caribbean were officially approved and formally overseen by Canadian customs agents. It went unnoticed that single boats operating out of ports along the Canadian shores of the Great Lakes made as many as four round trips to Cuba per day! These voyages were shortened considerably either by brief stopovers on the American shore or by mid-lake transfers to waiting American boats. That there was more alcohol flowing across Lake Erie than there was water flowing through it was a common remark of the day.

Profits from these ventures were considerable. Rocco Perri, the first Canadian Mafia don, was already involved in bootlegging on a small scale when the United States passed the *Volstead Act*. With Prohibition, he was able to expand his operation. His organization reportedly purchased a case of liquor for $18 in Canada and sold it for $120 to "importers" across the lake. Perri's smuggling operation apparently transported about 1000 cases every 24 hours, with profits exceeding $100 000 on a good day.

Under considerable pressure from the United States government, Canadian officials finally launched, in 1930, a major crackdown on the illegal export of liquor. With the sale of spirits by distilleries to wholesalers newly controlled by much stricter regulations, Perri and his contemporaries resorted to using illegal stills to manufacture their own alcohol. With quality and quantity down, however, profits declined.

The illegal export of alcohol from Canada into the United States finally came to an abrupt end with the repeal of Prohibition in 1933. This did not, however, eliminate the liquor smuggling. Rather, all that changed was the direction of the flow. The United States, with its new and extremely liberal liquor-control legislation, became a major source of high-quality alcohol products which were both less expensive and more readily available than their Canadian counterparts. The Canadian thirst for booze at bargain prices created a new opportunity for organized crime groups in Canada and the United States, and they began illegally transporting liquor north (Dubro, 1985). While this clandestine operation continues today, it is not a major activity for organized crime in either country.

The Prohibition era had several important effects on organized crime in North America. The creation of a large and lucrative market for contraband alcohol entrenched a rational, businesslike approach to illegitimate enterprises, broadened the scope of operations nationally and internationally, and firmly established the widespread corruption of law-enforcement personnel and politicians. By the time Prohibition was repealed and the market for illicit alcohol was eliminated, a large, tightly structured, and highly experienced criminal organization had already been established. Once created, organizations, whether they are law breaking or law abiding, do not voluntarily contract or dismantle themselves. They diversify by using their existing organizational structure, expertise, and web of contacts to exploit new market opportunities.

Prohibition also explains why Italians, unlike other ethnic groups before them, have not relinquished their dominant position in organized crime for more legitimate endeavours. Quite simply, Italians were in the right place at the right time. They were the dominant criminal group when Prohibition greatly expanded the market for an extremely profitable illegal commodity. Consequently, the Italian Mafia firmly established itself in organized criminal activities and did so with such success that it has been able to resist the encroachment of competing organizations. Moreover, the immense profits generated by organized crime reduced the allure of a purely law-abiding life (Abadinsky, 1985).

OTHER ORGANIZED CRIME GROUPS

While Italians continue their dominance, other groups have recently joined the ranks of organized crime. Some have come into direct competition with the Italian Mafia, while others have become involved as Mafia subordinates. Some work directly for the Mafia as drug pushers, numbers runners, or enforcers. A few, however, pay a licensing fee for permission to operate franchises in drug peddling, gambling, and prostitution. Like the Italians before them, many of these newer crime groups are bound together by a combination of ethnic and family ties. This is particularly the case for the Cuban, Puerto Rican, and Colombian groups. Others, like black gangs and renegade motorcycle gangs, band together primarily on the basis of earlier membership in youth gangs or of friendships forged in prison.

Four groups, in addition to the Italians, play major roles in organized crime in Canada: Asians, Colombians, Native people, and outlaw motorcycle gangs. Most prominent among the Asian gangs are the Chinese Triads or Tongs. Like the roots of the Italian Mafia, Camorra, and Ndrangheta, the origins of the Triads are located in a foreign country's past. The Triads transported their traditions to North America as Chinese immigration to this continent increased. Like the Black Hand movement, the Triads began in Canada by continuing the old-country traditions of extortion. Victims first came from the Chinese community; later, the Triads extended their activities to encompass the sale of drugs first to the Chinese and more recently to anyone having the necessary cash (Robertson, 1977; Bresler, 1980).

The Colombian presence is not as strong in Canadian as in American society. Nonetheless, the Colombian connection is a major conduit for illicit drugs in this country. Most cocaine in Canada can be traced to this source. The organizational structure of the Colombians is similar in many respects to that of the Italians. Colombian crime groups are virtually impenetrable because of their strong family ties, their Latino emphasis on *dignidad* or honour, and their notion of *hombria* — the equivalent of the Italian *omerta*. The Colombian crime groups also have a hierarchical authority structure and a specialized division of labour in which "enforcers" and "corrupters" are particularly important. The corrupter's function is to maintain smooth working relationships with customs and law-enforcement personnel in North America and Colombia. The role of the enforcer is to keep buyers in line and to ride herd on the competition. The Colombians are far more violent than their Italian counterparts. They regularly include women

and children among their victims, something the Mafia would be loath to do. The favoured weapon of Colombian gangs is the Uzi, a lightweight submachine gun. The group solidarity, the quick and easy resort to violence, and the frequent rotation of sales personnel in the United States and Canada combine to make the Colombian trade in illegal drugs extremely difficult to control (Abadinsky, 1985).

In recent years, Russian and Eastern European criminal organizations have become a growing problem in Canada, particularly in Ontario and Quebec. The police report that these organizations are involved in a variety of illegal initiatives. They are implicated in smuggling ecstasy from Holland to Montreal and distributing it in Toronto as well as in importing cocaine from several sites in the Caribbean into the United States and then across the border into Windsor. Police believe that Russian gangs have brought high-quality counterfeit diamonds into Montreal and Toronto from the United States. They have engaged in large-scale casino fraud at gambling houses in the southern United States, the Bahamas, Aruba, and the Dominican Republic and transmitted the ill-gotten gains to Toronto. Police report that these groups are involved in forging immigration documents and smuggling illegal migrants into the country and that they are implicated in schemes to create high-quality counterfeit credit cards for distribution and fraudulent use in Europe, Venezuela, and the United States (Skelton, 2000).

According to Beare (1996), Aboriginal organized crime groups originally became involved in schemes aimed at smuggling cigarettes from the United States into Canada. These initiatives have recently been expanded to include alcohol and firearms smuggling and illicit gambling operations. Canadian cigarettes cost a great deal more than their American counterparts. When Canadian cigarette manufacturers exported far more of their product to the United States than that market could absorb, Mohawks on the Akwesasne and Regis reserves seized the opportunity to smuggle back across the international border the unsold excess supply, which they then distributed at prices lower than those charged by legitimate vendors in Ontario and Quebec. The expansion of this smuggling infrastructure is of considerable concern to law-enforcement officials since these networks and routes, once established, are easily modified to accommodate the illegal transport of other commodities such as illicit drugs, weaponry, and illegal aliens.

What began as the illegal transport of guns to support militant Mohawk groups, for example, is becoming a profit-generating enterprise involving the supply of weapons to various gangs and other organized crime groups. The strengthening of links between Aboriginal and other organized crime groups is a matter of considerable concern to Canadian law enforcement (Beare, 1996).

A number of geographical, social, and economic factors facilitate illegal activities on Native reserves. First, reserve locations straddle the borders of Canada and the United States and the provinces of Ontario and Quebec. This situation creates jurisdictional disputes among law-enforcement agencies. Second, Aboriginal groups claim rights to certain tax-free statuses and the right to self-government. Third, legitimate economic opportunities on reserves are severely limited. Finally, the history of Aboriginal groups in this country is fraught with the kind of economic exploitation and institutional discrimination that boiled over into the Oka crisis of 1990 (Beare, 1996).

Renegade motorcycle gangs in North America date back to the early 1940s. In July 1947, the American Motorcycle Association organized a large gathering of motorcyclists in the town of Hollister, California. When members of rival gangs at the rally clashed, the affair quickly exploded into a riot. To distance itself from this incident, which was immortalized in the 1954 Marlon Brando film *The Wild One*, the American Motorcycle Association issued a statement claiming that 99 percent of its members were law-abiding motorcycle enthusiasts. The renegade "one percenters" as they referred to themselves, formed a number of outlaw gangs, of which the Hells Angels is the most infamous (Stamler, 1987; Wolf, 1991).

Like the structure of other crime groups, the organization of outlaw bikers is hierarchical. It consists of national clubs, with local chapters each having presidents, vice-presidents, secretary-treasurers, sergeants-at-arms, enforcers, and road captains. The revenues of Canadian biker gangs come from a range of crimes, including extortion, prostitution, and drug trafficking. In particular, Canadian motorcycle bands specialize in manufacturing and distributing synthetic chemical substances such as LSD. While the major motorcycle gang in Ontario is the Outlaws, Canadian chapters of the Hells Angels dominate much of the rest of the country. Neither the Outlaws nor the Hells Angels, however, control all Canadian territory. Quebec reportedly has at least 30 different motor-

cycle bands engaging in illegal activity. Many gangs have direct links to their counterparts in the United States and co-operate closely with them in drug operations and other mutually beneficial undertakings. Motorcycle gangs are difficult to prosecute successfully because of their tight internal discipline, their quick resort to violence and murder (especially against suspected informers), and their considerable geographic mobility (Abadinsky, 1985). A Hells Angels member wanted by the RCMP can easily seek safety in the clubhouses of his California comrades.

The Hells Angels now have chapters located in all provinces, most recently Ontario. In a conversion known as a "patchover," members of smaller gangs such as Satan's Choice and the ParaDice Riders have abandoned their former colours to join the Hells Angels with its more than 180 chapters worldwide. The gang's expansion represents an effort to take advantage of economic opportunities inherent in Canada's lucrative drug trade and to secure market share in the face of competition from the Rock Machine and their Texas-based allies, the Banditos. In an attempt to minimize the impact of competition from other gangs, particularly their Quebec rivals the Rock Machine, the Hells Angels are now making their presence felt as far north as Nunavut. Drug-related conflicts between these and other rival gangs were responsible for approximately 150 deaths in Canada between 1994 and 2000.

The Hells Angels and other such groups have proven difficult to control in recent years for several reasons. First, they use a cellular structure. There is no real pyramid of control and each cell is highly autonomous. Second, they do not communicate regarding business either over the phone or inside buildings. They talk on the street where it is difficult for law-enforcement agencies to monitor communications. Third, the Hells Angels now have the resources to hire expert legal and accounting assistance. Finally, gang members appear to have infiltrated police organizations. In so doing, they have acquired sensitive law-enforcement information that has rendered police efforts to control gang activities ineffective (Appleby and Ha, 2000; Gatehouse, 2000b; Cherry, 2000; Woods, 2000).

Like other organized crime groups, outlaw motorcyclists are attempting to improve their public images and to make investments in legitimate business. In recent years, some chapters have participated in organized and highly publicized charity drives. They

Box 14.3
ANGELS RAISE LITTLE HELL IN QUIET SUBURBS

Were it not for the three Harleys parked out front, the two-storey white stucco house with the trimmed lawn and shrubs wouldn't stand out in the residential, east Vancouver neighbourhood.

The house is a Hells Angels clubhouse, one of several in British Columbia's Lower Mainland. Most are located in quiet bedroom communities such as Langley, Coquitlam and Pitt Meadows.

There are no wild parties. Police are never called to break up brawls. The club's aging members, sometimes dressed in suits, meet there to socialize and talk business.

To add to their benign image, only a handful of B.C. Hells Angels have criminal records, a point the bikers often make when they complain of police harassment and persecution.

But B.C.'s Hells Angels aren't benign. Police say they have a secure grip on one of the most lucrative drug trades in North America: the cultivation and sale of the province's homegrown and highly potent marijuana.

Hells Angels are also linked to cocaine trafficking.

RCMP Inspector Kim Clark, who heads the province's proceeds-of-crime unit, said the Hells Angels are key players in the so-called grow-op industry, estimated to be worth $4-billion to $10-billion a year.

But to date, police and Crown attorneys can't point to any significant convictions of Hells Angels for drug trafficking.

While he was attorney-general, B.C. Premier Ujjal Dosanjh acknowledged that the Hells Angels operated with impunity in the province, saying the gang had succeeded in intimidating police, Crowns and journalists.

"This started out as a very insignificant problem in the early 1970s," Mr. Dosanjh said two years ago. "If we had been doing our job, the problem wouldn't have grown to the extent it has."

Today, police haven't improved their track record with Hells Angels, despite the establishment two years ago of the Organized Crime Agency, a 100-officer unit, charged with fighting outlawed gangs.

"There has not been an effective, co-ordinated police strategy to deal with Hells Angels," said Inspector Andy Richards, who heads the agency's outlaw biker gang unit.

Members of the Hells Angels met in Winnipeg this weekend, participating in an integration ceremony of another bike gang.

Police believe members of the Los Bravos biker gang were integrated with the local Hells Angels chapter, hidden behind blue tarps strung up to thwart police surveillance of their clubhouse.

In the past, competing police departments have been reluctant to share their information and commit big resources to lengthy investigations, Insp. Richards added.

Law enforcement's spotty track record may improve. Later this fall, two Hells Angels members from Vancouver's east-end chapter are to stand trial on several counts of trafficking cocaine and conspiracy to traffic cocaine.

In the past, police have also alleged that Hells Angels and their associates had taken jobs at ports in Vancouver and Halifax to smuggle drugs into Canada, a charge the ports denied.

The B.C. Hells Angels are also the world's wealthiest. There are about 90 members in seven chapters across the province and other chapters regularly hit them up for cash. Recently, the B.C. Hells Angels sent out a fax to other chapters gently asking them to stop requesting loans.

Insp. Clark said Hells Angels have avoided prosecution because they're rich, well-connected and shrewd. They conduct their business outside to avoid wiretaps. And they have expert legal advice.

Outspoken B.C. Hells Angel Ricky Ciarniello has openly challenged police to name any Angels involved in a criminal activity. According to Mr. Ciarniello, Hells Angels members and their associates are regularly harassed by police.

New Tenants

When driving through an industrial park in Kingston, Ont., it is easy to overlook No. 4, 621 Justus Drive. Its new tenants, however, are not easily missed; they are the Rock Machine, a local branch of Quebec's notorious motorcycle gang.

The gang uses the building's inconspicuous exterior to operate its clubhouse, which doubles as an after-hours pub under the façade of an upholstery repair shop.

Kingston is being eyed closely by biker gangs like the Hells Angels and the Rock Machine because of its strategic location between Toronto, Ottawa, and Montreal.

As well, its location on the St. Lawrence River makes for simple smuggling of contraband goods across the border with the United States.

The infamous Hells Angels have a regular presence in Canada's largest province, but have no official clubhouse. That's why they are envious of the Rock Machine's Kingston digs. The Rock Machine also has one other site in Ontario, located in Toronto.

Across Ontario, there are about 500 members in 11 outlaw motorcycle gangs.

Discussion Questions

How have the Hells Angels grown from an "insignificant problem" in the 1970s to a major problem in 2000? Is the newly formed Organized Crime Agency likely to change matters?

Source: Jane Armstrong, *Globe and Mail*, July 14, 2000, p. A5. Reprinted with permission from the *Globe and Mail*.

have also banded together to publicly denounce police and to charge them in court with unlawful harassment. Motorcycle gangs now invest heavily in many legitimate businesses, including bike shops, bars, towing companies, and tourist resorts.

ORGANIZED CRIME ACTIVITIES

Criminal organizations engage in three fundamental types of money-making enterprises: tactical crime, illegitimate business, and legal business. The relative importance of these income-generating strategies has shifted somewhat since organized criminal operations first took root in North America (Rhodes, 1984).

TACTICAL CRIME

When the Mafia first appeared in Canada during the latter part of the nineteenth century, the principal fundraising activity involved criminal gangs preying upon members of their own ethnic group. In recent times, this activity has taken the form of selling "insurance" against physical injury, death, property loss, and labour unrest. Other forms of tactical crime are blackmail and arson (Dubro, 1985).

At present, tactical crimes are not major sources of income for most organized crime groups. Criminal organizations now undertake tactical initiatives primarily to protect their other illegal business interests. Through the use of violence, clients are persuaded to co-operate, informants and witnesses are intimidated into silence, rule breakers are punished, and in extreme cases, those posing a serious threat to the organization are liquidated.

For the Mafia, the use of violence is rare. It is a tool of last resort for several reasons. First, there is not much of a lucrative market for services of a purely tactical nature. Second, violent acts tend first to kindle public indignation and then to draw unwanted attention from law-enforcement agencies. While threats are commonplace, violence itself is usually bad for business (Reuter, 1984).

The primary tactical strategy now used by criminal organizations is corruption. The targets of graft include national and local politicians, members of the judiciary, and the police. Politicians at any level of government may be corrupted through bribes and illegal campaign contributions. Similarly, judges, prosecuting attorneys, police officers, and customs officials are routinely offered hefty payoffs in return for "throwing" cases in court, dropping charges, failing to prosecute properly, and ignoring criminal activities like gambling and drug smuggling. Criminal organizations often conceal graft and illegal campaign contributions by using foreign bank deposits and by carrying out seemingly legitimate transfers of company shares.

To understand the dynamics of corruption, it is necessary to recognize two things. First, the sale of illegal goods and services results in a gargantuan profit margin. Organized crime has an enormous amount of money available to pump into bribes. Second, most of the illegal goods and services supplied by organized crime fill an intense public demand. Very large numbers of "law-abiding" people voluntarily and without question purchase illegal goods like drugs and pornography and illegal services like gambling and illicit sex.

While few Canadians would accept any amount of money to turn a blind eye to murder, rape, or robbery, some politicians, court personnel, and police officers have little difficulty accepting bribes to ignore illegal goods and services that large numbers of the population want, see as comparatively innocuous, and are willing to tolerate. When authorities discover corruption and when the media publicize it, the dismissal of the few "bad apples" in the otherwise healthy political and law-enforcement barrels usually placates an indignant public. Furthermore, the leaders of organized crime know that public support for initiatives against them is unlikely to be intense as long as their illegal activities remain nonviolent.

ILLEGITIMATE BUSINESS

The provision of goods and services prohibited by law but nonetheless highly desired is a major source of income for organized crime. Insatiable demand and a monopolized market combine to generate enormous profits from gambling, narcotics, loansharking, prostitution, pornography, and bootlegging. These "victimless" crimes produce satisfied customers far more often than they produce disgruntled or injured victims. Satisfied customers rarely complain to the police. A lack of complainants further facilitates the continuation of illegal business.

Gambling

A major illegal income earner for organized crime in North America is gambling. Estimates of the proceeds generated from this source are the matter of considerable speculation, but the amounts involved are substantial. Canadian law restricts betting on horses, games of chance, and lotteries. Underworld betting operations offer a number of distinct advantages over those run legally. First, illegal gambling operations are more extensive, giving people more opportunities to place wagers. Second, betting limits are usually much higher. Finally, governments cannot tax the winners in these clandestine gambling operations.

Two forms of gambling that are illegal in this country but that are extremely popular nonetheless are "numbers games" and "bookmaking." In a numbers game, gamblers select a number, usually between 0 and 999. They then register the selected number with a "runner," who ensures that selections are recorded at a central command post, called a "bank." The winning number can be determined in a number of ways, but the most common method is to choose the last three digits of the total daily winnings at a certain race track.

Bookmaking involves laying wagers on horse races and sporting events. There are several advantages for betters using the "bookie" system. Bookies often offer the only means of wagering on sporting events, are readily contacted, and can arrange easy credit. Moreover, their system precludes the necessity of reporting winnings to Canada Customs and Revenue Agency for income tax purposes (Reuter, 1984; Tyler, 1981).

Loansharking

Usury laws in Canada govern the rates of interest that lending institutions can charge to borrowers. Banks and trust companies often provide loans only to persons with acceptable credit ratings, collateral, or both. Not everyone needing money meets these requirements, and for them the services of a loan shark often prove enticing.

Loansharking involves lending money at rates of interest exceeding those permitted by law. Interest rates charged on relatively small loans can be enormous. Where the loans are larger — $20 000 and higher — or where the customer is well known to the loan shark, interest rates may be reduced to as little as 1 percent per week. While even this rate is far above that charged by legitimate banks, loans from loan sharks have the advantage of being granted with few questions and few conditions. All that is required is agreement on a repayment schedule.

Borrowers are usually seeking funds to revive a failing business, to pay off gambling debts, or to secure immediate cash for investment. Investments range from "hot deals" on unexpected shipments of illicit drugs or firearms to bargains on stock-market shares temporarily priced below the going rate. Before banking machines, some people turned to loan sharks for no other reason than because they urgently needed money late at night, on Sunday, or during a holiday, when banks were closed.

Although loan sharks occasionally accept property titles or business holdings as security for a loan, usually all that is required is verbal assurance from the borrower that the loan will be repaid. While some loan sharks have "foreclosed" on legitimate businesses, this practice is relatively rare. Security usually takes the form of the borrower's bodily health or life. Nevertheless, most borrowers repay loan sharks as agreed, not out of fear, but because they know that

Box 14.4
SMUGGLERS GO INTERPROVINCIAL

The federal government's sustained attack against the smuggling of contraband cigarettes into Canada has created a new multimillion-dollar crime problem.

Many smugglers are switching from international to interprovincial smuggling of cigarettes because the profits are high, the chances of getting caught are low, and even if they are caught the likelihood of going to prison is minimal.

"Interprovincial smuggling is costing millions and millions of dollars in lost taxes," Inspector John Ferguson, head of the RCMP's economic-crime unit in British Columbia, said in an interview. "It's a huge problem. People don't realize how serious it is."

He said British Columbia, where cigarette prices are among the highest in Canada, has been particularly hurt by the growth of interprovincial smuggling. Profits are so high it has attracted different organized-crime elements who are starting to fight among themselves for dominant positions in the trade.

"It's big business," he said. "And that's why they're in it, because it is such big business. When they get caught, they usually get fined and that's it. They rarely go to jail."

Groups as diverse as the Mafia, Russian mobsters, bikers, Chinese triads and other ethnically based organized gangs are starting to compete, with a serious potential for increased violence.

"The Iranians are going to be fighting with the Asians, who are going to be fighting with Russian organized crime and the bikers, or whoever," Insp. Ferguson said. "To a degree, they are already fighting amongst themselves here. Shootings and so on have taken place. It's just a question of time before it gets to a larger scale. ...

"The thing has really scary connotations to it. There is an element of criminal activity in this that goes far beyond buying a cheap smoke on the corner."

British Columbia, because of its high tobacco taxes and large population, is a major market for smuggled cigarettes. Insp. Ferguson said it is hard to say what percentage of cigarettes reach the province through interprovincial smuggling compared to international smuggling, but added: "I sort of have the gut feeling that it is a 50-50 split."

Superintendent Yves Juteau, head of the RCMP's customs-and-excise branch in Ottawa, said the force

is trying to help affected provinces. "It's very hard to define [the extent of the problem] right now," he said, "but, yes, there is an increased problem in interprovincial smuggling."

Cigarettes are smuggled interprovincially by road, through mail-order operators (who take orders by letter, 800 phone numbers and E-mail), by commercial couriers and in airline baggage. The smugglers have little fear of the law.

Smugglers, for example, regularly fly on commercial flights between Toronto and Vancouver, checking two dozen suitcases or more at a time, each packed with 50 cartons of cigarettes.

"They have people out here go out to the airport," Insp. Ferguson said, "and they pick them up [off the baggage carousel]. They know we can't have enough police there to catch them all. So they run up in a group of 20 or 30 people, grab the bags, and start running in all directions."

The surge in interprovincial smuggling of tobacco products has its origins in the crisis the federal government faced in 1994, when international cigarette smuggling from the United States into Canada reached crisis levels.

At the time, most of the smuggled cigarettes were entering Canada through Ontario and Quebec. It was estimated that two out of three cigarettes smoked in Quebec had been smuggled into Canada and that one of three smoked in the rest of the country was contraband. The police were overwhelmed by the magnitude of the problem.

Ottawa cut federal taxes on cigarettes in February, 1994, to reduce the price advantage of smuggled cigarettes. Ontario and Quebec, the two most affected provinces, cut their provincial cigarette taxes.

As a result, smuggled cigarettes are no longer readily available in Ontario and Quebec, which have the cheapest cigarettes in Canada, but they are commonplace in other provinces, where taxes have remained high.

A legal carton of cigarettes, for example, costs $26.40 in Ontario, compared with $48.55 in B.C. and $50.62 in Newfoundland. It is a problem that has captured the attention of the Auditor-General of Canada.

"Because of differences in the price of cigarettes, particularly between those provinces that lowered their tobacco taxes and those that did not, interprovincial smuggling of cigarettes has emerged as a new threat to revenue, primarily provincial revenue," Auditor-General Denis Desautels reported to Parliament in September, 1996.

"Of particular concern to the Western provinces is the illegal interprovincial movement (for example, by mail) of tobacco products originating from Ontario and Quebec, which is reportedly contributing to a decline in their tobacco tax revenues."

Kenora, Ont., where a legal carton of cigarettes sells for $26.40, is little more than a two-hour drive from Winnipeg, where Manitoba taxes push the price of a carton up to $43.66, providing a comfortable margin of profit for a smuggler.

"In the months prior to February, 1994, there was virtually no interprovincial smuggling here [from Ontario], because our tax rates were virtually the same," said Peter Murphy, manager of investigations for the Manitoba Finance Department. "Today, probably 95 per cent of the cigarettes smuggled into Manitoba are interprovincial."

Earlier this month, the Newfoundland government was forced to take steps to keep residents of western and southern Labrador from crossing the border into Quebec to buy cheaper cigarettes. Newfoundland dropped the local price of a carton of cigarettes in Labrador near the Quebec border by $16 to stem the flow of lost tax revenues. Elsewhere in the province, a carton still sells for $50.62, which means cigarettes remain a smuggling problem, both from the French islands of St-Pierre and Miquelon and from interprovincial smuggling.

Unlike those in British Columbia, Newfoundland smugglers are not connected to organized mobs, RCMP Corporal Lloyd Holmes said from St. John's. Instead, expatriate Newfoundlanders who have migrated to Ontario and Quebec smuggle cigarettes to the province.

Police and provincial tax officials say they face a losing battle in trying to win support for their efforts.

"We're trying to get the media involved locally to educate the public as to why they should not buy smuggled cigarettes," Insp. Ferguson said. "We have an almost insurmountable task ahead of us. I don't think the public realize the ramifications of what they are allowing to take place. It's not a victimless crime. Profits go to organized crime and they put them into drugs, gun running, prostitution, you name it."

Only rarely do the courts give their full backing to enforcement efforts. A recent decision by Madam Justice Marvyn Koenigsberg of the B.C. Supreme Court appears to be a rare instance of judicial support. She rejected the appeal of two Vietnamese against convictions in Vancouver for smuggling cigarettes both internationally and interprovincially. The pair were fined a total of $47,150 or three years imprisonment in default.

"It was suggested by the defence that the offence here was not serious or at least not as serious as a drug offence," Judge Koenigsberg wrote, "since it only involved a financial loss of tax revenue as opposed to the human suffering associated with criminal endeavour. I cannot agree.

"The market for contraband cigarettes arises because of increased taxes on cigarettes. These taxes are imposed in an attempt by government to influence smokers not to smoke by making cigarettes expensive. In turn, the increase in price, by increasing taxes brings revenue into government coffers to begin to offset the health care costs of smoking. To the extent that contraband cigarettes are available this government effort is undermined."

A B.C. tax official, who spoke on the condition that he was not named, said the province estimates its lost tax revenues from smuggled cigarettes is between $100-million and $125-million a year. The province pays the salaries and expenses of 12 RCMP officers assigned full time to interprovincial smuggling.

"If we had reduced our taxes in conjunction with Quebec and Ontario in February, 1994, to this point we would have lost $260-million [in revenues]," said Mr. Murphy. He heads a team of 27 investigators.

A major stumbling block for enforcement agencies, police or provincial tax investigators is that interprovincial smuggling is largely a provincial offence and not taken seriously as a criminal offence.

In New Brunswick, a Mountie in Fredericton said, smugglers know that even if they go to prison they will be released on parole after serving the bare minimum of their sentence, because cigarette smuggling is considered a low-priority offence compared to crimes of violence.

Last November, two men were convicted in Corner Brook, Nfld., after a lengthy investigation into a group that smuggled cigarettes from Ontario and Quebec. One man was fined $220,000 but given until Dec. 31, 1999, to pay the fine or go to prison for 4½ years. A second man was fined $170,000 and given the same lengthy amount of time to pay his fine or go to prison for 3½ years. Both men may appear in court on Dec. 31, 1999, and ask for an extension of time to pay their fines.

In Manitoba, tax investigators say they cannot get prison sentences for interprovincial smuggling of cigarettes.

A major method of smuggling cigarettes has been through mail-order systems. Until recently, a province that received smuggled cigarettes by mail could not prosecute the mail-order house in another province. The new federal Tobacco Act that came into force in April now makes it a federal offence to sell cigarettes by mail without a licence.

Discussion Questions

What are the main causes of interprovincial cigarette smuggling? What, in your opinion, is the most serious consequence of this illicit trade? Is law enforcement the answer? Should taxes across provinces be equalized? Would that solve the problem? Or would prices have to be lowered to U.S. levels in order to prevent international smuggling? What consequences for health care are involved in lowering cigarette prices?

Source: Peter Moon, *Globe and Mail*, July 28, 1997, p. A1. Reprinted with permission from the *Globe and Mail*.

they will likely require similar loans again in the future. Failure to repay within the agreed-upon time, when accompanied by an adequate excuse, normally results in an extension with interest. While harassment and threats are common experiences for miscreant debtors, bodily harm as an inducement to pay is a last resort. Loan sharks rarely have their delinquent debtors killed — they know it is impossible to collect money from a corpse (Abadinsky, 1985; Reuter, 1984).

Racketeering

Racketeering involves the extortion of money from law-abiding citizens and legitimate organizations and businesses. Racketeers sell "protection" to clients, "insuring" them against personal injury or death, against property damage and destruction, or against interference with legitimate business and commercial activity. If the insurance money is not paid, mobsters victimize the persons refusing the service. Common inducements include threatening or injuring family members, burning down homes, destroying industrial machinery, and scaring off customers. Racketeering on a small scale involves intimidating individual citizens and owners of small businesses such as restaurants, laundries, and corner stores. On a large scale, racketeers strike fear in the hearts of business executives, corporate owners, and union leaders alike.

Labour racketeering involves the direct and indirect extortion of money from a union, from the businesses and industries employing a union's members, or from both simultaneously. The mob either infiltrates key positions in organized labour or uses coercion and bribery to ensure that union leaders co-operate. Once they control key posts, organized criminals are in a position to plunder union pension funds, to negotiate union contracts, and to control the activities of union members. By controlling the work of the union rank and file, mobsters can extort money from any organization that employs union workers.

Criminal organizations can directly victimize unions through the outright theft of pension funds. Less blatantly, however, they can simply require that corrupted union officials use pension investments to grant loans to crime-controlled business concerns. These cut-rate loans have returns on interest far below those earned on legitimate investments. Mobsters may also insist that the money from union pension funds be lent out to designated borrowers without any collateral. The borrowers' shaky enterprises ultimately fail, leaving the union "holding the bag." Finally, many loans issued in this fashion go to persons who, from the start, have no intention of repaying. Regardless of how the union's funds are dispersed by organized crime, the inevitable result is a substantial loss to workers' future benefits.

Other forms of labour racketeering victimize not only unions but also the companies employing union workers. One of the most common schemes involves criminal organizations extorting money from employers in the form of "strike insurance." In return for guarantees that organized labour will not engage in work disruptions such as slowdowns and strikes, the mob requires companies to pay a substantial fee. Strike insurance is particularly common in trucking and construction businesses.

In another common racket, organized crime extracts money from employers while indirectly fleecing labour groups. An employer pays organized crime a retainer in return for assurances that contracts negotiated with unions will reflect the best interests not of the union but of big business. Having misrepresented these disadvantageous settlements, corrupt union officials recommend acceptance of these "sweetheart contracts." The final form of racketeering involves simple but large-scale theft. Criminal gangs, with the co-operation of union members, steal large quantities of goods or machinery from plants and warehouses. Workers either look the other way (for a fee) or aid and abet the crime (Abadinsky, 1985; Reuter, 1984).

Drugs

While the Mafia deals in most types of drugs, smaller crime groups are more specialized. The Chinese Triads in Vancouver, Toronto, and Montreal have concentrated on importing heroin from the Golden Triangle area of southeast Asia. Colombian criminal networks smuggle cocaine into Canada from South America. It is estimated that about 75 percent of the cocaine that comes into Canada comes from Colombian sources. The manufacture and distribution of synthetic drugs (e.g., LSD and methamphetamines) in Canada are largely controlled by outlaw motorcycle gangs. These gangs, however, are heavily involved in the street-level trafficking of virtually all forms of contraband drugs (Stamler, 1987).

Mafia and Camorra groups are now responsible for smuggling into North America much of the heroin produced in the Golden Crescent countries of Iran, Afghanistan, and Pakistan, as well as the Golden Triangle. Most cocaine enters North America through the efforts of drug cartels in the South American countries of Ecuador, Bolivia, Peru, and Colombia. While marijuana and hashish are now grown hydroponically in Canada and the United States, much of it is shipped into Canada by Colombian and Jamaican criminal networks (Inciardi, 1986).

Other Activities

Organized crime also embraces such diverse money-making schemes as stealing cars for eventual resale, counterfeiting currency, stocks, and bonds, distributing pirated records and tapes, and manufacturing and distributing pornographic movies. Declining profits in some traditional areas of vice have diminished the role of organized crime in bootlegging and prostitution (Abadinsky, 1985).

Insurance and bankruptcy frauds are other popular activities. In the former case, a criminal organization purchases properties and insures them heavily. The mob subsequently hires professional arsonists to torch the premises and then pockets the insurance money. In bankruptcy fraud, organized crime buys a controlling interest in a reputable retail business, making only a small down payment. It then uses the company's good reputation to purchase on credit a large inventory of goods ostensibly intended for sale to bona fide consumers. These goods, as yet unpaid for, are sold at bargain prices. After the discount sale, the newly purchased company declares bankruptcy.

LEGAL BUSINESS

The vastness of the proceeds from illegal business presents criminal organizations with a number of unique problems. Since increasing profit margins is the name of the game, it makes the most sense for organized crime to invest its ill-gotten gains in acquisitions that will show a substantial monetary return. Making more and more money by expanding illegal business endeavours, however, at some point becomes almost impossible. First, broadening the scope of illegal enterprise usually requires an expansion of territory, which in turn brings the growing operation into unwanted conflict with other criminal organizations. Gang wars are simply not good for business. Second, expansion into additional illegitimate ventures often increases the law-enforcement efforts of the police. Organized crime circumvents both of these difficulties when it sinks its funds in money-making operations that are perfectly legal.

Over the years, criminal organizations have invested in a plethora of legitimate business interests, including hotels, bars, restaurants, construction firms, trucking companies, and a host of others. Investments in legal commerce and industry provide an air of legitimacy and respectability. Moreover, legal enterprises can be used as fronts for illegal operations.

The enormous profits generated by illegal business are difficult for organized criminals to conceal completely. The Canadian government requires citizens not only to pay income tax but also to report the sources of their earned income. Visible profits from illegal operations present a serious dilemma. On the one hand, taxes must be paid to avoid prosecution for tax evasion. On the other hand, criminals cannot declare the source of their income.

Out of this quandary has sprung a new law-enforcement strategy called "net worth investigation" (Rhodes, 1984). Police have recently begun to examine the material quality of the lifestyles of suspected underworld figures. They then compare the observed standard of living with the suspect's reported income. When the suspect lives well but pays few taxes, the government can initiate criminal proceedings for tax violations. From the point of view of organized criminals, a desirable solution to this problem is to purchase legitimate businesses and to claim, through some creative bookkeeping, that these legitimate enterprises are the criminals' primary sources of income. Legitimate businesses that are losing money represent convenient tax write-offs.

Channelling illegally acquired funds through legitimate enterprises is known as "money laundering." One of the most popular techniques of processing illegal profits involves the use of foreign banks. First, a criminal group deposits drug or gambling profits in a number of Canadian banks. Then it quickly transfers these funds overseas to financial institutions in a country with strict bank-secrecy laws. In a country such as the Bahamas, stringent regulations permit the revelation neither of the identity of account holders nor of the balances held in their accounts. Many of these countries also offer the added advantage of low or nonexistent taxes on foreign funds. "Dirty" money is laundered when crime figures in Canada write cheques on anonymous foreign bank accounts to purchase legitimate Canadian companies.

Another laundering technique involves transferring money from a protected foreign bank into an account held in the name of a "paper company" (one that exists on paper only) in a country like Panama. The criminal organization then "borrows" funds from this paper company and invests in legitimate business. In effect, the organized crime group takes out a loan from itself. To add insult to injury, the interest on these loans is frequently tax deductible. The list of transactions among foreign bank accounts and paper companies in different countries is often very long and extremely complex (Abadinsky, 1985). The resultant impenetrable maze makes it almost impossible to discover the origins of monies invested in Canada.

Once organized crime invests in legitimate businesses, it turns profits in a number of different ways. First, underworld organizations invest in operations that are not only law-abiding but also lucrative. Second, even though these acquired businesses are legitimate, organized crime can avail itself of the option of improving its edge over law-abiding competitors by engaging in illegal tactics. There is some

evidence, for example, that mobs in the United States have taken control of some companies contracting with government and industry for contracts to dispose of various forms of toxic waste (Block and Scarpitti, 1985). Unconstrained by the law, companies process these chemical wastes in dangerous but inexpensive ways. Popular cost-cutting techniques for dealing with deadly chemicals include long-term storage in warehouses, discharging waste into city sewers and nearby water systems, burial in unmarked pits in landfill sites, and dumping in wilderness areas. Because legitimate waste disposal companies obey the law, they incur higher operating costs. As a consequence, they cannot compete effectively with the mob-owned and -operated competition. Continued losses eventually force law-abiding disposal companies out of business altogether. Finally, organized crime groups routinely invest in enterprises showing yearly financial losses. In so doing, they enjoy a variety of tax breaks that governments routinely accord to the owners of ailing companies.

Another reason for organized crime's diversification into legitimate businesses involves concerns for family progeny. Children whose fathers are in the mob, like the children of other wealthy parents, frequently attend prestigious schools and become well educated. Rather than follow in their fathers' footsteps, many move on to work in family-controlled but legitimate enterprises. There are two basic reasons for this transition. First, the children may disapprove of their fathers' criminal connections or their parents may wish to shield them from the negative aspects of work in a criminal organization. Second, illegal business enterprises and their proceeds are difficult to inherit. This problem is particularly acute when the offspring are female. Mob traditions completely deny women any possibility of assuming control over the criminal businesses operated by the family. This makes sensible the acquisition of legal businesses that can be much more easily passed from one generation to the next (Anderson, 1979).

A THEORY OF ORGANIZED CRIME

One of the most prominent explanations of organized crime is Bell's (1962) **"queer ladder of mobility"** perspective. Bell's approach borrows from Merton's (1938) strain theory of deviance and crime. Merton considered everyone in North American society to be preoccupied with monetary and material success. Not everyone, however, has equal access to legitimate means of achieving these goals in socially approved ways. Those whose high aspirations cannot be realized legitimately because they cannot get a good education or cannot land a good job are compelled either to accept their plight and conform or to adapt in some nonconforming way.

When people accept society's goals but reject the legitimate means through which these goals can be attained, they innovate. In so doing, they undertake deviant or illegal means in the pursuit of their objectives. As Bell argues, innovation, or the resort to criminal enterprise, is a means to upward mobility. In this endeavour, rewards are maximized through planning, skill, sophistication, and, most importantly, organization. When many innovators come from similar origins or belong to the same group, individual mobility is transformed into group mobility.

Bell begins by noting that various ethnic groups coming to the United States have historically found themselves confronted with an inhospitable labour market that discriminates against and excludes them. Denied legitimate avenues to betterment, they have innovated by adopting criminal means of amassing capital. In the process, they have climbed upward, rung by rung, on the parallel but illegitimate "queer" mobility ladder. Bell observes that once a particular group has attained wealth and power, it gradually becomes more and more respectable and eventually abandons the criminal for the legitimate means to wealth. As one ethnic group becomes legitimate and abandons the life of crime (usually after about three generations), another moves in at the bottom of the queer ladder to begin its climb to respectability. This process is referred to by Ianni (1974) as **ethnic succession**.

Ethnic succession occurred originally as crime groups moved from tactical crime through illegitimate business into legitimate enterprises. In the past 100 years, the process that began with the pioneers of capitalism, the British and the Scots, has subsequently involved a series of other groups in sequence — the Irish, the Jews, the Italians, the blacks, and the Puerto Ricans. The most recent entries at the bottom of the ladder are the Mexicans, the Cubans, and the Colombians.

The major criticism levelled at the theory of ethnic succession is that the Italians appear not to be relinquishing their control over underworld enterprises. Critics maintain that newer organized-crime groups are not displacing the Italians but rather are working for them by running franchises or engaging in commercial activities in which the Italian Mafia has no interest (Lupsha, 1981). The passage of more time may shed additional light on this controversy. One development that may interfere with the process of succession is the lucrative market provided by the trade in illicit drugs. This illegitimate market is so massively profitable that criminal organizations may find their willingness to depart significantly diminished (Abadinsky, 1985).

THE CONTROL OF ORGANIZED CRIME

Organized crime has proven difficult to control for several reasons. In the first place, many generally law-abiding people enjoy placing bets, getting high on cocaine, watching pornographic movies, and hiring kinky sex. For the most part, these criminal acts lack people who see themselves as victims. When crime is "victimless," the numbers complaining to the police and willing to serve as prosecution witnesses are low.

The criminal activity of organizations like the Mafia, the Triads, and motorcycle gangs is highly rational. Not only do these groups carefully plan their illegal ventures, they employ the talents of specially trained persons. A Mafia assassin, for example, knows precisely how to execute people without getting caught. Criminal organizations also make extensive use of experts in legitimate professions, including corporate attorneys, criminal lawyers, and tax accountants. Enthusiastic consumers, rational planning, and the use of skilled expertise combine to make organized criminal activity difficult to suppress.

The structure and the subculture of criminal organizations unite to protect them from the encroachment of police. The hierarchical division of labour, with its word-of-mouth communication, distances criminal leaders from the long arm of the law. With little written down, evidence is hard to come by. In addition, the strong emphasis on loyalty and silence, the quick resort to intimidation, and the willingness to murder if necessary diminish the enthusiasm and spirit of co-operation among complaints, witnesses, and informants (Cressey, 1969).

Another extremely important protective strategy is the mounting of vigorous initiatives aimed at corrupting politicians, court officials, and police officers. Criminal organizations bribe police on the street to

Box 14.5
LAUNDERING LAW CALLED A BURDEN

Canada's banks will face a huge bureaucratic burden when they are forced to comply with the recently passed federal money laundering legislation, a major consulting firm says.

The new law, which received royal assent on June 29, spells out that banks and other institutions that handle financial transactions must record and report all large cash transfers.

The threshold for reporting is expected to be set at $10,000 although detailed regulations won't be published until later this year.

The institutions must also report any transaction, regardless of its size, if they suspect it is being used for money laundering.

While the banks already voluntarily alert the RCMP to suspicious transactions, the new law will force them to systematically report to a new agency, the Financial Transactions and Reports Analysis Centre of Canada.

The new law doesn't just affect banks. It covers all institutions that handle large amounts of cash, including credit unions, casinos, currency changers, and insurance companies. Penalties for not reporting large or suspicious transactions are steep: up to five years in jail or a $2-million fine.

This will mean a massive effort to train individuals to recognize potential money laundering activity, and a huge amount of paperwork to track the thousands of large cash transactions that take place at banks every day, said Stephen Schneider, manager of KPMG Investigation and Security Inc., a unit of consultant KPMG.

"The banks are going to be bogged down in paperwork," Mr. Schneider said at a briefing for reporters yesterday. They'll have to keep better records, get to know their clients more thoroughly, and train their staff so potential money laundering activities are recognized, he said.

The banks have a huge incentive to document the processes they use to detect money laundering, Mr. Schneider said. That's because the new law says that if a case of money laundering slips through undetected, the financial institution will be off the hook "if they establish that they exercised all due diligence to prevent its commission."

Gene McLean, security director at the Canadian Bankers Association, said yesterday that it will not become clear just how much extra work and expense will be involved until the regulations are published. "We support the legislation in principle," he said, but the banks want to make sure the new federal agency is not "buried in a blizzard of paperwork."

Despite the potentially increased costs, the new rules are essential if Canada is to fight the huge financial drain from money laundering, said Chris Mathers, president of KPMG's corporate intelligence unit. Money laundering effectively hides criminal income, he said, and "unreported income subverts economies." He described laundering as the "No. 1 threat to our way of life," and suggested the problem is economically more damaging than the trade in illicit drugs.

KPMG said current estimates suggest about $600-billion (U.S.) is laundered globally every year, and as much as $17-billion (Canadian) of that takes place in Canada.

Bill Knight, president of the Credit Union Central of Canada, said yesterday that he supports the changes, even though they will increase administrative expenses. "Clearly, it adds regulatory costs," Mr. Knight said, "but it's good for the whole industry. I want [to effectively erect] a sign that says 'Canada is off limits to money laundering.'"

To keep extra costs under control, credit unions will try to use their own internal expertise to handle the new system, rather than hiring external consultants like KPMG, Mr. Knight said.

The new law will also require individuals and businesses to tell Canada Customs when they are moving large amounts of money across the border. The threshold for this reporting is expected to be $15,000.

One reason why Ottawta created the new law, Mr. Schneider said, was that is was under pressure from other developed countries to improve its procedures. Money laundering has become a huge international priority, he said.

The United States has had a mandatory reporting system since the 1970s, he said.

Discussion Questions

How effective is this initiative likely to be in the control of organized crime? Who will pay for its implementation?

Source: Richard Blackwell, *Globe and Mail*, July 13, 2000, p. B2. Reprinted with permission from the *Globe and Mail*.

ignore victimless crimes. More importantly, they pay off politicians and more senior criminal justice officials to ensure the inefficient allocation of law-enforcement resources and the relaxation of enforcement policies (Rhodes, 1984).

Criminal law itself poses problems for the control of organized crime. With few exceptions, it is designed to cope with an individual committing a specific offence rather than with an organization planning or perpetrating a series of offences. Criminal law does not concentrate on the control of large-scale criminal conspiracies (Hills, 1980). Being the member of an organized crime group in Canada, for example, is not in itself a crime.

Obtaining a conviction for a particular violation under current criminal law requires proving beyond a reasonable doubt the coincidence of *mens rea* (intent) and *actus reus* (an act). Unfortunately, the conspirators in organized criminal activity are often far removed from the commission of an offence. This "distance" makes proving intent, an act, and their coincidence difficult if not impossible. Furthermore, even when senior conspirators are convicted of individual crimes, the court often metes out minimal penalties because they often have only minor criminal records or none at all. Moreover, they may well have made legitimate contributions to their communities (Rhodes, 1984).

Criminal law in a liberal democracy like Canada places considerable emphasis on ensuring that rules of due process protect the civil liberties of citizens. Due-process regulations safeguard the individual's right to privacy and protect Canadians from unreasonable search and seizure, unwarranted visual and electronic surveillance, and entrapment. In order to search, seize, watch, or conduct a sting operation, law-enforcement officials must normally demonstrate that they have reasonable cause to believe that a serious crime has been or is about to be committed. Hunches and inchoate suspicions that a person might be involved in a criminal organization are legally insufficient for these purposes. While protecting the rights of citizens, due process also makes it extraordinarily difficult to crack down on organized crime (Rhodes, 1984).

Other aspects of Canadian law have impeded the curbing of organized crime. For example, confidentiality rules have allowed Canadian banks to resist disclosing to the authorities information contained in their records. Also, while it is illegal under the *Criminal Code* to possess the proceeds from a crime,

the penalties upon conviction for such possession did not until recently include provisions for the confiscation of assets.

In addition to their susceptibility to corruption, a number of other aspects of the police undermine their ability to deal effectively with organized criminal activity. First, police officers are generally trained to deal with street crime, which tends to be comparatively simple. Police training academies do not equip officers to deal with complex crimes involving conspiracy, fraud, money laundering, and planned bankruptcy. Tracing the transfer of funds through complicated networks of national and foreign bank accounts and investment companies requires highly skilled personnel, whom police forces find in short supply (Rhodes, 1984).

Second, the jurisdictions of various police forces overlap considerably both nationally and internationally. An operation against organized criminal activity may require the careful co-ordination of RCMP, provincial, and municipal police forces and, on occasion, the law-enforcement agencies of other nations. Jurisdictional disputes, agency rivalries, lack of communication and co-ordination, and the failure to share intelligence information all too frequently undermine co-ordinated action (Rhodes, 1984).

Third, most criminal offences covered by the *Criminal Code* involve reactive policing. Police generally respond to crime on the basis of the reports of victims, witnesses, or both. But organized criminal activity frequently lacks both victims laying complaints and witnesses volunteering evidence. This circumstance leaves the police with little choice but to abandon reactive techniques in favour of "proactive" strategies, which involve actively ferreting out criminal organizations and gathering evidence against them over long periods of time. To accomplish this, police routinely employ several methods, including visual and electronic surveillance, undercover infiltration, paid informants, and sting operations.

Proactive policing, because of its intrusive nature, inevitably runs up against a number of obstacles. First, many civil libertarians view with suspicion the powers exercised by police in placing persons under surveillance and in covertly infiltrating groups. Such circumstances, they argue, increase the potential for the violation of individual civil liberties. Critics of law enforcement are quick to point out the ease with which such laws can be and are abused by police (Rhodes, 1984).

The practice of using informants has also subjected the police to criticism. Informants frequently have criminal records, and their offences have often been serious. Sometimes, police pay informants for their information or pave the way for their "snitches" to plead guilty to offences less serious than those actually committed. Police may go so far as to grant snitches complete immunity from prosecution. Assertions that these are often the only means by which evidence can be gathered against organized crime figures do not sit well with many Canadians. The public finds distasteful the knowledge that informants not only profit from their crimes but are dealt with leniently (Abadinsky, 1985).

Finally, proactive techniques are generally time-consuming and costly. But legislators and the public are seldom patient; they want immediate results for their law-enforcement dollar. Securing the political will and public financing for expensive and protracted organized crime investigations is difficult enough, and the problem is exacerbated by the uncertain success of such crime-control operations (Rhodes, 1984).

Recommended responses to organized crime range from decriminalization to stepping-up law-enforcement efforts. None of these "solutions" is without problems, and all are controversial. Proponents of decriminalization argue that the questions are not whether people will be able to acquire a banned good or avail themselves of a prohibited service, but from whom, under what conditions, and at what price.

The market for illicit goods and services does not change much in response to price changes. Demand is constant. Narrowing or eliminating negative sanctions for such activities as usury, drugs, pornography, and prostitution and implementing government supervision through regulation, licensing, and zoning would effectively shatter the monopolies now held by organized crime groups. Proponents of decriminalization argue that it would drastically cut the profits of criminal organizations and raise the likelihood that organized crime groups would vacate many markets. They point out that eliminating the black market would substantially reduce its economic and social costs, which include the enrichment of criminals, the loss of tax dollars, the diversion of law-enforcement resources from serious crime, the corruption of officials, and the disrespect for criminal justice engendered by unenforceable laws and institutional corruption (Hills, 1980).

The public is unlikely to support decriminalization, however. Too many people see the prohibited goods and services not only as an integral part of the "crime problem" but also as issues of morality. Many Canadians already feel that the criminal laws are too limited and that law enforcement is too lax. A large number would vehemently oppose loosening constraints on drugs, commercial sex, and gambling on the grounds that such a liberal approach would breed violence and moral degeneration. Rather than favouring liberalization of existing measures, there is considerable support among the Canadian public for cracking down more heavily on these offences. Even if liberalization were to occur, it is unlikely that decriminalization would end organized crime. If history provides any lesson, it is that criminal organizations would merely shift their operations to the provision of goods and services that governments simply could not legalize.

Many Canadians favour increased law enforcement as the best way to control organized crime. Perhaps the greatest obstacle facing this strategy is financial; the costs of increasing the numbers of police, providing officers with the latest equipment, and improving the training of police officers, Crown attorneys, and judges are large. Underwriting the expenses of lengthy police investigations and trying complex cases before the courts are immensely expensive (Abadinsky, 1985).

A cheaper route to combatting organized crime is to alter existing law. Expanding the powers of the criminal justice system would make it easier to investigate, prosecute, and punish members of organized crime groups. These new measures add a more organizational focus to the current individualistic emphasis of Canadian criminal law. Along with new legislation, advocates suggest that special programs be instituted to facilitate the prosecution of organized crime. These strategies have been widely implemented in the United States, and a review of the American experience is instructive.

In 1970, the United States enacted the *Organized Crime Control Act*, which contained the "Racketeer Influenced and Corrupt Organization" provisions, better known as the "RICO statutes." These new statutes substantially increased electronic surveillance, search and seizure, and the confiscation of individual and group assets. RICO laws prohibit participation in a "pattern of racketeering," the demonstration of which only requires a conviction for two run-of-the-mill street crimes included in a list of potential racketeering offences. In its original formulation, RICO

Box 14.6
ASSET MANAGEMENT AND SHARING

The Proceeds of Crime legislation was passed with the expectation that it would enable the police to take away the illicit proceeds and property of convicted criminals. Unfortunately, no adequate provision was made for the management and maintenance of the goods seized by police. The difficulty arises from the time lag between the freezing and seizure of the goods and the completion of the legal processes that determine the guilt or innocence of the suspect. Upon a suspect's conviction, the goods determined to be the "proceeds of crime" can be forfeited. However, if the person is declared innocent, the property must be returned — and returned in good order. Court cases can take months or years to complete, and most types of property require professional handling to ensure that they retain some value for whoever assumes ultimate ownership.

The old RCMP line "Never seize anything that eats" should have been applied to the infamous "Ski Montjoie" case — the case that pushed the government to create an asset management and sharing regime. In 1990, the RCMP seized the Ski-Montjoie facility in North Hatley, Quebec. Police investigations had shown that this resort had been obtained through the importation of multi-tonne shipments of marijuana from Jamaica to Florida. The drug money was routed through Switzerland and then "loaned" to the traffickers by a Swiss company. The traffickers were said to have put over $7 million into the resort, which upon seizure had a market value of approximately $4.5 million.

In addition to the difficulties associated with keeping the resort in adequate condition pre-forfeiture, the federal government faced unanticipated legalities in the form of legitimate creditors whose claims for payment exceeded $2.5 million. The ski facility's operating companies were insolvent at the time of the seizure. A judge in Quebec appointed a lawyer to administer the facility (another major expense for the federal government). As of 1995, with an asset management group in charge, the ski facility is actually breaking even — but it still cannot be sold because of the significant decrease in land values in the area.

The liability aspect of the Proceeds of Crime legislation (which falls to the attorney general) makes it particularly essential that all seized property be professionally maintained pending the termination of the court process. A 1990 memorandum of understanding between the RCMP and National Health and Welfare stipulated that the RCMP was to maintain the property pre-forfeiture, that is, until a verdict was given. If conviction and forfeiture were decided by the courts, National Health and Welfare was to maintain, sell, or otherwise dispose of the property, with the revenue going into the General Revenue Fund. The first flaw in this scenario was the naive assumption that a policing organization would be able (or even willing) to take on professional property maintenance responsibilities. The second flaw was the expectation that provincial and municipal governments would enthusiastically encourage their police forces to assist the RCMP in completing these expensive and prolonged Proceeds of Crime investigations — and then stand by and watch as the forfeited proceeds were handed over to the General Revenue Fund. Professional maintenance of the property and a mechanism for sharing the proceeds with different agencies or levels of government were soon recognized to be essential to the successful handling of seized assets.

In addition to the conflicts arising within its own borders, Canada faced relentless pressure to share seized proceeds with foreign jurisdictions. The United States seemed particularly eager to share proceeds of crime with Canadian agencies and similarly share in Canadian seizures arising from joint-force operations or other collaborative efforts. U.S. Customs advertise the extent to which their own seizures pay for their law enforcement costs, and law enforcement officers south of the border boast of the vehicles and other property — including cash — that police forces are able to keep for their own use after forfeiture. A "Miami Vice" approach to law enforcement seems attractive to police forces feeling themselves strapped for funds. However, Canadian government officials, some Canadian police forces, and an increasing number of U.S. officials have expressed concerns that the choice of which cases to pursue can be biased by the vested interest of a police department that is in a position to benefit materially from the decisions that are made. Particular controversy centres on the civil *in rem* forfeiture cases, where goods are seized without a person having been found guilty of an offence.

While it is hard to convince some police departments that costs incurred during investigations should come out of their regular budgets without any additional recompense from seizures, it is easier to warn them that evidence from the United States indicates that jurisdictions short of resources tend to build the "expectation" of seizures into the budget process. With varying degrees of subtlety, U.S. police-force budgets are reduced in the expectation that some resources from the seizure of illicit proceeds will be accrued during the year. The upshot is that police forces become operationally reliant on making significant seizures, which again increases the likelihood of bias in enforcement practices. The police may target specific cases not for material gain, but merely to maintain existing resources and viability.

The police are by no means the only group to exhibit a proprietary interest in illicit proceeds. With only minor exceptions, each group (police, community, levels of government) consulted by Canadian government officials on the question of who should share in the distribution of these proceeds named itself as the most worthy candidate. Criminal sanctions have never been so utilitarian!

At one stage government officials were equating the seizure of funds to "priming" the pump that would gush drug prevention programs, treatment, and rehabilitation facilities, with a proportion feeding back into the expensive police investigations that would then produce more dollars. One of these pumps plus a couple of government-run casinos should produce all of the revenue Canada requires! It remains too early to know the potential extent of the forfeiture and sharing.

Discussion Question

While forfeiture and sharing appear to be appropriate strategies in the effort to control organized crime, what are some of the potential pitfalls associated with these approaches?

Source: Margaret Beare, *Criminal Conspiracies: Organized Crime in Canada* (Toronto: Nelson, 1996), pp. 171–73. Reprinted with permission of Nelson Thomson Learning, a division of Thomson Learning.

did not directly address money laundering. Such a provision, the *Money Laundering Control Act*, was introduced sixteen years after the initial passage of the Act (Beare, 1996).

Two departures from ordinary criminal law are worth noting. First, the RICO provisions make it a crime to *be* a racketeer. Second, the scope of the acts committed, rather than their seriousness, determines the severity of the legal sanction. Penalties for conviction as a racketeer are far more severe than those for conviction on individual criminal code offences. Sanctions include fines of up to $25 000, imprisonment for up to 20 years, or both. In addition to imposing fines and imprisonment, RICO statutes enable victims to bring civil actions against racketeers in the form of "triple damage suits," which require racketeers to compensate victims for three times the harm done to businesses and property; a victim who has lost $3000 can sue for $9000 (Rhodes, 1984).

The RICO provisions have met with a good deal of criticism from those whose primary concern is the preservation of individual civil liberties. While U.S. law (and Canadian law) fails to provide precise definitions of "organized crime," "racket," and "racketeer," it empowers prosecuting attorneys to use every conceivable legal tactic to secure convictions against accused persons. Vague legal definitions encourage broad interpretations of the law. Imprecise definitions give the courts considerable latitude in determining who is an ordinary criminal and who is involved in racketeering. Given the severe sanctions attached to RICO convictions, the ramifications for the accused are considerable (Abadinsky, 1994). As one might expect, American courts have invoked RICO statutes to convict persons who are not members of the kinds of organized crime groups described in this chapter.

Another problem with the RICO provisions concerns their invocation of civil proceedings. Civil law is more flexible than criminal law; the rules of evidence are more relaxed, and standards of proof are lower. Using civil law to prosecute a case permits the more stringent due-process rules of criminal law to be bypassed. It is thus possible for people who would never be convicted under criminal law to be found liable in a civil proceeding (Rhodes, 1984).

Expanding the use of such tactics as electronic surveillance also presents problems. Most tapped conversations involve discussions of noncriminal matters.

Box 14.7
GANG-RELATED CHARGES DROPPED AGAINST ALLEGED WARRIORS

The first major test of Canada's new antigang law limped to a conclusion of sorts yesterday, with the Crown dropping gang-related charges against 12 alleged Manitoba Warriors in exchange for pleas of guilty in cocaine trafficking.

The original accused, 32 aboriginal men and one aboriginal female, one Caucasian man and one black man – were rounded up in October of 1998 and directly indicted under 1997 federal legislation designed to thwart organized crime.

The joint federal-provincial prosecution of the 35 alleged Manitoba Warriors was touted as the first major test of the 1997 law.

But of the 35, only two people – minor players – actually pleaded guilty to participating in a criminal organization and had extra time tacked to their jail terms.

So after 20 months of pretrial wrangling and after spending an estimated $7-million for a custom-built courthouse, legal-aid fees, prosecutors and sheriff's officers, the matter never actually got to trial and the antigang law remains untested.

In the end, the Crown secured 32 convictions on drug charges and offered two complete stays in exchange for testimony. The case of one accused, Sheldon Clarke, remains undecided. The dozen men who pleaded guilty yesterday to cocaine trafficking and conspiracy charges will be sentenced next week. The trafficking charges involve peddling small quantities of cocaine in various hotels in Winnipeg.

"With these pleas entered, the Crown will enter stays on the other charges against these men," prosecutor Bob Morrison told Court of Queen's Bench Judge Nathan Nurgitz yesterday.

All who had earlier pleaded guilty were jailed for periods of six months to six years on drug-related charges.

Denied bail, the accused were routinely transported from a downtown jail to the specially built suburban Winnipeg courthouse during nearly two years of pretrial appearances. Yesterday, armour-clad guards stood vigil over video cameras while the accused sat chained to the floor in cubicles as each man stood to plead guilty.

Critics, including Phil Fontaine, National Chief of the Assembly of First Nations, called the case a gross abuse of civil rights. Mr. Fontaine and others complained the case was discriminatory since the accused faced a reverse onus to qualify for bail, yet the majority of them were too impoverished to post a surety.

Roland Penner, former Manitoba attorney-general, now a professor of law at the University of Manitoba, described the case yesterday as "entirely unwise and misconceived from the beginning."

Describing the case as politically motivated, expensive and constitutionally invalid, Prof. Penner said the federal antigang law is redundant because it is similar to various conspiracy laws, "which are sometimes called the shabbiest weapon of the prosecutorial arsenal."

"I don't think it would stand up [to a constitutional challenge]," Prof. Penner said. "It was really misconceived by both the previous government and the present government ... preventive detention under another name smells bad."

David Deutscher, also of the U of M's law faculty, said the case was too complex with too many accused and too many charges for it to have a chance of success. "Quite obviously it didn't succeed," he said. "In my view this law [in 1997] was a political reaction to some problems the federal government was having in Quebec [with gang wars]."

At one time, there were a dozen prosecutors and more than 30 defence lawyers appearing in the super-secure Winnipeg court, which was built by the previous Tory government at a cost of $3.3-million. Yesterday, there were 10 defence lawyers and three crown prosecutors in the sprawling courthouse.

Under the 1997 law, an offender is to be sentenced both for the crime and for participating in organized-crime. The sentences are to be served consecutively. The maximum penalty is 14 years in prison.

At the time of the mass arrests, which police dubbed Operation Northern Snow, Vic Toews, then Manitoba's justice minister, said the government had no choice but to prosecute. "We have to support the federal antigang legislation. I wouldn't say what's motivating us here is the economics," he said.

NDP Justice Minister Gord Mackintosh, who questioned the previous government's decision to build the courthouse without first testing the legislation, said yesterday the government would not use the building again as a courthouse. He said the government will try to find a new tenant or sell the building.

Discussion Questions

Does this case bode well for Canada's efforts to address the problems posed by organized gangs? What do you think might have gone wrong?

Source: David Roberts, *Globe and Mail*, July 6, 2000, p. A3. Reprinted with permission from the *Globe and Mail*.

When crimes are discussed, they are usually minor. Not only are wiretaps and planted bugs an invasion of privacy, but the costs per conviction of this form of intelligence gathering are staggering (Abadinsky, 1985; Rhodes, 1984).

In an effort to strengthen law-enforcement effectiveness in the control of enterprise crimes committed by organized criminal groups in Canada, Parliament has recently passed several RICO-like pieces of legislation designed to "target upwards" or to attack organized crime in its upper echelons by shifting emphasis from the person committing an offence to the proceeds generated from it. The 1989 *Proceeds of Crime Act*, for example, contains 24 offences designated as enterprise crime, including bribery, book-making, procuring, extortion, counterfeiting, money laundering, and certain drug violations. The *Proceeds of Crime Money Laundering Act* (1991) requires financial institutions such as banks, credit unions, loan companies, and foreign-exchange houses to retain certain records for a five-year period to facilitate police investigations. The *Seized Property Management Act* (1993) authorizes the federal government to manage property seized and restrained in connection with criminal offending and to dispose of property when the courts order forfeiture. Factors hindering the success of law-enforcement initiatives under this legislation include inadequate resources, lack of experience in prioritizing cases, deficient knowledge of forensic analysis, resistance on the part of police to include nonpolice agencies in investigations, and insufficient international co-operation in intelligence sharing (Beare, 1996).

The Canadian government introduced an anti-gang law in 1997. The law specifies that individuals can be sentenced to a maximum of fourteen years for participation in organized criminal activity as well as additional years for a particular crime. Those found guilty serve their sentences consecutively rather than concurrently. Participation in a criminal organization involves the conspiracy or commission of an offence for the benefit of, at the direction of, or in association with, a criminal organization where the crime involved has a maximum sentence of five or more years (Roberts, 2000). The law stops short of making it an offence to belong to an organized criminal group (Appleby and Ha, 2000).

Winning the co-operation of witnesses and informants is another major obstacle confronting those trying to gather evidence on organized criminal activities. Both witnesses and informants are highly vulnerable to intimidation and assassination at the hands of enforcers. Witness-protection programs and informant immunity are two strategies that help overcome the reluctance to participate in criminal proceedings. Witness protection involves providing those testifying against underworld figures with new identities and with relocation to new areas. In 1995, Canada tabled a bill to create a national Witness Protection Program. Its purposes are relocating witnesses, changing their identities, and providing them with subsistence or maintenance funding. The program is projected to contain between 80 and 100 witnesses at any one time and to cost approximately $3.4 million annually (Beare, 1996). Such programs, however, are not without their problems. Because they have "ceased to exist," government witnesses face the discontinuation of pensions and social security and the loss of their credit ratings. Furthermore, any subsequent use of their fingerprints for identification purposes is dangerous (Rhodes, 1984).

Using informants is particularly problematic. Informers are usually former members of criminal organizations and, as such, they have usually committed crimes for which they have neither been charged nor convicted. It is not unusual for governments to grant informants immunity from future prosecution in return for information. However, their testimony presents two major problems for law enforcement. First, the credibility of their evidence is frequently highly questionable. Often they have long histories of lying and perjury. Second, high-profile media exposés often follow testimony by informers. That known criminals, some of whom have committed serious offences, are allowed to go free creates a crisis of confidence among the public. Insult is added to injury if it becomes known that the absolved have also been paid for their testimony out of the public purse (Rhodes, 1984).

The American experience with legislative change and the intensification of law enforcement suggests a number of caveats regarding the control of organized crime in Canada. Extreme care must be taken to ensure that civil liberties are not sacrificed, that programs facilitating the testimony of witnesses and informers adequately meet their needs, and that public confidence in the criminal justice system is not compromised.

SUMMARY

Sociologists have brought to light several popular misconceptions about organized crime. They argue that organized crime historically is less an alien conspiracy than a logical outcome of North American capitalism. Their research has also ignited a debate about the extent to which organized crime is "syndicated" nationally and internationally. Some have argued that the sinister syndicate is little more than a hollow image manipulated by governments and law-enforcement agencies to garner support from a fearful public for more comprehensive and expensive policing initiatives. Syndicate or not, few dispute the fact that organized crime affects enormous numbers of people, directly and indirectly, by delivering highly desired goods and services, both legal and illegal.

Definitions of organized crime are vague. Definitional disputes hinge mainly on questions concerning the size and degree of co-ordination among criminal groups and the precise nature of the acts in which they engage. Organized crime groups are quite diverse, and their money-making enterprises are quite varied. Given the controversies surrounding the development of precise definitions, criminologists have opted for cataloguing the traits of criminal organizations. Key characteristics include a hierarchical and specialized division of labour, a quasi-bureaucracy in which communication is confined to word of mouth, and a subculture whose cornerstones are conspiracy and secrecy. Membership in criminal groups is con-

fined to males on the basis of kinship, ethnic ties, or the possession of an impressive criminal record. Crime groups use sponsorship and apprenticeship to induct and socialize new members. They seek to monopolize either through controlling all illegal business in a particular region (geographic dominance) or through controlling the trade in a particular good or service (sector dominance). Organized crime protects its business interests through extortion, corruption, or both.

The economic, physical, psychological, and moral costs to society that result from organized criminal activity are staggering. Direct money losses to ordinary citizens accrue from such illegal practices as fraud, large-scale theft, loansharking, and the drug trade. Indirect economic costs include the bill for law enforcement, taxes forgone on illegitimate revenues, and higher prices for legitimate goods and services stemming from unfair competitive practices and labour racketeering.

The syndicate and confederation perspectives are the two principal views of organized crime in North America. The syndicate approach sees big-league organized crime as an affair involving hierarchically organized underworld families, whose activities are orchestrated and mediated by an elected commission. In this view, the family is unified around a strong set of subcultural bonds whose cornerstones are honour, loyalty, and secrecy. Alternatively, the confederation perspective conceives of organized crime as a much more loosely connected client–patron contact system characterized by shifting roles and obligations.

There are three types of organized criminal enterprises. Tactical initiatives involve the judicious application of violence and the widespread use of corruption to facilitate commercial enterprise. Illegal businesses tap an extensive market of illicit goods and services for which there is a seemingly insatiable demand. Gambling, loansharking, racketeering, and drugs have given rise to monopolies of enormous wealth and power. Other less lucrative but nonetheless popular activities range from large-scale theft to the manufacture and distribution of pornography. Finally, organized crime has become increasingly involved in legal commerce to avoid territorial disputes, to launder its gargantuan illegal income, and to provide both legitimate work and a means of inheritance for its progeny. Underworld crime groups enjoy special advantages in their competition for legitimate markets. These include massive amounts of money for investment and quick resort to illegal tactics where necessary.

Bell's "queer ladder of mobility" concept is based on the notions of innovation contained in Merton's version of anomie. Bell explains organized crime in terms of ethnic groups' experiences of blocked legitimate opportunity in the face of high aspirations. The changing dominance of a series of ethnic groups in organized crime is accounted for through the notion of ethnic succession. Groups that achieve success by criminal means gradually switch over to legitimate money-making pursuits and, in the process, make room for other deprived segments to follow in their footsteps.

Organized crime is difficult to control for a variety of reasons, including the scope of its market, the victimless nature of much of the crime involved, and the calculated rationality of its perpetration. Criminal organizations communicate internally by word of mouth, strongly emphasize conspiracy, loyalty, and silence, retain the services of legal and criminal specialists, and make extensive use of intimidation and corruption.

Criminal law is not well suited to controlling the enterprises of illegal organizations. Broadening the scope of the law and increasing the powers of the police under RICO-type provisions engender the risk of civil liberties violations. For the police, cases involving organized crime are frequently very complex, extremely time consuming, and receive inadequate economic and personnel support. Jurisdictional overlap makes co-ordinating operations difficult, and the necessity of proactive measures increases the risk of the entrapment defence. Finally, both the use of informants and the decriminalization of morals offences are unpopular strategies with the Canadian public.

DISCUSSION QUESTIONS

1. Discuss the social and economic costs of organized criminal activities.

2. Discuss the development of organized crime in Canada.

3. Why is organized crime difficult to control? Explain.

4. How is organized criminal activity related to laws that govern society's morals? How might decriminalization of morality offences change the nature of organized crime?

5. What implications for the erosion of civil liberties are inherent in initiatives aimed at the control of organized crime?

WEB LINKS

Nathanson Centre for the Study of Organized Crime and Corruption
http://www.yorku.ca/nathanson/
   The Web site of this research centre includes a definition of organized crime, quarterly newsletters, a bibliographic database, news updates, and a great list of links.

Major Issues Relating to Organized Crime: Within the Context of Economic Relationships
http://www.lcc.gc.ca/en/themes/er/oc/nathan/
   This paper, prepared by Margaret E. Beare and R.T. Naylor for the Law Commission of Canada, re-examines the idea of organized crime and concludes that the term "organized crime" serves to camouflage differences and misdirect enforcement efforts.

Organized Crime Impact Study
http://www.sgc.gc.ca/epub/pol/e1998orgcrim/e1998orgcrim.htm
   Highlights of a study on the economic and commercial impacts of organized crime in Canada prepared for the Ministry of the Solicitor General of Canada by Samuel D. Porteous.

Organized Crime in Canada
http://www.cisc.gc.ca/Cisc2000/coverpage2000.html
   This annual report by Criminal Intelligence Services of Canada covers a variety of organized crime groups and activities. To find out more about CISC, go to http://www.cisc.gc.ca.

Federal Action Against Organized Crime
http://canada.justice.gc.ca/en/news/nr/2000/doc_25605.html
   A summary of initiatives taken by the federal government in the 1990s to combat the problem of organized crime.

RECOMMENDED READINGS

Beare, M. (1996). *Criminal Conspiracies: Organized Crime in Canada.* Toronto: Nelson.
   Provides a detailed assessment of economic aspects of organized crime and its control in Canada.

Charbonneau, J.P. (1976). *The Canadian Connection: An Exposé on the Mafia in Canada and Its International Ramifications.* Ottawa: Optimum.
   This is a classic work on organized crime in this country. It provides some very interesting historical data on Canadian organized crime and its links to criminal groups in other countries, such as the United States in particular.

Abadinsky, H. (2000). *Organized Crime* (6th ed.). Chicago: Nelson Hall.
   An American text on organized crime that provides an excellent overview of the topic.

Block, A.A., and F.R. Scarpitti. (1985). *Poisoning for Profit: The Mafia and Toxic Waste in America.* New York: William Morrow.
   Examines how organized crime has infiltrated a legitimate industry with potentially disastrous consequences.

Chin, K. (1990). *Chinese Subculture and Criminality: Non-Traditional Crime Groups in America.* London: Greenwood Press.
   Discusses the involvement of the Chinese in American organized crime and emphasizes the role of subculture in facilitating involvement in criminal enterprises.

Handelman, S. (1995). *Comrade Criminal: Russia's New Mafiya.* New Haven: Yale University Press.
   Discusses the emergence of Russian organized crime in the wake of the dissolution of the former Soviet Republic. Addresses the impact of Russian mobs on crime in North America.

Lavigne, Y. (1987). *Hells Angels: Taking Care of Business.* Toronto: Deneau and Wayne.
   Provides some interesting insights into this famous renegade motorcyle gang and their Canadian operations.

Wolf, D.R. (1991). *The Rebels: A Brotherhood of Outlaw Bikers.* Toronto: University of Toronto Press.
   Presents an ethnographic study of a biker gang and its involvement in comparatively minor crime in two prairie provinces.

Chapter 15

Business Crime

The aims of this chapter are to familiarize the reader with:

- definitions of business crime
- the distinction between white-collar crime and corporate crime as types of business crime
- sources of information on business crime in Canada
- the social and economic costs of business crime
- the nature of white-collar crime: fraud, embezzlement, computer crime, illegal securities trading, and professional misconduct
- the commission of corporate crime and the victimization of consumers, employees, and the public
- selected theories of business crime: differential association, conflict theory, and deterrence
- issues surrounding the control of business crime

INTRODUCTION

When asked whether they are concerned about levels of crime in their city, province, or country, almost half of all Canadians respond in the affirmative. Many also fear that they themselves might become victims of a serious crime such as burglary, armed robbery, rape, assault, or even murder. While a few Canadians do fall prey to these crimes every year, many more become the victims of equally if not more serious forms of socially injurious activity. The cost of street crime pales in comparison with the losses incurred through embezzlement, computer crime, business fraud, pro-

fessional misconduct and malpractice, false advertising, the marketing of unsafe products, the exposure of employees to dangerous working conditions, income tax evasion, price fixing, illegal mergers, industrial espionage, political corruption, and environmental pollution (Goff and Reasons, 1978). The principal victims of "suite crime" include businesses, consumers, employees, the public at large, and governments (Ermann and Lundman, 1982).

A single corporate violation can adversely affect the well-being of a staggering number of people. Moreover, the wrongdoing of higher-status workers and the business organizations for which they work is frequent and the recidivism rate for those convicted is high. Despite these unsettling facts, Canadians barely notice the stealing, maiming, and killing carried out by the hands of professional and business elites. Indeed, many of the injurious acts classified as white-collar, corporate, or "suite crime" are not prohibited by the *Criminal Code* of Canada.

This chapter focuses on two fundamental types of illegal conduct in business: white-collar crime and corporate crime. Following a discussion of the definition of business crime, the principal sources of data on this form of misconduct are described. The costs that deviance in business circles inflicts on Canadians are examined, and several prominent forms of white-collar and corporate crime are discussed in detail. The insights into this form of illegality contained in three sociological theories — differential association, conflict theory, and deterrence theory — are explored. The chapter concludes by assessing the prospects for controlling business crime in Canada.

DEFINING BUSINESS CRIME

Edwin Sutherland, an American criminologist, was the first to coin the term "white-collar crime" (Sutherland, 1940, 1949). In his early writings, he emphasized that white-collar crime differs from common street crime in several ways. White-collar crime, unlike street crime, is concentrated among the middle and upper classes. White-collar offenders are employed in prestigious occupations requiring education, hard work, and a shirt and tie — hence the term white collar. Sutherland designated white-collar crimes as illegalities committed by respectable people acting within their occupational roles. This conceptualization seriously challenged the prevailing notion that the principal predictor of involvement in criminal activity was lower-class standing. While the idea of white-collar crime is widely accepted today, Sutherland's perspective was a radical departure from the traditional views of crime in the 1930s and 1940s.

Sutherland's initial conceptualization is now somewhat outmoded. Initially, Sutherland intended "white collar" to convey high status, but now many jobs requiring a white shirt and tie are not prestigious. Moreover, some criminologists have argued that many white-collar crimes are not really crimes at all, but activities that large numbers of merchants, professionals, and business leaders consider "sharp" business practices that are at worst unethical. Unless the law specifically prohibits certain tactics, these critics say, they cannot be called crimes. At present, comparatively little business wrongdoing is prohibited by criminal law (Simon, 1999).

Finally, there has been some confusion about identifying the victims of white-collar crime. The victim of embezzlement, computer crime, and fraud is usually the company for which the criminal works. However, consumers of goods and services, company employees, and members of the public are victims of the injurious actions of the businesses for which white-collar criminals work. Among these harmful activities are price fixing, health and safety violations, and environmental pollution.

Despite a few conceptual problems, Sutherland made a major contribution by sensitizing criminologists and the public to the fact that crime is not confined to the lower classes. Following Sutherland's original conceptualization, this chapter uses the term "business crime" to convey three points: business criminals have relatively high status, they commit their crimes for commercial gain, and they do so in the performance of work roles. To eliminate potential confusion, it considers business crime as consisting of two basic types: white-collar or professional crime and corporate crime. The distinction is based upon who benefits from the violation and who its victims are.

In white-collar or professional crime, high-status workers engage in violations directly for their own benefit. The principal victims of white-collar crime are the employing organizations themselves. In crimes committed by professionals, the victims are usually those who pay for the service — clients, insurance companies, or governments. As with white-collar crime, the perpetrators of corporate crime are individuals or groups employed by legitimate organizations. The acts in question involve the violations of civil, administrative, or criminal law. The major difference between white-collar and corporate crime, however, is that corporate crime involves employees carrying out corporate illegalities *on behalf of* the corporation and in accordance with formally specified corporate goals (Clinard and Yeager, 1980; Simon and Eitzen, 1990).

Most criminologists now consider corporate wrongdoing as crime, even though many of these actions are not technically infractions of criminal law. The fact that such violations are costly in physical, economic, and social terms and that some form of penalty is provided by federal law, provincial statute, or municipal ordinance is sufficient to define the violations as crimes. Although the principal victims of corporate crime are employees, consumers, members of the general public, and other corporations, these victim groups are not mutually exclusive; a corporate violation may adversely affect members of all four constituencies.

White-collar and corporate criminals victimize people both directly and indirectly. For example, embezzlers steal directly from banks. Through acts of industrial espionage, corporations steal directly from other corporations. In both cases, the losses incurred by businesses are recouped through some form of increased charges to customers and clients. Passing along the costs of crime to consumers, taxpayers, and members of the public is indirect victimization.

Many white-collar crimes are dealt with under the *Criminal Code* — simple fraud and embezzlement are prohibited under criminal law and carry penalties ranging from approximately two to ten years. Criminal law, however, seldom covers corporate

Box 15.1
COMBINES LAW REVISITED

Some of corporate Canada's most spectacular successes in shaping laws in its own interests are not products of the "bad old days" of the 19th century; they came in the 1980s. The recent history of the Combines Investigation Act (now the Competition Act) stands as a case in point. Business power was able to stall amendments to the totally moribund mergers and monopoly provisions of the act for nearly twenty years, from 1969 to 1986, and in the end corporate interests were given carte blanche to write their own revisions. It is instructive to examine the lawmaking process over this period. The ineffectiveness of the statutes on merger and monopoly in effect in 1969 was originally signalled in the *Interim Report on Competition Policy*, published by the Ministry of Consumer and Corporate Affairs. This was superseded by a White Paper (another discussion stage), out of which came sample legislation in 1970. To say that business did not like the reforms suggested would be a severe understatement. More accurately, "all hell broke loose," according to Ian Clark, Deputy Minister of Consumer and Corporate Affairs (Clark, 1989). The Liberal government of Pierre Trudeau, responsible for the legislation, was blasted in the editorials and boardrooms of the nation, and took the heat from disaffected corporate officers on informal levels as well. Three Ministers of Consumer and Corporate Affairs were appointed and deposed in short order; several versions of the bill were put forth, each weaker than its predecessor, but in the end business resistance proved impossible to overcome.

The result was that the Liberal government admitted defeat by declaring victory. It divided the proposed legislation in half, dropping the proposed changes to mergers and monopolies and retaining those in less sensitive areas. Thus, Stage I Amendments, as they were called, passed into law on January 1, 1976. They called for increased maximum fines for false advertising, extended price-fixing regulations to cover services as well as products, and prohibited a range of new sales practices such as bid-rigging, pyramid selling, and bait and switch techniques. Stage II Amendments, on the other hand, had a more onerous "rite de passage." Several more versions of the act and a change of government, from the Liberals to the Progressive Conservatives under Brian Mulroney, were necessary before a revised act was passed in 1986. However, the new act bore little

resemblance to the original 1969 proposals, for the officially stated aim in 1969 was to restrain monopolistic practices through law to better protect the consuming public. The 1986 regulations were part of a very different agenda.

To overcome the roadblocks that had bedevilled the Liberals, the Conservative government, on its election in 1984, set up a committee to recommend revisions in the law on mergers and monopolies. The committee was composed largely of members of the corporate elite; the Canadian Manufacturers Association, the Canadian Chamber of Commerce, and the Business Council on National Issues all had their delegates. One of its first acts was to cease holding public inquiries. (It was feared that consumers and workers' groups, aided and abetted by the Canadian media, might cause trouble or lead the government to abandon its newfound "objectivity" and "impartiality.") Politically, the government had a lot of credibility riding on the success of these efforts, since its ability to cooperate with business and run the country efficiently had been a central election promise. Committee members, a blue-ribbon group of business people, proceeded to meet with senior officials of the Department of Consumer and Corporate Affairs on a weekly basis to work out a new competition policy. Representatives of the Grocery Products Manufacturers of Canada and the Canadian Bar Association were added to the original group at a later stage, but representatives of labour and consumer interests were kept off the committee. As the deputy minister phrased it: "The Consumers Association of Canada and interested academics were also consulted" (Clark, 1989:9). The committee never made any pretence of being truly representative.

The resulting legislation, which became law in June 1986, took the form of a Competition Act. It was expressly and explicitly designed not to control business offences, but to improve and facilitate corporate operations. Criminal sanctions were taken out of the merger/monopoly sections, for business argued that the stigma of criminality was inappropriate to handle the well-meaning but occasionally unfortunate acts of corporations and their executives. The public interest, as a criterion for assessing a particular merger or monopoly, was exorcised. The new act adopted an explicitly compliance-centred approach (Goldman, 1989:3). It focused on the provision of a stable and predictable climate for business; business prosperity was its major goal; and meaningful punishment for offenders was virtually removed. Such results, of course, are exactly what one would expect from this kind of legislative process. If committees of armed robbers were routinely appointed to devise criminal laws, one would expect that they too would design legislation to advance their own interests.

Discussion Question

Snider's tracing of the development of the Competition Act of 1986 provides some useful insights into the role of power in the creation of law. From Snider's perspective, what are the principal lessons to be learned from her analysis of this process?

Source: Laureen Snider, *Bad Business: Corporate Crime in Canada* (Toronto: Nelson, 1993), pp. 108–10. Reprinted with permission of Nelson Thomson Learning, a division of Thomson Learning.

crime. Rather, regulatory agencies controlled by the municipal, provincial, and federal governments codify corporate offences and police their violation. Federal Acts, some of which have been in place since the late 1800s, offer Canadians the most protection against corporate wrongdoing. The greatest jurisdiction over the major statutes that limit corporate offending once fell just on the federal Ministry of Consumer and Corporate Affairs (Casey, 1985) but now it also falls on Industry Canada.

Until 1986, the most important of the regulatory statutes was the *Combines Investigation Act*, which prohibited unfair competitive practices among corporations. Specific violations of the *Combines Investigation Act* included conspiring or acting to limit competition by restraining trade, creating monopoly conditions, improperly merging companies, and advertising falsely. Sanctions for violating these statutes included jail sentences of up to 5 years, a fine of up to $1 million, or an Order of Prohibition, which instructed a convicted company to cease and desist the illegal activity. Failure to comply with an Order of Prohibition could result in the guilty parties being imprisoned for up to two years (Snider, 1978; Goff and Reasons, 1978).

In the entire history of the *Combines Investigation Act*, the Crown registered only two convictions under its anti-competition sections. Only one of these, the conviction of the Eddy Match Company, involved a large corporation. In 1951, the courts convicted Eddy of "predatory pricing," a practice whereby a business drops its prices to drive its competitors into bankruptcy. Once it had bankrupted its opposition, Eddy took over their operations, thus illegitimately consolidating its monopoly (Dalglish, 1990).

In 1986, the Canadian government replaced the anti-competition sections of the *Combines Investiga-*

tion Act with the *Competition Act*. The *Competition Act* contains two categories of offences — criminal and reviewable. Criminal offences include bid-rigging, the striking of illegitimate agreements among banks, conspiracy, discriminatory and predatory pricing, and deceptive trade practices. Conspiracy to restrict trade carries a maximum fine of $10 million or five years' imprisonment. Unfair trade practices such as false advertising can result in fines of $25 000 or prison terms of five years. Mergers, abuse of a dominant position (monopoly), and market restriction are reviewable matters to which criminal sanctions do not apply. Canada's attorney general possesses the discretion to decide the manner of proceeding in each particular case. The emphasis is on a compliance-oriented approach of a voluntary nature. As with the *Combines Investigation Act*, Orders of Prohibition remain an option. Failure to comply with such an order can result in a sentence of two years. In association with the Bureau of Competition Policy, a Competition Tribunal consisting of four judges and up to eight laypersons (drawn largely from the corporate sector) now decides whether companies have abused their monopoly powers (Snider, 1993). The new legislation differs from the old by invoking civil law to control anti-competitive practices. Convictions under civil law do not require the same stringent burden of proof that must be established for a criminal conviction.

Several other statutes govern corporate activity. The *Weights and Measures Act* ensures that the weights and measures of goods purchased by consumers are accurate and honestly reported. It also prohibits tampering with automobile odometer readings. The *Hazardous Products Act* forbids the advertising, sale, or import of unsafe products. The *Food and Drug Act* makes the manufacture, sale, or import of unsafe food or drugs illegal. Also prohibited under this Act are the adulteration of food and the illegitimate substitution of one product for another. The maximum penalties for violating the rules and regulations set forth in these acts range from maximum fines between $5000 and $1 000 000 to two- and three-year periods of imprisonment (Snider, 1978).

Sanctions for violating federal regulations include warnings, forced recalls, injunctions, fines, and imprisonment. Enforcement, however, usually involves administrative nonprosecutorial strategies. Furthermore, authorities direct most of their efforts at smaller retail businesses. Fines are small, and incarceration is virtually unheard of. With respect to the *Combines Investigation Act*, and now the *Competition Act*, the most popular sanction has been the Order of Prohibition.

SOURCES OF INFORMATION ON BUSINESS CRIME IN CANADA

Business crime that is known and makes its way into official records represents only the tip of the iceberg. Victims of business crime are usually unaware of their losses. Consequently, no one reports these illegalities and no one pressures the authorities for action. Even in cases of employee fraud and embezzlement, company directors often ask miscreant workers to resign quietly. They often wish to avoid criminal charges; the costs of adverse publicity about inadequate company security outweigh the benefits of reporting the crime and prosecuting the culprit.

Even though business crime is difficult to uncover, there is little doubt that much more occurs than meets the eye. Because only a few commercial offences fall under the direct purview of criminal law, Uniform Crime Reports contain relatively little data on violations perpetrated in business circles. Victimization surveys do not gather information about whether respondents have been preyed on by businesses. Even if such questions were posed, the victims of business crime are usually ignorant of their victimization. Self-report crime investigations almost never include businesspeople and professionals in their samples, and even when they do, survey instruments include few if any questions of this nature.

None of the three levels of government in Canada systematically collects and compiles information on commercial offences. While the Americans do a much better job, their performance is also far from perfect.

Inadequate record-keeping makes it virtually impossible to compute rates of business crime with any accuracy (Ellis, 1987; Snider, 1978).

Information on the misconduct of professionals such as physicians and lawyers is equally difficult to unearth. Professions are self-regulating and their members are bound together by a code of ethics that, if violated, is supposed to result in the discipline or punishment of miscreant practitioners. However, critics of the professions argue that ethical codes are in reality codes of silence that protect rather than sanction wrongdoers. Professional norms discourage the criticism of colleagues to such an extent that an open discussion of dubious professional practices by doctors, dentists, and lawyers is rare (Halmos, 1973).

While few in number, sources of data on business crime do exist. Reports of the federal department of Consumer and Corporate Affairs, for example, contain information on illegal mergers and monopolies, false-advertising cases, and the fines levied when convictions are registered. Workers' compensation boards provide information on work-related injuries. The only other sources of information are the proceedings of occasional public inquiries and various anecdotal reports, many of which are of questionable quality (Ellis, 1987).

Very few social scientists have initiated independent studies of commercial crime. Business and professional wrongdoing is understudied largely because of serious impediments to front-line research. First and foremost, access to data on corporate activity of any sort is extremely difficult to obtain. Businesses and professional associations are very secretive and extremely powerful. Even when authorized government agencies demand information, corporations frequently refuse to provide data or react so slowly that the accumulation of information becomes enormously time consuming and frustrating (Simon and Eitzen, 1990; Clinard and Yeager, 1980). American researchers faced with these problems have been able to use the U.S. *Access to Information Act* to force corporations to comply with their requests. The equivalent Canadian legislation, passed in July 1983, has made access to some business information easier, but it seems that the Canadian *Access to Information Act* lacks the teeth of its American counterpart (Casey, 1985). To date, researchers have not pursued this avenue with any great success.

Perhaps the second most important barrier to investigating business crime is the considerable complexity of corporations and their operations. To fully comprehend the organization and operation of business requires knowledge of several disciplines, including political science, corporate law, civil law, administrative law, economics, accounting, data processing, and the theory of complex social organizations. Few social scientists have the necessary interdisciplinary expertise (Clinard and Yeager, 1980).

Finally, it is a truism that what gets funded gets researched (Simon and Eitzen, 1990). Funding for research on business and professional wrongdoing, from both public and private sources, has been lacking until recently. With increasing public and consumer activism surrounding issues of health, safety, economics, and global pollution, there is now much greater support for research on the socially harmful actions of businesspeople, professionals, and corporations. As a result, more studies of this type are likely to be undertaken in the future. It is perhaps not surprising that relevant Canadian investigations are both recent (since 1978) and small in number (fewer than a handful).

THE COSTS OF BUSINESS CRIME

While accurate estimates of dollar losses attributable to business crimes are extremely difficult to determine, most projections underestimate the magnitude of the figures. Economic analysts put the annual Canadian losses due to embezzlement, computer crime, commercial fraud, unnecessary auto repairs, unneeded home improvements, price fixing, illegal corporate mergers, false advertising, and other business crimes at something in excess of $4 billion (Toole, 1986). American studies provide a point of comparison, suggesting that while average losses to victims in robberies amount to less than $500, losses accruing from white-collar and computer crime routinely range in the neighbourhood of $300 000 to $400 000. Some estimates pegged the amount of money illegitimately billed by medical personnel to federally and provincially funded health-insurance plans at about $400 million (Toole, 1986; Wilson, Lincoln, and Chappell, 1988).

Not only are Canadians directly preyed upon by unscrupulous white-collar workers and businesses, they are also indirectly victimized in at least two ways. First, losses from illegal acts such as fraud, embezzlement, and corporate espionage are invariably passed on to consumers in the form of higher prices and to the public in the form of higher taxes. Furthermore, the costs associated with the Canadian government's efforts to catch, convict, and chastise business wrongdoers are also borne by Canadian taxpayers. Second, businesses often write off their legal defence costs as tax losses. The result is diminished revenue to the Government of Canada that, as a rule, is compensated for by individual taxpayers. Few Canadians realize the extent to which they are paying for white-collar and corporate crime.

Many Canadians perceive business crime solely as property crime and see its costs entirely in economic terms. The result is an inclination to view commercial crime as a less serious problem than street crime. Street crime raises images of interpersonal violence, while suite crime does not. This is a grave misperception — business crime is frequently violent. The volume of assaults and murders in Canada pales in comparison with the number of injuries, debilitating and life-threatening diseases, and deaths attributable to business enterprises and professions engaging in unsafe practices, marketing dangerous products, violating workplace safety regulations, and polluting the air, the water, and the land.

A cursory examination of some data on deaths related to work drives home the point that business wrongdoing can be considered violent. Death in the workplace ranks third, after heart disease and cancer, as a major killer of Canadians. Canadian criminologist Charles Reasons and his colleagues (1981) point out that people are killed on the job at a rate ten times the Canadian murder rate. They estimate that almost 40 percent of industrial "accidents" are a result of working conditions that are both unsafe and prohibited under existing law. About 25 percent, they argue, are attributable to conditions that, while not illegal, are dangerous nonetheless.

It is not only workers who become the victims of business violence. People who buy defective merchandise and who use unneeded and potentially dangerous services are also at risk. Estimates of traffic fatalities due to unsafe vehicles range up to 50 percent. Many operations performed by doctors in this country are unnecessary. All surgery carries some risk, and some patients do develop complications and suffer unduly. A small percentage die (Wilson, Lincoln, and Chappell, 1988).

While the violence perpetrated by businesses and professionals is both real and potentially devastating, it differs from the violence of street crime. In a

Box 15.2
COMPETITION BUREAU ISSUES WARNING AGAINST
AIRLINE 'MONOPOLY'

The federal competition watchdog would strongly consider issuing a cease-and-desist order against Air Canada's "unregulated monopoly" if Parliament granted it the power to do so, a senior competition official told a Senate transport committee examining proposed legislation.

The new Air-Canada/Canadian Airlines behemoth is causing concern because of suspected predatory pricing tactics against WestJet Airlines, and Raymond Pierce, assistant deputy competition commissioner, told senators yesterday: "If we had the cease-and-desist powers today we would be looking seriously at using them ... Essentially what we have here is an unregulated monopoly."

Laura Cooke, a spokeswoman for Air Canada, said the bureau struck a deal with the airline in December that contained many assurances for customers, including guaranteed seat sales.

"We have agreed to conditions that were placed upon us by the Competition Bureau. In large measure we've already demonstrated we are a responsible carrier. When the legislation is passed, we will comply to the letter of the law."

The new legislation, as drafted, would give the competition commissioner power to intervene with a cease-and-desist order against airlines reasonably suspected of predatory pricing, and Air Canada's actions on the Toronto-Moncton route, where it faces competition from WestJet, are of great concern, Mr. Pierce said.

Dave McAllister, a senior case officer added: "Airlines is the number one priority in the [Competition] Bureau right now."

WestJet has filed a complaint with the bureau, saying Air Canada flooded the market with extra seats and slashed fares after the Calgary-based airline announced it would offer a discount service between Moncton, N.B., and Toronto.

Air Canada denies it did anything wrong.

Under current competition law, the bureau can build a case and take it to the Competition Tribunal for a ruling, but the process takes months or even years. In the meantime, the competitor could be driven out of the market. The legislation is expected to become law by summer.

Mr. Pierce said the bureau is actively considering three complaints against Air Canada, including the one concerning WestJet.

He would not name the other two, citing confidentiality.

But he was blunt in his remarks to the committee, saying Air Canada is essentially unregulated because it faces pricing oversight only on its highest and lowest fares, and because of its sheer size.

"New entrants will face a formidable competitor," he said. "Air Canada is very, very much overwhelmingly dominant in this market."

And he repeated the bureau's view that three things must be brought about in order to create true competition: raising foreign ownership restrictions to 49% from 20%, which would allow small competitors greater access to foreign capital; allowing U.S. airlines to market flights between Canadian cities that pass through U.S. destinations as single tickets; and giving foreign carriers the right to set up Canadian subsidiaries to fly only within Canada.

"The bureau maintains that a truly competitive market can only be achieved by opening up the market," said Mr. Pierce.

The federal government has rejected the suggestions on the grounds they would harm Air Canada as it tries to absorb Canadian Airlines and its massive debt.

But Mr. Pierce said, given the airline's huge market share, such fears are misplaced.

"The bureau does not harbour any concerns about the financial future of Air Canada," he said.

The government's airline legislation provides some other consumer protections, including creating a complaints ombudsman and a mechanism to monitor pricing.

"This bill is a step in the right direction," Mr. Pierce said. But, he added, "Legislation alone does nothing to attract new competition to the market.

"The bureau remains concerned about the state of competition."

Discussion Questions

Given your reading of this case, how effective is Canada's Competition Act? What improvements, if any, are necessary?

Source: Ian Jack, *National Post*, June 7, 2000, p. A2. Reprinted with permission from the *National Post*.

common violent crime such as an assault, the illegal act is separated from its result by a relatively short period of time — perhaps seconds. In suite crime, the result may occur years after the initial illegal act. For example, pulp and paper companies dump mercury into river systems. Fish ingest the mercury, and people consume the tainted fish. Gradually poisoned, victims increasingly lose control of their muscles and those who are seriously contaminated eventually die. The process takes years. Furthermore, the time span may now extend to centuries. Scientists note that the wastes created by weapons manufacture and nuclear energy production may not just haunt future generations but perhaps kill them as well. The expanding time gap separating act and outcome has given rise to new terms in the study of violence, such as "postponed violence" and "intergenerational crime" (Hagan, 1986).

WHITE-COLLAR CRIME

White-collar criminals generally act illegally in their own best interests and victimize the individuals and organizations that employ them. Among the more common **white-collar crimes** are fraud, embezzlement, computer crime, and illegal security trading. The principal victims are usually corporations, gov-

ernments, banks, stock exchanges, smaller commercial businesses, and the clients of professionals.

FRAUD

Fraud involves any attempt through deceit or falsehood to obtain goods, services, or financial gain without legitimate rights. It comprises a wide variety of offences ranging from simple credit card theft to complicated electronic money transfers. According to the Uniform Crime Reports (UCR), frauds account for about 7 percent of all property crimes. In 53 percent of cases known to police, fraud perpetrators victimized commercial enterprises. In an additional 28 percent, they victimized banks or other financial institutions. As Figure 15.1 shows, with some exceptions, officially recorded fraud offences have decreased in recent years, especially in the area of cheque fraud. Credit card frauds, however, have increased. The overall rate of fraud (297 per 100 000 population) declined by 5 percent in 1999, the eighth consecutive annual decrease.

The principal contributing factor to the decrease in total fraud offences has been a significant reduction in the number of cheque frauds. In the late 1970s, cheque fraud represented about 70 percent of officially recorded frauds, while it currently represents

FIGURE 15.1

TRENDS IN FRAUD RATE, CANADA, 1977-1996

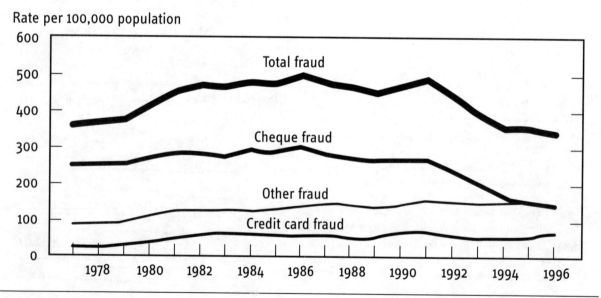

Rate per 100,000 population

Janhevich, D. (1998a). The Changing Nature of Fraud in Canada. *Juristat Service Bulletin* 18(4). Ottawa: Canadian Centre for Justice Statistics, Statistics Canada, p. 4, Cat. No. 85-002.

about 40 percent. Credit card fraud, however, grew dramatically (143 percent) from the late 1970s to the late 1990s.

Table 15.1 shows that, for 1996, the median dollar loss for an incident of fraud was $480. Nearly 70 percent of cases where the dollar amount was known involved a loss of less than $1000. Nonetheless, about 1 percent of incidents involved frauds in excess of $100 000 and some involved amounts running into the millions of dollars (Janhevich, 1998a).

Some frauds, not all of which are reported to the police, are very costly. The Insurance Bureau of Canada and the Insurance Crime Prevention Bureau, for example, estimate that 10 to 15 percent of automobile, household, and commercial claims are inflated or fabricated, costing approximately $1.3 billion annually. The Canadian Bankers Association calculates that credit card frauds involving major companies such as Visa, Mastercard, and American Express generate costs in excess of $80 million annually. Counterfeiting alone generates about one-third of these costs. This amount is a substantial increase from the $72.6 million lost in 1995 and the $28.9 million recorded in 1990. When businesses are victims of

TABLE 15.1

FRAUD OFFENCE BY DOLLAR VALUE OF PROPERTY STOLEN, 1996

Dollar Value Grouping	% Cheque Fraud	% Credit Card Fraud	% Other Fraud	% Total Fraud
<100	12	14	34	19
100–199	13	8	8	11
200–499	27	21	13	21
500–999	20	20	10	17
1 000–4 999	20	30	16	21
5 000–9 999	4	4	7	5
10 000–99 999	3	2	10	5
100 000 and more	–	–	2	1
Total[2]	100	100	100	100
Median amount	$462	$585	$325	$480

Source: Janhevich, D. (1998a). The Changing Nature of Fraud in Canada. *Juristat Service Bulletin* 18(4). Ottawa: Canadian Centre for Justice Statistics, Statistics Canada, p. 5, Cat. No. 85-002. Data from Canadian Centre for Justice Statistics, *Revised Uniform Crime Reporting Survey, 1996.*

Represents a non-random sample of 154 police agencies accounting for 47% of the national volume of crime. The data are not nationally representative.

[1] Excluded are cases where although a fraud took place, the amount was unknown or no amount was stolen. These incidents represented 22% of the total

[2] Due to rounding, totals may not add up to 100.

– Amount too small to be expressed

Box 15.3
FACTS ABOUT INSURANCE FRAUD

In June 1994, the IBC-backed Canadian Coalition Against Insurance Fraud was founded to implement a series of actions to try and reduce the annual $1.3 billion cost of property and casualty insurance fraud. With its more than 60 members, the Coalition represents groups affected by fraud including the private insurance industry, police and fire services, consumer advocacy groups and public auto insurers. Actions aimed at curbing the high toll of insurance "scams" include public awareness, changing business practices, improved investigative and enforcement techniques, improved understanding of the problem, and changes to the legal and regulatory environment.

The Coalition defines insurance fraud as: *any act or omission with a view to illegally obtaining an insurance benefit* – in other words, any action where claimants receive money that they were not entitled to. The Coalition's efforts have produced the following:

- Insurance fraud includes a wide array of activities: completely fabricated claims, exaggeration or padding of genuine claims, false statements on insurance applications, and all types of internal fraud.

- Insurance fraud costs approximately $1.3 billion and an additional $1 billion per year in police and fire resources. Health costs to victims and fire fighters are other unmeasured costs.

- In North America, insurance fraud is estimated to be second to illegal drug sales in the source of criminal profits.

- All insurance fraud is a crime – including "opportunistic" actions like exaggerating a genuine claim.

- In a 1996 public opinion poll regarding insurance fraud, 43% of Canadians agreed it was easy to successfully defraud an insurance company; 78% understood that fraud had an impact on the cost of insurance; and 50% believed it was common to exaggerate claims.

Discussion Questions

Why is insurance fraud such a costly problem? Who are its victims? How great an impact do you think insurance fraud has on the price of insurance? Given the breadth and seriousness of insurance fraud, what specific measures might be undertaken to reduce its incidence?

Source: Insurance Bureau of Canada, Canadian Coalition Against Insurance Fraud, 1996. In Janhevich, D. (1998a). The Changing Nature of Fraud in Canada. *Juristat Service Bulletin* 18(4). Ottawa: Canadian Centre for Justice Statistics, Statistics Canada, p. 7, Cat. No. 85-002.

fraud, shareholders, employees, creditors, and the general public are all adversely affected, since these economic crimes in particular cause the price of goods, insurance premiums, taxes, and the overall cost of living to increase.

There are several explanations for the recent decreases in fraud coming to the attention of the police. First, changes in both consumer behaviour and technology have altered the structure of opportunity for this crime. New methods of payment, such as credit cards, automated teller machines, automated bill payment, and direct withdrawals, have reduced the use of cheques and thus cheque fraud has decreased. Second, the types of fraud and the means by which they are executed have changed significantly. Newer fraud types are more difficult for businesses and police to detect in part because of the growing complexity of computer-based technology. Third, stable or declining police budgets have rendered the task of apprehension even more challenging. It is difficult for police to secure resources for combating fraud when the public is much more concerned with violent crime and more traditional property offences. Finally, the business sector often retains the services of private policing and security agencies to investigate frauds. They do so to retain greater control over case processing and publicity. Businesses are often reluctant to reveal their vulnerability to the public for fear of tarnishing their images (Janhevich, 1998a).

Most but certainly not all of the culprits are employees, and their thefts are often substantial. In an apartment-flipping exercise known as "the Greymac affair," for example, Leonard Rosenberg defrauded investors of $132 million. At the time, it was the largest fraud in Canadian history. Lawyer Julius Melnitzer was arrested in 1991 for a $75 million scheme involving bogus land deals, fraud, and forgery. Sentenced to 9 years, he was released on parole after serving a third of his sentence. After Len Gaudet's company collapsed in 1987 with a debt of $60 million, an investigation revealed that he had looted the company coffers of more than $12 million. He was sentenced to 8 years (Greenwood, 1996).

John Jaffey began laying the groundwork for his white-collar crime in the late 1980s. After creating a false identity using the birth certificate of a deceased person, he began diverting clients' funds into secret bank accounts opened under his alias. Telling his family that he was going away on business, Jaffey disappeared into thin air. His role in the $1.6 million fraud and theft was uncovered when police retrieved data supposedly erased from his computer's hard-drive. In addition to showing that he had stolen $100 000 from his own mother, the disk identified where he had deposited the cash and where he had gone into hiding. Jaffey was apprehended, convicted, and sentenced to five years (Greenwood, 1996).

White-collar fraud ranges in seriousness from the misuse of expense accounts, travel allowances, and company cars to the theft of enormous sums of money through deception and manipulation. Embezzlement is a type of fraud in which the criminal first steals money from an organization and then hides the theft by altering its financial records.

EMBEZZLEMENT

One of the oldest and most frequently committed forms of white-collar crime is embezzlement. According to research conducted by Cressey (1971), embezzlement involves three distinct stages. First, potential embezzlers have "unsharable" problems that cannot be discussed with other people because of pride or shame. Typical unsharable problems are gambling debts, mistresses with expensive tastes, and appetites for alcohol or other drugs.

In addition to the unsharable problem, Cressey emphasizes the opportunity factor. Embezzlements hinge on the aspirants being acutely aware of their probable success. Usually they occupy positions of trust, from which access to cash can be easily obtained without raising suspicion. White-collar workers, by virtue of their seniority, often know both the most vulnerable points in their employers' accounting systems and how to execute and conceal their thefts.

The final characteristic of the model embezzler, according to Cressey, is the capacity for rationalizing the theft as something other than a crime. Most embezzlers see their illegitimate appropriations as short-term loans; they fully intend to pay back the misappropriated funds before company officials notice that the money is missing.

Nettler's (1974) research on embezzlers offers a different picture. Nettler found that only one out of the six cases that he examined conformed to Cressey's ideal type. Five of Nettler's embezzlers either gave reasons for their thefts other than the unsharable problem or confessed their problem to others. Other rival and perhaps more intuitive explanations of white-collar crime come from police and bank authorities. The "detective's theory" calls upon police to look for the three Bs — babes, bets, or booze — along with a tendency for the culprits to live beyond their means. The "auditor's theory" suggests that, given desire and opportunity, anyone may steal. Bank authorities are particularly watchful of people with opportunity (Nettler, 1978).

Perhaps the most infamous case of embezzlement in Canada occurred in Toronto during the early 1980s. An assistant manager of the Bay and Richmond branch of the Canadian Imperial Bank of Commerce, Brian Molony, managed to "borrow" $10 395 800 (Can.) and $5 081 000 (U.S.) between September 15, 1980, and April 26, 1982. Molony's modus operandi involved giving out loans to phony customers, using some of the borrowed money to pay the interest on previous illegitimate loans, and gambling the rest in Las Vegas and Atlantic City.

For quite some time before Molony's arrest, police were wiretapping Toronto bookie Mario Colizzi. Colizzi had been providing gambling services to a "Mr. Brown." On one occasion, Molony alias Brown gave his real name over the phone. The voice was recorded by police, who recognized it as belonging to the gambler Brown. Police subsequently traced Molony and had him followed.

After Molony arrived in Atlantic City, police tailed him to a casino and watched him lose over $1 million on one night. He flew home the next day, was picked up by Toronto police for speeding, and was eventually charged with embezzlement.

Molony was a trusted bank employee and marked for promotion. He came from an upstanding Toronto family (his father was a doctor), and he excelled in school. His flaw, however, was compulsive gambling.

Box 15.4
NET CRIME CHALLENGES LAW ENFORCEMENT

The Internet makes life easier – and more profitable – for individuals pursuing legitimate activities in business, the arts and education. Not surprisingly, it also makes life a lot richer for individuals pursuing illegal activities. Catching these cyber criminals, however, requires cyber cops.

In Halifax, there is now a special unit with 16 police officers trained in the art and artifice of Internet crime. They were all trained by Sgt. Bill Cowper, once known throughout the city as the Internet Cop. "Police services and law enforcement agencies are generally aware of [technological] changes and the need to adapt to those changes, but that level of awareness is not where it should be. Preparing for the new society will be a monumental task," says Sgt. Cowper, a special projects officer with the Halifax Regional Police.

In preparation for the new world of Internet crime, the Halifax police force also hired two computer forensic officers, individuals who can get inside a seized computer and find out what is on file – and what has been erased. In addition, the province's public prosecution service has trained a Crown attorney to deal with Internet-related prosecutions. In the past two years, about 200 cyberspace crimes have been investigated. Of these case, 18 were prosecuted.

This is only the beginning, predicts Sgt. Cowper. "There is going to have to be a dedicated unit of specialists within every police force. Those specialists are going to have to train the street-level cops."

The need for such comprehensive cop coverage reflects the growing use of the Internet as a warm and welcoming place for crime to flourish, although Halifax is a particularly hot spot, with a well-educated, Internet-savvy population.

Sgt. Cowper estimates that law enforcement officers are currently only finding out about 10% of Internet crime, and perhaps as little as 1%. The reason? Embarrassment and confusion. Many victims are reluctant to come forward; many are not sure whom to call with their complaint.

There are really two types of Internet crime, says Teresa Scassa, an associate professor of law at Dalhousie University. First, there are old crimes that are proliferating on the Net. Then there are new crimes unique to cyberspace.

Child pornography is perhaps the best-known example of the former. "We're seeing that the Internet is making the distribution of child pornography much easier. It's a problem for law enforcement," says Ms. Scassa. "Most police officers are not computer literate. In order to fight this type of crime you need a certain level of computer literacy. You also need to be able to testify with respect to the chain of evidence. [Again] you need a certain amount of technical expertise."

You also need the patience of a saint. Working through jurisdictional red tape and innumerable time zones complicates investigations and increases tension. If an individual in Halifax, for example, is running a child pornography site on the Internet, but is using an Internet Service Provider in the United States to mask his identity, the Halifax police first must approach the U.S. federal Justice Department. Once cleared, they proceed to the state level, then to a local district attorney.

There are also thorny legal issues, notes Ms. Scassa. Police in Belgium, for example, recently posted pornographic photos of children in an effort to identify them. In the old days, pornographers needed access to photo processing equipment. Now, with the advent of digital cameras, child pornographers can work from the relative security and privacy of their basement or garage, making detection much more difficult.

New crimes arising as a result of the Internet include hacking into secure sites and creating computer viruses. "A lot [of this activity] is traditionally done by people who want to show off or make a point. It posed a problem in court. It didn't fit into the criminal code," notes Ms. Scassa. It does now. Canada has enacted new legislation to deal with "mischief to data."

Parents are concerned about a different form of terrorism – the bullying that goes on among young children, which the Internet fosters by allowing communication to be anonymous. "There's a fundamental shift in how we as a society communicate with each other. We're seeing it first and foremost among our young people," says Sgt. Cowper. "Our dynamics were face to face in groups. Now kids can come home and speak to 100 people all at the same time."

The one certainty about Internet crime, he adds, is that it is going to grow. "You can't stick your head in the sand. Our economic well-being has shifted from a brick and mortar environment to a click and mortar environment."

The criminals, it seems, are following suit.

Discussion Questions

Who has the upper hand: cyber criminals or cyber police? Consider the record of 200 investigations and 18 prosecutions (convictions are not mentioned). Is the success rate likely to improve in the near future? Why or why not?

Source: Donalee Moulton, *National Post*, June 19, 2000, p. E12. Reprinted with permission from the author.

Indeed, his defence hinged on this "condition." Criminal lawyer Edward Greenspan argued that Molony suffered from an illness (a type of impulse control) recognized by the American Psychiatric Association. Molony, he pointed out, was addicted to the high-stakes action and did not care about the money. As evidence for this argument, Greenspan pointed out that Molony had salted away for future use exactly none of his ill-gotten gains. In the end, losses to the bank totalled $10.2 million plus interest. Molony, sentenced to 6 years, served 2 (Ross, 1987).

In the past, embezzlement required expertise in accounting only. Given the recent advent of electronic data processing in financial record keeping, successful embezzlement now requires expertise in computer programming.

COMPUTER CRIME

There are three ways in which people use computers in the pursuit of criminal objectives. First, law breakers use computers to facilitate the operation of existing criminal enterprises. In pursuit of illegal ends, the computer serves as a mechanism for the creation, storage, manipulation, and communication of information. More sophisticated criminal organizations currently use computers to maintain records of drug trafficking finances and distribution networks. Second, criminals employ computers as tools to enhance the results of traditional criminal initiatives. Using these technologies to counterfeit money and documents is one example of committing a long-standing offence in a new way. Other examples involve relatively new forms of crime, such as the distribution of child pornography, the orchestration of confidence schemes, and the establishment of illegal gambling networks on the Internet. Finally, computers can be used as weapons to compromise the integrity of other computer systems. Such cases usually involve the theft of information or services or the willful damage of other computer networks (Adler, Mueller, and Laufer, 2001; Goodman, 1997).

Many computer security experts point out that amateur hackers are not their major problem. The greatest threat to computers and data often originates from within a company rather than from outside its boundaries. The person most likely to violate computer security is not a nerdy teenager in some distant locale but a disgruntled current or past employee. Simon and Hagan (1999) observe that about 80 percent of computer crime is committed by insiders, most of whom are employees.

Since computer crime is both difficult to detect and underreported, estimates of its actual cost are hard to arrive at and are probably conservative. Nonetheless, the losses are staggering, particularly since a single attack can simultaneously strike multiple victims in many distant places. In 1997, 563 American corporations, government agencies, financial institutions, and universities responded to a Computer Security Institute survey. Three-quarters of these respondents reported financial losses in the previous year directly attributable to compromises in their computer security. Approximately 250 organizations lost $24.9 million in financial fraud losses, $22.7 million as a consequence of telecommunications fraud, $21 million in proprietary information theft, $4.3 million due to sabotage of data or networks, $12.5 million from computer viruses, and $6.1 million from the theft of laptops. The accounting firm Ernst & Young recently estimated the yearly cost of computer crime in the United States at somewhere in the $3 billion to $5 billion range. According to the British Banking Association, the price tag for computer fraud globally comes in at about $8 billion a year. Worldwide losses from software piracy alone total about $12 billion (Adler, Mueller, and Laufer, 2001; Schmalleger, 1999; Simon and Hagan, 1999).

Box 15.5
VIRUS: THE HUNTERS AND THE HUNTED

Anthony Carathimas, an intense, dark-haired college student, is writing his first computer virus. His eyes locked on his computer screen at Sandia National Laboratories' Livermore branch, he types tentatively:

Cat virus»/etc/profile

When the program is complete and Carathimas launches it, he'll be instructing his computer to make a copy (cat) of the virus file he is creating and add it (») to another file (/etc/profile), which manages the user profiles of everyone with an account on that computer system.

Carathimas writes two more lines and is done. Most viruses are short, but Carathimas' program is just three lines of code. It does the job, however: It reproduces.

That is the defining characteristic of a computer virus. Viruses can do more: delete files from a victim's hard drive and send themselves out to others via e-mail, for instance. But at the core, a virus is simply a program that makes copies of itself.

The virus that Carathimas has written — a popular term is "malware," a combination of "malicious" and "software" — produces a message that appears on the screen: "This is the virus." The screen soon fills with the message, line after line, the virus replicating itself so fast that the computer eventually crashes.

Carathimas writes a new line of code that will render his creation more like the destructive viruses that make headlines:

rm-rf/&

This one is a killer. If a computer follows those instructions, it will delete every file on its hard drive. The "rm" is a standard housekeeping command used to delete files. The "r" in "rf" tells the computer to act recursively, working through every subdirectory; the "f" tells the machine to force the action, to refuse to take no for an answer when the computer attempts to protect the files.

Fred Cohen glances over Carathimas' shoulder and sees the lethal instructions.

"No damage, please," Cohen tells Carathimas.

Cohen, a rumpled, freewheeling Sandia researcher, is generally credited with first applying the term "virus" to describe reproducing computer programs back in 1983. He supervises the 30 or so students in his 18-month-old College Cyber Defenders programs as they try their hands at writing viruses. The idea is to show just how easily viruses can be made and how easily they can be blocked. But at Cohen's request, Carathimas deletes the line just as he might delete an ill-advised sentence from a school essay.

How hard is it to write a virus? No harder than ordering dinner at a provincial French restaurant. The biggest hurdle is knowing enough of the language.

"Any idiot can write a virus — and lots of idiots have," says Steve White, a computer-security researcher at International Business Machines Corp.

That's why viruses are increasingly common. About 40,000 have been identified since 1984, most of them in the past few years. One of them, attached to the "love bug" e-mail message sent earlier this year, reached multi-millions of computers around the world.

Computers run because software tells them what to do, and malware is no different in that from the programs that enable people to write letters, create spreadsheets and view photos.

The most direct way to talk to a computer is in what's known as machine language, the string of ones and zeroes in which a PC's microprocessor "thinks." Higher-level languages allow programmers to write the "source code" of their programs in something approximating words, with a vocabulary and syntax that can be learned by anyone willing to crack open a book or take the right classes, by using a simple word-processing program.

As viruses have evolved, the most striking aspect about them is how much faster they have become. Some of the earliest viruses that attacked IBM PCs, in the days before the Windows operating system, targeted specific program files or the first software routines that a computer goes through when it is turned on, the "boot" files.

Most of those viruses were written in a low-level programming code that was very close to machine language. The introduction of Microsoft Corp.'s Windows and its successors changed all that. Windows 95 automatically scans the boot sector for viruses, all but eliminating that threat. So the virus writers shifted their focus.

The biggest crop of viruses today attack via "macros," the automated commands used in such programs as Microsoft Word and Excel. Macros are small programs that can be used to format a document quickly, for example, or insert a letterhead at the top of a note, and Microsoft has gone a long way to make them easy to write.

Macros run automatically when users open their files, and travel with documents when they are appended to e-mail messages. The arrival of macro viruses hastened the spread of viruses. They took mere weeks to get around, hitchhiking on documents sent from victim to victim, most often via e-mail. But the bugs still had to wait for someone to send the infected file in order to spread.

Like almost all viruses, the one Carathimas has written is very specific. It will run on Unix, the operating system he is using. He and his fellow students at Sandia National Laboratories don't need to overcome the security measures built into many computer operating systems the way that malicious outsiders do. But if these students had to, they could do it the same way that "script kiddie" virus writers do, by grabbing ready-written chunks of code from

Internet sites devoted to the craft of virus writing and putting them together like Lego blocks.

To Cohen, one of the most alarming prospects is a virus that improves on early efforts at simulating evolution, a program that changes its own code as it goes along. That kind of program would be much harder to detect since it would offer no consistent signature for virus hunters.

So far, though, Cohen isn't impressed with what he has seen from amateur virus makers.

"There are no ... really clever viruses, not yet, and may never be. There may be a limit to the amount of effort people are willing to put into doing malicious things."

Discussion Questions

Is there a limit on the effort people are willing to put into doing malicious things? What motivates computer vandals? Can they be stopped? What does the future hold for this form of crime?

Source: John Schwartz, *Toronto Star*, July 10, 2000, p. D5. © 2000, *The Washington Post*. Reprinted with permission.

Among the more serious and costly computer crimes are software piracy, credit card fraud, sniffing out passwords, industrial espionage, mail bombing, virus dissemination, and illegal network entry.

Software piracy ranges from friends sharing and occasionally copying software to fraudulent practices on an international scale. In the latter schemes, software is replicated and marketed as the original product often at bargain prices. The illegal production of computer software is very big business in Southeast Asia and especially in Hong Kong. In this part of the world, pirated copies of popular business software are sold for considerably less than their retail cost. "Software pirates" unlawfully reproduce and use software. Their illegal enterprises result in losses to software manufacturers of billions of dollars per year. American manufacturers have discovered hundreds of illegal copies of their software being used by legitimate firms such as Britain's General Electric or Atari Taiwan Manufacturing Company. According to the Software Publishing Association, about half of all software in use around the world has been copied in violation of the law (Adler, Mueller, and Laufer, 2001; Schmalleger, 1999).

Consumers are increasingly using computers and the Internet to transact business by ordering and paying for merchandise on-line. Computers facilitate credit card fraud in two ways. First, a stolen credit card can be used to purchase goods on-line. Since perpetrators need not expend valuable time and energy moving from one store to another, they can maximize their takes before the card is inactivated. Also, since there is no physical contact with sales staff who might suspect fraud and alert authorities, culprits are more able to extend their run of thievery. Second, credit card numbers can be taken directly from the Internet while customers are purchasing goods or services. To do so, criminals use programs similar to those designed to steal passwords. An alternative method of stealing credit card numbers involves accessing computers located in credit bureaus or financial institutions and copying the desired information (Adler, Mueller, and Laufer, 2001; Schmalleger, 1999).

Entry into a computer system often requires a user password. "Password sniffers" are programs that record the names and passwords of network users as they are logging on to their systems. Acquisition of such confidential information permits unauthorized personnel to access unlawfully the computer and the information contained therein. It is not unusual for illegally obtained passwords to be sold to other parties for illicit purposes.

At a time when information is power, rivals in business and industry have considerable interest in securing information detailing their competitors products and marketing strategies. Technologically sophisticated spies use computers to gather confidential information, often without leaving a trace of their intrusion. Since these "cyber spies" are able to work from a considerable distance, the likelihood of their detection is significantly reduced.

"Mail bombs" are common means of attacking other computer systems. The process involves programming one computer to bombard another with information, usually in the form of e-mail. Mail bombs often shut down computers and networks because the amount of information is too voluminous for the receiving computer to accommodate.

"Viruses" are rogue programs that copy themselves onto other programs or disks, altering or destroying data. They can spread from one machine to another as users download data from networks via modem or direct link. Viruses may also spread through the exchange of floppy disks, CD-ROMs, or magnetic tapes among computers. Most viruses are hidden in executable computer software or in the boot sectors of floppy or hard disks.

Polymorphic viruses are especially destructive. A polymorphic virus uses advanced encryption to construct operational clones of itself. Since polymorphic viruses have the ability to alter themselves once they have infected a computer, they are able to circumvent most security devices that depend on scanning to identify viruses.

Among other techniques used by computer criminals to accomplish their ends are the "salami technique," "logic bombs," "trojan horses," "worms," and "spoofing." The "salami technique" is a form of embezzlement used to steal miniscule slices from the assets of a great many individuals and organizations and to transfer these slices to the embezzler's account. "Logic bombs" are computer programs that are timed to execute a specific task, such as printing a message or deleting information, on a certain date. "Trojan horses" are subprograms concealed in host programs. They may be viruses, bombs, or other harmful codes. "Worms" are self-contained programs that spread across computer networks. "Spoofing" involves gaining external access to a different computer by forging the Internet address of a friendly machine so a computer criminal can install damaging programs (Adler, Mueller, and Laufer, 2001; Schmalleger, 1999; Hagan, 1998; Simon and Hagan, 1999).

Gaining illegal network access is commonly known as "hacking." Some hackers do not have criminal gain as their objective, but rather break into a network as a means of demonstrating their superior computing ability. Especially exhilarating is being able to bypass security measures. These mischievous hackers enter a computer system and "nose around," often exiting without leaving a trace of their illegal instrusion.

Other hackers, however, are more malevolent. Their objective is to alter, steal, or destroy vital, confidential, and protected data. These hackers commit computer vandalism by breaking into a network, modifying operating structures, erasing files, altering passwords, or planting destructive viruses.

Most high-tech offenders, and especially computer hackers, are young, highly intelligent, white males from middle-class backgrounds. Socially, however, they tend to be withdrawn and tend to associate mainly with others who share their fascination for electronics and computer-related pursuits. Some see themselves as part of a counterculture that is combatting censorship, making information freely available, and throwing down the gauntlet to large and powerful corporations (Adler, Mueller, and Laufer, 2001).

Distinctions among types of hackers can be made on the basis of both personality and lifestyle. "Pioneers" are fascinated by the evolving technology of telecommunications. Their mission is to explore this technology, letting it take them where it may. "Scamps" are hackers with a sense of fun who intend no harm by their actions. Hackers motivated by their joy in the discoveries that they make after breaking into new computer systems are "explorers." The more distant geographically and the more secure the target systems are, the greater the excitement that explorers experience in breaking into them. "Game players" enjoy defeating software or system copy protection and especially look for systems with games to play. For game players, hacking itself becomes a game. "Vandals" are malicious hackers who deliberately cause harm for no apparent material gain. "Addicts" are classic computer "nerds" who are literally addicted to hacking and to computer technology (Schmalleger, 1999; Maxfield, 1985).

Box 15.6
MICROSOFT FINDS PIRATE SOFTWARE SITES

A new search engine working 24 hours a day, seven days a week has found thousands of Web sites — including more than a dozen in Canada — selling illegal software, Microsoft Canada Co. announced yesterday.

The search engine is the latest salvo in Microsoft Corp.'s battle to stop the theft, counterfeit and illegal sale of computer programs, an activity that costs the Canadian software industry an estimated $2.5-billion a year in lost revenues.

"You can run, you can try to hide but the tool is very intelligent and very fast about seeking out anybody who is conducting anything that's illegal," said Diana Piquette, anti-piracy manager at Microsoft Canada.

Microsoft identified 686 suspicious Web sites in a single day this week, more than were found in an average month using the manual approach, Ms. Piquette said.

The system also automates the process of sending legal "take down" warnings to the suspicious Web sites. About 90 per cent of the time, the sites remove the suspected illegal software but if they don't — or if they put it back later — the system helps Microsoft keep track and begin further legal action, she said.

Eight Canadian sites were sent notices Tuesday, the first day the system was in full operation. Including searches in the days leading up to the launch, 17 suspect sites were found in Canada, Ms. Piquette said.

The system is so new it's impossible to know what percentage of suspect sites are taken to court, she said.

Last week, an Ottawa man who pleaded guilty to software piracy was handed the stiffest sentence to date in Canada.

Scott Etheridge, 28 was fined $7,500 and sentenced to 12 months of house arrest, 12 months of probation and 200 hours of community service for violating Canada's Copyright Act.

Discussion Questions

Is this type of technology the best answer to fighting high-tech crime? Are technological approaches likely to be very successful? Why or why not?

Source: *Globe and Mail*, August 3, 2000, p. B9. Reprinted with permission from Canadian Press.

Computer criminals evade detection and prosecution relatively easily for several reasons. First, computer criminals carry out their illegal activities without geographic limitations. It is very difficult to trace their criminal activity and identify perpetrators, since cyber space has replaced physical space as the scene of the crime. Offenders can launch their missions from any computer terminal and often from the comfort and privacy of their own homes. By the time their intrusions are detected, if they are detected, the cyber criminals have already moved on to new targets. Second, computer criminals are very highly skilled and are continually developing and refining innovative forms of illegal conduct. Third, few law-enforcement agencies are adequately equipped to detect the computer crimes occurring within their jurisdictions. While technology changes very quickly, law-enforcement methods are both reactionary and traditional. They do not keep pace with new developments. Fourth, although some police departments have created specialized computer-crime units, they are often inade-quately funded, poorly trained, and abysmally under-staffed. Most police departments lack specialized computer-crime units and their officers are unskilled in the investigation of such crimes. People who are knowledgeable in computer applications frequently take positions in the private sector where remuneration is much better. Fifth, computer crime is not a major priority for many police departments. Police agencies are inclined to focus their attention and resources on traditional law-enforcement pursuits, such as the control of violent, property, and public-order crime. These are domains about which the public expresses high levels of concern. Many police officers choose their occupation to help eradicate what they consider to be "real" crime. Finally, prosecutions are too infrequent and penalties too light to act as much of a deterrent to computer crime.

Some experts predict a worsening of the computer-crime problem in the near future. Not only is the technology proliferating at a remarkable pace but various countries around the globe are about to face the impact of the first generation of children who have grown up using computers. The increased sophistication of hackers from this group may very well escalate considerably the incidence and deleterious impact of various forms of computer crime as members of this generation are tempted to commit more serious offences (Adler, Mueller, and Laufer, 2001; Schmalleger, 1999; Simon and Hagan, 1999).

ILLEGAL SECURITIES TRADING

Illegal securities trading involves stock brokers taking advantage of privileged information to make money solely for themselves rather than for their clients. There are three basic types of illegal trading. "Insider trading" entails either passing along to others confidential market information or using it oneself to buy and sell for personal gain. Another popular scheme involves allotting lucrative new issues of stocks and bonds to favoured clients before information on these stocks and bonds is made public. Finally, in "front running," traders make purchases in advance of pending stock trades and then benefit from the upward pressures on share prices generated by the volume buying. Although these schemes are difficult to prove, the Securities Exchange Commission prohibits them (Walmsley, 1987).

In 1990, the Ontario Securities Commission compelled a former federal Liberal cabinet minister, James Richardson of Richardson Greenshields of Canada Ltd., to pay $550000 after finding him guilty of insider trading violations. Richardson broke provincial securities laws by short-selling shares of a Kingston, Ontario, company just weeks before it went bankrupt in 1989 (Maclean's, July 2, 1990). At the time, the penalty was the severest of its type in Canadian history.

CRIME IN THE PROFESSIONS

Professionals such as doctors, lawyers, and dentists also defraud their clients. Among their repertoires of illegitimate practices are providing inadequate service, performing unnecessary but lucrative procedures, overcharging clients, and billing insurance companies and government plans for work not actually done. Physicians' illegitimate activities include unnecessary operations, sexually abusing patients, conducting gang visits, and fee splitting. Gang visits involve spending a few minutes checking large numbers of hospitalized patients and then billing the government for a series of lengthy hospital examinations. Fee splitting involves paying off other physicians for patient

referrals (Wilson, Lincoln, and Chappell, 1988; Reasons and Chappell, 1985).

In an investigation of the legal profession in Canada, Reasons and Chappell (1985) reported that many lawyers either provide substandard service or demonstrate unbridled incompetence. Others overcharge clients and mismanage their finances. Reasons and Chappell also pointed out that law societies usually reserve meaningful sanctions only for lawyers who misappropriate clients' funds. Lawyers whose misdeeds are discovered tend to be in financial difficulty; the reasons range from bad investments to alcoholism and gambling. Crooked lawyers tend to be marginal in the legal profession, engage in solo practice, and do most of their work in estates, real estate, and minor litigation. Their clients are usually individuals, and much of their work is of the "one-shot deal" variety. Reasons and Chappell argue that lawyers are especially likely to engage in crooked activities when tough economic times are exacerbated by an oversupply of legal practitioners.

As Sutherland first emphasized, white-collar criminals are first and foremost respectable people occupying positions of trust. Research shows that white-collar and street criminals share only one similarity — both tend to be male, although this may be changing. Otherwise, white-collar and lower-class lawbreakers differ significantly. The former are older, well educated, married, have children, and are in the top 40 percent income bracket.

The perpetration of white-collar crimes is supported by common misperceptions (Simon and Eitzen, 1990; Clinard and Yeager, 1980; Ermann and Lundman, 1982). First, many people, white-collar workers included, fail to perceive white-collar crime as "crime." The word "crime" is usually associated with lower-class violence, so altering financial figures, playing a few games with computers, and manipulating stocks do not seem to qualify as "real crime." This perception allows "respectable" people both to steal with a clearer conscience and to go relatively unpunished when caught.

White-collar criminals often prey on large organizations with big budgets. The size, wealth, and impersonal nature of insurance companies, banks, commercial businesses, and governments make them easier to steal from because there is no victim in the traditional sense. The criminals and the public alike believe that no one is seriously hurt because the victims are not ordinary people. Many who would not dream of stealing a few dollars from an old-age pen-

Box 15.7
LAWYER SENTENCED TO PRISON FOR FRAUD

Although he gambled away $1.2-million of their money, some of his 21 victims stood by lawyer Jorden Kolman, even writing letters of support extolling his good character.

But Mr. Justice William Gorewich of the Ontario Court of Justice sentenced Mr. Kolman, 35, to three years in a penitentiary yesterday for fraud over $5,000.

While the 15 letters from victims and members of the legal profession showed that Mr. Kolman has not been abandoned, Judge Gorewich said he had more important principles to consider in determining the sentence.

"Mr. Kolman took a huge amount of money in a short period of time and caused incalculable misery by what he did," Judge Gorewich said during the sentencing hearing in a small Newmarket courtroom.

He also ordered Mr. Kolman to repay the Law Society of Upper Canada the $1.2-million it has spent compensating the victims.

The judge remarked that lawyers are the "protectors of society" and as such hold a privileged position. He said Mr. Kolman should have known when he started skimming money to feed his gambling habit that he faced the possibility of serving time in a penitentiary.

Judge Gorewich gave Mr. Kolman a week to help the Law Society clear up the paperwork connected with his case before he begins serving his sentence.

Donna Pistillo, who attended yesterday's hearing, was not among the victims who wrote to the court praising Mr. Kolman as a "good and upfront person." Mr. Kolman stole more than $300,000 from the estate of the Pistillos, who were family friends.

"We're happy he's going to jail because he's a lawyer and is in a position of trust," Ms. Pistillo said outside the courtroom.

Other victims included Osgoode law professor Alan Young, who lost $100,000 when he hired his former student to handle the sale of his house. He was not at yesterday's sentencing.

Mr. Kolman showed no emotion when the judge pronounced the sentence. He pleaded guilty in November and during a sentencing hearing earlier this year sought a reduced sentence because of his gambling addiction.

Judge Gorewich said yesterday that Mr. Kolman has sought treatment for his addiction.

Discussion Questions

The amounts stolen were substantial. How do you account for the sentence of three years? Does the punishment fit the crime?

Source: Gay Abbate, *Globe and Mail*, June 21, 2000, p. A3. Reprinted with permission from the *Globe and Mail*.

---

sioner would consider taking thousands from General Motors. When victims are impersonal and vaguely defined entities, the illegal acts tend to become something other than crime.

People who believe that they are underpaid, that their contributions are unappreciated, and that they are being unfairly passed over for promotion develop feelings of frustration and animosity that may be expressed in criminal action. Resentment encourages biting the hand that feeds. Disgruntled white-collar and professional workers see the proceeds from embezzlement and fraud either as a well-deserved fringe benefit or as rightful compensation for having been somehow wronged.

Research on computer crime indicates that, for many, turning an unlawful profit through this form of

illegal conduct is of secondary importance. Many computer criminals are highly motivated solely by the challenges of beating computer security systems. The first challenge is committing the crime, and the second is not being found out. Computer criminals are often very gifted people; few are caught, and those who are apprehended are seldom prosecuted. Indeed, some employers have gone so far as to recruit computer criminals to redesign the security systems that they have managed to crack (Farquhar and Gomme, 1981).

CORPORATE CRIME

Corporate criminals act on behalf of their employing organizations to maximize profits and, in so doing, cause financial and physical harm to consumers, company employees, and the general public. The three types of **corporate crime** are determined by the identity of the victim: consumers, employees, or the public.

CONSUMERS AS VICTIMS

To maximize profits, some organizations, businesses, and professional associations employ illegitimate tactics to steal money from unsuspecting customers, clients, and investors. One of the most common forms of commercial crime is consumer fraud — a form of lawbreaking that entails deceiving consumers about either the type or the quality of a good purchased or service performed. Misleading investors about the financial solvency of a company or about the investment potential of stocks or bonds is another form of consumer fraud.

Incidents of consumer fraud in Canada are legion, and the amounts of money involved are substantial. In 1981, Atlantic Securities of Halifax suffered a $273 000 collapse after executives of the company misrepresented its finances to regulatory authorities. In another case, the Re-Mor Investment Management Corporation of Niagara Falls defrauded customers of close to $7 million. Officials had promised their clients secure endowments, but instead had invested much of the money illegally.

In 1985, a Kitchener, Ontario, real estate operator was convicted of fraudulent activity that had taken place over more than fifteen years and had involved a large number of investors. The realtor sold farmland at inflated prices after leading buyers to believe that the land would soon be developed. This illegal operation netted more than $8 million. In a $24 million real estate fraud involving the Argosy Financial Group of Canada Ltd., many of the 1000 unlucky investors lost the lion's share of their life savings. After a preliminary inquiry that lasted seven months in 1986, the founder of Consumer's Distributing Company and a stock promoter pleaded guilty to fraud charges. The two were accused of co-operating to purchase and sell Consumer's shares to mislead potential investors into thinking that there was significant market activity in the stock (Toole, 1986).

Toronto-based RT Capital Management Inc., associated with the Royal Bank, manages $37 billion worth of pension funds on behalf of major corporations such as Air Canada, Noranda Inc., and IBM Canada Ltd. In 2000, the Ontario Securities Commission (OSC) found RT Capital Management

guilty of an illegal trading practice known as "juicing" or the "high close" — a practice that artificially inflated the values for some of RT Capital's pension funds.

On 53 occasions between October 1998 and March 1999, RT Capital brokers purchased shares in companies listed on the Toronto Stock Exchange just before the market closed at 4:00 P.M. The goal, according to the OSC, was to manufacture or maintain an "uptick" in the closing price, or alternately, to stop or correct a "downtick." In one case, traders bought 1200 shares of Multibank NT Financial Corp. at $103 per share. The price on the previous trade, however, was only $90. In effect, traders artificially boosted the value of every Multibank share by $13. In total, traders used the "high close" to elevate the value of their portfolios by nearly $38.6 million.

In almost every case, brokers engaged in "juicing" at the end of the month, a time when portfolios are assessed for use in compiling quarterly statements for clients. Since capital management companies base their fees on the value of shares, RT Capital was able to increase their charges to clients in light of the funds' apparently improved performance. Brokers also stood to realize personal gain for meeting or exceeding performance objectives. They also earned bonuses based on growth in the portfolios for which they were responsible.

Some critics of the industry maintain that securities firms mount intense pressure to meet performance objectives and offer employees lucrative bonuses for doing so. Such inducements encourage brokers to bend or break the rules by embracing tactics such as juicing and high closing. The consequence, according to the OSC, was that RT Capital clients did in fact pay higher fees due to the manipulation of stocks.

The OSC discovered the juicing scheme when a series of high close month ends came to the attention of Toronto Stock Exchange (TSE) market surveillance officials. They established the identities of those who were buying and selling and discovered that RT Capital was involved in the majority of the transactions. Because the traders involved knew that the exchange was monitoring late trades, they colluded with over a dozen outside brokers to cover up the illegal transactions. OSC officials uncovered their misconduct by monitoring a taping system installed at RT Capital in early October 1998. The purpose of this system was to record conversations between company traders and outside brokers, a routine measure

Box 15.8
IN B.C., SECURITIES CRIME OFTEN PAYS

Convicted stock market manipulators in British Columbia often dodge their punishment because regulatory authorities are unable to collect the fines that are levied against them, according to the province's securities commission annual report.

That's why there are often huge discrepancies between fines and other penalties imposed against people convicted of securities offences in any given year and the amounts the British Columbia Securities Commission is able to collect from them.

For example, the BCSC imposed total penalties of $4.3-million in the year ended March 31, 2000, but was able to collect only $1.5-million of that amount, the report says.

And despite growing efforts by the securities industry to increase investor awareness, enforcement officials say they don't expect the situation to improve in the near future.

"It's the nature of the business," BCSC executive director Steve Wilson said. He said there are a number of reasons for the discrepancy between the fines assessed and the amounts collected.

When fines are imposed on individuals who flout securities rules, they are based on the significance of the infraction and the amount of money involved, rather than on the ability of the respondents to pay.

For example, the BCSC is unlikely to ever recover all of the $1.8-million it imposed on Eron Mortgage Corp., Eron president Brian Slobogian and vice-president Frank Biller because the company is bankrupt, Mr. Slobogian is living in the United States and Mr. Biller has declared personal bankruptcy.

Regulators also say they often forgo revenue they could have received from administrative penalties, to ensure that investors who lose money in illegal stock market schemes recover some of their money.

Enforcement officials are also hampered by the fact that the individuals they have to deal with are often very adept at hiding their assets in other jurisdictions and offshore accounts.

"The folks we do business with use every trick in the book to evade our investigation efforts," Mr. Wilson said. "By the time we get around to some of these guys, the cupboard is pretty clean."

In some cases, executives accused of bilking investors out of millions avoid paying the penalty simply by not showing up at hearings to give evidence. Eron's Mr. Slobogian, who was ordered to pay $300,000 in administrative penalties by the BCSC, didn't appear at recent hearings in Vancouver to respond to the allegations against him.

Gary Stanhiser, the Seventh Day Adventist pastor who masterminded an offshore investment scheme where 300 investors lost at least $11-million, has lalso eluded Canadian authorities by staying in the United States.

Securities industry officials say it's difficult to make comparisons between the situation in British Columbia and other jurisdictions because in Quebec, for example, penalties are dealt with by the courts.

An in Ontario, individuals who are found to have contravened provincial regulations are penalized through settlements that become payable once they're signed.

For example, the Ontario Securities Commission has already received the $3-million that RT Capital Management Inc., Royal Bank of Canada's pension management arm, agreed to pay last week for manipulating stock prices.

Discussion Questions

What measures might be reasonably undertaken to ensure that securities crime does not pay? Are criminal sanctions a viable approach?

Source: Peter Kennedy, *Globe and Mail*, July 27, 2000, p. B5. Reprinted with permission from the *Globe and Mail*.

in the industry to ensure the avoidance of errors. RT Capital employees, however, did not know that the system was also recording internal communications.

Following a year-long investigation by the TSE and OSC, allegations were made public on June 29, 2000. While RT Capital could have requested a complete hearing before a securities commission panel, at which both sides could summon witnesses and present evidence, it chose to negotiate a quick settlement and to pay the resultant fine. In this way, the company avoided having the tapes and other incriminating evidence become public (Jenish, 2000).

The OSC fined RT Capital $3 million and removed the chair of the company. The brokers involved received individual penalties ranging from one-month suspensions to lifetime bans on trading securities. Six employees resigned and another retired. Others involved in the high closing scheme received suspensions of up to 2.5 months. They were also levied fines totaling $390 000.

Some analysts of the securities industry expressed disappointment that the OSC's sanctions were not more severe, noting that a fine of $3 million is less harmful than a "parking ticket" to a company connected to an institution like the Royal Bank, which made $1.7 billion in profits in 1999. They maintain that the OSC should have levied a larger fine and imposed more severe sanctions on RT Capital's directors and senior executives as a way of sending a message concerning the importance of effective corporate governance. According to the OSC investigation, the six-member board of the company convened irregularly and rarely. More serious is the fact that senior executives failed to oversee the trading practices of portfolio managers and the traders who worked under their direction (Jenish, 2000).

In addition to being victimized by fraud, consumers of goods and services also fall prey to other illegal but firmly established business practices, including false advertising, price fixing, and the marketing of unsafe products. False advertising, in which companies make exaggerated, deceptive, and false claims about their products, is very common. It is also one of the most frequently prosecuted business crimes in Canada.

While not unusual, it is against the law for companies or other organizations to collaborate in setting prices for goods and fees for services. Rather than agree to set artificially inflated rates, companies are supposed to allow charges to be established through free competition on the open market. All other things being equal, the existence of open competition should result in lower prices for goods and services. While most Canadian companies convicted of price fixing have been small, there is little doubt that large organizations are also involved. Under the *Competition Act* of 1986, several multinational petroleum companies, including Shell, Imperial, and Sunoco, have been convicted of this offence (*Toronto Star*, March 15, 1989).

Finally, many sociologists maintain that, while not strictly illegal, the power of professional associations to set minimum fees for specific services represents lit-tle more than the fixing of prices among practitioners. Where provincial law societies and medical associations have been able to set the fees levied by their members for each particular service performed, competition on the basis of the cost of the service is eliminated. The result, critics argue, is that the client will ultimately have to pay more than if practitioners competed on the basis of fees charged. This is a particularly relevant point in occupations like law. The legal profession currently operates mostly on a fee-for-service basis. At the same time, there is an oversupply of licensed practitioners. Free economic competition among the multitude of licensed lawyers, if it existed, could reduce legal fees.

Despite government regulations, the marketing of products such as adulterated foods, unsafe drugs, and defectively designed and constructed automobiles is not as rare as one might think. Supermarkets wash tainted foods, shoot them full of water and food colouring, and repackage and sell them to unsuspecting consumers. Furthermore, many meats, vegetables, and fruits contain potentially dangerous chemical additives to increase shelf life, enhance taste, and improve appearance. Some additives may be linked to a variety of diseases, including cancer (Simon and Eitzen, 1990; Snider and West, 1985).

Many drugs intended for both medical and nonmedical use also constitute a hazard to the health of humans. Some medical drugs brought on the market in Canada and the United States have been inadequately tested. In some cases, researchers have falsified drug tests to shorten the time between a drug's development and sale, even though inadequate testing and falsifying test results are illegal (Braithwaite, 1984).

Some widely marketed and very profitable nonmedical drugs, while legal, are lethal. Multinational tobacco companies such as Rothmans, Imperial, and Macdonald produce millions of cigarettes containing the highly addictive drug nicotine. The Canadian Medical Association and other scientific bodies estimate that cigarette smoking kills at least 35 000 Canadians yearly (Lung Association, 1987a).

One widely owned and frequently dangerous product is the automobile. Estimates of the percentage of vehicular deaths attributable to poor design or failed equipment range up to 50 percent. The most infamous dangerously constructed car is the Ford Pinto. Because of the untimely deaths of Pinto drivers, Ford became the first corporation in history to be charged with murder (Dowie, 1977).

During the 1960s, Ford created the Pinto to capture a larger share of the small-car market in North America. The company rushed the car into production with a deadly design defect. To preserve the Pinto's large trunk capacity, designers located the gas tank in such a way that the Pinto occasionally exploded when struck from the rear. The tendency to blow up in a ball of fire upon impact first appeared in Ford's crash tests and was later confirmed when the cars came into use on the highway. Faced with a growing number of lawsuits over the fiery Pinto deaths, Ford executives undertook a "cost–benefit" analysis to determine the economic feasibility of a recall.

Ford calculated the costs to recall all affected Pintos at $11 per car. The total bill would have been about $137 million. Ford estimated that the costs of paying off on lawsuits for deaths, injuries, and damages would be considerably less expensive — about $49.5 million. Comparing costs, Ford decided not to issue the more expensive recall but to pay the suits instead. Estimates of the costs to Ford for a single Pinto death were in the neighbourhood of $200 000. Simple arithmetic suggests that Ford's savings would have been about $87 million. About 500 people lost their lives or were maimed in Ford-made balls of fire. Indicted for the murder of three people in Indiana in 1978, Ford was eventually acquitted (Hagan, 1986).

EMPLOYEES AS VICTIMS

Many businesses and corporations routinely place their employees at unreasonable risk. The dangers encountered include disabling and frequently lethal diseases, physical injury and perhaps permanent disability, and death. Sometimes these risks come about through corporate negligence and sometimes as a result of deliberate executive decisions. Regardless of why these sorts of incidents occur, the costs are substantial. Those permanently injured must change their lifestyles forever. Family members who lose loved ones through death on the job endure emotional trauma and a lower standard of living due to the loss of a breadwinner.

Workers' compensation board data enabled Ellis (1987) to estimate that the corporate death rate is six times greater than the street death rate. Other researchers believe that only about 33 percent of all work-related accidents can be attributed to the carelessness of workers. In more than 60 percent of work-related mishaps, employers can be held responsible either because working conditions were illegal and dangerous or, while technically within the law, were nonetheless unsafe (Reasons, Ross, and Paterson, 1981).

According to Reasons and his associates (1981), the numbers of life-threatening incidents are enormous and difficult for workers to avoid. Because they come disproportionately from lower-class backgrounds, most employees doing high-risk work cannot change jobs easily. It is not unusual for these lower-class employees to receive higher-than-average pay for their dangerous work. The high wages, especially in economically depressed regions, reduce the likelihood that workers will complain vigorously about unsafe working conditions.

When "accidents" happen, industries that have failed to follow recommended health and safety standards withhold information, deny responsibility, and cover up their wrongdoing. Because of the considerable power wielded by many of these corporations, they are able to suppress information that is not in their best interests.

Health and safety violations are particularly prominent in a handful of industries. Mining is one of the most dangerous (Simon and Eitzen, 1990). Investigations routinely follow cave-ins, explosions, and other mining accidents. Moreover, a good deal of medical research has charted the onset and progression of mining-related lung diseases and cancers. Subsequent reports frequently identify the health and safety violations of employing organizations as contributing causes. Coal mining is infamous for the "black lung" that has killed thousands of miners over the years. The disease is caused by the inhalation of coal dust. In the small Newfoundland community of St. Lawrence, the major livelihood for residents was the mining of fluorspar. Few families in this community have been spared at least one slow agonizing death from the lung disease caused by exposure to this substance. Leyton (1975) reports that even after the mines were closed, one in three households contained a former miner who was "dying hard."

In September 1988, Curragh Resources of Toronto announced that it would operate a $127 million coal mine near Stellarton, Nova Scotia. The following day, Donald Cameron, then Nova Scotia's industry minister, pledged a $12 million provincial loan for the Westray mine, a project that promised to create about 300 jobs. A week later, provincially owned Nova Scotia Power Corporation announced a fifteen-year deal to purchase 700 000 tons of coal a year at a price between

$60 and $74 a ton. The next day, Cameron confirmed that Nova Scotia would purchase an additional 275 000 tons annually whether or not it needed the coal. In July 1989, Curragh halted construction of the mine when federal funding arrangements fell through. In the fall of 1990, the Bank of Nova Scotia loaned the project $100 million and the federal government guaranteed 85 percent of the loan.

The first of numerous cave-ins occurred on May 23, 1991, when the roof along a 24-metre stretch of tunnel collapsed. No one was injured in the 1000-ton rock fall. The Labour Department conducted an investigation and the company retained a team of consultants to study the problems. In a July letter to the province's labour minister, a Liberal MLA warned that the mine was extremely dangerous. The minister responded that Nova Scotia officials were doing as good a job at Westray as they were at other Nova Scotia mines. On July 29, 1991, the province's director of mine safety received the first written report from one of his inspectors stating that there were serious safety concerns at Westray, including excessive accumulations of coal dust and methane gas.

At the end of August, the first trainload of coal made the trip from Westray to a Nova Scotia Power generating station 11 km away. On September 11, 1991, more than 500 guests gathered for the mine's official opening. Premier Cameron, Curragh Chief Executive Clifford Frame, and federal Revenue Minister Elmer MacKay, the region's MP, were on hand to cut the ribbon. On October 18, 1991, officials from the Labour Department met to discuss roof conditions. Seven rock falls had occurred and three of these had taken place in the previous three weeks. In November, the Labour Department issued a written order instructing the company to ensure that miners were not working in sections of the mine at risk of collapse.

After another cave-in in December, miner Carl Guptill refused to work under what he considered to be unsafe conditions. After being asked to assist in clearing the area, he complained that the light on his helmet was not working. His shift boss told him to work in the dark. He tripped and injured his back and shoulder. On December 10, Guptill lodged a formal complaint with the Labour Department, reporting not only his injury but the safety hazards at the mine. On December 16, Guptill met with provincial inspector Albert MacLean and, according to Guptill, informed him of his concerns about coal dust levels, methane gas, and overloaded tractors. Later, MacLean denied that Guptill conveyed any information about safety concerns.

In March 1992, an organizer from the United Steel Workers of America met with miners and discussed the formation of a union. In an internal report, the organizer reported that safety was the primary issue in the organizing drive, hinting that miners might be killed on the site in the near future. Later that same month, another cave-in released methane gas in the southwest section of the mine, causing the area to be abandoned temporarily. Air samples showed that methane readings approached the level at which explosions occur.

On April 2, MacLean sent a memo to his direct superior reporting on a visit two days earlier to the southwest section of the mine. He reported high levels of methane but stated that the mine manager was in control of the situation. On April 29, the Labour Department ordered Westray officials to remove the coal dust from the mine and to install a system to eliminate further accumulations. On April 30, Nova Scotia Power issued a complaint stating that Westray was falling far short of its production targets.

On May 9, 1992, at 5:18 in the morning, methane exploded in the southwest section of the mine, killing 26 miners. On May 15, Premier Cameron took the necessary steps to begin an inquiry. In 1993, Curragh declared bankruptcy.

The Westray inquiry brought to light a number of disquieting findings. The chief mine inspector admitted giving Westray management advance notice of inspections. An electrical engineer testified that the mine manager had refused the installation of air-monitoring equipment in the area of the explosion, presumably because the alarms would have been going off constantly. The government did not follow up on its compliance orders; there were no prosecutions, no fines, and no halts in production. Miners were intimidated and threatened with dismissal to discourage their refusal to enter a dangerous workplace. Miners lacked experience and their training was woefully lacking. Clifford Frame, Curragh founder, controlling shareholder, and CEO, could not be compelled to testify because of jurisdictional problems with subpoenas.

Westray's general and underground managers went to trial in February 1995 on charges of manslaughter and criminal negligence causing death. Charges were subsequently stayed. In March 1997, the Supreme Court ordered that these Westray officials be retried (Estok, 1996; Wells, 1996; R. Williams, 1996).

Medical research has implicated as causes of various types of cancer many chemicals currently in widespread use. Although exposure to many of these chemicals produces effects only over the long term, the risks are often enormous. In the United States, for example, the National Cancer Institute and the National Institute of Environmental Health Services estimate that close to 40 percent of all cancers are triggered by factors in current or former work environments. Tataryn (1986: 155–56) highlights the considerable cancer risks faced by employees working with toxic substances:

> (A risk of 2 indicates a doubling of the cancer risk.) Arsenic has a risk ratio of 2–8 for lung cancer. Benzene has a risk ratio of 2–3 for leukaemia. Coal tar pitch volatiles and coke oven emissions have a risk ratio of 2–6 for cancer of the lung, larynx, skin, and scrotum. Vinyl chloride has risk ratios of 200, 4, and 1.9 respectively for hemangiosarcoma (a malignant tumour of cells lining the cavities of the heart), brain, and lung cancer. Chromium has risk ratios of 3–40 for lung and larynx cancers. Nickel has risk ratios of 5–10 for lung cancer. Petroleum distillates have risk ratios of 2–6 for lung and larynx cancers.

Asbestos, a fire-resistant substance, is an ingredient in cement pipes, cement board, insulation, brake linings, and many other household and industrial products. Asbestos fibres are also deadly. Asbestosis, or "white lung," is a respiratory disease that destroys the lungs. Mesothelioma is a rare form of cancer that is also directly linked to asbestos exposure. Despite considerable debate over the years, it is now accepted that there is no level of exposure to asbestos that can be considered safe (Ermann and Lundman, 1982). Tataryn describes the long controversy regarding the setting of "safe" limits:

> The ways and means of eliminating asbestos dust have therefore long been a subject of controversy. Doctors, health professionals, and governments have joined companies and unions in pitched battles over establishing asbestos dust standards. The official "safe" exposure level has been lowered in fits and starts. Since the early 1900s, asbestos workers have been repeatedly assured that existing standards protect their health. Each time, diseased and dead bodies suggested otherwise. After such tragedy was uncovered, another official "safe" level of exposure was pronounced. (p. 157)

The gap separating the exposure of a worker to this lethal substance and the time of his or her death ranges from about 10 years to 30 years, depending on levels of exposure and the ability of the body to resist affliction.

During the 1980s, the United States Environmental Protection Agency proposed a ten-year ban on asbestos production. The result of such a ban was to further reduce the economic well-being of towns such as Thetford Mines, Quebec, that were already plagued by economic depression and chronic unemployment. While perhaps not surprising, it was nonetheless ironic that the very workers who suffered at the hands of negligent corporations such as Johns-Manville fought to keep asbestos on the market and to keep the mines operating. Faced with job losses, workers are often willing to tolerate some "acceptable" level of risk. The problem in this case was that there is no level of exposure below which workers can be reasonably assured that they will not contract one of the fatal asbestos-related diseases. By the end of the 1980s, many governments around the world placed a total ban on the use of this product (*Maclean's*, July 17, 1989).

At the beginning of the 1980s, news first broke of the potential for vast oil development off the eastern shores of Canada. The Hibernia discovery heralded the possibility of Canada's poorest province, Newfoundland, becoming one of its richest. Amid the euphoria of the time, oil exploration and drilling companies renewed their exploration off the Grand Banks by using semi-submersible drilling rigs. One of these, the *Ocean Ranger*, was widely touted as not only one of the biggest but also as one of the best in the world.

On February 15, 1982, the coast of Newfoundland was battered by a storm that some observers said was powerful enough to move buildings on their foundations. On that evening, the Ocean Ranger, prophetically nicknamed the "Ocean Danger" by offshore workers, capsized and sank, taking to their deaths 84 people, 53 of them Newfoundlanders.

In the inquiry that followed, investigators placed the responsibility for the *Ocean Ranger* tragedy squarely on the drilling companies and the Newfoundland and Canadian governments. From the official report, House (1986:184–85) summarizes the major reasons why the Ocean Ranger sank:

> (1) The rig was inadequately designed and constructed. (2) It had been inadequately inspected.

Box 15.9
A TRAGICALLY REPEATING PATTERN

When the Thetford asbestos issue flared again during a 1975 strike, Dr. Cartier openly stated that, on humanitarian grounds, he had not always informed workers suffering from asbestosis of the full extent of their illness: "I figured it was in their best interests to stay at their jobs. Besides, they didn't want to be reported ill and transferred to a lower-paying job where they might have earned as much as 50 dollars less a week." Cartier also noted that "even if they had left their work completely and gone on to drive cabs, for instance, it might not have arrested the progressive effects of asbestosis."

Paul Filteau, general manager and secretary of the Quebec Asbestos Mining Association, the organization which represents the Quebec asbestos industry, says the companies never encouraged Cartier to be wary of "medico-legal problems" when he examined Thetford workers and gave workers with impaired lungs "A" classifications. But Filteau admits that the companies' clinic had not always informed the workers about the state of their health: "Cartier told the workers they were all right, let them go back to their jobs, and, if he thought the case serious, recommended that they visit their family doctor. But the companies never told him to do this. It was his decision. We never interfered."

Neither did the Quebec government. This clinic's X-ray records were supposedly subject to government inspection. Until 1972, however, the government-appointment doctor responsible for monitoring the X-ray records of clinics in eastern Quebec was Dr. Paul Cartier. In the case of Thetford Mines, then, Cartier was in effect inspecting his own work.

The evidence continues to mount that asbestos companies hid from workers the diagnoses that they were suffering from asbestos-related diseases. They hid this until the men finally became physically disabled and the sickness could no longer be denied. In 1949, Dr. Kenneth Wallace Smith, then the medical officer for Johns-Manville Canada Inc. in Asbestos, Quebec, filed a health report with the asbestos company's head offices in the United States. The report indicates that Dr. Smith discussed the potential asbestos danger with Johns-Manville (JM) executives and recorded their reaction, which, according to Smith, was: "We know that we are producing disease in employees who manufacture these products and there is no question in my (our) mind that disease is being produced in non-JM employees who may use certain of these products." Smith noted in his report that asbestosis was "irreversible and permanent" and added "but as long as a man is not disabled it is felt he should not be told of his condition so that he can live and work in peace and the company can benefit by his many years of experience."

Discussion Questions

Could Johns–Manville executives be prosecuted under criminal law? Why would this course of action be unlikely?

Source: L. Tataryn, "A Tragically Repeating Pattern: Issues of Industrial Safety," in K. Lundy and B. Warme (eds.), *Work in the Canadian Context: Continuity Despite Change*, 2nd ed. (Toronto: Butterworths, 1986). Reprinted with permission of Butterworths Canada Ltd., through the Canadian Copyright Licensing Agency (CANCOPY).

(3) It had failed to meet the requirements specified for it in its last U.S. Coast Guard inspection. (4) Canadian federal safety regulations and enforcement procedures were inadequate. (5) Newfoundland provincial regulations were equally inadequate. (6) The operating manual for the rig was deficient. (7) The crew (Americans as well as Newfoundlanders and other Canadians), especially those responsible for ballast control, were poorly trained in operating procedures. (8) The lifeboats and other lifesaving equipment on the rig were inadequate. There were, for example, no survival suits for the crew. (9) The crew was poorly trained and drilled in lifesaving practices. (10) The standby vessels and helicopters that serviced the rigs in the area were not provided with lifesaving equipment. (11) The crew of the Ocean Ranger's standby vessel, the Seaforth Highlander, was not trained in lifesaving procedures. (12) The too little, too late efforts of Canadian search and rescue offices lacked preparedness and displayed "no sense of urgency."

House further points out that

> because they did not understand the basic principles of the ballast control system as a whole, and because they have not been trained to deal with emergency situations (in particular, they had been led to believe that manual devices could be used to close valves when in fact they opened them), ballast control room operators, in their desperation to right the rig after it had sustained an initial list, actually contributed to its capsizing. Because of their inadequate training and equipment, the crew of the *Seaforth Highlander* were subjected to the horror of witnessing at close hand a lifeboat capsize with its crew who were swept away to certain death.... [T]he oil and drilling companies have been allowed to get away with labour practices offshore that would not have been permitted onshore. A powerful coalition of financial interests between national governments and multinational corporations has dictated that the more mundane interests of offshore workers for safe working conditions be given low priority. The same constellation of interests has been at play within Canada, with the struggles among federal, provincial, and corporate power wielders overriding the less obvious conflict of interests between workers and managers in both industry and state. (p. 185)

The Public as Victims

In the long run, perhaps the most serious form of corporate crime involves the victimization of the general public through the destruction of the environment. Environmental pollution of land, air, and water may be the most serious social problem facing the world today. Along with dreaded diseases like cancer, genetic damage and birth defects are being linked to many of the toxic chemicals now firmly entrenched in ecological systems. Globally, increased levels of industrial pollution have triggered environmental changes. The release into the atmosphere of a group of chemicals known as CFCs, for example, is eroding the ozone layer that protects life from the sun's harmful rays. The reduction of protective ozone, in turn, is expected to increase human exposure to the cancer-causing ultraviolet rays of the sun. Furthermore, scientists anticipate that the warming of the earth through the greenhouse effect will bring drought in some areas of the world and, due to the melting of polar ice, flooding in others (Schneider, 1989).

Pollution is not a new problem; humans have always contaminated their environment. What has made pollution such a major problem recently is the massive growth in human population and the concomitant development of industrial technology. Not only are there more people to wreak havoc on the earth's ecosystems, their fuels, machines, and chemicals have vastly increased the severity of environmental destruction. While individuals, municipalities, and industries all pollute, industries are unquestionably the worst offenders. Unlike individuals and municipalities, a multitude of industrial operations create, use, and dispose of large quantities of extremely toxic chemicals and radioactive material (Commoner, 1990). Moreover, industry markets products that seriously contaminate the environment. In Los Angeles and Denver, for example, automobiles are the major source of polluted air. Similarly, the decomposition of aerosol cans and of styrofoam food and beverage containers has contributed greatly to the destruction of the ozone layer (Rifkin, 1991).

Every year, Canadian industries generate 3 million tonnes of hazardous wastes, including dioxin, mercury, and pesticides. About half of this amount comes from Ontario. Each type of toxic waste requires a different disposal technique, and very few disposal facilities operate safely. Canadian industries face relatively few regulations, and the few controls that do exist differ from one province to another. Furthermore, even where regulations exist, enforcement is frequently lax (Janigan, 1985).

There are many examples of the way in which industrial pollution has affected or will affect Canadians. In Northern Ontario, the Reed Pulp and Paper Company so polluted the English–Wabigoon river system with mercury that the catching and eating of fish from those waters had to be banned by the government. Unfortunately, the prohibition of fishing was not instituted before some Native Canadians dependent on the fish for food developed Minamata disease. Not only were significant numbers of them poisoned, but since fishing was a major source of livelihood for Native people in this area, the ban seriously eroded their traditional economic base (Macdonald, 1991).

PCBs present a pollution problem in much the same way as mercury does. PCBs are extremely toxic, build up in live tissue, and increase in concentration as they move up the food chain. Moreover, it can take 25 years for the cancers and birth defects associated with PCB contamination to show up. Until the federal government banned them in the late 1970s, PCBs

Box 15.10
U.S. WASTE DUMPERS SKIP SENTENCING

Three Americans who dodged their trial may never have to face the jail sentences and heavy fines levied against them yesterday for illegally dumping hazardous waste into Toronto Harbour.

Prosecutor Jerry Herlihy said the total of 16 months in jail they received, along with the more than $1.13 million in fines, added up to one of the stiffest sentences ever imposed for environmental offences in Ontario.

But Craig Dallmeyer, founder of Aquatech Blue, Robert Weddle, the former plant manager, both of Pennsylvania, and co-owner Morgan Whitely, of Virginia, weren't in court yesterday to hear Mr. Justice Joseph Bovard pass sentence on them.

When the three men failed to show up in June, the trial was held in their absence. They are believe to be outside the country and can't be extradited for breaking provincial laws.

Contacted by phone, Dallmeyer said, "I have no remorse because I did nothing. It's that simple." He called the Canadian justice system "corrupt."

Bovard found the three men deliberately committed more than 20 violations of Ontario's Environmental Protection and Water Resources Act, including:

- Dumping hazardous waste into a storm sewer which emptied into the Keating Channel between the Don River and the harbour.

- Pumping industrial waste into the city's sanitary sewers leading to the treatment plant at Ashbridge's Bay.

- Filling a 6-million-litre storage tank beyond capacity, causing it to bulge and eventually overflow.

- Keeping 4 million litres of waste in an old storage tank that was supposed to be kept empty, while telling ministry officials it wasn't being used.

- Failing to install approved equipment to treat hazardous waste.

- Falsifying reports to the ministry.

- Failing to test incoming waste to see if the facility could treat it.

During the trial, which began June 12, Bovard heard evidence that a rusty orange industrial waste storage tank maintained by the company was filled so far beyond its legal limit it bulged to the extent that employees nicknamed it "the pumpkin."

He cited an incident in which an Aquatech employee working near the tank was covered in oil from "head to toe" when the tank unexpectedly overflowed.

Bovard said a stiff punishment was warranted because the actions of the three men were deliberate, flagrant and dishonest.

Discussion Questions

Is the punishment sufficient? What measures could be undertaken to improve punishment and deterrence in cases such as this one?

Source: Harold Levy, *Toronto Star*, August 5, 2000, p. A8. Reprinted with permission – The Toronto Star Syndicate.

---

were used widely in the manufacture of plastics, paints, and cosmetics and as both an insulator and coolant in electrical equipment (Elsworth, 1990). Durable and extremely difficult to destroy, there are huge stockpiles of this deadly liquid in Canada. Awaiting their disposal, companies have stored these toxins in aging tanks and transformers nationwide. PCBs are often housed under poorly monitored conditions on the sites where they were originally used (Janigan, 1985).

Spills have occurred when PCBs have been moved. One such incident occurred when 100 gallons of the substance splashed from a transformer anchored to a flatbed truck travelling along a 150-km stretch of the Trans-Canada Highway east of Kenora in Northern Ontario. Following this incident, the Trans-Canada Highway had to be closed for a cleanup that took five days to complete. The contaminated gravel and asphalt dug up from the highway itself had to be stored as toxic waste (Elsworth, 1990; Janigan, 1985).

One of the areas in Canada where pollution is most acute is in the industrialized heartland of southern Ontario, adjacent to several of the Great Lakes. The lakes contain about 20 percent of the world's fresh water. Millions of Canadians and Americans use this giant reservoir of fresh water for drinking, irrigation, and recreation. Nevertheless, scientists have identified in the waters of the Great Lakes over 1000 toxic chemicals, among the more deadly of which are PCBs, dioxin, mirex, benzopyrene, toxaphene, and hexachlorobenzene. The sources of these chemicals include factories, chemical dumps, sewage-treatment and nuclear power plants, farmers' fields, and even the surface air, which itself is filled with effluent from the smokestacks of nearby industries. If all such pollution were stopped immediately, it would take decades for Lake Ontario to flush itself out through natural means. For the larger and deeper Lake Superior, natural cleansing could take centuries (Ohlendorf, 1985b; Ashworth, 1986).

More than five million Canadians and Americans draw their drinking water from Lake Ontario, the most polluted of the Great Lakes. The Niagara River, described by scientists as a "toxic bath," provides about 83 percent of the tributary flow into that lake. At dozens of locations, industrial and municipal wastes are dumped into the river. These sites, known as "point sources," release 1400 kg per day of priority pollutants (described as dangerous by the U.S. Environmental Protection Association) into the Niagara. Ninety percent of these extremely dangerous wastes come from ten sites, nine of which are in the United States. Nonpoint sources of pollution are those lacking discharge vents made by human hand. Within a 4.5 km belt of New York state adjoining the river, there are 164 hazardous-waste landfill sites known to have PCBs, dioxin, and mirex buried in them. From 61 of these sites, chemicals are seeping through the surrounding limestone into the Niagara River. Seventeen such waste-disposal dumps are on the Canadian side of the river. Authorities consider leaching imminent in five of them if a cleanup is not done (Malcolmson, 1987).

Another major pollution problem facing sections of Canada and the United States is acid rain. Industries and utilities that burn fossil fuels, coal in particular, release high levels of sulphur dioxide from their smokestacks into the air. Sulphur dioxide emissions are particularly heavy in the U.S. midwest and the Ohio Valley. In Canada, Inco smelters in Copper Cliff, Ontario, and Thompson, Manitoba, are the major offenders. The sulphur dioxide released into the atmosphere combines with nitrogen oxide and eventually falls in the form of acid rain, which is killing aquatic plant life and fish in lakes across the country. Scientists estimate that 80 percent of the lakes within 160 km of industrialized southern Ontario are dead

or dying. Furthermore, as the soil becomes acidic, trees also die. The threat to recreation and timber-based economies is considerable (Gordon and Suzuki, 1990; Rifkin, 1991).

THEORIES OF WHITE-COLLAR AND CORPORATE CRIME

DIFFERENTIAL ASSOCIATION

The pioneering theory in the field of business criminality was Sutherland's differential association. Sutherland (1949) sought, by focusing upon the individual rather than the organization, to explain why some businesses break the law while others do not. He argues that the causes of elite crime are the same as those of lower-class crime. People learn to break the law when they develop an excess of definitions that promote illegality. They acquire this "excess of favourable as opposed to unfavourable definitions" in association with others who hold pro-crime attitudes. In business, veteran workers socialize their less-seasoned colleagues; the latter adopt the skills and ideologies of the former. If veterans' definitions of the situation support unethical and illegal conduct, the lessons transmitted to their associates will reflect this predisposition. Alternatively, if the lessons promote ethical and law-abiding behaviour, the resulting conduct is likely to follow the letter of the law.

Business organizations are largely controlled by "dominant coalitions" of the company's most powerful executives and senior officers (Thompson, 1967). Unethical and illegal practices among subordinates are especially likely when members of dominant coalitions make it known that they tolerate, condone, or even expect their workers to engage in illegitimate activities to achieve organizational objectives.

Sutherland points out that the learning involved in differential association extends to a corporation's competition in a snowball-like fashion (Albanese, 1987). Commercial enterprises and industries in competition with one another learn that illegal conduct is necessary to stay in business. In this fashion, Sutherland explains how business illegality proliferates.

CONFLICT AND DETERRENCE THEORIES

Where Sutherland's theory explained business crime in terms of the conduct of individuals, more recent frameworks have concentrated on the roles of organizations, the state, and the law. From this vantage point, corporate crime can perhaps be best understood in terms of a combination of conflict and deterrence theories.

Simon and Eitzen (1990) develop a conflict theory of corporate crime that emphasizes the distribution of power in society as the key causal factor producing business crime. Borrowing from the work of American conflict theorist C. Wright Mills, they begin by arguing that a society's powerful economic and political (and in the United States, military) institutions are controlled by a power elite, who come from privileged backgrounds and command a disproportionately large share of society's social and economic rewards, specifically wealth, power, and prestige. Most of the power elite are upper-middle-class professionals or upper-class businesspeople who share a pro-business and pro-development ideology. Membership in the political and economic elites is restricted to a relatively small number of people and is largely interchangeable. It is not unusual for members of the elite working in the political realm at one time to assume high-ranking positions in business at another time, or vice versa.

When wealth and power are concentrated in a relatively small elite class, it is not surprising that members of this group play a large role in determining broader societal objectives. A small but powerful elite controls society's economic and political institutions, which in turn affect society's secondary institutions — the family, the education system, the church, and, perhaps most important of all, the media. According to Simon and Eitzen, these secondary institutions are the major socializing forces in contemporary capitalist society. The news and entertainment media, for example, provide the public with diversion and distraction and in the process send several important messages. First, they present the image that crime is a lower-class phenomenon and that it is among the world's most serious problems. Second, media promote the idea that business and capitalist social orders exemplify competition and individual freedom. Although it is not perfect, capitalism is better than its alternatives. Comparatively little social improvement is required in capitalist democracies.

While the corporate community in the United States is highly concentrated, in Canada it is even more so. The consequence of a high level of corporate concentration is that a small number of companies account for a very large share of the gross domestic product, either directly through their own commercial activities or indirectly through their influence on the smaller businesses and industries that provide so many of the country's goods and services. Large corporations choose where, when, and how much to invest. They are free to stay in a country or move elsewhere. It is their prerogative to hire, promote, lay off, or fire employees. These privileges translate into considerable power over workers who are dependent upon business and industry for their livelihood. Furthermore, the ability to engage in these business practices with little if any interference, Simon and Eitzen argue, ensures that power elites have the full attention of municipal, provincial, and federal governments. These governments depend upon business for their own well-being. An inadequate business and industrial base creates disgruntled voters and produces fewer workers, who earn lower salaries. Where such circumstances prevail, governments are left with less of a population to govern and with less of a financial base in land and income taxes.

Problems for governments become particulary acute during economic recessions. Corporations in search of profit can easily relocate to regions with abundant cheap labour, low taxes, easier access to raw materials, and few costly health, safety, and pollution regulations. In tough economic times especially, corporations tend to grow larger and more powerful not through expansion but through buyouts and mergers. Not only do buyouts and mergers create no jobs, they often result in job loss. Corporate relocation and consolidation can fuel unemployment and inflation and, in the process, further diminish the state's tax base.

When economic times are tough, governments are in a difficult position. Business and industry demand that the state provide assistance for their capital accumulation or suffer the consequences of an unhealthy economy. Typically, corporations insist on such "concessions" as tax relief, lucrative government contracts, loans and guarantees, and a relaxation of legislation that might further erode profits. The legislation at issue usually concerns investment practices, health and safety, and pollution. The state, however, must maintain legitimacy in the eyes of its citizens. The promotion of social order and harmony depends on the state's commitment to social programs that alleviate the pains of poverty, unemployment, and poor health. Where program demands exceed tax and other revenues, governments run up deficits.

Caught in a trap, legislatures have three solutions, none of which holds much appeal. First, they can raise the taxes paid by citizens. This is not a tactic greeted with enthusiasm by taxpayers. Second, governments can cut social programs. These measures target society's poor and underprivileged and create "crises of legitimacy" that can cause disruption, which, if sufficiently severe, can disrupt economic production. Such austerity measures also run the risk of necessitating ever more coercive measures on the part of the state and its police. Under such conditions, Simon and Eitzen argue, the state is increasingly called upon to maintain order through force. Finally, governments can solve the legitimacy problem by increasing the share of the bill for social programs that is paid by business and industry. Ever mindful of profits, corporations seldom if ever respond favourably to such initiatives.

According to conflict theory, three conditions set the stage for business crime: a small, similarly circumstanced, interchangeable economic and political power elite; corporate concentration, affluence, and global mobility; and the fiscal crisis of the state. For the state, accumulation (the creation of conditions conducive to corporations' production of profit) routinely takes precedence over legitimation (the effective maintenance of social programs). The precedence of accumulation over legitimacy explains why the state has relatively few laws prohibiting corporate crime, why it does not meaningfully enforce the statutes that do exist, and why corporate offenders are dealt with very leniently (Simon and Eitzen, 1990).

Deterrence theory provides some useful insights into why business crime flourishes in Canada, and much of this chapter's concluding section focuses on the plethora of reasons why crimes in business and professional circles are so difficult to curb. Suffice it to note at this point that corporate crime is a rational form of misconduct that occurs because it pays. Profits outweigh penalties. First, if the illegality is prohibited at all, the sentences meted out are not severe. Second, it is by no means certain that offenders will be caught and punished. Third, if they are apprehended, it can literally take decades before the cases are decided in the courts. In the absence of severity, certainty, and celerity, it is hardly surprising that corporate wrongdoing is so prevalent in Canada and other capitalist democracies.

CONTROLLING BUSINESS CRIME

Misconduct in business flourishes for a multitude of reasons. The business community is engaged in a relentless drive for profits. Commercial crime is rational, and rational crime is very difficult to control. Both a high level of corporate concentration and the structure of the corporation itself conspire against an effective response. Finally, the inadequacy of regulations, inattention on the part of both lawmakers and law enforcers, and the tolerance displayed by a misinformed and, until recently, uninterested public are other factors that facilitate business and professional misconduct.

PROFIT

Corporations are in business to make money. The wise use of profits dictates that executives invest these funds for a return, use them to expand existing enterprises, or put them into the purchase of new businesses, which in turn can generate income for the parent company. Many businesspeople firmly believe that the primary if not the sole responsibility of a company is to earn dividends for its shareholders. Truly ethical conduct and adherence to meaningfully competitive business practices is a surefire recipe for reduced profit margins. Ensuring that employees work under safe conditions siphons funds away from investment and expansion. Money tied up in training programs, safety equipment, and air cleaners neither earns interest nor contributes to increased production. Furthermore, safety equipment, once purchased, must be maintained. Faced with initial cash outlays and unending maintenance payments, the cheapest route is to replace the disabled, the injured, the sick, and the dying with new recruits. Preserving the environment from the ravages of toxic waste is similarly costly (Clinard and Yeager, 1980; Simon and Eitzen, 1990).

When measures to improve health and safety standards for workers are suggested to industry, companies routinely claim that the technology to implement the new standards is years away. Businesses habitually ask that standards be lowered and that they be given more time to comply with the new regulations. Both of these corporate strategies aim to minimize the potential profit reductions that forced implementation of new health and safety standards entails (Clinard and Yeager, 1980).

RATIONALITY

Those who commit white-collar and corporate crimes frequently do so with meticulous planning, carefully weighing anticipated benefits against potential costs. Criminal businesspeople and professionals are very intelligent and very well trained. Because they know what they are doing and pay considerable attention to detail, they are frequently successful. They also know that the proceeds generated by business crime dramatically outweigh the costs of discovery. Corporate executives are keenly aware that the chances of getting caught are small. They know that the likelihood of being convicted is even smaller and that the probability of being fined severely is minuscule. Indeed, fines are so small that business executives generally think of them as modest licensing fees (Clinard and Yeager, 1980). Finally, they know that the chances of imprisonment are virtually nonexistent. With such a low risk of negative sanction, there is little or no deterrent to this form of illegal conduct. Consequently, the high recidivism rates for most business crimes should come as no surprise (Goff and Reasons, 1978).

CORPORATE CONCENTRATION

Corporate Canada is highly concentrated (Casey, 1985). A relatively small number of very large companies, run by a handful of corporate directors, control a large portion of economic activity. Less than 1 percent of Canada's corporations control 50 percent of industrial sector property and profit and account for more than one-third of total sales. In 1985, 32 family dynasties generated $123 billion in revenues. The magnitude of this figure becomes clear with the knowledge that the federal government's revenues in the same year were about $80 billion. Certain sectors are especially concentrated. In the petrol industry, 58 percent of retail outlets are controlled by only four multinational companies. Canada's "big five" control 90 percent of bank assets and, in manufacturing, 2 percent of corporations control 80 percent of assets (Snider, 1993).

Not only is the corporate elite small, the directorships of companies interlock. A single individual may sit on the governing board of several corporations and financial institutions. Small numbers and interlocking directorships facilitate communication and, as criminologists have suggested, make conspiracy very possible if not likely. Conspiring to fix prices, merge companies, and create product shortages is facilitated by close ties and surreptitious communication among corporate directors (Ermann and Lundman, 1982).

ORGANIZATIONAL STRUCTURE AND VALUES

The organizational structure and its operational values and norms also promote wrongdoing. The success of a business often requires attaining a short-term goal — usually the immediate realization of profit. Executives' raises, bonuses, and promotions depend on their meeting these myopic objectives. Many corporate decisions emphasize short-term considerations over long-term effects. Increasing profits in the here and now takes precedence over any deleterious impacts on the economy, consumers, workers, and the environment that may materialize only years down the line. Indeed, the gap separating an executive decision from its harmful consequence is often so large that the businessperson is promoted, transferred, retired, or even dead by the time the victims feel the impacts (Ermann and Lundman, 1982).

The law seldom if ever holds corporations directly responsible for their executives' actions. Senior officials pressure their subordinates to get results. Company authorities set out aims and objectives for junior executives and expect the junior executives, encouraged through the corporate reward structure, to meet these goals any way they can. Business leaders, both by accident and by design, frequently keep themselves in the dark about the means adopted by subordinates to accomplish their assigned tasks. Neither the senior executives nor the corporation itself are expected to subject juniors to close enough supervision to ensure the observance of ethical codes and government regulations.

Even when violations occur, governments seldom hold corporate leaders responsible for the harmful conduct of their subordinates. With orders given from the top down and with the top not knowing the details of what underlings are doing, those in charge can and do argue that they cannot be held responsible for the injurious actions of their junior personnel. Furthermore, corporate officers cannot be sued as individuals and therefore cannot be held personally accountable for their companies' wrongdoings. Even when the courts convict a corporation and publicly hold its officers directly responsible for their decisions, businesses seldom punish their miscreant executives by demoting or firing them (Clinard and Yeager, 1980; Ermann and Lundman, 1982).

Corporations are, to a very large extent, secret organizations. Officers of the company fight hard to keep information confidential. Legal evidence usually depends on corporate records, and corporate records are protected under business law. Consequently, corporations can frequently delay or resist the efforts of police and courts to gain access to "confidential

Box 15.11
EXECUTIVE JAILED FOR WASTE SPILL

The operations manager of a waterfront oil recycling company was jailed yesterday for 90 days after admitting the company spilled hazardous chemical waste into Toronto Harbour.

Gerrard Lee, 36, of North York, a past director of Aquatech Blue Ltd., pleaded guilty to the dumping charge under the provincial Water Resources Act.

Lee also pleaded guilty to allowing chemical waste to be mixed in a storage tank designated only for used oil, falsifying company records and deceiving a provincial environment ministry inspector.

He was charged in August, 1997, along with the company, its two co-owners and a former plant manager following a year-long environment ministry investigation.

Lee started working for the company in late 1995 and was added to the board of directors — the only Canadian — in July, 1996. The other principals in the case live in the U.S.

Ministry inspections during the fall of 1996 and spring of 1997 found spills from the company's plant on Cherry St. at the east end of the harbour had seeped into storm sewers.

Rain water flushed the oils into the Keating Channel, which links the Don River with the harbour, an Ontario Court of Justice was told by ministry prosecutor Jerry Herlihy.

At the ministry's request, Aquatech hired a drainage consultant that found several catch basins leading to the sewer were filled with oil.

The report recommended pumping out the catch basins and rerouting the oil to company equipment that separated waste oil from water.

Lee doctored the consultant's report and removed all references to the oil in the catch basins before sending the report to ministry inspector Pearl Shore, Herlihy said.

Aquatech Blue set up a used oil recycling operation at a former oil refinery in the city's portlands

district. It expanded to include industrial chemical waste treatment in April, 1996.

The company's operating permit required the used oil and industrial waste to be kept separately but they were combined in one large storage tank on the company's property, Herlihy said.

The company was also required by the ministry to use a specific piece of Colloid Environmental Technologies equipment for treating the industrial waste.

During an August, 1996, inspection by Shore, Lee pointed to a large, blue machine on the property and said it was the Colloid equipment.

The company, however, did not purchase the Colloid equipment until four months later, Herlily said.

Lee told The Star he was flattered when he was offered a directorship with the company.

"My experience at Aquatech should provide a valuable lesson to anyone who is offered a director-ship in a company — think long and hard before you accept," said Lee, who now works for a cap manu-facturing company.

"This turned out to be a terrible mistake on my part," he said.

Lee will be allowed to serve his jail term on weekends.

Aquatech Blue, company founder Craig Dallmeyer of Pennsylvania, co-owner Morgan Whitely of Virginia, and former manager Robert Weddle of Pennsylvania are to go to trial Monday.

The ministry has said it will seek jail terms for the three Americans if they are convicted.

Discussion Questions

Are illegalities of this type rare? Is Mr. Lee's penalty just? What sentence would you have recommended and why?

Source: Brian McAndrew, *Toronto Star*, June 9, 2000, p. B1. Reprinted with permission — The Toronto Star Syndicate.

information." Big business routinely justifies its delays and denials by claiming that any information dis-closed outright might fall into the hands of the competition. Sensitive information in the hands of competing organizations, the argument goes, under-

mines the legitimate business interests of the accused corporation (Clinard and Yeager, 1980; Simon and Eitzen, 1990).

Professions such as medicine, law, and dentistry are equally difficult to regulate. Although they have codes of ethics, the professions are self-governing autonomous bodies. Ultimately, this means that members are accountable only to one another. Disciplinary boards of these high-status and powerful occupations are understaffed and operate with low budgets. Tribunals drawn from the membership conduct their investigations in secret, behind closed doors. With the regulated and the regulating coming from the same ranks, conflicts of interest are inevitable. Full enforcement of the rules is mitigated by the board's fears of alienating a profession's membership. This has led some observers to insist that professions have drawn up their codes of ethics more to protect their own interests than the interests of their clients.

Professionals are insulated from legal action by the public in several ways. Lawyers' victims, for example, must make their complaints in writing. Many people are unaware of where to direct formal accusations, and provincial law societies lack both the jurisdiction and the will to take much action in any but the most blatant cases of abuse. That lawyers have strong ties to busi- ness and political elites does little to increase their accountability. In 1982–83, for example, 32 percent of the members of Parliament in Canada were lawyers (Reasons and Chappell, 1985).

RATIONALIZATIONS

Businesspeople possess handy rationalizations that allow them to maintain noncriminal self-images and justify their harmful acts (Clinard and Yeager, 1980; Ermann and Lundman, 1982). First, they define business crime as something else. Embezzlement becomes borrowing. Price fixing becomes market stabilization. Bribery becomes lobbying. Many businesspeople feel that their actions cause little damage. Illegitimately squeezing one consumer for a few extra dollars on the price of a car is hardly going to drive that single buyer into poverty. The few extra dollars from one consumer, however, translate into millions from the many. Those extra millions, the thinking goes, make it possible to expand the company and the economy.

Another frequent rationalization is the argument that because most companies are cutting corners illegitimately, others must do the same to remain competitive. Executives state their positions in the following terms. If one plant adheres to pollution cleanup directives while another does not, the cleanup costs to the former will eventually drive it out of business. Companies going out of business darken the nation's economic future. Consequently, businesses have little choice but to pollute. This is the price of a healthy economy and a high standard of living.

Industries producing toxic wastes often claim that technology will eventually be developed to permit the safe disposal of these dangerous substances. Nuclear waste from power plants and weapons production, for example, cannot be destroyed and will remain deadly for centuries. Not surprisingly, critics of the nuclear industry have emphasized the dangers of continuing to create certain types of toxic wastes while there is no known way of safely disposing of them. Given the current state of technology, the nuclear industry can only store its toxic residue. There are serious doubts as to how safely and for how long this radioactive waste can be stockpiled.

Many Canadians inside or outside the business world staunchly believe in and support capitalism. Many business leaders who strongly adhere to the free-enterprise ideology view as unnecessary interference the creation of laws governing corporate action in areas of finance, health and safety, consumer rights, and pollution control. They argue that regulatory enforcement does nothing but generate unnecessary, costly, and time-consuming red tape and paperwork. Such sentiments are hardly conducive to corporations co-operating in the creation and implementation of laws protecting workers, consumers, and the public.

Finally, many companies, particularly those employing large numbers of workers, tend to view their employees as impersonal entities rather than people. From the management perspective, employees become either machines or extensions of machines. As a result, employers tend to think of diseased, disabled, and dead workers, particularly the unskilled, as easy to replace if the necessity arises. This reasoning makes it difficult to ensure the health and safety of employees (Ermann and Lundman, 1982).

INADEQUATE REGULATION

Government laxness also fuels corporate criminality. Many laws governing important and potentially harmful corporate action are weak. Inadequate regulation is partly a product of the close and sometimes conspiratorial connections between members of economic and political elites. In some cases, legislators do not introduce regulations; in others, they create laws but render them powerless by the way in which they are worded or by the inadequate penalties attached to them (Snider, 1978).

When they exist, conspiratorial links allow members of economic elites to influence politicians through either legal or illegal tactics. While business may legitimately lobby politicians to act in its best interests, corporations may cross the line by offering bribes, illegal campaign contributions, or other inducements (Clinard and Yeager, 1980; Simon and Eitzen, 1990). More often, however, business leaders influence politicians indirectly in a nonconspiratorial fashion. Members of political and business elites usually share the same upper-class background. An examination of the backgrounds of three recent Canadian prime ministers is suggestive. Brian Mulroney was an extremely successful "self-made" businessman, Pierre Trudeau was a millionaire, and John Turner was a corporate lawyer. Part and parcel of this common background is a built-in pro-business stance reflecting the belief that corporate development and economic expansion are inherently good. Not only do cabinet ministers and prominent politicians tend to have business and affluence in their blood, many hold stock in big-business enterprises and have sat or will sit on the boards of governors of large companies and financial institutions (Ermann and Lundman, 1982).

It is also by no means unusual for corporate officials to be appointed as civil servants. As industrial experts, they advise government on issues related to their particular corporate sector. Furthermore, industry occasionally hires civil servants away from government. Many politicians and civil servants thus find themselves in positions to benefit from the accumulation of profits by corporations. Such cross-fertilization calls into question the neutrality and integrity of government (Clinard and Yeager, 1980; Snider and West, 1985).

Laws governing corporate activity are very complex and difficult to enforce. Under the current system, law applied to corporations must treat them as individuals or, in legal terms, "intangible persons" (Clinard and Yeager, 1980). The state holds corporations responsible in the same way under the same law that it applies to individual citizens. Suppose a company is convicted of murder. The penalty for first-degree murder in Canada is life in prison, while in some of the U.S. states it is death. Imprisoning or executing a corporation raises obvious problems. The major difficulty posed by the juristic person concept concerns the question of who is to be held responsible and punished for the misconduct of an organization.

A second problem connected with the use of criminal law in the control of corporate wrongdoing is the requirement that the Crown prove guilt beyond a reasonable doubt. To establish guilt in a criminal case, the Crown must demonstrate not only that the accused perpetrated a prohibited act but that the act was carried out with criminal intent. In cases of corporate wrongdoing, this is seldom simple (Clinard and Yeager, 1980; Simon and Eitzen, 1990; Ermann and Lundman, 1982).

Intent refers to the outcome that the accused had in mind when he or she committed the act. A woman who points a gun at her husband's head and pulls the trigger intends to end his life. The intent and the act in this example are coincident. In many cases of corporate wrongdoing, however, intent and the coincidence between act and intent are virtually impossible to prove. Businesses do not market unsafe products or pollute the environment to kill innocent people. Rather, they do so for reasons of economic gain. Their specific intent is to earn money, not to commit murder. At best, under current criminal law, corporations can be accused of negligence, a much less serious offence with comparatively weak sanctions. Moreover, the fact that long periods of time often separate the initial act from its harmful impact makes it difficult for the Crown to establish coincidence between the act and the guilty mind.

Government agencies are reluctant to prosecute business conglomerates for several reasons. Cases brought by the state against corporations are usually very complex and lengthy. The financial costs of such protracted proceedings are enormous. Moreover, police officers with the necessary investigatory training and Crown prosecutors and judges well versed in both corporate and criminal law are relatively few. By contrast, corporations regularly employ large numbers of very highly trained and very talented corporate lawyers (Clinard and Yeager, 1980; Simon and Eitzen, 1990). Although Canada, like other nations, suffers from a paucity of law-enforcement personnel trained to cope with white-collar and corporate crime, some changes are occurring with the rise of a new crime-control specialty known as "forensic accounting." Nonetheless, the budget to fight corporate crime pales in comparison with the resources allocated to controlling street crime.

Corporations discourage strict regulatory enforcement by applying political pressure. Although government agencies have mandates to investigate corporate deviance, they have traditionally had little or no power to enforce sanctions. After completing their investigations and submitting their reports, regulatory bodies generally refer cases to the office of the attorney general. Because the decision to prosecute normally rests with either the federal or a provincial attorney general, it is particularly susceptible to political considerations (Snider, 1978).

The survival of the nation-state — of its revenue, social welfare, education, and military, and, most directly perhaps, of the political party in power — is dependent on the potential for private-sector profit. To survive, nations must attract capital and discourage its flight. Politicians are therefore keenly aware that governments are routinely voted out of power over issues concerning economic stagnation and unemployment. For these reasons, legislatures are reluctant to take initiatives that might cause business to cut back, move out, or close down. Corporations threatening to cut costs by moving operations from North America to Third World countries that have no labour laws and no pollution regulations often capture governments' undivided attention. The vulnerability of government is a major bargaining chip in the efforts of business to avoid prosecution, conviction, and severe penalty (Snider and West, 1985).

Corporations influence the creation of the very laws designed to regulate them. The *Combines Investigation Act*, which until recently governed restraint of trade in Canada, was worded in such a way as to be virtually unenforceable. Conviction for restraining trade required the Crown to prove that a corporation conspired to restrict trade "unduly." The degree of restriction suggested by the word "unduly" was sufficiently imprecise as to make it difficult if not impossible to define. In the United States, by comparison, prosecutors need only prove that a restraint of trade took place. With regard to the power of corporations to render regulations unenforceable, Snider comments, "Let us not forget that the power to get legislation written which cannot challenge most practices of the giant firms is perhaps the most important kind of power" (Snider, 1978:155).

Even with the changes embodied in the new *Competition Act* of 1986, convictions may be no easier to obtain. To gain a conviction, the tribunal must agree that a business controlled the Canadian market for its product, that it engaged in anti-competitive behaviour, and that its anti-competitive activities actually restricted competition. The new Act does not outlaw monopolies. Rather, it prohibits corporations with monopolies from "abusing" their power. If convicted, a corporation can be ordered to end its anti-competitive practices (Dalglish, 1990).

The penalties meted out to corporations upon conviction have traditionally been less than exacting. Indeed, the severity of the sentence appears inversely related to the size of the corporate enterprise. The government launched no prosecutions for illegitimate mergers under the *Combines Investigation Act* between 1923 and 1960. Between 1960 and 1972, 3572 mergers took place in Canada. Only nine resulted in prosecution under the *Combines Investigation Act*, and only three resulted in conviction (Casey, 1985; Snider, 1978). As Snider (1978) notes, the degree of case attrition "strains credulity." Between 1952 and 1972, the government registered 157 convictions against 50 corporations, the vast majority of which were small or medium in size. One-half of these companies were recidivists, with an average record of 3.2 decisions against them. Among chronic offenders were Simpsons Sears and the T. Eaton Company, with four or five convictions each. The courts meted out no jail sentences. The most popular penalty under the *Combines Investigation Act* was the Order of Prohibition, an edict that simply requires that the company cease and desist its unlawful activity (Snider, 1978).

The most frequently enforced section of the *Combines Investigation Act* was the one governing false advertising, a relatively innocuous offence. The average fine upon conviction was something under $1000. Most fines for the violation of other sections were trivial. Given the immense profits that could result from breaking the rules, the fines amounted to little more than economical "licensing fees." No one was jailed under the Act until 1974. In that case, a small business operator, not a member of the economic elite, was imprisoned for his second offence (Snider, 1978).

Table 15.2 shows the number of criminal cases opened (excluding the numerous cases pertaining to unfair trade practices), the number referred to the attorney general for further action, and the number of prosecutions and other proceedings commenced for two periods that predate the new legislation (1982–84 and 1984–86) and for one period immediately following its implementation (1986–88). The figures indicate a sharp drop in the number of cases referred for further action (from 44 and 48 to 24) and in the number of legal proceedings launched (from 37

TABLE 15.2

SANCTIONS FOR CRIMINAL MATTERS (EXCLUDING TRADE PRACTICES) BEFORE AND AFTER COMPETITION ACT

	Number of Cases	Referred to Attorney General	Prosecutions or Other
1982–84	441	44	37
1984–86	506	48	36
1986–88	475	24	23

Source: Bureau of Competition Policy, Industry Canada, *Competition Policy in Canada: The First Hundred Years* (Ottawa: Consumer and Corporate Affairs, 1989), p. 59. Reproduced with the permission of the Minister of Public Works and Government Services Canada, 2001.

and 36 to 23). Snider (1993:155) points out that while the time period covered is short and only a restricted range of offences is examined, "a decline of 50% in the number of cases referred and a similar drop in the number of proceedings commenced does not bode well from an enforcement perspective."

Table 15.3 shows a dramatic rise in enforcement activity in the area of unfair trade practices, specifically misleading advertising and price misrepresentation, over the past 25 years. The number of files opened rose from 33 in 1968–69 to 12 374 in 1987–88. Case attrition rates, however, have remained consistently high. An extremely small number of cases opened result in recommendations to the attorney general that charges be laid. The number of convictions actually registered is even lower. Furthermore, from the

TABLE 15.3

PERCENTAGE OF FILES RESULTING IN CHARGES: MISLEADING ADVERTISING/PRICE MISREPRESENTATION

	Number of Files	Referred to Attorney General	Convictions
1968–69	33	n.a.	13
1973–74	4 387	123	70
1978–79	8 091	174	119
1983–84	10 091	181	138
1987–88	12 374	113	84

Source: Bureau of Competition Policy, Industry Canada, *Competition Policy in Canada: The First Hundred Years* (Ottawa: Consumer and Corporate Affairs, 1989), p. 60. Reproduced with the permission of the Minister of Public Works and Government Services Canada, 2001.

pre-revision period (1983–84) to the post-revision period (1987–88), there was a substantial drop both in the number of matters referred to the attorney general for further action (from 181 to 113) and in the number of convictions recorded (from 138 to 84). Once again, Snider notes that there has been insufficient time to discern a clear trend.

Upon conviction, the courts are often lenient in their treatment of white-collar and corporate criminals. In many cases, the conviction is for a first offence and the guilty party is usually of "good character," having a family, holding a good job, belonging to a church, and having contributed to the community. There is also a tendency for persons convicted of business crime to have co-operated fully with the authorities. Trial judges frequently believe that, for upper-class offenders, the publicity surrounding trial and conviction, the subsequent damage to reputation, the loss of status in the community, and perhaps the forfeiture of a job or a licence to practice are sufficient punishments. Finally, because white-collar and corporate criminals do not conform to the stereotypical image of the criminal, the public and the courts are more tolerant of their misdeeds (Clinard and Yeager, 1980).

That the laws related to corporate offending are so ineffectual raises the question of why they exist in the first place. Unenforceable law can perform a vital function for those against whom it is aimed. One effect of the impotent laws governing corporate misconduct in Canada is to lull the public into complacency. The very existence of regulations falsely reassures Canadians that they are adequately protected from corporate wrongdoing when, due to lack of meaningful enforcement, they are not. The underfunding of regulatory agencies that often accompanies periods of government budget restraint, of course, paves the way for corporations' risk-free profit accumulation (Snider, 1993).

LACK OF PUBLIC CONCERN

The ambivalence of many Canadians is another major reason for the ineffectual control of corporate crime. Public tolerance of white-collar and corporate crime is the product of several factors. First, corporate wrongdoing and its costs to employees, consumers, and the general public have historically given rise to little social concern. Many forms of corporate wrongdoing have only recently become illegal. Second, victimization is diffuse. People are usually unaware that businesses have stolen from them. Canadians are equally ignorant of the fact that business organizations often bear both moral and legal responsibility for the diseased conditions, debilitating injuries, or untimely deaths of workers, consumers, and members of the public. Consequently, citizens generally have not put pressure on politicians to create and apply laws governing harmful corporate activity. Fourth, white-collar and corporate crime appear to most Canadians to be nonviolent and hence not serious (Clinard and Yeager, 1980). Canadians fear crime in the streets, not crime in the suites. Finally, the collapse of communism and the move on the part of former communist countries to develop market economies have simultaneously elevated confidence in capitalism and undermined efforts to limit its deleterious impacts (Snider, 1993).

The family, the school, and the media combine to socialize Canadians from an early age to place a high value on hard work, entrepreneurship, and economic development and to have a healthy respect for business in general. Canadians learn that pollution in an industrialized nation is a "necessary" trade-off for a high standard of living. Canadians are also led to believe that existing laws adequately protect their health and safety, preserve free-market activity, and guard against environmental pollution. At the same time, they are told over and over again that domestic violence, sexual assault, child abuse, robbery, and illegal drug use are "real" crimes. Not only do these infractions represent the real crime problem, people believe that they rage on at epidemic proportions and threaten the very fabric of Canadian society. Conversely, the media — powerful sources of information and shapers of public opinion — say little about corporate crime. There are several underlying reasons for this silence. Big business owns many of the news and entertainment media. Moreover, what media it does not own it influences indirectly through its payouts of enormous sums of money as remuneration for advertising. Put simply, the media are reluctant to bite the hand that feeds (Snider, 1978).

SUMMARY

While Canadians are more fearful of street crime, suite crime is much more costly in terms of money and physical well-being. Incidents of business crime are frequent, and recidivism rates are high. Few of the many forms of business crime are prohibited by the *Criminal Code*. Some are banned in the statutes of regulatory agencies, and some are not covered by any law.

The concept of white-collar crime was developed initially by American criminologist Edwin Sutherland to describe illegal acts committed by higher-status people in the course of their work. Problems with this initial conceptualization of white-collar crime were created by the gradual decline in the status of many white-collar jobs, by the fact that some injurious activities on the part of white-collar workers were technically not crimes, and by the lack of specificity in the categorization of white-collar crime victims. Sutherland's major contributions were to focus attention on the fact that people from advantaged social segments engage in socially harmful activity. Sutherland drove home the point that crime is not the exclusive domain of the underprivileged.

In an effort to clarify Sutherland's initial conceptualization, criminologists have rather arbitrarily provided new names for the illegal activities of workers in higher-status occupations. This chapter has used the term "business crime" to encompass all types of illegality perpetrated by higher-status employees and has subdivided this conduct into two types, based on perpetrator and victim characteristics. White-collar crime refers to the commission of illegal acts against employing organizations or bill-paying clients and customers. The perpetrators are higher-status workers acting independently in their narrow self-interests. Corporate crime refers to socially harmful acts of executives on behalf of the organization employing them and in line with organizational goals. The principal victims of corporate crime are consumers, company employees, and members of the general public. These victim categories, however, are not mutually exclusive.

Canadian governments have directed a variety of legislation at controlling business crime. The *Criminal Code* prohibits some white-collar offences. Most of the legislation aimed at corporate wrongdoing is contained in regulations set out in the *Weights and Measures Act*, the *Hazardous Products Act*, the *Combines Investigation Act*, and, most recently, the *Competition Act*. Violators can be fined, imprisoned, or ordered to cease and desist. The record of enforcement in this century shows few convictions, paltry fines, and almost no instances of incarceration. The most popular sanction is the Order of Prohibition.

Perpetrators of white-collar crimes such as embezzlement, computer crime, and securities violations and perpetrators of corporate crimes against consumers, employees, and the public differ from street criminals in tending to be older, to be better educated, and to have families. Regardless of status, however, most criminals are male. White-collar predation is bolstered by rationalizations that it is not "real" crime, that there is no victim, and that miscreant workers somehow wronged by their employers are justified, on that basis, in doing damage. For one type of white-collar illegality — computer crime — challenge plays a key role in criminal motivation. In a pioneering work in criminology, Cressey argues that nonsharable problems, opportunity, and the ability to rationalize are necessary conditions for embezzlement. Nettler's research, however, disputes this assertion.

Differential association provides an account of business crime that focuses on the individual. The theory suggests that businesspeople learn the necessary techniques and rationalizations for commercial crime from their associates. Especially when those in authority convey definitions of the situation that favour breaking the law, employees are likely to engage in business deviance and the practices are likely to become widespread. Furthermore, competing organizations transmit among one another similar pro-deviance definitions of the situation and in this process, business crime snowballs.

A more structural explanation of business crime is offered by conflict theory, which emphasizes the centrality of economic and political power elites in capitalist democracies. Under capitalism, businesses and industries are driven first and foremost to realize profits. Since governments depend on corporations for their survival both materially and at the polls, the state must promote the interests of the capitalist class. The state's role in this process is to create conditions favourable to the accumulation of wealth by business, while maintaining legitimacy in the eyes of the populace. Society's agencies of socialization, particularly the media, facilitate the process by presenting an image of crime as a lower-class phenomenon while depicting capitalist enterprise only in positive terms. Thus, attention is shifted away from the business wrongdoing and the shortcomings of the capitalist system. The tendency for the state to favour accumulation over legitimacy sets the stage for understanding why legislation and enforcement are ineffective means of controlling business misconduct. As deterrence theory would predict, without some measure of severity, certainty, or celerity in the dispensation of justice, it is hardly surprising that business crime continues unabated.

Given the power and influence of higher-status workers and the organizations for which they work, white-collar and especially corporate crime are extremely difficult to control. The unbridled pursuit of profit in the short term, the existence of ineffective sanctions, corporate concentration, and the tendency to plan meticulously combine to set the stage for successful wrongdoing. An enforcement-proof corporate structure emphasizing short-term goals, disavowal of knowledge by senior executives, limited executive liability, secrecy, and a plethora of subcultural rationalizations add to the likelihood that business crime will be frequent, profitable, and go unpunished. The focus of criminal law on individual crime makes it unsuitable for prosecuting delinquent organizations. Moreover, businesses can exert enormous political pressure to influence the wording of regulations and to affect the way in which they are enforced. Finally, business crime flourishes unabated because the public is either ignorant of its occurrence or misinformed about its seriousness. In any case, Canadians have historically been much more tolerant of crimes in the suites than of crimes in the streets.

DISCUSSION QUESTIONS

1. Discuss the social and economic costs of "crime in the suites" compared with "crime in the streets."

2. Explain why business crime has been so difficult to control in Canada.

3. Identify the major types of computer crime and explain their operation. Why is computer crime so hard to control? What are the prospects for combatting this crime in the near future?

4. Is the public perception of corporate wrongdoing changing? Why might such changes be taking place now? What implications do such changes have for the control of corporate wrongdoing?

5. How might economic growth and economic decline affect both the illegal conduct of businesses and government initiatives to control such wrongdoing?

WEB LINKS

Competition Act
http://laws.justice.gc.ca/en/C-34/index.html
Full text of the *Competition Act*.

Types of White Collar Crime
http://www.ckfraud.org/whitecollar.html
This page, from the U.S. National Check Fraud Center, provides brief definitions of various white-collar and corporate crimes.

Economic Crime Prevention
http://www.rcmp-grc.gc.ca/html/ecbweb.htm
This section of the RCMP site provides information on the latest schemes and scams, as well as various types of consumer and business fraud.

Transparency International Canada
http://www.transparency.ca/index.html
Transparency International Canada is a voluntary not-for-profit organization whose purpose is to inform the business community, the government, and the general public of the effects of corruption in the international marketplace and to provide support and resources for public- and private-sector initiatives to prevent corrupt business practices. The Readings and the Corruption Index sections are of special interest.

Corporate Responsibility Campaign
http://www.dwatch.ca/camp/corpdir.html
The Corporate Responsibility Campaign, organized by Democracy Watch, a non-profit Canadian citizen advocacy organization, aims to push for solutions to the problem of the lack of accountability of large corporations operating in Canada. The Web site includes reports, recommendations, and media releases.

RECOMMENDED READINGS

Calavita, K., H.N. Pontell, and R.H. Tillman (1997). *Big Money Crime: Fraud and Politics in the Savings and Loan Crisis.* Berkeley: University of California Press.
> Documents one of the largest financial crises and the most costly bailout in the history of the United States. Argues that embezzlement was standard operating procedure for American financial institutions.

Clinard, M.B., and P.C. Yeager. (1980). *Corporate Crime.* New York: Free Press.
> Thoroughly examines American corporate crime. The authors point out the causal relevance of both corporate structure and the structure of economic opportunities in explaining how and why some businesses are more criminal than others.

Goff, C., and C.E. Reasons. (1978). *Corporate Crime in Canada: A Critical Analysis of Anti-Combines Legislation.* Scarborough: Prentice-Hall.
> This is the classic study of corporate crime in Canada. It provides an analysis of the development and implementation of the anti-combines legislation in force until 1985.

Goold, D., and A. Willis. (1997). *The Bre-X Fraud.* McClelland and Stewart.
> Discusses a recent and high-profile case of fraud in Canada's mining industry.

Hills, S.L. (1987). *Corporate Violence: Injury and Death for Profit.* Totowa, NJ: Rowman and Littlefield.
> A series of readings that emphasize the violent and deadly side of corporate wrongdoing.

McCormick, C. (1999). *The Westray Chronicles: A Case Study of Corporate Crime.* Halifax: Fernwood.
> Collection of papers forming a case study of events, causes, and the consequence of the Westray mine explosion. Emphasizes the problems associated with attributing legal responsibility for the disaster.

Pearce, F. and L. Snider (1995). *Corporate Crime: Contemporary Debates.* Toronto: University of Toronto Press.
> Presents debates surrounding several contemporary issues in the study of corporate wrongdoing including the role of business interests in shaping legislation, the history of penalties associated with Canada's competition laws, and the rising power of multinationals and the problems for enforcement that result.

Reasons, C., and D. Chappell. (1985). "Crooked Lawyers: Towards a Political Economy of Deviance in the Profession." in T. Fleming (ed.), *The New Criminologies in Canada: State, Crime, and Control.* Toronto: Oxford University Press.
> Provides an analysis of misconduct in Canada's legal profession and identifies underlying structural causes.

Reasons, C.E., L.L. Ross, and C. Paterson. (1981). *Assault on the Worker. Occupational Health and Safety in Canada.* Toronto: Butterworths.
> This is a Canadian classic on corporate wrongdoing that emphasizes the potentially violent and lethal nature of elite deviance.

Snider, L. (1993). *Bad Business: Corporate Crime in Canada.* Scarborough: Nelson.
> Presents an overview of issues related to corporate crime in general and in Canada in particular. Builds on Snider's pioneering work in this area up to the introduction of Canada's *Competition Act*.

Tonry, M., and A.J. Reiss. (1993). *Beyond the Law: Crime in Complex Organizations.* Chicago: University of Chicago Press.
> A series of readings exploring various aspects of illegal conduct in a variety of complex organizations.

Wilson, P.R., R. Lincoln, and D. Chappell. (1988). "Physician Fraud and Abuse in Canada: A Preliminary Examination." *Canadian Journal of Criminology* 28:129–46.
> Provides an analysis of physician fraud in the context of Canadian health care that remains relevant given recent efforts by the Canadian Medical Association to strengthen penalties for such abuses.

CHAPTER 16

MENTAL ILLNESS

The aims of this chapter are to familiarize the reader with:

- the complexities of defining mental illness
- the official position of the Canadian government on the nature of mental disorder and mental health
- the difficulties experienced by epidemiologists in estimating the incidence and prevalence of mental illness
- differences among physiological, psychological, and sociological approaches to mental disorder
- historical change in the perceptions of mental illness and in society's response to those affected
- the Freudian perspective, its remedies, and the views of its critics
- contemporary classifications of mental disorder according to the *DSM IV*
- the demographic distribution of mental illness
- the experience of institutional treatment
- life outside the mental-care facility
- the processing of the mentally ill by officials of the criminal justice system
- sociological theories of mental disorder

INTRODUCTION

Most Canadians have little exposure to people who are publicly identified as mentally disordered. Their images of mental illness and its prevalence come from media depictions, which routinely portray the mentally disordered as ignorant, dirty, unpredictable, and dangerous (McIlwraith, 1987). Day (1985) analyzed the images of mental illness in a number of Canadian

newspapers and concluded that most commentaries and articles depict the mentally ill as dangerous (95 percent), unproductive (86 percent), violent (84 percent), and dependent either upon others or upon social services (76 percent). The media also misinform the public when they suggest that various types of mental disorders, such as amnesia and multiple personality disorder, are quite common, when in fact they are very rare (McIlwraith, 1987). Furthermore, while the personalities of serial killers, mass murderers, and child molesters are routinely assessed in reference to psychological distress, in reality very few of the individuals who suffer from mental disorder are entirely incapable of functioning in society, and fewer still are violent and dangerous (Teplin, 1985). Nonetheless, it should come as no surprise that "mentally ill" is a designation that most people strenuously attempt to avoid.

This chapter begins by assessing the extent and impact of mental illness. It discusses physiological, psychological, and sociological perspectives on mental disorder and examines the problems of defining and measuring mental illness. It then explores the major psychiatric classifications of this form of deviance and documents its various demographic correlates. The process of being designated as mentally ill is investigated in some detail. This discussion is followed by an examination of issues concerned with treatment and cure. The chapter concludes with a brief description and critique of the **medical model** of mental illness and an assessment of the contributions to the understanding of mental disorder that have been made by macro and micro social theories.

Box 16.1
TEST PROJECT TEAMS CRISIS UNIT, POLICE

Toronto police and mental health workers have joined forces to deal more sensitively with mentally ill people – and, it's hoped, defuse situations that might otherwise end in police shootings.

Starting tomorrow, police officers in Scarborough's 42 Division will be required to call a local mental health crisis unit for cases involving an "emotionally disturbed person," Inspector Gary Ellis said.

The initiative partners officers with the Scarborough Mobile Crisis Unit, a division of the New Dimensions of Community Living program (NDCL) created by the health ministry.

Ellis, a member of the New Dimensions board, agreed to a pilot project in his division over the next six months.

Coroner's inquests into the deaths of schizophrenics Wayne Williams and Edmund Yu, both shot and killed by police, contributed to his strong feelings about the need for the program.

"It's heavy on my mind always," Ellis said. "They're in the wheelchair of the mind. How would you feel with someone who's disabled in another way, having to use force on them? This is no different."

When it gets a call, the Mobile Crisis Unit will send out a team of two: a psychiatric nurse/social worker and a crisis intervention worker. They'll be able to do on-site mental status assessments, explain the person's mental status to police and help calm the situation.

On Wednesday, laminated cards carrying the crisis unit's phone number were attached to the dashboards of 42 Division cruisers. The cards explain how to fill out a report for evaluation and tracking.

At the end of the pilot project, Ellis said, a decision will be made about whether to pursue the program at all 17 Toronto police divisions.

Julie, a psychiatric nurse at the Mobile Crisis Unit who has been riding with police to get acquainted, says the idea of combining units has been well-received. Crisis workers do not disclose their last names, for safety reasons.

"The families have always been pleased to see us," she said. "We've had no complaints about service."

Over the past three months, officers and mobile crisis workers have gone together to certain calls, on a voluntary basis.

Recently, when a young man stood baying at the moon in the streets of Toronto, instead of being arrested he was taken to a hospital, diagnosed as psychotic and given treatment.

The service is also practical, as it lets officers leave a mentally ill person in a professional's care while they return to patrol.

Julie said the crisis unit can provide the mentally ill with access to long-term care, support services, education for their families and support groups.

The program is not without controversy, however.

The mobile unit has only a dispatcher and the two-person team on duty during each of three daily eight-hour shifts, Julie said. That means incoming calls must be prioritized.

The project also drew criticism at last weekend's "Alternatives to the Use of Lethal Force" conference, where some psychiatric survivors said it would be better for a person with experience of mental illness to go on such calls than a mental health worker.

The main point, Ellis said, is not "who comes along," but the fact that "attempts are being made to fix the problem."

Discussion Questions

Identify the unique problems faced by police officers encountering mentally disordered people on the street. Is this program a good idea? Is it likely to solve the problem in the long term?

Source: Heather Greenwood, *Toronto Star*, June 30, 2000. p. B5. Reprinted with permission – The Toronto Star Syndicate.

DEFINING MENTAL ILLNESS

Mental illness as a form of deviance and mental health as a form of conformity are difficult to define. Some psychiatrists argue that mental illnesses, variously termed psychological disorders, psychopathologies, and abnormal behaviours, are concrete, real, and objective. They define as mentally healthy those people who possess integrated personalities. These people can correctly perceive the world, can adjust to their environment, and can accommodate change within their social worlds (American Psychiatric Association,

1987; Davison and Neale, 1990; Health and Welfare Canada, 1988). Failure on any of these points constitutes a degree of mental disorder.

From the objectivist stance, behaviour that exceeds community tolerance and is inappropriate to the circumstances in which it occurs ranges, on the basis of seriousness, from eccentricity to full-blown mental disorder. The breadth of this definition has led to the "medicalization of deviance" (Conrad, 1981). **Medicalization** refers to the tendency to transform a wide variety of nonconforming behaviours into medical problems. At an extreme, the notion is that all people who steal, burn down buildings, overindulge in drugs and alcohol, enjoy sex with partners of the same sex, abuse children, or murder other people are mentally unbalanced and need medical treatment. To the extent that these claims are considered valid, the power of the medical professions is expanded considerably.

At the other end of the scale are social scientists who argue that mental illness does not exist. The concept of mental illness, they maintain, is abstract, obtuse, and culturally relative. Psychiatric definitions contain words like "inappropriate" and "community tolerance," which unavoidably render definitions of mental health and mental disorder culturally relative. Simply put, professionals determine what behaviours represent illness on the one hand and eccentricities or mental health on the other. Such evaluations, sociologists point out, are influenced by the moral and ethical positions of the professionals (Szasz, 1974; Scheff, 1984).

To support the "**myth of mental illness**" claim, social researchers cite evidence that psychologists and psychiatrists cannot agree on who is mentally ill and who is not, that they cannot agree on their diagnoses of the maladies plaguing the same individual, and that they cannot accurately predict whether patients diagnosed as mentally ill will be dangerous to themselves or others in the future. Sociologists adopting this **relativistic** view of mental illness point out that mental disorders are inferred from nonconforming behaviours, which in themselves classify the person as disordered. Whether or not such nonconformity is defined as mental illness depends largely on context and to some extent on pure chance (Szasz, 1974; Scheff, 1984).

Most sociologists adopt a position between these two poles. They accept that the symptoms of mental illness are real and frequently seriously debilitating,

but they also point out that social definition and the attachment of stigma to nonconforming behaviour play important roles in individuals' developing mental problems, in their remaining ill for long periods of time, in their inability to benefit from treatment, and in their inability to recover. While biological abnormalities and psychological traumas cause some mental illnesses, stigmatization frequently exacerbates these problems.

A document entitled *Mental Health for Canada: Striking a Balance* sets out the federal government's position on the nature of mental health and mental disorder (Health and Welfare Canada, 1988). According to this document, mental health comprises four qualities: psychological and social harmony and integration, a sound quality of life and general well-being, self-actualization and growth, and effective personal adaptability. Health and Welfare Canada divides mental disability into two basic categories on the basis of its seriousness. Mental disorders are more serious, while mental-health problems are less so. The department recognizes the former as medically diagnosable illnesses that result in significant impairment on three dimensions: cognition, affectivity, and relations. Cognition comprises the abilities to perceive, to learn, to reason, and to imagine. Affectivity involves moods, feelings, and emotions. The ability to relate refers to effective interaction with other persons and the environment and to one's ability to communicate properly. The official position of the federal government is that mental disorders result from biological, developmental, and psycho-social factors and that mental illness needs to be managed, like physical disease, with programs that promote prevention while facilitating diagnosis, treatment, and rehabilitation.

Less serious mental-health problems are those that disturb the integrative links among individuals and interfere with their assimilation in groups and social environments. According to the government, mental-health problems accrue from the combination of stress and inadequate coping skills.

Health and Welfare Canada recognizes that knowledge about mental disorders such as schizophrenia, Alzheimer's disease, and manic depression is limited. It also recognizes that the management of mental disorders is more difficult than that of physical diseases. Finally, the relationship between mental illness and poverty is acknowledged. On the last point, the department suggests that poverty is either a cause that helps trigger mental illness or an aggravating condition that prolongs and worsens the symptoms of distress (Health and Welfare Canada, 1988).

THE EXTENT AND IMPACT OF MENTAL ILLNESS

Rates of mental disorder, like those of other illnesses, are calculated from data generated by epidemiological studies. **Epidemiology** is a field of science devoted to describing the distribution of diseases, mental and otherwise, as they manifest themselves in societal segments and across geographical areas. Consequently, epidemiology also permits the identification of social and cultural factors that may contribute to certain types of mental disorders (Cockerham, 1989). Epidemiological studies establish "prevalence rates" and "**incidence rates**." The former rate counts the total number of cases of mental illness in a given population, while the latter rate counts only new cases occurring in a designated time span, usually one year (Gallagher, 1987).

Few areas in the sociology of deviance or the sociology of health and illness present as many obstacles to measurement as does mental disorder. In their efforts to enumerate cases of mental illness, epidemiologists rely on two basic sources of information, official data from hospital and clinic records and data from population surveys. Using hospital records to estimate the prevalence of mental illness presents familiar problems. People treated for mental disorder do not represent all those who are actually ill. At best, they represent a subset of those in distress. In areas with more mental-health-care facilities and personnel, with more affluent and insured citizens, and with positive attitudes toward the mentally ill, the numbers of people who are treated and officially counted will be inflated. Conversely, in economically depressed regions with fewer hospitals, fewer private practitioners, and negative attitudes toward the mentally ill, the numbers treated and recorded will be artificially low. Also problematic is the sometimes considerable variation in patient diagnoses from one psychologist or psychiatrist to another. Health-care professionals frequently disagree in their assessments of the same patients (Cockerham, 1989; Gallagher, 1987).

An additonal problem is that different studies use different counting procedures and that many of these measurement techniques are imprecise. Using mental-hospital admissions, for example, does not allow the researcher to differentiate between three persons being admitted (new cases) and one person being admitted on three different occasions in the same month. Another official measure, the length of hospitalization, may have much less to do with the severity of illness than with the development and availability of drugs, out-patient services, and community mental-health programs. While such data are published by the Canadian government, they are useless for estimating the proportions of the population affected by various disorders. It is also impossible, for this reason, to meaningfully compare regions or social segments with respect to the distribution of mental illness in Canada.

Surveys overcome several of these difficulties to some extent, and consequently researchers refer to estimates made on this basis as "true prevalence rates." The first step in the survey approach is to interview a sample of respondents. In the second stage, psychiatrists evaluate the interview responses and diagnose the interviewees' degree of impairment. Unfortunately, variation in the diagnoses made by psychiatrists remains a problem in these studies (Cockerham, 1989; Gallagher, 1987).

In the light of these difficulties, estimates of the distribution of mental illness are crude and must be interpreted cautiously (Dohrenwend, 1975). Often, Canadian projections are made on the basis of limited information. In other cases, they are extrapolated from American data.

The exact number of people afflicted with mental disorders is difficult to ascertain because only a minority of people suffering from psychological problems ever come to the attention of the Canadian health care system. Most experts agree that mental disorder is by no means rare. Estimates suggest that as many as 80 percent of the population may experience at least mild forms of distress at some point in their lives while as many as 10 percent may become seriously depressed (Gallagher, 1987; Cockerham, 1989). Menzies (1991) estimates that privately and publicly operated institutions in Canada contain more than 25 000 patients and that approximately a million more Canadians are involved in some form of therapy for mental disorder. He also points out that doctors treat even larger numbers of Canadians for the effects of stress. The multitude of persons who might benefit from therapy but never seek it out must also be considered. Nonetheless, Canadians annually utilize 4.5 million days of care in psychiatric institutions. Although this number is smaller than in the past, the decline is due to an increase in community care and not a reduction in the prevalence of mental disorder (Statistics Canada, 1991).

Despite the large numbers affected in some way by these maladies, researchers and mental-health caregivers admit that the causes of disorders remain shrouded in mystery. Effective strategies of treatment, while elusive, are seldom inexpensive. The total bill to provincial health-care systems in Canada is enormous, even though the number of Canadians receiving care is much smaller than the number in need of some form of assistance.

Mental disorder can be a source of considerable distress not only for those afflicted but for their families and friends as well. Depression, neuroses, and psychotic episodes can transform life into a nightmare. Mental disorder undermines marriages, erodes the quality of parenting, adversely affects performance on the job, and makes the establishment and maintenance of friendships difficult if not impossible. Moreover, the stigma of being identified as a "mental case" exacerbates these difficulties.

A recent trend in the field of mental health has also caused problems. As a result of growing concerns over the violation of patients' civil liberties, the ineffectiveness of institutional care, and the rising costs of hospitalization, mental-health-care facilities have been releasing patients back into the community (Bloom, 1973). Many of those returning seem incapable of caring for themselves adequately and join the ranks of the poor, the destitute, and the homeless across Canada and the United States. As a result, many mentally distressed people have become members of a highly visible and often homeless underclass. Furthermore, many run afoul of the law and are imprisoned for minor offences such as vagrancy and disorderly conduct (Gove, Tovo, and Hughes, 1985).

PHYSIOLOGICAL, PSYCHOLOGICAL, AND SOCIOLOGICAL PERSPECTIVES ON MENTAL DISORDER

The study of mental illness is a domain shared principally by medical researchers and practitioners, psychologists, and sociologists. Physiologists and some physicians investigate and treat the genetic, anatomical, and chemical origins of mental distress. They examine genes, brain tissue, and other components of the central nervous system. Some biological and family-history inheritance research, for example, suggests that certain genetic abnormalities may be involved in some cases of depression and schizophrenia. Similarly, biochemists have unearthed evidence linking low levels of serotonin and high levels of dopamine to schizophrenia. They have also found that low levels of epinephrine are associated with depression. Moreover, the fact that some forms of mental illness can be effectively controlled through drug therapy lends weight to the assertion that chemical imbalances play a causal role in certain types of disorder. Finally, brain autopsies point to tissue degeneration as a cause of senile dementia and Alzheimer's disease (Spitzer and Wilson, 1975).

Psychologists and many psychiatrists approach mental disorder differently. They see mental illness as an "intra-psychic" problem, the origins of which can be located in childhood, when the personality is being formed. From the intra-psychic perspective, mental disorder occurs either because of faulty family socialization practices or because of some trauma during childhood. Some psychologists emphasize the destructive role of overprotective, neglecting, domineering, or warring parents. Others cite the deleterious effects of maternal-love deprivation, which may occur, for example, in institutional settings (Meissner, 1985).

Sociological investigations of mental illness proceed in one of two directions. Some sociologists focus on structural factors involved in the production of stress, while others focus on the labelling process and the negative impacts of social stigma (Gallagher, 1987).

A number of social forces create stress for Canadians. First and foremost among these factors are the fast pace, competitive outlook, and social isolation of life in an industrialized capitalistic society. Economic recession, unemployment, and the unexpected severing of bonds to family members and peers generate stress that can result in psychological impairment. Restrictions in social roles also produce stress. Children's departure from home can be traumatic for women whose identity has been derived exclusively from motherhood. Elderly people whose self-esteem has been intimately linked to their work may experience stress when they are forced to retire. Regardless of its source, an undue amount of stress is not conducive to good mental health.

Sociologists working in the symbolic interactionist tradition concentrate on the impact of being

Box 16.2
DIARY REVEALS DIFFICULTY OF LIFE WITH A SCHIZOPHRENIC

Brenda Sawyer's 34-year-old brother Sam is a schizophrenic.

Sam was diagnosed 20 years ago. He has been in and out of hospitals at least 30 times in the past 10 years, Brenda says, and the system seems unable to keep him long enough to help him.

Brenda and her mother have been dealing with Sam's problems for years. Sam lives with his mother because he is unable to care for himself.

"The burden is very great for us," says Brenda. "Frustration is never-ending. The sad realization is we are unable to help Sam because of the system."

She says that the bottom line of most advice she gets is to cut Sam out of their lives.

"How can I do that? He's my brother, I love him, no matter what. If I don't take care of him, who is going to?"

The following is a partial diary of what the Sawyers have dealt with in the past few weeks. Their names and some locations have been changed to protect their privacy.

Friday, March 31: On this date, Sam signed himself out (of the local psychiatric hospital). He went to my mother's apartment and began to verbally abuse her, yell and scream, and ask for money.

Tuesday, April 11: Sam told my mother he was going to leave town. He was going to a welding job in Montreal; he was going to Washington, D.C.; he was going to Atikokan. He was totally disoriented and hallucinating.

Wednesday, April 12: At 10 A.M., my mother got a reverse-charge call from Sam in North Bay. He said he had gone to hospital to be admitted but had been refused, and had been given an appointment to go to the crisis centre to see a psychiatrist at 3 P.M. He told her he had taken pills, but did not know how many he had taken, and also that he could not see clearly.

A captain from the Salvation Army came to visit my mother. He was returning Sam's clothes. Sam had dropped them off at the Salvation Army and said he would not need them. The captain said that Sam was in desperate need of mental assistance.

Thursday, April 13: On this day I made 11 separate phone calls to different hospitals, clinics, police, and to the MP and the MPP for the area to see what help or direction or suggestions I could get. Nobody could help.

Friday, April 14: My mother received a call from Sam at 1:30 A.M. He had hitchhiked to Montreal. He was calling to say he had no money and no place to stay: Could she do something for him? I called the local police to see if they could help by getting a court order to pick him up. They said they had no jurisdiction in Quebec and that Sam would have to commit a crime before the police could get involved.

Saturday, April 15: Sam called at 12:30 A.M., 7 A.M., 9:30 A.M. He had no money and no place to stay: What could we do? I called the Queen St. Mental Health Centre in Toronto and they told me to get Sam to the Douglas Hospital in Montreal. Then a transfer could be arranged to a hospital near home. Sam called at 10:30 A.M. and we told him to go to the Douglas.

The Montreal police called at 11 A.M. to say that Sam had gone to the Douglas Hospital but was refused admission because the hospital had no background on him and there was a shortage of beds. At 8 P.M. Sam called to say he was in a hostel. He was still the Holy Ghost.

Monday, April 17: Sam called after lunch. He said he had been to the welfare office and was going to the ocean to get well. We asked him to phone a counsellor who had helped him in the past. He said he couldn't because he had three letters in his name and the counsellor had six letters.

I spoke with a lawyer at 4 P.M. to see what I could do to get Sam committed or get help for him. He told me there is a dramatic gap in the legal system when dealing with a person with an illness such as this. He told me there was absolutely nothing I or he, as a lawyer, could do to help Sam.

Thursday, April 20: Sam called and said he was in Charlottetown, P.E.I. He said welfare in Montreal had given him money to get there and for food. Now he needed money again. He also wanted to get out of there.

- Sam keeping a can of gasoline in the closet in his bedroom and threatening to blow my mother up.

- Sam calling me on the phone and threatening to slit my throat and my 4-year-old's throat.

- Sam needing to leave the washroom door open while going to the bathroom because he was scared.

My mother got a postcard from him this week. It read "Dear Mom: I'm in Charlottetown, P.E.I. The weather is great here. It's raining now and I'm nearly broke ... I'm thinking of going into the ministry (sic). I'm called a God. A witness of the olive tree is my ministry, God Bless...."

Discussion Questions

What personal costs are borne by the family and friends of the mentally disordered? How might Sam's needs be better met? Is involuntary confinement an acceptable answer in this case? Is Sam dangerous?

Source: Lindsay Scotton, *Toronto Star*, May 8, 1989, p. C6. Reprinted with permission – The Toronto Star Syndicate.

labelled mentally ill. Interactionists point out that the extent to which people consider behaviours "normal" or "abnormal" is relative and varies among different cultures. They also highlight the importance of the negative reactions to the mentally ill. They argue that the attachment of stigma, the feelings of inadequacy, guilt, and anxiety that stigma produces, and the corrosive impacts of the resulting negative self-image combine to undermine mental stability (Cockerham, 1989).

HISTORICAL CONCEPTIONS OF MENTAL DISORDER

Conceptions of mental illness have evolved and changed over time. Members of primitive societies thought that mental disorder resulted from magic spells that at some times were benevolent and at other times malevolent. When they thought demonic forces were at work, they attempted to exorcise the evil spirits from the human body. Common techniques to achieve this ranged from prayer to torture and execution. One popular means of ridding the body of an unwanted spirit was "trephination," in which a hole was punched in the skull of the possessed and a pointed stick was used to encourage the devil to flee (Davison and Neale, 1990).

During the Middle Ages, Europeans gradually came to view the mentally disordered as either directly possessed by the devil or experiencing God's punishment for their sins or those of their parents. Many of these unfortunates were labelled as witches and warlocks. Thought to possess supernatural powers, they were systematically persecuted by banishment, burning at the stake, and beheading.

During the eighteenth century, a gradual decline occurred in the brutal treatment of the mentally ill. The painful practices of earlier times gave way to physical confinement. Saved from physical torture and exe-

cution, the disordered were chained to prison walls along with convicted felons, where they lived and often died in deplorable conditions. Few were ever released back into society (Davison and Neale, 1990).

The nineteenth century saw the development of special institutions called "asylums," and over time, the introduction of more humane approaches to treatment. Spearheading this reform movement was a Frenchman, Philippe Pinel. Under his direction, the mentally ill in institutions were unchained, bathed, and given the freedom to walk the grounds around their institutions. Treated with a measure of kindness, many appeared to recover. Pinel's reforms were widely adopted, but their success was short-lived. Conditions in asylums deteriorated as the numbers of patients grew dramatically (Bromberg, 1975).

Notions about the causes of mental illness also changed during this period. Demonological accounts of mental disorder gave way during the eighteenth century to biological explanations, which in turn were largely supplanted during the nineteenth century by Sigmund **Freud's** development of the psychoanalytic framework (Meissner, 1985). Freud's psychoanalytic approach to understanding the causes of mental illness stressed the importance of personality development and the unconscious mind.

Freud understood the personality as consisting of three interdependent parts: the **id**, the **ego**, and the **superego**. The id represents an individual's instinctual drives, which Freud believed were rooted in the unconscious. The superego, on the other hand, is a person's sense of morality. It translates external social norms governing good conduct into a person's conforming behaviour and sense of "doing the right thing." Mediating the id's base impulses and the superego's sense of propriety is the ego. According to Freud, the ego balances a person's instinctual desires for sex (id), for example, with a sense of what is proper (superego).

Freud maintained that these components of personality develop in stages as a person passes through childhood. Each of the stages, the **oral**, the **anal**, and the **phallic**, are characterized by certain needs that must be met for personality development to proceed normally. Mental disorder, Freud suggested, occurs as a consequence of an individual's psychic growth being abnormally arrested or "fixated" at a particular stage. Psychoanalysts also believe that the stage at which people become fixated largely determines the type of mental illness they experience. Some psychoanalysts cite fixation at the oral stage as a prime factor in the production of schizophrenia, while others believe that anal and phallic fixations generate certain forms of obsessive and compulsive behaviours.

Because mental disorder has its roots in fixation at a particular stage of personality development, one treatment strategy utilized by psychoanalysts is to "regress" patients, through hypnotic and other techniques, back in time through their unconscious minds. When patients reach the developmental stage at which the disturbance was first experienced, analysts encourage patients, while regressed, to deal with the original trauma (Meissner, 1985).

Criticisms of psychoanalytic theory are intense. Critics charge that the theory is overly deterministic and view its assertion that the stage is set for mental illness in childhood by the parents' child-rearing practices as extreme. They also maintain that psychoanalytic theory ignores traumas experienced in adulthood. Moreover, psychoanalytic approaches treat mental disorder as purely an intra-psychic phenomenon, thereby overlooking the contributions of biogenetics and labelling perspectives to the explanation of some forms of disturbance. Finally, the sequence of developmental stages through which the person must pass appears to vary among cultures. For this reason, critics argue that, at best, psychoanalytic explanations and treatments of mental distress may be limited to middle-class people of European descent (Cockerham, 1989; Gallagher, 1987).

CONTEMPORARY CLASSIFICATIONS OF MENTAL ILLNESS

People are considered mentally disordered when they are distressed or psychologically disabled. Medical practitioners and social scientists in Canada classify different types of mental illness on the basis of their symptoms. They follow the guidelines outlined in the American Psychiatric Association's fourth edition of the *Diagnostic and Statistical Manual of Mental Disorders*, commonly called the DSM IV. The list of disorders is a long one (American Psychiatric Association, 1987; Davison and Neale, 1990).

Disorders first evident in infants, children, and adolescents include mental retardation and various learning and communication disorders. *Delirium, dementia, and amnestic and other cognitive disorders* have a variety of causes. Some of these maladies are caused by brain injuries or degenerating brain tissue; the senility brought on by Alzheimer's is an example. Delirium is produced by substance intoxication or withdrawal, and some forms of dementia result from HIV disease, Parkinson's disease, and Huntington's chorea. *Substance-related disorders* involve the abuse of drugs and alcohol (see Chapter 13).

Schizophrenia, personality disorders, and mood disorders, among the most serious of mental illnesses, account for the majority of mental-hospital admissions. *Schizophrenic disorders* are the most common of the psychoses. Schizophrenics fail completely or intermittently to connect with reality and often live in their own fantasy worlds. Although practitioners routinely misdiagnose schizophrenia, researchers still estimate that it affects as many as 1 percent of North Americans at some point in their lives. Since the prospects for recovery are not great, the patient population is large. Most schizophrenics are relatively young at onset (between the ages of 20 and 40) and the majority come from lower-class backgrounds. The most common of a broad range of symptoms for this disease are the inability to express emotion, disjointed trains of thought, hallucinations, the simultaneous expression of opposing emotions, the inability to experience pleasure, the use of new words for familiar objects, the repetition of the words of those with whom conversations are being conducted, and the mimicking of others' actions. While persons suffering from this disorder often exhibit bizarre behaviours, they do not, as is commonly thought, possess split personalities. Multiple-personality disorder is a different form of mental illness altogether.

Among the *personality disorders* are paranoid personality disorder and obsessive-compulsive personality disorder. Psychiatrists classify paranoid disorders as "single delusions." Paranoids falsely believe that some individuals or organizations have it in for them. The list of enemies may include family members, friends, the police, organized criminals, and the government. Paranoids are suspicious and fearful. Common paranoid delusions are persecution, jealousy, and grandeur. When they feel persecuted, paranoids believe that some individual or group has set about to ruin their reputations, to destroy their chances of achieving certain goals, or to harm them physically. Although most paranoids know that those around them do not take their delusions seriously, they remain undeterred in their convictions.

Many people experience mild forms of paranoia from time to time. The precise numbers of those more seriously debilitated by this disorder are difficult to determine, partly because, given the suspicious natures of those afflicted, they tend not to seek help. For this reason, they do not become officially counted. Paranoid personality disorder appears to develop relatively late in life and to be concentrated among urban dwellers, the divorced, and migrants.

One of the most devastating disorders, from society's point of view is *antisocial personality disorder*, also known as *psychopathy* or *sociopathy*. **Psychopaths** and sociopaths are persons devoid of conscience and incapable of feeling remorse. While this personality disorder has been detected in large proportions among incarcerated people, by no means do all criminals suffer from this malady. The vast majority of convicted criminals can form affective relationships with other people and are capable of feeling both guilt and remorse.

Mood disorders involve the kinds of mood swings characteristic of depression. When they are depressed, people feel worthless, hopeless, and guilty. Depression varies in intensity. In its milder forms, it is the "common cold" of psychiatric ailments and affects almost everyone on occasion. In its more severe forms, however, particularly when it is juxtaposed with episodes of mania, depression appears to hit hardest people from middle- and upper-class backgrounds. The severity and frequency of manic-depressive attacks seems to increase with age.

Anxiety disorders manifest themselves in anxiety states. These anxiety attacks occur irrationally and in the absence of real stressors. While anxiety disorders result in unwanted distress, people experiencing them do not as a rule lose touch with reality, nor do they engage in behaviour that seriously violates prevailing norms of social conduct. The distress and its physical consequences are neither transitory nor caused by physiological abnormalities. Physiological symptoms

of anxiety disorder include tremors, heart palpitations, nausea, fatigue, muscle tension, insomnia, and sexual dysfunction. Chronic unhappiness, feelings of inadequacy, oversensitivity, and shyness are the central psychological symptoms of this form of mental disorder. Mild forms of anxiety disorder are the subject of a plethora of popular self-help manuals that advocate many strategies for coping with the stresses and strains of everyday life. Divorce, pregnancy, unemployment, and death of a family member or friend are common stressors for adults. Children appear susceptible to stress and anxiety from such everyday events as family dissolution, changes of school, or the birth of siblings.

One type of anxiety disorder is called phobias. Phobias are intense irrational fears. Although phobics generally recognize the irrationality of their terrors, they are powerless to ignore them. Among the more common of the phobias are intense fears of heights (acrophobia), of open spaces (**agoraphobia**), of closed confines (**claustrophobia**), of water (aquaphobia), of strangers (xenophobia), of animals (zoophobia), and of dead bodies (**necrophobia**).

Obsessive and **compulsive disorders** are another two types of anxiety disorders. **Obsessions** comprise recurrent and unwanted thoughts that people cannot get out of their minds. Compulsions produce in people recurrent needs to perform certain actions. Examples of these illnesses include brooding over obscure and abstract subjects (obsessive rumination), rearranging the letters used to spell words into their alphabetical order (alphabetizing), washing the hands repeatedly, or going through a long, complex routine before leaving the house. The prognosis for recovery from these maladies is not good, and their severity appears to increase with age.

When psychiatrists attribute physical disabilities such as paralysis, blindness, and deafness to psychological rather than organic causes, they call the illness a *somatoform disorder*. Also included in this group are hypochondriacs who, without grounds, fear that minor discomforts are signalling the onset of serious physical disease.

Dissociative disorders include memory loss unrelated to physical disease or trauma (amnesia) and multiple-personality syndrome, which is a dramatic but exceedingly rare form of mental illness. Persons with multiple-personality disorder have two or more distinct personalities, only one of which is present at any given time. The behaviour of people suffering from this disorder alters when one of their personalities assumes dominance. Not only have researchers noted distinct changes in personality, in some cases they have documented physiological changes as well. These physical alterations include different brain wave patterns, different heartbeats, and even changes in eye colour. Most treated cases of multiple-personality disorder involve highly intelligent women. Some psychologists and psychiatrists believe that this disorder is brought on by experiences of severe stress such as those produced by battering.

People who develop attachments to socially unacceptable sex objects or who develop problems associated with gender identity are grouped into a category called *sexual and gender identity disorders*. Defining a sex disorder is particularly difficult because there is considerable disagreement about what constitutes an abnormal sexual practice. Conservative definitions consider as deviant and worthy of treatment people committing any sexual act that violates an existing law. Liberal definitions suggest that sexual acts performed by consenting adults are normal and healthy. Many mental-health professionals fall between these two poles, defining sex acts as symptomatic of mental disorder when they are engaged in compulsively or when they create feelings of internal distress.

From the latter perspective, sexual disorders encompass several sets of stressful obsessions. Psychiatrists define paraphilia as a set of disorders involving unusual activities or symbols, the latter of which comprise objects and surroundings not normally associated with sexual excitement. Examples of paraphilia include using particular objects (fetishism), craving sexual contact with children (**pedophilia**), craving intercourse with a corpse (**necrophilia**), displaying oneself to unwilling observers or watching unsuspecting people in sexually stimulating situations (exhibitionism and voyeurism), and intentionally inflicting or experiencing pain in sexual activities (sadism and masochism). Psychiatrists employ a second category, gender identity disorder, to classify persons who are uncomfortable with their anatomical sex identity. Transsexualism is a condition wherein people who are biologically male or female believe that they are psychologically and emotionally members of the other sex. A final grouping of sexual disorders, which psychiatrists term psycho-sexual dysfunction, includes various sex problems involving inhibited sexual desire, arousal, or orgasm. Among these functional problems are erectile dysfunction (commonly called impotence), anorgasmia (sometimes called frigidity), premature ejaculation, involuntary vaginal spasms interfering with intercourse, and hypersexuality. For hypersexual persons, the sex drive is overly strong and results in a compulsive need for frequent sex, perhaps with many partners. In women the problem is called "nymphomania" and in men "the Don Juan complex."

People suffering from **fetishism** require an inanimate object, such as a piece of fur, a life-size rubber doll, or a certain person's underwear, to achieve orgasm. Sometimes the object is used in the sexual act, and sometimes it is not. Most people suffering from this disorder are males, and many are adolescents.

Pedophiles also tend to be male, but they are usually older — often in their thirties. Their preferred targets for sexual exchange are children of either the same or the opposite sex. Pedophilia is a particularly worrisome sexual disorder. It has the potential for serious psychological harm to the child, both from the sexual experience with the pedophile and from the often hysterical reaction of parents and other onlookers. Pedophiles are seldom violent and are frequently known to the youthful objects of their desires. It is not unusual for the sexual exchanges to occur in the home of either the pedophile or the child. Sexual acts range from stroking through manual and oral stimulation to, in some instances, anal or vaginal intercourse.

Voyeurs and exhibitionists are almost always male, and the latter, in particular, are often between their teenage years and their thirties. Voyeurs are obsessed with watching others, usually strangers, either in various states of undress or engaged in some form of sexual activity. Part of their thrill is generated by the high risk of capture. Many exhibitionists expose themselves ritualistically in similar surroundings, to similar onlookers, and at roughly the same time of day. Frequently referred to as "flashers," some wear outfits especially designed for the occasion. Flashing regalia is made up of long overcoats, shirts with short tails, and pant legs extending from the ankle upwards to the knee and secured by knee-bands. The costume is designed in such a way that vital parts remain unencumbered. Incidents of exhibitionism increase during the summer. This sexual disorder accounts for a disproportionately high number of arrests for sexual misconduct.

Sadists and masochists can be categorized into two basic types, depending on the form of pain administered or received. To be stimulated sexually and to achieve orgasm, some must inflict or experience physical pain. For others, the pain can take the form of humiliation or some combination of pain and humiliation accompanied by being tied up or chained (bondage). A minutely small number of sadists (necrosadists) cannot enjoy sex without killing their partners. Some necrosadists experience sexual fulfillment by watching someone being murdered on celluloid, in what is now commonly known as the "snuff" film. While data remain sketchy, some social scientists believe that the gender of sadists (initiators) and masochists (recipients) reflects traditional sex roles — sadists are predominantly male, while some masochists are female.

Transvestites "cross dress," or clothe themselves in the attire of members of the opposite sex. Research suggests that transvestites are male, but this finding may be due to the fact that it is neither unusual nor unacceptable for females to dress in masculine attire. Few transvestites are homosexual.

Transsexuals possess a strong aversion to their biological sex characteristics. They believe that they are male or female personalities trapped in opposite-sexed bodies. Most transsexuals strongly desire to change their anatomical sex to match their personalities and attempt to do so both with and without surgery. Sex-change operations are difficult to obtain, and transsexuals are often refused this form of treatment. Health-care institutions usually deny the requests for sex-change operations on psychological, moral, and religious grounds and because of concerns over medical malpractice suits.

Until relatively recently, the American Psychiatric Association classified homosexuality as a psycho-sexual disorder. Most Canadians and Americans remain woefully ignorant of the facts regarding homosexuality, and many express an irrational fear of homosexuals. This homophobia has been exacerbated by the AIDS crisis.

Research indicates that between 5 and 10 percent of the population is gay and that, aside from sexual preference, homosexuals and heterosexuals as aggregates are indistinguishable from one another. Contrary to popular belief, homosexuals as a group are not emotionally disturbed and are not inclined to desire sexual relations with children. Neither are homosexual males likely to be any more effeminate than heterosexual males. Furthermore, homosexuality is unrelated to family background, education, occupation, ethnicity, or any other demographic variable.

Homosexuality is now officially viewed by mental-health professionals as a lifestyle rather than a disorder. This change in official position has occurred for several reasons. First, research shows that most gays and lesbians are not unhappy with their sexual identities. Second, it has become clear that the psychological problems of being identified by oneself and others as homosexual are substantially reduced in communities where this form of sexual expression is socially accepted.

Eating disorders include **anorexia nervosa** and **bulimia**. Bulimia usually involves overeating in a binge, followed by a "purging" of the ingested food either by vomiting or by using laxatives. Anorexia nervosa is a disorder wherein the person limits food intake to dangerously low levels. Anorexics literally starve themselves because, regardless of how thin they become, they consider themselves overweight. These disorders, which appear to be on the increase, most often affect young females from middle-class backgrounds. Moreover, most who are diagnosed with these disorders are Caucasian.

In a study of bulimia among Canadian university students, Piccinini and Mitric (1987) discovered that a significant number of students in their sample met the *DSM III* diagnostic criteria. Their study showed that almost 15 percent had engaged in bulimic behaviour and that half that percentage did so at least once a week. These findings are in line with most studies of college females. It is commonly estimated that bulimia affects about 10 percent of the student body. As Piccinini and Mitric point out, however, these enumerations are probably low. The guilt and shame that surround this disorder probably results in underreporting, which in turn translates into a conservative enumeration of cases.

Finally, *disorders of impulse control* refer to psychopathologies in which individuals cannot restrain their actions. Psychologists consider some people "addicted" to gambling. Others have uncontrollable urges to set fires (**pyromania**) or to steal things (**kleptomania**).

THE DEMOGRAPHIC DISTRIBUTION OF MENTAL DISORDER

SEX

Both official and survey data in North America indicate that women, since the end of World War II, have become more susceptible than men to mental disorder (Dohrenwend and Dohrenwend, 1976). Social scientists account for this shift in several ways. Some point to changes in structural factors and role conflicts, both of which produce stress. Others cite reasons that have little to do with any real change among women. They argue that socialization and the broadening of types of disorders are the key explanatory variables (Nadelson, 1983).

Women's roles have become more stressful. Women continue to do most of the domestic and childcare work within the home, even though they are gainfully employed in the labour force. Furthermore, women, more than men, are intimately involved in the lives of those around them. Consequently, they are more likely to experience within themselves any suffering endured by those they care for. From another point of view, females, because of their socialization to dependence, are simply more likely than males to admit and to display to others their feelings of distress. Moreover, women are more comfortable seeking the advice and assistance of professionals. For men, on the other hand, social norms require that they be stoic and deny emotional weakness. When men violate such norms by confessing a mental disorder, they are subject to considerably more stigma than are women. Finally, the range of mood and anxiety disorders has expanded greatly in recent decades. It is precisely to these disorders that women may be most susceptible (Nadelson, 1983; Gove and Tudor, 1973; Phillips and Segal, 1969).

The types of mental illness also vary for males and females. While males and females experience schizophrenia in equal proportions, many more men than women are psychopathic. Women, on the other hand, are over-represented among those suffering from anxiety and mood disorders. In particular, many women experience middle-age depression. Depression is especially acute when the woman is not employed in the paid labour market outside the home and when her marital relationship is not good (Gallagher, 1987).

MARITAL STATUS

For both males and females, being single — whether due to never marrying, separation, divorce, or the death of a spouse — increases the chances of mental disorder. Being single also reduces the likelihood of making a timely recovery. Indeed, some researchers suggest that marital status is the best single predictor of the probability of experiencing mental illness (Gove, 1972).

Males are particularly hard hit by being single because they usually find themselves much more cut off from networks of social support than are single women. Single females receive more support both from other women and from men. Because they are socialized to compete with one another, men receive less support from their male friends. Men are also taught to hide their emotions, particularly from others of the same sex. When people are forced to join the ranks of the single through separation or divorce, the hardship for men more than for women takes the form of emotional distress alone. For women in the same situation, economic survival is often equally if not more important. When males are single because they never married, it is not unusual for them to be depressed because they feel rejected and inadequate (Pearlin and Johnson, 1977).

GEOGRAPHICAL MOBILITY

Data indicate that there is a tendency for foreign-born people to be over-represented among the mentally ill. This pattern is perhaps not surprising; many sources of stress confront migrants from other nations. First, many immigrants experience "culture shock." If the cultural difference between the old country and the new is great, immigrants experience more stress. In comparison with their younger counterparts, older newcomers often find adjustment to a new host culture particularly difficult. Moving into a neighbourhood already densely populated with members of one's own ethnic group is a cushion against the development of mental disorder, as is the length of one's stay in the new country. The chance of an immigrant's becoming mentally ill declines with the time spent in the new surroundings. It also appears that the reason for leaving one's homeland influences the development of disorder. When individuals leave their native lands as a matter of personal choice, they experience less psychological trauma than when they are forced out. Forced migration is the common experience of many recent refugees to Canada.

In addition to experiencing culture shock, many migrants to Canada face significant discrimination in the job and housing markets. Furthermore, employment discrimination can also cause downward social mobility. The stresses experienced by downwardly mobile immigrants are particularly acute when the reason for migrating was the pursuit of a better life (Gallagher, 1987).

RURAL-URBAN RESIDENCE

Rates of mental illness appear to be marginally higher in urban than in rural settings. Explanations of the link between city living and higher rates of mental disorder involve both quality-of-life factors and a self-selection process. Many people living in urban sprawls are isolated in a highly competitive and impersonal atmosphere. Moreover, high population density is stressful. On the other hand, people who are already mentally unstable may gravitate to urban areas in an attempt to survive (Srole, 1972; Morgan, 1972; Kolb and Brodie, 1982). These displaced people often join the burgeoning ranks of North America's home-less "street people." Another factor contributing to the urban concentration of mentally disordered people is the disproportionately large number of treatment facilities and therapists in cities. Finally, it may also be that rates are higher in cities simply because of the increased visibility of the mentally disordered in urban settings.

AGE

The chances of being treated for mental disorder increase with age. Canadian males and females living to the age of 90 have a 24 percent and 20 percent chance, respectively, of being hospitalized (Johnson, Cooper, and Mandel, 1976). For those over the age of 55, a growing number of strains are conducive to depression in particular. Retirement, children leaving home, degenerating appearance and physical prowess, the departure or death of a spouse, and age discrimination each contribute to feelings of social isolation and stress for those in their "golden years." People surviving long enough to be called elderly also run increased risks of becoming impaired either by senility or by Alzheimer's disease.

SOCIAL CLASS

Social scientists are keenly interested in the importance of social class in the development of mental illness. This is largely the case because family interaction patterns, a variable considered central in a child's personality formation, are known to vary with class. In rearing their children, lower-class families tend to emphasize the importance of conformity and obedience, while middle- and upper-class families are more likely to stress independence and flexibility of thought along with self-sufficiency. The ways in which lower-class parents control their offspring also differ from those of the middle and upper classes; the former rely more on physical discipline while the latter depend more on reasoning and psychological punishment (Bronfenbrenner, 1958).

The likelihood of becoming mentally disordered decreases both with higher education and with membership in higher-status occupations (Johnson, Cooper, and Mandel, 1976). Lower-status jobs tend to be alienating. Workers in unskilled and semi-skilled jobs often feel powerless to control their work and isolated from management and co-workers. They often see little meaning in their work and are able to identify neither with the organization employing them nor with the occupation itself (Blauner, 1964). Worse still, however, is unemployment, which almost totally cuts people off from society's reward structure. For adults, the nature and quality of their work determines their social status, which in turn determines the economic and social rewards that they can enjoy. The deprivations of lower-class people with respect to income, power, and prestige erode self-concept and produce strains that, as psychologists and psychiatrists point out, are linked to the development of mental disorders (Liem and Liem, 1978).

Social scientists explain the relationship between class and disorder in three fundamental ways: stress, social reaction, and drift. The stress explanation emphasizes the deprivations disproportionately endured by lower-class people. The disadvantaged endure hardships not experienced in the same degree by the more affluent. These deprivations include malnutrition, family dissolution, violence and other forms of abuse, and inadequate educational opportunities. The grimmer the conditions, the more likely the occurrence of disorders involving complete breaks with reality.

The social reaction approach highlights the effects of the social distance separating middle-class mental-health caregivers from their lower-class clients. The cultural biases of middle- and upper-class professionals result in their definition of lower-class behaviours, which they find more foreign, as "disordered." The manifestation of similar "symptoms" in persons from higher-class backgrounds, sociologists suggest, would more likely be interpreted as merely "eccentric" and not needing treatment. Finally, some sociologists maintain that class position is more a consequence than a cause of mental illness. They argue that people who become mentally disordered lose their abilities to function effectively in the workforce and experience downward social mobility as a result. Such persons drift from a higher to a lower status. This downward drift may then exacerbate their feelings of isolation and estrangement (Schwab and Schwab, 1978; Liem and Liem, 1978).

It is unlikely that any one of the stress, social reaction, or drift explanations fully accounts for the relationship between social class and mental disorder. It is more probable that these processes operate in combination with one another.

Membership in one social class or another not only affects the likelihood of experiencing mental illness, it also influences the type of disorder and the form of treatment. Becoming psychotic, psychopathic, and phobic is more likely for people in the lower classes. On the other hand, anxiety and some forms of depression are more common among people from the middle and upper classes (Dohrenwend, 1975).

THE TREATMENT OF MENTAL ILLNESS

Since the 1950s, there has been a transformation in the treatment of mental disorder in Canada. More emphasis is now placed upon caring for a larger portion of the patient population in community settings through out-patient care strategies. This transition has come about through the development of a wide range of drugs to alleviate the symptoms of disorder. Drug therapy has permitted patients to function more effectively without constant care and monitoring. Nevertheless, the mental hospital is still a major component of treatment for mental disorders in this country.

BECOMING A MENTAL PATIENT

People who become mental patients pass through a sequence of stages that can be conceived of as a career (Goffman, 1961). Often, the first stage involves the buildup of stress brought on by a variety of potentially traumatic life events. Psychologists have developed stress rating scales that assign numbers ranging from 1 to 100 to reflect the magnitude of the readjustment problems posed by certain everyday happenings and circumstances. Among less severe stressors are taking a vacation (13), going home for Christmas (12), and moving (20). Job-related stressors include working in shifts (16), trouble with the boss (23), added responsibilities (29), getting fired (47), and retirement (45). At the high end of the scale are distressing events that can profoundly affect family and home life. Examples of these are getting married (50), death of a close family member (63), getting divorced (73), and death of a spouse (100) (Holmes and Rahe, 1967).

In the face of an accumulation of these stressors, whether or not one is struck by mental disorder depends to some extent upon one's personal resilience and social support network. Some people thrive on overcoming adversity, and some find significant meaning in all events, whether good or bad. They see potentially devastating blows more as interesting sources of personal growth than as crushing setbacks. Furthermore, people who are highly integrated into tightly knit families and supportive friendship groups are better equipped to fend off mental disorder.

The common reaction of family members to the initial onset of the symptoms of mental disorder is to ignore them. Research indicates that spouses and children withdraw from their afflicted family members while at the same time taking over the family responsibilities normally performed by the mentally debilitated person. Families often do not seek outside help until one of several conditions arises. Increases in the frequency, persistence, and seriousness of the symptoms is a major factor in hastening the recruitment of professional assistance. When the mentally ill person can no longer function, has become visibly disturbed, and has begun to engage in behaviours that exceed community tolerance, even the most accepting and protective of family members and friends must take action. Two additional factors affecting whether treatment is sought are the extent to which the mentally disabled persons themselves think that they have a serious problem and the degree to which treatment services are readily available in the community (Gallagher, 1987).

The community response to the mentally disordered person is all too often fraught with ignorance, fear, and stigma. Being defined as mentally ill frequently results in so much rejection that people needing assistance do not seek it out. Many believe that the trauma of being treated and stigmatized is greater than the pain of continuing personal distress. Often, disturbed individuals do come to the attention of authorities. It has not been unusual, for example, for those considered homicidal, suicidal, or dangerous either to others or to themselves to be committed to mental institutions involuntarily. In recent years, however, controversies have arisen around the well-known and widespread ambiguities of many psychiatric assessments of dangerousness and around patients' due-process rights more generally (Menzies, 1991).

Critics of mental-health-care delivery point out that once someone is reported by family members or residents of the community as mentally disordered, professional caregivers tend to operate rather uncritically on the assumption that the person is indeed significantly impaired. Mental-health professionals tend to adopt this position for several reasons. First, their inclination is that it is better to risk hospitalizing those with relatively minor problems than to deny those who might injure themselves or others the benefits of lengthy observation, diagnosis, and, if necessary, treatment. Historically, the prevailing belief has clearly been that hospitalization could do no harm and that it might help. As a result, many people have been admitted to mental hospitals with little careful psychiatric assessment or vigilant judicial review. Involuntary commitment has been a probable fate for those whose petitions were instigated by people in the community rather than by family members. The old and those lacking money, social status, and supportive family and friends have been particularly vulnerable to involuntary commitment (Rushing, 1971; 1978).

Recent concerns with the civil liberties of mental patients in Canada and the United States have resulted in some legislative changes. First, new legislation emphasizes that only those who are clearly a danger to either themselves or others can be committed. Second, the law requires mental patients to be informed both of the potential benefits and of the possible risks of certain kinds of treatment. They must be permitted the right to refuse treatment.

The new civil liberties legislation is not entirely without problems. The adoption of these practices may mean that fewer people who require treatment will receive it. Furthermore, many still-disturbed ex-patients who appear incapable of properly caring for themselves are finding their way onto the streets of large urban centres (Gallagher, 1987).

In response to problems created by de-institutionalization, legislators have drafted bills intended to tighten up mental-health laws. Their efforts are aimed at ensuring that those with serious disorders who pose a danger to themselves or others receive necessary treatment. Such legislation is contained in Ontario's "Brian's Law," named after Brian Smith, an Ottawa sportscaster killed in 1995 by a man suffering from severe mental illness. The new statute amends the *Mental Health Act* and the *Health Care Consent Act* to address directly recommendations issued by a number of inquest juries. The law is designed to assist people with severe mental illnesses in gaining access to appropriate care while at the same time ensuring the safety of the public. To accomplish this goal, the revised Act permits the use of community treatment orders

(CTOs), legal agreements that direct appropriate treatment in the community for those who have serious mental illnesses.

Specifically, CTOs expand the grounds for committal for individuals who suffer from serious mental disorders and who have a history of repeated hospitalization. They permit community treatment for involuntary psychiatric patients who consent to a community treatment plan as a condition of their release from psychiatric facilities. The law requires that patients report regularly to mental-health caregivers. It can also require that patients take prescribed medication or be re-hospitalized against their will. The new legislation also makes it possible for substitute decision-makers, such as family members, to make treatment and hospitalization choices where patients are deemed incapable of doing so. The law also removes the requirement that police "observe" disorderly conduct before taking a person into custody. Patient safeguards under the legislation include various rights of review concerning such matters as the original necessity of the CTO and the incapacity of the patient to consent to treatment. Also provided for are the right to seek advice and entitlement to appointed counsel.

Critics have raised several issues about the Ontario law. First, they note that the legislation over-emphasizes the link between mental illness and violent behaviour and therefore reinforces stereotypes. In reality, observers point out that when it comes to violent crime, more mentally ill people are victims rather than perpetrators. Second, they argue that the Act reduces the right of informed consent. The law has the potential of undermining the civil liberties of the mentally disordered especially where it forces treatment upon those who present no real danger to themselves or others. Finally, enforcement of the Act requires levels of support above and beyond what is currently available. Critics highlight the need for additional beds and other community resources and express concern about whether adequate support will be forthcoming from fiscally conservative governments (Hendley, 2000; Government of Ontario, 2000).

THE EXPERIENCE OF TREATMENT

Treatment for mental illnesses is different from treatment for physical illnesses. The mission of health-care workers dealing with people with physical illnesses, for the most part, is to make them well. Those working with the mentally disordered, however, must not only promote their patients' recovery but ensure that their disordered charges harm neither themselves nor others. The expectations placed upon caregivers who work with the mentally ill are twofold: treatment and control (Cockerham, 1989). For a variety of reasons, these goals are contradictory and, this being the case, one often assumes primacy over the other. Unfortunately, because of a widespread tendency for the mentally disordered to be viewed as unpredictable and potentially dangerous, control often takes precedence over rehabilitation. Patients subjected to control frequently challenge authority. Caregivers meet this challenge by asserting themselves in an effort to curb rebellion and maintain order. As a result, patients and hospital staff become alienated from one another. Patients find it hard to muster the necessary enthusiasm for participating in their own recovery, and hospital staff find it difficult to empathize with their patients. This outcome is particularly problematic because both patient participation and sympathetic caregiving are crucial to rehabilitation.

In the earlier decades of this century, observers depicted mental hospitals as medieval "snake pits"; endless confinement was accompanied by treatment that was at best inhumane and at worst brutal. With custody as their main purpose, mental institutions exhibited uninteresting architectural designs, bleak surroundings, and melancholy atmospheres that reflected the depression and feelings of hopelessness that the institutions were supposed to cure. Meaningful therapy was virtually unheard of. In some instances, little has changed over the years (Gallagher, 1987).

Writing about mental institutions in the early 1960s, American sociologist Erving Goffman (1961), in his book Asylums, described these hospitals as "**total institutions.**" For institutions to be "total" in Goffman's terms, they must meet certain specified criteria. First, all aspects of patients' lives are conducted in the same place under the same single authority. Second, inmates carry out their daily round of activities in the immediate company of similarly circumstanced others. Staff treat institutionalized persons identically and require them to perform the same tasks together. Third, all phases of a day's routine are tightly regimented, rigidly timed in sequence, and governed by formal rules developed and administered by officials. Finally, a single rational plan guides the institution's fulfillment of its goals.

While few would suggest that no efforts are made to treat disorders, mental institutions in Canada continue to emphasize the control of patients. Hospitalization often means the effective segregation of patients from the outside world. Life in these settings tends to be highly routinized. Patients rise in the

---

Box 16.3
MENTALLY ILL 'ROTTING IN JAIL,' CROWN SAYS

Mentally ill people charged with criminal offences are "rotting in jail" because of a shortage of hospital beds necessary for assessment or treatment, a Metro crown attorney says.

"People are rotting in jail, waiting for treatment," crown attorney Michael Leshner said, adding that the system is "so broken" that exasperated judges have subpoenaed hospital administrators to explain why prisoners can't get treatment.

"The system appears to be broken because of a chronic shortage of beds," he said.

The problem is so severe that a rare top-level meeting between judges and hospital officials has been scheduled for next week to discuss ways of fixing it.

"The beds are there but the funds aren't available to open them up or service them," Judge Walter Gonet of the Ontario court, provincial division, who is also the regional senior judge for Metro, said yesterday.

"Jail is not a proper place for the mentally ill," he said. "If it's a matter of money, then let's decide who's going to accept the cost of fixing the problem."

Dr. Sam Malcolmson, clinical chief of forensic services at the Queen St. Mental Health Centre, said next Wednesday's meeting won't be a cure all. "We're going to try to make the system work better where we can and submit proposals to various ministries," Malcolmson said.

"There will be adjustments and improvements, but if you're asking whether we can fix what's wrong, the answer's straightforward – no, we can't."

The problem has been especially acute in the Greater Toronto Area since about 1995.

MENTAL HEALTH CRISIS

When one public servant has to plead with an Ontario judge to force another public servant to discharge his responsibility, something must be terribly amiss at Queen's Park.

Yet that's what happened Tuesday when crown attorney Michael Leshner asked Judge Walter Gonet to order Dr. Sam Malcolmson, clinical chief of forensic sciences at the Queen Street Mental Health Centre, to find a bed for a woman who has spent three weeks in jail awaiting a psychiatric assessment to determine whether she is fit to stand trial.

Pointing out that the case is one of dozens in which people referred by courts for psychiatric assessment can spend up to seven months in jail waiting their turn, Leshner told court the practice contravenes federal law requiring humane treatment of the mentally ill.

Ordering Malcolmson to find a bed immediately, Judge Gonet added his own concern that in the woman's case, the time she already has spent in jail may be longer than the sentence she would receive if convicted of cocaine possession.

Malcolmson found a bed by bumping someone else. Blaming the shortage of beds on budget restraint imposed on Queen Street by the Ministry of Health, he said that to accommodate the courts, the centre would have to turn away other people who need help.

Since Health Minister Jim Wilson – the only person with the power to solve the bed-shortage problem –

was not in court, Leshner encouraged the judge to send "a clear message to the policy makers that we are in crisis here."

Wilson got the message. To avoid being tagged the minister who jails the sick, Wilson opened up 40 beds in the medium-secure unit of the new Whitby Mental Health Centre – a unit that has stood empty ever since the facility opened nine months ago. But that stopgap measure has by no means alleviated everyone's concerns.

With the Health Services Restructuring Commission recommending the closing, downsizing or merging of five of the province's 10 psychiatric hospitals, Dr. James Young, Ontario's chief coroner, warns that "if we squeeze the system further before we put in place the necessary community supports, we'll take what's already a very bad situation and make it many times worse."

Instead of waiting for the next crisis in mental health, Wilson ought to spell out exactly what community supports he's planning to compensate for the anticipated reductions in institutional space.

Discussion Questions

What social, political, and economic factors might be associated with the decline in mental-health services in Ontario and in particular in the Toronto area since 1995? What does the editorial "Mental Health Crisis" suggest about the role of politics in the provision of proper care to the mentally disordered?

Source: Nicolaas van Rijn, "Mentally Ill 'Rotting in Jail,' Crown Says," *Toronto Star*, June 20, 1997, p. A7; Toronto Star editorial, June 27, 1997, p. A26. Reprinted with permission – The Toronto Star Syndicate.

---

morning, eat, receive medication, perhaps participate in therapy, smoke, watch TV, eat some more, and return to bed. Particularly as time passes, many patients carry out this routine by rote. They do so without stimulation from the outside, as family members and friends cease to visit and stop sending letters.

Sometimes the controls on patients are even more restrictive. Some are physically restrained, some are sedated with drugs, and some are subjected to solitary confinement, aversion therapy, and electro-shock. For many patients, being cut off from the outside world for prolonged periods of time produces "dependency syndrome" (Cockerham, 1989). Inmates suffering

from dependency syndrome cease, for all intents and purposes, to show any possibility of functioning outside the institutional environment.

Mental-hospital staff are organized hierarchically, with psychiatrists having the most power. Psychologists and social workers occupy the second tier of authority, followed by psychiatric nurses and ward aides. Nurses, and particularly ward aides, often lack intensive formal training in psychiatric practice.

At the bottom of the authority hierarchy, of course, are the patients. Goffman (1961) provides a penetrating observation on the relationship between staff and patient groups:

In the total institution there is a basic split between a large managed group conveniently called inmates and a small supervisory staff. Inmates typically live in the institution and have restricted contact with the world outside the walls; staff often operate on an eight-hour day and are socially integrated into the outside world. Each grouping tends to conceive of the other in terms of narrow hostile stereotypes, staff often seeing inmates as bitter, secretive, and untrustworthy, while inmates often see staff as condescending, highhanded, and mean. Staff tends to feel superior and righteous; inmates tend, in some ways at least, to feel inferior, weak, blameworthy, and guilty (7).

Those with the greatest degree of expertise, the psychiatrists, spend comparatively little time with patients. Rarely do they provide institutionalized people with individual therapy. Rather, they spend most of their time either giving or certifying medical orders and executing the multitude of higher-level administrative tasks necessary to keep the hospital bureaucracy running smoothly. Nurses occupy intermediary positions of authority and more frequently deal directly with patients, but it is the least-trained and least-powerful of the caregivers, the ward aides, who have the most contact with the mentally disordered. The aides frequently know the patients best and consequently often exert considerable influence in the decisions made by psychiatrists. Aides also occupy a position between the patients and the professionals, which gives them great power over the lives of patients. Among other things, aides influence the access that patients have to psychiatrists, the privileges they enjoy, and, indirectly, their chances of being discharged (Gallagher, 1987).

When the mental-hospital staff normally in contact with patients are poorly qualified and financial constraints are such that there are too few of them on the wards, they cannot provide proper care. These conditions occur routinely and undermine staff morale. Over time, the lack of success in treating the mentally ill under such conditions breeds a sense of futility. The staff become disenchanted with the institution emzploying them and the efficacy of psychiatric treatment. Negative staff attitudes toward patients, employers, and psychiatry are not conducive to treating and rehabilitating patients (Gallagher, 1987).

Despite problems with institutional approaches, however, mental hospitals do offer some advantages over other strategies, and thus they are unlikely to disappear entirely. Sometimes hospitalization is desirable because it removes patients from environments that have caused or contributed to their mental disorders in the first place. Second, hospitalization does permit caregivers to continue, monitor, and assess treatment more easily. Finally, some disordered persons, such as those with irreparable organic injury or disease and those judged violent and criminally insane, do require confinement (Cockerham, 1989). The darker side of necessary confinement is that some mental hospitals have employed inhumane practices such as isolation rooms and electro-shock, not as treatments, but as punishments for violating institutional rules. There have also been instances of psychosurgery and potentially dangerous drug therapies being used as means of social control (Weicker, 1985).

TREATMENT MODALITIES

There are three major treatment modalities for mental disorder: psychotherapy, organic therapy, and custodial care (Gallagher, 1987). **Psychotherapeutic** techniques involve the verbalization of the patients' problems, either on a one-to-one basis or in a group context, under the supervision of a psychologist or psychiatrist. Organic treatments are physiological and include electro-shock, drugs such as tranquillizers and antidepressants, and psychosurgical procedures such as lobotomy. Patients generally qualify for custodial care under two conditions. The mentally disordered go into custody if they are diagnosed as dangerous to themselves or others or if there appears to be little hope of recovery. The latter is the major reason why people wind up in custodial treatment programs.

Higher-class patients are more likely to undergo individual psychotherapy. As one descends the socioeconomic continuum, one is more likely to experience the less expensive group therapy. Organic therapies such as electro-shock and psychosurgery have been most often applied to lower-class patients. Most people in custodial facilities come from socially and economically disadvantaged backgrounds.

The relationship between type of treatment and social class position occurs partly as a result of selection and discrimination and partly as a result of the social distribution of mental illness (Gallagher, 1987). The receipt of individual psychotherapy often depends on having the social and economic means to seek out and employ professional services. Group therapy is less expensive and is more often a feature of the hospital services provided to the less affluent. The success of psychotherapy depends on the language capacity of patients, and verbal facility is greater among better-educated, higher-class persons. Verbal approaches also work best when the social distance separating doctors and patients is minimal. Consequently, psychologists and physicians select as prime candidates for this form of treatment patients who are verbal, intelligent, well educated, and successful. Such processes as patient self-selection, professional choice, and institutional discrimination do not provide a full account of the class–treatment relationship, however, because type of illness is also class related. Psychoses and personality disorders are not only concentrated among people from the lower classes, they are less amenable to psychotherapy and more often require organic and custodial responses.

CURED?

The challenges for mental patients who leave hospital begin before their release. First, long hospital stays encourage institutional dependency, which in turn increases the likelihood of readmission. Second, to be released from an institution, patients often must demonstrate that they are "cured" or at least have experienced some improvement. An experiment conducted by American researcher David Rosenhan (1973) suggests that convincing hospital staff that one is well may not be easy. Rosenhan sent research associates, whose identities were concealed, to several psychiatric institutions. He instructed his researchers to complain of hearing strange voices. Once admitted, they were to behave normally and immediately seek release. On average, it took the new patients nineteen days to gain their freedom. Some were detained for almost two months. Rosenhan's "plants" tended to be released, not as "cured," but as "in remission." This outcome is not uncommon; mental patients free of their troublesome symptoms are often diagnosed as "in remission" rather than fully recovered. Finally, positive attitudes on the part of patients' families appear to be more important in their being released than is their psychological condition. If the families oppose patients' requests for release, petitions are unlikely to be granted (Greenley, 1972).

Upon release, a minefield of potential problems must be negotiated by the ex–mental patient. Demonstrating wellness in the institution is one thing; avoiding relapse on the outside is quite another. Returning to stressors such as isolation and broken families, which may have contributed to the initial onset of disorder, is hardly conducive to remaining well (Gallagher, 1987).

Another major problem confronting people who are publicly defined as mentally ill is the attachment of "**stigma**" (Goffman, 1963). Sociologists define stigma as negative social worth and point out that it literally "spoils" people's identities. The strength of stigma varies by type of mental disorder and with the type of response that resulted in its creation in the first place. People with more bizarre and visible symptoms, such as those associated with schizophrenia, and people who have been involuntarily committed to a mental hospital are more stigmatized than are individuals whose symptoms are hidden and who have been treated in the community as out-patients.

The stigma experienced by mentally disordered people originates in erroneous beliefs held by the public and created and buttressed by inaccurate media depictions. Many Canadians view most mentally disordered people as dangerous, violent, unpredictable, and bizarre. The image of violence, which is patently false, is nurtured by entertainment media depictions of crazed lunatics. News media also make a habit of reporting criminals' histories of psychiatric care if they have any. The fact that the vast majority of murderers and rapists have no such history is overlooked.

There are two additional aspects of stigma that affect the mentally disordered. First, many people believe that mental problems, especially minor ones, are not true illnesses. While missing work because of a bad cold is legitimate, telling the boss that one will not be at work because one is depressed is not. Second, many people view mental illnesses as completely incurable. Thus, a diagnosis of mental disorder becomes a label for life. The consequences can be serious for the executive who cracks under the stress of overload at work or for the dentist overcome by depression. Taking time off to recover from the illness highlights the problem. The recovered executive may not receive any further demanding assignments from an employer, and the dentist may not regain patients lost during the recovery period. Whatever the response, the result is often rejection and low levels of tolerance, especially among those with the least amount of education (Gallagher, 1987; Cockerham, 1989).

Ex-patients need some place to go and something to do. A supportive home environment is particularly important to recovery. Family support is typically greater for married women and children than it is for married men. Social norms permit women and

Box 16.4
THREAT TO FREEDOM IN MENTAL HEALTH BILL

If a government amendment is adopted, the Ontario Mental Health Act will allow people to be forcibly confined and medicated in order to avert "substantial mental deterioration." This represents a radical addition to the existing criteria under which no such coercion may occur unless "serious bodily harm" or "imminent and serious physical impairment" is anticipated.

For years, certain psychiatrists and the families of many schizophrenics have attacked the existing law as too narrow. According to them, many mentally ill people — not dangerous, suicidal or physically impaired — have nevertheless been suffering the agonies of their various disorders without anyone being able to help. These disordered people are seen as being too incapacitated to seek or accept help. And, since coercion is not permissible, the families feel a sense of hopelessness. The government amendment is designed to relieve this suffering.

But the proposal could authorize state coercion in many other situations as well. The government bill contains no definition for "substantial mental deterioration." Nor does the bill attempt to limit these terms to any officially recognized disorders. But even if it did, the outcome would be hopelessly vague.

Much controversy rages over the categories of psychiatric diagnosis recommended by the most authoritative source, the American Psychiatric Association (APA). Leading journals have charged the APA recommendations among other things, with "sex bias," "biased diagnostic criteria," a susceptibility to "ideological, political and market influences," and "excessive" reliance "on the prejudices of the day." It appears, therefore, that the diagnosis of mental disorder is, at the very least, contentious.

The issue, however, is not the character or ability of the mental health professionals; it is the nature of their discipline. The discipline is influence by ideological factors. Some years ago, for example, homosexuality was listed among the mental disorder. It is no longer there.

To a great extent, the decisions to include it and to remove it were ethical rather than clinical. As much as psychiatric egalitarianism is to be welcomed, it must nevertheless be realized that the issue was more ideological than scientific. Could it, therefore, be that, but for the passage of a few years, the government's amendment would have authorized the forced confinement and medication of homosexuals in order to prevent their further "mental deterioration?"

Under the proposal, such confinements would also require that prospective patients lack the capacity to consent to treatment. But how often can anyone adequately discern the limits of another person's competence? In this regard, consider a comment in the winter 1999 issue of *Psychiatric Quarterly*: "Currently, there exists no standardized method to establish competency, either in psychiatric or in medical patients."

For all these reasons, those of us involved in the mental-health reforms of the late 1970s urged a more restrictive approach to the powers at issue. There was a growing realization that the ability to distinguish unacceptable pathology from acceptable nonconformity was a value-laden exercise. But, since the ability to recognize an urgent situation is less encumbered with ideological baggage, pressures developed for any powers of coercion to be limited, as much as possible, to such circumstances. Hence, the narrower committal powers in the existing law.

At the time, we had no illusions that these reforms would produce a good outcome. Indeed, in situations concerning mental illness, it is not possible to have a good outcome. We believed, however, that the approach we advocate would be significantly less bad than the open-ended power than then existed.

This government amendment threatens to restore the discredited situation of that earlier era. Where the criminal law is concerned, our society would never stand for a power to incarcerate based on such ill-defined criteria. In view of its comparable impact on human freedom, why should our mental health law be so much looser?

Discussion Question

Discuss the contentious nature of this bill. Can you offer a better solution that would accomplish the goals of the new Mental Health Act, while at the same time minimizing its potential negative consequences?

Source: Alan Borovoy, *Toronto Star*, June 19, 2000, p. A15. Reprinted with permission of the author.

children to be dependent on other family members while requiring to a much greater extent that husbands perform and be self-reliant. Having a job is also important because employment, particularly if the work is meaningful, boosts self-esteem and facilitates contact with others who, presumably, are more healthy mentally (Maguire, 1983). Particularly in periods of high unemployment, however, it is not unusual for other workers and labour unions to oppose programs that provide work for out-patients. Such well-meaning initiatives, so beneficial to the mentally ill, can reduce the scarce opportunities available to the able-bodied and able-minded.

Social service programs that assist ex–mental patients with their re-entry into the community are problematic in several respects. In some communities, they do not exist. In others, they are of dubious quality, consisting simply of placement in boarding houses. In other cases, community mental-health counsellors are so overworked that they cannot provide effective therapy. Even where community programs are of high quality, there is no assurance that released patients will attend therapy sessions. Once away from under the watchful eyes of hospital attendants, there is no guarantee that out-patients will continue to take necessary medication. Where these problems result in the return of symptoms, the relapse generates the potential for rejection by a hostile community, and the downward cycle begins anew (Cockerham, 1989; Gallagher, 1987).

As with other areas of deviance that are treated as medical afflictions (drug abuse and alcoholism), one of the responses to problems posed by mental illness has been the creation of self-help groups. These organizations provide a combination of information, public education, and support services and engage in fundraising activities. The Canadian Friends of Schizophrenics and the Canadian Alzheimer Society provide assistance both for those afflicted and for their families. The Anorexia Nervosa and Bulimia Foundation of Canada is a relatively new self-help and support group that began with one chapter in Western Canada and expanded throughout the country. This organization has patterned its program on the "12-step" approach pioneered by Alcoholics Anonymous.

LIFE OUTSIDE THE INSTITUTION

Effectively treating the mentally ill by placing them in institutions has proven to be an elusive achievement.

The enterprise has consistently been plagued by the imprecision of psychiatric diagnoses, the debatable usefulness of various treatment modalities, the inadequate training and heavy workloads of hospital staff, the public's misconceptions and prejudices about mental illness, and the overriding concern with maintaining secure custody. Escalating health-care costs and current policies favouring government budget restraint only serve to exacerbate these problems. Finally, some investigations stress the deleterious effects of long-term institutionalization, including apathy, extreme submissiveness, and utter dependence, accompanied by a deterioration of personal-care habits.

Some studies suggest that some patients treated in mental hospitals fare no better than if they were cared for in the community. Coupled with rising concerns about the growing intrusion of the state into the lives of its citizens and about the necessity of preserving the civil liberties of a wide range of relatively powerless groups, findings such as these have produced a gradual shift from in-patient to out-patient care. They have resulted in a reduction both in the numbers of in-patients and in the lengths of their institutional stays. Because of the overcrowding in some facilities and the reduction in expenses associated with community treatment, governments have not been entirely unsupportive of these **de-institutionalization** measures (Cockerham, 1989).

These trends, which began in North America in the 1960s, solved some problems while creating others. Critics of these liberal policies argue that the more stringent civil liberties legislation has released or kept out of institutions many mentally ill people who suffer from serious conditions such as schizophrenia and paranoia and who could benefit greatly from hospital treatment. They further point out that de-institutionalization has not only contributed to the problem of homelessness across North America, but because of the increased visibility of some mentally ill people, it has also exacerbated negative community responses to the mentally disordered.

The problems posed by de-institutionalizing the mentally disabled while at the same time failing to provide adequate support are as apparent in Canada as in other Western nations. Kearns and Taylor (1989) investigated the daily life experiences of 66 people with chronic mental disabilities who were involved in three mental-health programs in Hamilton, Ontario. Their findings echo those of American research on

Box 16.5
REMARKABLE TORONTO COURT FILLING MUCH-NEEDED NICHE

Something curious is happening in a provincial courtroom at downtown Toronto's Old City Hall.

As each defendant is escorted by a police officer to the dock, the justice on the bench greets him or her by asking, "How are you?" After this unorthodox salutation, the judge asks if the person is aware of where he is and the possible consequences of a criminal trial.

A large, bluff-looking man, Judge Edward F. Ormston has other surprises in store this day as well. When a homeless young man accused of assaulting someone in a men's hostel rambles on at considerable length, almost incoherently, Judge Ormston doesn't interrupt; indeed, he appears to glean something useful from the disjointed monologue.

In other instances, the judge asks Dr. Eva Chow, a forensic psychiatrist who is on duty throughout this session of the court, to meet privately with the defendant then and there to make an assessment.

This is a session of Mental Health Court, one of the only such facilities in North America and in its manner of proceeding the sole example on the continent. Those accused who have severe illness such as schizophrenia, bipolar illness and major depression have in Toronto a unique option.

"It's a non-adversarial court with a lot of participation from almost everybody in the courtroom," explains Judge Ormston in his chambers. "This has allowed the bulk of the work to be done much more efficiently."

And humanely. Without Mental Health Court, those accused with serious mental illness would be kept in the cells of Old City Hall until a judge could send them to a psychiatric hospital for evaluation and then back to jail when their fitness had been determined.

It meant extended incarceration for any minor charge before they were even heard and then subsequent delays.

"People with this sickness were spending extraordinary amounts of time in jail for stealing an apple," remarks Judge Ormston, adding the petty theft of food is indeed a common example of lawbreaking among this distressed population.

Probation officers, prison guards, nurses attached to the system, lawyers and judges all felt that the justice system wasn't working well for disturbed people who were often, as Judge Ormston puts it, "Mad not bad, sick not dangerous."

Dr. Richard Schneider, a clinical psychologist and criminal lawyer who is counsel to the Ontario Review Board, says he had advocated such a court since 1995.

"Obviously, when you're dealing with a so-called normal accused you can make certain assumptions that don't apply when you're dealing with the mentally ill," says Dr. Schneider, who teaches at the University of Toronto.

When the mentally ill would be up on criminal charges in the usual manner, he comments, "you'd go to court and the clerks wouldn't know what to do, the crown attorneys didn't know the law [when mental illness was involved], the judges didn't know how to proceed."

Along with the specialized legal knowledge that everyone attached to Mental Health Court has, there is a particular kind of emphasis found in Judge Ormston's handling of the session. There are questions to those accused about their medication, housing, appointment dates with therapists; directives to court clerks to look into hospital bed availability; time taken to explain to family members present what is happening and why.

"Judge Ormston is a very sensitive, caring, humane judge," Dr. Schneider says. "He is prepared to go the extra distance and listen to things that a lot of other judges would not. To make a court like this work you have to be creative, you have to be patient."

No court can furnish the needs of Canada's mentally ill, of course. Indeed, many of these people end up in the courts, says Judge Ormston, because "basically the criminal justice system has become the social system of last resort."

With psychiatric hospitals closing and community resources often lacking, tragic numbers of mentally ill end up with the law.

"Police are forced to criminalize people in order to get them treatment," Judge Ormston says. Many of those accused before him, he adds, had gone off their medication before the alleged incident, perhaps wanting to avoid the side effects of the drugs or lacking the dispensing fee for the pharmacy. "The police try to get these people into the hospital and they can't, so they end up arresting them" says Anita Barnes, program manager for Mental Health Court support services. "We are creating this huge forensic system unnecessarily."

Even if the crown attorney drops the charges out of compassion, the mentally ill accused do not end up with treatment, simply cycling back through the justice system.

Here, with a team of social workers attached to the Mental Health Court effort, "we try to get them housing, get them ID, whatever they need," Barnes says. "We give them Starbucks coffee, we give them [subway] tokens and we don't bug them."

Concluding a case this afternoon, Judge Ormston hands down this advice to the somewhat rumpled young man before him: "You work hard at getting well and taking your meds and keeping in touch with your social worker."

Pausing before releasing the defendant, the judge adds: "You're looking much better."

Discussion Questions

What social and economic forces have given rise to innovations in dealing with the mentally ill who run afoul of the law? Are they likely to be effective in the long run? Why might their impact be minimal?

Source: *Globe and Mail*, June 12, 2000. Special Interest Supplement: Mood Disorders and Mental Health, p. C3. Reprinted with permission from the *Globe and Mail*.

similar community mental-health initiatives. Most patients were single; 65 percent had never married and 20 percent were, at the time of the study, no longer married. Most of their incomes were based on social assistance and welfare programs and averaged less than $6000 per year. Most (59 percent) had either been unemployed for the past two years or had never held a job.

The researchers argue that clients' low incomes reduce their range of meaningful life activities and necessitate their congregating "on the street." Not only were participants generally unable to bolster their self-worth through employment, few of their friends were drawn from the wider community. Most of their associates were themselves mentally disordered. Furthermore, clients reported "funny looks" and "put downs" from members of the community more generally. The lifestyles of the participants consisted of unrestricted time coupled with restricted access to places. Their collective experience was one of stigma, impoverishment, boredom, and "killing time" in public places. Kearns and Taylor concluded that this disordered state was exacerbated by poverty, unemployment, limited social networks, and negative public attention.

THE MENTALLY ILL AND THE CRIMINAL JUSTICE SYSTEM

Particularly in urban centres, responding to problems posed by the mentally ill has become a significant aspect of the work of police and the corrections system. Widely held stereotypes of mentally disordered

people as dangerous and society's continuing intolerance of the mentally ill in the community form the basis of a problem that has been exacerbated in recent years by several long-term trends. De-institutionalizaton, mental-health-care funding cutbacks, and changes in the law governing patients' rights to live in the community and to refuse psychiatric treatment have increased the likelihood of police encounters, arrest, and incarceration. Citizens frequently call upon the criminal justice system to take action in situations involving mentally ill individuals, especially when they exhibit clear signs of mental disturbance.

Two legal principles govern police involvement with the mentally ill. First, police have the power and responsibility to ensure the safety and welfare of the public. Second, the doctrine of *parens patriae* dictates protection for those with mental and physical disabilities. Where persons are either dangerous to themselves or others or unable to provide for their basic needs, police must initiate emergency psychiatric apprehensions.

Officers encountering an irrational person creating a disturbance have three options: they can deliver the person to a mental hospital; they can arrest and transfer the person to jail; or they can resolve the situation informally. The latter measure in particular requires that police serve as "street-corner psychiatrists." Bureaucratic obstacles and the legal difficulties associated with commitment and treatment often thwart the initiation of an emergency hospitalization. In addition, many psychiatric facilities are over-burdened. Consequently, it is by no means uncommon for the mentally ill to wind up in jail.

In a process referred to as the "criminalization of mentally disordered behaviour," mental-health professionals observe that people who were previously treated within the mental-health-care system are more often now being transferred into the criminal justice system. In the face of bureaucratic and legal impediments to making mental-health referrals, arrest is a more straightforward and reliable way for police to remove a problem person from the community. Those who cannot be accommodated, for whatever reason, by the mental-health-care system must be accepted by the criminal justice system, which is unable to turn away clients. Consequently, jails and prisons have increasingly become long-term repositories for people with mental disorders (Teplin, 2000).

A U.S. study on this issue demonstrated that the probability of arrest was 67 percent greater for suspects exhibiting signs of mental disorder than for those who did not appear to be mentally ill. Police arrested 47 percent of disordered suspects compared to only 28 percent of "healthy" suspects. Researchers concluded that mentally ill citizens in the study were considerably more likely to be treated as criminals (Teplin, 1984).

That mentally ill persons are criminalized is of considerable concern because the criminal justice system is not designed for the provision of mental-health care. Furthermore, arrest labels a mentally ill individual as "criminal" and increases the likelihood of that person being arrested again in cases of future disorderliness. Once incarcerated, jail is by no means an ideal treatment centre for mentally ill people. The noisy, crowded, and criminogenic environment of jail settings works against even the recognition of mental disorder let alone its effective treatment. Budget constraints in the mental-health-care field may be shifting the financial burden from hospitals to jails and prisons.

Improved responses to these problems require that policies be modified and resources more effectively allocated to ensure that governments protect the civil rights of the mentally ill, while the same time providing the most humane and effective treatment available. Many de-institutionalized adults can be productive members of the community if they live in structured settings where they are encouraged to take their medications regularly. Funding to support those who have been de-institutionalized should be sufficient to meet more adequately the needs of the mentally ill who must cope with their maladies in a comparatively unstructured community context. Greater co-ordination between mental-health-care facilities and criminal justice system agencies would also facilitate more effective responses and treatment. Community-based treatment programs require enhancement to meet the needs of minor offenders, while programs based in correctional institutions need to be expanded to meet the needs of more serious offenders. Police and correctional officers require special training and clear procedural guidelines for dealing appropriately with an expanding mentally disordered clientele (Teplin, 2000).

SOCIOLOGICAL THEORIES OF MENTAL ILLNESS

THE MEDICAL MODEL

Sociological perspectives on mental disorder have arisen largely in response to the medical model. The medical model of mental illness is premised upon the idea that mental disorders are symptoms of psychic disturbances that have medically treatable causes. According to this approach, the sources of mental illnesses can be found in the fields of physiology, biochemistry, and genetics. Medical treatments appropriate to maladies brought about by biological, chemical, and genetic causes include drug therapy, electro-shock, and psychosurgery.

The medical model has dominated psychiatry for many years. Its persistence can be explained partly by evidence that medical treatments are effective for some disorders and partly because its practitioners (medical doctors) have been extensively trained to believe in the value of the model. The fact that the medical community, which is strongly committed to the medical model, is an extremely powerful occupational group has done nothing to erode the pre-eminence of this approach.

Sociologists dispute the validity of the medical model by citing evidence that mental disorders are not randomly distributed across the population but appear to be related to demographic and social variables such as socioeconomic status, sex, marital status, education, religion, and weakened social bonds. They also argue that the definition of mental illness is affected by culture.

CONFLICT AND ANOMIE INTERPRETATIONS

Although conflict theory, a macro-level approach, has so far been used sparingly to explain mental disorder, it does have some utility. Conflict approaches, especially those in the Marxist tradition, focus on the importance of work in the lives of individuals. Work is a central social activity for several reasons. It represents the means by which society distributes its economic and social rewards. In Canada, one's income and material well-being depend largely upon one's job. Also dependent upon one's work are social rewards such as prestige and power. A related point is that work affects a person's identity and self-esteem. To a large extent, we are what we do for a living.

Conflict theorists point out that much work in our society is conducted under exploitative conditions characterized by rationalization (being broken down into its constituent parts) and routinization (repetitive tasks). Workers, especially those at the bottom of the status hierarchy, are isolated and alienated on the job and are marginalized in the society by low incomes and uncertain and perhaps intermittent employment. These persons are disproportionately vulnerable to poverty, slum living, and job loss. In turn, each of these conditions is conducive to stress and, as a consequence, to mental disorder.

Merton's theory of anomie also briefly addresses the relationship between low socioeconomic status and mental disorder. Merton presents a typology of the possible adaptations to structural conditions wherein everyone is encouraged to aspire highly but only some are provided with the legitimate means of attaining their goals. One of Merton's categories is retreatism, and one of the groups he cites to exemplify this category is the mentally disordered. Facing the greatest levels of social strain and possessing the fewest resources with which to cope, it is the poor who are most likely to reject both socially lauded goals and socially approved means of goal attainment. In essence, retreatists drop out of society and into their own worlds of fantasy and hallucination. The relationship between social class standing and mental disorders such as schizophrenia supports not only the strain explanation but also the account provided by conflict theory.

SYMBOLIC INTERACTIONISM

Labelling theorists, principally Thomas Scheff (1984) and Thomas Szasz (1974), have vehemently attacked the medical model. In his account of mental illness, Scheff introduces the concept of "residual rule breaking." He points out that a very large number of norms are relatively unequivocal, easily comprehended, and straightforwardly responded to. If someone breaks a

rule, a negative response can be marshalled in various degrees as punishment. Talking loudly to friends in a library, for example, can result in disapproving looks from adjacent bookworms or a few harsh words from the librarian. Some social norms, however, are so deeply imbedded as social convention that they represent what many might consider "natural" behaviour. People are usually supposed to talk with other people and, from time to time under certain circumstances, to themselves. People who engage lamp posts, parking meters, and trees in spirited debate are another matter altogether. When people violate fundamental rules that fall into this "natural" residual category, they run the risk of being designated by onlookers as somehow unnatural, as "ill."

In keeping with the interactionist perspective, Scheff points out that the designation of residual rule violation as mental disorder is affected by a series of contingencies. These contingencies include the status of the actor, the degree of understanding and tolerance displayed by the audience, the type of residual rule being violated, and the setting in which the violation occurs. Some contingencies hasten the application of the label "mentally ill." Others provide alternative "rational" explanations for a person's unusual behaviour that militate against his or her being labelled "disordered."

Scheff also highlights the importance of pervasive cultural stereotypes regarding the forms that craziness can assume. Stereotypes of the mentally ill and their disorders are deeply imbedded in our culture and strongly reinforced by news and entertainment media. These widespread cultural stereotypes not only pattern onlookers' reactions to the mentally disturbed, they also form the orientation that guides the actions and shapes the identity of those defined as "crazy."

Scheff argues that, once stigmatized as mentally ill, especially if formally stigmatized, it is extremely difficult for a person to renounce the label. Consider again the experience of the subjects in Rosenhan's research. Once the sane were admitted to insane places and began to behave normally, it took them between 7 and 52 days to gain their freedom. Even then, they were released because hospital personnel considered them "in remission" rather than cured. Similarly, research by Krohn and Akers (1977) provides some support for the labelling perspective rather than the medical model. They determined that, holding psychiatric condition constant, extra-psychiatric factors such as socioeconomic status, family connections, marital status, and legal representation affect the likelihood of a person's commitment, whether the commitment is voluntary or involuntary.

Szasz (1974) presents the more radical argument that mental disorder is not illness at all, but rather, that it is a myth. Szasz begins with the observation that certain criteria are necessary for any phenomenon to be considered a disease. First, there must be a physical lesion of some sort. This requirement cannot be met in many if not most types of mental disorder. Second, he argues that while physical symptoms are objective and independent of cultural forces, the same cannot be said of mental symptoms. The latter are subjective and dependent on culture for their meaning and interpretation.

Szasz argues that mental illnesses are really symptoms of "problems of living" that are subject to definition in the context of competing values. The standards through which behaviour is labelled disorder are social, psychological, ethical, and legal, rather than medical. Rather than being something one "has," mental illness is something one "does" or "is." Its symptoms are a matter of social judgement regarding how well a particular action fits the concept of "normal" in a given circumstance and in a particular cultural milieu. In Szasz's view, psychiatrists are agents of social control whose principal function is to preserve the status quo.

While social scientists have contributed many insights to the understanding of mental illness, those giving credence to the medical model are not without substance in their criticism of the labelling approach. There is evidence that biological, chemical, and genetic factors play some role in some disorders. There is more to mental illness, the critics argue, than labelling alone.

SUMMARY

Arriving at an acceptable definition of mental illness has been extremely contentious. Objectivists maintain that mental illness is concrete and can be delineated from mental health on the basis of prevailing community standards. Relativists point out that such standards are both vague and subject to change. Nonconforming unusual behaviour is targeted, especially by professional groups, as disorder. In this way, much deviance has been medicalized — transformed by psychiatrists into medical maladies requiring remedy under their expert supervision.

Relativists point out that even professionals, let alone laypersons, cannot agree on who is mentally fit and who is incompetent. The medical community is famous for its inability to make predictions about the future behaviour of those designated as disordered. The intermediary position, taken by most, accepts that some forms of mental disorder are real but also takes account of the definitional process, especially when the symptoms are less than severe. The comparatively few extreme cases are relatively easier to categorize than the comparatively large number in which symptoms are mild and indistinct.

Mental illness is one of the most difficult forms of deviance to enumerate. Official information is deficient because it only counts those treated. Official data are also sensitive to a host of confounding factors, including locations of institutions and health-care personnel, the distribution of affluence, public tolerance or indignation, and variable definitions and diagnoses. Hospital admissions are useless as an indicator because they cannot differentiate between old cases (readmissions) and new cases. Data derived from surveys suffer from the varying assessments and definitions applied by medical personnel. Canadian data on the distribution of mental illness are weak. Therefore, discussions of estimates and correlates must be considered with caution.

Three predominant perspectives inform the understanding of the causes and consequences of mental disorder for individuals and society. Physiological approaches emphasize genetics, anatomical damage, and chemical imbalances, while psychological perspectives highlight the roles of deficient socialization and emotional trauma on the retardation of normal personality development in childhood. Sociological perspectives approach the understanding of mental disorder in two ways. The first explores the impacts of social structure (e.g., age, social isolation, unemployment), while the second investigates the deleterious impacts of the labelling process (the application of social stigma).

Historically, perspectives on mental incapacity have changed dramatically. In the past, people believed that the disordered were either possessed by demons or being punished for their own or their parents' sins. Demonological accounts gave way first to biological and later to psychoanalytic explanations. With differing interpretations of causes, different "treatments" have evolved, moving from torture through institutional confinement to, most recently, de-institutionalization.

The intentions of de-institutionalization were to release into the community people who were capable of functioning adequately in society, thereby reducing the dehumanization and stigma to which they were subject. While treatment in the community, as it is currently conducted, is less expensive, one of its negative effects has been to contribute to the growing problem posed by the homeless fending for themselves on the streets of North American cities.

Psychoanalytic theory and its attendant treatment program, called psychoanalysis, was formulated by Sigmund Freud. The Freudian perspective, which emphasizes personality development and the unconscious mind, has been very influential in the evolution of modern psychiatry. Freud envisaged the personality as comprising three parts — the id (animal instinct) and the superego (moral conscience) are mediated by the ego. He considered a balance of these components essential to mental health. Imbalance and fixation on a developmental stage from childhood were the prime sources of disorder, the treatment of which could best be accomplished by regressing a patient back to the point in time where the problem initially manifested itself. Freudian theory, as a pioneering approach, has been heavily criticized for being extreme, overly deterministic, untestable, and culturally specific.

The list of different classifications for mental disorders is lengthy. The major categorizations are outlined in the DSM IV and include the following: (1) disorders first evident in infants, children, and adolescents (retardation, learning and communication disorders); (2) delirium, dementia, and amnestic and other disorders (intoxication, organic disease); (3) substance-related disorders (drugs and alcohol); (4) schizophrenia and other psychotic disorders; (5) personality disorders (paranoid personality disorder, antisocial personality disorder; (6) mood disorders (depression); (7) anxiety disorders (phobias, obsessive and compulsive disorders, somatoform disorders); (8) dissociative disorders (amnesia, multiple personality disorder; (9) sex and gender identity disorders (paraphilia, gender identity disorder, sex dysfunction); (10) eating disorders (anorexia nervosa, bulimia); and (11) impulse control disorders (behavioural addictions, kleptomania).

A number of points raised in the discussion of these maladies are important. First, mental illness is not rare. For example, mild depression is to mental illness what the common cold is to physical disorder. Second, a common error that people make when discussing multiple-personality disorder is to confuse this illness with schizophrenia. They are not the same thing. Third, homosexuality, once considered by the psychiatric community as a form of psycho-sexual disorder, is now properly regarded as within the bounds of normal sexual expression and, therefore, as a healthy lifestyle.

There are two fundamental approaches to accounting for the distribution of mental disorder in North America. The first approach views the relationship between demographics and disorder as real — for example, being old (age) or single (marital status) increases the risk of experiencing mental distress. The second approach sees the relationship between demographics and mental illness as more apparent than real. For example, females are no more distressed than males but simply feel more comfortable confessing their emotional and psychological problems. Higher-class people are no less disordered than lower-class people. Rather, because they can afford private treatment, their mental illnesses are unrecorded. With such caveats in mind, available evidence suggests that more males than females are sociopaths, that more females than males suffer from mood disorders, and that males and females are schizophrenic in more equal numbers. Being single is the best predictor of mental disorder, especially for males. Other less powerful predictors are living in a city, being a recent immigrant, and being elderly. Class position is related to many types of disorder, particularly the more severe forms. The three accounts of the class–disorder correlation involve stress, social reaction, and drift. The three primary forms of treatment — psychotherapy, organic therapy, and custodial care — are also class-related, with the latter two approaches used predominantly where patients have comparatively few social and economic resources.

Becoming a mental patient takes the form of a career. The process begins with the experience of stress. Two important career contingencies are the presence or absence of internal personal resilience and external social support. Families and friends ignore the disordered conduct until the afflicted person can no longer function, at which point action is taken. Stigma is brought on by formal recognition, treatment, and perhaps even involuntary commitment. The possibilities of commitment have increased of late with passage of statutes such as Brian's Law.

While there has been movement toward de-institutionalization in recent years, the mental hospital has and continues to be the predominant provider of care for the mentally disordered. Much of the research on this institution has emphasized one or the other of two sets of problems. The first approach highlights the tension between the contradictory goals of treatment and control and points out how these competing objectives widen the gulf separating caregiver from patient. The second perspective emphasizes the deleterious effects on patients of life in total institutions that are inadequately financed and are operated by poorly qualified staff with low morale.

Questionable success rates, stories of patient abuse, and high operating costs have fuelled a massive shift to out-patient care. This transition has solved some problems and created others. Most specifically, the movement has been credited with increasing the ranks of "street people," many of whom cannot adequately care for themselves. Such individuals pose unique challenges for police and correctional personnel.

DISCUSSION QUESTIONS

1. Discuss the complexities plaguing definitions of mental health and mental disorder.

2. Explain the principal differences in the approaches to mental illness causation taken by physiologists, psychologists, and sociologists. Within the sociological approach, discuss the two principal perspectives used to investigate mental disorder.

3. Explain how society's view of the causation and treatment of mental illness has changed over time.

4. Treatment and control are competing goals in the response to mental illness. Is this state of affairs necessary? How might this conflict in goals be reduced? What implications for patients, for mental-health caregivers, and for government might emerge from efforts to reduce the conflict in goals?

5. What are the positive and negative effects on Canadian society of the de-institutionalization of many mentally disordered people? How do these benefits and liabilities reflect or mesh with the vested interests of professionals, politicians, social activists, patients, and their families?

WEB LINKS

Canadian Mental Health Association
http://www.cmha.ca
> The CMHA Web site contains much information, including useful pamphlets on various aspects of mental health and mental illness. Click on "Research" and then "Publications." To view these pamphlets, you will need a copy of Acrobat Reader.

Internet Mental Health
http://www.mentalhealth.com
> Internet Mental Health is a free encyclopedia of mental-health information, designed by Dr. Philip Long and programmed by Brian Chow. It contains a description of over 50 mental disorders, on-line diagnosis, research findings, bulletin boards, and more.

About Mental Health
http://www.camh.net/mental_health/index.html
> This section of the Centre for Addiction and Mental Health site includes papers on many types of mental illness.

Mental Health
http://www.hc-sc.gc.ca/hppb/mentalhealth
> This section of the Health Canada Web site includes information and papers on Canada's mental health service systems and on specific mental-health problems and disorders, such as anxiety disorders, mood disorders, physical–mental health interactions, and schizophrenia.

Mental Illness and Violence: Proof or Stereotype?
http://www.hc-sc.gc.ca/hppb/mentalhealth/pubs/mental_illness/index.htm#tc
> This paper examines the relationship between mental illness and violence, using studies conducted in Canada and the United States.

RECOMMENDED READINGS

Gallagher, B.J., and C.J. Rita. (1995). *The Sociology of Mental Illness* (4th ed.). Englewood Cliffs, NJ.: Prentice-Hall.
An American text that provides an excellent overview of mental illness and society's response to it.

Globe and Mail. (2000). Special Interest Supplement: Mood Disorders and Mental Health. (June 12):C1–C6.
A series of articles on breaking issues on mental disorders and their treatment in Canada.

Goffman, E. (1961). *Asylums: Essays on the Social Situation of Mental Patients and Other Inmates*. New York: Doubleday.
This is the pioneering work on mental hospitals. Issues raised by Goffman in this early work remain highly relevant to current concerns about dealing effectively and justly with the mentally disordered.

Menzies, R.J. (1989). *Survival of the Sanest: Order and Disorder in a Pre-Trial Clinic.* Toronto: University of Toronto Press.
Provides an in-depth analysis of the workings of a pre-trial clinic involving mentally ill individuals caught up in the criminal justice system.

Rosenhan, D. (1973). "On Being Sane in Insane Places." *Science* 179:250–58.
A classic piece on attitudes toward and treatment of the mentally ill.

Shimrat, I. (1997). *Call Me Crazy: Stories from the Mad Movement.* Vancouver: Press Gang.
Discusses issues concerning mental disorder in Canada from a perspective that is critical of the psychiatry movement. Presents alternative responses to disorder that go beyond psychiatric hospitalization.

Scull, A., C. MacKenzie, and N. Hervey. (1997). *Masters of Bedlam: The Transformation of the Mad Doctoring Trade.* Princeton: Princeton University Press.
Uses a case study approach to examine how structural forces in a particular historical context shaped the lives of "mad doctors" and their work in the asylum. Shows how current central issues are similar to those of the past.

Absolute liability: A form of legal liability in which intent does not have to be proven. Absolute liability is seldom found in criminal law but is common in administrative law and regulatory law. For example, if a fisher is found with undersize lobster in the hold, the fisher cannot argue that there was no intent to catch or keep the undersize lobster.

Actus reus: One of the two components legally necessary to constitute a crime, the other being *mens rea*. *Actus reus* refers to the physical component of a crime: the act of committing the crime (e.g., actually breaking into a car and stealing the stereo).

Age-segregated society: A society organized around age categories and where contact between age groups is limited. Social roles and physical locations of individuals are determined by age. For example, youths attend school while adults work at occupations. Youths have limited interaction with adults other than their parents and teachers.

Aggregate: Large collective of individuals who share one or more common characteristics, but who do not interact, communicate, or work together. To study aggregates, sociologists sum up the individual characteristics of these collectives. How many women are there? What is their average GPA? Is there an association between these two characteristics? When this approach is taken, the researcher is typically dealing with the groups as the unit of analysis.

Agoraphobia: A form of anxiety disorder in which a person experiences intense fear of open spaces or being in public.

Anal stage: From Freud's model of infant psychological development, the stage when the infant's erotic pleasure is centred in the bowels and anus. The infants' experience with this stage as they interact with parents and caregivers is thought to have a profound effect on the formation of personality. If an infant is handled with warmth and naturalness and there is no demand that the bowel movements be controlled, then the child will simply become controlled as it develops and wishes to be like older children and adults. The freedom of this stage is thought to encourage personality traits of spontaneity and generosity. In contrast, premature strictness from adults can bring earlier control, but it will also encourage a fear of spontaneity, a desire for personal control and possessions, and distrust of others. Though controversial, this portrait Freud paints has become part of our language and culture, and it is taken for granted that we must often look into the earliest infant experiences of individuals to try to understand the psychological forces behind their crimes or other social behaviours.

Androcentrism: A view of the world that focuses on the roles and life experiences of men and ignores or denies the separate experience of women. Feminism can be seen, in part, as a critique of androcentrism and as an effort to analyze and make apparent the distinct social situation and perspectives of women.

Anger rape: Sexual assaults that are unusually motivated by hate and frustration. These assaults are more brutal and there is an urge to demean and humiliate.

Anomie: Literally "without norms," a term referring to a social situation in which social norms and values are unclear or confused. Originally developed by Émile Durkheim (1858–1917) to describe a social condition in which individuals lack a sense of social regulation, anomie can occur for a variety of reasons. Durkheim's main concern was that it would arise in modern societies that are complex and impersonal. In modern societies, people are acutely interdependent, but they lack intimate social contact with each other. In such situations, people lose a sense of connection to others and social solidarity breaks down. The concept can also be helpful in partially understanding the experience of colonized Aboriginal peoples. As their traditional values are disrupted, they do not identify with the new cultural values imposed upon them: they lose a sense of authoritative normative regulation. American sociologist Robert Merton used the term more narrowly to refer to a situation where people's goals — what they wanted to achieve — were beyond their means. Merton argued that societies like the United States, which stress material success as the central goal for individuals, create anomie among those who do not believe in their chance of success through conventional avenues (a good education, good job, good income, etc.). In this situation, people are induced toward unconventional routes to attain wealth — including crime. They want to win the game without regard to the rules. In this context, anomie arises from normative conflict or dissonance. More recently, the term has been used in a more individually-focused way to talk about problems of immigrant youth when faced with a new culture or about the identity crises that often erupt during the age transition from youth to adult.

Anorexia nervosa: A form of mental disorder in which individuals are obsessed with their body image and weight and proceed to starve themselves regardless of their actual bodily condition. Sufferers can recover from the illness, but treatment is difficult and often fails, resulting in serious illness or death.

Atavism: A tendency to reproduce ancestral type in plants or in animals; to resemble one's grandparents or great-grandparents more than parents. This concept was used by Cesare Lombroso (1835–1909) to describe a type of criminal he called the born criminal. The atavistic criminal was one representing an earlier stage of human evolution (thus representing the ancestral type more than the parental type). This ancestral type was identified by Lombroso through several stigmatized physical characteristics — including the length of ear lobes and fingers and the bone structure of the head. This supposed physical degeneracy was associated with moral degeneracy, and thus more frequent criminal behaviour. Research established that these physical stigmata were not found to be especially associated with criminals and this particular theory of criminality was rejected.

Attachment: Affective personal ties to others. In Travis Hirschi's work, aspects of the "social bond."

Automatism: A rarely used legal defence in which the accused, while sane, claims to have committed an offence involuntarily because of a psychological or physical condition.

Beliefs: The degree to which an individual believes in conventional values, morality, and the legitimacy of law. In Travis Hirschi's work, aspects of the "social bond."

Bourgeoisie: From the French meaning a citizen of a city (burgh). In feudal times, the cities were the place of trade and business and became populated by a growing class of merchants, professions, and craftspersons. These city dwellers were legally free and came to be seen as having a social status between the serf and peasant classes and the land-owning aristocratic class. The economic interests and social attitudes of this new middle class came into conflict with the restrictions of feudalism and aristocratic rule and eventually they were able to grasp power and transform social values. Politically, they are associated with the bloodless revolution of Great Britain in 1688, which established parliamentary superiority over the Crown and the French Revolution in 1789. This new class also had a distinctive lifestyle of domestic refinement, literacy, and respectability that came to be referred to as "bourgeois." The term bourgeois class, or bourgeoisie, was used by Marx to refer to the corporate or capitalist class in modern societies that he claimed was the ruling class.

Bulimia: A mental disorder associated with food and body image. The person with this disorder will engage in binge eating followed by periods of vomiting or using laxatives.

Capital punishment: Execution of the offender as a punishment for crime. The root of the word capital is Latin and refers to the head, *capo*, the locus of life. Capital punishment is widely imposed in world societies, but not in the countries of western Europe or Canada. The last hanging in Canada took place in 1962, after which the Canadian government routinely advised the Governor General to commute any death sentences to life imprisonment. Capital punishment was formally abolished by changes to the law in 1976. A free vote was held in the House of Commons in 1987 and the majority supported the continued abolition of the death penalty.

Capitalism: An economic system in which capital (the goods or wealth used to produce other goods for profit) is privately owned and profit is reinvested so as to accumulate capital. Capitalism is based on free markets and free consumer choice. It is assumed that people acting as free individuals will make choices in the marketplace that will lead to optimal personal and social benefit and to the most rational and effective use of economic resources.

Case law: Equivalent to the term "common law." Previously decided cases or precedents are the main source, along with

statutes, of Anglo-Canadian and American law. Quebec has a civil law system where decisions are based on a legal code. Judges in Quebec are not bound by precedent and are free to apply the principles of the code in deciding civil cases. The criminal law in Quebec, as in other provinces, is established by the Criminal Code and the decisions of Quebec courts are referred to by other judges in deciding criminal cases. Decisions made in previous cases are binding on judges if the facts of the case are similar and if the decision was made by a superior court of the same province. Judgments made by courts outside a province may be referred to in cases, but only decisions of the Supreme Court bind judges in all provinces.

Cause: Those factors that produce a particular effect (e.g., influences that might cause an individual to commit a crime). Causal analysis is a positivist approach to criminology. In order for something to be a cause it must meet three criteria: (a) the cause must happen before the effect; (b) there must be a correlation between the causal variable and the effect variable; (c) all other possible reasons for the correlation must be examined, tested and discarded.

Celerity: The speed with which guilt is determined and punishment is administered after the commission of an offence. It is thought that punishments provide greater deterrence when there is greater celerity.

Census: A count of all of the members of a population. For example, a count of all Canadians or a count of all federal inmates. A census study is usually too large to be economically viable as a database for researchers; instead, a sample is used.

Certainty: In deterrence theory, it is argued that criminal law and punishment effect greater deterrence when there is a strong probability that the offender will be caught.

Chicago School: The world's first school of sociology, established at the University of Chicago in 1892. It had a major influence on the development of social research and theory. Chicago's exceptionally rapid population growth and urban expansion provided a fruitful opportunity to develop and test theories about the effects of urbanism on culture and social relationships. In criminology, the school focused on the social causes of urban crime and its prevention. The school has a macro perspective that examines the ecology of the city and a micro perspective that focuses on differential association of individuals.

Class: The term is used in various ways in sociology. It usually implies a group of individuals sharing a common situation within a social structure, usually their shared place in the structure of ownership and control of the means of production. Karl Marx (1818–1883), for example, distinguished four classes in capitalist societies: a bourgeois class that owns and controls the means of production; a petite bourgeoisie of small business and professionals; a proletariat of wage workers; and a lumpenproletariat of people in poverty and social disorganization who are excluded from the wage-earning economy. In land-based economies, class structures are based on an individual's relationship to the ownership and control of land. Class can also refer to groups of individuals with a shared characteristic relevant in some socioeconomic measurement or ranking (for example, all individuals earning over $50 000 per year). It then has a statistical meaning rather than a meaning based on social relationships. While class is extensively used in discussing social structure, sociologists also rely on the concept of status, which offers a more complex portrait in which individuals within a class can be seen as having quite differentiated social situations.

Class faction: Usually used by political economy theorists in discussion of the corporate class to acknowledge significant segmentation of this class. It is commonly linked to such distinctions as that between finance-based capital and industrial-based capital, each viewed as having different interests and perspectives. This is a useful concept in avoiding the simplistic view that the "corporate class" is a necessarily unified group.

Classical school of criminology: Considered to be the first formal school of criminology, classical criminology is associated with eighteenth and early nineteenth century reforms to the administration of justice and the prison system. Associated with authors such as Cesare Beccaria (1738–1794), Jeremy Bentham (1748–1832), Samuel Romilly (1757–1818), and others, this school brought the emerging philosophy of the Enlightenment — liberalism and utilitarianism — to the justice system, advocating principles of rights, fairness, and due process in place of retribution, arbitrariness, and brutality. Critical criminologists see in these reforms a tool by which the new industrial order of capitalism was able to maintain class rule through appearing to apply objective and neutral rules of justice rather than obvious and direct class domination through coercion. Criminal law is stated in terms of moral universals rather than being seen as rules that simply protect the interests of property holders. The claims to fairness in the justice system provide a sense of legitimation for the state and the order it represents.

Classless society: A society that does not have a hierarchy of different social classes and in which individuals have similar resources of wealth, status, and power. It is found in simple hunter–gatherer societies (like the pygmies of the Democratic Republic of Congo [Zaire]), and is also a socialist vision of a future society founded on collective ownership of the means of production.

Claustrophobia: A mental disorder characterized by fear of being in confined spaces.

Commitment: The degree to which an individual pursues conventional goals. In Travis Hirschi's work, aspects of the "social bond."

Compulsive disorder: A form of mental disorder in which a person exhibits recurrent needs to perform certain actions. Individuals may, for example, repeatedly wash their hands, wipe door knobs, repeat certain words, or rearrange objects into a certain order.

Conflict subculture: A community subculture characterized by violence and conflict. This subculture arises in neighbourhoods that are cut off from the mainstream of society and that are not able to provide access either to legitimate opportunities or to illegitimate opportunities.

Containment theory: A theory developed by Walter Reckless in which he uses the term containment much as others use the term controls. Containments include a strong ego, a sense of personal responsibility, and ability to accept disappointment and frustration. These personal traits "contain" pressures towards deviance and thus stabilize the individual. Outer containments would include parental rules, school regulations, and supervision by adults.

Corporate crime: A crime committed by corporate employees or owners to financially advantage a corporation. It may involve acts like committing fraud, polluting the environment, making unsafe products, and permitting dangerous work environments.

Correlation: Sometimes simply called "association." Criminologists working in the positivist perspective tend to look at the social world in terms of variables (anything that varies within a population or group rather than being constant). Everyone in a classroom is a student so that is a constant; however, there is variation between class members in, for example their sex, age, income, GPA, religion and ethnic heritage. If one gathers information from the whole class on these variables, we might begin to see that some variables vary (are associated) in patterned ways. People with a particular ethnic heritage may tend to be more religious than those from other heritages. This would suggest a correlation; as one variable varies, so does the other. If there were more students of that particular ethnic heritage in the class, then religiosity for the group would also increase. If one goes up and so does the other, this is referred to as a positive correlation. If one variable goes up and the other down, this is called a negative or inverse relationship. For example, crime rates decrease as age increases.

Crime: Crime is a subset of what has been defined as deviance, but the relationship is not hard and fast. Some social scientists prefer to define crime as a violation of the *Criminal Code*. Other broaden the boundaries to include violation of other laws intended to protect the public and still others define it to include any socially harmful actions. Criminologists usually define crime as a violation of law but not exclusively criminal law.

Crime funnel: The image of a "funnel" refers to the much lower number of crimes detected and punished by the criminal justice system (coming out the bottom) than the number actually committed (going in the top). In this model, it is assumed that crime is an objective occurrence; it is thought to exist when certain illegal acts take place. This is what is called a "realist" definition of crime. Symbolic interactionists and phenomenologists, however, see "crime" as something created and defined by processes of social interaction, interpretation, and official response. They reject both the "realist" assumption and the concept of the crime funnel.

Crime rates: A method of expressing the amount of crime in relation to the population. For example, we might say there are 3 murders per 100 000 people in Canada. By using the relationship to population and standardizing this (per 100 000), researchers are able to compare crime rates across jurisdictions.

Criminal law: Laws enforced by state prosecution that prohibit and provide punishment for acts or omissions that are regarded as damaging to the public and to the social order of the society. In Canada, criminal law is principally contained in the *Criminal Code*, originally passed by Parliament in 1892.

Criminal subculture: A culture of a group or neighbourhood where crime is seen as normal and even justifiable and where there is easy access to criminal activities. Young people exposed to this subculture can become socialized into it and adopt criminal behaviour as a way of living.

Criminogenesis: The creation and causation of crime. Some social conditions or structures can be seen as creating crime. Just as hospitals can create disease like infections among their patients, so might prisons or even courts or youth correction centres be "criminogenic."

Criminogenic conditions: The social conditions that lead to or cause crime. Poverty in neighbourhoods may underlie a rise in street muggings, for example, or prison institutions might unintentionally provide inmates with socialization into a continued criminal life style.

Crisis of legitimacy: A condition in which the government or political order of a community does not command sufficient commitment or authority to govern by general consent. The government, or anyone in authority, is no longer seen as legitimate. In these situations, there may be civil unrest or revolution, or governments may start to rely on force rather than consent to maintain their rule. From a political economy perspective, there is a major source of a legitimation crisis in the economic transformation of the world in conjunction with a globalization process that to many seems dominated by international corporations. This transformation raises the possibility that citizens will see the economic system with its growing concentration of power for corporations and international bureaucracies as illegitimate and will reject governments that attempt to accommodate this new world economic order.

Culture conflict: A conflict of cultural values and norms that may arise between differing interest groups within a society. Some of these interest groups are distinct cultures or subcultures that have come into being through immigration or territorial expansion. Frequently, the dominant culture excludes the minority culture and creates the perception that the new culture is inferior. This may lead to members of the dominant group feeling free to discriminate, and the minority group may come to internalize a sense of inferiority.

Dark figure of crime: The amount of crime that is unreported or unknown. The total amount of crime in a community consists of crimes that are known or recorded plus the dark figure of crime. Criminologists have used differing methods (like victimization surveys) to try to decrease the amount of unknown or unrecorded crime. The idea of a dark figure of crime is based on a positivist approach to criminology and a realist assumption about crime.

Date rape: A sexual assault of a person, typically a woman, while on a date. This type of assault is usually of the form called "power rape."

Decriminalization: Removing a prohibited activity from the *Criminal Code*, thus making it non-criminal. The activity may continue to be regulated or controlled through other legal mechanisms.

Defining the situation: The process through which humans go when trying to comprehend the social situations in which they find themselves. Social interactions are given meaning by people as they interpret the social world and negotiate with others. The concept is associated with symbolic interactionism and phenomenology and is in contrast to macro-structural studies. The structural views tend to focus on the situation individuals are in rather than on the processes by which they define their situation. The term was first used by W.I. Thomas (1863–1947).

Definition of the situation: *See* Defining the situation.

De-institutionalization: The movement of chronic mental patients from custodial care to community care. It was thought that patients would be better off in the community and that community care would be cheaper than institutional care. Many communities found that their resources were inadequate, and uncared-for patients began wandering the streets.

Deterrence: As used in criminal justice, crime prevention achieved through the fear of punishment. Deterrence theory refers to the set of beliefs and assumptions that lead a researcher to predict that fear of punishment will prevent crime.

Deterrence — general: As used in criminal justice, crime prevention achieved through instilling fear in the general population through the punishment of offenders. *See* deterrence — specific.

Deterrence — specific: As used in criminal justice, crime prevention achieved through instilling fear in the specific individual being punished, such that he or she refrains from future violation of the law. Also referred to as individual deterrence.

Deviance: Deviance is constituted by the reactions of observers to an action. Something is labelled deviant because an individual or groups takes offence and reacts negatively, usually in a controlling fashion.

Deviant career: In common use, "career" refers to the sequence of stages and positions that people move through during their employment in an occupational sector. This model of stages has also been applied to analyzing the course of an individual's involvement with deviant or criminal activity.

Differential association: Developed by Edwin Sutherland in the 1930s, this was a radical explanation for criminal behaviour, since it argues that crime, like any social behaviour, is learned in association with others. The phrase "differential association" simply means that people have different social situations and thus learn different things. What is learned is cultural material. If an individual regularly associates with criminals and is relatively isolated form law-abiding citizens, then he or she is more like to engage in crime. First the individuals learn some specific skills need to commit crime (how to open a locked vault), and second, ideas that justify and normalize crime. This concept leads directly to a subcultural theory of crime that asserts that not all groups in society uphold the same values or norms and for some groups crime is normative. The effect of association depends on variables like priority, frequency, and duration.

Differential identification: A concept that extends the theory of differential association by suggesting that in order for a person to be influenced by criminal traditions the person must identify with the definitions of deviance held by those who see crime or deviance as acceptable.

Differential illegitimate opportunity: In Cloward's and Ohlin's extension of Robert Merton's theory of anomie, they note that just because access to legitimate opportunity is restricted for some individuals, this does not mean these individuals have access to illegitimate opportunity. Access to illegitimate opportunity is also structured; some individuals have access to these opportunities and some do not. Access to illegitimate opportunity is usually structured by the kind of neighbourhood the individual lives in.

Differential opportunity: In Robert Merton's theory of anomie, access to the opportunities to use legitimate means to achieve cultural goals is structured. Access is restricted for some groups of individuals and these persons are more likely to be motivated to turn to crime or deviance in order to achieve the cultural goals.

Dissociative disorders: A form of mental illness in which a person becomes dissociated from his or her life. Examples of this would be amnesia (other than that form caused by trauma or organic disease) and multiple-personality disorder.

Double doctoring: The practice of those with a drug addiction of visiting two or more doctors in order to obtain prescriptions for drugs that have some street value or have non-medical uses.

Double failure: In Ohlin's and Cloward's extension of Robert Merton's theory, a condition in which access to both legitimate opportunity and illegitimate opportunity is restricted. In addition, individuals do not possess the physical characteristics or bravado to be successful in a conflict subculture. Experiencing this double failure, these individuals are predicted to turn to forms of retreatism, like drug use or alcoholism.

Double rape: The experience of rape victims during police investigations and court proceedings where their credibility is questioned and they are treated as if under trial rather than the accused.

Due process: A central concept of the criminal justice system that gives priority to values and practices that protect the rights of the offenders from the coercive power of the state. This protection includes, in principle, strict regulation of police enforcement and investigation procedures, independent and impartial judicial process, and imposition of proportional and justifiable punishment.

Duration: In differential association theory, the length of the exposure to association with deviant values, viewed as a factor in determining whether this exposure will affect the person's chances of becoming committed to those values.

Duress: A legal defence available to an accused for crimes less serious than murder or kidnapping. The accused must prove to the court that he or she was coerced by someone into committing the crime and that the consequence of not doing so would be immediate and irreparable serious harm to the offender or another person. For example, someone who smuggles drugs to prevent the murder of an abducted child.

Ecological school: Developed by criminologists in the early part of the twentieth century, this research looks at the relationships of various areas of a community to each other and the ways in which particular forms of behaviour may flourish in some communities and not in others. Central concepts are symbiosis and invasion, dominance and succession, ideas linked to the Chicago school.

Egalitarian family: A family system based on equality and without dominating authority. It is in stark contrast to a patriarchal family, in which obedience and duty to the senior male is imposed on all members. It usually refers to an equal relationship between the adult partners, though it can also refer to a permissive, rather than authoritarian, parent–child relationship. In North American families, this family form is most likely to be found among young and well-educated couples. The term "symmetrical family" is sometimes used as an equivalent. The idea is in many respects an ideal, rather than descriptive of typical family relationships.

Ego: In psychology, the term refers to the self-identity. In Freud's psychoanalytic theory, the ego is the outcome of the individual's struggle to adapt his or her basic drives (the "id") to the imperative control of society and culture (the "superego"). Between their drives and the coercive influence of social expectation, individuals create a sphere of unique personality.

Enlightenment: A philosophy that provided the foundation for the classical school of criminology. The enlightenment period focused on the idea of the natural rights of the individual and on the importance of reason in establishing policy and practice.

Enslavement hypothesis: The claim that drug users can be so overpowered by drugs as to become permanently addicted after one or two exposures. There is little evidence to support this hypothesis.

Entrapment: A legal defence available to an accused. The accused must prove to the court that he or she was induced by law enforcement agents to commit a crime that he or she would not otherwise have contemplated.

Epidemiology: A term used largely in medical sociology and in describing the study of the occurrence and distribution of diseases. Such investigations look for changes in the frequency of occurrence (or incidence) and association of diseases with particular physical or social locations. Epidemiological research can be conducted on crime — viewed as analogous to a disease of society — and a host of other social problems.

Ethnic succession: The process of successive waves of immigrants establishing themselves in a society. The most recent immigrants sometimes find illegal activity as a vehicle of economic success and social mobility. They fill the deviant and criminal positions that were once occupied by other ethnic groups now successful in legitimate enterprises.

Explanation: All science provides explanation by means of a theory that will usually specify causal relationships according to some law or pattern.

Extralegal characteristics: The non-legal characteristics of individuals or of social situations that shape law-enforcement or judicial decisions.

Feminist theory: There is not a single feminist theory, but all share in an attempt to understand the unique social, economic, and political position of women, with the objective of liberation from status inequality. Feminist theory challenges the claim to objectivity of previous social science and calls it into question as being male-centred and a component of the hegemonic rule of patriarchy.

Fetishism: A form of sexual disorder in which the person becomes sexually aroused by inanimate objects, such as underwear, fur, leather or rubber, or becomes erotically fixated on a non-sexual area of the body like the feet, the hair or the hands.

Feudalism: A system of economic and social organization found historically in diverse areas of the world, including China, Japan and other parts of Asia, Africa, South America and many countries of eastern and western Europe. In western Europe, feudalism was at its height around 1000 to 1500. The system was founded on a web of military obligations between powerful overlords and their vassals. Vassals, who were usually landlords of knightly rank, owed duties of military service in return for grants of land (fiefs) from the overlord. The land, and the military obligations, were usually passed from father to son. The usual economic foundation of the system was the feudal manor, an agricultural organization that included a central farm owned by the landlord and small land holdings for a class of bonded farm labourers (serfs). The serfs were required to work the central manorial farm and to provide the lord with produce and money payments in return for their own rights to land use. The system gradually declined as cities and towns grew, money became the basis for economic transactions, and power became centralized in nation states under monarchies. Loss of rural population from plague also hastened the end of this system of economic organization, especially in England.

First-degree murder: An offence under the *Criminal Code* of Canada. To be charged with this offence, one of three conditions must be met: (1) the killing is planned and deliberate; (2) it involves killing a police officer or prison personnel on duty; or (3) the killing was committed during the commission of certain other criminal offences, e.g., armed robbery.

Formal control: Those controls or restrictions placed on individuals by authorized agents of control like police, courts, or school principals. These controls are linked to deterrence theory.

Freud: Sigmund Freud (1856–1939) was the founder of psychoanalysis, the theory that the shaping of an individual's personality occurs in childhood and is influenced by experiences in physical development and erotic exploration. Psychoanalysis also advocates therapeutic treatment of psychological disturbances through the recovery of infant and childhood traumatic experiences and their reinterpretation by the now mature ego.

Functionalism: Also known as structural functionalism or the consensus perspective. In the social sciences, functionalism is associated with teleological explanation: explaining the existence of features of society by reference to their end results. Society is thought to resemble complex forms of organic life, like the human body. Any individual aspect of culture and of social institutions and social organization is then assumed, in a stable and efficiently running society, to contribute to the working of the society as a whole. Just as the function of the heart or lungs can be understood in relation to their purpose of maintaining the human body, so can the functions of the principal features of society be understood by how they support the whole. Functionalism is useful in thinking about how culture, social structures, principal institutions and social organization are related, but because it focuses on reproducing the existing society, functionalism tends to be conservative in its perspective.

Functions of deviance: From a functionalist perspective, most aspects of society must serve a positive role in supporting society's efficient working or they would not persist. These positive roles are typically stated in terms of encouraging solidarity and integration, and bringing stability. Émilie Durkheim (1858–1917), who is associated with this perspective, was the first to ask what could be the positive social function of crime, a persistent aspect of many societies. Durkheim argues that it serves the function of clarifying moral rules and establishing the moral boundaries of the community. In a sense, crime allows the community to flex its moral muscles and refresh its commitment to guiding values.

Gateway hypothesis: The claim that the use of soft drugs inevitably leads to the use of harder drugs. There is little evidence to support this hypothesis, though this assumption shapes criminal law penalties for soft drug offences, especially in the United States.

Generalized other: A term used by George Herbert Mead (1863–1931) to refer to an individual's recognition that other members of his or her society hold specific values and expectations about behaviour. Individuals then react to these assumed expectations of others when they socially interact, thus orienting themselves to the norms and values of their community or group.

Gross population counts: Used to calculate crime rates on the basis of a gross count of the population of the area in question. The rate is expressed as the incidence of occurrences within that population: for example 1 in 100. This statistic can be misleading when comparing the rates in different communities, since some communities may have more or less of those population members who are higher risk for committing crime. Some may have a high percentage of seniors, whose crime rate is low, while others may have more young people whose crime rate is high.

Guardianship: An aspect of the routine activities approach to understanding crime and, in particular, victimization. This approach argues that three key factors are required for crime to happen: a motivated offender, a suitable target, and ineffective guardianship of that target. Effective guardianship involves security precautions like locks on bikes or security lights in the backyard. Measures like these should reduce the risk of being victimized.

Homicide: The killing of one person by another person. Not all homicides are classified as murder or as manslaughter, since they may lack criminal intent.

Humanism: Often contrasted to positivism, which sees the individual as an object subjected to external social forces. Humanism starts from the assumption that each individual has consciousness, and therefore, has a will, intent, and desires, all of which also contribute to shaping the situation of the individual.

Hypothesis: A supposition or claim that can be tested by the use of measurable evidence. The claim is investigated by examining the relationship between variables, for example, smoking and the incidence of lung cancer. In the classic model of science, testable statements are deduced from a theory, and research is undertaken to provide evidence to support or refute that theory.

I: Term introduced by George Herbert Mead (1863–1931) to refer to the aspect of identity, or self, that reacts uniquely in social interaction to the expectations of others. Individuals each have different experiences and emotions, and their social behaviour can be spontaneous and unpredictable.

Id: In the work of Sigmund Freud (1856–1939), founder of psychoanalysis, the id represents the basic drives and psychic energies of humans as biological organisms. It is untouched by culture and encompasses all that is primitive, natural and pre-civilized in human passions and energies. Freud claimed that the psychic turmoil that humans have experienced in gaining self-consciousness and control of the unconstrained passions of the id remains buried in the unconscious minds of all individuals.

Ideology: A linked set of ideas and beliefs that uphold and justify particular patterns of social relationships. For example, a socialist ideology promotes a transformation of a society based on capitalism, with private ownership and unequal distributions of wealth, into one based on collective ownership and economic equality. A liberal ideology, in contrast, claims that capitalism is the most moral and desirable form of social organization and that capitalism benefits the community as a whole. A patriarchal ideology asserts claims that justify male domination over women in society. A racist ideology claims that people can be classified into distinct races and that some races are inferior to others. Although there is often a dominant ideology in a society supporting its present values and organization, there can also be counter-ideologies that advocate transformation of social relationships.

Incidence: A contrasting term to prevalence. Incidence tells us the frequency of occurrence of some event during a particular time period. For example, there were 581 criminal homicides in 1997, or the rate of crime for one year is higher than for the previous year.

Industrialization: The process of developing an economy founded on manufacturing, using powered technologies. The process of industrialization is associated with the urbanization of society, an extensive division of labour, a wage economy, differentiation of institutions, and growth of mass communications and mass markets. Many western societies are now described as post-industrial, since much economic activity is based on the product of services, knowledge, or symbols rather than physical goods.

Infanticide: An offence under the *Criminal Code* of Canada involving the killing of a child under the age of one year by a mother who has not fully recovered from the effects of childbirth. This is an unusual provision in criminal law because it takes into account the subjective situation of the offender. Anyone other than the mother who committed this offence would be charged with homicide.

Informal control: All of those social controls not included under "formal controls." These would include attachment to parents, community influence, peer-group involvements, or achieving success and prestige in school.

Infrastructure: In Marxist theory or political economy theory, refers to the base or economic foundation of society upon which the culture and social institutions of society are built. Also referred to as the mode of production, this infrastructure includes the technical forces of production and the social arrangements that people enter into to carry out production. It is assumed that most aspects of culture and social organization, including law, ideology, class relations, and political institutions, reflect and are shaped by the mode of production.

Inner containment: Those psychological characteristics that insulate an individual from pressures to commit criminal or deviant acts. They include a sense of personal responsibility, commitment to moral standards, a secure ego, positive self-image, and an ability to cope with frustration.

Inner controls: Those regulations or controls on behaviour that have been internalized through socialization and thus appear to come from inside. In Hirschi's theory, beliefs are an example of inner controls.

Instrumental Theory of Marxism: A perspective claiming that the state's role in society is chiefly shaped by an intimate connection between the capitalist class and the organizations and personnel of the state bureaucracy and political system.

Intensity: In differential association theory, the extent of emotional involvement of individuals with people for whom crime is an acceptable form of behaviour.

Intent: Anticipation of the direct consequences of one's act or failure to act. Criminal law distinguishes this from motive (*see* motive) and it also distinguishes between specific intent and general intent. Specific intent means purposefully and knowingly committing an act with full awareness of its result. General intent refers to those situations in which an individual commits a more serious offence in the process of committing a less serious offence. For example, someone is killed in the act of robbery. The law assumes specific intent for the more serious offence.

Involvement: The degree to which an individual is active in conventional activities. In Travis Hirschi's work, aspects of the "social bond."

John: A customer or client of the sex trade, usually of a prostitute.

Kleptomania: A mental disorder motivating compulsive stealing. The objects stolen often have little or no value to the offender.

Labelling perspective: The view that deviance is not inherent in an act or behaviour, but is simply whatever is labelled or named as deviant. Since law is culturally and historically variable, what is crime today is not necessarily crime yesterday or tomorrow. For example, in 1890, it was legal to sell and use opium, but illegal to attempt suicide. Today, the law is reversed. This shows that deviance is not an objective category, but is created by a process of labelling by law makers and law enforcers. If, therefore, deviance is just a label, it makes sense to ask: where does the label come from? How does the label come to be applied to specific behaviours and to particular individuals? The first question leads to a study of the social origins of law. The second question leads to an examination of the actions of labellers, such as psychiatrists, police, coroners, probation officers, judges, and juries.

Latent function: In functionalist analysis, most aspects of society are thought to serve some function (or role). Sociologists are interested not only in manifest functions, those that are intended or predicted, but also in the incidental or unintended outcomes or latent functions, those that are not intended or predicted. While the manifest function of punishment is retribution and deterrence, the latent function may be to promote community solidarity by creating a moral division between normal citizens and a deviant "them."

Left idealism: A form of instrumental Marxism that sees criminals as victims of a capitalist system. Criminal activity is seen as a form of political resistance or an outcome of deprivation. By diminishing individual responsibility for criminal actions, this approach seems to find solutions only in the transformation of the capitalism system into one of socialist equality.

Left realism: A criminological perspective that focuses on the working class as victims of street crime, state and corporate crime, and women as victims of male crime. By asserting that official studies of crime underestimate victimization of the working class and other marginal groups, they supported community-controlled research as a method of getting at the "reality" of the experience of the marginalized. Social policies to reduce victimization of marginal communities, involve communities in crime prevention, return political control to local communities, and increase police accountability following from this beginning point. Left realism can be contrasted with left idealism, which, while also believing that the structure of capitalism is causative of crime,

tends to see working class crime as acts of rebellion or political resistance. This can be seen as a romantic or idealistic view.

Levels of analysis: There are three levels of analysis: the micro, the meso, and the macro. Each of these refers to distinct types of questions asked by social scientists and to distinct forms of analyzing questions. *See* Units of analysis.

Liberal conflict perspective: An approach that assumes that society consists of a plurality of competing interest groups. This differs from a more radical or Marxist perspective that sees power concentrated in the hands of the economic elite and see most fundamental conflict as class conflict. In a liberal theory, the solutions to conflict do not involve major social change but may require education, increased opportunities for disadvantaged groups involved in conflict, or new laws to increase penalties for forms of group conflict (e.g., race-based assaults or gay-bashing).

Liberal feminism: A form of feminism that argues that the liberal principles of equality, freedom, and equality of opportunity must be fully extended to women. This form of feminism does not call for specific structural changes to society. Neither patriarchy nor capitalism are identified as the enemies of women. It is an inadequate support for liberal values like equal opportunity that is seen as the problem.

Lifestyle–exposure perspective: A theory of victimization that acknowledges that not everyone has the same lifestyle and that some lifestyles expose people to more risks than others. If you usually go to bed early, you are less at risk than if you visit a bar every night.

Looking-glass-self: Developed by Charles H. Cooley (1864–1929) to describe the social nature of the self and the link between society and the individual. This image compares social interaction to looking in a mirror and thus seeing ourselves from outside as others see us. The term is comparable to George Herbert Mead's more influential concept of the "me."

Lumpenproletariat: Karl Marx's term to describe a large class of unemployed slum dwellers and homeless people surviving on scavenging or crime in the urban industrial centres of capitalist societies. It can be thought of as a subculture of those not needed in the economic system, disorganized, powerless, and riven by internal conflicts.

Macro-level analysis: Analysis centred on the broad cultural and structural features of society. It is assumed that examination of these characteristics or features will, for example, explain why men have a higher crime rate than women or why the United States of America has a higher homicide rate than Canada.

Mala in se: An act that society sees as inherently evil or criminal because it affronts basic morality and damages individuals and society. Murder, for example, is regarded as criminal in itself, even if it were not prohibited by law. Law reform commissions have recommended that the criminal law be reserved only for this type of act. At present, there are still apparently victimless crimes prohibited by criminal law.

Mala prohibita: An act that is deemed to be wrong or even criminal only because it is prohibited. There is nothing inherent to the act to make it criminal. It is commonly argued this is the case with laws against soft drugs like marijuana. Possession is claimed to be not wrong in itself, but only criminal because it is prohibited.

Manifest function: In functionalist analysis, most features of society are thought to serve some function (or role). Manifest function refers to intended or predicted outcomes. For example, the manifest function of the imprisonment of violent offenders is the protection of public safety.

Manslaughter: A category of homicide that would be thought of as murder except that the killing occurred in the heat of passion, caused by sudden and active provocation. This category also includes negligently causing death by reckless disregard for the safety of others.

Marital rape: Sexual assault occurring within a marital or equivalent relationship. Usually, these assaults rare of the form called "power rape."

Marxism: The philosophical, political, economic, and sociological ideas of Karl Marx (1818–1883) and his collaborator Friedrich Engels (1820–1895). Also used more generally to refer to work in the social sciences and humanities that employs theories and concepts from Marx's and Engels's original writings. The core Marxist claim is that historical eras can be distinguished from each other by their distinct modes of production. These modes of production then shape the whole society, exerting a primary influence over society's social relations, politics, law, and intellectual ideas.

Marxist feminism: A form of feminism that believes that women's oppression is a symptom of a more fundamental form of oppression. Women are not oppressed by men or by sexism, but by capitalism itself. If all women are to be liberated, capitalism must be replaced with socialism. In Friedrich Engels' (1820–1895) writings, women's oppression originated with the development of private property and of regulated family and marital relationships. Men's control of economic resources developed with settled society and the consequent growth of separate spheres of life for the two sexes. In capitalist societies, women become segregated into the domestic sphere and men into the outer world of paid work. Economic and social inequality between the sexes is increased, and women's subordination in marriage, the family, and society in general is intensified. Engels assumed that socialist revolution, through which the means of production becomes common property, would result in the development of equal access to paid work for both men and women, and consequently, gendered inequality between the sexes would disappear.

Mass murder: The killing of several people by one individual at roughly the same time.

Master status: A status that overrides all others in perceived importance. Whatever other personal or social qualities individuals possess, they are judged primarily by this one attribute. "Criminal" is an example of a master status that determines the community's identification of an individual. A master status can also arise form other achieved or ascribed roles.

Material forces of production: In Marxian terms, the materials used in the production of goods and to the tools, knowledge, and techniques used to transform these materials. It does not include the class structure of the economy, which is termed the "relations of production".

Me: A concept of George Herbert Mead (1863–1921). The "me" is guided and shaped by the culture of an individual's society or groups, which is internalized and acts to direct and control behaviour. Mead suggests an image of an internal dialogue taking place within the individual between a socially shaped "me" and his or her more spontaneous and ego-focused "I."

Mechanism of social control: The way groups control and direct the behaviour of their members. In any group, whether a society, gang, church, or club, control is exercised through mechanisms of approval and disapproval, rewards and punishments, and a framework of rules. Examples of these controls are frowning at a child, criticizing, denying a bank loan, arresting, convicting, or stigmatizing.

Medical model: A model of mental illness or other form of deviance that assumes it is a symptom of some underlying disturbance that can be identified and treated. It is associated with positivism because it claims that the disturbance, for example schizophrenia or psychopathology, can be objectively defined.

Medicalization: Redefinition of deviant behaviour from a legal or social problem into something under the control of the medical profession.

Mens rea: The mental component that, along with a criminal act (*actus reus*), is necessary to constitute a crime. The act must be done with conscious, rational, and wilful criminal intent to be one of gross negligence or recklessness.

Meso-level analysis: The form of analysis that examines the "units" between the individual and the larger structure of the society, it usually refers to the subcultural groups of society.

Micro-level analysis: The form of analysis that examines the individual. It asks why individuals were motivated to commit their crimes. Questions of this type are typically answered by psychology or psychiatry.

Misogyny: The hatred of women.

Mistake of fact: A defence in which the accused argues that the action was a consequence of an honest error. For example, a shopper really thought he or she had paid for the groceries.

Mistake of law: An ineffective defence in which an offender argues he or she did not know the act was against the law. Ignorance of the law is not a defence, since all citizens are presumed to know the law.

Mitigating circumstances: Aspects of the context in which a crime was committed that may be seen to reduce the offender's degree of responsibility and thus reduce the severity of the punishment.

Mood disorders: A form of mental disorder in which the individual experiences abnormally intense or prolonged periods of sadness, especially without sufficient apparent cause. Major depression involves severe, debilitating negative feelings. In bipolar disorder, depression alternates with mania, or periods of excitement and over-confidence.

Motivated offenders: To be motivated is to be ready to engage in a particular experience or action. While some people are motivated to attend college and pursue success, others are motivated to crime for reasons like drug dependency, poverty, or lack of self-control. This motivation may need something to turn it into action, such as a scholarship to go to college or an unlocked car with the keys in it.

Motive: The underlying reason for committing a crime; it may be material gain or some form of psychological satisfaction. Motive should be distinguished form the notion of intent.

Myth of mental illness: A term coined by Szasz (1974), who intended to challenge the medical model of mental disorders by suggesting that mental disorders typically have no objective problems that can be identified, there are no injuries, or physical symptoms. If there are no objective signs of mental illness, then it must be just a label typically applied to what Szasz calls ordinary "problems of living."

Necrophilia: A mental disorder in which a person has a strong desire for sexual acts with a corpse.

Necrophobia: A form of anxiety disorder in which a person has an exaggerated fear of dead bodies.

Neoclassical perspective: A shift away from the central assumption of the classical school brought about by the developing field of psychiatry. The central assumption of the classical school was that all individuals had equal degrees of freedom or will, and thus all could be held equally responsible for their criminal actions. There was no need for considering mitigating circumstances, the age of the offender, or his or her ability to form moral intent. The neoclassical school recognized the complexity of individual motivation and those factors, such as mental illness, that may restrict the ability to exercise free will.

Neutralization techniques: Those techniques that a person who engages in deviant or criminal activity uses to neutralize the feelings of guilt or moral conflict that might arise. Gresham Sykes and David Matza (1957) identified five such techniques: denying responsibility, denying that the injury to others is real, denying that the victim is really a victim, condemning those who condemn one, and appealing to higher loyalties to justify one's actions.

Nonrandom sample: A sample from a population in which each member of the population did not have an equal chance of being selected. Therefore, it cannot be claimed to represent the popula-

tion. For example, it would be difficult to conduct a random sample study of drug users in a population-based survey because it is impossible to identify the elements of the population.

Norm: A relatively precise rule, shared by others in the society, that specifies appropriate conduct in social situations. Norms are usually linked to more generalized values. For example, while respect for the elderly is a social value, it is a norm to give up one's bus seat for an elderly person.

Objectivism: One of the two opposing ways of thinking about crime; the other is subjectivism. Objectivism assumes that norms and laws are precise, external to the individual, and merely applied by police and other agents of social control in the process of identifying the naming crimes. Crime is thought to be independent of the subjectivity of both the accused and the official actors involved. This approach is criticized for treating social actors as objects who simply follow rules and for ignoring the processes of definition and negotiation that are always involved in any social interaction.

Obsession: A form of mental disorder in which individuals have recurrent and unwanted thoughts they cannot get out of their mind.

Oedipal complex: A concept of Sigmund Freud, founder of psychoanalysis. Freud argued that infants of both sexes have intense erotic desires principally directed toward their mothers. Girls develop through transferring this erotic energy to the father and later to other male figures. Infant boys, in contrast, see the father as a rival for their mother's attention and affection, and develop a deep desire to displace him and become their mother's lover themselves. This desire must be repressed, and Freud saw this as achieved through the castration complex, a fear that rivalry with the father may lead to the loss of the sexual organ the child has discovered in the phallic stage of development. The concept derives from the ancient Greek legend of King Oedipus, who unknowingly killed his father and then became lover and husband of his mother. Upon discovering this terrible secret, his mother killed herself and he blinded himself to finish his life wandering in exile.

Official data: Counts of crime that come from the recording processes of agencies of the criminal justice system. Police, for example, record crimes and these records become the official counts (data) of the amount of crime or the fluctuations in rates of crime.

Omerta: Originating in Sicily, this term refers to a conspiracy of silence and a code of values of "manliness," distrust of authorities, and preserving the honour of the family.

Operant conditioning: Concept associated with behaviourist B.F. Skinner to refer to learning that occurs through consequences or responses. The conditioning is achieved either by changing or omitting a response that reinforces or punishes a particular behaviour.

Oral stage: The earliest stage in Sigmund Freud's model of infant psycho–sexual development. Within each human there is an energy called the libido, which becomes attached to objects that give sensual or sexual satisfaction. As the infant develops, this energy moves from the mouth, to the anus, and finally to the genitals. At the oral stage, the infant's libido is focused on the breast or bottle, which brings satisfaction and nurturance. Freud assumed that the handling of this stage of development could permanently shape personality, depending on how the breast or bottle was given or withdrawn.

Organic mental disorders: Those forms of mental disorder that have physical or anatomical causes, for example, brain injury or degeneration of brain tissue found in various forms of dementia such as Alzheimer's disease.

Outer containment: Those characteristics external to the individual that may prevent the individual from engaging in crime. These might include parental rules, supervision, and the expectations of rule-abiding friends.

Outer control: Regulations or controls on behaviour that are external to the individual. For example, the presence of the police or a parent, or various forms of punishment imposed by the courts.

Over-representation: The presence of a group in a sub-set of the population in greater numbers than its proportion of the general population. For example, if a group makes up 20 percent of the population, it then should compose 20 percent of offenders or victims or those in prison, and it will be over-represented if its number is higher. Examples of over-representation include the higher percentage of men in prison compared to women or the proportion of sexual offences with female victims.

Participant observation: The act of observing the behaviour and recording the norms and values of groups while participating as fully as possible in their life and activity. Seen as a way to overcome the methodological problem in the social sciences that overt observation without participation may change the behaviour of the actors being observed.

Patriarchy: Literally "rule by the father," but more generally refers to a social situation in which men are dominant over women in wealth, status, and power. Patriarchy is associated with a set of ideas, a "patriarchal ideology" that acts to explain and justify this dominance, and attributes it to inherent natural differences between men and women.

Pedophilia: A form of sexual disorder in which a person is sexually aroused by children.

Phallic stage: From Sigmund Freud's model of infant psychosexual development, the period when the sexual energy of the libido becomes focused in the penis. A fear that rivalry with the father for the love of the mother will lead to loss of this organ arrives with the castration complex. This fear causes the repression of the erotic desire for the mother and increased identification with the father. It is at this time that the period of latency begins, where the intensity of the libido diminishes to develop again at puberty with the emergence into the adult genital stage of sexuality.

Pimp: A person who is not a prostitute but who lives off the avails of prostitution. Researchers have identified types of pimps, each with a somewhat different relationship to the prostitute: the "loser," the "Name," and the "bodyguard."

Polarization of classes: In Marxian analysis, the inevitable historical process of the class structure becoming increasingly separated. Over time, it is argued, the secondary classes of capitalism (the self-employed and the residual aristocracy, etc.) will disappear and be absorbed into either the bourgeoisie or the proletariat. The class structure will come to consist only of these two classes and the lumpenproletariat, and the disparity in their conditions will increase.

Politicality: A characteristic of criminal law, referring to the fact that criminal law is always the outcome of a political process.

Positivism: A classic model of the relationship between science and society found in the writings of August Comte (1798–1857). Comte begins by assuming that history has order and meaning, and he argues that societies must evolve through three stages: theological, metaphysical, and positive (or scientific). Each of these stages is paralleled by an intellectual evolution of the human mind. The developed positive or scientific human mind, among whom the most privileged was the sociologist, would use the scientific method to arrive at an understanding of the universal laws of social development. Comte argues against a democratic discourse on the problems of society, claiming that political organizations are always committed to a particular viewpoint. Instead, science must guide society because only it can rise above narrowness and special interests and understand the world impartially. Positivism, therefore, places science in a privileged position; assumes the possibility of a scientific understanding of human and social behaviour; assumes the separation of knowledge and power; and assumes the possibility of objectivity and impartiality. Positivism shaped sociology for 100 years. All of the assumptions that Comte makes are now rejected by postmodernists. In much contemporary social science debate, positivism has become a term of abuse.

Postmodernism: A complex term with rather different meanings in diverse contexts like architecture, literary criticism, and art or the social sciences. In the social sciences, its key focus is a rejection of the central assumptions of the modern world contained in what is described as the "enlightenment project: a belief in progress, the objectivity of science, and the possibility of uncovering universal truths." Postmodernists hold that social theory has always imposed meaning on historical events (think of the writing of Marx), rather than simply providing for the understanding of the empirical significance of events. Some of the implications of this postmodern rejection of the claims of science are that history has no meaning or purpose and that what is true or not true is entirely relative, since science lacks ability to test theories according to universal scientific principles. By excluding the idea of a unitary reality, we are left with a fragmented world with multiple subjective realities, a suspicion of science or authoritative claims, and many groups involved in identity politics in order to impose their reality on others. The current of postmodernist thinking can be identified in sociology in social constructionism, ethnomethodology, and labelling theory.

Power rape: A sexual assault in which the offender tries to emotionally possess his victim. Attackers often see the assaults as a "seduction," believing that the sexual dominance of women is expected and accepted.

Power–control theory: An explanation for gender differences in criminality, building on the idea that social control is stratified within the family. It claims that girls have traditionally been subjected to more social control than boys because they identify more closely with the role modelling and socialization provided by their mothers as principal caregivers. Now that mothers are increasingly involved in the workplace, this may decrease their social control activity and affect the willingness of girls to violate norms.

Private domain: *See* public domain.

Psychoactive drugs: Drugs capable of altering the functioning of the brain and the central nervous system. They can affect perception, attention span, memory, dexterity, and respiratory and cardiovascular functioning.

Psychopath: Antisocial personality disorder. Psychopaths tends to be lacking in what is considered conscience, are unable to form emotional attachments (even to friends or family), are quite impulsive, and are only self-interested. It is doubtful that psychological therapy can change this condition.

Psychotherapeutic: Intended to cure or alleviate mental disorders. Typically, treatment centres on getting patients to verbalize their problems so they can see them with greater objectivity and insight, thus making them able to change their attitudes and behaviour. This approach works best if patients have good verbal skills.

Public domain: The public and private domains are separate spheres of social life. The private domain encompasses the intimate relations of family and the public domain includes work, state organizations, and other formal institutions. Feminists see the private domain as shaped by familial patriarchy and the public domain by social patriarchy. In criminology, the relationship between these spheres is central to the power–control theory.

Pyromania: A form of compulsive disorder in which a person gains satisfaction by repeatedly setting fires.

Qualitative data: The type of data produced by research methods like participant observation and case studies. These result in a narrative and descriptive account of a setting or practice. These methods are a form of interpretive sociology and reflect a rejection of positivism.

Quantitative data: Information gathered by methods that allow for the measurement of variables within a collection of people or groups and result in numerical data subjected to statistical analysis.

Queer ladder of mobility: In this context, the term queer has the traditional meaning of unconventional or unacceptable. The phrase is another statement of Merton's theory that everyone desires mobility and financial success, and those without access to legitimate means may choose to achieve this through deviant means like crime.

Radical feminism: A perspective within feminism that differs from traditional Marxism in arguing that women's oppression is older than class oppression, is harder to transform, causes more harm, and is more pervasive in society. It is argued that the situation of women provides a model for understanding other forms of oppression like racism and class domination. Some radical feminists claim that biology lies at the root of this oppression and that it can be eliminated only when women transform their relationship to reproduction. Within criminology, this perspective is concerned with the description and analysis of the content of law and practices of law-enforcement that serve to maintain male dominance in society.

Random sample: A set of members of a population selected in such a way that each element of the population has an equal, and known, chance of being drawn for the sample. This ensures that the distribution of population characteristics corresponds to the assumptions of probability theory, and allows inferences to be drawn about the population.

Rape: An act in which a man has sexual intercourse with a woman who is not his wife and who has not given lawful consent. The original meaning of "rape" is to steal and carry off the belongings of another. Historically, women were considered the property of their fathers or their husbands, and virginity was all important prior to marriage as was fidelity after marriage. Sexual assault or even sex outside of marriage was therefore considered a violation of a man's property. The Statute of Westminster (1275) formalized this offence and laid the foundation that carried forward into modern times: it made rape an offence against the state and defined intercourse with a child, consented to or not, as statutory rape. It also declared that a woman was partially responsible unless she resisted the attack and established the long-lasting rule that a husband could not be charged with rape of his wife. Canadian rape laws were changed in 1983, and the more broadly defined offence of sexual assault was added to the *Criminal Code*.

Rape shield law: Enacted in 1983, this legal provision prohibited the interrogation of a victim of sexual assault about past sexual history with anyone except the accused. In 1991, this law was found unconstitutional, as it could result in the exclusion of relevant evidence and infringe the accused's right to a fair trail. In 1992, Parliament passed a new law that restricted the admissibility of evidence about past sexual history, but did not prohibit it.

Rationalization: Within symbolic interactionism, the term has the everyday sense of the word and refers to providing justifications or excuses for one's actions. The concept of neutralization techniques developed by G. Sykes and D. Matza provides an example of this.

Reasonable man: The concept is gender neutral and should be "reasonable person." It refers to a legal test found in both civil and criminal law that is used to determine liability for the consequences of actions and inactions. For example, in determining liability in tort or criminal law, it is important to ask whether a person acted reasonably or could have been expected to foresee the possible consequences of his or her actions or inaction.

Recent-complaint rule: An expectation that a victim of rape or another offence should report the incident at the first reasonable opportunity. This rule was referred to in assessing evidence that the offence or rape actually took place. It is now recognized that victims may need a period of recovery before they are emotionally able to report offences.

Reference group: From social psychology, this is the group people compare themselves to or refer to in evaluating themselves. For example, some people might compare their income to the medical profession or their family situation to that of their neighbours.

Reintegrative shaming: Shaming that brings a person to acknowledge wrongdoing, but offers community support and forgiveness rather than stigmatizing the offender. This is seen as a way to avoid creating a deviant status through labelling.

Relativist: In relation to mental illness or other forms or behavioural deviance, this term draws attention to the fact that these conditions cannot be precisely and objectively defined and identified. Rather, mental illness or deviance is relative, since application of these labels depends on a complex process of interactive interpretation and negotiation.

Retreatism: The response of individuals when they recognize they lack legitimate opportunities and do not have the physical or personality characteristics to be good at crime. They give up aspirations for success and retreat into drugs or passivity.

Retribution: From the idea of retribute, meaning to return or to receive in recompense and the Biblical sense of deserved and just. The term is now used exclusively to refer to punishment deserved because of an offence and fitting its seriousness. Punishment is justified because the offender must give up an amount of money, personal freedom or comfort equivalent to the harm or loss done to others. Retribution is distinguished form revenge and retaliation.

Ritualism: A response to restricted access to legitimate opportunities among those strongly socialized to conformity. They adapt to their apparent failure by reducing their aspirations and they act as if aspiring to cultural goals but have little expectation of success.

Role convergence: The process of women's social roles becoming more similar to those of men. Since men have higher crime rates than women, this development is thought to partly explain the rising crime rates of women.

Routine activities theory: The argument that exposure to crimes is an expected outcome of routine activities and changing social patterns. For example, those who like to go out in the evening are more likely to be robbed or assaulted than those who remain at home. This is similar to lifestyle–exposure theory.

Sadistic rape: A form of sexual assault in which the offender imposes bizarre violent acts designed to cause pain and to disfigure the sex organs.

Sampling: The process or method of drawing a sample from a population. This process can be based on random selection that gives each member of the population an equal probability of being selected, or it may be based on selection to reflect certain characteristics of interest in the population. Many statistical tests assume a process of random selection.

Scientific method: The body of methods and techniques of analysis used in the sciences to develop theories and conduct tests of hypotheses. These methods attempt to discover the causes of things or the relationships between variables. They assume the existence of discoverable, measurable, and objective evidence that will lead to the development of theory and formulation of scientific laws. The key principles are gathering data by observation and research, formulation of theory and hypotheses, testing by experiment, replication of tests to ensure consistent results, and avoidance of personal bias and prejudgement. A theory or hypothesis must be stated in a testable form to have scientific status: it must be clear enough that it can be disproven. The principles of scientific method have been influential in the social sciences, but they are inappropriate in some areas of investigation, often cannot be strictly applied where they do have relevance, and may divert attention from the interpretive and negotiated qualities of social action.

Second-degree murder: Killings that do not meet one of the three conditions required to be charged with first-degree murder. The distinction between first- and second-degree murder is often vague and disputable.

Secondary deviance: As used by Edwin Lemert, deviant behaviour that flows from a stigmatized sense of self; the deviance is thought to be consistent with the character of the self. A person's self can be stigmatized or tainted by public labelling. Secondary deviance is contrasted to primary deviance, which may be behaviourally identical to secondary deviance but is incorporated into a "normal" sense of self.

Self: A concept associated with Charles H. Cooley and George Herbert Mead suggesting that our sense of self or identity is not something biological or innate, but is formed in social interaction with others. We must see ourselves from the outside as others see us before we are able to create a sense of self-consciousness.

Self-report crime surveys: A method for measuring crime that can overcome the problem that official crime data reflects only recorded and reported crime. It involves a survey of a sample population asking if they have committed a crime in a particular period of time. This has been a good method for criminologists to determine the social characteristics of "offenders."

Serial killing: Murder of a number of individuals by a single person on separate occasions over a period of weeks, months, or years. Usually associated with psychopathic offenders.

Sexual assault: Generally defined as an assault, not necessarily including penetration, that has as its consequence a violation of the sexual integrity of the victim. In 1983, this replaced the offence of rape in the *Criminal Code*. The *Criminal Code* specifies three types of sexual assault: sexual assault, aggravated sexual assault, and sexual assault with a weapon. These categories are distinguished by the level of seriousness of the act.

Sexualization: A perspective on women's deviance or crime that links it to sex or to gender roles.

Shadow line: The central metaphor of this book, it suggests that the division or line between good and evil is never clear-cut and unchanging, but tends to be shifting and blurred as though viewed in the shadows.

Social bond: The degree to which an individual is integrated into the values and institutions of the community. Involvements in family, school, workplace, or group are all elements of the social bond.

Social class: Refers to a group of individuals sharing a common situation within a social structure. This may be a shared location in the structure of ownership and control of the means of production or possession of similar economic resources and opportunities. Class can also refer to groups of individuals with a shared characteristic relevant in some socio-economic measurement or ranking (for example, all individuals earning over $50 000 a year), it then has a statistical meaning rather than referring to social structure.

Social control theory: An explanation of why most people are law-abiding. It looks at those aspects of society that restrain or inhibit criminal behaviour. These include the controls exerted by family, schools, peer groups, work situation, or moral conscience. Most conventional theories, in contrast, try to explain why some individuals are not law-abiding.

Social relations of production: The class structure of a society, consisting of the social relationships that people enter into in the production or delivery of goods and services. In the Marxist perspective, these relationships involve ownership of resources and control of work by one social class and the subordination of others. It is the pattern of economic class relations that is presumed to shape the entire culture and social structure of the society.

Specificity: In criminal law, the requirement that the characteristics of criminal behaviour and punishment for offences be precisely identified.

Status frustration: Albert Cohen's theory that crime is committed by young, lower-class males as an expression of their frustration when they realize that they are not going to achieve status, respect and recognition in the middle-class environment of the school.

Status offence: A delinquency or crime that can only be committed by people occupying a particular status. The *Juvenile Delinquents Act* (replaced in 1984), for example, created criminal offences of school truancy, incorrigibility, sexual immorality, and violations of liquor laws. Only young people could be charged with or found to be in a state of delinquency because of these behaviours. Under this law, approximately 20 percent of young girls coming to youth court did so because their sexual behaviour was considered delinquent but very few boys were ever charged with this offence.

Statutory rape: Sexual intercourse with an underage person with or without consent.

Stigma: As used by Erving Goffman (1922–1982), a differentness about an individual that is given a negative evaluation by others and thus distorts and discredits the public identity of the person. For example, physical disability, facial disfigurement, stuttering, a prison record, being obese, or not being able to read, may become stigmatized attributes. The stigma may lead to the adoption of a self-identity that incorporates the negative social evaluation.

Stigmata: Physical signs of some special moral position. While the term has Christian origins, Cesare Lombroso used it to refer to physical signs of the state of atavism, a morally and biologically inferior person lower on the evolutionary scale. Sociologist Erving Goffman, avoiding a primary focus on physical signs, developed this into the notion of stigma, a set of social, moral or physical attributes that can produce shame in the individual because of society's response to these features.

Structural Marxism: An approach to understanding the role of the state within a conflict or Marxist perspective. The state is seen as captured by the structure of capitalism and, while having a degree of autonomy or freedom from the dominant class of society, the state finds it must act so as to reproduce the economic and social structures of capitalism. This approach typically sees the state doing this through attending to three functions: capital accumulation, legitimation, and coercion.

Structure, social: The patterned and relatively stable arrangement of roles and statuses found within societies and social institutions. Points to the predictable patterns of organization, activity and social interaction found in societies and social institutions. This relative stability of organization and behaviour provides the quality of predictability that people rely on in every day social interaction. Social scientists refer to aspects of social structure to account for criminal behaviour at the meso- and macro-level of analysis.

Subculture of violence: Concept developed by Wolfgang and Ferracuti (1967) to account for variations in the frequency of violence by groups or in particular regions. It is argued that groups with high rates of violence have been socialized into a distinctive culture and have developed a different perspective.

Subjectivism: Subjectivism emphasizes the complexity of the process of social construction of societal norms and the differential application of these rules. These rules and their application are thought to be socially constructed and are understood as flowing from the wishes, desires, political motivations, and stereotypes held by agents of social control. The focus is on the subjectivity of actors and how they interact to create meaning.

Substantive law: The portion of the *Criminal Code* that specifies the acts that constitute crimes and what the punishments shall be. Often contrasted to procedural law, which lays out the rules that agents of the state must follow in investigating and convicting offenders.

Superego: In Sigmund Freud's theory of the personality, the component that represents the internalized social norms or conscience.

Superstructure: A term from Marxist social analysis central to the materialist concept of history and social development. Marx argues that the fundamental base of any society, which permeates and shapes all its legal, political, and intellectual characteristics, is the social relation of production: the social and technological way that production is organized and carried out. These relations of production provide the social foundation on which develops the superstructure of legal and political relations and human intellectual ideas and consciousness.

Symbolic interactionism: A sociological perspective that stresses the way society is given life and meaning through the interactions of individuals. Unlike both functionalist and conflict perspectives, it is a micro-level analysis that focuses on the way that individuals, through their interpretations of social situations and behavioural negotiation with others, give meaning to social interaction. George Herbert Mead (1863–1931), a founder of symbolic interactionism, saw interaction as creating and recreating the patterns and structures that bring society to life. More recently, however, there has been a tendency to argue that society has no objective reality aside from individual interaction. This latter view has been criticized for ignoring the role of culture and social structure in giving shape, direction, and meaning to social interaction.

Target suitability: A target refers to a person or a property that an offender may approach to commit a crime. Unlit homes, hidden by hedges or fences, are more likely to be identified as targets than those with a resident guard dog or garden lighting.

Terrorism: The calculated stimulation of fear through threatening or actual use of cruelty, destruction, killing, or assaults. What is defined publicly as terrorism is often determined by political motivations.

Theory: A system of ideas used to explain something. All sciences use theory to understand and analyze the social or natural world. Theory can be thought of as providing a conceptual model of some aspect of life. An example is Darwin's theory of evolution and of the processes of organic development from simple to complex forms. Or, like Durkheim, we may have a theory that explains differences in the crime rates of societies by referring to social and normative integration. In these examples, theory consists of a set of concepts, definitions of these concepts, assertions about their relationship, a set of assumptions, and various claims to knowledge. In the classic model of how science is conducted, the scientist may begin with a theory, deduce a hypothesis from the theory and then test it. Theory may also be constructed to explain observations and then, in turn, be used to derive testable hypotheses. The practice of science always involves theory testing.

Total institution: From Erving Goffman, this is an institution that encompasses the individual physically and psychologically,

cutting him or her off from outside relationships or communication and exerting control over both thought and behaviour. Such institutions can bring about resocialization where individuals become detached from their previous sense of identity and are reshaped to internalize new values and behaviour. Examples include religious orders, mental institutions, prisons, and army training camps.

Transitional zone: In Shaw's and McKay's analysis of the distribution of crime within a community, that part of the city surrounding the downtown or central core that is being allowed to deteriorate because development and a rise in land prices is expected. Buildings are allowed to fall into disuse and these areas become attractive to the poor, the disturbed, and the transient, who are said to contribute to crime and social disorganization.

Transsexualism: A mental condition in which people who are biologically male or female identify themselves psychologically and emotionally as members of the other sex. They often engage in cross-dressing and some seek to achieve body characteristics of the other sex through hormonal treatments or surgery.

Uniform crime reports: Since 1961, Canada has had a uniform crime reporting system developed by Statistics Canada and the Canadian Association of Chiefs of Police. This system is designed to provide a measure of reliability and consistency for crime statistics by establishing a standard set of police procedures for collecting and reporting crime information.

Unit at risk: Objects that are convenient targets of crime. Criminologists partly account for the high crime rates in modern societies by noting that there are more units at risk in modern societies than in others. It is much easier and more rational to steal an automobile than a horse and cart. Or, compare a mainframe computer with the small personal computers that we can now carry in a bag. Objects like those are much more likely to be stolen, and today, more people have more of them.

Unit of analysis: The things that researchers are comparing or examining when looking for patterns are referred to as the units of analysis, or the units to be analyzed. The most frequent unit of analysis is the individual, used when researchers look for patterns among a number or sample of individuals. One might look for patterns between individual attributes like education and income. If research is conducted to compare groups, then the group is the unit of analysis. For example, one might compare the placement of men and women in income rankings. Patterns can also be sought in things like newspaper stories, advertisements, types of social interaction, or speech utterances. In these cases, the unit of analysis would be what Earl Babbie has called social artefacts. In this text, three units of analysis are associated with three levels of analysis: the individual with the micro-level, the subcultural group with the meso-level, and the whole population or society with the macro-level.

Urbanization: The movement of people from rural areas into towns and cities. The growth of city-living is associated with industrialization; in western societies and North America, it occurred very rapidly. Urbanization and its consequences were a main focus of the Chicago School, since Chicago itself was an example of phenomenally rapid growth and was seen as a laboratory of sociological research.

Victimization surveys: A survey of a random sample of the population in which people are asked to recall and describe their own experience of being a victim of crime.

Victim-precipitated homicide: A killing in which the person killed has him- or herself initiated or escalated the violence that has led to the person's death.

Victimless crime: The conventional conception of crime is that there must be a victim of the criminal behaviour who experiences harm. Behaviours like illegal gambling, drug use, and selling sex appear not to have victims, and people are willing participants. Many argue that acts of this nature should not be regulated by criminal law.

Watch style of policing: A style of policing that focuses on resolving situations informally, if possible, rather than according to standardized procedures of enforcement. This leads to greater discretion among constables and less reporting.

White-collar crime: Originally a term of Edwin Sutherland in 1945, referring to illegal activities committed to benefit businesses and corporations. Most corporate acts, like false advertising, anti-trust violations, environmental pollution, or dumping products on the market below cost, are not regulated by criminal law but by regulatory laws of various kinds. The term now generally used for this type of act is corporate crime or organizational crime. Criminologists now use the term white-collar crime in reference to illegal acts committed for personal gain by people in positions of trust. For example, making personal long-distance calls on an employer's account or billing for fictitious travel expenses.

Women's movement: A broad term for a range of social and political organizations and activities, like research, writing, and criticism, aimed at advancing the status of women and overcoming cultural marginalization of women's perspectives and social experience.

"A Brief History of Sex Worker Activism in Toronto." on-line: <<http://www.walnet.org/csis/groups/swat/torontohistory.html>>

Abadinsky, H. (1985). *Organized Crime* (2nd ed.). Chicago: Nelson Hall.

———. (1994). *Organized Crime* (4th ed.). Chicago: Nelson Hall.

Adler, F. (1975). *Sisters in Crime: The Rise of the New Female Criminal.* New York: McGraw Hill.

Adler, F., G.O.W. Mueller, and W.S. Laufer. (2001). *Criminology* (4th ed.) New York: McGraw Hill.

Adler, P. (1985). *Wheeling and Dealing: An Ethnography of an Upper Level Dealing and Smuggling Community.* New York: Columbia University Press.

Adler, P.A., and P. Adler. (1997). *Constructions of Deviance: Social Power, Context, and Interaction.* Belmont, CA: Wadsworth.

Agar, M., and R.C. Stephens. (1975). "The Methadone Street Scene: The Addict View." *Psychiatry* 38:381–87.

Akers, R.L. (1980). "Further Critical Comments on Marxist Criminology." In J.A. Inciardi (ed.), *Radical Criminology: The Coming Crisis.* Beverly Hills: Sage.

———. (1985). *Deviant Behavior: A Social Learning Approach.* Belmont, CA: Wadsworth.

———. (1997). *Criminological Theories: Introduction and Evaluation* (2nd ed.). Los Angeles: Roxbury.

Akman, D., and A. Normandeau. (1967). "The Measurement of Crime and Delinquency in Canada." In R.A. Silverman and J.J. Teevan (eds.), *Crime in Canadian Society* (2nd ed.). Toronto: Butterworths.

Albanese, J.S. (1987). *Organizational Offenders: Understanding Corporate Crime* (2nd ed.). Niagara Falls: Apocalypse Publishing.

———. (1996). *Organized Crime* (3rd ed.). Cincinnati OH: Anderson.

Albini, J. (1971). *The American Mafia: Genesis of a Legend.* New York: Appleton, Century, Crofts.

Alexander, B. (1990). *Peaceful Measures: Canada's Way Out of the "War on Drugs."* Toronto: University of Toronto Press.

Allen, G. (1985). "The Crisis Over Water." *Maclean's* (August 26):34–37.

Allen, R. (1991). "Preliminary Crime Statistics, 1990." *Juristat Service Bulletin* 11(9). Ottawa: Canadian Centre for Justice Statistics, Statistics Canada.

American Psychiatric Association. (1987). *Diagnostic and Statistical Manual of Mental Disorders* (3rd ed.). Washington, DC: American Psychiatric Association.

———. *Diagnostic and Statistical Manual of Mental Disorders* (4th ed.). Washington, DC: American Psychiatric Association.

Amir, M. (1971). *Patterns of Forcible Rape.* Chicago: University of Chicago Press.

Anderson, A.G. (1979). *The Business of Organized Crime.* Stanford, CA: Hoover Institution Press.

Anderssen, E. (2000). "Police Trace Past Movements of Alleged Killer." *Globe and Mail* (June 26):A3.

Appleby, T., and T.T. Ha. (2000). "Bikers Expand Crime Empire." *Globe and Mail* (July 24):A1, A5.

Archer, D., and R. Gartner. (1984). *Violence and Crime in Cross-National Perspective.* New Haven, CT: Yale University Press.

Ashworth, W. (1986). *The Late Great Lakes: An Environmental History.* Toronto: Collins.

Avio, K.L., and C.S. Clark. (1976). *Property Crime in Canada: An Econometric Study.* Toronto: University of Toronto Press.

———. (1978). "The Supply of Property Offences in Ontario: Evidence on the Deterrent of Punishment." *Canadian Journal of Economics* 11:1–19.

Babbie, E. (1973). *Survey Research Methods.* Belmont, CA: Wadsworth.

Badgley Committee. *See* Committee on Sexual Offences Against Children and Youths.

Bailey, W.C. (1974). "Murder and the Death Penalty." *Journal of Criminal Law and Criminology* 65:416–23.

Bales, R.F. (1962). "Attitudes Toward Drinking in the Irish Culture." In *Society Culture and Drinking Patterns.* New York: Wiley.

Ballard, M. (1987). "On the Safe Side: Holdup Review, 1986." *Canadian Banker* 94(3):47–48.

Barber, J. (1986). "The New Drug Crusade." *Maclean's* (September 29):36–39.

Barber, M. (1985). "A Troubled Community." *Maclean's* (July 1):10–11.

Barlow, H.D. (1995). *Crime and Public Policy: Putting Theory to Work.* Boulder, CO: Westview.

Beare, M. (1996). *Criminal Conspiricies: Organized Crime in Canada.* Toronto: Nelson.

Beccaria, C. (1963 [1764]). *On Crimes and Punishments.* New York: Bobbs Merrill.

Becker, H.S. (1963). *Outsiders: Studies in the Sociology of Deviance.* New York: Free Press.

———. (1964). *The Other Side: Perspectives on Deviance.* New York: Free Press.

Bell, D. (1962). *The End of Ideology.* New York: Free Press.

Benjamin, H., and L. Masters. (1964). *Prostitution and Morality.* New York: Julian.

Berger, P. (1963). *Invitation to Sociology: A Humanist Perspective.* Garden City, NY: Doubleday Anchor Books.

Bergman, B. (1989). "Sisterhood of Fear and Fury: Intimations That Marc Is Not Alone." *Maclean's* (December 18):18–19.

Bernard, T.J. (1984). "Control Criticisms of Strain Theories: An Assessment of Theoretical and Empirical Adequacy." *Journal of Research in Crime and Delinquency* 21:353–72.

Bernstein, J., E. Adlaf, and A. Paglia. (2000). *Drug Use in Toronto — 2000.* on-line: <<http://www.city.Toronto.on.ca/drugcentre/rgdu00/rgdu1.htm>>

Besserer, S. (1998). "Criminal Victimization: An International Perspective." *Juristat Service Bulletin* 18(6). Ottawa: Canadian Centre for Justice Statistics, Statistics Canada.

Besserer, S., and C. Trainor. (2000). "Criminal Victimization in Canada, 1999." *Juristat Service Bulletin* 20(10). Ottawa: Canadian Centre for Justice Statistics, Statistics Canada.

Bird, H. (1985). *Not Above the Law: The Tragic Story of JoAnn Wilson and Colin Thatcher.* Toronto: Key Porter Books.

Bissland, T. (1986). *Buxbaum.* Toronto: Dell.

Black, D.J. (1970). "The Production of Crime Rates." *American Sociological Review* 35:733–47.

Blackwell, J. (1988a). "Canada in a Global Setting: Notes on the International Drug Market." In J.C. Blackwell and P.G. Erickson (eds.), *Illicit Drugs in Canada: A Risky Business.* Scarborough: Nelson.

———. (1988b). "An Overview of Canadian Illicit Drug Use Epidemiology." In J.C. Blackwell and P.G. Erickson (eds.), *Illicit Drugs in Canada: A Risky Business.* Scarborough: Nelson.

———. (1988c). "Sin, Sickness, or Social Problem?: The Concept of Drug Dependence." In J.C. Blackwell and P.G. Erickson (eds.), *Illicit Drugs in Canada: A Risky Business.* Scarborough: Nelson.

Blackwell, J.C., and P.G. Erickson. (1988). *Illicit Drugs in Canada: A Risky Business.* Scarborough: Nelson.

Blaise, C., and B. Mukherjee. (1987). *The Sorrow and the Terror: The Haunting Legacy of the Air India Tragedy.* Markham: Viking.

Blauner, R. (1964). *Alienation and Freedom: The Factory Worker and His Industry.* Chicago: University of Chicago Press.

Block, A.A., and W.J. Chambliss. (1981). *Organizing Crime.* New York: Elsevier.

Block, A.A., and F.R. Scarpitti. (1985). *Poisoning for Profit: The Mafia and Toxic Waste in America.* New York: William Morrow.

Bloom, B.L. (1973). *Community Mental Health: A Historical and Critical Analysis.* Morristown, NJ: General Learning Press.

Blumer, H. (1969). *Symbolic Interactionism.* Englewood Cliffs, NJ: Prentice-Hall.

Bondanello, P., and J. Bondanello. (1979). *Dictionary of Italian Literature.* Westport, CT: Greenwood Press.

Bonger, W. (1916). *Criminality and Economic Conditions.* Boston: Little, Brown, and Company.

Bordua, D.J. (1961). "Delinquent Subcultures: Sociological Interpretations of Gang Delinquency." *Annals of the American Academy of Social and Political Science* 338:119–36.

Boritch, H. (1997). *Fallen Women: Female Crime and Justice in Canada.* Toronto: Nelson.

Bowers, W.J. (1984). *Legal Homicide: Death as Punishment in America, 1964–1982.* Boston: Northeastern University Press.

Box, S. (1981). *Deviance, Reality and Society.* New York: Holt, Rinehart and Winston.

Boyd, N. (1988a). "Canadian Punishment of Illegal Drug Use: Theory and Practice." In J.C. Blackwell and P.G. Erickson (eds.), *Illicit Drugs in Canada: A Risky Business.* Scarborough: Nelson.

———. (1988b). *The Last Dance: Murder in Canada.* Scarborough: Prentice-Hall.

———. (1991). *High Society: Legal and Illegal Drugs in Canada.* Toronto: Key Porter.

Boyle, C. (1984). *Sexual Assault.* Toronto: Carswell.

Braithwaite, J. (1984). *Corporate Crime in the Pharmaceutical Industry.* London: Routledge and Kegan Paul.

———. (1989). *Crime, Shame, and Reintegration.* Cambridge: Cambridge University Press.

Brannigan, A. (1984). *Crimes, Courts and Corrections: An Introduction to Crime and Social Control in Canada.* Toronto: Holt, Rinehart and Winston.

Brantingham, P., and P. Brantingham. (1981). "Notes on the Geometry of Crime." In P. Brantingham and P. Brantingham (eds.), *Environmental Criminology.* Beverly Hills, CA: Sage.

———. (1984). *Patterns in Crime.* New York: Macmillan.

Brantingham, P., S. Mu, and A. Verma. (1995). "Patterns in Crime." In M.A. Jackson and C.T. Griffiths (eds.), *Canadian Criminology: Perspectives on Crime and Criminality* (2nd ed.). Toronto: Harcourt Brace.

Bresler, F. (1980). *The Chinese Mafia.* New York: Stein and Day.

Brickman, J. (1980). *Winnipeg Rape Incidence Project.* Winnipeg: Canadian Association of Sexual Assault Centres.

Bromberg, W. (1975). *From Shaman to Psychotherapist.* Chicago: Henry Regnery.

Bronfenbrenner, U. (1958). "Socialization and Social Class Through Time and Space." In E.E. Macoby (ed.), *Readings in Social Psychology.* New York: Holt, Rinehart and Winston.

Brownmiller, S. (1975). *Against Our Will: Men, Women, and Rape.* New York: Simon and Schuster.

Bruno, A. (1993). *The Ice Man: The True Story of A Cold Blooded Killer.* New York: Dell.

Bryan, J.H. (1965). "Apprenticeships in Prostitution." *Social Problems* 12:287–97.

Bureau of Justice Statistics. (1979). *Computer Crime.* Washington, DC: U.S. Department of Justice.

Burgess, A.W., and L.L. Holmstrom. (1974). "Rape Trauma Syndrome." *American Journal of Psychiatry* 131:981–86.

Burgess, E. (1925). "The Growth of a City." In R.E. Park and E. Burgess (eds.), *The City.* Chicago: University of Chicago Press.

Burgess, R., and R.L. Akers. (1966). "A Differential Association-Reinforcement Theory of Criminal Behavior." *Social Problems* 14:128–47.

Came, B. (1989). "Montreal Massacre." *Maclean's* (December 18):14–17.

CAMH. *See* Centre for Addiction and Mental Health.

Canadian Centre for Justice Statistics (Statistics Canada) (CCJS). (1985). Canadian Crime Statistics, 1984. Ottawa: Minister of Supply and Services Canada.

———. (1987). *Homicide in Canada, 1976–1985: An Historical Perspective.* Ottawa: Minister of Supply and Services Canada.

———. (1989). *Homicide in Canada, 1988*. Ottawa: Minister of Supply and Services Canada.

———. (1990). *Canadian Crime Statistics, 1989*. Ottawa: Minister of Supply and Services Canada.

———. (1996). *The Justice Data Factfinder*. Ottawa: Statistics Canada.

———. (1999). Sex Offenders. *Juristat Service Bulletin* 19(3). Ottawa: Canadian Centre for Justice Statistics, Statistics Canada.

———. (2000). Justice Factfinder, 1998. *Juristat Service Bulletin* 20(4). Ottawa: Canadian Centre for Justice Statistics, Statistics Canada.

Canadian Press Newswire. (January 24, 1997). "Morin to Get $1.25 M in Compensation."

Canadian Profile 1999: Highlights. (1999). Canadian Centre on Substance Abuse. Ottawa. on-line: <<http://www.ccsa.ca/cp99high.htm>>

Canadian Security Intelligence Service. (1995). *Public Report and Program Outlook*. Ottawa: Ministry of Supply and Services.

Canadian Urban Victimization Study (CUVS). (1983). *Bulletin 1—Victims of Crime*. Ottawa: Solicitor General of Canada.

———. (1984a). *Bulletin 2—Reported and Unreported Crimes*. Ottawa: Solicitor General of Canada.

———. (1984b). *Bulletin 3—Crime Prevention: Awareness and Practice*. Ottawa: Solicitor General of Canada.

———. (1985a). *Bulletin 4—Female Victims of Crime*. Ottawa: Solicitor General of Canada.

———. (1985b). *Bulletin 5—Cost of Crime to Victims*. Ottawa: Solicitor General of Canada.

———. (1985c). *Bulletin 6—Criminal Victimization of Elderly Canadians*. Ottawa: Solicitor General of Canada.

———. (1986). *Bulletin 7—Household Property Crimes*. Ottawa: Solicitor General of Canada.

———. (1987). *Bulletin 8—Patterns of Violent Crime*. Ottawa: Solicitor General of Canada.

Caplan, L. (1984). *The Insanity Defense and the Trial of John W. Hinckley, Jr.* Boston: David R. Godine.

Carman, A., and H. Moody. (1985). *Working Women: The Subterranean World of Street Prostitution*. New York: Harper and Row.

Carriere, D. (2000). Youth Court Statistics, 1998/99 Highlights. *Juristat Service Bulletin* 20(2). Ottawa: Canadian Centre for Justice Statistics, Statistics Canada.

Carrithers, D.W. (1985). "The Insanity Defense and Presidential Peril." *Society* 22:22–27.

Casey, J. (1985). "Corporate Crime and the State: Canada in the 1980's." In T. Fleming (ed.), *The New Criminologies in Canada: State, Crime, and Control*. Toronto: Oxford University Press.

CCENDU. (1997). *Canadian Community Epidemiology Network on Drug Use: Executive Summary*. Toronto: Addiction Research Foundation.

CCJS. *See* Canadian Centre for Justice Statistics.

Centre for Addiction and Mental Health (CAMH) (2000). *Ontario Student Drug Use Survey: Executive Summary*. Ottawa: Centre for Addiction and Mental Health on-line: <<http://www.camh.net/understanding/ont_study drug_use.html>>

Chalmers, L., and P. Smith. (1988). "Wife Battering: Psychological, Social, and Physical Isolation and Counteracting Strategies." In Arlene Tigar McLaren (ed.), *Gender and Society: Creating a Canadian Women's Sociology*. Toronto: Copp Clark.

Chambliss, W. (1978). *On the Take*. Bloomington, IN: University of Indiana Press.

Chambliss, W., and R. Seidman. (1982). *Law, Order and Power* (2nd ed.). Reading, MA: Addison-Wesley.

Chappell, D., R. Geis, and G. Geis. (1977). *Forcible Rape: The Crime, the Victims, and the Offender*. New York: Columbia University Press.

Chappell, D., G. Geis, S. Schafer, and L. Siegal. (1971). "Forcible Rape: A Comparative Study of Offenses Known to the Police in Boston and Los Angeles." In J.M. Henslin (ed.), *Studies in the Sociology of Sex*. New York: Appleton, Century, Crofts.

Charbonneau, J.P. (1976). *The Canadian Connection: An Exposé on the Mafia in Canada and Its International Ramifications*. Ottawa: Optimum.

Charon, J.M. (1985). *Symbolic Interactionism* (2nd ed.). Englewood Cliffs, NJ: Prentice-Hall.

Cherry, P. (2000). "Ontario Gangs Join Hells Angels: Smaller Gangs Change Colours in Quebec Ceremony. *National Post* (December 30).

Chesney-Lind, M. (1986). "Women and Crime: The Female Offender." *Signs* 12:78–86.

Chilton, R. (1964). "Continuity in Delinquency Area Research: A Comparison of Studies of Baltimore, Detroit, and Indianapolis." *American Sociological Review* 29:71–83.

Chin, K. (1990). *Chinese Subculture and Criminality: Non-Traditional Crime Groups in America*. London: Greenwood Press.

Chisholm, P. (1988). "A Dangerous Trail." *Maclean's* (October 31):40–41.

Cicourel, A. (1968). *The Social Organization of Juvenile Justice*. New York: Wiley.

Clark, I.D. (1989). "Legislative Reform and the Policy Process: The Case of the Competition Act." Address given to the National Conference on Competition Law and Policy in Canada. Toronto, October 24–25.

Clark, L., and D. Lewis. (1977). *Rape: The Price of Coercive Sexuality*. Toronto: Women's Educational Press.

Clark, M. (1985). "Taking Aim at Takeovers." *Maclean's* (April 29):36.

Clark, R. (1971). *Crime in America*. New York: Pocket Books.

Clark, S., and D. Hepworth. (1994). "Effects of Reform Legislation on the Processing of Sexual Assault Cases." In J. Roberts and R. Mohr (eds.), *Confronting Sexual Assault: A Decade of Legal and Social Change*. Toronto: University of Toronto Press.

Clinard, M.B. (1964). *Anomie and Deviant Behaviour*. New York: Free Press.

Clinard, M.B., and D.J. Abbot. (1973). *Crime in Developing Countries*. New York: Wiley.

Clinard, M.B., and R.F. Meier. (1989). *Sociology of Deviant Behavior*. Chicago: Holt, Rinehart and Winston.

———. (1998). *Sociology of Deviant Behavior*. (10th ed.) New York: Harcourt Brace.

Clinard, M.B., and P.C. Yeager. (1980). *Corporate Crime*. New York: Free Press.

Cloward, R., and L. Ohlin. (1960). *Delinquency and Opportunity*. New York: Free Press.

Clugston, M. (1985). "Terror in the Capital." *Maclean's* (March 25):17–18.

Cockerham. W.C. (1989). *Sociology of Mental Disorder* (2nd ed.). Englewood Cliffs, NJ: Prentice-Hall.

Cohen, A. (1955). *Delinquent Boys: The Culture of the Gang*. New York: Free Press.

———. (1966). *Deviance and Control*. Englewood Cliffs, NJ: Prentice-Hall.

Cohen, L., and M. Felson. (1979). "Social Change and Crime Rate Trends: A Routine Activities Approach." *American Sociological Review* 44:588–608.

Comack, A.E. (1985). "The Origins of Canadian Drug Legislation: Labelling Versus Class Analysis." In T. Fleming (ed.), *The New Criminologies in Canada: State, Crime, and Control*. Toronto: Oxford University Press.

Commercial Sex Information Service (CSIS). (1999). *Rights Groups*. on-line: <<http://www.walnet.org/csis/groups/index.html>>

Committee on Sexual Offences Against Children and Youths (CSOACY). (1984). *Sexual Offences Against Children: Report of the Committee on Sexual Offences Against Children and Youth*. Ottawa: Minister of Supply and Services.

Commoner, B. (1990). *Making Peace with the Planet*. New York: Pantheon.

Conklin, J.E. (1972). *Robbery and the Criminal Justice System*. Philadelphia: Lippincott.

Conrad, P. (1981). "On the Medicalization of Deviance and Social Control." In D. Ingleby (ed.), *Critical Psychiatry*. Middlesex: Penguin.

Cook, P.J. (1980). "Research in Criminal Deterrence: Laying the Groundwork for the Second Decade." In N. Morris and M. Tonry (eds.), *Crime and Justice: An Annual Review of Research*. Chicago: University of Chicago Press.

Cooley, C.H. (1902). Human Nature and the Social Order. New York: Scribner's.

Corelli, R. (1986). "Frustrations in the Drug War." *Maclean's* (September 29):42–43.

Correctional Services Canada. (1986). *Basic Facts About Corrections in Canada*. Ottawa: Minister of Supply and Services Canada.

Cotterrill, R. (1984). *The Sociology of Law: An Introduction*. London: Butterworths.

COYOTE Homepage on-line: <<http://www.freedomusa.org/coyotela/index.html>>

Cressey, D.R. (1955). "Changing Criminals: The Application of Differential Association Theory." *American Journal of Sociology* 61:116–20.

———. (1969). *Theft of a Nation*. New York: Harper and Row.

———. (1971). *Other People's Money: A Study in the Social Psychology of Embezzlement* (2nd ed.). Belmont, CA: Wadsworth.

Cristie, N. (1989). *Beyond Loneliness and Institutions: Communities for Extraordinary People*. Oslo: Norwegian University Press.

Crook, N. (1984). *Report on Prostitution in the Atlantic Provinces*. Working Papers on Pornography and Prostitution Report No. 12. Ottawa: Department of Justice.

Crutchfield, R., M. Geerken, and W. Gove. (1982). "Crime Rates and Social Integration: The Impact of Metropolitan Mobility." *Criminology* 20:467–78.

CSIS. *See* Canadian Security Intelligence Service.

CSOACY. *See* Committee on Sexual Offences Against Children and Youths.

Currie, E. (1993). *Reckoning: Drugs, the Cities, and the American Future*. New York: Hill and Wang.

CUVS. *See* Canadian Urban Victimization Study.

Dahrendorf, R. (1959). *Class and Class Conflict in Industrial Societies*. Stanford, CA: Stanford University Press.

Daily. (1999). "Control and Sale of Alcoholic Beverages." *The Daily*. Ottawa: Statistics Canada. on-line: <<http://www.statcan.ca/Daily/English/000622/d000622b.htm>>

Dalglish, B. (1990). "The Test of Competition." *Maclean's* (July 16):30–32.

Daly, K., and M. Chesney-Lind. (1988). "Feminism and Criminology." *Justice Quarterly* 5:497–538.

Darwin, C. (1927). *The Origin of Species*. New York: Macmillan.

Davis, K. (1937). "The Sociology of Prostitution." *American Sociological Review* 2:744–55.

Davis, N. (1978). "Prostitution: Identity, Career and Legal-Economic Enterprise." In J.M. Henslin (eds.), *The Sociology of Sex*. New York: Schocken.

———. (1980). *Sociological Constructions of Deviance*. Dubuque, IO: Wm. C. Brown.

Davis, S. (1993). "Changes to the Criminal Code Provisions for Mentally Disordered Offenders and Their Implications for Canadian Psychiatry." *Canadian Journal of Psychiatry* 38:122–26.

Davison, G.C., and J.M. Neale. (1990). *Abnormal Psychology* (5th ed.). New York: John Wiley and Sons.

Day, D. (1985). "Portrayal of Mental Illness in the Media: A Content Analysis of Canada's Newspapers." *Network* 5:20–21.

Deitz, M.L. (1983). *Killing for Profit: The Social Organization of Felony Homicide*. Chicago: Nelson Hall.

Deitz, P. (1986). "Mass, Serial, and Sensational Homicide." *Bulletin of the New York Academy of Medicine* 62:477–491.

DeKeseredy, W.S. (1988). "The Left Realist Approach to Law and Order." *Justice Quarterly* 4:635–40.

DeKeseredy, W.S., and M.D. Schwartz. (1991). "British Left Realism on the Abuse of Women: A Critical Appraisal." In H.E. Pepinsky and R. Quinney (eds.), *Criminology as Peacemaking*. Bloomington and Indianapolis: Indiana University Press.

Denisoff, R.S., and D. MacQuarie. (1975). "Crime Control in Capitalist Society." *Issues in Criminology* 10:109–19.

Department of Justice. (1985). *Sexual Assault Legislation in Canada: An Evaluation*. Ottawa: Supply and Services Canada.

Depew, R. (1986). *Native Policing in Canada: A Review of Current Issues*. Ottawa: Solicitor General of Canada.

Desroches, F.J. (1990). "Tearoom Trade: A Research Update." *Qualitative Sociology* 13:39–61.

Dohrenwend, B.P. (1975). "Sociocultural and Social-psychological Factors in the Genesis of Mental Disorders." *Journal of Health and Social Behavior* 16:365–92.

Dohrenwend, B.P., and B.P. Dohrenwend. (1976). "Sex Differences and Psychiatric Disorders." *American Journal of Sociology* 81:1447–54.

Dolphin, P. (1988). "Hidden Addictions: The Increasing Abuse of Prescription Drugs." *Maclean's* (December 12):N2–N4.

———. (1989). "A Global Struggle: Drug Police Are Fighting the Odds." *Maclean's* (April 3):48–49.

Douglas, J.D. (1977). "Shame and Deceit in Creative Deviance." In E. Sagarin (ed.), *Deviance and Social Change*. Beverly Hills: Sage.

Dowie, M. (1977). "Pinto Madness." In S.L. Hills (ed.), *Corporate Violence: Injury and Death for Profit*. Totowa, NJ: Rowman and Little Field.

Dubro, J. (1985). *Mob Rule: Inside the Canadian Mafia*. Toronto: Totem Books.

———. (1992). *Dragons of Crime*. Markham: Butterworths.

Dubro, J., and R.F. Rowland. (1988). *King of the Mob: Rocco Perri and the Women Who Ran His Rackets*. Markham, ON: Penguin.

Duchesne, D. (1997). Street Prostitution in Canada. *Juristat Service Bulletin* 17(2). Ottawa: Canadian Centre for Justice Statistics, Statistics Canada.

Durkheim, É. (1951). *Suicide: A Study in Sociology*. New York: Free Press.

———. (1962). *The Rules of Sociological Method*. New York: Free Press.

Eaton, W.W. (1986). *The Sociology of Mental Disorders* (2nd ed.). New York: Praeger.

Edgerton, R.B. (1978). *Deviance: A Cross Cultural Perspective*. Menlo Park, CA: Cummings.

Egger, S.A. (1998). *The Killers Among Us: An Examination of Serial Murder and Its Investigation*. Upper Saddle River, NJ: Prentice-Hall.

Ekstadt, J.W., and C.T. Griffiths. (1988). *Corrections in Canada: Policy and Practice* (2nd ed.). Toronto: Butterworths.

Elliott, D., and S. Ageton. (1980). "Reconciling Race and Class Differences in Self-Reported and Official Estimates of Delinquency." *American Sociological Review* 45:95–110.

Elliott, D., and D. Huizinga. (1983). "Social Class and Delinquent Behavior in a National Youth Panel." *Criminology* 21:149–77.

Ellis, D. (1987). The Wrong Stuff: An Introduction to the Sociological Study of Deviance. Don Mills, ON: Collier Macmillan Canada.

———. (1988). "Urine Testing: A Critical Appraisal." *Canadian Journal of Criminology* 30:261–71.

Ellis, D., and A. Choi. (1984). *Video Arcades and Student Behavior*. Toronto: Toronto Board of Education.

Elsworth, S. (1984). *Acid Rain*. Pluto Press.

———. (1990). *A Dictionary of the Environment*. Paladin.

Empey, L.T. (1982). *American Delinquency: Its Meaning and Construction*. Homewood, IL: Dorsey Press.

Environics Research Group. (1998). *Focus Canada Environics 1998-1*. Ottawa: Environics.

Erickson, P.G., E.M. Adlay, G.F. Murray, and R.G. Smart. (1987). *The Steel Drug: Cocaine in Perspective*. Toronto: D.C. Heath.

Erikson, K.T. (1962). "Notes on the Sociology of Deviance." *Social Problems* 9:307–14.

———. 1966. *Wayward Puritans*. New York: Wiley.

Ermann, M.D., and R.J. Lundman. (1982). *Corporate Deviance*. New York: Holt, Rinehart and Winston.

Estok, D. (1996). "This Is World War III: A Chronology of Events Leading to the Westray Explosion." *Maclean's* (July 15):24–25.

Faith, K. (1993). *Unruly Women: The Politics of Confinement and Resistance*. Vancouver: Press Gang.

Faris, R.E. (1967). *Chicago Sociology, 1920–1932*. San Francisco: Chandler.

Farquhar, W., and I.M. Gomme. (1981). "The Terminal Fix: Learning to Compute." Paper presented at the annual meetings of the Canadian Sociological and Anthropological Society, Halifax, Nova Scotia.

Farrell, R., and V.L. Swigert. (1982). *Deviance and Social Control*. Dallas: Scott, Foresman and Company.

Farrington, D., and E. Dowds. (1985). "Disentangling Criminal Behavior and Police Reaction." In D. Farrington and J. Gunn (eds.), *Reactions to Crime: The Public, Police, Courts, and Prisons*. Chichester: Wiley.

Fattah, E.A. (1972). *A Study of the Deterrent Effect of Capital Punishment with Special Reference to the Canadian Situation*. Ottawa: Information Canada.

Fedorowycz, O. (1996). Homicide in Canada, 1995. *Juristat Service Bulletin* 16(11). Ottawa: Canadian Centre for Justice Statistics, Statistics Canada.

———. (1999). Homicide in Canada, 1998. *Juristat Service Bulletin* 19(10). Ottawa: Canadian Centre for Justice Statistics, Statistics Canada.

———. (2000). Homicide in Canada — 1999. *Juristat Service Bulletin* 20(9). Ottawa: Canadian Centre for Justice Statistics, Statistics Canada.

Fehr, K.O. (1988a). "The Dealer's Choice: An Introduction to Street Drugs." In J.C. Blackwell and P.G. Erickson (eds.), *Illicit Drugs in Canada: A Risky Business*. Scarborough: Nelson.

———. (1988b). "Making Connections: Drugs, Mind, and Body." In J.C. Blackwell and P.G. Erickson (eds.), *Illicit Drugs in Canada: A Risky Business*. Scarborough: Nelson.

Felson, M., and L. Cohen. (1980). "Human Ecology and Crime: A Routine Activities Approach." *Human Ecology* 4:389–406.

Ferry, J., and D. Inwood. (1982). *The Olson Murders*. Langley, BC: Cameo Books.

Finkelhor, D. (1981). "Four Preconditions of Sexual Abuse." In D. Finkelhor (ed.), *Child Sexual Abuse: Theory and Research*. New York: Free Press.

———. (1984). *Child Sexual Abuse: New Theory and Research*. New York: Free Press.

Fleischman, J. (1984). *A Report on Prostitution in Ontario*. Working Papers on Pornography and Prostitution Report No. 10. Ottawa: Department of Justice.

Fleming, T. (1983). "Criminalizing a Marginal Community: The Bawdy House Raids." In T. Fleming and L.A. Visano (eds.), *Deviant Designations: Crime Law and Deviance in Canada*. Toronto: Butterworths.

Fox, J.A., and J. Levin. (1994). *Overkill: Mass Murder and Serial Killing Exposed*. New York: Dell.

Francis, D. (1988a). "Crackdown on Corporate Culprits." *Maclean's* (August 29):9.

———. (1988b). "Harsh Measures Against Drugs." *Maclean's* (September 12):9.

Frank, N. (1987). "Murder in the Workplace." In S.L. Hills (ed.), *Corporate Violence: Injury and Death for Profit*. Totowa, NJ: Rowman and Little Field.

Fraser Committee. *See* Special Committee on Pornography and Prostitution.

Freeze, C. (2000). "Previous Night Like Any Other On the Street." *Globe and Mail* (July 7):A3.

Freud, S. (1961 [1930]). *Civilization and Its Discontents*. New York: Norton.

Friedrichs, D.O. (1980). "The Legitimacy Crisis: A Conceptual Analysis." *Social Problems* 27:540–55.

Gabor, T., M. Baril, M. Cusson, D. Elie, M. LeBlanc, and A. Normandeau. (1987). *Armed Robbery: Cops, Robbers, and Victims*. Springfield, IL: Charles C. Thomas.

Gadd, J. (2000). "Law Against Marijuana Struck Down in Ontario." *Globe and Mail* (August 1):A1, A7

Gagnon, L. (1985). "A Dark Flirtation with History." *Maclean's* (October 21):5–7.

Gallagher, B.J. (1987). *The Sociology of Mental Illness* (2nd ed.). Englewood Cliffs, NJ: Prentice-Hall.

Gatehouse, J. (2000a). "Incident Joins Spate of High-profile Domestic Violence." *National Post* (July 7):A7.

———. (2000b). "Hells Angels Corner the Drug Market in Nunavut." *National Post* (July 10):A1, A6

Gemme, R., A. Murphy, M. Bourque, M.A. Nemeh, and N. Payment. (1984). *A Report on Prostitution in Quebec*. Working Papers on Pornography and Prostitution Report No. 11. Ottawa: Department of Justice.

Gerson, L., and D. Preston. (1979). "Alcohol Consumption and the Incidence of Violent Crime." *Journal of Studies on Alcohol* 40:307–12.

Gibbons, D.C. (1982). *Society, Crime and Criminal Behavior*. Englewood Cliffs, NJ: Prentice-Hall.

Gibbs, J.P. (1966). "Conceptions of Deviant Behavior: The Old and the New." *Pacific Sociological Review* 9:9–14.

———. (1975). *Crime, Punishment and Deterrence*. New York: Elsmere.

Gibson, L., R. Linden, and S. Johnson. (1980). "A Situational Theory of Rape." *Canadian Journal of Corrections* 22:51–65.

Giffen, P.J., and S. Lambert. (1988). "What Happened on the Way to Law Reform?" In J.C. Blackwell and P.G. Erickson (eds.), *Illicit Drugs in Canada: A Risky Business*. Scarborough: Nelson.

Gillis, C., C. Eby, and J. Gatehouse. (2000). "Why Take the Kids With You?" *National Post* (July 7):A1, A7.

Glaser, D. (1956). "Criminality Theories and Behavioral Images." *American Journal of Sociology* 61:433–44.

Glassner, B. (1982). "Labeling Theory." In M.M. Rosenberg, R.A. Stebbins, and A. Turrowitz (eds.), *The Sociology of Deviance*. New York: St. Martin's Press.

Glassner, B., and B. Berg. (1980). "How Jews Avoid Alcohol Problems." *American Sociological Review* 45:647–64.

Glock, C. (1967). *Survey Research in the Social Sciences*. New York: Russell Sage Foundation.

Glueck, S. (1956). "Theory and Fact in Criminology." *British Journal of Delinquency* 7:85–98.

Goff, C., and C.E. Reasons. (1978). *Corporate Crime in Canada: A Critical Analysis of Anti-Combines Legislation*. Scarborough: Prentice-Hall.

Goffman, E. (1961). *Asylums*. Garden City, NY: Doubleday Anchor Books.

———. (1963). *Stigma*. Englewood Cliffs, NJ: Prentice-Hall.

Goldman, C. (1989). "The Impact of the Competition Act of 1986." Address given to the National Conference on Competition Law and Policy in Canada. Toronto, October 24–25.

Gomme, I.M. (1985a). "Predictors of Status and Criminal Offences Among Male and Female Adolescents in an Ontario Community." *Canadian Journal of Criminology* 27:157–59.

———. (1985b). "On the Statistical Testing of Causal Ordering in Delinquency Research." *Canadian Review of Sociology and Anthropology* 22:574–78.

———. (1986a). "Fear of Crime Among Urban Canadians." *Journal of Criminal Justice* 14:249–58.

———. (1986b). "Strain and Adult Crime: The Use of Self Report Measures." Paper presented at the annual meetings of the Academy of Criminal Justice Sciences, Orlando, Florida.

———. (1987). "Popular Views of Justice in Canada." Paper presented at the annual meetings of the American Society of Criminology, Montreal, Quebec.

———. (1988). "The Role of 'Experience' in the Production of Fear of Crime." *Canadian Journal of Criminology* 30:67–76.

Gomme, I.M., M.E. Morton, and W. Gordon West. (1984). "Rates, Types, and Patterns of Male and Female Delinquency in an Ontario County." *Canadian Journal of Criminology* 26:313–24.

Gomme, I.M., and L.G. Richardson. (1991). "All the Leaves Are Brown and the Sky Is Grey: A California Nightmare Writ Large." Paper presented at the annual meetings of the American Society of Criminology, San Francisco, California.

Goode, E., and N. Ben-Yehuda. (1994). *Moral Panics: The Social Construction of Deviance*. Cambridge, MA: Blackwell Publishing.

Goodman, M. (1997). "Why the Police Don't Care About Computer Crime," *Harvard Journal of Law and Technology* 10:465–94.

Goold, D., and A. Willis. (1997). *The Bre-X Fraud*. Toronto: McClelland and Stewart.

Gordon, A., and D. Suzuki. (1990). *It's a Matter of Survival*. Toronto: Stoddart.

Gordon, M.T., and S. Riger. (1989). *The Female Fear*. New York: Free Press.

Goring, C. (1913). *The English Convict: A Statistical Study*. London: His Majesty's Stationery Office.

Gorman, C. (1988). "Why It's So Hard to Quit Smoking." *Time* (May 30):59.

Gottfredson, M.R., and T. Hirschi. (1990). *A General Theory of Crime*. Stanford, CA: Stanford University Press.

Gove, W.R. (1972). "The Relationship Between Sex Roles, Marital Status, and Mental Illness." *Social Forces* 51:34–44.

———. (1980). *The Labelling of Deviance: Evaluating a Perspective* (2nd ed.). Beverly Hills: Sage.

Gove, W.R., M. Tovo, and M. Hughes. (1985). "Involuntary Psychiatric Hospitalization: A Review of the Statutes Regulating the Social Control of the Mentally Ill." *Deviant Behavior* 6:287–318.

Gove, W.R., and J. Tudor. (1973). "Adult Sex Roles and Mental Illness." *American Journal of Sociolology* 78:812–35.

Government of Ontario Press Release. (2000). *Ontario introduces Brian's Law for better mental health and safer communities*. April 25. on-line: <<http://www.newswire.ca/government/ontario/english/releases/April2000/25/c6778.html>>

Gray, J. (1971). *Red Lights on the Prairies*. New York: Signet.

Gray, M. (1986). "The Horror of Child Murders." *Maclean's* (August 11):40–41.

Green, E., and R. Wakefield. (1979). "Patterns of Middle and Upper Class Homicide." *Journal of Criminal Law and Criminology* 70:172–81.

Greenberg, D.F. (1980). "Delinquency and the Age Structure of Society." In David F. Greenberg, *Crime and Capitalism*. Palo Alto, CA: Mayfield.

Greenland, C., and E. Rosenblatt. (1975). *Murder Followed by Suicide in Ontario*. Hamilton: McMaster School of Social Work.

Greenley, J.R. (1972). "The Psychiatric Patient's Family and Length of Hospitalization." *Journal of Health and Social Behavior* 13:25–37.

Greenwald. H. (1970). *The Elegant Prostitute*. New York: Walker.

Greenwood, J. (1996). "Rogues' Gallery." *Financial Post Magazine* (February):46–52.

Griffin, S. (1971). "Rape: The All-American Crime." *Ramparts* (September):26–35.

Griffiths, C.T., and S.N. Verdun-Jones. (1989). *Canadian Criminal Justice*. Toronto: Butterworths.

Griffiths, C.T., D. Wood, E. Zellerer, and J. Simon. (1994). *Aboriginal Policing in British Columbia*. Report prepared for the Commission of Inquiry, Policing in British Columbia. Victoria BC: Ministry of the Attorney General.

Groth, N., and J. Birnbaum. (1979). *Men Who Rape: The Psychology of the Offender*. New York: Plenum.

Guerry, A. (1831). *Essai sur la statistique morale de la France*. Paris: Chez Crochard.

Gunn, R. and R. Linden. (1997). "The Impact of Law Reform on the Processing of Sexual Assault Cases." *Canadian Review of Sociology and Anthropology* 34:155–74.

Hacker, J. (1994). *Crime and Canadian Public Policy*. Scarborough: Prentice-Hall.

Hackler, J.C., and C.T.L. Janssen. (1985). "Police Killings in Perspective." *Canadian Journal of Criminology*. 27:227–32.

Hagan, F.E. (1986). *Criminology: Theories, Methods, and Criminal Behavior*. Chicago: Prentice-Hall.

Hagan, F. (1998). *Introduction to Criminology* (4th ed.) Chicago: Nelson Hall.

Hagan, J. (1975). "Setting the Record Straight: Toward the Reformulation of an Interactionist Perspective in Deviance." *Criminology* 13:421–23.

———. (1985). *Modern Criminology: Crime, Criminal Behavior, and Its Control*. New York: McGraw Hill.

———. (1987). "White Collar and Corporate Crime." In R. Linden (ed.), *Criminology: A Canadian Perspective*. Toronto: Holt, Rinehart and Winston.

———. (1989). *Structural Criminology*. New Brunswick, NJ: Rutgers University Press.

———. (1991). *The Disreputable Pleasures: Crime and Deviance in Canada* (3rd ed.). Toronto: McGraw-Hill Ryerson.

Hagan, J., A.R. Gillis, and J. Chan. (1980). "Explaining Official Delinquency: A Spatial Study of Class Conflict and Control." In R.A. Silverman and J.J. Teevan (eds.), *Crime in Canadian Society* (2nd ed.). Toronto: Butterworths.

Hagan, J., A.R. Gillis, and J.H. Simpson. (1985). "The Class Structure of Gender and Delinquency: Toward a Power-Control Theory of Common Delinquent Behavior." *American Journal of Sociology* 90:1151–78.

Hagan, J., and R. Peterson. (1995). *Crime and Inequality*. Stanford, CA: Stanford University Press.

Hagan, J., J.H. Simpson, and A.R. Gillis. (1979). "The Sexual Stratification of Social Control: A Gender Based Perspective on Crime and Delinquency." *British Journal of Sociology* 30:25–38.

———. (1987). "Class in the Household: A Power Control Theory of Gender and Delinquency." *American Journal of Sociology* 92:788–816.

Hagedorn, J. (1988). *People and Folks: Gangs, Crime, and the Underclass in a Rustbelt City*. Chicago: Lakeview Press.

Halmos, P. (1973). "Introduction." In P. Halmos (ed.), *Professionalization and Social Change*. Staffordshire: University of Keele Press.

Handelman, S. (1995). *Comrade Criminal: Russia's New Mafiya*. New Haven: Yale University Press.

Harries, K.D. (1990). *Serious Violence: Patterns of Homicide and Assault in America*. Springfield, IL: Charles C. Thomas.

Harris, A.R. (1977). "Sex and Theories of Deviance: Toward a Functional Theory of Deviant Type Scripts." *American Sociological Review* 42:3–16.

Harris, M. (1986). *Justice Denied: The Law versus Donald Marshall*. Toronto: Totem Books.

———. (1990). *Unholy Orders: Tragedy at Mount Cashel*. Toronto: Penguin.

Hartnagel, T. (1987). "Correlates of Criminal Behavior." In Rick Linden (ed.), *Criminology: A Canadian Perspective*. Toronto: Holt, Rinehart and Winston.

Hawaleshka, D. (1997). "A High Tech Tool for Police." *Maclean's* (March 24):56–57.

Hawley, A.H. (1986). *Human Ecology*. Chicago: University of Chicago Press.

Health and Welfare Canada. (1988). *Striking a Balance*. Ottawa: National Health and Welfare Canada.

Hendley, N. (2000). "Volunteers Against Involuntary Drugs." *National Post* (July 8):F2.

Hendrick, D. (1996). *Canadian Crime Statistics, 1995*. Juristat Service *Bulletin 16(10)*. Ottawa: Canadian Centre for Justice Statistics, Statistics Canada.

Herold, E.S. (1984). *Sexual Behaviour of Canadian Young People*. Markham, ON: Fitzhenry and Whiteside.

Hess, J.H., and H.E. Thomas. (1963). "Incompetency to Stand Trial: Procedures, Results, and Problems." *American Journal of Psychiatry* 119:713–20.

Heyl, B.S. (1979a). *The Madam as Entrepreneur: Career Management in House Prostitution*. New Brunswick, NJ: Transaction.

———. (1979b). "Prostitution: An Extreme Case of Sexual Stratification." In F. Adler and R.J. Simon (eds.), *The Criminality of Deviant Women*. Boston: Houghton Mifflin.

Hickey, E.W. (1991). *Serial Murderers and Their Victims*. Belmont, CA: Brooks Cole Publishing.

———. (1997). *Serial Murderers and Their Victims* (2nd ed.). Belmont, CA: Wadsworth.

Higgins, P.C., and R.R. Butler. (1982). *Understanding Deviance*. New York: McGraw Hill.

Highcrest, A. (1997). *At Home on the Stroll: My Twenty Years as a Prostitute in Canada*. Toronto: Knopf.

Hills, S.L. (1980). *Demystifying Social Deviance*. New York: McGraw Hill.

———. (1987). "Introduction." In S.L. Hills (ed.), *Corporate Violence: Injury and Death for Profit*. Totowa, NJ: Rowman and Littlefield.

Hinch, R. (1983). "Marxist Criminology in the 1970's: Clarifying the Clutter." *Crime and Social Justice* 19:65–74.

———. (1988a). "Enforcing the New Sexual Assault Laws: An Exploratory Study." *Atlantis* 14:109–15.

———. (1988b). "Inconsistencies and Contradictions in Canada's Sexual Assault Law." *Canadian Public Policy* 14:282–94.

———. (1994). *Readings in Critical Criminology*. Scarborough: Prentice-Hall.

Hindelang, M., M. Gottfredson, and J. Garofalo. (1978). *Victims of Personal Crime*. Cambridge, MA: Ballinger.

Hippchen, L.J. (1978). *Ecologic-Biochemical Approaches to the Treatment of Delinquents and Criminals*. New York: Van Nostrand Reinhold.

Hirschi, T. (1962). "The Professional Prostitute." *Berkeley Journal of Sociology* 7:33–49.

———. (1969). *Causes of Delinquency*. Berkeley: University of California Press.

Hirschi, T., and M. Gottfredson. (1983). "Age and the Explanation of Crime." *American Journal of Sociology* 89:552–84.

Hobson, B.M. (1987). *Uneasy Virtue: The Politics of Prostitution and the American Reform Movement*. New York: Basic Books.

Hoigard, C., and L. Finstad. (1992). *Backstreets: Prostitution, Money, and Love*. University Park: Pennsylvania State University Press.

Holmes, R.M., and J. De Burger. (1988). *Serial Murder*. Newbury Park, CA: Sage.

Holmes, R.M., and S.T. Holmes. (1994). *Murder in America*. Thousand Oaks, CA: Sage.

———. (1998). *Serial Murder* (2nd ed.) Thousand Oaks, CA: Sage

Holmes, T.H., and R.H. Rahe. (1967). "The Social Readjustment Rating Scale." *Journal of Psychometric Research* 11:213–25.

Holmstrom, L., and A. Burgess. (1978). *The Victim of Rape: Institutional Reactions*. New York: John Wiley and Sons.

———. (1983). *The Victim of Rape* (2nd ed.). New Brunswick, NJ: Transaction Books.

Homer, F.D. (1974). *Guns and Garlic: Myths and Realities of Organized Crime*. West Lafayette, IN: Purdue University Press.

House, D. (1986). "Working Offshore: The Other Price of Newfoundland's Oil." In K. Lundy and P. Warme (eds.), *Work in the Canadian Context: Continuity Despite Change* (2nd ed.). Toronto: Butterworths.

Humphreys, L. (1970). *The Tearoom Trade: Impersonal Sex in Public Places*. New York: Adeline.

Ianni, A.F.J. (1972). *A Family Business*. New York: Russell Sage.

———. (1974). *The Black Mafia: Ethnic Succession in Organized Crime*. New York: Simon and Schuster.

Inciardi, J.A. (1980). *Radical Criminology*. Beverly Hills: Sage.

———. (1984). *Criminal Justice*. New York: Harcourt Brace Jovanovich.

———. (1986). *The War on Drugs: Heroin, Cocaine, Crime, and Public Policy*. Mountainview, CA: Mayfield.

———. (1987). *Criminal Justice* (2nd ed.). New York: Harcourt Brace Jovanovich.

———. (1991). *The Drug Legislation Debate*. Newbury Park, CA: Sage.

Jacobs, D. (1980). "Marxism and the Criticism of Empiricism." *Social Problems* 27:467–70.

Jamieson, K.M. (1994). *The Organization of Corporate Crime: Dynamics of AntiTrust Violations*. Thousand Oaks, CA: Sage.

Janhevich, D. (1998a). The Changing Nature of Fraud in Canada. *Juristat Service Bulletin* 18(4). Ottawa: Canadian Centre for Justice Statistics, Statistics Canada.

———. (1998b). Violence Committed by Strangers. *Juristat Service Bulletin* 18(9). Ottawa: Canadian Centre for Justice Statistics, Statistics Canada.

Janigan, M. (1985). "The Trail of Toxic Disaster." *Maclean's* (April 29):14–17.

Jenish, D. (1993). "A Trail of Brutality: Investigation into a String of Rapes and Killings Led Police Teams in Ontario to a Young Man Once Known as Both 'Caring' and 'Kind.'" *Maclean's* (March 1):22–23.

———. (1994). "The Final Chapter: How Strong Is the Case Against Paul Teale?" *Maclean's* (April 18):23.

———. (1995). "The Jury Finds Bernardo Guilty of First Degree Murder." *Maclean's* (September 11):18–23.

———. (1996). "Bungling the Case: An Inquiry Concludes That Paul Bernardo Could Have Been Stopped." *Maclean's* (July 22):40–41.

———. (1997). "How Did It Happen?" *Maclean's* (March 10):19.

———. (2000). "Breach of Trust." *Maclean's* (July 31):28–30.

Jenkins, P. (1988). "Serial Murder in England 1940–1985." *Journal of Criminal Justice* 16:1–15.

Jenness, V. (1989). "Serial Murder in the United States 1900–1940: A Historical Perspective." *Journal of Criminal Justice* 17:377–92.

———. (1993). *Making it Work: The Prostitutes' Rights Movement*. New York: Aldine de Gruyter.

Jensen, G.E., and D.G. Rojek. (1980). *Delinquency: A Sociological View.* Lexington, MA: D.C. Heath.

Johnson, D.R., and L. St. Peter. (1976). "Marital Role Education and Mental Disorder Among Women: A Test of an Interaction Hypothesis." *Journal of Health and Social Behavior* 17:295–301.

Johnson, G., J. Cooper, and J. Mandel. (1976). "Expectation of Admission to a Canadian Psychiatric Institution." *Canadian Psychiatric Association Journal* 14:296–98.

Johnson, H. (1986). *Women and Crime in Canada.* Ottawa: Solicitor General, Canada.

———. (1995). Children and Youths as Victims of Violent Crime. *Juristat Service Bulletin* 15(15). Ottawa: Canadian Centre for Justice Statistics, Statistics Canada.

———. (1996a). "Sexual Assault." In V. Sacco and L. Kennedy (eds.), *Crime Counts.* Toronto: Nelson.

———. (1996b). Violent Crime in Canada. *Juristat Service Bulletin* 16(6). Ottawa: Canadian Centre for Justice Statistics, Statistics Canada.

Johnson, H., and V. Sacco. (1991). "The Risk of Criminal Victimization: Data from a National Study." In R.A. Silverman, J.J. Teevan, and V.F. Sacco (eds.), *Crime in Canadian Society.* Toronto: Butterworths.

Johnson, S., L. Gibson, and R. Linden. (1980). "Alcohol as a Contributing Factor in Forcible Rape." In R.A. Silverman and J.J. Teevan (eds.), *Crime in Canadian Society* (2nd ed.). Toronto: Butterworths.

Johnson, W. (2000). "Reefer Madness Redux." *Toronto Star* (August 2):A17.

Johnstone, L. (1989). *Users and Abusers of Psychiatry: A Critical Look at Traditional Psychiatric Practice.* London: Routledge.

Kaihla, P. (1989). "A Lethal Choice for Murder." *Maclean's* (December 18):16.

Kanin, E.J. (1984). "Date Rape: Unofficial Criminals and Victims." *Victimology: An International Journal* 9:95–108.

Katz, S., and M.A. Mazur. (1979). *Understanding the Rape Victim: A Synthesis of Research Findings.* New York: Wiley.

Keane, C., A.R. Gillis, and J. Hagan. (1989). "Deterrence and Amplification of Juvenile Delinquency by Police Contact: The Importance of Gender and Risk Orientation." *British Journal of Criminology* 29:336–52.

Kearns, R.A., and S.M. Taylor. (1989). "Daily Life Experiences with Chronic Mental Disabilities in Hamilton Ontario." *Canada's Mental Health* 37:1–4.

Kinnon, D. (1981). *Report on Sexual Assault in Canada.* Ottawa: Canadian Advisory Council on the Status of Women.

Kirby, C., and T.C. Renner. (1986). *Mafia Assassin: The Inside Story of a Canadian Biker, Hitman, and Police Informer.* Toronto: Methuen.

Kleck, G., and S. Sayles. (1990). "Rape and Resistance." *Social Problems* 37:149–62.

Klein, D. (1973). "The Etiology of Female Crime: A Review of the Literature." *Issues in Criminology* 8:3–29.

Klein, M.W., and C.L. Maxson. (1989). "Street Gang Violence." In N.A. Weiner and M.E. Wolfgang (eds.), *Violent Crime, Violent Criminals.* Beverly Hills: Sage.

Klockars, C. (1979). "The Contemporary Crisis of Marxist Criminology." *Criminology* 16:477–515.

Knox, D. (1984). *Human Sexuality.* St. Paul, MN: West Publishing.

Kolb, L.C., and K.H. Brodie. (1982). *Modern Clinical Psychiatry* (10th ed.). Philadelphia: Saunders.

Kong, R. (1998). Breaking and Entering in Canada, 1996. *Juristat Service Bulletin* 18(5). Ottawa: Canadian Centre for Justice Statistics, Statistics Canada.

Kooistra, P. (1989). *Criminals as Heroes: Structure, Power, and Identity.* Bowling Green, OH: Bowling Green State University Popular Press.

Kornhauser, R. (1978). *Social Sources of Delinquency: An Appraisal of Analytic Models.* Chicago: University of Chicago Press.

Krohn, M.D., and R.L. Akers. (1977). "An Alternative View of the Labelling Versus Psychiatric Perspectives on Social Reaction to Mental Illness." *Social Forces* 56:341–61.

LaFree, G.D. (1989). *Rape and Criminal Justice: The Social Construction of Sexual Assault.* Belmont, CA: Wadsworth.

Laing, R.D. (1985). *Wisdom, Madness, and Folly: The Making of a Psychiatrist.* New York: McGraw Hill.

Landau, S. (1974). "Rape: The Victim as Defendant." *Trial* 10:19–22.

Lane, B., and W. Gregg. (1994). *The Encyclopedia of Mass Murder.* London: Headline.

Laufer, W.S., and J.M. Day. (1983). *Personality Theory, Moral Development, and Criminal Behavior.* Lexington, MA: Lexington Books.

Lautt, M. (1984). *A Report on Prostitution in the Prairie Provinces.* Working Papers on Pornography and Prostitution Report No. 9. Ottawa: Department of Justice.

Laver, R. (1985). "A New Reign of Terror." *Maclean's* (July 8):20–23.

Lea, J., and J. Young. (1985). *What Is to Be Done About Law and Order: Crisis in the Eighties.* Harmondsworth: Penguin.

LeBlanc, M. (1975). "Middle Class Delinquency." In Robert A. Silverman and James J. Teevan (eds.), *Crime in Canadian Society.* Toronto: Butterworths.

Lefebvre, H. (1968). *The Sociology of Marx.* New York: Random House.

Leibow, E. (1967). *Tally's Corner.* Boston: Little, Brown, and Company.

Lemert, E.M. (1967). *Human Deviance, Social Problems and Social Control.* Englewood Cliffs, NJ: Prentice-Hall.

Lenton, R.L. (1989). "Homicide in Canada and the USA: A Critique of the Hagan Thesis." *Canadian Journal of Sociology* 13:163–78.

Lenzer, G. (1975). *Comte and Positivism.* New York: Harper.

Levi, M. (1991). *Customer Confidentiality, Money Laundering, and Police–Bank Relationships: English Law and Practise in a Global Environment.* London: Police Foundation.

Levin, J., and J.A. Fox. (1985). *Mass Murder: America's Growing Menace.* New York: Plenum Press.

Leyton, E. (1975). *Dying Hard: The Ravages of Industrial Carnage.* Toronto: McClelland and Stewart.

———. (1986). *Hunting Humans: The Rise of the Modern Multiple Murder.* Toronto: McClelland and Stewart.

Liazos, A. (1972). "The Poverty of the Sociology of Deviance: Nuts, Sluts, and Perverts." *Social Problems* 20:103–20.

Liem, R., and J. Liem. (1978). "Social Class and Mental Illness Reconsidered: The Role of Economic Stress and Social Support." *Journal of Health and Social Behavior* 19:139–56.

Linden, R., and C. Fillmore. (1981). "A Comparative Study of Delinquency Involvement." *Canadian Review of Sociology and Anthropology* 18:343–61.

Liska, A. (1987). *Perspectives on Deviance* (2nd ed.). Englewood Cliffs, NJ: Prentice-Hall.

Lofland, J. (1969). *Deviance and Identity*. Englewood Cliffs, NJ: Prentice-Hall.

———. (1984). *Analyzing Social Settings*. Belmont, CA: Wadsworth.

Lombroso, C. (1972). *Criminal Man*. Montclair, NJ: Patterson Smith.

Low, P.W., J.C. Jeffries, and R.J. Bonnie. (1986). *The Trial of John W. Hinckley, Jr.: A Case Study in the Insanity Defense*. Mineola, NY: Foundation Press.

Lowman, J. (1984). *Vancouver Field Study of Prostitution*. Working Papers on Pornography and Prostitution Report No. 8. Ottawa: Department of Justice.

———. (1990). "Notions of Formal Equality Before the Law: The Experience of Street Prostitutes and Their Customers." *Journal of Human Justice* 1:55–76.

———. (1991). "Prostitution in Canada." In M.A. Jackson and C.T. Griffiths (eds.), *Canadian Criminology: Perspectives on Crime and Criminality*. Toronto: Harcourt Brace Jovanovich.

———. (1995). "Prostitution in Canada." In M.A. Jackson and C.T. Griffiths (eds.), *Canadian Criminology: Perspectives on Crime and Criminality*. Toronto: Harcourt Brace.

Luckenbill, D. (1977). "Criminal Homicide as a Situated Transaction." *Social Problems* 25:176–86.

Lung Association. (1986). *You're Young, You're Female, and You Smoke*. Canadian Lung Association.

———. (1987a). *Cigarette Smoking*. Canadian Lung Association.

———. (1987b). *Second Hand Smoke*. Canadian Lung Association.

Lupsha, P.A. (1981). "Individual Choice, Material Culture, and Organized Crime." *Criminology* 19:3–24.

Luske, B. (1990). *Mirrors of Madness: Patrolling the Psychic Border*. New York: Aldine de Gruyter.

Lyman, M.D., and G.W. Potter (1997). *Organized Crime*. Upper Saddle River, NJ: Prentice-Hall.

Macdonald, D. (1991). *The Politics of Pollution*. Toronto: McClelland and Stewart.

MacDonald, S.B. (1989). *Dancing on a Volcano: The Latin American Drug Trade*. New York: Praeger.

MacKenzie, H. (1987). "Hard Choices on Crime." *Maclean's* (July 13):6–7.

MacLean, B. (1986). "State Expenditures on Canadian Criminal Justice." In B. MacLean (ed.), *The Political Economy of Crime: Readings for a Critical Criminology*. Scarborough: Prentice-Hall.

Maclean's (July 17, 1989). "Asbestos Ban." *Business Notes*, p. 25.

Maclean's (January 29, 1990). "Standing on Guard Against a Virus." p. 13.

Maclean's (July 2, 1990). "Record Penalty." *Business Notes*, p. 51.

Maguire, K., and A. Pastore. (1995). *Sourcebook of Criminal Justice Statistics, 1995*. Washington: Bureau of Justice Statistics.

———. (2000). *Sourcebook of Criminal Justice Statistics 1999*. Washington: Bureau of Justice Statistics.

Maguire, L. (1983). *Understanding Social Networks*. Beverly Hills, CA: Sage.

Makin, K. (1992). *Redrum: The Innocent*. Toronto: Penguin.

Makkai, T., and J. Braithwaite. (1994). "Reintegrative Shaming and Compliance with Regulatory Standards." *Criminology* 32:361–86.

Malcolmson, R. (1987). "Niagara in Crisis." *Canadian Geographic* 105(5):10–19.

Mann, C.R. (1996). *When Women Kill*. Albany: SUNY Press.

Mannheim, H. (1972). *Pioneers in Criminology* (2nd ed.). Monclair, NJ: Patterson Smith.

Maris, P., and M. Rein. (1973). *Dilemmas of Social Reform* (2nd ed.). Chicago: Adeline.

Marshall, J. (1982). *Madness: An Indictment of the Mental Health Care System in Ontario*. Toronto: O.P.S.E.U.

Marshall, W.L., and S. Barret. (1990). *Criminal Neglect: Why Sex Offenders Go Free*. Toronto: Doubleday.

Martin, R., R.J. Mutchnick, and W.T. Austin. (1990). *Criminological Thought: Pioneers Past and Present*. New York: Macmillan.

Marx, G.T. (1981). "Ironies of Social Control: Authorities as Contributors to Deviance Through Escalation, Non-enforcement, and Covert Facilitation." *Social Problems* 28:221–46.

Masters, J. (1987). "Prenatal Child Abuse." *Maclean's* (May 17):40.

Matsueda, R., and K. Heimer. (1987). "Race, Family Structure, and Delinquency: A Test of Differential Association and Social Control Theories." *American Sociological Review* 52:826–40.

Matthews, R., and J. Young. (1986). *Confronting Crime*. London: Sage.

Matza, D. (1966). *Becoming Deviant*. Englewood Cliffs, NJ: Prentice-Hall.

Mawby, R. (1979). *Policing the City*. Westmead: Saxon House.

Maxfield, J. (1985). "Computer Bulletin Boards and the Hacker Problem." EDPACS, the *Electric Processing Audit Control and Security Newsletter*. October:31–2.

Maxson, C.L., M.A. Gordon, and M.W. Klein. (1985). "Differences Between Gang and Non-gang Homicide." *Criminology* 23:209–22.

Maxwell, M.A. (1984). *The Alcoholics Anonymous Experience*. New York: McGraw Hill.

McCaghy, C.H., and T.A. Capron. (1997). *Deviant Behavior: Crime, Conflict, and Interest Groups*. Boston: Allyn and Bacon.

McConnell, M.L. (1991). "Protecting Public Places: Prostitution, Pollution, and Prohibiting a 'Perfectly Legal' Profession." *National Journal of Constitutional Law.* 1:197–223.

McCord, W., and J. McCord. (1960). *Origins of Alcoholism*. Stanford, CA: Stanford University Press.

McDonald, L. (1979). "Crime and Punishment in Canada: A Statistical Test of the Conventional Wisdom." In E. Vaz and

A. Lodhi (eds.), *Crime and Delinquency in Canada*. Scarborough: Prentice-Hall.

McIlwraith, R.D. (1987). "Community Mental Health and the Mass Media in Canada." *Canada's Mental Health* 35:11–17.

McIver, M. (1987). "New Campaigns in the War on Drugs." *Maclean's* (June 7):44.

McKay, S. (1985). "Coming to Grips with Random Killers." *Maclean's* (July 8):44–45.

McKenzie, D., and E. Single. (1997). *Alcohol. Canadian Profile, 1997: Alcohol, Tobacco, and Other Drugs*. Toronto: Addiction Research Foundation and Canadian Centre of Substance Abuse.

McKenzie, D., and B. Williams. (1997). *Licit and Illicit Drugs. Canadian Profile, 1997: Alcohol, Tobacco, and Other Drugs*. Toronto: Addiction Research Foundation and Canadian Centre of Substance Abuse.

McKenzie, D., B. Williams, and E. Single. (1997). Introduction. *Canadian Profile, 1997: Alcohol, Tobacco, and Other Drugs*. Toronto: Addiction Research Foundation and Canadian Centre of Substance Abuse.

McLeary, R., B. Neinstedt, and J. Erven. (1982). "Uniform Crime Reports as Organizational Outcomes." *Social Problems* 29:361–72.

McNamara, R.P. (1995). *The Time's Square Hustler: Male Prostitution in New York*. Westport, CT: Praeger.

McNichol, A. (1983). *Drug Trafficking: A North South Perspective*. Ottawa: North-South Institute.

Mead, G.H. (1943). *Mind, Self and Society*. Chicago: University of Chicago Press.

Meissner, W.W. (1985). "Theories of Personality and Psychopathology: Classical Psychoanalysis." In H. Kaplan and B. Sadock (eds.), *Comprehensive Textbook of Psychiatry* (4th ed.), Vol. 1. Baltimore: Williams and Wilkins.

Meithe, T.D., M.C. Stafford, and J.S. Long. (1987). "Routine Activities/Lifestyle and Victimization." *American Sociological Review* 52:184–94.

Menzies, K. (1982). *Sociological Theory in Use*. London: Routledge and Kegan Paul.

Menzies, R.J. (1989). *Survival of the Sanest: Order and Disorder in a Pre-Trial Clinic*. Toronto: University of Toronto Press.

———. (1991). "Mental Disorder and Crime in Canada." In M.A. Jackson and C.T. Griffiths (eds.), *Canadian Criminology: Perspectives on Crime and Criminality*. Toronto: Harcourt Brace Jovanovich.

Merton, R.K. (1938). "Social Structure and Anomie." *American Sociological Review* 3:672–82.

———. (1957). *Social Theory and Social Structure*. New York: Free Press.

———. (1968). *Social Structure and Anomie*. New York: Free Press.

———. (1971). "Social Problems and Social Theory." In R.K. Merton (ed.), *Contemporary Social Problems*. New York: Harcourt Brace Jovanovich.

Messner, S.F., and J.R. Blau. (1987). "Routine Leisure Activities and Rates of Crime: A Macro Level Analysis." *Social Forces* 65:1035–51.

Messner, S., and K. Tardiff. (1985). "The Social Ecology of Urban Homicide: An Application of the Routine Activities Approach." *Criminology*. 23:241–67.

Mickleburgh, R. (2000). "Air India Suspect Charged." *Globe and Mail*. (October 28) online: <<http://www.globeand ma.../config-neutral&slug=wairindia2&date=20001028& archive=RTGA>>

Micucci, A.J. (1986). "Public Support for the Death Penalty in Canada." Paper presented at the annual meetings of the American Criminology Society, Atlanta, Georgia.

Middleton, R. (1962). "Brother–Sister and Father–Daughter Marriage in Ancient Egypt." *American Sociological Review* 27:603–11.

Miller, W.B. (1962). "The Impact of Total-Community Delinquency Control Project." *Social Problems* 10:168–91.

Mills, C.W. (1943). "The Professional Ideology of Social Pathologists." *American Journal of Sociology* 69:1965–80.

———. (1956). *The Power Elite*. New York: Oxford University Press.

Ministry of Indian Affairs and Northern Development. (1980). *Indian Conditions*. Ottawa: Government of Canada.

Mitchell, B. (2000). "Sniffer Dog Hit by Passenger." *Toronto Star* (June 13):B4.

Monachesi, E. (1973). "Cesare Beccaria." In H. Mannheim (ed.), *Pioneers of Criminology* Montclair, NJ: Patterson Smith.

Moore, R.J. (1985). "Reflections of Canadians on the Law and the Legal System: Legal Research Institute Survey of Respondents in Montreal, Toronto, and Winnipeg." In D. Gibson and J. Baldwin (eds.), *Law in a Cynical Society? Opinion and the Law in the 1980's*. Calgary: Carswell.

Morgan, G. (1972). "Mental and Social Health and Population Density." *Journal of Human Relations* 20:196–204.

Moyer, S., and P. Carrington. (1989). *Street Prostitution: Assessing the Impact of the Law*. Ottawa: Minister of Supply and Services.

Moyer, S., F. Kopelman, C. LaPrairie, and B. Billingsley. (1985). *Native and Non-Native Admissions to Provincial and Territorial Correctional Institutions*. Ottawa: Solicitor General of Canada.

Murphy, E.F. (1922). *The Black Candle*. Toronto: Thomas Allen.

Murray, G.F. (1988). "The Road to Regulation: Patent Medicines in Canada in Historical Perspective." In J.C. Blackwell and P.G. Erickson (eds.), *Illicit Drugs in Canada: A Risky Business*. Scarborough: Nelson.

Nadeau, C. (2000). *Wrongful Convictions: The Case of David Milgaard*. On-line: <<http://www.ace.acadiau.ca/soci/ agt/soci3703/crimepunish2000/wrongful.htm#The Case of David>>

Nadelson, C.C. (1983). "The Psychology of Women." *Canadian Journal of Psychiatry* 28:210–18.

Naffine, N. (1988). *Female Crime: The Construction of Women in Criminology*. Boston: Allen and Unwin.

National Commission on Marijuana and Drug Abuse. (1973). *Drug Use in America*. Washington, DC: U.S. Government Printing Office.

National Institute on Drug Abuse (NIDA). (2001). *Nicotine Addiction*. Maryland: National Institute on Drug Abuse Research Report Series. online: <<http://www.nida. nih.gov/ResearchReports/Nicotine/nicotine2.html# addictive>>

National Drug Test. (1988). Toronto: CTV, MC Productions Inc.

Nettler, G. (1974). "Embezzlement Without Problems." *British Journal of Criminology* 14:70–77.

———. (1978). *Explaining Crime* (2nd ed.). New York: McGraw Hill.

———. (1982). *Criminal Careers, Part Two: Killing One Another.* Cincinnati: Anderson.

———. (1984). *Explaining Crime* (3rd ed.). New York: McGraw Hill.

Newton, M. (2000). *The Encyclopedia of Serial Killing.* New York: Checkmark Books.

Nichols, M. (1987). "Should the State Kill?" *Maclean's* (June 29):14–17.

Nieradzik, K., and R. Cochrane. (1985). "Public Attitudes Towards Mental Illness: The Effects of Behavior, Roles, and Psychiatric Labels." *International Journal of Social Psychiatry* 31:23–33.

North, D. (1985). "James Cross Remembers." *Maclean's* (October 21):10–12.

Nye, F.I. (1958). *Family Relationships and Delinquent Behavior.* New York: John Wiley.

O'Brien, R.M. (1985). *Crime and Victimization Data.* Beverly Hills, CA: Sage.

O'Hara, J. (2000a). "Abuse of Trust." *Maclean's* (June 26):16–21.

———. (2000b). "No Forgiving." *Maclean's* (June 26):22–3

Ohlendorf, P. (1985a). "A Crisis in Canada's Chemical Valley." *Maclean's* (December 8):54–56.

———. (1985b). "The Deteriorating Great Lakes." *Maclean's* (August 26):38–39.

Ohlin, W. (1980). *Escape from Utopia.* Santa Cruz, CA: Unity.

Olson, Steve. (1985). *Alcohol in America.* Washington, DC: National Academy Press.

O'Reilly-Flemming, T. (1996). *Post-Critical Criminology.* Scarborough, ON: Prentice-Hall.

Overall, C. (1992). "What's Wrong with Prostitution?: Evaluating Sex Work." *Signs* 17:705–24.

Packer, H.L. (1968). *The Limits of the Criminal Sanction.* Stanford, CA: Stanford University Press.

Park, R.E. (1952). *Human Communities.* Glencoe: Free Press.

Parker, D.B. (1989). *Computer Crime: Criminal Justice Research Manual.* Washington, DC: National Institute of Justice.

Parker, G. (1987a). *An Introduction to Criminal Law* (3rd ed.). Toronto: Methuen.

———. (1987b). "Crime, Law, and Legal Defences." In R. Linden (ed.), *Criminology: A Canadian Perspective.* Toronto: Holt, Rinehart and Winston.

Parker, R.N. (1995). *Alcohol and Homicide: A Deadly Combination of Two American Traditions.* Albany: SUNY Press.

Parker, R.N., and A.V. Horwitz. (1986). "Unemployment, Crime, and Punishment: A Panel Approach." *Criminology* 24:751–73.

Parsons, T. (1951). *The Social System.* New York: Free Press.

Pearlin, L.I., and J.S. Johnson. (1977). "Marital Status, Life Strains, and Depression." *American Sociological Review* 42:704–15.

Pepinsky, H.E. (1991). "Peacemaking Criminology and Criminal Justice." In H.E. Pepinsky and R. Quinney (eds.), *Criminology as Peacemaking.* Bloomington, IN: Indiana University Press.

Pepinsky, H.E., and R. Quinney. (1991). *Criminology as Peacemaking.* Bloomington, IN: Indiana University Press.

Pfohl, S. (1985). *Images of Deviance and Social Control: A Social History.* New York: McGraw Hill.

Phillips, D.L., and B.E. Segal. (1969). "Sexual Status and Psychiatric Symptoms." *American Sociological Review* 34:58–72.

Phillips, D.P. (1980). "Airplane Accidents, Murder, and the Mass Media: Towards a Theory of Imitation and Suggestion." *Social Forces.* 58:1001–04.

Piccinini, H., and W. Mitric. (1987). "Self-Esteem Levels of Female University Students Who Exhibit Bulimic Behavior." *Canada's Mental Health* 35:15–19.

Piven, F.F. (1981). "Deviant Behavior and the Remaking of the World." *Social Problems* 28:489–508.

Polk, K., and W. Schafer. (1972). *Schools and Delinquency.* Scarborough: Prentice-Hall.

Polsky, N. (1969). *Hustlers, Beats and Others.* New York: Anchor Books.

Porteous, S. (1998). *Organized Crime: Impact Study (Highlights).* Ottawa: Solicitor General of Canada.

Posner, M. (1985). "The Tragic Last Voyage of Flight 182." *Maclean's* (July 1):43.

Prus, R., and S. Irini. (1988). *Hookers, Rounders and Desk Clerks: The Social Organization of the Hotel Community.* Salem: Sheffield.

Prus, R., and C.R.D. Sharper. (1977). *Road Hustler: The Career Contingencies of Professional Card and Dice Hustlers.* Lexington, MA: Lexington Books.

Prus, R., and S. Vassilakopoulos. (1979). "Desk Clerks and Hookers: Hustling in a 'Shady' Hotel." *Urban Life* 8:52–71.

Quetelet, A. (1842). *A Treatise on Man and the Development of His Faculties.* Edinburgh: W. and R. Chambers.

———. (1984). *Research on the Propensity for Crime at Different Ages.* Cincinnati: Anderson.

Quinney, R. (1970). *The Social Reality of Crime.* Boston: Little, Brown, and Company.

———. (1973). *Critique of the Legal Order.* Boston: Little, Brown, and Company.

———. (1977a). *Class, State, and Crime.* New York: McKay.

———. (1977b). "The Study of White Collar Crime: Toward a Reorientation in Theory and Research." In G. Geis and R.F. Meier (eds.), *White Collar Crime: Offenses in Business, Politics, and the Professions.* New York: Free Press.

Rand, A. (1987). "Transitional Life Events and Desistance from Delinquency and Crime." In M.E. Wolfgang and T.P. Thornberry (eds.), *From Boy to Man: From Delinquency to Crime.* Chicago: University of Chicago Press.

Rashke, R. (1981). *The Killing of Karen Silkwood.* Boston: Houghton Mifflin.

Rasmussen, P., and L. Kuhn. (1976). "The New Masseuse: Play for Pay." *Urban Life* 5:271–92.

Reasons, C., and D. Chappell. (1985). "Crooked Lawyers: Towards a Political Economy of Deviance in the Profession." In T. Fleming (ed.), *The New Criminologies in Canada: State, Crime, and Control.* Toronto: Oxford University Press.

Reasons, C.E., L.L. Ross, and C. Paterson. (1981). *Assault on the Worker: Occupational Health and Safety in Canada.* Toronto: Butterworths.

Reckless, W.C. (1973). *The Crime Problem* (3rd ed.). New York: Appleton Century Crofts.

Renner, K.E., and S. Sahjpaul. (1986). "The New Sexual Assault Law: What Has Been Its Effects?" *Canadian Journal of Criminology* 28:407–13.

Reuter, P. (1984). *Disorganized Crime: Illegal Markets and the Mafia.* Cambridge, MA: MIT Press.

Rhodes, R.P. (1984). *Organized Crime: Crime Control vs. Civil Liberties.* New York: Random House.

Ribordy, F. (1980). "Culture Conflict Among Italian Immigrants." In Robert A. Silverman and James J. Teevan (eds.), *Crime in Canadian Society* (2nd ed.). Toronto: Butterworths.

Rifkin, J. (1991). *Biosphere Politics: A New Consciousness for a New Century.* New York: Crown Publishers.

Roberts, D. and R. Ubha. (2000). "Wrongfully Convicted Sophonow Ready to Forgive." *Toronto Star* (June 9):A3.

Roberts, G. (2000). "Anti-Gang Test Case Moving Slowly." *Globe and Mail* (July 3):A2.

Roberts, J. (1994). Criminal Justice Processing of Sexual Assault Cases. *Juristat Service Bulletin* 14(7). Ottawa: Canadian Centre for Justice Statistics, Statistics Canada.

Roberts, J., and R. Gebotys. (1992). "Reforming Rape Laws." *Law and Human Behavior* 16:555–73.

Roberts, J.V., and C. Grimes. (2000). Adult Criminal Court Statistics 1998–99. *Juristat Service Bulletin* 20(1). Ottawa: Canadian Centre for Justice Statistics, Statistics Canada.

Robertson, F. (1977). *Triangle of Death: The Inside Story of the Triads.* London: Routledge and Kegan Paul.

Rogers, J.W., and M.D. Buffalo. (1974). "Fighting Back: Nine Modes of Adaptation to a Deviant Label." *Social Problems* 22:101–18.

Rootman, I. (1988). "Epidemiological Methods and Indicators." In J.C. Blackwell and P.G. Erickson (eds.), *Illicit Drugs in Canada: A Risky Business.* Scarborough: Nelson.

Rosenberg, M. (1968). *The Logic of Survey Analysis.* New York: Basic Books.

Rosenhan, D.L. (1973). "On Being Sane in Insane Places." *Science* 179:250–58.

Rosnoff, S., H. Pontell, and R. Tillman. (1998). *Profit Without Honor: White Collar Crime and the Looting of America.* Upper Saddle River, NJ: Prentice-Hall.

Ross, G. (1987). *Stung: The Incredible Obsession of Brian Molony.* Toronto: Stoddart.

Rossi, P.H., E. Waite, C. Bose, and R.E. Berk. (1974). "The Seriousness of Crimes: Normative and Individual Differences." *American Sociological Review* 39:224–37.

Rubin, J., and N. Friedland. (1986). "Theater of Terror." *Psychology Today* (March):18–28.

Ruch, L., S. Chandler, and R. Harter. (1980). "Life Change and Rape Impact." *Journal of Health and Social Behavior* 21:248–60.

Rushing, W.A. (1971). "Individual Resources, Societal Reaction, and Hospital Commitment." *American Journal of Sociology* 77:511–25.

———. 1978. "Status Resources, Societal Reactions, and Type of Mental Hospital Admission." *American Sociological Review* 43:521–33.

Russell, D.E.H. (1975). *The Politics of Rape.* New York: Stein and Day.

———. (1984). *Sexual Exploitation: Rape, Child Sexual Abuse, and Workplace Harassment.* Beverly Hills: Sage.

Sacco, V. (1986). "An Approach to the Study of Organized Crime." In Robert A. Silverman and James J. Teevan (eds.), *Crime in Canadian Society* (3rd ed.). Toronto: Butterworths.

———. (1995). "Media constructions of crime." *Annals of the American Academy of Political and Social Science.* 535:141–154.

Sagarin, E. (1975). *Deviants and Deviance.* New York: Praeger.

Sanday, P.R. (1990). *Fraternity Gang Rape: Sex, Brotherhood, and Privilege On Campus.* New York: New York University Press.

Sanders, W.B. (1980). *Rape and Woman's Identity.* Beverly Hills: Sage.

Sansfacon, D. (1985). *Prostitution in Canada: A Research Review Report.* Ottawa: Department of Justice.

Sasson, T. (1995). *Crime Talk: How Citizens Construct a Social Problem.* New York: Aldine de Gruyter.

Saunders, E. (1988). "Women in Canada." In D. Forcese and S. Richer (eds.), *Social Issues* (2nd ed.). Scarborough: Prentice-Hall.

Sauvé, J. (1999). Impaired Driving in Canada — 1998. *Juristat Service Bulletin* 19(11). Ottawa: Canadian Centre for Justice Statistics, Statistics Canada.

Savoie, J. (1999). Youth Violent Crime. *Juristat Service Bulletin* 19(13). Ottawa: Canadian Centre for Justice Statistics, Statistics Canada.

Schatzman, L., and A. Strauss. (1973). *Field Research: Strategies for a Natural Sociology.* Englewood Cliffs, NJ: Prentice-Hall.

Scheff, T. (1984). *Being Mentally Ill* (2nd ed.). Chicago: Aldine.

Schlegal, K., and D. Weisburd. (1992). *White Collar Crime Reconsidered.* Boston: Northeastern University Press.

Schmalleger, F. (1999). *Criminology Today.* Upper Saddle River, NJ: Prentice-Hall.

Schneider, S. (1989). *Global Warming: Are We Entering the Greenhouse Century?* New York: Random House.

Schrag, C. (1962). "Delinquency and Opportunity: Analysis of a Theory." *Sociology and Social Research* 46:165–75.

Schur, E.M. (1971). *Labelling Deviant Behavior.* New York: Harper.

———. (1973). *Radical Non-Intervention: Rethinking the Delinquency Problem.* Englewood Cliffs, NJ: Prentice-Hall.

———. (1979). *Interpreting Deviance.* New York: Harper and Row.

———. (1984). *Labeling Women Deviant.* New York: Random House.

Schwab, J., and M. Schwab. (1978). *Sociocultural Roots of Mental Illness.* New York: Plenum.

Schwartz, M.D., and D.O. Friedrichs. (1994). "Postmodern Thought and Criminological Discontent." *Criminology* 32:221–46.

Schwendinger, H., and J. Schwendinger. (1975). "Defenders of Order or Guardians of Human Rights." In I. Taylor and J. Young (eds.), *Critical Criminology*. London: Routledge and Kegan Paul.

———. (1983). *Rape and Inequality*. Beverly Hills: Sage.

SCPP. *See* Special Committee on Pornography and Prostitution.

Sellin, T. (1938). *Culture Conflict and Crime*. New York: Social Science Research Council.

Sex Workers' Alliance of Vancouver. (2000). SWAV's *Aims and Principles*. on-line: <<http://www.walnet.org/csis/groups/swav/swav.hmtl>>

Shaffir, W., R. Stebbins, and A. Turowetz. (1980). *Fieldwork Experience: Qualitative Approaches to Social Research*. New York: St. Martin's Press.

Shaver, H. (1988). "A Critique of Feminist Charges Against Prostitution." *Atlantis* 14:82–89.

———. (1993). "Prostitution: A Female Crime?" In E. Adelberg and C. Currie (eds.), *In Conflict with the Law: Women and the Canadian Justice System*. Vancouver: Press Gang.

Shaw, C., and H.D. McKay. (1931). *Social Factors in Juvenile Delinquency*. Washington: U.S. Government Printing Office.

———. (1969 [1942]). *Juvenile Delinquency and Urban Areas*. Chicago: University of Chicago Press.

Sheehy, G. (1971). *Hustling*. New York: Delacorte.

Shimrat, I. (1997). *Call Me Crazy: Stories from the Mad Movement*. Vancouver: Press Gang.

Short, J. (1976). *Delinquency, Crime and Society*. Chicago: University of Chicago Press.

Silverman, R.A. (1980). "Measuring Crime: A Tale of Two Cities." In Robert A. Silverman and James J. Teevan (eds.), *Crime in Canadian Society* (2nd ed.). Toronto: Butterworths.

Silverman, R.A., and L. Kennedy. (1993). *Deadly Deeds: Murder in Canada*. Scarborough: Nelson.

Silverman, R.A., J.J. Teevan, and V.F. Sacco. (1991). "Measurement of Crime and Delinquency." In R.A. Silverman, J.J. Teevan, and V.F. Sacco (eds.), *Crime in Canadian Society*. Toronto: Butterworths.

Simon, D.R. (1999). *Elite Deviance* (6th ed.) Boston: Allyn and Bacon.

Simon, D.R., and D.S. Eitzen. (1990). *Elite Deviance* (3rd ed.). Boston: Allyn and Bacon.

Simon, D.R., and F.E. Hagan. (1999). *White Collar Deviance*. Boston: Allyn and Bacon.

Simon, R.J. (1975). *Women and Crime*. New York: Lexington.

Simpson, G. (1969). *Auguste Comte*. New York: Crowell.

Simpson, S.S. (1989). "Feminist Theory, Crime, and Justice." *Criminology* 27:605–32.

Single, E., L. Robson, X. Xie, and J. Rehm. (1997). *The Costs of Substance Abuse in Canada: Highlights of a Major Study of the Health, Social and Economic Costs Associated with the Use of Alcohol, Tobacco, and Illicit Drugs*. Toronto: Addiction Research Foundation and Canadian Centre of Substance Abuse.

Skelton, C. (2000). "Immigration Canada Unable to Weed Out Russian Mobsters." *National Post* (June 7):A7.

Skogan, W. (1975). "Measurement Problems in Official and Survey Crime Rates." *Journal of Criminal Justice* 3:17–32.

———. (1976). *Sample Surveys and the Victims of Crime*. Cambridge, MA: Ballinger.

Smandych, R. (1985). "Marxism and the Creation of Law: Re-Examining the Origins of Canadian Anti-Combines Legislation, 1890–1910." In T. Fleming (ed.), *The New Criminologies in Canada: State, Crime, and Control*. Toronto: Oxford University Press.

Smart, C. (1976). *Women, Crime and Criminology: A Feminist Critique*. London: Routledge and Kegan Paul.

Smart, R.G., and A.C. Ogborne. (1986). *Northern Spirits: Drinking in Canada Now and Then*. Toronto: Addiction Research Foundation.

Snider, L. (1978). "Corporate Crime in Canada: A Preliminary Report." *Canadian Journal of Criminology* 20:142–68.

———. (1993). *Bad Business: Corporate Crime in Canada*. Scarborough:Nelson.

Snider, L., and W.G. West. (1980). "Special Control: Crime and Conflict in Canada." In R.J. Ossenberg (ed.), *Power and Change in Canada*. Toronto: McClelland and Stewart.

———. (1985). "A Critical Perspective on Law in the Canadian State: Delinquency and Corporate Crime." In T. Fleming (ed.), *The New Criminologies in Canada: State, Crime, and Control*. Toronto: Oxford University Press.

Solomon, P.H. (1983). *Criminal Justice Policy: From Research to Reform*. Toronto: Butterworths.

Solomon, R.R. (1988a). "Canada's Drug Legislation." In J.C. Blackwell and P.G. Erickson (eds.), *Illicit Drugs in Canada: A Risky Business*. Scarborough: Nelson.

———. (1988b). "The Noble Pursuit of Evil: Arrest, Search, and Seizure in Canadian Drug Law." In J.C. Blackwell and P.G. Erickson (eds.), *Illicit Drugs in Canada: A Risky Business*. Scarborough: Nelson.

Solomon, R.R., and M. Green. (1988). "The First Century: The History of Non-Medical Opiate Use and Control Policies in Canada, 1870–1970." In J.C. Blackwell and P.G. Erickson (eds.), *Illicit Drugs in Canada: A Risky Business*. Scarborough: Nelson.

Solomon, R.R., E. Single, and P. Erickson. (1988). "Legal Considerations in Canadian Cannabis Policy." In J.C. Blackwell and P.G. Erickson (eds.), *Illicit Drugs in Canada: A Risky Business*. Scarborough: Nelson.

Sourina, J.C. (1990). *A History of Alcoholism*. Cambridge, MA: Basil Blackwell.

Spears, J. (1990). "Marshall Feels Pretty Satisfied with $700,000 in Compensation." *Toronto Star* (July 6):A3.

Special Committee on Pornography and Prostitution (SCPP). (1985). *Pornography and Prostitution: Report of the Special Committee on Pornography and Prostitution*. Ottawa: Department of Justice.

Spitzer, R.L., and P.T. Wilson. (1975). "Nosology and the Official Psychiatric Nomenclature." In H. Kaplan and B. Sadock (eds.), *Comprehensive Textbook of Psychiatry* (2nd ed.). Vol. 1. Baltimore: Williams and Wilkins.

Sproule, C.F., and D.J. Kennett. (1988). "The Use of Firearms in Canadian Homicides 1972–1982: The Need for Gun Control." *Canadian Journal of Criminology* 30:31–38.

———. (1989). "Killing with Guns in the U.S.A. and Canada, 1977–1983: Further Evidence of the Effectiveness of Gun Control." *Canadian Journal of Criminology* 31:245–52.

Srole, L. (1972). "Urbanization and Mental Health: Some Reformulations." *American Scientist* 60:576–83.

Srole, L., and T.S. Langner. (1969). "Protestant, Catholic, and Jew: Comparative Psychopathology." In S.C. Plog and R.B. Edgerton (eds.), *Changing Perspectives in Mental Illness*. New York: Holt, Rinehart and Winston.

Stamler, R. (1987). "Organized Crime." In R. Linden (ed.), *Criminology: A Canadian Perspective*. Toronto: Holt, Rinehart and Winston.

Statistics Canada. (1985). *Canada Year Book*. Ottawa: Minister of Supply and Services.

———. (1991). *Canada Year Book*. Ottawa: Minister of Industry, Science, and Technology.

———. (1993). *Violence Against Women Survey*. Ottawa: Ministry of Supply and Services.

———. (1996a). *Mortality: Summary List of Causes*. Ottawa: Ministry of Industry.

———. (1996b). *Vital Statistics Compendium*. Ottawa: Ministry of Industry.

———. (1999). *General Social Survey*. Ottawa: Ministry of Supply and Services.

Stebbins, R.A. (1987). "Interactionist Theories." In R. Linden (ed.), *Criminology: A Canadian Perspective*. Toronto: Holt, Rinehart and Winston.

Steffensmeier, D. (1978). "Crime and the Contemporary Woman: An Analysis of the Changing Levels of Female Property Crime, 1960–1975." *Social Forces* 57: 566–84.

———. (1980). "Sex Differences in Patterns of Adult Crimes, 1965–1967: A Review and Assessment." *Social Forces* 58:1080–1108.

Steffensmeier, D., and R. Terry. (1975). *Examining Deviance Experimentally: Selected Readings*. Sherman Oaks, CA: Alfred Publishing.

Stephens, R.C. (1987). *Mind Altering Drugs: Use, Abuse, and Treatment*. Newbury Park, CA: Sage.

Strauss, A. (1987). *Qualitative Analysis for Social Scientists*. New York: Cambridge University Press.

Sumner, M. (1981). "Prostitution and the Position of Women: A Case for Decriminalization." In A. Morris (ed.), *Women and Crime*. Cropwood Conference Series No. 13. University of Cambridge: Institute of Criminology.

Sutherland, E. (1940). "White Collar Criminality." *American Sociological Review* 5:1–12.

———. (1947). *The Principles of Criminology* (3rd ed.). Philadelphia: Lippincott.

———. (1949). *White Collar Crime*. New York: Holt, Rinehart and Winston.

Sutherland, E., and D. Cressey. (1970). *Principles of Criminology*. New York: Lippincott.

———. (1978). *Criminology*. Philadelphia: Lippincott.

Swigert, V.L., and R.A. Farrell. (1976). *Murder, Inequality and the Law*. Lexington, MA: D.C. Heath.

Sykes, G., and D. Matza. (1957). "Techniques of Neutralization: A Theory of Delinquency." *American Sociological Review* 22:664–70.

Szasz, T. (1974). *The Myth of Mental Illness* (2nd ed.). New York: Harper and Row.

"Taking a byte out of crime." (1990). *Lotus Quarterly* 5(1): 27-28.

Tallmer, M. (1987). "Chemical Dumping as a Corporate Way of Life." In S.L. Hills (ed.), *Corporate Violence: Injury and Death for Profit*. Totowa, NJ: Rowman and Little Field.

Tannenbaum, F. (1938). *Crime and the Community*. Boston: Ginn.

Tataryn, L. (1979). *Dying for a Living: The Politics of Industrial Death*. Canada: Deneau and Greenberg.

———. (1986). "A Tragically Repeating Pattern: Issues of Industrial Safety." In K. Lundy and P. Warme (eds.), *Work in the Canadian Context: Continuity Despite Change* (2nd ed.). Toronto: Butterworths.

Taylor, A. (1993). *Women Drug Users: An Ethnography of a Female Injecting Community*. New York: Clarendon Press.

Taylor, I., P. Walton, and J. Young. (1973). *The New Criminology: For a Social Theory of Deviance*. London: Routledge and Kegan Paul.

Teplin, L.A. (1984). "Criminalizing the Mentally Disordered: The Comparative Arrest Rate of the Mentally Ill." *American Psychologist* 39:794-803.

———. (1985). "The Criminality of the Mentally Ill: A Dangerous Misconception." *American Journal of Psychiatry* 142:593–98.

———. (2000). "Keeping the Peace: Police Discretion and Mentally Ill Persons." *National Institute of Justice Journal* (July):8-15.

Thio, A. (1973). "Class Bias in the Sociology of Deviance." *American Sociologist* 8:1–12.

———. (1975). "A Critical Look at Merton's Anomie Theory." *Pacific Sociological Review* 18:139–58.

———. (1988). *Deviant Behavior* (3rd ed.). Boston: Houghton Mifflin.

Thomas, C.W., and J.R. Hepburn. (1983). *Crime, Criminal Law and Criminology*. Dubuque, IA: Wm. Brown Publishing.

Thomas, J. (2000). Adult Correctional Services in Canada, 1998–99. *Juristat Service Bulletin* 20(3). Ottawa: Canadian Centre for Justice Statistics, Statistics Canada.

Thompson, D. (1997). *Greed: Investment Fraud in Canada and Around the Globe*. Toronto: Viking.

Thompson, H. (1972). *Hell's Angels*. New York: Random House.

Thompson, J.D. (1967). *Organizations in Action*. New York:McGraw Hill.

Tittle, C.R. (1969). "Crime Rates and Legal Sanctions." *Social Problems* 16:408–23.

———. (1975). "Deterrence or Labeling." *Social Forces* 55:579–96.

Tittle, C.R., and A.R. Rowe. (1974). "Certainty of Arrest and Crime Rates: A Further Test of the Deterrence Hypothesis." *Social Forces* 52:455–62.

Tittle, C.R., W.J. Villemez, and D.A. Smith. (1978). "The Myth of Social Class and Criminality." *Social Forces* 43:643–56.

Toby, J. (1980). "The New Criminology Is the Old Baloney." In J.A. Inciardi (ed.), *Radical Criminology: The Coming Crisis*. Beverly Hills: Sage.

Toch, H. (1977). *Living in Prison: The Ecology of Survival*. Indianapolis, IN: Bobbs Merrill.

Tonry, M. (1995). *Malign Neglect: Race, Crime, and Punishment in America*. New York: Oxford.

Tonry, M., and A.J. Reiss. (1993). *Beyond the Law: Crime in Complex Organizations*. Chicago: University of Chicago Press.

Toole, D. (1986). "Why the Boss Steals." *Maclean's* (April 29):22–25.

Toronto Star (March 15, 1989). "Price Fixing Brings Shell $100,000 Fine."

Toronto Star (May 1, 1995). "Terrorists: Not Only in America." p. A17.

Toronto Star (January 10, 1997). "India and Canada to Fight Terrorism." p. A18.

Tournier, R.E. (1979). "Alcoholics Anonymous as Treatment and as Ideology." *Journal of Studies on Alcohol* 40:230–39.

Trainor, D. (1984). "Chinese Immunity to Alcohol Being Tested." *The Journal (Addiction Research Foundation)* 10.

Trebach, A.S. (1987). *The Great Drug War*. New York: Macmillan.

Tremblay, S. (1999). Illicit Drugs and Crime in Canada. *Juristat Service Bulletin* 19(1). Ottawa: Canadian Centre for Justice Statistics, Statistics Canada.

———. (2000). Canadian Crime Statistics, 1999. *Juristat Service Bulletin* 20(5). Ottawa: Canadian Centre for Justice Statistics, Statistics Canada.

Trevethan, S. (1993). *Police-reported Aboriginal Crime in Calgary, Regina, and Saskatoon*. Ottawa: Canadian Centre for Justice Statistics, Statistics Canada.

Troiden, R.R. (1979). "Becoming Homosexual: A Model of Gay Identity Acquisition." *Psychiatry* 42:362–73.

Turk, A. (1969). *Criminality and the Legal Order*. Chicago: Rand McNally.

Tyler, G. (1981). "The Crime Corporation." In A.S. Blumberg (ed.), *Current Perspectives on Criminal Behavior* (2nd ed.). New York: Knopf.

Tyler, T., and H. Levy. (2000). "Anguish Ends for Wrongly Convicted Man." *Globe and Mail* (June 9):A1, A7.

United States Department of Justice. (1985). *FBI Uniform Crime Reports*. Washington DC: United States Department of Justice.

Vaillant, G. (1983). *The Natural History of Alcoholism*. Cambridge: Harvard University Press.

Vallee, B. (1986). *Life with Billie*. Toronto: Seal Books.

Van den Hagg, E. (1975). *Punishing Criminals: Concerning a Very Old and Very Painful Question*. New York: Basic Books.

Van Truong, M., G. Timoshenko, D. McKenzie, and E. Single. (1997). *Tobacco. Canadian Profile, 1997: Alcohol, Tobacco, and Other Drugs*. Toronto: Addiction Research Foundation and Canadian Centre of Substance Abuse.

Vaz, E. (1965). "Middle Class Delinquency: Self-Reported Delinquency and Youth Culture." *Canadian Review of Sociology and Anthropology* 2:52–70.

Vaz, E., and A. Lodhi. (1979). *Crime and Delinquency in Canada*. Scarborough: Prentice-Hall.

Venturi, F. (1972). *Italy and the Enlightenment*. New York: New York University Press.

Verdun-Jones, S. (1979). "The Evolution of the Defences of Insanity and Automatism in Canada from 1843 to 1979: A Saga of Judicial Reluctance to Sever the Umbilical Cord to the Mother Country?" *University of British Columbia Law Review* 14:1–73.

———. (1989). *Criminal Law in Canada: Cases, Questions and the Code*. Toronto: Harcourt Brace Jovanovich.

———. (1991). Commentary. "Regina v. Swain" and "Chaulk v. The Queen." *International Bulletin of Law and Mental Health* 2:19–23.

Verdun-Jones, S., and G.K. Muirhead. (1982). "The Native in the Criminal Justice System: Canadian Research". In C. Boydell and I. Connidis (eds.), *The Canadian Criminal Justice System*. Toronto: Holt, Rinehart and Winston.

Vetter, H.J., and G.R. Perlstein. (1991). *Perspectives on Terrorism*. Pacific Grove, CA: Brooks Cole.

Visano, L.A. (1987). *This Idle Trade*. Toronto: VitaSana Books.

Vold, G.B. (1958). *Theoretical Criminology*. New York: Oxford University Press.

Vold, G.B., and T.J. Bernard. (1979). *Theoretical Criminology* (2nd ed.). Oxford: Oxford University Press.

———. (1986). *Theoretical Criminology* (3rd ed.). Oxford: Oxford University Press.

———. (1998). *Theoretical Criminology* (4th ed.). Oxford: Oxford University Press.

Vold, G.B., T.J. Bernard, and J.B. Snipes. (1998). *Theoretical Criminology* (4th ed.). Oxford: Oxford University Press.

Wachs, E. (1988). *Victim-Crime Stories: New York City's Urban Folklore*. Bloomington, IN: Indiana University Press.

Waldron, R.J. (1989). *The Criminal Justice System* (4th ed.). New York: Harper and Row.

Wallace, B. (1989). "The Make-up of a Mass Killer." *Maclean's* (December 18):22.

Walmsley, A. (1987). "Explosive Questions About Trading." *Maclean's* (June 30):22–25.

Warr, M. (1993). "Age, Peers, and Delinquency." *Criminology* 31:17–40.

Warr, M., and M. Stafford. (1991). "The Influence of Delinquent Peers: What They Think and What They Do." *Criminology* 29:851–66.

Watts, A.D., and T.W. Watts. (1981). "Minorities and Urban Crime." *Urban Affairs Quarterly* 16:423–36.

Weber, M. (1967). From *Max Weber: Essays in Sociology*. H. Gerth and D.W. Mills (eds.). New York: Oxford University Press.

Weicker, L.P. (1985). "Dangerous Routine." *Psychology Today* 19:60–62.

Weisberg, D.K. (1985). *Children of the Night: A Study of Adolescent Prostitution*. Lexington, KY: D.C. Heath.

Wells, S. (1996). "Running for Cover." *Maclean's* (July 15): 22–26.

West, D.J. (1982). *Delinquency: Its Roots, Careers, and Prospects*. London: Heineman.

West, W.G. (1979). "Trust Among Serious Thieves." *Crime and/et Justice* 7/8:239–46.

———. (1980). "The Short-Term Careers of Serious Thieves." In Robert A. Silverman and James J. Teevan (eds.), *Crime in Canadian Society* (2nd ed.). Toronto: Butterworths.

———. (1983). "Serious Theft as an Occupation." In T. Fleming and L.A. Visano (eds.), *Deviant Designations: Crime Law and Deviance in Canada*. Toronto: Butterworths.

———. (1984). *Young Offenders and the State: A Canadian Perspective on Delinquency*. Toronto: Butterworths.

Western Report. (1995). "It's the RPC and 69% of the Public vs the Media: That's the Split as Reform Defies the Jury of the Press and Calls for a Return to the Death Penalty." (July 31):10.

White, J.R. (1998). *Terrorism: An Introduction*. Belmont, CA: Wadsworth.

Williams, B., M. Van Truong, and G. Elmoshenko. (1997). *Drug-related Crime in Canada. Canadian Profile, 1997: Alcohol, Tobacco, and Other Drugs*. Toronto: Addiction Research Foundation and Canadian Centre of Substance Abuse.

Williams, F., and M. McShane (1994). *Criminological Theory* (2nd ed.). Englewood Cliffs, NJ: Prentice-Hall.

Williams, R. (1996). "Westray Never Again." *New Maritimes* 15:7–12.

Williams, S. (1997). *Invisible Darkness: The Strange Case of Paul Bernardo and Karla Homolka*. Toronto: Little Brown.

Wilson, A.V. (1993). *Homicide: The Victim/Offender Connection*. Cincinnati, OH: Anderson.

Wilson, J.Q. (1975). *Thinking About Crime*. New York: Basic Books.

———. (1978). *Varieties of Police Behavior*. Cambridge, MA: Harvard University Press.

Wilson, P.R., R. Lincoln, and D. Chappell. (1988). "Physician Fraud and Abuse in Canada: A Preliminary Examination." *Canadian Journal of Criminology* 28:129–46.

Wilson-Smith, A. (1985). "Quebec's State of Siege". *Maclean's* (October 21):12j–12l.

Winick, C., and P. Kinsie. (1971). *The Lively Commerce*. Chicago: Quadrangle.

Wolf, D.R. (1991). *The Rebels: A Brotherhood of Outlaw Bikers*. Toronto: University of Toronto Press.

Wolfgang, M.E. (1958). *Patterns in Criminal Homicide*. Philadelphia: University of Pennsylvania Press.

———. (1973). "Cesare Lombroso." In H. Mannheim (ed.), *Pioneers of Criminology*. Montclair, NJ: Patterson Smith.

Wolfgang, M.E., and Franco Ferracuti. (1967). *The Subculture of Violence: An Integrated Theory in Criminology*. London: Tavistock.

Wood, C. (1989). "A Deadly Plague of Drugs." *Maclean's* (April 3):44–47.

———. (2000). "Fighting Net Crime." *Maclean's* (June 12): 38–40.

Wood, D., and C.T. Griffiths. (2000). "Patterns of Aboriginal Crime," In R.A. Silverman, J.J. Teevan, and V.F. Sacco (eds.), *Crime in Canadian Society*. Toronto: Harcourt Brace.

Woods, A. (2000). "Hells Angels Moving Into Ontario, Say Police." *Toronto Star* (December 30).

Wright, C. (1991). Homicide in Canada, 1990. *Juristat Service Bulletin* 11(15). Ottawa: Canadian Centre for Justice Statistics, Statistics Canada.

Wright, C., and J.P. Leroux. (1991). Children as Victims of Violent Crime. *Juristat Service Bulletin* 11(8). Ottawa: Canadian Centre for Justice Statistics, Statistics Canada.

Yablonski, L. (1965). *The Tunnel Back: Synanon*. New York: Macmillan.

Young, J. (1986). "The Failure of Criminology: The Need for a Radical Realism." In R. Matthews and J. Young (eds.), *Confronting Crime*. London: Sage.

Zimring, F.E., and G.J. Hawkins. (1973). *Deterrence*. Chicago: University of Chicago Press.